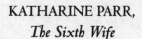

"Absolutely stunning . . . I was completely gripped from the first page to the last. Katheryn emerges from the pages of this beautifully realized portrayal as beguiling, vivacious, and, in the end, tragically naïve. Her story, as a young woman who fell prey to the ruthless scheming of the men around her, still resonates today, and Alison Weir tells it with characteristic verve and stunning period detail."
—TRACY BORMAN, author of *The Private Lives of the Tudors* and *Henry VIII and the Men Who Made Him*

"A wonderful book . . . Katheryn Howard is, for me, the most tragic of Henry VIII's wives, and in her latest novel, Alison Weir covers her life from its early beginnings of impoverished nobility, her family wholly dependent on royal patronage, to her short period as queen, a position she had been pushed into, used as a pawn by her power-hungry family, though she lacked the intellect or sophistication to negotiate its pitfalls. The novel conveys the heart-rending pathos of a young woman executed, whose only real crime was her naïveté and her desire to be loved. It is a profoundly moving story that lingers long after the last page is turned."
—ELIZABETH FREMANTLE, author of *Queen's Gambit* and *The Poison Bed*

ANNA OF KLEVE,
The Princess in the Portrait

"The title of Weir's perceptive latest entry in her acclaimed Six Tudor Queens series . . . signals a new, original view of Henry VIII's fourth wife. . . . Political, legal, and religious matters are dexterously illustrated. . . . A richly satisfying portrait of a woman who made the best of limited choices."
—*Booklist*

"There is an Anne of Cleves we all think we know—the dumpy fourth wife so uninspiring that Henry VIII couldn't even consummate their marriage. Alison Weir gives us a radically different *Anna of Kleve*—one who is definitely hiding some secrets under her thick, unbecoming German gown. It takes a writer of Weir's skill to make us believe her fantasia on the established story. But more importantly, it takes a historian of Weir's experience—her familiarity with the sources and the period detail—to use this compelling fiction to cast a revealing fresh light on the real historical figure."
—SARAH GRISTWOOD, author of *Blood Sisters* and *Game of Queens*

"This is an outstanding novel, the most intriguing so far in Weir's Six Queens series. . . . Weir tells her story with passion, a strong emotional pulse and an excellent knowledge base, creating a novel which will keep her readers page-turning."

—*Historical Novels Review*

JANE SEYMOUR,
The Haunted Queen

"Highly recommended for fans of the period . . . As with the earlier novels in the Six Tudor Queens series . . . Weir focuses tightly on the sole perspective of her protagonist, thereby finding enough relatively fresh territory to keep even die-hard Tudor buffs interested. A fascinating afterword sheds light on Weir's departures from the confirmed historical record and on the additional research she did for this novel, including an investigation of how exactly Jane died."

—*Library Journal* (starred review)

"Best-selling Weir's impressive novel shows why Jane deserves renewed attention. Without any dull moments, Weir illustrates Jane's unlikely journey from country knight's daughter to queen of England. . . . This third volume in Weir's exceptional Six Tudor Queens series offers new angles on its earlier subjects. . . . From the richly appointed decor to the religious tenor of the time, the historical ambience is first-rate. With her standout novel in the crowded Tudor-fiction field, Weir keeps the tension high, breathing new life into a familiar tale and making us wish for a different ending."

—*Booklist* (starred review)

"Jane Seymour the shy mouse type? Think again! This superb book, the result of deep and meticulous new research, brings her to astonishing life—she is vibrant and determined, and she sets the king's court on fire. The fascinating secrets of the Seymour family are deftly explored, the world of the Court painted anew—and Jane's romance with the king is an absolute revelation. Wonderfully written with sympathy and grace, this gripping book gives us the real third wife and shows her struggle to stay true to herself and survive in the toughest of worlds. A magnificent novel."

—KATE WILLIAMS, author of *Becoming Queen Victoria*

ANNE BOLEYN,
A King's Obsession

"This Anne is clever and clear-sighted. . . . Those sympathetic to Boleyn tend to stumble at her documented spite towards Katherine of Aragon and Mary Tudor, but Weir roots this bad behaviour in understandable insecurity, as the King's ardour for her wanes and the longed-for son does not arrive. This tale of Anne's ascent and demise cannot escape comparisons with Hilary Mantel's Wolf Hall series, which deals with the same events. Weir's version is . . . detailed, immaculately researched and convincing. She is particularly interesting on Anne's probable exposure to early feminist writings."
—*The Times*

"*Anne Boleyn, A King's Obsession* is beautifully written, exquisitely detailed, and gives readers a more down-to-earth picture of the often maligned Anne. . . . Don't miss this series."
—*Romance Reviews Today*

"This is a well-written and fast-paced novel that should appeal to fans of Tudor-era fiction looking for a fresh look at one of the period's most popular protagonists."
—*Library Journal*

"A marvelous book—Anne comes alive and leaps from the page, fascinating, enthralling, full-blooded—you can't help but fall in love with her. A brilliant evocation of the period—and a knife-edge moment in British history. Wonderful."
—KATE WILLIAMS, author of *Becoming Queen Victoria*

"As with all her books Weir makes history come alive as no one else. Her novels are biographical but with that comes that extra magic ingredient of a vividly imagined fictional framework that takes the reader there. I enjoyed it enormously. I finished it late last night and genuinely couldn't put it down. I'm still reeling from the horror of that final paragraph, which kept me awake for the rest of the night. Brilliant!"
—BARBARA ERSKINE, author of *Lady of Hay*

KATHERINE OF ARAGON,
The True Queen

"Opulent . . . Weir is uniformly excellent at conveying the chaotic emotional give and take of the relationship [between Henry and Katherine]. . . . Katherine carried herself with a nobility she clearly intended to speak well to posterity. Alison Weir's novel captures that nobility better than any biography ever has."
—*Christian Science Monitor*

"As always, Weir demonstrates a keen eye for crafting dramatic scenes of beautiful, accurate detail, instilling in the reader a vivid sense of being there. . . . If this greatly impressive inaugural installment is any indication, Tudor lovers have much to look forward to."
—*Booklist* (starred review)

"Vividly detailed . . . Weir brings considerable expertise to her fictional retelling of the life of Katherine of Aragon. . . . [The author] portrays her sympathetically as both credulous and steely."
—*Kirkus Reviews*

"[Weir's] fresh approach to Henry's first wife [is] a wonderful place to start for those unfamiliar with Katherine's story. Weir's portrayal is far from that of a weak, victimized woman, but one of a courageous, strong, devoted queen fighting for her life and rights. An easy, quick read to begin the series."
—*RT Book Reviews*

BY ALISON WEIR

FICTION

SIX TUDOR QUEENS:

Katherine Parr, The Sixth Wife
Katheryn Howard, The Scandalous Queen
Anna of Kleve, The Princess in the Portrait
Jane Seymour, The Haunted Queen
Anne Boleyn, A King's Obsession
Katherine of Aragon, The True Queen

The King's Pleasure
The Last White Rose
The Marriage Game
A Dangerous Inheritance
Captive Queen
The Lady Elizabeth
Innocent Traitor

NONFICTION

ENGLAND'S MEDIEVAL QUEENS:

Queens of the Age of Chivalry
Queens of the Crusades
Queens of the Conquest

The Lost Tudor Princess: The Life of Lady Margaret Douglas
Elizabeth of York: A Tudor Queen and Her World
Mary Boleyn: The Mistress of Kings
The Lady in the Tower: The Fall of Anne Boleyn
Mistress of the Monarchy: The Life of Katherine Swynford,
Duchess of Lancaster
Queen Isabella: Treachery, Adultery, and Murder in Medieval England
Mary Queen of Scots and the Murder of Lord Darnley
Henry VIII: The King and His Court
Eleanor of Aquitaine: A Life
The Life of Elizabeth I
The Children of Henry VIII
The Wars of the Roses
The Princes in the Tower
The Six Wives of Henry VIII

The Last White Rose

The Last
White Rose

A NOVEL OF
ELIZABETH OF YORK

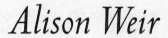

Alison Weir

 BALLANTINE BOOKS | NEW YORK

2023 Ballantine Books Trade Paperback Edition

Copyright © 2022 by Alison Weir
Book club guide copyright © 2023 by Penguin Random House LLC

Published in the United States by Ballantine Books, an imprint of Random House, a division of Penguin Random House LLC, New York.

BALLANTINE is a registered trademark and the colophon is a trademark of Penguin Random House LLC.
RANDOM HOUSE BOOK CLUB and colophon are trademarks of Penguin Random House LLC.

Originally published in hardcover in the United States by Ballantine Books, an imprint of Random House, a division of Penguin Random House LLC, and in the United Kingdom by Headline Review, an imprint of Headline Publishing Group as *Elizabeth of York, The Last White Rose,* in 2022.

ISBN 978-0-593-35505-3
Ebook ISBN 978-0-593-35504-6

Printed in the United States of America on acid-free paper

randomhousebooks.com
randomhousebookclub.com

1st Printing

For Shelley Tucker, in loving memory,
and to Father Luke (Rev. Canon Anthony Verhees),
who has always been an inspiration

O royal maid,
Put on your regal robes in loveliness.
A thousand fair attendants round you wait,
Of various ranks, with different offices,
To deck your beauteous form. Lo, this delights
To smooth with ivory comb your golden hair,
And that to curl or braid each shining tress
And wreath the sparkling jewels round your head,
Twining your locks with gems; this one shall clasp
The radiant necklace framed in fretted gold
About your snowy neck; while that unfolds
The robes that glow with gold and purple dye,
And fits the ornaments with patient skill
To your unrivalled limbs; and here shall shine
The costly treasures from the Orient sands:
The sapphire, azure gem that emulates
Heaven's lofty arch, shall gleam, and softly there
The verdant emerald shed its greenest light,
And fiery carbuncle flash forth rosy rays
From the pure gold.

—"EPITHALAMIUM," GIOVANNI DE' GIGLI

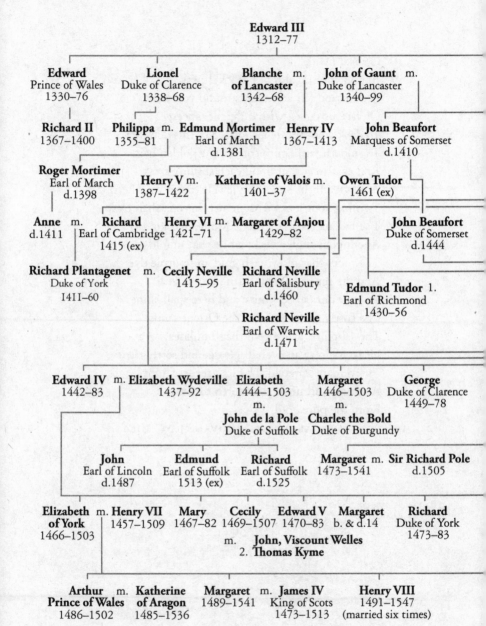

Edward III
1312–77

Edward
Prince of Wales
1330–76

Lionel
Duke of Clarence
1338–68

Blanche m.
of Lancaster
1342–68

John of Gaunt m.
Duke of Lancaster
1340–99

Richard II
1367–1400

Philippa m. **Edmund Mortimer**
1355–81   Earl of March
d.1381

Henry IV
1367–1413

John Beaufort
Marquess of Somerset
d.1410

Roger Mortimer
Earl of March
d.1398

Henry V m. **Katherine of Valois** m. **Owen Tudor**
1387–1422   1401–37   1461 (ex)

Anne m. **Richard**
d.1411   Earl of Cambridge
1415 (ex)

Henry VI m. **Margaret of Anjou**
1421–71   1429–82

John Beaufort
Duke of Somerset
d.1444

Richard Plantagenet m. **Cecily Neville**
Duke of York   1415–95
1411–60

Richard Neville
Earl of Salisbury
d.1460

Edmund Tudor 1.
Earl of Richmond
1430–56

Richard Neville
Earl of Warwick
d.1471

Edward IV m. **Elizabeth Wydeville**
1442–83   1437–92

Elizabeth
1444–1503
m.
John de la Pole
Duke of Suffolk

Margaret
1446–1503
m.
Charles the Bold
Duke of Burgundy

George
Duke of Clarence
1449–78

John
Earl of Lincoln
d.1487

Edmund
Earl of Suffolk
1513 (ex)

Richard
Earl of Suffolk
d.1525

Margaret m. **Sir Richard Pole**
1473–1541   d.1505

Elizabeth m. **Henry VII**
of York   1457–1509
1466–1503

Mary
1467–82

Cecily
1469–1507
m.
John, Viscount Welles
2. **Thomas Kyme**

Edward V
1470–83

Margaret
b. & d.14

Richard
Duke of York
1473–83

Arthur m. **Katherine**
Prince of Wales **of Aragon**
1486–1502   1485–1536

Margaret m. **James IV**
1489–1541   King of Scots
1473–1513

Henry VIII
1491–1547
(married six times)

Katherine Swynford
1350–1403

Edmund
Duke of York
1341–1402

Thomas
Duke of Gloucester
1355–97

Joan Beaufort m. **Ralph Neville**
d.1440   Earl of Westmorland
d.1425

Margaret m. **Sir Henry Stafford** **Jasper Tudor** m. 2 **Katherine** m. **Henry Stafford**
Beaufort   d.1471   Earl of Pembroke   Wydeville   Duke of Buckingham
1443–1509   Duke of Bedford   1483 (ex)
   3. **Thomas Stanley**   d.1495
     Earl of Derby
     d.1504

m. **Isabel Neville**   **Richard III** m. 2. **Anne Neville** m. 1. **Edward of Lancaster**
1451–76   1452–85   1456–85   Prince of Wales
                         1453–71

Edward of Middleham
Prince of Wales
d.1484

Edward
Earl of Warwick
1475–99

m. **Anne Mowbray**   **Anne**   **George**   **Katherine**   **Bridget**
1472–81   1475–1513?   Duke of Bedford   1479–1527   nun at Dartford
         m.   1477–9   m.   1480–?
      Lord Thomas   **William Courtenay**
      Howard   Earl of Devon

Elizabeth   **Mary** m. **Louis XII, King of France**   **Edmund**   **Katherine**
1492–5   1496–1533   2. **Charles Brandon**   Duke of Somerset   b. & d.15
               Duke of Suffolk   1499–1500

PART ONE

Princess

Chapter 1

1470

"Wake up, Bessy! Wake up!"

Elizabeth stirred, roused by the unfamiliar whisper. What was her mother the Queen doing here, shaking her? It was usually Lady Berners who came to wake her with a smile and a "Good morning, my lady Princess." But Mother was not smiling, and Lady Berners, holding a candle aloft, was standing in the doorway with Mistress Jakes, the wet nurse, who had baby Cecily in her arms. With them was Grandmother Rivers, holding a sleepy little Mary by the hand. They were all dressed for outdoors. But it was still dark and, beyond the narrow window, there was no sign of dawn breaking.

"What's wrong?" Elizabeth asked, instantly awake.

"Shh!" the Queen hissed, putting a finger to her lips. "We must all be very quiet. Get up and I'll put you into some warm clothes."

Mother was dressing her? Her lady mother, whose queenly hands never deigned to do everyday tasks? Something must be badly amiss.

Mother gave a faint smile. "I and my sisters had to shift for ourselves before I became queen." She lifted Elizabeth's night-rail over her head, put on her smock and her green woolen winter gown and wrapped her cloak around her, pulling the hood down over her face. Then she took her own cloak from Grandmother Rivers and wrapped herself in it, concealing her swollen belly. She turned to the other women. "Let us go." There was an urgency in her lowered voice.

"My lady, what's happening?" Elizabeth asked, completely bewildered.

"Hush! I will tell you later. Now, not a word. We all have to be very quiet."

The four women hurried the children through the Lanthorn Tower, holding their breath as they passed the open door of the room where the sentries, who were supposed to be on watch, were—luckily—snoring soundly. And then they were out on the wall walk and hurrying down the stairs and along Water Lane, to the postern gate of the Tower of London, which had been left ajar.

"Thank God for a loyal guard," Mother breathed. Tightly holding Elizabeth's hand, she led her down the Queen's Stairs to the wharf, where several small craft were tied up. Lady Berners hailed a boatman.

"Westminster Stairs!" she said.

"Right-ho," he answered, taking the baby from her as she boarded. The Queen and Elizabeth followed, with Grandmother Rivers, the wet nurse, and Mary climbing on deck last. The boatman adjusted his oars and pulled out into the Thames.

The water was black and sinister. Elizabeth shivered with fear and the chill of the early-October night. Around them, London slept. From the darkness came the distant voice of the watch: "Three o'clock, and all's well."

"If only it was," Grandmother whispered.

Elizabeth was desperate to know what was wrong, but she obeyed her mother and kept silent, wondering why they were going to Westminster at this time of night.

"It's late for you good ladies to be out," the boatman observed as they passed Baynard's Castle, where Elizabeth's Grandmother York, who was far sterner than Grandmother Rivers, lived. Did she know about this adventure they were having? Maybe she was asleep, like everyone else.

"We are going to my daughter, who is travailing with child as we speak," Lady Berners said. "I've had word that things are critical."

Elizabeth was surprised, for Lady Berners's married daughter Anne had only just had a baby, while the other daughter was as yet unwed—and Lady Berners had always impressed on her that it was wrong to tell lies.

"We'll get you there quickly, then," the boatman said kindly, and began rowing harder. Elizabeth saw the women exchange glances.

Soon, she could make out the sprawling bulk of the palace of Westminster looming ahead. The boatman pulled in at the jetty and then they were hurrying up the stairs, huddling together as they hastened alongside the wall that enclosed the palace yard. Elizabeth was disappointed when they did not enter the gate, but instead moved away from the palace; she had been entertaining fond notions that they were going to her father the King, who would make whatever was wrong right again. It was a long time since she had seen him. She and her two little sisters had been staying with Mother in the Tower palace for what seemed like ages.

They were passing Westminster Abbey now and walking through St. Margaret's churchyard. Soon it became appallingly clear that Mother was heading for the great sanctuary building that stood opposite. It was grim and stark, like a church in form, but exuding menace, not holiness. Young as she was, Elizabeth knew that bad people lived there, murderers and thieves. Once, after she had had a nightmare about being trapped in there, Lady Berners had explained that anyone could claim sanctuary, which meant that no one could arrest them or bring them to justice because they were on holy ground, under the protection of St. Peter.

Holy ground it might be, but it was an evil place and Elizabeth was terrified of going there. Tears came as she shrank, whimpering, from the prospect.

"Hush," Mother said, her grip tightening.

Elizabeth was too frightened to heed her. "But why are we going here, my lady? We haven't done anything wrong. We're not thieves."

"Bessy, be quiet. I will explain everything soon."

A hand descended on Elizabeth's shoulder. She looked up to see her grandmother smiling down at her. "God is surely watching over us, child," she said. "He will provide for the best."

They had reached the stout oak door now and Elizabeth, trembling, saw her mother hesitate, then rap on it with the iron knocker.

After what seemed like an age, a monk opened the door. "God be with you, my sisters. Whom do you seek?"

"Alas, Brother," Mother said, "we are not here as visitors. We have come to claim sanctuary."

There was a pause while the monk stared at them all. "Are you debtors? I cannot credit that such fine ladies can be guilty of any crime. And there are children with you—we don't admit—"

"I am your Queen," Mother said, putting on that icy look that quelled most people, "and I and my children are in danger. The King has fled the realm and my lord of Warwick and the Duke of Clarence are marching on London. I beg of you, grant us sanctuary."

Elizabeth listened in confusion. Father had fled his kingdom? And why did they have to run away from her godfather Warwick and her uncle Clarence? She had been vaguely aware that there had been quarrels in the family, and she knew that her mother hated both men, but she had no idea why.

"Her Grace is near her time," Grandmother said.

"Pray come in and sit down while I fetch Father Abbot," the monk invited, looking nervous.

As they entered the building, Elizabeth peered about her, frightened lest she see desperate men materializing out of the dimness, but, to her relief, the vast chapel-like space was almost deserted. There were just two sleeping forms, wrapped in their cloaks, lying on the straw at the far end.

Mother sank down on the bench just inside the door. Her *froideur* had vanished and there were tears on her cheeks. "I cannot believe this is happening," she whispered.

"Don't cry, my lady," Elizabeth pleaded, as her grandmother gathered the stricken Queen to her bosom and three-year-old

Mary started wailing. Lady Berners bent to comfort her, a whimpering Cecily still in the crook of her arm.

"You must leave, Lady Berners," the Queen said, recovering herself and reaching for the baby. "They will not be interested in you."

"But the children, Madam," the governess protested as both Elizabeth and Mary clung to her skirts, crying.

"Don't leave us!" they begged.

"It is an order," the Queen said. "I would not have you shut in with us when you don't need to be. It is different for Mistress Jakes." She looked at the wet nurse. "I cannot let her go. As soon as the situation improves, I will send for you. Quiet, children! You will have me and Grandmother Rivers to look after you, and you will see Lady Berners soon."

"As your Grace wishes," Lady Berners said, but Elizabeth could see that she was not happy about leaving. "I dare say I will find an inn tonight, and tomorrow I'll go to Windsor, trusting that my husband is still constable of the castle."

"God go with you," the Queen said. "Pray for us!"

Elizabeth watched, stricken, as her beloved governess walked away. Then she saw the monk returning with the familiar figure of Abbot Milling, a rotund gentleman in a plain black habit with a kindly moon of a face beneath his tonsure. She had met him several times when visiting Westminster Abbey.

"Your Grace, it grieves me to see you here," he greeted Mother, holding out his hands and squeezing hers. "Things have come to a pretty pass when the blameless Queen of England is driven to seek sanctuary with common criminals."

"Father Abbot, you will have heard the news," said the Queen, bending her head for his blessing. "In this world, we reap what we sow. I would not see what was staring me in the face. And now I, and these innocent little ones, must pay the price."

"It is a sad thing when might must prevail over right," the Abbot observed. "You did not make Warwick and Clarence commit treason."

"No, but I unwittingly helped to give them grounds." Elizabeth wondered what Mother meant, but the Queen was still speaking. "Father Abbot, will you let me register myself as a sanctuary woman? If it had not been to keep my children safe, I would not have come here."

"Madam," he replied, "you may of course claim sanctuary, and Brother Thomas here will register your names. But I would not hear of you lodging in this place with murderers and thieves. I insist that you all stay as my guests at Cheyneygates, my own house."

"I can never thank you enough, Father." Elizabeth saw tears of relief in her mother's eyes. Meekly, she took Mary's hand as they all followed the Abbot back to the abbey. He led them through a gateway by the west door, then turned toward the cloisters. Under an archway, he opened another door and led them up a steep flight of stairs into a beautiful house that smelt of incense and beeswax.

"Your Grace shall have my three best rooms," he told Mother. "The beds are made up and I will send my servants with towels and other necessities for your comfort. If you need anything more, do tell them."

When Elizabeth saw the chambers they were to occupy, she felt much better. The Abbot was a great prince of the Church and lived accordingly. She and her sisters were to lodge with the Queen in a sumptuous bedchamber furnished with a great tester bed and two small pallet beds, all made up with bleached white linen and velvet counterpanes. Abbot Milling told them that the large room he called the Jerusalem Chamber, which was hung with rich tapestries and was almost as magnificent as the state apartments at Westminster, would serve as Mother's great chamber. Grandmother was to have the Abbot's hall, which had a minstrels' gallery and was no less splendid than the rest of the apartment.

Gratefully, Elizabeth lay down on her pallet, while her mother tucked the bedclothes in. A few feet away, Mary was already asleep, her fair curls tousled on the pillow. Elizabeth watched as the Queen ordered the wet nurse to help with her buttons, stripped to her smock and climbed into the big bed. The nurse pulled out a truckle bed and lay on that, cradling Cecily in her arms.

"Mother, what is happening?" Elizabeth asked, keeping her voice low.

"Bessy, go to sleep. I will tell you in the morning. I'm too tired now."

Soon, the room was filled with the sound of even breathing and the occasional snuffle from the baby. But Elizabeth lay awake thinking, trying not to fret about tonight's strange adventure and what it meant.

She had known she was important for as long as she could remember. She was nearly five years old and the eldest daughter of a golden king and a beautiful queen, and she lived in wondrous glittering palaces, just like a princess in a fable. She had been called Elizabeth after her mother, who often wore the jeweled brooch that Father had given her to mark her birth. In normal circumstances, Mother was a remote figure to her daughters, an elegant, graceful goddess who sat on a throne and sometimes descended on the nursery in a cloud of floral perfume, swishing her fabulous damask skirts, her neck like a swan's under the shaven hairline and the gauze-covered hennin.

Mother was remote and regal, but Father was fun, a towering, boisterous figure with a twinkling eye and a merry laugh that belied his narrow, watchful eyes. He was the handsomest man in the world, and everyone adored him, especially his children. His court was famed far and wide for its grandeur; it bustled with great lords and ladies and visitors from all four corners of the earth. Elizabeth had often felt fit to burst with pride, having such a strong and splendid father. Now she wondered if he would ever come back to sit on his throne. Would she even see him again? Where was he?

Elizabeth's everyday world was not her father's magnificent court, but the nursery at Sheen Palace, where kindly, plump Lady Berners held sway, ruling the children and their nurses, rockers and household servants with effortless authority. As the daughter of the King, whose person was sacred and who had been appointed by God to rule England, Elizabeth had been drilled regularly in good manners and warned of the dangers of disobeying Heaven's commands and falling into sin. She always tried very hard to be good and win Lady Berners's smiles of approval.

That good lady often beamed when she saw how protective her charge was of her younger sisters, whom she adored. When Elizabeth was not kneeling by the cradle, rocking Cecily to sleep, she and Mary would run about the palace, playing ball or tag in the courtyards, or stand in an oriel window watching the boats pass by on the Thames, craning their necks to see if they could glimpse their father's favorite residence, the great palace of Westminster, which lay some way upstream. His sun-in-splendor badge was prominent among the heraldic antelopes, swans, harts, hinds and lions that adorned the state rooms at Sheen.

"Do you know that once, before a battle, he saw three suns in the sky?" Elizabeth had told a wide-eyed Mary. "It was a good omen, as he won the battle."

The pattern of their years had long been established, as had their simple faith in God; daily, the chaplain came to school them in their catechism and explain the pictures and writings in their psalters. On feast days and holy days, they made their offerings at Mass. At Lent, they fasted. On Maundy Thursday, they gave gifts to the poor. On Good Friday, they crept to the Cross on their knees. At New Year, they received Yuletide gifts, and on Twelfth Night they were allowed to join the feasting and revelry at court, highly excited at the naughty antics of the Lord of Misrule. Remembering this, Elizabeth shut her eyes tightly and prayed to God to let her return to her pleasant life. Send Father home, she pleaded.

Her trips to court had always been the highlight of her year, but, to her disappointment, she and Mary were only summoned there for celebrations and state visits, when the King liked to show them off to his guests. On these occasions, they joined their mother's household and enjoyed the rare privilege of her teaching them manners, music, singing, dancing, embroidery, and anything else needful to make them ornaments of the court, as she put it. Mother was strict about the proper observance of the courtesies—Elizabeth had once seen her keep Grandmother Rivers on her knees before her for a very long time. The child reveled in being at the center of the court and dressing up in miniature versions of the rich clothes worn by the Queen; already, she was adept at managing long court trains.

Most of all, she loved spending time with her parents. She had been enjoined to show them the highest reverence, not only because they were royal persons and exalted above everyone else, but also because she had been taught that children must revere, honor, and obey their father and mother, and be dutiful toward them all their lives. She must greet them with curtseys, wait to be spoken to before she addressed them, and conduct herself properly in their presence. Usually, though, her father would dispense with formality and lift his daughters high in his arms, twirling them about and kissing them. He took the time to talk to them about their childish concerns, and to play games with them. Mother, on the other hand, seemed chiefly concerned that they behaved well. She would not allow her ladies to make a fuss of them in case they were spoiled. But she did want the best for them, which Lady Berners said was the most important part of being a good mother.

Elizabeth now remembered, with a pang, how, each evening at court, before they went to bed, she and Mary knelt before their parents and asked for their blessing, which was always given gladly and made her feel safe and loved. She had long wished that she could live at court all the time. Now she wondered if she would ever go there again.

Still she could not sleep. She lay there thinking back on the weeks before their flight to sanctuary and recalling something she had heard her attendants saying as she played in the garden at Sheen one hot afternoon.

"Warwick hates the Queen and, if this child she carries is another daughter, I dread to think what will happen." That was Lady Berners. "The King needs an heir. I always thought it folly for him to marry for love and then promote all those greedy Wydeville relations. Not that I dislike *her*—she's a good mistress. But sometimes I can see why Warwick is disaffected."

"Warwick grows ever more arrogant," Mistress Jakes replied. "He must see the Wydevilles as a threat to his influence over the King."

"Aye, indeed. It's said he was furious when the Wydeville marriage scuppered that French match he was negotiating for the King. He would be in control of everything. My husband heard an Italian ambassador at Windsor joke that there are two kings in England, Warwick, and another whose name he had forgotten."

"Small wonder that Warwick has allied himself with Clarence. Now there's an untrustworthy rascal!"

There was a pause, during which Elizabeth heard her lady mistress mutter something about little pitchers, and then the talk turned to an entirely different subject. She had frowned, not fully comprehending the words she had heard, although they troubled her. Warwick was her godfather. Why did he hate her mother? Why had he fallen out with her father, after helping him to become king? Why was her uncle Clarence a rascal?

And now they were marching on London together, and her mother was so frightened that she had made them all run away in the night. Elizabeth lay there in the unfamiliar dark, unable to make sense of it all, and longing to know where her father was and when she would see him again.

In the morning, Mistress Jakes was all briskness and practicality. "I hope you agree, Madam, that the children should follow their daily routine as far as possible," she said, combing Elizabeth's red-gold hair as the little girl stood patiently, washed and laced into her green gown.

"I do agree," the Queen said, as Grandmother plaited her gilded tresses and bound them up high on her head.

"I think I make a fair tirewoman," she observed, admiring the result. "Yes, the children need the stability of their daily regimen."

At Mother's request, the Prior, John Eastney, came to celebrate Mass in the Abbot's private chapel. Elizabeth could not concentrate because she was desperate for the Queen to talk to her, as promised. The moment came after Mass, when two lay brothers brought them a generous breakfast of fresh bread, ale, meat, and eggs. After they had eaten, Mistress Jakes took Mary off to play in Grandmother's chamber, and the Queen leaned back in her high carved chair, regarding Elizabeth with an unusually sympathetic gaze.

"Daughter, for some time now I have done my best to spare you any unpleasantness, but you are a toward child and able, I am sure, to understand something of what has been happening and why we have had to seek sanctuary. It's a long story."

Elizabeth was seized with a feeling of dread. But Mother suddenly smiled in a wistful way. "The King your father married me for love. You may hear lots of foolish tales about it, but pay them no heed. My first husband, Sir John Grey, died fighting for the House of Lancaster in the late wars with the House of York, and I was left with two small boys—your brothers Thomas and Dickon—and no money."

Elizabeth was not close to her half-brothers, who had both inherited the Queen's fair coloring and good looks. They were a lot older than she—Thomas was fifteen and Dickon thirteen—and, being puffed up with their importance as members of the King's household, they tended to look down on little girls; but she tried to love them for Mother's sake.

"York was victorious," Mother was saying. "The pretended King, Henry of Lancaster, was overthrown, and your father took the throne as the true and rightful heir. My situation was desperate, for no one wanted to help a Lancastrian widow, so, when I heard that King Edward was hunting in Whittlewood Forest, not far from Grandmother's house at Grafton, where I was living, I decided to appeal to him for help. I waited for him by the wayside, holding my little boys by the hand."

Elizabeth had never heard this story. "Did he ride by? What did he say?"

The Queen smiled again and picked up the tiny bonnet she was embroidering. Her stitches were deft and neat, so unlike Elizabeth's. "He said he would help. And he fell in love with me. He was so tall, so debonair and so handsome that I was swept away. And when he asked me to marry him, I said yes at once. It was unheard of, a king marrying for love. They marry to make alliances with foreign princes or to bring peace or great trading treaties. We had to marry in secret because we knew that the nobility

would try to prevent us. Warwick wanted to marry your father to
a French princess. When we announced our marriage, he was furious, as were your father's brothers and many other lords. There
was an awful fuss. Everyone said that Father had married beneath
him in taking a Lancastrian commoner to wife; they chose to forget that Grandmother is a princess of the House of Luxembourg.
But he was deaf to their complaints. He extended his bounty to
my family and there were titles and great matches aplenty for my
brothers and sisters. That too caused a lot of muttering. But I was
too busy concentrating on being a good queen to let it bother
me." She paused, looking pensive. "I wish now that I had paid
more heed. Yet it was the King, not me, who promoted my relatives, and he had made me queen, so it was only right that I should
have had the respect I was due."

Elizabeth, agog at hearing these revelations, and really only
grasping the fact that her parents had married because they loved
each other, thought that people had been very unfair to Mother,
especially Warwick. "But why did they say that Father had married beneath him?"

The Queen sighed. "Child, you must understand that kings are
very special persons. They are called by God to rule and set above
their subjects. When a king is crowned, he is anointed with holy
oil and becomes a sacred being."

"Like the saints?"

"In a way." The Queen's smile faded. "Many hold that kings
should marry princesses so that their children are of royal birth
and of the highest blood, saying it is only fitting for those chosen
by God to rule. Thus you can understand why people did not approve of Father marrying me. And then I bore three daughters,
one after the other, so now they criticize me for not giving England a prince to inherit the throne."

"But you've got me!" Elizabeth piped up.

"I have indeed, and your father and I love you and your sisters
dearly, but it is against Nature for a woman to rule, so you cannot
succeed your father as queen."

Elizabeth had not given the matter any thought until now, but she felt somehow cheated. She was the King's eldest child; didn't that count for a lot?

Her mother shook her head, as if she had read her thoughts. "A king needs a son. He needs to know that the royal succession is secure." She patted her belly. "Let us hope that this little one is a boy. Alas, that he will be born in such perilous circumstances . . ." She sighed. "It is a sorry tale, but I must continue."

Elizabeth waited, while the Queen re-threaded her needle and the monks returned to take away the breakfast things. When they had gone, her mother spoke again.

"There grew great jealousy and bad blood between my family and Warwick over who should be the greatest power in the realm. Matters came to a head when your grandfather Rivers opposed Warwick over your aunt Margaret's marriage to the Duke of Burgundy. Warwick was against it; he had a deadly hatred of Burgundy then and was still pushing for an alliance with Burgundy's enemy, France. But my kinsmen persuaded the King to allow the marriage, and it took place. You are too young to remember the great celebrations."

Elizabeth could not, nor could she recall her aunt Margaret, her father's sister.

"That was the end for Warwick. It was what made him join forces with your uncle Clarence." Elizabeth had never taken to her fair-haired uncle George, a paler and less charming imitation of her father. On the rare occasions she had seen him, he had been a brooding presence with an unpredictable sense of humor that often made him sound angry. She much preferred her younger uncle Richard, Duke of Gloucester, who was quiet, but always kind, and treated her more like a favorite cousin than a niece.

"Uncle Clarence is jealous of your father." Mother made a moue of disgust. "He wants to be king himself and he has seized this new chance to plot again against his brother and sovereign. He's a fool. Your father has been more than generous to him, but that counts for nothing!" She snapped her fingers. "You remember Warwick's elder daughter?"

Isabel Neville. Elizabeth had met her at court, and her sister Anne, slender, pretty girls who were always whispering together.

"Warwick has no son," the Queen continued. "When he dies, his daughters will be the greatest heiresses in England, and your uncles have repeatedly sought them in marriage. The King always refused because he did not want Warwick to become too powerful. But, last year, Warwick gave Isabel to Clarence in marriage anyway, and they rose in arms against the King. Father was away from court for a long time—do you remember?" Elizabeth shook her head. "You were too young to know the truth, so we told you he was on a hunting progress, but he had been taken prisoner. Clarence was determined to seize the throne, and he and Warwick spread a wicked lie that the King was not his father's son and was not entitled to the crown. It's not true, of course."

Mother paused, and Elizabeth was appalled to see tears on her cheeks. Her serene mother, who never cried!

"That was not the worst of it. Warwick had your grandfather, Lord Rivers, and my brother John put to death." The Queen dabbed her eyes with a handkerchief.

Elizabeth's eyes widened with shock. She had seen her mother and grandmother weeping when they told her that her grandfather and uncle had died. But what did Mother mean, put to death?

"He had them killed," Mother said.

"How?"

"It's best you don't know," the Queen said. "Then they arrested Grandmother Rivers and accused her of witchcraft. They said she had used spells to bring about my marriage to the King and destroy Warwick."

Grandmother, sweet Grandmother—a witch? Elizabeth could not believe it. This was all too much to take in.

Mother laid down her embroidery. "None of it was true. They were just doing their best to ruin me and my family. Luckily, Grandmother had friends who complained to the King's Council, who dismissed the accusations. And then the King made Warwick release him and returned to London in triumph. That was when he betrothed you to Warwick's nephew, George Neville."

Elizabeth could just recall the betrothal ceremony, for which she had worn a shimmering white gown that had made her feel every inch the princess. She remembered her father telling her that her marriage would bring peace to England and ensure that if anything happened to him, the Nevilles would see that she and George became king and queen. But it would not happen for ages and ages because Father was still a young man and George, with his scrawny knees and shock of black hair, was only five.

Mother's voice drew her back to the present. "It was a great joy to me to see your father restored to power last year. He broke your betrothal to George Neville and denounced Warwick and Clarence as traitors, and they fled to France. Since then, they have been scheming to restore Henry of Lancaster. Henry's wife, the pretended Queen Margaret, our great enemy—and theirs, too, once—made an extraordinary turnabout and joined forces with them. She even agreed to let Warwick's daughter Anne marry her son, Edward of Lancaster, to cement this new friendship. Then we heard that Warwick and Clarence were raising an army to invade England. That was when I took you and your sisters to the Tower for safety. And now they are marching on London, which is why we came here last night, and why your father the King had to flee with Uncle Gloucester, with only the clothes on their backs, to seek help from our friends in Burgundy."

"Will Warwick and Uncle Clarence come here?" Elizabeth asked nervously.

"I do hope not!" her mother replied. "No knight worthy of his spurs makes war on women. And we are under the protection of the Church."

Just then, the Abbot entered the room and bowed to the Queen. "I trust that everything is to your Grace's satisfaction."

"You are being very good to us, Father," she replied.

"It is my pleasure, Madam. But I must tell you that, this morning, it has been cried in London that Warwick and Clarence are approaching the City with a large force."

Elizabeth felt panic rising as she saw her mother turn pale.

"Are we safe here, Father Abbot?" the Queen faltered.

"They will not dare to violate God's sanctuary!" the Abbot replied firmly.

Elizabeth tried hard not to cry. She was very frightened, but she was her father's daughter and must be brave.

Later that morning, she and Mary were playing with their dolls when the Abbot returned, looking worried. "Your Grace, Warwick's men are running amok in the City. Law and order have broken down. Mobs are looting and rioting unchecked—all in the name of Warwick! Some of our felons have left the sanctuary to infest the streets. Madam, I do not believe that any authority will be imposed until my lord of Warwick arrives."

Mother had risen to her feet, her eyes wide with alarm. "Father Abbot, I beg of you, get a message to the Lord Mayor, for he has charge of London's defenses. Entreat him not to resist Warwick's forces or do anything to provoke him, lest he harm the citizens and force his way into the abbey."

"Madam, be of comfort. I will do it," the Abbot promised, and hastened away.

Elizabeth was trembling with fear, but there was Mistress Jakes, firmly taking her and Mary by the hand to the pegs where their cloaks were hanging and then leading them downstairs to the Abbot's private courtyard, bidding them run about in the fresh air for a space. They played tag, and then hoodman blind. Elizabeth espied the Abbot at his window, waving at them. He was such a kindly, calm, and authoritative man, and somehow she knew that he would not let any harm come to them. Comforted, she began to enjoy the games—until she heard shouts in the far distance, and then she froze. But there was the Abbot again, smiling through the diamond panes and shaking his head in the direction of the noise, to show them that it was nothing to worry about.

At eleven o'clock, they were summoned indoors to dinner. Normally, it would have been served with great ceremony and, during it, improving and noble tales would have been read aloud to them. But today, in the Jerusalem Chamber, there were only the soft murmurs of the Queen and the other women. The lay brothers brought them food—honest, plain fare, given in charity, but nothing like the elaborate dishes they were used to.

After dinner, their faces washed, Elizabeth and Mary were sent to have a nap, although Elizabeth found it impossible to sleep, wondering what was happening a mile away in London. Gratefully, she arose when called and they went back to their playing. But she was aware of her mother watching the door, as alert as she herself was for any sounds of unrest. It disturbed her to see Mother so nervous; she was always a serene, regal presence in their lives. It felt as if her world was rocking around her. All she wanted was to be comforted and assured that all would be well.

Late that afternoon, they were given their usual milk and bread, and then everyone went to the Abbot's chapel for Vespers. There had been no news for hours now, and the monk who welcomed them could tell them nothing.

Afterward, Mother sank down wearily at the supper table, looking drawn. "What wouldn't I give to know what is happening out there," she murmured. "And where my lord the King is. I long to hear that he is safe. Dear God, how long are we going to be prisoners here?"

"Warwick and Clarence must arrive soon," Grandmother said.

"And then what?"

"Things will become clearer, Beth. Try to stay positive. Think of the children."

Mother's voice was shrill. "Stay positive? Think of what they tried to do to you."

A shadow crossed Grandmother's face. "I still have friends in high places."

"You hope!"

"My lady," Elizabeth piped up, "why not try to make friends with my lord of Warwick?"

Mother stroked her hair. "I wish it was as simple as that, sweeting."

"But then he might let us leave here and go back to the palace."

"I dare not leave here," Mother said. "Here, we are under God's protection."

Elizabeth tried hard to believe it.

After supper, there were disports as usual, for the children's sake. The women put on brave faces, sang songs and played hide-and-seek with them, then Mistress Jakes served the princesses their bedtime drink of aleberry and put them to bed. Normally, they could slumber safely, knowing that the outer gates to the palace were barred, the porters on watch, and the watchmen patrolling three or four times a night, checking every chamber. But here, there were no guards, no watchmen—only God and Father Abbot. Elizabeth lay awake fearfully for a long time, straining to hear if there were any unwelcome noises from outside. But all remained quiet.

"I wish I had brought more clothing with me," Mother lamented the next morning.

"We'll just have to make do with what we have," Grandmother said. "We can wash our smocks and rub down our gowns."

"That we have come to this—doing the work of laundresses!" Mother lamented, near to tears. She was still complaining when Abbot Milling arrived, his face grave.

"Your Grace, Warwick and Clarence have entered the City and taken control of the Tower. The Mayor sent me a message saying he had no choice but to come to terms with them. That is all I know for now, but I have dispatched two of our lay brothers to the City to find out what is happening."

Mother could eat no dinner and Elizabeth was not very hungry either. The tension in the room was palpable. It was only broken when Father Abbot returned in the afternoon.

"Your Grace, Warwick has restored order in the City, but I regret to tell you that he has proclaimed Henry the Sixth king once more. He has brought him from his prison in the Tower to the royal palace there."

Mother's glare was icy. "So he acts the kingmaker once again. He thinks he is above us all. Henry of Lancaster is no more fit to reign than baby Cecily here, even if he did have the right. His mind is gone. He is an idiot, poor man."

"But a dangerous one," Grandmother observed.

"No doubt the pretended Queen Margaret will cross from France and try to seize power in Henry's name, but it is Warwick who will rule here, and that fool Clarence," the Queen spat. "Henry will be their puppet, and they may use him to destroy me and mine. Do not forget what they did to my dear father and brother!"

Elizabeth shrank from her words. Mother was frightening her almost as much as the thought of Warwick and Uncle Clarence did.

"Madam, please." The Abbot's voice was firm. "There is more news, and it is to your advantage. One of my friends on the royal Council came to see me this afternoon. He had spoken to Warwick in the Tower. The Earl told him that he had little reason to love you, but he did not persecute women. Indeed, he has issued a proclamation forbidding his followers to defoul any churches or sanctuaries, on pain of death. So, be at peace, for you and your children are safe."

Elizabeth felt so relieved that she could have kissed the Abbot. But Mother looked doubtful. "I wish I felt safe, but the situation is so volatile. What of my unborn child? If it is a boy, will Warwick and Clarence see him as a threat to their regime? What shall I do, Father Abbot?"

"There is no question but that your Grace must stay here," he replied.

"But I have no money and lack many necessities. My friends have probably forsaken me, and who can say how long we will have to remain here?"

"God—and this abbey—will provide for you, never fear. And He has already shown His hand. Word of your plight has spread, thanks to our worthy lay brothers, and a loyal butcher, Master Gould, came here not an hour since, promising to donate half a beef and two muttons every week for the sustenance of your Grace's household."

"How very kind of him," Mother said, visibly moved. "It seems I am not without friends after all. And you, Father Abbot, have been the greatest of them. I can never thank you sufficiently for your kindness to us."

"Bless you, my daughter," the Abbot smiled. "Let us hope that your tribulations will soon be at an end."

Chapter 2

1470–1471

The abbey bells were tolling midnight on All Hallows Eve when Elizabeth was awakened by Mistress Jakes, who proceeded to move her, Mary, and their pallet beds into Grandmother's room, where Cecily slept in a plain wooden cradle the monks had fashioned for her.

"What's happening?" Elizabeth whispered nervously. "Is Warwick coming?" He had become the demon of her dreams.

"No, Princess. Your mother is brought to bed. By morning, God willing, you'll have a baby brother or sister."

That was good news. But, as the night wore on, it seemed that being brought to bed, whatever that meant, was a painful business. She could hear Mother moaning behind the firmly closed door. Later, the whimpers turned into ceaseless cries. She put her hands over her ears, terrified.

The door opened at one point and Lady Scrope arrived and spoke soothingly to her. Elizabeth remembered Mother's surprise when, three days ago, she had been informed that Henry of Lancaster's Council had appointed Lady Scrope to wait on her, and had also sent Mother Cobb, the midwife who had delivered Cecily, and the Queen's own physician, Dr. Sirego. Mother had expressed astonishment that the new regime had paid for their services. "Especially since the child might be a boy who will one day challenge Henry."

"Maybe they want to make friends," Elizabeth suggested, but Mother had shaken her head.

"Even if they do, I do not deal with usurpers."

That, Elizabeth thought, was not right. A kind word from Mother and this horrid nightmare might be over.

Lady Scrope looked in again later. Her voice was kind. "Are you still awake, my little lady? There is nothing to worry about. All is going well."

"But Mother is crying." Elizabeth was nearly in tears.

"It is normal. Travail is hard work. But it will not be long now. Try to sleep." She departed in a rustle of skirts.

Dawn brought the wail of a baby. Elizabeth was out of bed like a ball from a cannon and burst into her mother's chamber before anyone could stop her. But Mother was propped up on her pillows smiling, her silver-gilt hair fanned out about her shoulders.

"Bessy, you have a new brother," she said proudly. "A prince for England."

Elizabeth leaned over the cradle. Inside, snugly swaddled and gazing up at her, lay a tiny infant with rosebud lips and wide blue eyes. "He's beautiful!" she gasped. "Can I pick him up?"

"Not yet," the Queen said. "He needs to sleep now."

"What is his name?"

"Edward. It is fitting that he be called after the King." Elizabeth was disconcerted to see Mother suddenly dissolve into weeping. Of course, she was missing Father. How happy he would be when he knew he had a son to reign after him.

Grandmother, who was sitting by the bed, took Mother's hand. "Don't distress yourself, Beth."

"It seems cruel that this Prince we have longed for should be born during his father's exile," Mother sobbed.

Grandmother patted her cheek. "It may be a blessing, if our friends derive from it some hope and consolation and remain faithful to Edward."

"I pray they do!" Mother said fervently. "But what if Warwick sees the child as a threat?"

"It is not the child who is the threat—it is his father, and they do well to fear him. He will return soon to reclaim his throne, never doubt it. As for this little one, he is too young and helpless to be of any importance to them. They have enough trouble on their hands as it is, trying to reestablish Henry of Lancaster on a throne that isn't his."

That seemed to calm Mother. She asked Grandmother to take the baby and lay him in Elizabeth's arms. "Careful, now," she said. Elizabeth looked down at his cherubic face and lost her heart.

There was none of the pomp that had attended his sisters' baptisms when the little Prince was christened in the Abbot's house by Prior Eastney. There was no more ceremony than if he had been a poor man's son.

Grandmother and Lady Scrope were godmothers at the font; Abbot Milling and the tall, imposing Prior Eastney stood as godfathers. Elizabeth proudly carried the chrisom, the robe that was put on her brother after his christening to show that he had been purified from sin. Little Ned—for so they were calling him, to distinguish him from his father—made only a murmur as the Devil was driven out of him.

There was no royal churching ceremony for Mother, who, after making a speedy recovery, was quietly blessed by the Abbot with her small household looking on. By then, life seemed to have settled down. It was clear now that Warwick would make no move against them, yet still the Queen deemed it wise to remain in sanctuary.

"Leaving could be seen as provocation. It might make them wonder if we were making ourselves a focus of support for their enemies," she said, taking the baby from Lady Scrope and cradling him in her arms as she sat by the fire. "No, our security rests solely on the great franchise of this holy place. We must sustain our ordeal in patience." But, as the winter days grew ever shorter, she was often sorrowful, heavy-hearted, and anything but patient, railing against being confined and lamenting her lost husband and the royal life she had led. "When will it end?" she would cry. "When will Edward come?"

Elizabeth could not bear to hear her or see how her serene mother had been brought so low and become so fearful that the slightest disturbance made her jump. But there was always Grandmother, soothing and reassuring. She never gave up hope that all would soon be well, and Elizabeth felt comforted by that.

Time was beginning to drag. The adults left the girls much to themselves. Elizabeth and Mary would have liked to play with baby Ned, but he was often asleep. They grew bored with the few toys they had with them and weary of devising new games. Elizabeth longed for all the fine playthings that had been left behind at the Tower and Westminster. Christmas passed with muted celebrations, although the women did their best to make merry for the children's sake, and Master Gould delivered a fine goose for their table, while the Abbot gave them a plum pudding. In February, Elizabeth had her fifth birthday, and the monks baked her a cake. These were bright interludes in a monotonous existence. Eventually, though, the evenings began to draw out, and it was spring.

Abbot Milling regularly brought them news of events in the outside world. Having many friends in high places, he was well informed, and he had heard that the Duke of Burgundy, who had married Aunt Margaret, was helping King Edward to gather a fleet. But how reliable this information was, no one could say.

Then, one day in April, Father Abbot arrived in the Jerusalem Chamber with a broad smile on his face. "Your Grace, I have the best of news. The King has invaded and England is falling to him shire by shire. Gloucester and Earl Rivers march with him and the people are flocking to his banner!"

Mother's face was transformed, radiant. "God be praised! This is what I have prayed for."

"He has wrought a great work," the Abbot said.

"Father is coming home!" sang Elizabeth, as she and Mary joined hands and danced for joy around the room.

"I never lost faith that he would," Grandmother chimed in. "And I rejoice to know that my son Rivers is with the King."

"We must pray for a happy and peaceful outcome to this conflict, once and for all," the Abbot said. "But I think this news calls for a celebration. I will send you a ewer of my best Rhenish."

The next day, he returned.

"More excellent tidings, Madam. My lord of Clarence has abandoned Warwick and made peace with the King. And I have received from his Grace a very comfortable message for you. He bids you be of good cheer, for he means to prevail over his enemies."

Mother's face lit up again as she hugged her daughters. "God willing, we shall soon be reunited with your father. And, Father Abbot, we shall be a burden on you no longer."

He shook his head. "You have never been that. It has been an honor to shelter you in these difficult times."

When he had gone, Mother's smile slipped. "I shall never forgive Clarence for what he has done to us. Edward may have made peace with him, and I shall put on a friendly face for his sake, but I will never see Clarence as anything but an enemy."

Elizabeth didn't think she could forgive Uncle Clarence either.

Father marched into London two days later at the head of a great army, and no one stopped him. Gathered with her family in the Jerusalem Chamber, Elizabeth listened excitedly as the Abbot related how the King had entered St. Paul's Cathedral and reclaimed his throne.

"The people were rejoicing around him. He has them all at his feet. Truly, the hand of God is in this."

"Where is Warwick?" Mother asked.

"Fled! And poor Henry of Lancaster is back in the Tower. It

seems that King Edward means to be lenient. Henry is to be pitied, for he has not his wits about him and has been used by un-
scrupulous men for their own ends."

"I will pray for him," Grandmother said. "He was ever an innocent soul, even before his madness came upon him."

"The King will be here tomorrow," the Abbot said. "He will
come first to the abbey to give thanks for his restoration, and then
he will send for your Graces. I suggest that you start gathering
your belongings together."

In the morning, the Lord Chamberlain arrived at the Abbot's
house with some of Mother's ladies in attendance, their arms laden
with regal attire for the Queen and her children. Elizabeth was
jumping up and down when she was told that they were shortly
to be escorted to the palace of Westminster. It was wonderful to
be going home!

The large crowds gathered outside the abbey cheered loudly
when Mother, carrying the Prince in her arms, emerged from the
cloisters and led her daughters toward the palace. Elizabeth was
wearing her favorite crimson velvet gown, although it was tight,
for she had grown in the months since she had last worn it. She
smiled and waved at the people, feeling as if she was walking on
air, and they roared back, calling down blessings on her.

When they entered the palace and approached the White Hall,
the trumpets sounded. And there was Father, dressed in cloth of
gold and seated on his throne, a great triumphant grin on his
handsome face. As they walked toward him, through the ranks of
bobbing lords and ladies, he rose to greet them. Mother began to
curtsey, but he stepped forward and raised her up, staring in wonder at the babe in her arms.

"My son!" he said, awed. "My darling, you could not have given
me a better welcome-home gift. It is the greatest joy to see you,
and our princesses. I have missed you greatly."

"And I you, my lord." The Queen's voice faltered, and tears
streamed down her face. Father drew her into his arms.

"It is over now, Beth. We can look forward to a glorious future. We have a fair son, to our hearts' comfort and gladness. He is God's precious gift, and my most desired treasure."

He released Mother and bent to kiss Elizabeth and Mary tenderly, then Cecily, who was crowing in Grandmother's arms. "How you have all grown!" he remarked. "I'll have to find husbands for you all soon, won't I?" Elizabeth gazed up at him, hardly able to believe that her father, this tall, magnificent man with his glossy tawny hair and dazzling smile, was really here.

He returned her gaze. "My Bessy," he said. "You are dearer to me than ever." Patting her head, he turned to the Queen and took the baby from her.

"My lords and ladies, I present to you Edward, Prince of Wales, your future king!" he announced, to a resounding ovation. Elizabeth looked around her, thrilling to the sound. There was her uncle, the slight, dark-haired Duke of Gloucester, smiling broadly; having suffered exile with the King, he was now in the highest favor. There too was Uncle Rivers, Mother's debonair brother Anthony, beaming and clapping. And there was Uncle Clarence, the smile fixed on his face, as if he was putting it on. Elizabeth hoped he felt ashamed of himself and had learned his lesson, for Father had been truly merciful to him. But she would not think of his treachery now. They were all back together, the world had righted itself, and the future was beckoning.

Later that day, in the King's private closet, Elizabeth and Mary played on the floor with the toys they had joyfully retrieved from their coffers, while their parents sat talking, holding hands, and exchanging the occasional kiss. They were blissfully joyful to be reunited, and Mother looked so much happier.

"I intend to reward Abbot Milling for his kindness to you," Father said.

"He deserves it," Mother said. "I don't know how I would have got through these past months without him. People were so kind to us. That butcher, Master Gould, kept us well fed for five months at his own expense."

"He shall be rewarded, too, and those who attended you in childbed, my love."

Mother leaned forward and kissed him. "And I, my lord, by your leave, will found a chapel in Westminster Abbey and dedicate it to St. Erasmus, the protector of women in childbirth, in gratitude for the safe delivery of our son."

"By all means," Father beamed. "And now, we should depart for the City, and Baynard's Castle. My mother will be anxious to see us."

"She will be relieved that this nightmare is over."

Father paused, his face suddenly serious. "It's not over yet. Warwick is out there somewhere and must be dealt with. I've had news that Margaret is on her way from France with an army, and she too must be vanquished. Only then will I be safe on my throne."

Elizabeth looked up from her skittles and was disturbed to see the look of alarm on her mother's face. Would there be more fighting? She was terrified to think of what would become of them all if Father lost.

After rising from her curtsey to the King, Cecily Neville, Duchess of York, embraced him warmly. "You have come back safely to me, my son," she said, and kissed him, unable to stem her tears. Then she held out her arms.

"My dear children!" she smiled, and Elizabeth and Mary ran to her. She was a more regal figure than Grandmother Rivers, and very grand and correct, yet she always unbent when she saw them.

"Now, go and look in the chest over there, and you might find something for your pleasure," she said. She always had treats secreted away for them, be it coins, comfits, or trinkets. Today, there was a gold pendant for each of them; Elizabeth's was set with amber, Mary's with a beryl. They thanked her joyfully.

The Duchess inspected baby Ned, who stared up uncertainly at her black-veiled head. "See how strong he is!" she remarked. "What a king he will make."

She bade Elizabeth and Mary go off and play, and they found themselves enjoying their first taste of freedom in ages, racing from room to room of the cavernous Baynard's Castle, playing tag, then looking down on the Thames from the battlements, watched over by a sturdy groom.

The next day was Good Friday, and they found it hard to sit still through the solemnities in chapel, even with Grandmother watching them like a hawk. She was very devout and expected her grandchildren to be, too. Elizabeth wondered what she thought about Clarence siding with Warwick. Had she forgiven him as heartily as Father had? It must have grieved her to see her sons bitterly at odds with each other.

That afternoon, the King summoned his lords to a council at Baynard's Castle. Afterward, Mother interrupted the children as they played with their poppets.

"Make haste, girls. Your father has commanded us to remove to the Tower of London. He wants to leave us in safety there while he rides north to deal with Warwick."

Elizabeth hated to think of Father going off to war again. As she helped Mistress Jakes to pack their traveling chests, she wished with all her might that he could stay with them. Their time together had been all too short. When it came to bidding him farewell on the jetty, she put on a brave face, as befitted a princess, and tried not to cry. But she could not help herself. Seeing her distress, he swung her up in his arms and kissed her tears away.

"Look after your little brother," he said. "I will return soon, never doubt it."

As Mother led her away to the waiting barge, Elizabeth twisted her head back and waved, wishing to keep the memory of Father's smiling face in her heart.

Both grandmothers accompanied them to the Tower, with the venerable Cardinal Thomas Bourchier, Archbishop of Canterbury, who had been charged to keep them all safe. And there, waiting for them in the Queen's lodgings, was Lady Berners, whom Mother had summoned as soon as she left sanctuary. Elizabeth flung her arms around her beloved lady mistress, who had been an ever-constant and reassuring presence for as long as she could remember. If Lady Berners had been with them in sanctuary, she knew she would not have felt so frightened.

The royal apartments in the Tower were older and not as palatial as those at Westminster, but they had bright wall paintings and a garden outside. As they waited impatiently for news, Elizabeth and Mary romped in the spring sunshine. Cecily toddled after them, trying in vain to keep up, while Avice Welles, Ned's wet nurse, sat on a bench, feeding him, and keeping an eye on his sisters.

They did not have long to live in trepidation. On Easter Sunday, Elizabeth was thrilled to see excited, mud-spattered messengers bringing the Queen tidings of a great battle at Barnet, north of London.

"The King is victorious!" they said, as the women and children clustered around. "Warwick is slain!"

Mother crossed herself. "So falls the mighty Kingmaker, our great enemy."

"The King is riding west, Madam, for Queen Margaret and her son have invaded and it is bruited that she means to cross the Severn to Wales and join forces with Jasper Tudor."

"That rebel!" Mother muttered. "Those Tudors are forever making trouble. Welsh upstarts! I pray that my lord intercepts Margaret before she reaches the Severn. May God keep him safe." Elizabeth silently echoed that prayer. Queen Margaret had often haunted her dreams as a terrifying specter intent on crushing Father and bringing the House of York to ruin. And her son, Edward of Lancaster, was a nasty young man, judging by the gossip she had overheard. Elizabeth wondered if his wife, Warwick's younger daughter Anne, had come to England with him. She could not help thinking badly of Anne for agreeing to marry him, although she knew that it was fathers and mothers who chose husbands for their children. At least, this time, Uncle Clarence was fighting for Father, alongside Uncle Gloucester.

They endured three anxious weeks before they heard of the King's triumph at Tewkesbury.

"It was a savage battle, your Grace," the messenger reported, "but Edward of Lancaster lies dead in the field and Margaret is taken prisoner. The King is on his way back to London."

Elizabeth felt a pang of sorrow for Margaret, who had lost everything. She saw Mother snatch up an outraged Ned from his cradle, as if she was imagining the horror of losing a precious child. Then she collected herself and turned to them, her eyes shining. "Praise be to God!" she breathed, as Grandmother Rivers hugged her and Grandmother York crossed herself and bent her head in prayer.

Elizabeth turned to Mary. "Isn't it wonderful news? Father is coming home!" She was dancing for joy.

The joy was short-lived. The next day, Mother looked up from her sewing. "What's that noise?" She rose and peered out of the window of her great chamber, which overlooked the Thames. "God save us!" she cried.

Elizabeth, who had been hosting a feast for the poppets, jumped up and joined her grandmothers, who had dropped their embroidery and hastened to the windows. Upstream, before London Bridge, were assembled numerous ships packed with great multitudes of men.

"That's the Bastard of Fauconberg's flag," Mother said in a strangled voice. "He is one of Margaret's most zealous supporters. Dear God, what is he about?"

She summoned the Lieutenant of the Tower, who came hurrying.

"Madam, I am aware of the danger. When the first ships appeared, I sent out scouts to discover what was going on. They heard Fauconberg boasting that he has come to dethrone King Edward and restore Henry of Lancaster."

"How dare he!" Mother cried. "Doesn't he know that the Lancastrian cause is lost?"

"We will resist them, Madam," the Lieutenant vowed, "but there are thousands of soldiers in those ships. The captains here think there must be mercenaries and pirates among them—the usual troublemakers. I fear that the fury of these malignants will not be easily repelled, but we may have time on our side, for it seems they are poised to attack London before they attempt the Tower."

Elizabeth began wailing in terror. Lady Berners put a hand on her shoulder. "We are safe here, child," she said.

"Never fear, my lady Princess," the Lieutenant assured her. "The citizens have closed the gates and are building barricades. The Lord Mayor has sent to say that he has dispatched fast riders to the King, urging him to come in all possible haste to the defense of the City and your Graces."

"Until then, we stand in the greatest jeopardy that ever was," Mother faltered. "The Bastard of Fauconberg will surely attempt the Tower, for King Henry is here."

Elizabeth froze. Lady Berners had said that they were safe! Now Mother was saying they were in danger. Who should she believe?

She was relieved to see that the Lieutenant seemed calm. "First, Madam, Fauconberg must breach London's defenses, for he who takes the capital takes the realm. I shall go now and order our defenses. We have a strong force here and are well stocked with ordnance. Do not worry."

Despite his brave words, they found themselves tense as bowstrings, awaiting news.

"It is always the lot of women to sit at home and wait," Mother fretted. "I wish I was a man and could be out there doing something."

"That would strike fear into them," Grandmother Rivers smiled.

"We must put our trust in God," Grandmother York said. "I am going to the chapel to pray."

"And I," said Mother, "am going to speak with Henry of Lancaster."

"What?" both older women chorused.

"I am going to make him see sense and order the Bastard to desist, to avoid bloodshed."

"I hope he has his wits about him," Grandmother York said, "but I fear you will be wasting your time."

"It is worth a try," Mother said, and summoned the Lieutenant again. He looked dismayed and tried to dissuade her, but she insisted. "Pray bring him here."

Presently, as Elizabeth watched warily, four men-at-arms arrived, escorting a shuffling figure in a dusty black gown. So this was Henry of Lancaster, her father's arch-enemy and rival. How pitiful he looked, with his straggly gray hair, gaunt features and eyes that darted nervously here and there—eyes that seemed strangely empty. He gave the Queen an uncertain smile, in which there was no more guile than in baby Ned's gummy grins, and Elizabeth saw that there was no harm in him.

Evidently, Mother thought the same, for her voice was gentle when she addressed him. "Sir Henry of Lancaster, your supporters are intent on attacking London and we all stand in great peril. Will you help us to repel them? A word from you might tip the scales."

Henry was looking about him. "Where is Margaret?"

"She is on her way here," Mother said.

"Is she with Warwick?"

"No, Sir Henry. Warwick is dead."

"I'm dead, too," the flat voice quavered. "Are you an angel?"

Elizabeth stared at the poor man. How could he be dead?

The Queen sighed. "Sir Henry, do you understand? There are multitudes outside who are bent on taking London in your name. Will you ask them to stop?"

He stared at her blankly. She shook her head, defeated.

"Take him back," she instructed the guards. Elizabeth watched the stooped figure walk off meekly between his jailers.

Mother could not keep away from the windows. The other women kept trying to shoo the girls away, but they were so preoccupied with what was happening outside that they soon gave up. Elizabeth spent hours with her nose pressed to the diamond panes.

"What's happening?" Mary's blue eyes were wide with fear. "I can't see." She was too little to look out.

"They are putting cannon on the Surrey bank," Elizabeth told her, fighting down panic. "Mother, why are they doing that?"

"The cannon aren't facing the Tower," Mother said. "It looks as if they are going to bombard the City."

And when they had taken that, they would turn their sights to the Tower. Elizabeth was tense with fear. What would become of them all? Were the Tower walls stout enough to protect them?

Soon, they saw smoke billowing.

"They've fired the bridge!" Grandmother Rivers cried. Elizabeth stared as the flames took hold and London Bridge began to burn. It was a fearsome sight, but not as terrifying as the deafening blasts of the cannon.

"They are aiming at Aldgate and Bishopsgate!" Mother shouted above the din, drawing her daughters close. Elizabeth clapped her hands to her ears and Mary started to wail. Soon, she, Cecily, and Ned were howling in unison, and the women had all to do to comfort them.

Elizabeth would not be dragged from the window. Horrified, she watched the furious assaults of the besiegers. But God had given the Londoners stout hearts and it was cheering to see them bravely defending their bridge.

The Bastard was clever, she saw. He sailed his ships down the Thames and began unloading multitudes of men right below her, on the Tower wharf. She ran screaming to the Queen, who was trying to calm the baby. Struck dumb by fear, Elizabeth could only tug at her mother's skirts and gesture at the window. And then there came even louder explosions as the cannon from the Tower thundered out in response to the attack. The noise was ear-shattering.

Thrusting Ned into Lady Berners's arms, the Queen ran to the casement. "Dear Mother of God, they're here! And I can see flames. They must have fired buildings nearby."

Elizabeth looked up at her elders. Fear was writ large on every face. Grandmother York began to say her rosary. But then there issued loud booms from the direction of Aldgate. The Londoners were fighting back with their great artillery! Before long, to everyone's astonishment and thankfulness, many of Fauconberg's men jumped into their boats and sailed away.

Elizabeth clung to her mother. Never, ever would she forget

this horrible day. Even now, there was fighting outside, and their ears were assailed by shouts and screams.

"Look! Anthony's come to the rescue!" Grandmother Rivers cried. They hurried to that window and saw below them Uncle Rivers and the Lieutenant of the Tower on their great destriers, leading a large force of men through the outer ward.

"They are going to the defense of the City," Grandmother breathed.

Uncle Rivers looked quite magnificent in his silver armor. Mother always said he was the perfect knight and embodied all the virtues of chivalry. If anyone could save London, it was he. Soon, there came more sounds of battle, fiercer this time, but gradually dying away.

They looked at each other. "Is it really over?" Mother whispered. Elizabeth hardly dared hope. She would have given anything to know what was happening out there. But everything remained quiet.

After what seemed like hours, Uncle Rivers and the Lieutenant and their men came clattering back, and presently they were shown into the Queen's chamber, all of them in a noisy good humor.

"The Bastard has fled," Uncle told them. "We chased his rebels as far as Stepney." He grinned. "I think we have cause for rejoicing, dear sister." He turned to the Lieutenant. "Some wine for everyone, I think! We have much to celebrate, and I am heartily relieved that his Grace will return to find his family safe."

He bent down to Elizabeth. "You've been very brave, my special girl!" How handsome he was, and how gallant! She owed her life to him. Her heart overflowed with love and gratitude.

Father was back! After six days of willing him to come, Elizabeth stood in the large bay window of the house in Cheapside from where the Queen and the ladies were watching the procession. She was bobbing up and down with impatience. The bells of London's churches were ringing out joyfully, and in the street below the excited crowds were packed tightly; all around, people were leaning out of windows hung with tapestries and painted cloths. When the clamor swelled to a roar, she craned out to see the King approaching—and there he was, looking like a god on his white charger, his breastplate gleaming and the crown on his helm catching the sunlight. Smiling broadly, he raised his hand to acknowledge the cheers, and bowed in the saddle when he saw his Queen and his children at the window. All too soon, he was gone, but there were the ranks of soldiers marching behind him still to cheer.

Suddenly, Elizabeth's attention was drawn to a black-clad woman sitting in a chariot surrounded by men-at-arms. Her face taut and ravaged, she was staring ahead, as if oblivious to the crowds around her.

"Margaret," Mother said grimly. So, this was the wicked Queen who had dared to raise arms against Father. How humiliated she must feel to be paraded, a captive, through London in shame.

"What will happen to her?" Elizabeth asked.

"Your father has been merciful," Mother said. "She will be sent home to France, which is more than she deserves. And good riddance!"

Elizabeth could not help feeling a little bit sorry for Margaret, for she had just lost her son in battle, and it was unlikely that she would ever see her lord again. "Where's Anne Neville?" she asked.

"I have no idea," the Queen replied.

When the procession ended, they rode to Westminster, where the King hosted a feast to celebrate his victory. It was wonderful to be back in the rambling old palace that sprawled along the north shore of the Thames. Elizabeth had been overjoyed to see once more the vast great hall, the soaring spires of St. Stephen's Chapel, the great towers and the new ranges of royal lodgings—all dear and familiar to her.

She was allowed to stay up and attend the feast, and wore her gold damask gown with the high waist and tight sleeves. She sat at the high table, feeling very important and enjoying the rich dishes offered her, which were much nicer than those served in the nursery. Next to her, lower down the table, Aunt Suffolk, Father's sister, who looked so like him, sat with Lord Stanley, a very rich northern baron. He was hearty and jovial, and very patient with a little girl who was doing her best to join in the adult conversation; and Aunt Suffolk was, as ever, kind and encouraging. But Father seemed preoccupied. Every time Elizabeth looked his way, he was deep in conversation with Uncle Gloucester and the Chamberlain, the florid-faced, genial Lord Hastings, his great friend and councillor. Before the meal was over, the three of them rose, bowed to the Queen, and took their leave. Mother looked disconcerted, but she continued to reminisce on the day's events with Grandmother York.

Elizabeth stifled a yawn. When Lady Berners came to take her to bed, she curtseyed to her mother and gratefully allowed herself to be led away. As she passed, she heard the Queen murmur to Grandmother, "It is for the best. He has no choice."

It was grown-up talk and meant nothing to her. But, over the next few days, which she spent with her siblings in the nursery and the Queen's privy garden, she became aware of adults talking in whispers, and of conversations abruptly ended when she drew near. She took to listening intently while she was playing, pretending to be absorbed in the game, and eavesdropping when the nurses were chatting and thought she was out of earshot. And that was how she found out that Henry of Lancaster was dead.

"It's all very mysterious," Mistress Jakes said. "They say my lord of Gloucester was at the Tower when it happened."

"Do you believe what was proclaimed, that Henry died of pure displeasure when he learned of the death of his son and the capture of his wife?" That was Lady Berners.

There was a pause. "It's possible. I knew of a man who dropped dead when they told him his wife had been run over by a cart."

"I do wonder, though. I heard that when Henry's body was displayed at St. Paul's Cathedral in his coffin, the blood was seeping through the boards onto the pavement. That sounds odd to me, as corpses don't bleed. But it would be wrong to draw conclusions. Remember who we serve."

"I do. But I can't help wondering if someone chose to crush the seed."

"I think we should change the subject," Lady Berners said, and they fell to discussing new clothes for Ned, for when he was out of his swaddling bands.

That poor madman, Elizabeth was thinking. Perhaps he was happy to depart his sad life and go to Heaven, but that bit about his bleeding on the pavement was horrible. She didn't understand what Lady Berners had meant, or why Uncle Gloucester had been at the Tower when Henry died, or Mistress Jakes's remark about crushing the seed.

"What does seed mean?" she asked Mother when she sought her blessing that evening.

"It is a grain that is sown, from which a plant or flower grows," Mother told her. Elizabeth was puzzled. That made no sense at all.

She would have liked to talk to Uncle Gloucester about it. He would surely be able to tell her what had happened in the Tower. But he never visited the Queen's chamber, at least not when Elizabeth was there, so she bided her time.

Her moment came when the King took a pleasure jaunt on the river with his family, all of them crammed into the luxuriously upholstered state-house of the royal barge, even little Ned. Mother allowed Elizabeth and Mary to go outside on deck, and Uncle Gloucester said he would keep an eye on them. They stood watching the other boats go past and marveling at the sights of London. It was so calm and peaceful after the terrible fighting of a few weeks ago. Elizabeth still shuddered to think of that.

The boat began rocking as it approached London Bridge, where the water was choppy. She saw Uncle Gloucester steady himself, and remembered that he had a crooked back, which he hid so well that no one could perceive his affliction, and which had not stopped him fighting bravely in battle.

A little later, she seized her moment. "Uncle, were you with Henry of Lancaster when he died in the Tower?"

He stared at her, frowning. "No, I was not, Bessy. Why do you ask?"

"I heard someone say that you were there."

"I was in the Tower, but on the King's business." Her eyes searched his serious face with the jutting chin, beak-like nose, and dark eyes. She knew he would not lie to her. He had always been loyal to Father and had shared his exile. Father said he had a sharp courage, high and fierce, and that there was no one he trusted more.

"I felt sorry for Henry of Lancaster," she said. "He was mad."

"He was, and he died of grief," Uncle Gloucester told her. "This war between York and Lancaster has taken a dreadful toll. When I was young, Warwick was as a father to me, especially after my own father was killed at the Battle of Wakefield. That was before you were born. But Warwick betrayed the King and our family. It was he who was responsible for all the recent bloodshed." He fixed his gaze on the shore, frowning. "It is as well that God took Henry of Lancaster when he did. A deposed king will always be a threat to his successor and a focus for rebellion." He smiled at her reassuringly. "But let us not dwell on sad matters, Bessy. You should be enjoying our day out. Look there, there's Placentia!" He pointed to the beautiful palace on the Thames shore at Greenwich.

Life had resumed its pleasant course. Father was back firmly on his throne, with his enemies defeated, never to rise again. And Mother's belly was swelling with another child.

Ned now had his own household within the palace, including a chamberlain, Master Vaughan, who carried him in public, and a chaplain, the mild-mannered Uncle Lionel, Mother's younger brother. In July, Elizabeth was present when the King formally created Ned prince of Wales and made his lords swear an oath of loyalty to him as his undoubted son and heir. She watched in pride as, led by Clarence and Gloucester, the nobility came forward one by one and paid homage.

By December, Ned had learned to walk. He was tottering toward Elizabeth's outstretched arms when Lady Berners arrived with a letter addressed to her. "The Queen says you may open it."

Elizabeth broke the plain seal. She could not yet read, so she handed the letter to the lady mistress.

"It's from the Countess of Warwick," Lady Berners said, her smile vanishing. "She begs you to intercede with the King on her behalf, for she claims that he and my lords of Clarence and

Gloucester have stolen her lands. Bessy, I think this should be shown to his Grace."

"I want to give it to him," Elizabeth said, inquisitive to know the story behind the letter.

"Very well," Lady Berners said.

Elizabeth handed Father the letter when he visited them after Vespers. Standing beside his chair, she watched his face darken as he read it. "She is a foolish woman and had no right to approach you, Bessy." He drew her onto his damask-clad knee. "I did not steal her lands. Her husband died a traitor, and she has been in sanctuary ever since. Warwick's vast lands should pass to his two daughters. I have allowed Uncle Clarence to take control of them, since he is married to Isabel. Uncle Gloucester wants to marry Anne now that she is widowed and, when that happens, I have ordered that the Warwick estates be divided between my brothers."

"But what of my lady of Warwick?" Elizabeth pitied her, for she knew how dreary life in sanctuary could be.

"Parliament will declare her legally dead, so that her daughters can inherit."

Elizabeth looked up at the King, troubled that someone could be declared dead when they weren't.

"She will not be left destitute," he assured her.

"So when is Uncle Gloucester going to marry Anne Neville?"

Father sighed. "That's a good question, Bessy. The problem is that she has disappeared. No one knows where she is."

"I suspect that Clarence does," Mother chimed in, stabbing her needle into her embroidery tambour.

"He denies it," the King countered.

"But who has the most to lose if Gloucester marries Anne? Clarence wants to keep the whole inheritance for himself."

"He would hardly go so far as to hide her away."

Mother looked exasperated. "My lord, you should learn to take a more realistic view of your brother. You were far too lenient when he treacherously supported Warwick. And he hates me and mine. He thinks my family jumped-up parvenus, and always has."

"I think this is a conversation that can wait until later," Father said, setting Elizabeth on the floor. "I expect you're looking forward to Christmas, Bessy. We're keeping it here at Westminster and there will be games and disguisings and banquets and mummings. I'm planning a fabulous celebration to make up for last year."

Elizabeth clapped her hands. "I can't wait!" she cried. But, when she lay wakeful in bed that night, it was not because of the coming Yuletide, but because she could not stop wondering where Anne Neville might be.

Chapter 3

1472—1475

Father often spoke of the splendors of Bruges, where he had spent his exile as a guest of the Duke of Burgundy. It was Burgundy this and Burgundy that, and Elizabeth soon learned that the Burgundian court led Christendom in magnificence as in art and fashion and manners.

Determined not to be outshone, Father spent lavishly on his own court, wanting to impress his subjects and foreign visitors with its splendor. Elizabeth became used to seeing workmen making endless improvements at Westminster and other royal palaces, rebuilding in the new red brick so favored in Burgundy, gilding paneling, installing stained glass, putting up exquisite tapestries, and hanging paintings by Flemish masters. Father was spending fortunes on the trappings of majesty, especially on extravagant clothes, costly jewels, and a sumptuous table. It thrilled Elizabeth to see it all, and she vowed to herself that if she ever married a king or a great prince, she would have a court such as this.

Wherever the court was in residence, she watched her father as he sat in state or moved effortlessly among his courtiers, ever genial and approachable. The common touch came naturally to him. She loved it when, seeing a man overawed by his royal magnificence, the King gave him courage to speak by laying a kindly hand upon his shoulder. She knew that, when roused to anger, Father could appear terrible to those who had offended him, but never to his children. And he often showed great tenderness toward Mother.

One day in early spring, Mother came to the nursery at Westminster and, great with child, eased herself down on the bench beside her. "You are six now, Bessy, and it is time for your education to begin. You must learn how to be the wife of a great prince, and all the accomplishments that become a queen. We will start with the most important things, which are honesty and chastity, qualities much admired by men." She launched into a long homily about what was expected of a young lady. "You must carry yourself with dignity, with a straight back and your eyes modestly lowered. There must be no more running in the palace."

That was to prove harder than Elizabeth had expected. She frequently forgot that she must not run or skip, as she had done freely up until now. Lady Berners often had cause to reprove her and constantly enjoined her to follow the example of her mother, who was the epitome of queenly deportment.

Lady Berners took some of the lessons, but it was Mother who taught Elizabeth to read and write. "You are fortunate, Bessy," Lady Berners told her. "In my day, it was frowned upon for a woman to know her letters. People feared it might lead to light behavior, such as writing love letters. But my father, God be thanked, was forward in his thinking, and now it is becoming accepted that an educated woman can still be a virtuous woman. Being able to read and write will equip you with the skills needed to run castles and palaces. You can write your own letters and your mind will be broadened by reading books."

Elizabeth had always been fascinated by books. Mother had regularly shown her some of the beautiful manuscripts in the royal library, and she had been captivated by the illuminated miniatures in them and the borders decorated with fantastic beasts and pretty flowers. Soon, she could read a lot of the words herself. It was a joy to enter the world of King Arthur, or discover the stirring story of St. George, England's patron saint, who had rescued a doomed princess from a horrible dragon.

Her lessons were not all from books. She spent time observing her mother ordering the servants and dealing with the officers who assisted her in her great responsibilities. She learned her numbers quickly so that when she grew up, she would be able to check her accounts. She had lessons in dancing, music, and needlework, and was allowed some leisure for play. Most days, she rode her pony, Galahad, with a groom in attendance. She loved being out in the park, letting her mount carry her away, the fresh air blowing her hair in all directions. Even though memories of past troubles sometimes invaded her dreams, she gave little thought to them in her waking moments. Life was peaceful now.

They were at Windsor Castle when, in April, Mother gave birth to a very pretty daughter called Margaret, after Aunt Margaret, the Duchess of Burgundy. Elizabeth fell in love instantly with her new sister, and she, Mary, and three-year-old Cecily made a great fuss of her, passing her from one to the other like a doll, and squabbling over who should hold her. Young Ned was a little put out at being displaced as the baby of the family, but he was more interested in roaring around on his wooden horse and wielding a toy sword than in petting a mewling, swaddled bundle.

Elizabeth remained intrigued by Anne Neville's disappearance. She could not comprehend how a great heiress could just vanish. Uncle Gloucester had never stopped searching for Anne. He was convinced that Uncle Clarence had secreted her away in one of his country manors, but all his inquiries—and, it was said, his bribing of his brother's servants—had come to naught.

"But then Fortune favored me," he told Father, and Elizabeth's ears pricked up as she played with Mary in the King's privy garden on the first warm day of spring. Mother was still lying in, and Lady Berners was maintaining a discreet distance from the royal brothers, who were seated on a stone bench, the King large and splendid in tawny velvet, Uncle Gloucester slight and pale-faced in black, but looking unusually exuberant.

"It occurred to me," he said, "that Clarence might be hiding Anne in his house in London. I went there this morning when I knew he was at court; I said I had come to collect some books I had lent him. His steward let me in, and I looked in all the rooms, pretending I could not find the books. But there was no sign of Anne. Then I went down to the service quarters, the only place I had not searched, although by then I had given up. I said I was thirsty and asked for a flagon of ale. It was busy; they were cooking dinner. By a stroke of luck, I saw this cook-maid chopping onions. She was gazing at me as if I was the Savior come again—and it was Anne. I could hardly believe it."

Father looked furious. "A sorry thing it is when one of the greatest heiresses in the kingdom is treated like a kitchen wench."

"I was outraged." Gloucester became animated. "I turned to the steward and said that the young lady was coming with me. He made some protest about asking Clarence's permission first, but I said that I would clear it with my brother. I just took Anne by the hand and led her out. When we were in the street, with my men-at-arms surrounding us, she burst into tears, thanking me over and over. I took her to the sanctuary at St. Martin-le-Grand, and there she lies still. Ned, I want to marry her as soon as I can obtain a dispensation from the Pope. As you know, we are closely related."

"And you shall marry her, and receive her lands." Father still sounded angry. "I intend to have words with Clarence, and there's no time like the present." He rose, his face like thunder.

The Lord Chamberlain appeared. "Your Grace, my lord of Clarence is craving an audience. He says it's urgent."

"Indeed, it is!" Father said grimly. "Bring him to me. Lady Berners, please take the princesses to the nursery."

But then Uncle Clarence appeared, his face red with fury. "What gave you the right to force yourself into my household?" he spat at Uncle Gloucester.

"Come now," Lady Berners said, pulling Elizabeth and Mary away, not even bidding them curtsey to the King. As she hurried them into the palace, they could hear angry shouting behind them. Father would win the argument, of course. He was the King, and none dared gainsay him, although it sounded as if Uncle Clarence was doing his best.

When Elizabeth next saw Uncle Gloucester, at Mother's churching, he winked at her. After the feast, she asked the King if her uncle was to marry Anne Neville.

"He is indeed, Bessy," he told her. "The Warwick estates will be divided between your uncles." No wonder Uncle Clarence had looked fit to explode!

The family gathered in the soaring glory of St. Stephen's Chapel at Westminster for the wedding, Elizabeth, Mary, and Cecily in matching gowns of grass-green velvet with laced bodices, black velvet cuffs, and gold chains, their hair loose as became young maidens. They stood at the front of the chapel, feeling very important among the noble throng of lords and ladies; even little Cecily tried not to fidget during the long nuptial Mass.

Elizabeth was excited to have a new aunt. Anne Neville was slender and quite beautiful, with full lips, wide eyes, and a cascade of russet hair. After the way Uncle Clarence had tried to deprive him of his bride and her inheritance, Uncle Gloucester deserved to be happy. And he did look so, smiling at Anne. The only sadness was that they would be moving to the north, where she owned many great castles, which were all Uncle Gloucester's now, of course. Elizabeth would be sorry to see them go.

There was no sign of Uncle Clarence and Aunt Isabel; they had pointedly missed the wedding and flounced off to their estates in the West Country. Elizabeth thought they were silly. Even Cecily would behave better than that!

At the end of May, Mother came into the nursery with a sad smile on her face and drew her children to her.

"Grandmother Rivers has gone to be with our heavenly Father," she said, the glint of a tear in her eye.

"Is she coming back?" Cecily lisped.

"No, sweeting. But one day we will all be together in Heaven, reunited in Christ."

Cecily looked none the wiser, but Elizabeth had long understood what death was and explained to her sister that Grandmother had gone to sleep and would never wake up. As the sad days passed, she came to feel her absence more and more. She had loved her grandmother's warm hugs, her wonderful tales of chivalric deeds long past, and her thoughtful gifts. Most of all, she would miss the love that radiated from her. They still had Grandmother York, of course, but she was very proud and a stickler for good and godly behavior. Elizabeth felt bereft.

In September, she was allowed to take part in the great celebrations held at Windsor in honor of the Lord of Gruthuyse, who had offered the King shelter and hospitality in Bruges during his exile. She first met him when Father brought him to the Queen's chamber, where she was playing at marbles and ninepins with Mother and the other ladies.

"Now here's a pleasant sight!" the King observed heartily to his guest, a thin man clad in a brilliant scarlet houppelande and bonnet, who smiled courteously and bent to kiss Mother's hand. When Father led him away for a private talk, a great banquet was laid out in the Queen's apartments, with every comfit, sucket, and sugary confection a child could dream of. Elizabeth stood eyeing it greedily, her mouth watering, until Uncle Rivers pulled her away.

"You may not partake until our guest and the King and Queen have been served," he admonished, although there was a twinkle in his eye. "Come now. You are to be seated at the royal table, so you must be on your very best behavior, my little Lady Princess."

Elizabeth nodded meekly. She would have done anything for Uncle Rivers.

The banquet went on for a long time, but Elizabeth enjoyed gorging herself on the delicious sweetmeats. Much of the adults' talk went over her head, but she joined in the laughter and listened avidly when Father boasted to the Lord of Gruthuyse how he was creating a Burgundian-style court in England, and of his plans to build a new chapel dedicated to St. George at Windsor.

As the evening wore on, Elizabeth began to feel a little sick. Her attention was drawn to the next table, where sat the stolid-looking young Duke of Buckingham and his docile wife, Mother's much younger—and very beautiful—sister Katherine. It was no secret that Buckingham did not like her and felt he had been forced by the King to marry beneath him. He had barely spoken a word to Katherine, but had chatted continuously to Lord Hastings and the other nobles at the table. When the dancing began, it was Elizabeth he asked to partner him. Reviving suddenly, she stepped out on the floor, holding his hand, and performed a *basse* dance without making a single mistake, as Father and Mother looked on approvingly. At the end of the dance, Buckingham made a courtly bow and escorted her back to her seat.

"Bravo, Bessy!" the King cried. And then he himself was whirling her about the room in a circle dance, in which everyone hastened to join. How wonderful it was!

Afterward, Elizabeth and the other ladies followed when the King and Queen did their guest the honor of conducting him to his lodging. She was sorry when she was told that it was time for the ladies to leave because the Lord of Gruthuyse wanted to have a bath.

She could not sleep that night. It had been a marvelous evening and she wanted to go on reliving the memories in her head, so that she could hold them for ever.

Christmas was approaching, and Elizabeth was eagerly anticipating the festivities. She and Mary were planning to stage a Nativity play in the Queen's privy chamber. She was to be St. Joseph, Mary was Our Lady, and baby Margaret the infant Jesus, while Cecily and Ned had been cast as cherubic-looking—and rather unruly—angels. Lady Berners helped them with their costumes and taught them new carols. Elizabeth was hoping that Father would come to watch.

"May I pick up Margaret?" she asked one afternoon in the second week of December, when they were preparing for a rehearsal.

"Yes, Bessy," Lady Berners replied. "If she's still having her nap, just wake her; her nurse won't want her up half the night."

Elizabeth skipped off happily into the bedchamber where her younger siblings slept and leaned over the gilded cradle. Margaret was still asleep, her little auburn head facedown on the pillow. Elizabeth pulled back the velvet counterpane, exposing the swaddled little body. Margaret did not stir. Elizabeth gently turned her over onto her back. The baby's lips were blue and her face had a dusky tinge.

Something was not right. Elizabeth ran into the next chamber.

"Lady Berners, come and look at Margaret. I think she's ill."

The lady mistress hurried to the cradle and took one look at the baby. "No!" she cried, crossing herself. Then she picked up the still infant, sat down and laid her on her lap, rubbing her back over and over.

"Mistress Welles, fetch the Queen!" she barked at the Prince's nurse. "Hurry! You children, out!"

Elizabeth shooed her siblings into the nursery. Her heart was pounding so fast that she could hardly catch her breath. She sank down amid the pile of props and costumes, trying not to cry, as Ned and her sisters regarded her curiously. But Mother was coming. Mother would make everything right again.

Mother arrived within two minutes and flew into the bedchamber. Then Elizabeth heard her howl of distress. "Dear God, not Margaret!"

Elizabeth and Mary stood with their weeping parents and watched the tiny coffin being lowered beneath the altar flagstones of St. Edward the Confessor's Chapel in Westminster Abbey. Father had his arm around Mother, who looked frozen, like an ice queen, white and drawn in her black gown and mourning hood.

Elizabeth had cried and cried since Margaret had been taken from them. She had asked repeatedly why she had died, but no one knew. The baby had not been ill and had taken her milk two hours earlier. "Even the physicians cannot explain it," Lady Berners said, dabbing her eyes.

Christmas went ahead as planned, but it was overshadowed by the tragedy. How could Elizabeth enjoy it when her mother and father looked so sad? The children had not the heart to perform the Nativity play, and no gifts, decorations, festive fare, or games could compensate for their loss. Elizabeth kept seeing that little gray face and wished with all her heart that she could hold Margaret again, just once. But wishing was useless. What good would it do?

In February, in the year of Our Lord 1473, she was taken to see the little altar tomb of gray marble that now stood before St. Edward's glittering shrine in Westminster Abbey. On it lay a shiny new brass showing Margaret as if she was a fully grown child.

"What does it say?" asked Mary, pointing to the inscription.

Father read it aloud: "'Nobility and beauty, grace and tender youth are all hidden here in this chest of death.'" His voice broke. "Children are so very precious. It is a dreadful thing to lose one."

"Compared to some families, we have been lucky," Mother said, "but the pain is unbearable, nonetheless. To have death take a child you have loved and nurtured and protected—it makes you feel so helpless."

She knelt before the tomb, weeping. Presently, Father raised her, and Abbot Milling said Mass. Elizabeth placed her hands together, closed her eyes tight and prayed for Margaret's soul. Surely she would not suffer purgatory for long? She had been too young to be naughty, bless her.

Elizabeth gazed down at the new baby and felt a great swell of love in her heart. He was tiny, but he was thriving.

"Richard," she repeated.

"Richard," her father smiled. "He shall be duke of York, like my father and his forebears, all the way back to Edmund of Langley."

"Who's Edmund of Langley?" she asked.

"The founder of the House of York, sweeting! Your great-great-grandfather. He was the fifth son of King Edward the Third and the first Duke of York. It is a proud title, never forget it. And this little knight will bear it now." He reached out a finger and gently touched his son's cheek as the infant lay in Mother's arms. She smiled up at him.

"The succession is assured, my lord. You have two heirs now."

"The most precious jewels in my crown!" he declared. "You have done me proud, my love."

The baby had come early, before Mother even had a chance to take to her chamber for her confinement. The family were being entertained by the town councillors of Shrewsbury when Mother had surreptitiously put her hand to the small of her back. Elizabeth saw her do it several times, then murmur something in Father's ear.

"Good sirs," he said, rising, "I regret to interrupt this most excellent feast, but the Queen's hour has come upon her sooner than expected."

There was a hurried scraping of chairs and a chorus of farewells, then the King had shepherded his family back to their lodging in the guest house at the Blackfriars. The sheriff's wife hastened after them and told Mother she would send a midwife. Not two hours later, Elizabeth had been summoned to meet her new brother. It was good to see her parents looking happy again.

In the autumn, the Queen took them all into the russet-hued palace garden by the Thames at Westminster and let them run about. Ned was three now, a handsome, sturdy boy with silver-gilt hair like Mother's and an angelic face. He loved to join his sisters in their boisterous games and trailed behind them everywhere. Baby York crowed at them from his nurse's arms.

But now Mother made them all sit down, and Elizabeth was aghast to be told that Ned was to have his own household at Ludlow Castle, near the Welsh border. It sounded so far away. And,

Mother said, he was to be lord president—when he couldn't even say the name—of the newly formed Council of Wales and the Marches. There he stood, smiling happily, uncomprehending of what was about to happen.

"But why, my lady? We want him to stay here," Elizabeth protested.

Mother smiled and drew Ned onto her lap. "Because he must learn how to be a king," she explained, kissing his head. "At Ludlow, he will be schooled in government and taught how to be a virtuous prince. Your father and I will also be sad to see him go, but he will be well looked after, and he could not have a better governor, for your uncle Rivers is being entrusted with his care and education."

Elizabeth was doubly sad to hear that she would be losing her elegantly fashionable uncle, too. She loved to watch him demonstrating his valor in the jousts or hear him speak of his pilgrimages to Rome and the shrine of St. James at Compostela. She was aware that there was a serious side to him. He was kind, just, and pious, and wore a hair shirt beneath his fine clothes, to remind himself of the frailty of the flesh. He had told her that his dearest wish was to go on a crusade against the Infidel. Well, that would have to wait now.

"I myself will be a member of the Prince's council," Mother was saying, "and my kinsmen will be there to serve him. Girls, don't look so sad. You will still see Ned. He will come to court whenever possible and spend all the great feast days with us. Remember that you yourselves will one day make great marriages and leave court, perhaps to live in another kingdom."

It was a sobering thought, and an alarming one. Elizabeth had grown up knowing that she would one day marry a king or a prince, but that was going to happen far in the future. What it might actually mean for her was something she had not considered. Aunt Margaret had been sent abroad to marry the Duke of Burgundy and had not returned to England since. The prospect of never seeing her parents again, or her brothers and sisters, and of leaving England and everything familiar, was horrible. And that it would really happen one day was brought home to her when, not long after the Prince's departure for Ludlow, Mother told her that Cecily was to be wed to the Scottish Prince James.

"He is only two years old, so it won't be for a long time," she said.

"Will I be a queen?" Cecily asked.

"When the Prince becomes king you will, but that won't be for many years yet," Mother said. "In the meantime, you will be brought up here and be called the Princess of Scots." Cecily smiled, showing a gap in her milk teeth. Poor little fool, Elizabeth thought, you would be weeping if you knew what this really meant.

Mother turned to her and Mary. "It is customary, I know, for princesses to be married in order of seniority, but Cecily has been chosen because she is nearest in age to the Prince." There was a pause, in which the Queen looked pained, and Elizabeth knew she was remembering that poor Margaret would have been exactly the same age as James.

In the spring of 1475, the court was at Windsor. The family were all together, apart from Ned, who was far away at Ludlow. He had visited from time to time, but never for long enough. Little York, therefore, had become the pet of his sisters.

Elizabeth had noticed over the past weeks that Father was getting fat. Gone was the glorious young man who had thrown her high in the air and whirled her around when she was little. He no longer participated in sports or jousting, preferring nowadays to go fishing. He ate far too much, that was the problem. She had overheard Lady Berners expressing concern about it and deploring his taking emetics so that he could gorge his stomach once more. Elizabeth was shocked to hear that. But, when she thought about it, she realized that he indulged himself in every way, reveling in the finer things in life—good food, lavish display, rich clothing, jewelry, and court festivals.

Servants loved to gossip about their betters and seemed to think that children were deaf to it. Elizabeth had learned that waiting a pace before passing an open door, or lingering over a flower bed, led to the discovery of all sorts of fascinating gossip. Sometimes, though, she wished she had hurried by. Sitting quietly in the nursery while her ladies tidied the bedchamber next door one morning, she was appalled to hear that Father was not only a glutton but an adulterer, and that everyone knew it.

At nine, she did not know exactly what adultery entailed. She had thought that it meant loving someone who was not your wife, but the tittle-tattle she overheard made her wonder if there was more to it than that.

She learned that her father kept three mistresses. She had understood that a mistress was a lady worshipped by a knight from afar, but that did not chime with the disapproving tone of the gossips, which suggested that there was something unpleasant about it. She could guess who one of these mistresses was, for the name "Shore's wife" kept cropping up. Elizabeth had seen the pretty, diminutive Mistress Shore about the court. For a goldsmith's wife, she was exquisitely dressed, well above her station, but the most memorable things about her were her merry smile, her ready laughter, and her kind eyes. Elizabeth could not comprehend how Father could love someone other than Mother, who was so beautiful; it was not right, but she understood why he liked Mistress Shore. She would not blame Mother if she hated her as much as some gossips said she did; others claimed it was beneath her dignity to notice.

Elizabeth also learned that her half-brothers, Thomas and Dickon Grey, were Father's companions in his debaucheries, whatever that meant, although it didn't sound very nice. Thomas was eleven years older than she was and Father had just created him marquess of Dorset and married him to an heiress, and Dickon had been knighted, but the age gap meant that she wasn't close to either of them. They were wild young men, determined to make their way in the world, and not interested in little girls.

Barging into the linen room in search of a clean kerchief, Elizabeth heard Lady Berners say to Mistress Jakes that the powerful Lord Hastings was the King's companion in crime. They fell silent when they saw her. She liked Lord Hastings, who was a loyal friend to Father, but it was obvious that he did not like the Wydevilles; he and Dorset had quarreled over the ownership of certain lands—and, she had heard, they were rivals for the love of Mistress Shore. "She certainly spreads her favors around," Lady Berners had once muttered. Elizabeth had thought that favors were what you won in games. It was all very mysterious.

She did not like to dwell on these matters. The relentless gossip unsettled her. But more unsettling was the prospect of Father invading France. Talk of war had been simmering for a while and preparations were now under way. He was in a bullish mood, bent on conquest; he would complete the work begun by those great hero-kings, Edward III and Henry V, and take the French throne. All England was praying for another victory such as Crécy or Agincourt. Despite her trepidation, Elizabeth's heart thrilled when she heard the stories of those long-ago battles.

The King finally departed, full of confidence, at the head of his army, and the summer dragged as they waited tensely for news of what was happening in France. When it came, it was not what they had been expecting to hear.

The royal messenger arrived when Elizabeth and Mary were sitting with the Queen in her privy chamber, looking at a beautiful illuminated manuscript of the wondrous tales of King Arthur—thrilling stories of love and chivalry. Elizabeth enjoyed these lessons with Mother, who had inspired her with a thirst for learning and even re-founded Queens' College in Cambridge. If only Mother could be more affectionate and demonstrative. As Elizabeth grew older, the Queen seemed to expect higher and higher standards of behavior and deportment and was becoming increasingly critical. Fortunately, Elizabeth was an avid pupil and did so well at her studies that Mother did bestow on her occasional words of praise, which she valued like manna from Heaven.

The Queen promptly disappeared with the messenger into her closet. When she emerged, her face was radiant.

"The King your father has decided to come to terms with King Louis, who is eager for peace and has offered a huge pension as an inducement."

"So there won't be a war?" Elizabeth asked.

"No, thanks be to God." Mother sat down. "Father is to meet with King Louis in three days. We must pray that they come to a good accord."

The King was home! The royal children stood impatiently with the Queen as they watched him ride triumphantly into the Upper Ward of Windsor Castle, resplendent in gold damask on a horse caparisoned in crimson. He swung himself heavily down from the saddle and embraced them as the courtiers cheered.

"The treaty is signed, and on better terms than I could have dreamed of," he told Mother, as they gathered in his privy chamber. "I have much to tell you."

Seating himself in his high-backed chair, he called for wine and marchpane, then leaned his head back as his fool, the disreputable Scoggin, sidled over and knelt at his feet.

"Going to tell the Queen what you got up to in France?" he murmured, grinning.

"Oh, be off with you!" Father cuffed him good-naturedly, as Mother laughed in a brittle, unsmiling way. Father played with the little ones and made much of York, who was nearly two now. Then he called for Lady Berners to take all the children away except for Elizabeth. "For what I have to say concerns you, Bessy."

Elizabeth felt no stirrings of concern. She sat quiet on her stool as Father turned to Mother. "I met Louis on the bridge of Picquigny; we parleyed through a wooden trellis and hammered out the terms of the treaty. Then peace between England and France was proclaimed."

"You got your pension?" Mother asked.

"Oh, yes. As I said, I have done well out of it. And Bessy, France has never had an English queen, but, to seal this new friendship, you are to be betrothed to King Louis's son, the most illustrious Dauphin Charles. When he succeeds father, you will be queen of France. It is a great destiny and I hope you are pleased that I have arranged such a grand marriage for you."

France? Queen of France? Elizabeth heard Mother's joyful gasp. She was stunned and somewhat appalled, for marriage would mean the end of her happy life in England and, worst of all, leaving those she loved. And yet, deep inside her, excitement bubbled. France was not so very far away, and she would love to be a queen one day.

"I am pleased, Father," she stammered, "but I hope I shall not be leaving you for ages and ages."

"You will go to France in three years' time, when you are twelve and of marriageable age. That will give you time to get accustomed to the idea."

"This is a marvelous match for you," Mother exulted, her eyes sparkling. "What a triumph of diplomacy, my lord! What did you have to concede to bring that old spider to the point?"

"I renounced my claim to Aquitaine in favor of the Dauphin," Edward grinned, "an empty concession, since England lost Aquitaine in the late French wars. It is to be part of Bessy's dower. After your marriage, child, King Louis will assign you an annual income of sixty thousand pounds so that you can be maintained in a manner befitting the future queen of France."

Mother's jaw dropped. "That's fifteen times the dower you settled on me."

Father shrugged. "France is a far wealthier kingdom, my love. Bessy can look forward to a life of luxury."

Elizabeth was still struggling to come to terms with the new future mapped out before her. But three years was a long time, and anything might happen to prevent the marriage. She half wanted it to, yet she also felt a small shock of dismay at the thought of her glorious prospects being snatched away.

"What is the Dauphin like, Father?" she asked.

"He is five years old, so four years younger than you, but he will grow."

"Is he handsome?" she asked.

"I have not seen him," Father replied, "but I have heard good reports of him. We will send for his portrait and then you can see him for yourself."

Elizabeth could not help reveling in being addressed as "Madame la Dauphine" and treated with the honors and deference due to a future queen of France. She squealed with delight when she saw the new gowns in the French fashion spread out on her bed. She was less enamored of being made to work harder on her French lessons.

"You must be fluent," Mother insisted. "What would King Louis think if we sent you to him unable to converse in his tongue?" But Elizabeth struggled; she could memorize words, but stringing them together was beyond her. She feared she would never be fluent.

"Come, Madame la Dauphine," Lady Berners reproved. "You won't work it out staring into space!"

Mother, even more than Father, was overjoyed about the marriage, and bursting with pride. "I have written to King Louis to ask him if he wishes us to send you to France on your twelfth birthday or later that year," she related. Suddenly, three years did not seem all that long and if Elizabeth did go on her birthday, it would be more like two and a half years. She suddenly became aware of time creeping up on her. Wherever she went, whoever she met, she could not stop thinking that, one day, it would be for the last time. This England, this land she loved, would no longer be her home.

"You must learn to be, and think, like a Frenchwoman," Mother exhorted her, "yet you must never forget England's interests." It sounded rather contradictory. Elizabeth had no idea how she would manage it. But she must do her duty; she had been brought up to know what was expected of her.

"A queen ought to be chaste, wise, and well mannered," Lady Berners told her during one of her improving lectures. "Her wisdom must be apparent in deeds and good works, and in what she says. You must never betray any secrets. And you must always be humble and modest." Elizabeth was learning these lessons well. She had stopped romping with her siblings and begun concentrating on carrying herself like a queen. Madame la Dauphine must be dignified and move through life serenely, as her mother did.

"Emulate the Queen!" Lady Berners exhorted. "You could not have a better example before your eyes."

* * *

In the midst of a cold snap in November, Mother gave birth to another fair daughter, Anne. A new nurse, Mistress Butler, appeared in the royal nursery at Sheen, and Elizabeth and Mary were promoted to the Maidens' Hall, a beautiful apartment created at Westminster specially for them. There were sculpted moldings around the windows, bright tapestries on the walls, and a Turkey carpet on the floor of the great chamber.

It was pleasant, sitting at table before a roaring fire, doing lessons with Lady Berners, working on their embroidery, or playing chess and backgammon. Elizabeth allowed herself to cherish the notion that she would never leave England and that she could remain at Westminster, cocooned in this safe and pleasant room where she felt truly happy. She was closer to Mary than to any of her other siblings; being near in age, they naturally gravitated together. They helped each other with their studies, played together endlessly and, at night, often crept into each other's beds to lie there in the darkness and giggle. Elizabeth didn't want to grow up. She wanted to stay like this forever.

A week before Christmas, when they were making New Year's gifts amid a pile of scraps of fabric and ribbons, Lady Berners walked in, carrying a basket of biliments, buttons, and some sparkly oddments.

"You might be able to use these," she said. "The Queen your Mother looked them out for you. There's—"

Without warning, she fell to the floor like a stone, dropping the basket and sending its contents scattering everywhere.

"Lady Berners?" Elizabeth jumped up and ran to her, falling to her knees. "Lady Berners, wake up! What's wrong? Oh, Mary, she won't wake up!" She shook the governess again and again.

Mary knelt beside her and they stared down at the familiar, loved face, which now looked distorted, as if it had been dragged down on one side. Lady Berners was breathing, but she was not conscious. Distraught, Elizabeth called their maids, who came running from the bedchamber and regarded the prone figure with frightened eyes.

"Fetch help!" she cried. "Hurry!"

Dr. Sirego, the Queen's physician, was quickly summoned, and Mother, just out of childbed, came hastening after him.

"Oh, no," she said, taking one glance at the prone form on the floor. "Come, girls, let the doctor see to Lady Berners." She took their hands.

Dr. Sirego fell to his knees, his swarthy face all concern. Presently, he looked up. "There is nothing I can do, your Grace. The poor lady is with God now."

They cried for hours. Nothing anyone said could console them. For as long as Elizabeth could remember, Lady Berners had been a constant, loving, reassuring presence in her life—and now she was gone and there was a huge hole in their world. Mother did her best to comfort them, but it was not the same, for—apart from that long-ago time in sanctuary—she had never looked after them daily or soothed their childish hurts as Lady Berners had. And now Agnes Butler was to care for them, until a new lady mistress could be found. Elizabeth liked the rosy-cheeked Agnes, but she was no substitute for Lady Berners. Life, she thought miserably, would never be the same again.

Chapter 4

1476–1478

In the new year of 1476, Father took his family to see Master Caxton's new printing press in his shop near Westminster Abbey. Uncle Rivers had told them about Caxton, who had published a devotional work he himself had translated, *The Dictes and Sayings of the Philosophers*; it had been the first book ever printed in England. Now Father was Caxton's patron. Elizabeth stood by the great press, engrossed, watching the master arranging the metal letters, spreading them with ink, then impressing them on the paper. He was so deft, so fast.

"It is marvelous that book-learning can now be disseminated by such a process," Father observed. "You can print many copies in a day, whereas it takes months for a manuscript to be completed."

"Master Caxton, I should like to commission some books from you," Mother said. "Would you print them for me?"

"It would be an honor, your Grace." The handsome, gray-bearded printer bowed.

"I was thinking of the history of Troy and Jason and the Golden Fleece," Mother said.

"I am at your Grace's service," he smiled.

Elizabeth wandered around the shop. She passed Lord Hastings standing in a corner, deep in conversation with Uncle Lionel, who was visiting the court. She stood a little apart, looking at the new books displayed on the table. The men were speaking quietly— but not quietly enough.

"He lives at Amboise, away from his father's court, because his health is poor," she heard Hastings say. "I've warned the King: the boy might have a pleasant disposition, but he is stunted in height and feeble in body and mind. Some think he is too foolish to make a good king. What sort of husband will he be?"

Elizabeth froze. Were they talking about the Dauphin? Stunted . . . feeble . . . foolish? No! Surely not.

"It is a brilliant match, though," Uncle Lionel said. He was as single-mindedly ambitious as the rest of Mother's kin.

"Aye, but would you wish such a fate on your daughter?"

"Bessy knows her duty. The crown of France will compensate for her husband's shortcomings," Lionel murmured.

She had heard enough. Had Father known these things when he consented to her betrothal? Surely he would not have agreed to it if he had?

She did not want to hear any more. Trembling, she returned to her parents, desperate to talk to her father and find out the truth.

After an eternity, they returned to the palace. The King was about to go to a council meeting, but Elizabeth tugged at his sleeve.

"Father, can you spare a moment, please."

He smiled down at her. "What's the matter, Bessy? You look troubled."

She repeated what she had heard, the words coming out haltingly. "I couldn't help overhearing," she ended.

Father was frowning. "They should not have been discussing such matters where others could hear them. It is true that the Dauphin has had spells of poor health, which is why King Louis does not subject him to a demanding education, but I am assured that he is well mannered and known for his sweet nature. You should not pay heed to gossip, Bessy. I would not have betrothed you to an idiot, future king or not, so do not fret."

"I won't, Sir," she replied. "I'm glad I talked to you."

"So am I," Father agreed. "And now I'm going to have strong words with Lord Hastings." He smiled grimly.

The July sun beat down on Elizabeth's head as she stood with Mary and their parents before the entrance to the churchyard at Fotheringhay, waiting for the funeral cortège. They were surrounded by an august company that included Uncle Clarence, Uncle Rivers, Dorset, standing stiffly apart from Lord Hastings, and many other noblemen. The princesses were wearing mourning robes and veils of deep blue, the color of royal mourning, in a style similar to that worn by their mother. There was an air of forced courtesy; Elizabeth could sense the hostility emanating from lords who were at odds with each other, especially Uncle Clarence, who wore a perpetual look of discontent these days.

Today, the royal House of York was burying its dead—the grandfather and uncle Elizabeth had never met. Many times, she had heard how, sixteen years ago, the Duke of York and his seventeen-year-old son, the Duke of Rutland, had fallen at the Battle of Wakefield and been meanly interred at Pontefract by the victorious Lancastrians.

Now, Father was having them laid to rest with all due honors in the collegiate church founded by Edmund of Langley, the first Duke of York, near the magnificent castle of Fotheringhay, one of the House of York's most palatial seats. Elizabeth shuddered, imagining what a gruesome task it must have been for the men who had exhumed the bodies and placed them in new coffins.

The procession was approaching now, with Uncle Gloucester, in deepest black, riding at the head of it, followed by many peers and officers of arms. Here was the first funeral chariot, drawn by six horses in sable caparisons charged with the royal arms of England. On the coffin lay an effigy of the late Duke of York, garbed in an ermine-furred mantle and cap of maintenance. Despite it being broad daylight, the bier was ablaze with candles and guarded by an angel of silver bearing a crown of gold, to signify that the Duke had been the rightful King of England.

Elizabeth saw tears in Uncle Gloucester's eyes.

"It is sad that Richard did not know our father better," the King murmured. "He was only eight when he was killed. He was born here in the castle, did you know?"

Elizabeth nodded, watching as Uncle Rutland's hearse made its stately way toward them. When the chariots drew to a standstill, Father bowed his head in humble obeisance to his father's coffin, and laid his hand on it, weeping. Then the biers were wheeled into the church, and Elizabeth and Mary followed after the King and Queen, trailed by the great procession of clergy and lords. Father entered his closed pew, while Uncle Clarence, Uncle Gloucester, and the officers of arms took up their positions around the hearses, their heads bowed in reverence. Mass was sung and the King's chamberlain, on his behalf, laid seven palls of cloth of gold on the coffins. Then everyone retired to the castle for the night.

The next day, Elizabeth and Mary again donned their mourning. Today, the burial was to take place and a great feast would follow. As they stood by the gatehouse, waiting for their parents, Uncle Gloucester joined them, pulling on his gloves.

"This has been a solemn occasion for you both, but I am glad to see you here," he told them.

"We miss you at court," Elizabeth said. He was rarely there these days, being preoccupied with affairs in the north. Earlier that summer, Elizabeth had been happy to hear that Anne had borne him an heir at last, at Middleham Castle in Yorkshire.

"How are Aunt Anne and cousin Edward?" Mary asked.

"Anne is well," the Duke said, "but Edward is delicate. I pray that the good Yorkshire air will do him good and give him strength." He looked pained for a moment. "Come, the King and Queen approach."

On the short walk from the castle to the church, Elizabeth was astounded to see huge crowds of people lining the narrow road and packed into the churchyard.

"There must be at least five thousand here," Father marveled, as he nodded and bowed to left and right.

"It is touching that they have come to pay their respects," Mother replied.

"More likely they've come for the free food," Father muttered.

Elizabeth too was eagerly anticipating the feast. The three funeral Masses seemed to go on forever, but, at last, she and Mary rose and followed their parents to the altar rail to offer their Mass pennies, bowing to the catafalques as they did so. Behind them came the diminutive figure of Margaret Beaufort, the Dowager Countess of Richmond, now the wife of Lord Stanley. She smiled at them kindly.

"It will soon be over," she murmured. Elizabeth liked Lady Stanley, who was known for her piety and wisdom. She was a plain, thin-faced woman, but always richly dressed. Elizabeth knew that she was descended from the House of Lancaster, and that her son, Henry Tudor, Earl of Richmond, had gone into exile after the King's victory at Tewkesbury. Henry's father had died before he was born, and Father had once said that the Lady Margaret had shown good sense in later marrying Lord Stanley, who had been loyal to the House of York since switching his allegiance from York to Lancaster and back again in the late wars. Lord Stanley was now a prominent member of the King's Council and steward of the royal household. He was here today, broad and imposing in his mourning robes. He too smiled at her encouragingly.

Back in her place, Elizabeth watched as the bodies of York and Rutland were interred in the church, where Father was planning to build fine tombs for them. Then it was over, and they were walking out into the sunshine to greet the multitudes. The King and Queen began distributing alms, and Elizabeth and Mary helped them, speaking courteously to the recipients. Then they were free to mingle among the people, enjoying the feast that had been laid out in tents and pavilions by the road and in the vast castle courtyard. The royal cooks had excelled themselves—there were capons, cygnets, herons, rabbits, and all kinds of tasty meats. The feasting went on well into the evening, until a lot of the men got rather drunk and Mother frowned and told Elizabeth and Mary to go to bed.

"I like Lady Stanley," Elizabeth said the next day, as she dined with her parents in her mother's solar.

"She is a good woman," Father said, carving more beef for himself. "But she is ambitious for her son."

"Isn't he in Brittany?"

"Yes, he was spirited away by his uncle, Jasper Tudor, after Tewkesbury and is now at the court of Duke Francis. He must be nearly twenty now."

"I expect his mother wishes he was with her," Elizabeth reflected.

"That would make life a lot easier," the King sighed. "I could then keep an eye on him. Abroad, he is free to plot against me. He is the only man left of Henry the Sixth's blood, and I fear he covets my throne."

Mother drew in her breath.

"How dare he!" Elizabeth cried.

Father took another slice of pigeon pie. "He thinks he has a better claim. He is descended from King Edward the Third on his mother's side—"

"From bastard stock!" Mother interrupted. "The Beauforts are descended from the children Katherine Swynford bore John of Gaunt before they wed." John of Gaunt had been a younger son of Edward III and the ancestor of the House of Lancaster, but Elizabeth had not heard of Katherine Swynford.

"They were legitimated by statute when old Gaunt married Katherine," Father explained. "Lady Stanley is their great-granddaughter. There is some doubt as to whether the Beauforts have a legal claim to the throne, but Richmond pretends he is the natural heir of Henry the Sixth, who was descended from Gaunt's first wife. And if he chooses to press his claim, his mother's loyalty to the House of York will go flying out the window. She is a clever woman, and subtle—not to be trusted, much as I like her. I would dearly like to snare Richmond."

Elizabeth shivered. She had not realized that the House of Lancaster still posed a threat to her father.

Mother dabbed her napkin delicately to her mouth. "Tell Bessy *how* you plan to snare him." There was an edge to her voice.

Father grimaced. "Bessy, you must never reveal what I am going to tell you, not even to Mary. Promise me."

Elizabeth crossed herself. "I promise, Father."

"Then know that I am sending an embassy laden with gold to the Duke of Brittany, to request that he sends Richmond back to England. My envoys will tell him that I intend to arrange a marriage for him that will unite the houses of York and Lancaster—the implication being that I am offering one of your sisters."

"Who?" she asked.

The King grinned. "None of them, of course. It is a ruse to lure him back to England, where I can place a watch on him."

"Do you think he will come?"

"He's a wily fellow, but he might find the offer irresistible. An English princess is a great prize."

Weeks, then months passed, but there was no news from Brittany, and soon other things took precedence in Elizabeth's mind. Lady Berners had not been replaced, for Mother was tutoring her now—or would do so until she grew too heavy with this latest child, her eighth. At ten years old, Madame la Dauphine now had her own ladies-in-waiting and maids-of-honor, as became the future queen of France. Cecily, now seven, had joined her and Mary in the Maidens' Hall.

In November, when the three girls were playing a game of riddles, Mother appeared and drew Elizabeth into the window alcove.

"We have had news from Brittany," she murmured. "Richmond is said to be ill, but your father doubts it, for the Duke of Brittany has committed him to sanctuary in a church in Saint-Malo, which suggests he fears for his safety. The King believes that Lady Stanley somehow found out the truth about the proposed marriage. We don't know how. You didn't tell anyone, did you?"

"No, my lady, of course not."

"I knew you wouldn't, but it is a mystery, and a worrying one. Now Henry has slipped through Father's fingers and will be even warier of attempts to entice him back to England. So the King has offered Duke Francis a pension as an inducement to keep him in Brittany."

"Lady Stanley won't be happy about that," Elizabeth observed.

"Well, she has probably brought it on herself," Mother said briskly. "Come, let us join your sisters." She rose and they went to sit with Mary and Cecily at the table. "I have some good news," she revealed. "Your father has found a bride for Ned. She is the Infanta Isabella, the eldest daughter of the Spanish sovereigns, Ferdinand, King of Aragon, and Isabella, Queen of Castile, and she is the same age as Ned. It is a great match, for the sovereigns have united Spain under their rule and are highly regarded throughout Christendom."

Did Ned know? Elizabeth wondered. He had been at court recently; he had grown tall for his age, but was still angelically beautiful, and she wished he were still here, so that she could talk to him and find out if he was happy at the prospect of his marriage. She wondered what the Infanta Isabella was like, then reminded herself that Ned was only six and would not be getting married for years, so she herself might not even be in England when his bride arrived. The thought made her shiver.

News of the new alliance was an uncomfortable reminder that the time for her departure for France was drawing ever nearer. In just fifteen short months, she would be twelve. The realization gave her a panicky feeling. She knew her duty, so she could never tell her parents how she felt, but she had often confided her unhappiness to Mary, huddled up to her in bed at night. She was now praying that King Louis would decide that his son was not ready to be married and postpone the evil moment. But that, she thought, fighting back tears at the sight of Mother playing with her sisters, was not likely to happen.

To Father's joy, the new baby, who arrived in March 1477, was a lusty boy, called George after England's patron saint, and given the grand title of duke of Bedford. Elizabeth knew heartfelt relief when Mother came safely through her confinement. Last year, Aunt Isabel, Uncle Clarence's wife, had died in childbed, and it had brought home to Elizabeth just how perilous bearing children could be. In Isabel's case, matters had been made worse by Uncle

Clarence blaming her servant for the calamity and ordering her to be hanged. That had created a stir.

But little George was here, safe and healthy. His sisters, especially tiny Anne, made much of him, and even three-year-old York expressed approval.

"When will he be old enough to play at fighting?" he asked, leaning over the cradle. Mistress Welles, and Lady Dacre, who had been appointed to look after baby George, shook their heads at each other.

"My lord of York, you are a rascal," Lady Dacre told him. "Babies don't like to fight."

"May I hold him?" Elizabeth asked.

"Of course, Madame la Dauphine." Lady Dacre lifted up the swaddled bundle and laid him in her arms. Elizabeth gazed down at the bullish little face with its wide, unblinking eyes that seemed to contain a wealth of wisdom and wondered what mark this little one was destined to make in the world.

As she kissed him tenderly, it occurred to her that, within a couple of years, she might have a babe of her own to love, one like this, if God was good. Her twelfth birthday was now only eleven months off. Still she prayed that she would be allowed to stay in England a little longer. She did not feel ready for marriage. Mother had briskly explained what to expect in the nuptial bed, and Elizabeth shrank from it. Letting her stunted, foolish bridegroom— for so she thought of him, whatever Father had said—do that to her outraged her sense of modesty. But her monthly courses had not begun yet, so maybe there was cause to hope for a delay.

April brought the blossom to the trees and the annual feast of St. George at Windsor, attended by all the Knights of the Garter. This year was special, because Elizabeth, the Queen, and Aunt Suffolk were all to be made Lady Companions of the Order of the Garter, the highest honor Father could confer on them. Elizabeth had always thrilled to see him and the Knights mounted on horseback in their blue robes, and now she herself was to be part of the great procession. Wearing a gown and mantle of mulberry embroidered with garters, she rode in a chariot with her mother, her aunt and their ladies to St. George's Chapel, which still resembled a building site. There, amid the scaffolding, Mass was celebrated, as Elizabeth and the ladies looked down from the rood loft.

Afterward, they attended the great feast the King hosted in the magnificent St. George's Hall within the castle, a feast that had been held every year since the time of Edward III, who had founded the Order. The ladies did not eat with the Garter Knights, but entered the hall as the second course was being served. Elizabeth was awestruck at the splendor of the occasion, and the magnificence of her father, who was enthroned in solitary state at the high table, presiding over the august gathering. Collecting herself, she followed the Queen up to the gallery at the west end of the hall, where they watched the proceedings, and where a table had been set up for their own banquet.

Later that day, the King gathered his family and friends around him in his privy chamber for a private toast to the ladies. But, as he chatted and joked, circling the room with a goblet in his hand, Elizabeth saw that he was tense—and it was most apparent when he was talking to Uncle Clarence. At one point, it looked as if they were exchanging harsh words. She was delighted that Uncle Gloucester was here on one of his infrequent visits to court, but noticed him watching his brothers warily, his serious face creased in a frown. There was something amiss, she was sure.

She felt she could ask Uncle Gloucester, for he had always been kind to her and easy to talk to. Seeing him break away from Aunt Suffolk, she wove her way through the throng and joined him at the table on which an array of sweetmeats had been laid out.

"Some cordial, Bessy?" he asked, and she held out her goblet.

"Uncle," she said, "can I talk to you?"

He gave her that sad smile of his. "Of course. Is something troubling you?"

"It's Father and Uncle Clarence. They are arguing again. I don't trust Uncle Clarence."

Gloucester sighed. "They've been at odds since the Duke of Burgundy was killed in battle early this year. He left his duchy to his only child, Mary. You may know that the dukes of Burgundy have constantly striven to remain independent of the French crown. But King Louis has now declared the duchy extinct, saying it belongs to France."

"But what has that got to do with Uncle Clarence?" Elizabeth had just seen her father's face flush with anger at something Clarence had said.

"Your Aunt Margaret rashly suggested that he marry Mary of Burgundy, and he is all for it, since he stands to gain the duchy with all its riches. But your father has forbidden it, because such an alliance would threaten England's friendship with France and put your marriage in jeopardy."

Elizabeth's heart skipped a beat. She almost wished that Uncle Clarence would defy Father and marry Mary of Burgundy, so that King Louis would take offense and break her betrothal treaty—but what was she thinking? Never would she wish such ill fortune on Father. "So that's why they are so angry."

"There's more," Uncle Gloucester confided. "Since Clarence allied himself to Warwick and committed treason, the King has not trusted him—and who can blame him? Clarence is ambitious: he wants a crown."

Him, too! Elizabeth thought, remembering Richmond. Truly, she was beginning to understand how perilous it was to be a king.

"If Clarence marries Mary," Gloucester was saying, "he will gain a great power base, with the wealth of Burgundy at his disposal, and control over the North Sea coast. With all that behind him, he could challenge your father's right to the English throne. That is what the King fears, and he has thrown all possible impediments in Clarence's way."

Everything made sense now.

"But don't worry, Bessy. King Louis no more wants to see your uncle ruling Burgundy than your father does. Between them, they will scupper his plans."

Soon afterward, Uncle Clarence left court—in a fury, Elizabeth heard.

"It's hard to believe he's my brother!" Father seethed. They were at dinner with Grandmother York in her gloomy dining room at Baynard's Castle. "The things he said to me—unbelievable. I have never seen such naked jealousy."

"He was ever wayward," Grandmother recalled. "Remember that vile rumor he started when he abandoned you for Warwick. It cut me to the core. That he should impugn me, his own mother—and with no cause!"

Elizabeth was agog to know what she was talking about.

"He accused *my* mother of witchcraft," Mother said.

"He is an unnatural son. He shows scant respect for any of us."

"But this latest insult to the Queen is a step too far," the King said sternly. "I cannot let it pass."

"What has he said, Father?" Elizabeth persisted, trying to make sense of it all.

Father hesitated. "He has accused your mother of poisoning Aunt Isabel."

Elizabeth looked at the Queen, speechless.

"It's all right, Bessy," Mother said, patting her hand. "Your poor aunt died in childbed. She was not poisoned. As if I would do such a thing! But your uncle Clarence has never liked or approved of me or my kin, and he is determined to undermine your father."

"In charity, the most one can say is that he has convinced himself that poor Isabel was murdered," Grandmother said.

"But he keeps repeating the accusation, and in public, too," Father growled. "He claims that Isabel's servant administered the poison on the Queen's instructions. It was bad enough that he had the poor woman put to death, but now he has gone too far. And when one of his affinity was convicted and hanged for using sorcery against me and Ned, he had the nerve to defend him publicly before the Council, disparaging my justice!" He banged his fist on the table. "I am sorry, my lady mother, but I am sending him to the Tower."

There was a shocked silence. Then the Duchess spoke. "He has committed treason, my son, so that is where he should be. This tragedy is of his own making. But what will you do with him?" She could not disguise the fear in her voice. "I have buried five sons. I do not want to bury another."

"I will let him cool his heels in the Tower for a while," Father said. "When he is contrite, I will consider releasing him."

"Will he be put in a dungeon?" Elizabeth asked, imagining a dank, dark cell, and wondering how her uncle would cope; he, who was used to living in luxury.

"No," Father reassured her. "He will be confined to an apartment within the palace. Those of royal blood are not treated like common prisoners."

"And his children?" Grandmother asked. "Margaret and Warwick are so young."

"I will send them to Sheen. They can share the nursery with our children."

Elizabeth traveled to Sheen, poised to take her young cousins under her wing. When they arrived, she was waiting in the nursery to greet them. They looked forlorn and uncertain, two fair little waifs standing there mute as she kissed them. Poor mites, they had already lost their mother, and now their father was in prison.

Two-year-old Anne toddled over with a doll to show Margaret, and four-year-old York challenged little Warwick, half his age and barely half his size, to a fight with wooden swords, but Elizabeth shooed him away, seeing that Warwick was reluctant to play. She did not want to unsettle her cousins, who looked so unhappy.

"Come, you are most welcome here," she said, kneeling down and hugging them. "We are all excited about having you to stay, and you must think of yourselves as part of the family."

Four-year-old Margaret's pale face brightened. Elizabeth stood up and took them both by the hand. "Let's go and say hello to baby George," she said.

Uncle Gloucester had been right. King Louis had invaded Burgundy and seized it, plunging Father into a bad mood.

"I no more want Louis ruling Burgundy than I did Clarence," he muttered that evening at supper in the Queen's chamber. "Yet it is imperative that I maintain the alliance with France, so I have written to remind him of the treaty of amity between us, and of my desire to see you, Bessy, married to the Dauphin."

Elizabeth made herself smile, ashamed of her heart leaping at the prospect of the alliance foundering.

"I anticipate a favorable reply!" Father said.

But a week later, he came to the table in a foul temper. "I've heard from Louis," he growled. "He seems to have lost enthusiasm for our friendship. My spies tell me he is thinking of marrying the Dauphin to Mary of Burgundy."

Elizabeth's heart soared, but when she saw the grim disappointment written plain on Father's face, she felt guilty again.

"If the alliance falls apart, it will humiliate Bessy—and what of my pension?" he flared.

Mother reached across and laid a hand on his. "Louis has no need to marry the Dauphin to Mary. He holds Burgundy himself now."

"Yes, but their marriage would give legitimacy to it. I can see where his mind tends, the old spider. I'd probably do the same myself, were I in his place. But fear not, Bessy, I will do everything in my power to save the alliance and your marriage. I intend to offer Uncle Rivers as a husband for Mary of Burgundy."

Mother beamed. "She could not make a more fitting match!"

Elizabeth sat there, thinking. Nothing was ever certain when it came to royal marriage alliances, and treaties could be broken or ignored if a better offer presented itself. Her future was by no means certain—and, for all that her conscience troubled her, she rejoiced in that.

One hot August day, the King joined the Queen and their children in her privy garden, his handsome face jubilant.

"Mary of Burgundy has married Maximilian of Austria," he announced. "He is the husband her father chose for her."

Mother gasped.

"Who's Mathimilian?" lisped young York.

"He is the son of the Holy Roman Emperor." Father sank down heavily on the stone bench where the Queen and Elizabeth were at their embroidery. "We have Aunt Margaret to thank. She has worked indefatigably to oust the French from Burgundy, and triumphed. This is tremendous news, for Maximilian has made it clear that he will not tolerate their presence and is bent on driving them out. I'd love to have seen the look on Louis's face when he heard of the marriage. Mark my words, he will now turn back to England for friendship! My agents report that he fears I will marry you, Bessy, into the Imperial house and thus forge a new alliance with Burgundy against France. He is frantically planning strategies to avert that threat." He rubbed his hands in glee.

"The only way to counter it is to hold to his alliance with us," Mother said.

"Indeed," Father chuckled. "It looks like the wedding is on again, Bessy!"

Elizabeth's heart plummeted.

She was astonished when Mother told her that York, now four years old, was to be married. Her first thought was, Heaven pity his intended—for her brother was a mischievous and boisterous imp who ruled the nursery through sheer charm and force of will.

"The bride your father has chosen is Anne Mowbray, the late Duke of Norfolk's heiress. She is five, so they are close in age, and she is very pretty. The marriage will bring York the rich Norfolk estates and provide for his future." Elizabeth suppressed a smile. York would care little for the prettiness of a little girl or the vastness of the lands that were coming to him; like all small boys, he was preoccupied with martial games and evading lessons.

"They are so young," she said.

"I know," Mother replied, "but it will be years before they can live together. The Lady Anne is going home to Framlingham Castle with her mother, the Dowager Duchess, after the ceremony. What matters now is that the Norfolk inheritance is secured."

Elizabeth looked forward to the wedding. Seven-year-old Ned, who had come up from Ludlow for Christmas, was staying on for the celebrations, which meant that the royal children could be together for longer. And they were all to have new clothes. And Uncle Gloucester was coming south for the nuptials. It was going to be a great occasion!

On 15 January 1478, the royal family gathered in St. Stephen's Chapel in the palace of Westminster. The King took his place in the royal pew, while his younger children fidgeted on an adjacent bench beneath a cloth-of-gold canopy, ignoring Grandmother York's muttered reproofs. Elizabeth sat marveling at the vaulted ceiling of sky blue studded with gold stars, which soared a hundred feet above her head. She studied the murals, familiar to her since infancy, of angels, kings, and religious scenes in vivid scarlet, green, and blue. They were partly concealed because the chapel walls had been hung with azure cloth embroidered with gold fleurs-de-lis, just like the French royal arms. And that, like so much else these days, reminded her that she would soon be going to France. Her twelfth birthday was less than a month away.

But there was little time to brood, for trumpets were heralding the arrival of the Queen, who escorted her son to the altar, where she put his hand in that of the handsome, statuesque Dowager Duchess of Norfolk and enjoined him sternly to stand still. Then two great lords, Uncle Rivers and John de la Pole, Earl of Lincoln, Aunt Suffolk's son, led in Anne Mowbray. Elizabeth stared. She had never seen such a lovely child, or such vivid red hair. Shimmering in cloth of silver, the little bride carried herself well and executed a perfect curtsey to the King, who stood up and took her hand, ready to give her away at the altar.

When the bride and groom led the august company out of the palace, Uncle Gloucester scattered gold and silver coins among the crowds outside. The bridal party then entered Westminster Hall, where they were served spices and wine. York was looking bored, but cheered up considerably when the tournament began, and bounced up and down in the royal stand, roaring his approval of the victors, as the King looked on indulgently and Anne Mowbray smiled sweetly at everyone.

Afterward, they all repaired to the vast Painted Chamber for the nuptial feast. The royal family seated themselves at the high table with the bride and groom at the King's right hand, as foreign ambassadors, lords, ladies, knights, and squires took their places at the lower tables, and a procession of servants in the murrey-and-blue livery of the House of York entered with the first course. Everyone clapped as the little Duchess of York was named "Princess of the Feast."

Later, there was dancing, and the King and Queen led out York and his bride to the floor. Uncle Gloucester rose and offered Elizabeth his hand. It was thrilling to be dancing before the court in her beautiful golden gown, while her uncle, his twisted spine hidden, cut an elegant figure in his short houppelande of maroon velvet.

"It seems strange that Uncle Clarence isn't here," she observed.

"Indeed, it does," he said, frowning. "But let us not dwell on sad things on such a glorious day. You have a birthday soon, don't you, Bessy?"

"Yes, Uncle." The prospect brought the familiar feelings of dread. Yet neither Father nor Mother had said anything more about sending her to France, and she shrank from asking when it would be because that might make it horribly real.

"Time for you to be married!" Uncle Gloucester smiled, then paused, looking hard at her face. "Am I getting the feeling that you are not too happy about that?"

Before she could answer, the King's squire, Humphrey Brereton, appeared, bowing. "My lady Princess, the King's Grace requests your presence at the high table."

Elizabeth curtseyed to her uncle. "I'm sorry, I must go," she said. He bowed and followed her to the dais. As she took her place, the Kings of Arms entered and made obeisance before the bride.

"Will your Grace consent to present the prizes at the jousts tomorrow?" they asked.

Anne Mowbray had been well schooled. "I shall be delighted, good sirs," she replied, and made a pretty reverence to them.

"Bessy, will you assist your new sister?" the King asked.

"With pleasure," she smiled.

It was another fabulous tournament, despite the cold. Wrapped in furs, Elizabeth sat next to the little Duchess in the royal stand, guarding the gems that the Kings of Arms had given them to present to the victors; each was engraved with the initials of Anne and herself. They watched, tense with excitement, as the knights charged against each other, lances couched, gasped when one was unhorsed, and cheered the champions at the tops of their voices. Elizabeth was delighted when Sir Thomas Fiennes rode up to the royal stand, bowed in the saddle, and humbly asked if he could carry her favor. Feeling very grown-up, she handed him her kerchief, which he tied to his lance. And he won! Exulting, Elizabeth handed the prize to the little Princess of the Feast, who bestowed it on him, to much applause. Sir Thomas then kissed Elizabeth's kerchief and waved it aloft with a triumphant flourish.

"The honor, my lady Princess, is all yours!" he cried.

After the splendor of the wedding, a dark pall seemed to descend on Westminster. Elizabeth noticed royal councillors murmuring in corners and falling silent when she passed by. She feared that something ominous was afoot. Father was in a strange mood and rarely appeared at supper.

"He has weighty matters of state on his mind," Mother explained. She was as calm and serene as usual, keeping the conversation to the latest style of headdress and the antics of young York, which she related fondly. But there came an evening when the King appeared in a foul temper.

"Leave us!" he barked. The ladies rose from their curtseys and hastened after the servitors. Elizabeth was about to follow, but he stayed her. "No, Bessy. You are not a child any more. You ought to be aware of what is happening."

"My lord, tell us!" Mother urged. "You're making me nervous."

"It's Clarence," Father hissed, easing his bulk into his great chair at the head of the table. "Imprisonment in the Tower has proved no barrier to his scheming."

Mother had gone white. "What has he done?"

"He has continued falsely and traitorously to plot my destruction and the disinheriting of our children. By any reckoning, this is high treason. And he is still spreading that false and unnatural tale that I am a bastard and was not begotten to reign over England."

"That old calumny!" Mother was vehement. "He and Warwick dreamed it up between them to justify their rebellion. There's no truth in it, Bessy."

"But how could you possibly be a bastard, Father?" Elizabeth asked. She knew what the word meant.

"How indeed?" he snorted. "They claimed that I was the son of Grandmother York by an archer, conceived when my father was away fighting the French. Can you imagine your grandmother stooping so low? Of course, she has denied it vehemently. She is still deeply hurt that her own son spread such a tale. There is not a grain of truth in it, yet still Clarence insists there is. He has charmed someone in the Tower to pass on messages. But, thanks be to God, my spies are vigilant. The letters they showed me today leave me in no doubt of what is going on. The worst of it is that people might believe the story—and that could undermine my throne."

Mother looked shaken. "Clarence wants to be king. That's what drives him, Bessy. If your father and his issue are overthrown, he is next in line for the crown. He is a dangerous man." She turned to the King. "My lord, he *must* be dealt with! He has rebelled against you and spread this slander, he has publicly impugned your justice, and his scheme to marry Mary of Burgundy posed a major threat to you. He is a dangerous troublemaker and a threat to this realm's stability!"

"I know, Beth, I know! And that is not all. He is now questioning the validity of our marriage."

"What?" Mother cried. "How dare he!"

"He was ever rash," Father said. "When we were boys, our governor couldn't control him. Now, it is as if he is marshaling any and every argument to rob me of my rightful crown!"

"No!" Elizabeth cried.

"Edward, please, listen to me," Mother begged. "You have been too lenient with him. He is never going to stop. Look what happened when he joined forces with Warwick—you were *deposed*! What if some disaffected lords support Clarence in this? It could happen again!" Tears were running down her face. "I live in terror of that. I have not forgotten those awful months in sanctuary. Edward, I fear our children will never come to the throne unless Clarence is removed. I beg of you, heed me!" Elizabeth stared as Mother fell to her knees and grasped Father's hands. "I am begging you. He is dangerous."

The King's eyes blazed. "You are asking me to put my own brother to death."

"You must see that he has to be silenced!"

"There are other ways of doing that."

"Can I believe it, when he has circumvented his guards in the Tower?"

Father said nothing for a few moments. Elizabeth held her breath, fearing that Mother was right, and that the world would undoubtedly be a safer place without Clarence in it. But she was asking the King to do a truly awful thing.

"You speak truth," he said at length. "I cannot allow him to go on committing treason. He shall face justice and get what he deserves. I will have him attainted in Parliament."

"It is the right decision, dear heart," Mother said, and kissed him. "I know how difficult this is for you, but you have no choice."

Father rose, his face drained of its ruddiness. "I don't think I can face food," he said. "I bid you both good night. May God bless you."

When he had gone, Mother pushed her plate away. "Now you know what it is to be a king, Bessy. It is a hard thing—a terrible thing—I have asked of him, but he knows he must do it."

Three days before Elizabeth's birthday, Uncle Clarence was tried in Parliament, with Father himself sitting in judgment on him. Elizabeth waited with Mother for news, both of them on edge. The Queen had summoned Uncle Rivers and her kinsmen and friends, making no secret of wanting her family to be well represented in Parliament to counteract any threat from Uncle Clarence.

Late in the afternoon, the King arrived in the Queen's privy chamber, his countenance ashen.

"He is condemned," he told them. "He was defiant, but he could not refute the evidence. An Act of Attainder is to be passed against him. Bessy, you must know that the Act will deprive him of his life, titles, and estates, and the rights of himself and his heirs to the succession."

"Will he be executed?" Elizabeth whispered, horrified that Father had had to condemn his own brother.

"That is what Parliament requires," Mother said gently, putting an arm around her.

"Unless, of course, I exercise my prerogative of mercy," Father stated. "Maybe this judgment will be sufficient to make Clarence realize what a dangerous game he has been playing."

Mother flew at him, pummeling his chest with her fists. "No! You cannot give him yet another chance! That would be foolhardy beyond belief. He has committed treason again and again. Why should you show him mercy?"

"I shall not, Beth," he reassured her. "I shall do what needs to be done." Elizabeth had never seen him look so stricken. She was filled with an immense pity for him.

An hour later, while they were still talking in the Queen's chamber, an usher entered and bowed to the King.

"Your Grace, my lady of York is here, wishing to see you."

Father's face fell. "Oh, God. How can I face her?" he muttered.

"It must be done," Mother said, rising. "Send her in."

Grandmother York looked as if she had aged a hundred years. Holding herself stiffly, she curtseyed, as Father knelt for her blessing.

"I pray you deem me worthy of it after what has passed this day," he said.

"I give it freely," the Duchess said. "It is for God to judge, not I. I know what your brother has done, and that you have the security of a hard-won throne to consider." She took the Queen's chair by the fire, her back ramrod-straight, her aristocratic features a mask of tragedy. "It is a dreadful thing when brother plots against brother. A house divided must fall, but your brave decision today has ensured that the House of York will not perish." She paused, struggling to master her feelings. "Clarence has brought this upon himself. I do not come to beg for him, only to ask that you will not have him executed in public. Let it be done privately, in the Tower."

Father nodded, his expression grim. "It shall be as you wish, my lady mother."

Elizabeth listened, appalled. How terrible this must be for her grandmother. She watched, horrified, as that pillar of dignity began to crumple in sorrow.

Mother rose and shepherded Elizabeth out of the room. "This is no place for you," she murmured.

Elizabeth's twelfth birthday was a subdued affair, overshadowed by the tragedy that was taking place. She had heard nothing more of Uncle Clarence and was not even sure if he was still alive. Had Father taken the irrevocable step of having him executed in secret? It did not bear thinking about.

Nothing had been said about her going to France. Of course, Father was preoccupied with other things. As she sat at table in the Maidens' Hall, with York, Mary, and Cecily, who had come up from Sheen, she looked at their dear faces and prayed that she would be allowed to remain here for just a little longer.

She had invited Margaret and Warwick to sit on either side of her, for she wanted to be especially kind to them. Poor little things, they had no idea that their father was doomed. They had settled well into the royal nursery; the company of a happy group of children near in age had helped them to blossom and forget their sad circumstances. She vowed to do all she could to shield them from the dreadful deed that was about to happen. Some day, they would have to know about it, but not for a long time yet.

One frosty February morning, Elizabeth was in the nursery at Eltham, encouraging baby George to walk, when the other children came tumbling in, rosy-cheeked after playing in the gardens.

"I hope you stayed clear of the workmen," she said. Father was having a new great hall built, and her siblings had been told not to go near the scaffolding.

"We did," Cecily declared.

Four-year-old York pulled off his padded jerkin. "Bessy, did you know that Uncle Clarence was drownded in a butt of wine?" he asked.

"*What?*" Elizabeth asked, as Anne stared, wide-eyed.

"I heard the guards talking," York revealed.

Elizabeth was furious. How dare they speak of such things when the children were within earshot? It was as well that Clarence's two were playing in the bedchamber.

"What nonsense!" she exclaimed. "You should not listen to idle gossip."

"But it's true," York protested. "They said Father let him choose how he wanted to die, and he wanted to be drowned."

"I don't believe it!" she retorted. "Don't you dare repeat it in front of Margaret and Warwick."

As she spoke, she saw York's dismayed gaze move to the doorway, where the Clarence children stood. One look at their faces told her that they had heard what he had said. Then Margaret burst into tears. "I want my father!" she cried. "Tell me he's not dead!" That set Warwick off, too.

Elizabeth hastened to them and folded them in her arms. "I'm sure it's not true, but I will go and ask the King." She turned to Mary and Cecily, who were looking on, appalled. "Look after them," she bade them. "Keep them occupied."

She sped through the palace, around courtyards rimed with frost and along crowded galleries, until she reached the King's lodgings. The guards let her in and, fortunately, she found him alone in his closet, signing papers. He looked drawn and weary, and she noticed for the first time that there was gray in his thick auburn hair.

"Bessy! What's wrong?"

"Oh, Father!" She related to him what York had said, and how badly Margaret and Warwick had taken it. She willed him to dismiss it as nonsense, but his expression turned grave.

"Sadly, it is true," he said, to her horror. "Clarence did choose such a death. I'm sorry you had to find out that way, Bessy, and that his children heard it, too. But, believe me, sweetheart, I had no choice in the matter. I pardoned his treachery so many times, but he was out to destroy us all. He had to die. Sometimes, a king must do things from which he shrinks. I would give anything for things to have been otherwise." He drew her to him and held her tight, as if he was the one who needed comforting.

"What shall I say to the children?" she asked, dreading returning to the nursery with the awful news.

"Your mother will break it to them. I will send for her."

Mother arrived speedily. She nodded when Father explained what she must do and, as they walked back to the nursery, she ordered Elizabeth to go to the Maidens' Hall. "I intend to tell the children that their father did some very bad things and that Parliament said he had to die. I will say that the King had forgiven him many times, but that even he has to obey the law, and that he tried to give Uncle Clarence as kind a death as possible."

She drew Elizabeth into a window embrasure, her face set hard. "This is a terrible tragedy, but I am glad he is dead. He hated me and mine, you know. He despised us as low-born, and he was determined to ruin us. Don't forget, it was he and Warwick who executed your grandfather Rivers and your uncle John and accused Grandmother Rivers of sorcery. And Clarence has relentlessly impugned my marriage and, by implication, your legitimacy. I shall shed no tears for him. But I feel deeply sorry for his children. Young Warwick will suffer most, for his father's attainder has stripped him of his title and barred him from the royal succession."

"What will happen to them?" Elizabeth asked, her heart bleeding for the little boy.

"They are to be made wards of your brother Dorset." Mother had clearly been busy behind the scenes; she was always eager to secure lucrative wardships and offices for her family. "But they will stay at Sheen Palace with your brothers and sisters. Maybe you would like to go with them for a while."

Elizabeth felt hope burgeoning in her breast. Mother had spoken of her going to Sheen, not to France.

* * *

On the night before she left, Elizabeth supped with her parents in the Queen's chamber, and Uncle Gloucester joined them, wearing deep black and a mournful expression. When Uncle Clarence's name was mentioned, Elizabeth was astonished to see tears in his eyes—he, who usually kept his feelings hidden. She also noticed that he barely spoke to Mother, except to observe the courtesies. But he was as kind as ever toward Elizabeth.

"How are young Warwick and Margaret taking this?" he asked.

"They are much grieved," she told him. "It is a hard thing for such young children to bear. I think a change of place will help."

"It was a cruel necessity," Father observed, "and I was grateful, Richard, for your support in Parliament."

"Did he have to die?" Uncle Gloucester blurted out. "Could you not just have kept him in prison?"

"Richard, no prison walls could have stopped his evil scheming. He was a danger to us all."

"Yes, but when I backed you in Parliament, I did not think that you would take things this far. A king should show mercy, especially to his brother."

"Clarence showed no mercy to us!" Mother said sharply.

Uncle Gloucester ignored her. He kept his eyes fixed on Father.

"The Queen is right," the King said wearily.

Gloucester pursed his lips, as if he was about to say something, but had thought better of it. "What of Clarence's share of the Warwick inheritance?" he asked at length.

"It is yours," Father said, "as I promised."

Elizabeth wondered if that had been the price of Uncle Gloucester's support.

"I had not looked to come into it in such circumstances," her uncle replied, "but I will not deny that I am grateful."

"I am bestowing Clarence's earldom of Salisbury on your son." Father seemed to be placating his brother. "And I am appointing you Great Chamberlain of England in Clarence's place."

"Thank you," Uncle Gloucester replied quietly. Mother glared at Father, and Elizabeth wondered if she had wanted Clarence's estates for her own sons. Then a horrible thought occurred to her.

Did Uncle Gloucester know that Mother had pressed Father to execute Clarence? Did he think she had done it in revenge for the killing of her father and brother? Was that why he was being so cold toward her?

"I am returning to the north tomorrow," she heard him say, and felt saddened, for she would miss him.

"I shall be sorry to see you go," Father told him. "Of our mother's sons, only we two are left."

"There is much business to attend to," Gloucester reminded him.

"I appreciate that. Bessy, you should know that Uncle Gloucester governs very efficiently for me in the north. No king could have a more loyal lieutenant. But I sense you will not be sorry to go, Richard."

"I mean no offense, brother, but I prefer the good air of Yorkshire and Durham to the tainted air of the court."

Father's smile faded. "You have no enemies here now."

Gloucester raised his eyebrows. "It is forever tainted for me. I hope you understand that. But I will continue to serve you well in the north, and I will return to court when necessary."

They had given up all pretense of eating. Gloucester rose. "I will take my leave."

"Write to me," Father said, and the brothers embraced each other stiffly, before Uncle Gloucester bowed to the Queen and bent to kiss Elizabeth.

When he had gone, Mother broke her silence. "You know what taints the court for him? It is me and my blood. He blames me for Clarence's death."

"Beth, it is not that. He knows why Clarence had to die. I'm sure he does accept it."

"But he hates us Wydevilles, just as Clarence did. I believe that he, too, if he had the opportunity, would bring us to ruin."

Father reached for her hand. "If that were true, why would he be intent on avoiding the court?"

"Perhaps he fears me as much as I fear him, and that I will press you to get rid of him, as I urged you to eliminate Clarence."

The King sighed. "Beth, calm yourself. Richard loves me. Why would he hurt you? And he accords well with your brother Rivers. He knows that I alone bear the responsibility for Clarence's death."

It chilled Elizabeth to hear her father speak those words. She did not want to be reminded that he had sent his own brother to his execution.

The argument rambled on, but Mother would not be persuaded that Uncle Gloucester meant her no harm. In the end, Father became exasperated and rose to leave.

"Go to bed, Bessy," he said. "You have an early start for Sheen tomorrow." He gave her his blessing and hastened away. Elizabeth wondered if he was going to seek the company of the merry Mistress Shore, who would doubtless be a more congenial companion than Mother was right now.

Time at Sheen passed slowly. The children reveled in the spacious days and the coming of spring, running about in the park, free as birds, or pulling along a squealing little George in his miniature chariot, as their nurses looked on indulgently. Elizabeth and Mary often joined in their romps, or went for long rides along the Thames shore on their palfreys, enjoying the new-minted sun on their faces.

All through that summer, Elizabeth waited anxiously to be told that she was leaving for France. Whenever her parents visited, she was tense, afraid that the subject would be raised. But as time moved on, she began to hope that her marriage had been deferred— or might not go ahead at all. If that was the case, though, surely she would have been told?

In the middle of August, the King and Queen came again, arriving by barge as usual, to be greeted joyously by their children. After they had spent time with them and dined, Father settled down to a game of chess with Mary, while Mother took Elizabeth off for a ride in the park.

"You have gathered that you are not to go to France just yet," she said, as they skirted the palace green.

"I did wonder," Elizabeth replied. At the word "yet," her heart had sunk.

"Your Father still desires the match very much. The Duchess of Burgundy appealed to him for aid against King Louis, but he ignored her, for he will allow nothing to compromise your marriage. Yet we fear that Louis is by no means committed to it. He has made no arrangements for your coming. However, Father has sent an envoy to press him to conclude the espousals without further delay. He wants you to know that he is sparing no effort on your behalf."

Elizabeth once more felt guilty for hoping that the negotiations would come to nothing, especially since this marriage meant so much to Father—and to England. Yet, as the year moved on and the leaves died, she began to feel a little indignant. King Louis was obviously stalling. It was insulting, not only to her father, but also to herself.

When she and her siblings arrived at court for Christmas, the King summoned her to his closet.

"I want to talk to you about your marriage, Bessy," he said, looking vexed. "Before you join them in the hall for the bringing in of the Yule log, I must tell you that I've just seen the French ambassador, who had been instructed by King Louis to say that the Dauphin is too young to be wed at present, and that your dower will be paid only after the marriage is consummated, which will not be for six years yet."

Six years! If she could stay in England that long, she would go to France willingly when the time came.

Father was drumming his fingers on the table. "My councillors are furious at King Louis breaking the terms of the treaty and are urging me to repudiate it, but I will not. I mean to force him to keep to its terms. But, Bessy, I am not optimistic. France needs England right now, for Louis is terrified lest I support Maximilian in Burgundy. So why is he behaving so dishonorably over your marriage? I have to ask myself, is he truly committed to it? And the answer seems blatantly clear: he is not. Bessy, my sweet child, if it comes to your betrothal being broken, would you be very sad?"

"For myself, no," she admitted, "although I would be sad not to become queen of France. But I would be very sad for your sake,

Father, because I know this alliance means a lot to you. True happiness for me lies in doing your will."

The King stood up and embraced her. "My lovely Bessy. If I had my way, I would keep you with me forever. But your destiny is to wear a crown and I would not deprive you of that—nor England of a beneficial alliance. So we must hope that something can be salvaged from this diplomatic posturing. You can rely on me to make Louis see sense—even if I have to cross the Channel and beat him into submission!"

Making her way to the great hall, Elizabeth rejoiced in the delay in negotiations, but could not help looking forward six years hence, and seeing herself, at eighteen, bedding a sickly fourteen-year-old boy. She was nearly thirteen now. Beneath her court gown there were budding breasts, an aching belly (for her courses had recently begun), and a heart that beat faster when a handsome man addressed her. She had taken to gazing at her reflection in her silver mirror, liking the effect of red-gold hair and blue eyes and pleasing features. She did not have the glacial beauty of her mother, but she was pretty. Men paid her compliments. And her dreams were of love, of knights rescuing maidens and lovers plighting their troth, as in the romances she devoured. In these fantasies, the Dauphin had no place.

Chapter 5

1479–1483

They kept Easter and St. George's Day at Windsor. One evening, over a Lenten supper of fish in verjuice, Father began grumbling again about King Louis dragging his heels.

"He won't see reason. I've sent envoys to warn him that if he will not honor the treaty, I will ally myself with Maximilian."

Mother looked alarmed. "And then we will lose the alliance. My lord, do not provoke Louis! I want to see my daughter wearing the French crown."

"And so you shall, darling." Father smiled at her.

At that moment, Lady Dacre burst into the room without being announced, her mouth working in distress.

"Your Graces, I beg of you, come to the nursery, quickly!"

There was a scraping of chairs as they hastened to follow her, Elizabeth hurrying in the wake of her parents.

"It's my lord of Bedford," Lady Dacre panted. "He will not wake up!"

"No!" Mother cried, as Elizabeth began to tremble, remembering how her sister Margaret had died in her sleep seven years ago. Dear God, it could not be happening again—and to sweet little George, who was the dearest creature and had only just celebrated his second birthday. Mother of God, she prayed, not George, please!

Another funeral, another tiny coffin. This time, the mourners gathered in St. George's Chapel at Windsor. Mother was nearly prostrate, and an ashen Father was all concern because she was with child again. Elizabeth and Mary clung to each other, weeping silently, appalled to see her in such agony. How cruel life was!

It was a sad spring. A pall of grief hung over the royal family, and Elizabeth no longer had the will to care whether she would ever be sent to France. Negotiations were dragging on, as slow as a lumbering tortoise, and Father seemed to have lost the impetus to pursue them with any vigor.

In the summer, they moved to Eltham, and it was there, in August, that Elizabeth's sister Katherine was born. It was a comfort to her parents, who made much of this ninth addition to the family, and Elizabeth began to find pleasure in life again.

In February 1480, Father hosted a banquet in the White Hall at Westminster to mark her fourteenth birthday.

"You look beautiful, my illustrious maid of York," he complimented her in the antechamber beforehand, as she twirled before him in her purple velvet gown with the ermine-trimmed neckline and cuffs, and the bejeweled belt at hip level. "Here is your gift." He turned to Humphrey Brereton, who was holding a cushion, lifted from it a heavy gold collar and placed it around her neck. Mother stepped forward to fasten the clasp.

"It's gorgeous!" Elizabeth cried. "Oh, thank you!" She hugged and kissed them. "I will always treasure it."

"You look lovely," Mary said.

"Luminous!" the King chimed in. "It's not the jewels, but the sweetness in your face. The Dauphin may count himself fortunate indeed." There was an uncomfortable pause. Louis was still prevaricating, and Father, who had been muttering about war, remained reluctant to take an irrevocable step that would scupper the alliance for good.

But she would not think about that now. She would enjoy her special evening, and all the more so because Ned was up from Ludlow and Uncle Gloucester had come down from Middleham to celebrate with her. When she entered the hall and saw them standing together—nine-year-old fair-haired Ned, who was nearly as tall as their slight, dark-haired uncle—she hastened forward joyfully to embrace them.

The courtiers made obeisance as she passed, then clustered around her to offer their good wishes. Lord Stanley kissed her hand in the most affectionate fatherly manner, and Lady Stanley told her how beautiful she looked. In the flush of the moment, Elizabeth asked after her son Richmond, and saw a surprised smile light up the Lady Margaret's face.

"He is well," she said. "How kind of you to inquire."

Elizabeth hoped that her inquiry about Richmond had not been misinterpreted, and hastily changed the subject before moving on to greet Aunt Suffolk and her son Lincoln.

The next morning, she visited Grandmother York at Baynard's Castle. Now that she was older, she was not so overawed by the old lady, and they were quite affectionate together.

Today, when she was shown into the great chamber, she was astonished to see that Grandmother was not wearing her usual rich attire, but a sober black gown and wimple, very much like a nun's habit.

"My dear child!" the Duchess said, as Elizabeth rose from her curtsey and kissed the soft cheek proffered her. She poured some wine. "Don't stare at me, Bessy," she reproved gently. "I am sixty-five and need to look to the health of my immortal soul. I have enrolled myself as a Benedictine oblate."

"Are you become a nun?" Elizabeth asked, astonished.

"No, it means that I have dedicated myself to the service of God, while remaining in the world. I observe the daily Hours, I pray, and I read the Scriptures; I can wear secular dress, but it must be plain, as is fitting for one who has dedicated herself to religion. But I do not have to renounce my property or my noble rank."

Elizabeth had known that her grandmother was deeply devout—but that she should take it this far was surprising. "Will we be able to visit you?" she faltered.

"Of course, child. There is always time in my day for recreation. And, as you see, I am surrounded by worldly riches." She waved her hand at the treasures on display in her chamber, the tapestries, the buffet groaning with gold plate. "But I shall not be in London very often. Your visit is timely, for I am leaving for my castle at Berkhamsted tomorrow. It is more peaceful there."

Elizabeth wondered if Uncle Clarence's awful fate had prompted Grandmother's decision, but did not like to ask for fear of upsetting her. "I wish I could be as devoted a servant of God as you, my lady," she said, filled with awe.

"There are many ways of serving Him," Grandmother smiled. "Some choose to do so by prayer; others by doing what they were created for, marrying and rearing children. I was lucky. Your grandfather and I loved each other, and we were blessed with twelve offspring, though only four have been spared to me. It is because I was granted such worldly happiness that I feel able to embrace a life of prayer and thanksgiving. You, Bessy, are destined to marry. You can serve God by loving your husband and your children. That is a holy way of life, too. It is what Our Lord has called you to do."

Elizabeth derived some small comfort from that. Who was she to resist what God had planned for her? It was a step on the way to acceptance.

Sitting in the barge on her way back to Westminster, she resolved to try to be as pious as her grandmother. She had been touched to see the old lady's gaunt face light up when she spoke of her happy marriage. How could Uncle Clarence have leveled that slur about the archer at her? It was absurd, and cruel.

Another baby sister arrived in November, when the court was at Eltham. Grandmother asked for her to be called Bridget, for she

cherished a special devotion to St. Bridget of Sweden, the found-
ress of the Bridgettine order, and often visited their nunnery of
Syon, which lay by the Thames at Isleworth.

"It is not a royal name, but it is a holy one, and I'm happy with
that," Father said, as he sat by Mother's bed, cradling his new
daughter in his arms. "And we have decided to dedicate this child
to God. He has been bountiful in sending us ten offspring, and we
wish to show our thanks by giving one back to Him."

Elizabeth gazed down at the tiny sleeping face and felt a deep
pang of sadness. Had she thought herself in a poor case, marrying
the future King of France? This little one would never know married love or the joy of children and would never wear a crown until
she rose to Heaven. Her life would be one of bells and offices, her
heart and mind not her own, but bound by the rule of poverty,
chastity, and obedience. And yet it was not for her to gainsay her
parents' choice. Giving a child to God was a holy, awesome deed
that involved great sacrifice. Elizabeth was sure that they had not
reached such a decision lightly.

On the morning after the birth, she stood godmother to her
new sister at her christening in the chapel at Eltham, which was
packed with a huge throng of nobles and knights. Little Bridget
was borne in procession to the font in the arms of her other godmother, Lady Stanley, with Elizabeth following. At the moment
of baptism, a hundred knights and esquires lit their torches, and
the heralds donned their tabards. The baby was taken up to the
altar to be confirmed, and then into an anteroom where she lay
wide-eyed and peaceful as Elizabeth and Lady Stanley presented
their gifts; then she was brought back to the Queen's chamber to
be blessed by her waiting parents.

Seven-year-old York had carried himself very importantly at
the christening and managed to stay out of mischief (maybe the
stern gaze of Grandmother York had had something to do with
that), but his little wife, Anne Mowbray, had been absent. Nor
did she attend the Christmas celebrations.

"Her mother writes that she is unwell," the Queen said after
Twelfth Night. "The doctors do not know what is wrong."

York looked sad when he was told that Anne had died, but he

did not weep. They had hardly known each other. Her death caused merely a ripple in his young life, which resumed its usual course after her lavish burial in the new chapel of St. Erasmus, which the Queen had founded in Westminster Abbey in thanksgiving for Ned's birth.

Father spent the summer matchmaking. Anne, now five, was to marry the Archduke Philip of Burgundy, Maximilian's son. Evidently alarmed, King Louis stopped the King's pension and began preparing for war. England's alliance with France now looked decidedly precarious, and Elizabeth began to believe that her marriage would never take place.

Ned, now rising ten, was to wed four-year-old Anne, the heiress of Brittany. Mary, at fourteen, was betrothed to Prince John of Denmark, and King James was urging Father to send Cecily to Scotland to be betrothed to his son. Even two-year-old Katherine had her suitors, among them the Infante Juan, son of the Spanish sovereigns and the heir to their thrones, and Thomas Butler, Earl of Ormond, although Elizabeth knew he did not stand a chance against the Infante.

When she entered Father's great chamber one day, she found him poring over a map.

"If these marriages take place," he told her, "English influence will extend into France, Scotland, Denmark, Burgundy, the Empire, and Spain—and beyond." It was a breathtaking triumph of diplomacy, demonstrating to Elizabeth what a great monarch her father was. But the prospect of herself and her siblings living in different lands was so sad that she had to turn away so that Father would not see the tears in her eyes. All she could think of was that they might never see each other again.

The Scots were the first to place the grand chain of alliances in jeopardy. Over the border they streamed, emboldened by rumors that their ally, King Louis, was growing cold toward England. In retaliation, Father raised a great army.

"I suppose I won't be going to Scotland," Cecily said, frowning over her lute.

"You're lucky," Mary replied. "I wish I wasn't going to Denmark. And Bessy doesn't want to go to France."

"I don't think I will be," Elizabeth chimed in. "But Father is still hopeful. He has told King Louis that he will continue to uphold the treaty, so long as Louis restores his pension and sends an embassy to arrange my marriage to the Dauphin."

"Perhaps we'll be waving you off to France soon, then," Mary said, the tears in her eyes belying the flippant remark. "Dearest Bessy, I do not know how I will bear to see you go."

"Or I," Cecily added.

Elizabeth was so overcome at the prospect that she could not speak. She loved all her siblings, but Mary was closer to her than any of them, a friend, a confidante, and a sharer of girlish secrets. She would miss her most of all. And it could not be long now before one or the other of them was sent away.

Father was greatly relieved when King Louis confirmed their treaty and agreed to send envoys to make arrangements for Elizabeth's marriage, insisting that there be no further delays. Elizabeth found it a strain hiding her heavy heart. Wherever she went, whatever she did, she could not forget that time, for her, was running out.

She was surprised to find herself still in England in May 1482. Her marriage was taking an eternity to arrange.

"If they'd left it to us women, you'd have been married years ago," Mother muttered. "I don't know why men have to make things so complicated."

The Queen and her elder daughters were enjoying an outdoor picnic, seated at a table set up under a shady tree and laden with gold plate, meats, fruits, and marchpane. It was a warm day and the girls had rolled up their sleeves, but Mother had refused to discard her hennin. She never did anything to detract from her dignity as queen. It annoyed Elizabeth, but she understood that Mother constantly felt the need to compensate for her unroyal origins.

At sixteen, she often found herself looking at her mother with a critical eye. The Queen was so exacting and controlling, always carrying on about how Madame la Dauphine should behave, as if Elizabeth had not had it drummed into her all these years. Sometimes, Elizabeth did not like her mother at all. Then she would feel guilty, remembering that the Queen had suffered many tragedies, and that beneath that cool manner of hers, she really did love her.

Today, though, Mother was in a witty, laughing mood. Elizabeth loved these times. But Mary wasn't joining in.

"What's wrong?" she asked.

"I don't feel well," Mary said, shivering.

Mother felt her brow. "You're burning up, child," she said, looking anxious. "Go indoors and lie down, while I send for Dr. Sirego." Rising, she summoned the servants to clear away the table.

"I'll go and sit with her," Elizabeth volunteered.

"Do not get too close," Mother warned. "We don't want you catching anything."

"You mustn't worry, Mary," Elizabeth said, catching up with her sister. "I won't leave you, even if it's the plague. Which it won't be, of course, for there have been no cases reported. I'm sure it's just a summer cold."

"Yes, it's probably that," Mary agreed, "but I do feel ill."

Elizabeth helped Lady Dacre to put Mary to bed, then sent for some cordial and settled down to watch over her sister. Cecily brought books to while away the hours, and soon Mother arrived with the doctor.

"It is just an ague," he pronounced, having asked Mary several questions and examined her water. "She will be better in a few days."

Mary did not get better. Her fever worsened and she complained of pains in her chest. Presently she gasped that she could not breathe. Then nothing she said made any sense at all. Across the bed, Mother and Father's eyes met.

"We must send for Ned," Father said in a hoarse voice.

Elizabeth was distraught. She would not leave Mary's side, and kept falling asleep with exhaustion in her chair. All day long, she offered heartfelt prayers to God, beseeching him to spare Mary. "Don't let her die!" she pleaded.

Mother was ever present, too, holding Mary's hand or mopping her brow with a cool damp flannel, willing her to get better, her face a mask of anguish. And there, at last, was Ned, grown taller since Christmas and looking every inch the Prince with his angelic good looks.

"Fair sister . . ." he said, and dissolved into tears. For Mary looked a sad sight, with her hair all sweaty and her lips an alarming shade of blue.

Elizabeth slept in her chair that night. She woke to find Mother rocking a corpse in her arms, keening softly, her cheeks streaked with tears. She burst out wailing.

Father came running, summoned by the doctor. He folded Elizabeth in his arms and held her tightly. "She is with God now. You must be glad for her." His voice broke, and he turned to the bed. "Our sweet angel is at peace, Beth." He embraced both the Queen and his lost child, then gave way to the most piteous weeping.

For four days, Mary's embalmed body lay on a bier surrounded by candles in the great hall so that all might pay their respects. Elizabeth and her siblings kept vigil, turn by turn. Even York showed a solemn face. The King and Queen did not appear in public. They were bearing their great sorrow in private and comforting their younger children, who did not really understand their loss.

When it came to following the coffin to the nearby church of the Observant Friars, which Father had founded, Elizabeth froze. She could not face it. She was all used up. Her parents bade her and her sisters stay behind. They themselves would not be attending the obsequies; they could not face it. It was a black-clad Ned who followed Mary's coffin on its chariot bearing her arms and drawn by sable-trapped horses on the long journey to St. George's Chapel at Windsor, where she was laid to rest beside her brother George.

* * *

Summer seemed like a mockery that year. Elizabeth felt that the sun should not be shining on a world from which Mary was so, so absent. The days ran into each other, a blur of grief, with poignant reminders of her everywhere. Elizabeth tried to turn to Cecily to fill the gap their sister had left, but Cecily, loving and headstrong as she was, was not Mary, and might soon be leaving for Scotland. Elizabeth was learning the painful lesson that where there was love, there would some day be loss. She even found herself saddened by the news that the pretended Queen Margaret had died in poverty in France. It barely registered with her that Father had offered Richmond lands on condition that he return from exile to marry one of her sisters. But he did not come.

"He suspects a trap," Father said one evening as they sat in the privy garden after supper. "Yet, this time, I really did intend to receive him into favor, and I asked Lady Stanley to assure him of my good faith." He sighed. He had seemed ill at ease since joining them at table. Now, he turned to Cecily.

"It is not Richmond who troubles me. Cis, the Duke of Albany, King James's brother, is here, and he has warned me that James is no friend to me at heart, despite that groveling apology for the border raid. I am therefore breaking off your betrothal to his son."

Cecily did not look too sad about that. She had told Elizabeth that she had never expected to be queen of Scots. "Am I to marry Richmond?" she asked.

"No, you are to wed the Duke of Albany," Father told her, accepting a goblet of wine from Humphrey Brereton.

Dismay was writ large on Cecily's face. "So I am still to go to Scotland, but I will never be its queen."

Father's eyes glinted. "I would not be so sure about that. Albany means to challenge the Scottish throne, and he has assured me of his lasting friendship. I am raising an army to help him press his claim. You could yet be a queen, Cis."

Cecily still looked dubious.

"I'll believe it when it happens," she told Elizabeth as they climbed the spiral stair to the Maidens' Hall.

* * *

King Alexander (for so Albany now styled himself) marched north to Scotland at the head of an English army. With him rode Uncle Gloucester. There was rejoicing at Westminster when it became known that they had taken King James captive, but then came the news that Albany had come to terms with his brother. In July, Gloucester made peace with James, insisting that the Scots cede Berwick to England, which was a great triumph, Father said, because the border town had changed hands between the English and the Scots a dozen times already. Uncle Gloucester returned a hero, but he did not come south.

Cecily found herself once more betrothed to James's son, but then Albany made another attempt to seize the Scottish throne and once more sought English support, securing the promise of her hand in the process. In October, Edward finally called off her betrothal to the Scottish heir and sealed the pact with Albany.

"All these betrothals!" Cecily complained. "My head hasn't stopped spinning. And I doubt that any of them will come to something."

Elizabeth was thinking the same thing about her own betrothal. In March had come the dreadful news that Mary of Burgundy had fallen from her horse and died, whereupon her Flemish subjects, who had never taken to her husband Maximilian, had appealed to King Louis to help them oust him. Father had been uneasy ever since he heard. "It would be just like Louis to press his advantage," he muttered. "And then we can say goodbye to the French alliance."

Despite the uncertain situation, he ordered that Christmas be kept lavishly at Westminster.

"We'll have a grand display of magnificence, Bessy, and show everyone that England is not to be trifled with!" he declared, as they stood in the beautiful White Hall on Christmas Eve and watched the servants decorating it with holly, ivy, and bay. Elizabeth's younger siblings were capering around excitedly, even two-year-old Bridget, who danced over with a sprig of berries and would have popped them in her mouth had Elizabeth not swooped on them. "No, sweeting, they will make you ill." A tragic look appeared on Bridget's rosy face, but Father swept her up in his arms and showed her the massive kissing bough that hung from the ceiling. A seasonal scent of spices filled the air, calling to mind past Yuletides when Mary had been there with them. Elizabeth's smile froze. They would miss her dreadfully this year—and at all the festive seasons to come.

The King put Bridget down and she toddled off to help Cecily make a holly wreath. Elizabeth did not want him to see her weeping; she would not add to his own pain.

"I must go and look out my gown for tomorrow," she said. As she left the hall, she wondered if this would be the last Christmas she ever spent in England. She was nearly seventeen now, and ripe for marriage, yet somehow she could not imagine a future in France. Maybe that was just wishful thinking.

It was the most lavish Christmas ever. Father presided over a magnificent court packed with lords and ladies, and appeared in ever more splendid attire at Mass, at table, and when processing through the palace. His giant figure overshadowed everyone else as he sat enthroned before the noble company. The grandeur of his court proclaimed the mightiness of his kingdom; it was filled with riches and men from almost every nation, and Elizabeth was in a turmoil of pride, joy, grief—and fear that she would soon no longer be a part of it.

"What surpasses all else are those beautiful and most delightful children," she heard Lady Stanley say to Mother as they stood together helping themselves to sweetmeats at a banquet hosted by the King on the evening before Twelfth Night. Mother, looking radiant in green taffeta shot with cloth of gold, smiled at her.

"They really are the most lovely princesses," Lady Stanley continued, making Elizabeth wonder if she was still hoping for a bride for her son. "And the Prince—how he has grown!"

Elizabeth looked at her brother, now twelve and wearing a dazzling outfit of white cloth of gold. He was wolfing up comfits and chatting condescendingly with young York, whose gold plate was piled precariously high with goodies.

"We are very proud of him," Mother said. "And he is doing so well at his studies."

"You must miss him when he is away at Ludlow," Lady Stanley said. "I know I miss my Henry. I wish he would heed the King and return to England. Then he can take his proper place in the world." Elizabeth wondered what that might be.

She wandered over to her father, who was laughing heartily with Lord Hastings, Uncle Rivers, and Lord Stanley.

"Close your ears, Bessy, that was not a jest for a young lady," Father grinned.

Suddenly, there was Humphrey Brereton at his sleeve. "Your Grace, your envoy from France is here, wishing to speak to you. He says it is urgent."

Father sighed. "Well, gentlemen, duty calls. Bessy, I'll be back."

He disappeared through the throng of guests, who bowed and curtseyed as he passed.

"I hope it's not bad news," Elizabeth said.

"It may be good news," replied Hastings.

"Don't worry, Bessy," Uncle Rivers soothed. "Louis and Maximilian are probably at fisticuffs again. Come, let me tempt you to a goblet of that fine Bordeaux."

Father did not reappear that evening, and when Hastings, Dorset, Stanley, and other lords were summoned to his closet, Mother began to look anxious.

Elizabeth went over to her. "What's going on?"

"I don't know," the Queen said, "but it's not like your father to neglect his guests. He loves a gathering. I would go and find him, but I can't really leave."

"I can play hostess, Mother—or I could seek out Father."

"Go and look for him, Bessy. But if you find him closeted with his lords, best leave them be."

Elizabeth picked up her silver skirts and hastened along the gallery that led to the King's lodgings. At the door, the guards raised their halberds to let her through. The presence chamber was deserted, so she sped through to the privy chamber beyond it. She could hear shouting from behind the door of the King's closet. It was Father, sounding angrier than she had ever heard him.

"I mean it—this is war!" she heard him roar. "I'll not tolerate such an insult!"

There was a murmur of men's voices in response.

She knocked at the door. She had to know what this was about. The shouting stopped as a nervous-looking page opened it.

"Bessy!" Father exclaimed. He was flushed and breathing heavily, his face thunderous.

She swallowed, feeling that she should not be here. "My lady mother was wondering where you were," she faltered. Stanley, Rivers, Hastings, and Dorset were regarding her with pained expressions.

"Bessy," the King said heavily, "this concerns you more than anyone. Louis has abandoned us. You will not be marrying the Dauphin. That villainous spider has made an alliance with the Flemings and betrothed the Dauphin to Maximilian's daughter Margaret. Under this treaty, he gets to keep all of Burgundy except Flanders, which has been ceded to Maximilian. And he has stopped the pension he recently restored to me." The words came through gritted teeth. As Elizabeth tried to take it all in, the King began pacing the floor, still seething. "This treaty has left my careful foreign policy in shreds, but what really moves me is that you, my precious Princess, must suffer the humiliation of being publicly jilted."

She did not mind her betrothal being broken, but her relief at not having to go to France was suddenly tempered by burning shame. Everyone would know that she had been cast aside. Those who were ignorant of the circumstances might think it was because of some defect in herself. How could she face appearing in public? People would be looking on her with pity—or worse.

She could not speak. She stood there, frozen, no longer the future queen of France, and feeling horribly exposed.

Father fixed a furious gaze on his advisers. "I will take any means of obtaining revenge! Let Parliament be summoned so that this whole rigmarole of gross deceits can be made public. I *will* make war on France!"

When the lords had gone, he put an arm around Elizabeth's shoulders. She was shaking, trying not to cry.

"I'll deal with Louis and then I will find another husband for you, Bessy—a greater match."

She nodded, although what greater match could there be? It did not matter, though. She was staying in England—it was what she had wanted all along.

"Go now and find some pleasant pastime to take your mind off things," Father bade her. "And Bessy—hold your head high. It is not any lack in you that has caused this, only that spider's perfidiousness. Now I must send for your lady mother and break the news to her."

When Elizabeth was commanded to the Queen's chamber later, she found her white with anger. Lady Stanley and Aunt Rivers were doing their best to calm her down, assisted by a tiny, sweet-faced lady whom Elizabeth recognized as her aunt's cousin, Alice FitzLewis. Lord Rivers and Lord Stanley were standing in the window, shaking their heads in sympathy.

"It is cruel!" Mother seethed. "To bring the child up all these years to be queen of France, and then to have her jilted like this. It's abominable! She was to be a queen . . ."

"And she may be yet, Madam," Lady Stanley said, gripping her hands. "There are other kingdoms. France is not the greatest monarchy in Christendom."

"We both know it is," Mother snapped.

Lady Stanley regarded her evenly. "There is Spain. The heir to the sovereigns is not yet spoken for."

"He is still a babe in arms," Mother said dismissively. She looked up. "Bessy!" She held open her arms and Elizabeth went into them. Now the tears did come. It felt strange to have Mother soothing her like a baby; the Queen was not given to demonstrations of affection. Elizabeth felt awkward, for she was not a child anymore, but she endured having her cheek pressed to Mother's velvet-clad bosom and wriggled away when she had suffered enough maternal consolation. She saw Alice FitzLewis regarding her with understanding.

Lady Stanley watched her dry her tears. "This will all pass, Lady Bessy," she said kindly. "God must have something better in store for you."

"At least you have been spared having that universal spider for a father-in-law and a stunted idiot for a husband," Mother said viciously.

Elizabeth stared at her. Only a week ago, Mother had been extolling the virtues of the Dauphin. So it had been true. He *was* ugly and backward. Had Father been deceived? He must have known, or should have made it his business to know. But a fat pension and a French crown for his daughter had probably outweighed the drawbacks, in his view. She tried not to feel bitter.

Lady Stanley smiled at her. "It is not the end of the world, child. Marriage alliances are broken all the time. You are fortunate in still being with your parents at seventeen. I was wed at twelve to my first husband, Edmund Tudor. He died of plague the following year, leaving me with child. I bore my beloved son when I was thirteen, at great cost to myself. So you see, Lady Bessy, there are worse things in life than a broken betrothal."

"Yes, I see that there are," Elizabeth said. She must keep a sense of proportion.

Uncle Rivers and Lord Stanley joined them at the fireside.

"We'll give those dishonorable French a drubbing," Rivers declared. "They won't get away with treating our Bessy like that." He patted her shoulder.

Lord Stanley rested his avuncular gaze on her. "If there is ever anything I can do for you, Lady Bessy, don't hesitate to ask."

Mother looked irritated. Elizabeth put it down to her being vexed with King Louis, but later, lying in her bed, she wondered. Could the Stanleys be angling for a betrothal between herself and Richmond? Were they trying to ingratiate themselves with her?

Mother would not approve. She wanted Father to have no truck with Richmond. She had said he was not worthy of any of their daughters and believed he might regard marriage to one of them as a means to obtaining the crown. He was ambitious, and his mother was ambitious for him. According to Mother, Lady Stanley was not quite rational when it came to her son.

"I know what it is to love your children," she had said, "but she is obsessed. She holds that he is the true heir of Lancaster. He, who is descended from the double adultery of John of Gaunt and Katherine Swynford! Such notions are dangerous, Bessy. They threaten our house. The last thing we want is to see the wars between Lancaster and York break out again. We must be wary of such ambitions."

Elizabeth had long thought that a marriage between Richmond and one of her sisters would do much to bind York and Lancaster together. But she kept such thoughts to herself.

In February, Father summoned her to his closet. He kissed her and bade her be seated.

"You are looking a lot happier these days, Bessy," he observed.

"I am feeling better," she said. "It helps to know that the whole kingdom is on my side."

"Indeed, it is!" he replied. "Parliament has denounced King Louis. We will be arming for war soon. Do you know, I think that old spider is encouraging the Scots to break Cecily's betrothal too?"

"That's awful of him."

"Well, he will soon be taught a lesson. But I did not ask you here to talk about Louis. I want to talk to you about your marriage."

Her marriage? Had there already been a new proposal?

Father was regarding her speculatively from across his desk. "I am seriously considering a marriage between you and Richmond. It would be an effective means of removing him from under the nose of King Louis and securing his loyalty."

It made sense, of course. But, having spent the past eight years expecting to be a queen, her first reaction was that this match was not worthy of her.

"I have been talking to Lord and Lady Stanley, and to my bishops, and told them that I wish to bring this marriage to fruition. Your lady mother, I should warn you, is not keen on the idea. But what do you think, Bessy?"

She hesitated. Her mother's response was predictable, and she might yet put pressure on Father to abandon the idea. Elizabeth could well imagine how overjoyed Lady Stanley must be at the prospect of securing her hand for her son. She tried to remember all she had heard of Richmond and wished she had listened more when he was spoken of. All she really knew was that he was twenty-six, lived in exile in Brittany, and was a paragon of all the virtues—at least, his mother said he was.

"Well?" the King said, interrupting her thoughts.

"I was considering, Father. It would be advantageous for England." She had a mental picture of a crown rolling away from her. "But I am your humble daughter. I will do your pleasure in this, as in all things."

Father beamed at her. "I knew I could rely on you to take a sensible view, Bessy."

Nothing had been settled when they moved to Windsor for Easter, which fell on 1 April 1483. It was a chilly spring and Elizabeth was startled when, one evening at supper, Father announced that he was going out fishing on the Thames with Lord Hastings.

"Are you mad, my lord?" Mother said tartly. "It's damp and cold out there."

"I'm a soldier, Beth. I don't concern myself with trivialities such as weather."

Elizabeth realized, with a jolt, that he did not look like a soldier. He was fat and his narrow eyes were sunk in rolls of flesh. He had not fought a battle for years.

He ignored Mother's protests. He went out on the river regardless, with Lord Hastings in tow. Elizabeth wondered if this was a cover for an assignation with Mistress Shore, who was still regularly to be seen at court.

When they returned to Westminster after Easter, Father took to his bed with a chill, and Mother said, "I warned you!" When

Elizabeth paid him a visit, she found him sitting up and reading state papers. But, the next day, Mother said he had taken a turn for the worse.

"He is shaking with ague," she told her children. "I have summoned his physicians."

They waited anxiously in her chamber for news. Presently, the doctors arrived.

"It is as you feared, Madam," they said. "His Grace let the damp cold chill his guts and it has led to this sickness. We have prescribed some physick, but the malady will take its course. We do not think there is great cause for concern. It does not help that he is still angry with the King of France. We have advised him not to dwell on it."

Elizabeth guessed that his illness afforded Father long hours in which to brood. She had not realized he had taken the breaking of her betrothal so much to heart. Still, the doctors did not seem worried. He would be well soon. He had to get well, for it would soon be St. George's Day and the Garter feast. She was looking forward to that.

Elizabeth knelt by the King's bed, her siblings on their knees beside her, even two-year-old Bridget. Only Ned was absent, for there had not been time to summon him from Ludlow. Mother was on the opposite side, holding Father's hand. His confessor was anointing him with holy oil, intoning prayers, giving him Extreme Unction. She knew what it meant. Around her stood the great nobles of the realm, their faces solemn.

She could not stop trembling. She had been shocked at the sight of her father when she had hastened to his bedchamber this morning after receiving Mother's urgent summons. The apoplexy he had suffered had left his face all twisted. When he tried to speak, the words sounded horribly garbled. He was doomed. There was no escaping the fact.

This could not be happening. She knelt there, willing him to rally. God could perform miracles, and she was praying as hard as she could for one.

The priest finished his office and retreated to the foot of the bed to continue his prayers.

Suddenly, Father spoke. "I am dying," he croaked. "Lord Hastings."

Hastings moved in two strides to the bed. "Sire?"

"Take care . . . my son, my wife and ch-children, my goods and all that ever I had. Gl . . . Gl . . . I have . . . changed my will. Glo . . . is to be protector." He closed his eyes, exhausted with the effort of speaking.

"I will look after the Prince and see that your Grace's wishes are carried out," Hastings said, with tears in his eyes. "You can depend on me."

"I . . . thank you," the King murmured. "Stanley . . ."

Lord Stanley approached the bed and knelt. "Your Grace?" Like Hastings, he seemed genuinely moved to see his sovereign laid so low.

"Look to Bessy's w-welfare," Father gasped. "Be a f-father to her." He muttered something else Elizabeth could not hear. Stanley bowed his head and vowed to do the King's bidding, then rose and stood by her, as if to show that his paternal care began here. She felt bolstered by his bluff, hearty presence, but she did not want him to be a father to her; she wanted her own father, who was slipping away before her tear-filled eyes.

"Dorset, come," the King croaked. "This enmity between you and H-Hastings must . . . end. I command and entreat you both, whom I love, to be reconciled." His voice tailed away. Hastings and Dorset looked at each other warily from opposite sides of the bed.

"Here is my hand on it," Hastings said, walking across to Dorset.

"And mine," Dorset declared. They shook hands and gave each other the kiss of peace, but their eyes remained cold. Elizabeth wondered if they were still competing for the favors of Mistress Shore.

The King's eyes had closed. His face looked gray; his lips were blue. Gradually, his rasping breathing slowed—and then there was silence. Mother slid to her knees, grasping his dead hand, her shoulders heaving. The children began sobbing loudly. Elizabeth turned to Lord Stanley, who put his arm around her, drew her to him and let her weep until his doublet was sodden.

"I will be your protector now," he murmured. "You must look upon me as a second father."

Elizabeth barely heard him. She could not take her eyes from the still figure on the bed. That was her beloved father—dead. She could hardly believe it.

Mother rose, her beautiful face ravaged by tears. She bent and kissed the pale forehead. "He was only forty-one," she murmured. "Why, God, why?"

The priest regarded her with compassion. "We must not question His will, my daughter. Your husband is in His hands now and in hope of holy bliss."

Elizabeth was surprised when Lord Hastings reached out a hand to the Queen, to whom he had never shown much warmth. "Madam, you must be strong. You have your son to think of, and your other children."

"Yes," said Lord Stanley. "The King is dead. Long live the King! We must all offer allegiance to our new sovereign lord, King Edward the Fifth."

Mother visibly rallied. "You are right, my lords. We must ensure his smooth succession. But that can wait until tomorrow; we can leave the poor boy in ignorance for a little longer. He is only twelve. Today is for mourning my dear lord. Come to me, children." She held out her arms to them.

Chapter 6

1483

Late the next morning, wearing a simple black gown, Elizabeth obeyed a summons to the Queen's chamber and found her mother swathed in mourning clothes, a nun-like wimple and a black veil. With her sat Dorset and Uncle Lionel, who, by good fortune, had been visiting the court when Father died and had been able to stay and offer spiritual comfort.

"Be seated, Bessy," Mother instructed, quite calmly. "We have just been discussing the proceedings in the council meeting this morning. Ned is to be proclaimed king tomorrow. A new bidding prayer will be read in churches, enjoining all loyal subjects to pray for him and for me and all you children."

Elizabeth found it hard to think of her brother as king. He was so young. How would he rule?

"We have been reading your father's will," Mother went on. "He left you ten thousand marks for a dowry, on condition that you be governed by me in your choice of husband."

Elizabeth did not care about husbands. The future stretched ahead, bleak and sad, because Father was not here. She had barely slept last night, and this morning, when she arose, her legs could barely carry her.

"My lady, I will be guided by you. But who is to be regent until Ned comes of age?"

"The King's Council," Mother said firmly. "We Wydevilles and our following command the majority. We are in a strong position. Your uncle Rivers has control of the King, Dickon is in attendance on him, and your uncle Edward Wydeville commands the fleet. The Tower of London and the royal treasure and ordnance are in our custody. You and York and your sisters are in my charge. Thank goodness I ensured that the Prince's council at Ludlow was comprised of my blood and affinity."

It sounded, Elizabeth thought, dismayed, as if Mother was expecting opposition, as well there might be, for the Wydevilles had never been popular.

"You should tell Bessy about the codicil," Dorset said darkly.

"What codicil?" Elizabeth asked.

"The codicil to your father's will," Mother said. "He added it on his deathbed. It provides for your uncle Gloucester to act as lord protector during Ned's minority."

Elizabeth felt reassured. For many years now, Uncle Gloucester had been ruling the north loyally as Father's trusted lieutenant. He was the obvious choice.

Clearly, Mother didn't think so. "We cannot allow that to happen. He detests us—always has—and will do his best to overthrow us."

"But why does he hate you?" Elizabeth asked, feeling overwhelmed. She knew that Uncle Gloucester could be counted on to rule wisely and well, but now here was Mother making difficulties, and they didn't need more trouble at this sad time.

"He has always despised me and mine because he thinks we are ignoble upstarts who have been advanced beyond our merits. Like other lords I could name, he is jealous and resentful of the power and influence we command."

"But he has huge influence in the north. He's like another king. Father often said there has been no greater subject."

"That's what concerns us," Dorset said, "but Gloucester has another reason to hate our mother, for he holds her—and our kin— responsible for the death of his brother Clarence."

Mother said nothing. She did not have to. Elizabeth could remember her urging Father to remove Uncle Clarence once and for all. She could recall her saying that she had packed Parliament with those of her faction. She could see why Uncle Gloucester hated her for it. But Uncle Clarence had deserved death, surely? He had been dangerous.

"I have no intention of allowing Gloucester to seize power," the Queen said. "I have worked hard to ensure that everything is in place for the continuance and flowering of our supremacy when Ned comes to the throne. The councillors agreed today that they should govern for him, but that Gloucester should have a leading role rather than an autonomous one, because no regent ever laid down his office save reluctantly. The danger is that, if the entire government were committed to him, he might try to usurp the throne. My kinsmen voted for this proposal, for they are afraid that, if Gloucester governs alone, or seizes the crown, they might be put to death for their part in Clarence's death."

"We Wydevilles are so important that, even without Gloucester, we can make and enforce decisions," Dorset boasted.

Elizabeth saw that the rift between Uncle Gloucester and her mother's family was very serious indeed. But what of herself? She had Wydeville blood, yet her uncle had always been kind and affectionate to her.

Uncle Lionel rose and stoked the fire. "The position is this. Once the King is crowned, he can summon Parliament, then Parliament can confirm the arrangements for the regency. It is vital that Ned is crowned soon, to pre-empt Gloucester seizing power for himself."

"We have persuaded the lords to set a date, the fourth of May, for the coronation," Dorset said.

"That's about three weeks away," Elizabeth calculated. "Uncle Gloucester will surely be here by then."

"I doubt it," her half-brother replied. "We have not yet informed him of the King's death—and Middleham is many days' ride away. With luck, by the time he hears of it, Ned will be crowned."

Elizabeth's head was spinning. She had not realized that there had been such poisonous divisions and rivalry at her father's court. She could see why Uncle Gloucester had stayed in the north. It seemed dreadful that they had been plunged into a power struggle when they should be mourning poor Father. Her own feeling was that his will should be respected, and that Uncle Gloucester should be granted the regency. But then he might take revenge on Mother and her family for Clarence's death. Oh, it was a horrible, complicated situation. Yet it seemed wrong and deceitful not to inform him of his brother's passing, or the codicil.

"Ned will support us," Mother was saying. "He has been brought up by my kinsfolk from infancy. And he will be thirteen in five months' time. Henry of Lancaster was declared of age to rule on his sixteenth birthday, so thankfully it will not be a long minority. We just have to contain Gloucester for that short time."

Mother took Elizabeth and her other children to see Father's body lying in state in Westminster Hall. It was hard to believe it was him encased in that large coffin covered with rich palls and surrounded by candles. Elizabeth found it incomprehensible that she would never see him again.

Later, they watched from a window as the coffin was solemnly lifted into a barge and conveyed up the Thames to Windsor, where it was to be buried in St. George's Chapel. Neither the Queen nor the royal children were to be present; they would remain at Westminster for now. Mother had explained that, in accordance with royal custom, the funerals of kings were not attended by their female relations.

"We must mourn in private," she said.

Elizabeth found that spending time with her younger siblings provided a welcome distraction from her grief, although she was growing weary of young York's boisterous war games. He would never sit still for long and got bored when she tried to make him look at a book, so she usually ended up entertaining eight-year-old Anne and four-year-old Katherine. She was showing them how to sew garments for their dolls when she overheard Lady Dacre murmur to Mistress Welles that, according to the latest gossip, Lord Hastings had taken Elizabeth Shore as his mistress.

"He wasted no time!" Mistress Welles sniffed.

"He was much enamored of her while the King was alive. It was well known that they shared her favors. Maybe she now feels she needs a protector in Lord Hastings. My lord of Dorset is said to be furious at her not favoring him, and even more incensed against Hastings."

Elizabeth slipped to her knees and rescued a doll from the puppy that was trying to eat it. She hoped the women would not realize that she was listening. But they were at the other side of the room, sitting at table with their mending, and clearly unaware of how far their voices carried.

"And Lord Hastings, of course, is hostile to the Queen's entire kin, on account of this rivalry with Lord Dorset," Lady Dacre continued. "But there is no doubting his loyalty to our young King. As he loved the father, so he loves the son."

"Even though the boy has Wydeville blood."

"Aye, even so. I'll wager he'll try to keep the Queen from ruling, yet she and her faction seem firmly entrenched."

"I'll be glad when the boy is safely crowned and all strife brought to an end," Mistress Welles said.

So will I, Elizabeth thought fervently.

Mother burst into the Maidens' Hall, with Dorset in tow, as Elizabeth and Cecily jumped up and made hasty curtseys.

"Gloucester is on his way south," she told them. "Somehow he has learned of your Father's death."

"The means is not far to seek." Dorset's handsome, craggy face was livid with anger. "It was that viper Hastings, I have no doubt. He will stop at nothing to prevent us from wielding power."

Mother looked distracted. "I wonder if Ned is on his way. I sent fast messengers to Ludlow to summon him to London, and I can rely on Uncle Rivers and Dickon to make all possible haste. We need to get him crowned before Gloucester arrives." She began to pace in agitation, wringing her hands. "Dear God, I wish I knew where they were."

"My lady, please don't worry," Elizabeth urged. "Uncle Gloucester would not wish any harm to Ned, or any of us, and nor would my Lord Hastings."

"You would do well not to trust either of them," Mother retorted. "I can't see Gloucester tolerating us in power, and I *can* see him seeking revenge for Clarence's death. I tell you, if he reaches London, we are all in danger."

Elizabeth shivered. Mother had it all wrong. Uncle Gloucester had been ruling the north justly and well. Why should he not rule all England as wisely? She could not imagine him wreaking vengeance. It was just not in character. Mother was overwrought with grief, she decided.

Seeing her silent, Dorset's eyes narrowed. "Bessy, Gloucester is driven by hatred and ambition. Never doubt it. Remember how he colluded in the disinheriting of his mother-in-law so that he could gain her lands? And he's cunning, too. Look how he tracked down Anne Neville."

"I have grave misgivings about where his ambition will lead him," Mother cut in. She turned to her son. "What should we do?"

"We wait for Ned to arrive—and pray it will be soon!" he said.

"Very well. Children, you must hold yourselves in readiness, for there is no knowing what will happen."

Elizabeth was bewildered. In readiness for what?

Still she could not believe that Uncle Gloucester and Lord Hastings wished them harm or had any evil intent. Both had loved Father and been loyal to him. Surely they would not go so far as to take revenge on Mother?

Much perplexed, she tried to find Lord Hastings, hoping he would reassure her that he meant no ill to the Queen and did not suspect Gloucester of any disloyalty, but she could not locate him, so she sought out Lord Stanley, who was finishing dinner and chatting to some of his fellow councillors. He rose when he saw her and bowed.

"Lady Bessy! What can I do for you?"

"Father Stanley," she said, hoping that addressing him thus would win his confidence. "May I speak with you in private?"

"Of course." He led the way to a gallery with diamond-paned windows that overlooked a formal garden. "You look worried, Princess."

"I am. My lady mother told me that my lord of Gloucester is on his way south." She related what the Queen had said.

Stanley considered for a few moments. "If the Wydevilles fear Gloucester, then certain it is that he fears them, too. Your father's codicil expressed the wish that his brother act as lord protector and, as Gloucester will see it, that is his right. You can see, Lady Bessy, why he would wish to enforce it. To him, denying him that right must seem like a hostile act. Has it occurred to you that he might fear the consequences to himself if your mother's faction seize power for themselves?"

Elizabeth felt desperate. It was looking very much as if her mother and her following were to blame for this horrible situation. "Is there no way to make peace between the Queen and Gloucester?" she asked.

Stanley shook his head sadly. "I fear that enmity goes too deep on either side. If I may be frank, Gloucester has never loved the Wydevilles. He has never forgiven your mother for Clarence's death. There's no way around that. And your lady mother cannot change who she is or where she came from, or the part she played in Clarence's fall. It's a sad fact that the Wydevilles are not liked by the nobility or the people."

Elizabeth was silent for a while, thinking furiously. "But they have to work together. Uncle Gloucester is to lead the Council."

"Not if your lady mother can help it! She is doing all she can to pre-empt his taking up that office."

A distant church bell sounded outside. Stanley bowed. "I must go, Lady Bessy. The Council is to sit again in a few minutes. Try not to worry. I and my fellows will strive for a peaceful conclusion to all this strife."

* * *

Late that afternoon, Elizabeth received a summons from the Queen, who was waiting for her in her privy garden. It seemed that Mother had begun to turn to her and Dorset, the oldest of her children near at hand, at this time of trouble. It made Elizabeth feel very grown-up, but it also burdened her with grave matters that she felt should not be her concern—or not yet.

"I have had a letter from Gloucester," the Queen said. "He wishes to console me in my loss and assures me of his care and natural affection toward you, his brother's children."

Elizabeth was greatly relieved. She had known she could rely on Uncle Gloucester to do the right thing and ease the tensions between him and Mother.

"It is a most loving letter," she said. "You must feel better now."

Mother looked at her as if she were mad. "I most certainly do not! He has written to the Council, too, and demonstrated that he is not to be trusted. Oh, he is most reassuring. He writes that he has always been loyal to your father, and will be equally loyal to his brother's son, and to all his brother's children if—which God forfend—Ned should die. And there he unmasks himself and his intentions! Why should Ned die? Why even mention it? Unless, of course, he has been envisaging it, to his own advantage!" Mother was becoming distraught.

"My lady, you forget that if anything happened to Ned, York would be king."

"If he is allowed to live that long!" the Queen shrilled.

"May I see the letter?" Elizabeth asked. Mother handed it to her and she read it quickly. "But, my lady, Uncle Gloucester says he will expose his life to every danger so that I and my brothers and sisters might flourish in our father's realm. Is that not comforting?"

"No, Bessy, it is not, and the sooner you start seeing this man for what he is, the better. As long as there is breath in my body, I will never allow him to rule in this kingdom."

She was being unfair and irrational. If only she could see that Uncle Gloucester had the best aims and was paving the way for them to work amicably together. Elizabeth did understand her mother's fears, but was sure they were misplaced.

She prayed that Ned would arrive in London soon. It could not be long now, surely?

April was at an end, and still there was no sign of him. Neither Uncle Rivers nor Dickon had sent any news. Mother was panicking because there was no word of Gloucester's coming either. Where were they?

Elizabeth could settle to nothing. There was a sense of impending doom in the air. She was aware of tensions within the court, of a resolute sense of purpose in Lord Hastings, and the palpable hatred between him and Dorset. Lord Stanley seemed to be perpetually on the alert. Mother was taut with anxiety. The atmosphere had even got to the children, who were fractious and highly strung.

Elizabeth found it hard to sleep at night; when she did, she was haunted by disturbing dreams in which someone was chasing her. It was a man, someone she did not know, for she never saw his face.

The dream came again on the last night of April, but suddenly someone was shaking her awake, none too gently, and Mother's voice invaded her slumber.

"Bessy! You must wake up. There is no time to lose!"

It was as if she was four years old again and Mother was about to rush her off to the sanctuary. She struggled to come to, and saw that the Queen was just as distraught as she had been all those years ago, if not more so.

"What's wrong?" she mumbled, rubbing sleep out of her eyes.

Mother's voice shook. "Ned is taken, *and* my brother Rivers and Dickon, and other kinsmen of mine have been arrested and sent no man knows where, to be done with God only knows! Gloucester has destroyed us at a stroke! Get up, hurry! We must go into sanctuary again. It is the only safe place. Hurry, girl, hurry!"

Elizabeth was shaking from head to foot, her mind suddenly filled with vague and disturbing memories from twelve years earlier.

"Here, put this on." The Queen pulled a gown from a peg and

thrust it at her. "And hurry! Gloucester will soon be in London. There is not a minute to waste." She hurried away to rouse Cecily and then sped off to the nursery to collect the other children. "Wait for me in the White Hall!" she called over her shoulder.

"What's going on?" Cecily gasped, barely awake.

"Uncle Gloucester has seized Ned and Uncle Rivers and Dickon," Elizabeth said. "He is coming to London. I don't know any more. Hurry, get dressed. Mother is taking us to sanctuary."

"What?"

"There's no time for questions, Cis. Make haste."

They pulled on their clothes, summoned their maids, and helped to pack their belongings into chests, which grooms carried down to the White Hall. There, they witnessed a flurry of panicked activity. It seemed that every servant had been roused and impressed to carry the Queen's belongings to sanctuary. There were piles of stuff in the White Hall, and relays of people were carrying them out of the palace.

Mother and Dorset were standing in a corner, in urgent conversation with several lords. As Elizabeth joined them, she heard the Queen say, "We must raise an army! We must defend ourselves and free the King from Gloucester's clutches!"

"I don't see how that can be done," one of the men said.

"You can summon your affinities!" Mother retorted.

The nobles shifted uncomfortably, avoiding her gaze. One or two looked openly hostile.

"Why do you demur?" Dorset challenged them. "Where is your loyalty?"

"It is with the King, my lord," he was told. "And some of us think that our late sovereign's wishes should be respected, and that it would be more just that our young monarch should be governed by his paternal uncle than by his maternal kinsfolk."

Mother gave them a withering look. "Since you will not aid women and children in distress, and are heedless of the safety of your King, I must take the only course open to me. Come, my lord of York, and you, my daughters, we will go to the sanctuary, so that I can deliver you from this present danger. As for the King, I can only pray that God will watch over him." At that, she broke down. "Oh, Holy Mother, protect my innocents! Spare us from ruin and misfortune!"

The lords said nothing, but stood watching as the Queen led her party to the door, with Dorset and Uncle Lionel holding the younger children's hands. It was still dark outside, and servants continued to haul chests and bundles toward Westminster Abbey. As they walked the short distance, Mother began weeping profusely and bewailing her misfortune, which set off the little girls. Elizabeth couldn't help thinking that she was overreacting, and that she should be showing greater restraint in front of the children. It was horrible to see her so distressed, and she remembered how frightening it had been when she was a young child and they were in sanctuary before. Only York seemed unfazed, walking apart and behaving as if this was a great adventure. How soon he would be disillusioned, Elizabeth thought sadly.

She had never forgotten kindly Abbot Milling, but he was dead now, and she wondered if his successor would allow them to lodge in his house. She hated the prospect of staying in the grim sanctuary building, yet it was there that Mother led them.

They had no sooner registered themselves than Abbot Eastney appeared. He had aged little since the day he had stood godfather to Ned, and was still tall and thin, his face lean and serious beneath his white tonsure. He smiled at them kindly.

"My daughter, you and yours are welcome to use my house while you are here," he told Mother, as she knelt for his blessing. "Come, let us go in and get these children to bed."

"Thank you! Thank you!" she sobbed.

And so, once more, they were installed in the magnificent Cheyneygates, and Elizabeth again found herself lying on a pallet bed in the Queen's bedchamber. The only difference was that they were all much older and, sadly, poor Mary was not with them. Elizabeth still missed her terribly, and never more so than now. As she listened to Mother weeping, she wondered if this flight into sanctuary had really been necessary. Why was her mother convinced that Uncle Gloucester intended harm to them all?

"What exactly did happen today, my lady?" she asked.

Mother's sigh came out of the darkness. "I don't think I have the strength to recount it."

"My lady, I need to know!" Elizabeth had rarely spoken so forcefully to the Queen.

"And I do, too," said Cecily. "If we are in danger and have to stay here, we should be told why."

There was a pause. "Very well. As you know, someone—Lord Hastings, I believe—informed Gloucester of your father's death, and he rode south and met up with the Duke of Buckingham, who has never loved me or my blood. He thinks himself above us and has long resented having been forced to marry your aunt Katherine. Yet that was the King's doing, not mine."

Elizabeth wondered. Father had listened to Mother when she pressed him to do things. Again, she realized she was seeing her mother in a more critical light, and felt at once guilty and resentful.

"Of course, one would expect Gloucester, who also hates us, to ally himself to Buckingham," Mother spat. "And no doubt Hastings is in it too—and all of them bent on bringing us down." Elizabeth knew Buckingham quite well and had danced with him at court. He was a bullish, hot-tempered man, but most eloquent and persuasive. He would relish this chance of paying back the Wydevilles.

"But what happened?" She tried to bring her mother back to the point.

"Ned was on his way to London, in the charge of Uncle Rivers, Dickon, and an escort of two thousand men. Gloucester had ridden south and joined his forces with those of Buckingham—clearly this was all planned—and he surprised Ned's party at Stony Stratford. Uncle Rivers and the rest had no idea they were walking into a trap. They supped with Gloucester and Buckingham, and apparently it was all most convivial, but, the next day at dawn, Gloucester suddenly arrested Uncle Rivers, Dickon, and other officers of the King . . ." She began to sob. "They have been taken north as prisoners, and I fear I shall never see them again! And they have seized charge of Ned and are bringing him to London."

"Don't cry, Mother," Cecily said, as Elizabeth heard her feet pattering across the floor to the bed. "I'm sure they will be all right."

"Dear God, I pray so!" Mother burst out. "But I am in no doubt that Gloucester has intended my overthrow all along. And no one seems to be opposing him! On the contrary, many lords are hastening to join him. He had no right to seize the King, for he has not yet been confirmed as lord protector and has no legal mandate to act as he did. But Ned is too young to stand up to him."

Together, Elizabeth and Cecily tried to calm her, and eventually she drifted off into a fitful sleep. Back in bed, Elizabeth lay fretting. When it boiled down, Uncle Gloucester had only done what anyone appointed lord protector would reasonably do. He had taken the King under his protection. *He* had not driven Mother into sanctuary: she had chosen to come here. He had perhaps intended to reach an amicable arrangement with her once he got to London, but she had not waited to give him the chance, and now he might be angered—not to mention embarrassed—by her precipitate flight and the very public implication that she had something to fear from him.

Did he really pose a threat to them? She could not accept that. Father had never doubted his loyalty, and she wanted to believe the best of him. Even if he did hate her mother's family, he had never shown any animosity to her, and she prayed that he would never look upon her as an enemy, for she could never hate him as Mother did.

Long before dawn, the Queen was up, complaining that she could not sleep. Once roused, Elizabeth found that she too was wide awake and followed her into the Jerusalem Chamber. There she found a scene of total chaos, with exhausted servants still bringing the Queen's stuff. Chests, coffers, and packages were piled everywhere, and men were still staggering in with bundles trussed on their backs. Some were unloading carts below, their shouts echoing up the stairs. Others were even knocking a hole in a wall to make space for passing things through, as the Abbot looked anxiously on.

Mother seemed oblivious to it all. She sank down on the rushes, looking desolate.

"What is all this stuff?" Elizabeth asked, shivering in her night robe.

"It is what we will need for our stay in sanctuary," Mother said. "I remembered how little we had here before and decided to bring as many of our possessions as I could, for I fear we might be here for a long while."

"I do hope not," Elizabeth muttered fervently, seeing the anguished look on the Abbot's face. It seemed wrong for Mother to be worrying about her worldly goods when they were supposedly in danger.

In the midst of all this chaos, the Archbishop of York arrived, panting with the effort of mounting the stairs.

"Madam," he said, "I have brought you the Great Seal of England to hold on behalf of the King."

The Queen stared at it. It was the fount of royal authority.

"At least someone is on my side," she said. "Yet I have no power now, nor any means of exercising it. And this time there will be no King Edward coming to rescue me and my children." She fell to weeping again.

"Madam," soothed Archbishop Rotherham, "be of good cheer. This situation is not as bad as you seem to think it is. Lord Hastings has assured me that all will be well. He himself is not worried, and he truly believes that my lord of Gloucester has only the best intentions."

Elizabeth brightened, hearing that. Mother, she was sure, had overreacted. She herself had found it hard to believe that Lord Hastings, her father's closest friend and adviser, could ever be disloyal. He was a wise man, and if he thought that Uncle Gloucester's intentions were honorable, then they must be.

But Mother had burst into fresh tears. "Ah, woe to him!" she cried. "He is one of those that labor to destroy me and my blood. And the King is of my blood!"

The Archbishop frowned. "Madam, you see danger where there is none. I promise you, if they crown any other king than your son, we shall on the morrow crown his brother." With that, he handed her the Great Seal.

"Father, I thank you," she replied, belatedly kissing his ring. "This is a great comfort to me. But tell me, is there any word of my brother Rivers and my son Sir Richard Grey?"

"None as yet, Madam, but I am sure we will hear something soon. You should not worry. Gloucester is a just man."

Mother shook her head. "I wish I could believe it."

"Well, I do," the Archbishop countered. "I have had the cure of souls for many years and I think I am as good a judge of character as any."

It was dawn when he left, by which time Mother had calmed down somewhat.

Soon afterward, the Abbot returned. "Your Grace, you should know that the Thames is full of boats carrying my lord of Gloucester's servants. Some have disembarked and are watching to see if anyone approaches the sanctuary. One passerby was searched."

"I was right," Mother faltered. "Gloucester wants me out of the way. We are prisoners." She dabbed at her eyes and glared at Elizabeth. "He means no good to us. I told you!"

Elizabeth could not bear her mother always putting the worst construction on things or treating her as if she knew nothing. "Could it be that Uncle Gloucester fears you will plot against him?"

"I'm sure he does!" Mother was tart. "And I have every justification. I'll do whatever it takes to overthrow him."

There was no reasoning with her. Elizabeth picked up her book and said no more.

Three days later, the Abbot came again. "Madam, my lord of Gloucester has arrived in London with the King. Two of my lay brethren were in the City buying provisions and saw them riding through the streets, side by side, both wearing mourning. You will be pleased to hear that the Duke showed King Edward much respect and honor."

Elizabeth was relieved to hear it. Soon, Uncle Gloucester would give further proof of his good intentions, Mother would be reassured—and then they could leave sanctuary. All would be well. But the Abbot was regarding Mother speculatively.

"There's something you're not telling me," the Queen said.

"Maybe, Madam, there is something *you're* not telling *me*," he replied. "At the head of the procession, the lay brothers saw four wagons loaded with weapons bearing the badges of your Grace's brothers and sons, and there were criers walking with them, who made it known that these arms had been collected by my lord of Gloucester's enemies to use against him, to his utter destruction. Is it true?"

The Queen erupted. "No, it most certainly is not! Those weapons were being stored against a war with the Scots. The late King could have attested to that! Father Abbot, this is the proof of Gloucester's perfidy. He and Buckingham are seeking to arouse hatred against me and my kin, and to estrange public opinion from us."

"Maybe, Madam, the dukes did not realize that the weapons were for use against the Scots," the Abbot suggested, still looking doubtful. "In this current climate of suspicion, it might be easy to believe that they were intended for another purpose."

Mother shook her head vehemently. "No! Gloucester is out to ruin me. I know it!"

Abbot Eastney sighed. "I shall pray that Almighty God brings your Grace and my lord of Gloucester to a peaceful accord."

Elizabeth did not give her mother a chance to reply. "Tell me, Father Abbot, did the lay brothers say anything of the King's demeanor? He must be grieving for our father and perplexed by the great changes that have happened of late." She wished she could be with Ned and comfort him.

The Abbot smiled at her. "They were full of praise for him, my lady Princess. Judging by the acclaim of the crowds who had come flocking to see him, he has already won the love of his subjects. They said he had such dignity in his person and such charm in his face that, however much anyone might gaze, he could never weary the eyes of those who beheld him."

She could imagine it. Ned had such a sweet nature, and he was polite and scholarly, wise far beyond his age. He would make a great king.

Chapter 7

1483

Within days, they had unwillingly resigned themselves to the monotony of life in sanctuary. Their lives were now governed by bells and prayers. No servants had remained with them, for Mother was unable to pay them, and it was once more fortunate that she had lived as a commoner before she became queen. She helped her younger children to dress and made a desultory attempt to set lessons for them, although she was easily distracted and often asked Elizabeth or Cecily to take over.

Elizabeth thanked God for the presence of her siblings, who enlivened her existence and kept her occupied. She was glad that they were together, although it saddened her that Ned could not be there, and York had, several times, loudly proclaimed his desire to leave them and join his brother. Yet she was used to Ned being away at Ludlow, and surely they would see him soon.

York was already growing bored and restive, much to Mother's irritation. "Take him outside!" she commanded Elizabeth and Cecily, and they hastened to do so, lest she become further agitated. That morning, she had received an upsetting letter from Father's executors, who had declined to administer his will because she was holding his children in sanctuary, which meant that his bequests to them could not be carried out. Accordingly, Cardinal Bourchier had placed all the late King's assets under sequestration. Thus, Mother was penniless, and Elizabeth and her sisters could have no dowries. Not that anyone was thinking about their futures and there was no knowing whether the marriages that had been planned for them would still go ahead.

The palace of Westminster was just yards away, and yet it might have been on the moon. So near and yet so far! Still, Elizabeth told herself, watching York roaring around the Abbot's courtyard, things could be much worse. They could be in the common sanctuary with murderers and thieves instead of living in luxury in the Abbot's house.

When they returned indoors for dinner, Mother was again complaining about how she had been reduced to humble straits and that there was no kind butcher this time to supply her with meat. "Father Abbot has been most hospitable, but we cannot expect him to go on providing us all with food. I hate presuming on his charity! Oh, if your father could see us now!"

After dinner, Elizabeth got out her chess set and tried to play with York, who would not sit still and readily gave place to Cecily. She was fed up with her brother crashing about the place, always wanting to be up and doing something. Dorset and Uncle Lionel were trying their best to keep him amused, but even they couldn't channel all that energy. How different her two brothers were!

"Couldn't we take him for a walk, my lady?" she asked, giving up on the chess game. "The sanctuary boundaries extend for some way around the abbey."

"No!" Mother cried. "You could be seized. I will not allow it."

"I don't think so," Elizabeth sighed.

"You will not take the risk. Sanctuaries might be holy places, but they have been breached." There was an eloquent pause, and Elizabeth recalled that after the Battle of Tewkesbury, her own father had entered the nearby abbey and slain or dragged out the Lancastrians who had sought sanctuary there. Dorset had told her that years ago and said that, in war, rights were often overlooked, and that the King had only done what was necessary.

"But the sanctuary here enjoys the special protection of the King," she pointed out, and then realized her mistake.

"Who is in the power of Gloucester!" Mother retorted.

It was decided that Dorset should leave sanctuary and try to raise support for the Queen. He departed on a bright May day, planning to go into hiding until he could safely contact his friends, and promising to get word to Mother of the whereabouts of Uncle Rivers and Dickon.

Although she had urged him to go, Mother was bereft. "I have four sons, and I am cut off from three of them," she wept. "I can only pray that God keeps them safe."

Elizabeth did feel sorry for her, because she knew she was grieving for Father, but she was finding her constant emotional storms and her obsessive suspicions about Uncle Gloucester wearing. Couldn't she try to put on a brave face, especially for the younger children's sakes? Anne, Katherine, and Bridget were much affected by their mother's moods. Elizabeth worried about Bridget, who was different from other children in some way, although she could not exactly say why. Mother had not mentioned it, so maybe it was her imagination. Yet Bridget somehow seemed vulnerable, and Elizabeth's heart felt heavy when she remembered that her little sister was destined for a convent. But, she comforted herself, that might never happen now.

Abbot Eastney visited them faithfully every day and brought them what news he could. He was optimistic and clearly thought that Mother's fears were unfounded.

"The Council has recognized the Duke of Gloucester as lord protector," he told them, accepting the cup of wine Mother offered him, which had been left over from dinner.

"Since he has control of my son, they had no choice," the Queen muttered.

"But it was the late King's wish, Madam," Abbot Eastney pointed out, "and, from what I have heard, a wise choice. My lord of Gloucester has wasted no time. He has ordered that the laws of the realm be enforced in the name of King Edward the Fifth. He is having coins struck bearing the King's image, and he is insistent that all royal honors be paid to his Grace."

Mother looked doubtful. "And what of my other son and my brother Rivers?"

The Abbot hesitated. "I have just received some news. They are in custody in Yorkshire, Madam. Given that unfortunate discovery of the weapons, my lord of Gloucester fears that they might rise against him. But the Council has decided that they will not be prosecuted. When things settle down, I'm sure they will be released."

"Gloucester had no right to imprison them—he was not then lord protector!"

The Abbot sighed. "But the Council has now authorized it. Madam, there is good news. King Edward's coronation has been set for the twenty-fourth of June. Everyone is looking forward to it, and to the peace and prosperity that will surely follow. I was at court this morning and saw Lord Hastings, who was saying that he was overjoyed at this new world, and that nothing worse has happened than the transfer of the rule of the kingdom from two of your Grace's relatives to two of the King's, my lords of Gloucester and Buckingham, and it was our late sovereign lord's wish that Gloucester rule for his son. Madam, all seems set fair for the future. Do you not think that your flight into sanctuary was a little precipitate?"

"No!" Mother cried. "My Lord Hastings must be a man of limited imagination to pass over so glibly the tragedies and perils that have overtaken me and my family."

Abbot Eastney looked pained. "But there are no perils, Madam. And think how it looks to the world at large—the mother and siblings of the King seeking refuge in sanctuary, which carries with it the enormous implication that my lord of Gloucester bears you such ill will that you perceive yourself to be in danger. It is highly embarrassing for him—he, to whom your husband entrusted the rule of the kingdom. Will you not think again?"

"Absolutely not," Mother declared. "You and others may be taken in by that man's guile, Father Abbot, but I know him for my enemy!"

* * *

The next day, Elizabeth was trying to concentrate on her book, but Mother kept fretting about the whereabouts of Dorset and interrupting her. Her face lit up with expectancy when Abbot Eastney returned.

"Your Grace, I have learned that the King has been lodged in the Tower, as is customary for a monarch about to be crowned."

The royal palace within the Tower had been one of Father's favorite residences. Elizabeth could remember many happy times there. Ned would like it, although he might be a little lonely. If only they could all go and stay with him.

Mother wrung her hands. "Of course. It is a strong and secure fortress. Where better to immure a defenseless child?"

"Madam, please!" Abbot Eastney was unusually severe. "The Council has approved his being there. And I might add that the lords are becoming uneasy about your continuing in sanctuary. It reflects badly on the Lord Protector. The people are saying he does not take fitting care of your dignity or your safety. They are putting the worst construction on it."

"I care not what the people say. I will not leave and expose my children to danger. Already, he has two of my sons!"

Cecily put her arms around her. The Queen's shoulders were heaving.

"Please, Mother," Elizabeth pleaded, kneeling before her. "Let us leave here. I'm sure that everything will be all right."

"My lord of Gloucester will be so relieved to see you back at court that I'm sure he will bend over backward to make you welcome and do you all honor," the Abbot said.

"No!" Mother was adamant. "You think I fear too much—but I believe you all fear far too little!"

Late in May, Elizabeth was present when a deputation of councillors came to Cheyneygates and knelt before the Queen in the Jerusalem Chamber.

"Your Grace," their spokesman said, "the Lord Protector asks that you leave sanctuary with your children and assures you of your safety. Will you not come with us and return to court?"

Elizabeth was praying that Mother would agree, but she saw her mouth set in an angry line.

"Do you think I'm a fool?" the Queen cried. "I will not leave this place while my lord of Gloucester is free to do harm to me and mine! He has imprisoned my brother and my son. Is that not evidence of his malice?"

"He has imprisoned them, Madam, because he fears that the malice is all on the side of you and your family," one councillor said boldly. "But he would like to make peace with you, so that you can enjoy an honorable retirement as queen dowager. He intends you no harm."

"How can I believe his word? He is a villain! And I will not be shunted into retirement." Elizabeth watched, horrified, as her mother broke down in tears, and saw that she was not being difficult, but was genuinely frightened.

"Then, Madam, we can only conclude that you are hostile to the Lord Protector and that he is right to be wary of you and all your blood."

Several days passed. It was now June and the weather was warm. Elizabeth often took a chair and a book into the Abbot's courtyard, where York and her sisters could play their games around her.

Late one afternoon, when she returned upstairs to wash for supper, she heard the Abbot speaking urgently to her mother.

"Your Grace, Lord Hastings told me today that Gloucester has ordered the city of York to muster troops to march on London against you, your kin, and your adherents. Gloucester believes that you have intended all along to murder and utterly destroy him, my lord of Buckingham, and the old royal blood of this realm."

"Now you have it, Father Abbot—proof, if any were needed, of how deeply he hates me and mine." Mother sounded at her wits' end. "Why should I wish to destroy the old royal blood of this realm when it runs with my own in the King's veins? And what harm can we do Gloucester now? I am in sanctuary, powerless, and my kinsmen are scattered, either in prison or in hiding. At last, this traitor has betrayed his malice. He makes me the scapegoat for his own shady dealings. These accusations are merely an excuse to bolster his power with military force!"

There was a pause, and Elizabeth held her breath.

"In truth, Madam, I am concerned, but I fear that you have rather brought this on yourself."

"I—a defenseless woman?"

"Not so long ago, you had command of everything. Hardly defenseless, forgive me, but one who could be perceived as an enemy. I believe my lord of Gloucester fears that you are spending your time here plotting and secretly rallying your supporters."

"What supporters? He has dealt with anyone who might have helped me!"

"Dorset is yet free. And you cannot deny that you are looking to him to seize back power from Gloucester."

"If he can raise support."

"That isn't the point. It's the intention that counts. My advice now is to stay here. With these northern troops marching south, it is the safest place for you."

Realizing that the Abbot was leaving, Elizabeth hastened back downstairs, her heart pounding, remembering what her mother had said about people breaking sanctuary. Would Uncle Gloucester really go that far, with his armed force behind him? She could not believe it.

A week later, they were about to retire to bed when the Abbot appeared.

"I am sorry to disturb you so late, your Grace, but there is a gentleman here who wishes to speak to you." He stood aside to admit a cloaked man carrying a candle.

When he put back his hood, Elizabeth recognized Lord Hastings.

"Your Grace." He knelt before the Queen and tried to kiss her hand, but she snatched it away.

"I do not receive those who betray me," she hissed.

"Madam, I am no traitor. I served the late King faithfully and I will serve his son likewise. I came here because I must speak to you, and it took a lot of cunning to circumvent the scrutiny of Gloucester's men, who are watching who goes in and out of sanctuary. I have come to mistrust Gloucester's intentions. I fear he aims at the throne itself."

"No!" Mother wailed, her frosty manner dissolving. "It is what I have feared all along!"

"Why, my lord?" Abbot Eastney asked.

"I believe that these troops Gloucester has summoned will be used to effect a coup. Many at court suspect that his ambitions are focused on the crown."

"Belief? Suspicion? That is not evidence or proof." The Abbot sounded angry.

Hastings glared at him. "While there is the slightest doubt of his intentions, we must be on the alert. And I am truly convinced that his much-vaunted loyalty to his brother now counts for nothing, while I, who was faithful to King Edward, and will be to his son, to the death, am frozen out. My opinion now counts for nothing. I am shouted down in council. Buckingham's is the dominant voice. They will tolerate no dissent—and I fear that Gloucester has come to see me as an obstacle to his ambitions. Madam, I know you have no cause to love me, but I am your friend, and I urge you to heed my concerns. I swear I will do everything in my power to uphold and protect the King's rights."

Mother grabbed his sleeve. "Are you telling me that my son is in danger?"

"I will not lie to you, Madam. I fear he is. But I will keep him safe, I promise."

Elizabeth shivered. She was praying that Hastings was wrong.

"Let us hope that your concerns are unfounded," the Abbot said, clearly unconvinced.

* * *

Mother lay awake all night, weeping piteously. "I feel so helpless," she sobbed. "All my instincts urge me to protect Ned, but I cannot get near him. Even if I left here, they would not let me go to him." She dissolved in a fresh flood of tears.

Elizabeth did not know what to think. Lord Hastings had been one of her father's closest friends. Should she trust his instincts? Or was he angry at having to give place to Buckingham and looking for a return to power? Mother believed he had betrayed her plans to Uncle Gloucester, and certainly he had no cause to protect the Wydevilles. But somehow she believed that he was their friend, however mistaken he might be about Uncle Gloucester. Yet why was Abbot Eastney so skeptical?

She longed for this horrible situation to be resolved. She wanted to get out of sanctuary and feel normal again—and she wanted to believe the best of her uncle. It seemed incredible that he should bear such malice toward her mother, or that he was plotting to seize Ned's throne—especially after doing so much to establish him as king. She still believed that his intentions were honorable. It was living with someone who was convinced otherwise that made her doubt it.

In the middle of June, Elizabeth and Cecily finally persuaded Mother to sit with them in the courtyard. It was a pleasant day and the children were playing a noisy game of tag.

"Quietly!" Mother commanded. "You will disturb Father Abbot!" But they raced on, heedless. "Oh, well." She gave a faint laugh. "They are young, and it is not fair on them, being cooped up here."

Elizabeth sat in the sun, feeling in her pocket for the letter from Lord Stanley that the Abbot had given to her yesterday. She was not to worry, Stanley had written. There were tensions on the Council, but all was set fair for the King's coronation, and he himself was keeping a watchful eye open. If he could be of service to her and the King, he would not hesitate. It was reassuring to know that both he and Lord Hastings were looking out for them at court, and that Stanley was not taking such a pessimistic view as Hastings.

York was becoming boisterous and began pulling Anne's hair when he caught her. She slapped him in retaliation and things got rough to the point where Elizabeth had to separate them. "Play something different!" she admonished them.

"There's nothing else to play." York looked mutinous. "I wish Ned was here. I hate playing with girls. I'm bored."

"Then we'll do some lessons," she said.

"Oh, I've thought of something," he answered quickly. "Let's play hide-and-seek."

There weren't many places to hide, so they soon gave up and began running around again until Katherine hurtled into the Abbot, who had appeared in the archway.

"Steady now!" he warned her, smiling. Then his expression grew serious. "Your Grace, I must talk to you."

"Cecily, take the children upstairs," Mother commanded. They went, York protesting noisily. "What is it, Father Abbot?"

"There is no easy way to tell you this, Madam—but Lord Hastings has been executed."

Elizabeth gasped, shocked. Mother had clapped her hand to her mouth. "What?" she whispered.

"My lord of Gloucester summoned Hastings and others to a council meeting in the Tower this morning. There, he accused him of treason and had him summarily beheaded. It was done without judgment of law or justice. There was no trial by his peers, as there should have been."

"But why?" Mother's voice sounded strangled.

The Abbot sat down on Cecily's vacated stool. "No one quite knows. At court, it is said that Gloucester accused Hastings of plotting treason against him."

"Treason? You cannot commit treason against a lord protector, only against the King! Now you see that I was right. This man is a tyrant and will stop at nothing to get what he wants—and what he wants, Father Abbot, is my son's crown! One by one, he is removing or neutralizing all those who stand in his way. Me, my brother Rivers, my son Grey, and now Hastings, good, faithful Hastings!" Shocked as she was, Elizabeth was surprised at that. A week ago, Mother would have called him something rather different. "And who is to be next? My poor boy, who is shut up in the Tower in Gloucester's tender care?"

Abbot Eastney looked grave. He even reached out and laid his hand on the Queen's. "Madam, Lord Stanley, Archbishop Rotherham, and John Morton, the Bishop of Ely, were also arrested at that council meeting, but spared execution. They have been sent to Wales, where I assume they will be imprisoned."

Mother had turned pale. "Without trial?"

"Yes, without trial. Madam, I do fear that you were right all along. These are acts of tyranny, for which there is no justification."

"He will silence us all," the Queen whispered.

Elizabeth started to cry. For Lord Hastings, whom she had always liked. For her father, who, looking down from Heaven, would be appalled at the cruel fate that had overtaken his friend. For kind Lord Stanley, Bishop Morton, and Archbishop Rotherham, who had been hauled off to God knew what fate. But mostly she wept for herself and her family, knowing that those who would have protected and looked out for them had been silenced. She felt vulnerable and, for the first time, afraid. The strongest supporters of the King had been removed, without anyone making a protest. And this was all Uncle Gloucester's fault. Had Hastings and the rest been such a threat to him that he had felt it necessary to mete out this summary and brutal punishment? But then Hastings had been plotting his overthrow. She had heard it from his own mouth.

She had been certain that Uncle Gloucester was an honorable, upright man whose loyalty to her father had never been feigned, and who had had a special rapport with her and would do her no harm. She was struggling to come to terms with the fact that he had acted ruthlessly and cruelly outside the law and left her and her loved ones in jeopardy. And yet a part of her still believed that this tragic situation had arisen purely from unfounded suspicion on all sides. It was what she wanted and needed to believe, because if Uncle Gloucester really was determined to wrest the crown from Ned, what would happen to them all?

"Gloucester and Buckingham will do just as they please now, with no one to stop them," Mother was saying, her tone bitter. "Once these northern troops get here, there will be no stopping them. Hastings warned us of this. Father Abbot, what can we do? And how can I protect my sons and my brother and keep them safe from this tyrant?" She was weeping now, her face a mask of misery.

"We must pray, my daughter," the Abbot said gently. "We must trust in God to look after them and defend them from all ills."

"Where was God in the Tower this morning?" she shrilled.

The Abbot visibly recoiled. "I will pray for you all," he said, and left them.

To their dismay, they learned that the northern troops had arrived in London in fearful and unheard-of numbers, and were camped out on Finsbury Fields, north of the City.

"My lay brothers think all northerners are savages with tails," the Abbot said, smiling grimly.

"The Londoners have long hated and feared them," Mother observed, looking up from her embroidery. "Remember how they once barred the gates against Margaret of Anjou and her northern army?" She shuddered. "It is frightening to think what these men are here for. Does Gloucester think to force us from sanctuary or seize the throne by intimidation?"

"Maybe he fears that others are plotting against him," the Abbot suggested.

"But he sent for these soldiers before he fell out with Lord Hastings. No, Father Abbot, he set his mark at the throne from the first. He will get it by foul means if fair means fail."

"I pray it will not come to that."

"Come, Father, you know as well as I do that, in the late wars, might often triumphed over right. Terrible deeds were committed. Why should my lord of Gloucester scruple to overthrow a mere boy to make himself king?"

Sitting at the table, ostensibly playing chess with Cecily, Elizabeth winced to hear her mother railing thus. It frightened her, and still she hated to hear her speak of Uncle Gloucester as if he were a monster. Oh, if only she herself could talk with him, just for a short time, she was sure that all their doubts and fears would be resolved.

The next day, they were at meat when they heard the distant tramp of marching feet. As they stared at each other in alarm, it grew louder, and soon it seemed to be coming from all around them.

"What's that noise?" York asked.

"I don't know," Mother faltered, her hand shaking as she laid down her knife.

With uncustomary haste, the Abbot burst in. Elizabeth had never seen him so agitated. "Your Grace, the abbey is surrounded by my lord of Gloucester's soldiers. They are armed with swords and staves, and Cardinal Bourchier has just arrived, asking to see you."

"Why?" The Queen rose, her face pale against her widow's weeds. "Has he come to force us out of sanctuary?"

"He did not say, Madam. Will you see him? It might be politic."

"I will. Pray send him in." She seated herself in her high-backed chair, looking every inch the Queen. "You four, go outside and play," she ordered her younger children. "Bessy and Cis, come and stand beside me."

Cardinal Bourchier entered in a rustle of red robes and bowed to Mother, extending his ring for her to kiss. "God's blessings on you, my daughter," he greeted her. Elizabeth knew him well, for she was kin to this aristocratic old man who had somehow won and retained the confidence of both sides in the conflict between Lancaster and York, simply because he was committed to seeking a peace.

"Pray be seated, your Eminence," the Queen invited. "Will you take some wine?"

"Thank you." Abbot Eastney poured some. The Cardinal sipped it and cleared his throat. "Madam, I am sent here by the Lord Protector. He has expressed to the Council his concern that it would be improper for the King to be crowned in the absence of his brother, who ought to play an important part in the ceremony. But, Madam, I fear he believes that you are holding my lord of York here in sanctuary against his will."

Mother looked outraged, and opened her mouth to protest, but the Cardinal raised his hand. "Please hear me out. He wishes the Duke to be liberated, because this sanctuary was founded by his ancestors as a place of refuge, not of detention, and he is sure that this boy wants to be with his brother."

It was true, Elizabeth knew. York had made it quite clear. It was understandable that a lively nine-year-old was chafing against the constraints of being in sanctuary. He had often complained that he was cooped up in a household of women, and repeatedly expressed a wish to be with Ned.

Uncle Gloucester, the father of a son himself, was right. It *was* unfair to keep the boy confined in sanctuary.

"Madam," the Cardinal continued, "I am here to ask you to let York come with me and take his proper place in society. I promise you, no harm will come to him."

Mother was gearing for battle; you could see the hackles rising. "Your Eminence, you are too good a man to perceive malice in others, but I assure you I am in sanctuary for a very compelling reason, and recent events have shown that I was right to come here. My lord of Gloucester has silenced my friends. He has my brother and my sons in custody. But it is not enough to have the King in his power. He foresees that the Duke of York would by legal right succeed to the throne if his brother were . . . removed. I tell you, my lord, that I would be sending my son into danger if I let him leave this place."

The Cardinal spread his hands. "Madam, Madam, you are making too much of this! My lord of Gloucester has an uncle's tender regard for the King and his brother; he wishes them to be together at this time. York has no reason to be in sanctuary—whoever heard of a child claiming that benefit? You and your daughters have no need to be here either, but I understand your concerns, even if they are unfounded. No, wait, Madam, I have not finished. My lord of York will be restored to you after the coronation. My Lord Protector wants him to be there to save further embarrassment."

Mother's voice was icy. "Does it, then, take a large detachment of soldiers to escort my son to the Tower? Your Eminence, that seems to me like intimidation. You do not deny that there are men surrounding the abbey? We heard them arriving."

The Cardinal looked embarrassed and lowered his voice. "Madam, believe me, if you do not surrender the boy, he will be taken by force."

The Queen gripped the arms of her chair, her knuckles as white as her face. "He would not dare!"

There was a silence. Elizabeth could sense her mother's anguish. She was frightened herself, realizing, with a heavy heart, that she had been wrong all along about Uncle Gloucester. Did it really take armed force to enable a boy to attend a coronation?

"Please, Madam," the Cardinal said. "My lord of Gloucester is angered at your being here and is determined that the lad should leave. I am trying to mitigate his fierce resolve. You must understand that, if you do not agree, the consequences could be . . . unfortunate. This abbey is under siege. I do not wish to frighten you, but there could be violence. Far better that the Duke comes with me than that the sanctuary is violated."

Elizabeth was trembling so much that she feared she might faint. Tears were streaming down Cecily's face.

"How can you, then, assure me that my son will be safe?" Mother's voice shook.

"You must trust me, Madam, to ensure it. I do not believe that he is in danger, and I promise that he will return after the coronation."

"Very well," Mother capitulated. "I will surrender him to you, trusting in your Eminence's word. Elizabeth, go and fetch your brother. Cecily, help her to gather his things. Use the small chest."

She turned to the Abbot, who had been watching them with grave concentration. "Father, would you ask two of your lay brothers to carry it down?"

"Of course," he said, and left the chamber.

"I and my daughters will be staying in sanctuary," Elizabeth heard Mother say as she and Cecily left. "I know we will not be safe if we leave. I can only pray that your Eminence's trust in Gloucester's good intentions is not displaced."

Elizabeth stifled her tears and her fears as she packed York's clothes, his toys and games, his toy sword, and his bow and arrows. Even for the short time he was to be away, she would miss his company, his mischievousness, his pranks, and even the noise he made. He had enlivened their time in sanctuary.

But York himself was excited to be leaving. He had clapped his hands and cried, "At last!" when she told him that the Cardinal had come to fetch him and that he was going to join Ned in the Tower. He went skipping into the Jerusalem Chamber and patiently endured the Queen's desperate embrace.

"God bless and keep you, my sweet son," she wept. "It will not be long, I pray, until you are restored to me. Keep him safe, your Eminence, oh, please keep him safe—and my other poor lamb!"

"I will, your Grace," the old man said, making the sign of the Cross over her. "Now, come along, my lord of York."

Elizabeth watched as the two of them departed, York almost dancing by the Cardinal's side. Oh, to be nine years old again and blissfully unaware of the dangers—real or imaginary—that beset them.

The door closed. Mother sank to the floor, screaming out her agony. "Oh, my boy, my boy . . . Will I ever see you again?" And then they were all crying.

York had been gone for two days and Elizabeth could not stop fretting about him and Ned. How were they faring in the Tower? Were they happy? Were they being properly looked after? The worst of it was that there was no news. Even the Abbot had heard no word of them. Elizabeth was willing the time away until the coronation. Thousands would then see that her brothers were alive and well, and she would be reassured.

"It's not long to wait now," she said, trying to keep her mother calm. "Only eight days."

The Queen rounded on her. "You think Gloucester will allow Ned to be crowned? Don't be a fool, Bessy! His office of lord protector will lapse with the coronation and, when Parliament is summoned in the King's name, he runs the risk that he will not be reappointed. He has enemies and must have alienated people by his recent actions. No, he will not let the coronation go ahead." She burst into a fresh torrent of tears.

Elizabeth could not believe that. There would be an outcry, surely, if the King was not crowned. He had won the hearts of the people; he was his father's son, and Father had been popular. And he was the rightful heir! Mother was distracted, and allowances must be made for that.

"Gloucester may yet remove us all by force," the Queen fretted. "If anything happens to your brothers, you girls are the next heirs to York; he'll want you in his clutches, too."

"Nothing will happen to our brothers," Cecily sighed. "Ned will be crowned, you'll see, Mother."

"I wish I could believe it!"

Elizabeth knelt at the Queen's feet. "If Uncle Gloucester was going to take us, he would have done so by now. You fear him, my lady, but I'm sure he fears you, too, and that you would plot against him if you had the chance. Dorset is still free, and you have other kin who might help you."

For once, Mother listened. "You may have the right of it," she said at length, heaving a great sigh.

That evening, the Abbot joined them for supper. He seemed subdued and, after saying grace, made no move to carve the meat.

"I was at court today, Madam," he said. "I saw my good friend, the Bishop of Lincoln. He is a councillor, as you know, and a man of great learning and piety. We had a long talk in private. I hesitate to tell you this, but I think you should know that the King and York seem to have been moved to more secure accommodation within the Tower."

Mother rose, her face a mask of horror. "You mean they are in a dungeon?"

"No, they are in the White Tower. Last week, they were seen shooting and playing in the Lieutenant's garden. Since then, they have been seen only once or twice at the windows, and those windows are barred. What concerns me most is that all their attendants have been removed. Apparently, the only person who has been able to visit them is Dr. Argentine, the King's physician, and I have been trying to speak to him, with no success."

Elizabeth felt sick. How could she have deluded herself into believing that Uncle Gloucester was acting honorably? This was cruelty, no less. She took a gulp of wine to steady herself as Mother collapsed at the table in tears. "Are they ill? I am their mother! I should have been told! Oh, my poor boys, what has become of them? Why are they left to fend for themselves? What did they do to deserve such treatment?"

The Abbot shook his head. "They are blameless children, and it is inexcusable to deprive them of their servants. But they are not ill. Bishop Russell said only that the King had some problem with his teeth. And, if my lord of Gloucester had any malicious intentions toward them, he would hardly have permitted their physician to visit."

"Isn't what he has done evidence enough of his malice?" Mother spat. "Do you still not believe that he is plotting to seize the crown?"

Abbot Eastney looked grieved. "Alas, Madam, I do not know. There is speculation at court that he is. The Bishop had heard it, too. But there is surely no substance to it."

Mother raised a ravaged face. "I am helpless here. I can do nothing to protect my children. If Gloucester seizes the throne, we are lost. He has removed those who might oppose him. My sons are the last obstacle. You must know what has been the fate of deposed kings in this realm—they have all been murdered!"

"Madam, please!" the Abbot begged. "I cannot believe that my lord of Gloucester would contemplate destroying his brother's children."

"Then why has he deprived them of anyone who would have helped them?"

"Alas, I do not know. It seems cruel."

"They have never had to look after themselves," Elizabeth put in. "They probably can't even dress themselves properly, and York won't wash unless he's made to. If Ned has been prescribed physick for his teeth, he might forget to take it. Father Abbot, Dr. Argentine is the only person who can tell us how they are and how they are coping. For my lady mother's sake, please seek him out!"

"I will return to court tomorrow," the Abbot promised.

The following afternoon, Elizabeth was sitting alone in the courtyard, Katherine and Anne having been banished to the bedchamber after fighting and pulling each other's hair. Mother was lying down with a headache, and Cecily was with her, keeping an eye on Bridget.

It was hard to concentrate on her book when she could not stop thinking about her brothers. She was no longer so certain that Ned would be crowned. But were they actually in danger—or did Uncle Gloucester merely mean to keep them shut up in the Tower? She would not have been so worried had their servants not been removed; it was that, more than anything else, which seemed to bode ill.

Sitting below Abbot Eastney's open window, she heard voices coming from his study. He was talking to his deputy.

"Thank you for coming, Father Prior," she heard him say. "I'd value your advice. I have had some news, but the Queen is in a highly distressed state and I am not sure that she should hear it, for I would not upset her further. I went to court this morning to seek out Dr. Argentine, because he visited the princes recently and their mother and sisters wanted news of them."

Elizabeth held her breath, dreading what was coming next.

"He did not want to talk to me," the Abbot continued, "but I pressed him and he insisted we speak in his office, where he locked the door. Father Prior, he is a frightened man. He confided to me that the young King told him that, like a victim prepared for sacrifice, he sought remission of his sins by daily confession and penance because he believed that death was facing him."

There was an appalled silence. Elizabeth feared she would start wailing and never stop. It was bad enough being separated from her brothers, but knowing that they were alone and in fear was unbearable.

"That is not all," the Abbot continued. "When I was at court, I spoke with some of the councillors. One said he had been at the Tower, but had seen no sign of the King or his brother. It was as if they had been removed from men's sight. Others wept, saying they suspected that they had been done away with. It is speculation, of course, but these are wise men, experienced in government and privy to state secrets. They are not normally given to tears."

There was another pause. Elizabeth's heart was pounding so loud she feared they might hear it.

"It would be best to say nothing, Father Abbot," the Prior said at length. "Our poor Queen has enough to concern her as it is. I will pray for her, and for the King and his brother."

"I do fear for them," the Abbot confessed, "and I do now mistrust my lord of Gloucester's intentions. I wished to believe that he would act honorably, but each piece of news makes that more difficult. I hear that some citizens have armed, fearing that his northern troops might be used to subdue London. I have received no word about the coronation, which is imminent, so no preparations have been made in the abbey."

"I doubt there will be a coronation," the Prior said.

"I hope you are wrong." The Abbot's tone was pessimistic.

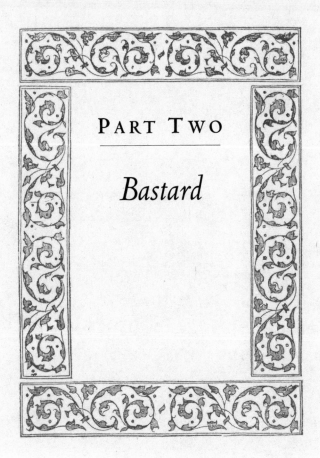

PART TWO

Bastard

Chapter 8

1483

The day set for the coronation arrived. It was now clear that it would not take place. Mother wept for hours, anticipating the worst. As that dreadful Sunday morning wore on, Elizabeth found it hard to maintain a cheerful face in her presence. She kept busy amusing her sisters, whose young lives should not be blighted like this, and playing chess with Cecily, but she was living with the constant fear that something terrible was about to happen. The Abbot had mentioned nothing of his conversation with Dr. Argentine to Mother, but each time he visited them, she anticipated that he would bring bad news.

Today, he wore that serious expression she had come to know so well.

"Your Grace, I am informed that a sermon has been preached at Paul's Cross that may have grave implications, for the preacher was Dr. Shaa, the Mayor's own brother. He took as his text 'Bastard slips shall not take root.' Forgive me, Madam, but he asserted that the late King was conceived in adultery."

Mother gave a contemptuous laugh. "That old calumny? Is it all that Gloucester can come up with to justify his ambitions? He knows as well as I do that it is not true."

"True or not, I have heard that the same sermon was repeated elsewhere in London. My lord of Gloucester seems to have so corrupted the preachers of God's word that they have not blushed to assert in public, without the slightest regard for decency or religion, that King Edward should be deposed at once, since he has no right to be king."

Mother leaped to her feet. "This is outrageous!"

"Indeed, it is." The Abbot looked disgusted. "And apparently the people thought so, too. I was told that most of them looked unconvinced; only a few nodded their approval."

"They will not tolerate such an injustice. The Duchess of York must be horrified. To be publicly proclaimed an adulteress—it is intolerable for a lady of her standing and piety! Gloucester must realize that this horse won't run. No one will take it seriously."

The Abbot appeared doubtful. "I am uneasy, Madam. Something is afoot. The lords are arriving for Parliament as we speak. The Duke of Buckingham is to address them and the commons at the Guildhall tomorrow; the citizens have been summoned and I am going myself. I will report to you on my return."

Monday morning dragged. No one could settle to anything. The abbey bells tolled the endless hours. When would the Abbot be back? What in Heaven was happening?

When Abbot Eastney finally walked into the Jerusalem Chamber, he looked drawn.

"Gloucester has been offered the crown," he told them.

"No!" Mother swayed in her chair. "No! He has no right!"

Elizabeth and Cecily hastened to support her. This was terrible, terrible. It could not be happening.

Shocked as she was, Mother gestured to the Abbot to sit down. "Tell me what happened," she whispered.

"When I arrived, Madam," he related, "the Guildhall was packed. The lords and bishops were there in force, and my Lord Mayor and the citizens of London. Then my lord of Gloucester appeared, and Buckingham read out an address, asserting that

King Edward's children are bastards because he was legally contracted to another lady at the time of his marriage to your Grace."

Elizabeth gasped, but Mother looked bewildered. "Another lady? That is preposterous."

"And many thought the same, for a low whispering broke out, like a swarm of bees. People looked at each other, aghast, scarcely able to credit it, and there was much muttering. But Buckingham held up a hand to silence them and entreated Gloucester that, as the next in line of succession, and the only certain and uncorrupted blood of Richard, Duke of York, he would accept the crown. He appeared reluctant, but Buckingham urged him to do so, arousing the people to acclaim him as their undoubted King. In the end, they did, which is not surprising, for there were great numbers of Gloucester's and Buckingham's armed retainers in the City, while three other lords told me afterward that they had been ordered to bring only a small escort to London."

"So they were intimidated into approving this treason," Mother retorted acidly. "And it sounds as if it has been in the planning for some time. But this . . . this slander about the late King committing bigamy must be addressed, and soon, for it is a wicked lie invented to satisfy Gloucester's ambition. Did he accept the crown?"

"Not yet. He asked for time to pray on the matter. The lords and commons are to wait on him tomorrow at Baynard's Castle."

"He has a nerve, visiting his mother's house after he has defamed her! Oh, this is a dreadful business. My poor sons! What will become of them?" She broke down, sobbing. Elizabeth found herself crying, too. How could Uncle Gloucester do this to them? It flouted every law of loyalty and decency.

"Your sons are still in the Tower, Madam. I imagine that Gloucester will leave them there. They are children and cannot rise against him."

"But others could rise on their behalf! When my son Dorset hears . . ."

"I think not," the Abbot said sternly. "Who would now dare to resist the combined might of Gloucester and Buckingham? And, to be plain, some might think it better to have a grown man with a proven record of service in government and the field of battle on the throne rather than a child. That said, if Gloucester takes the crown, it will be an act of usurpation, and I am ready to speak out against it."

"No, Father Abbot. I would not have you put yourself in danger." Mother rose and began pacing, her train swishing behind her. "But these proceedings must be challenged! The allegations about my children's legitimacy are unfounded. Where are the proofs?"

"Buckingham did not produce any, Madam. He merely stated that Bishop Stillington of Bath had revealed that he had solemnized a marriage between the late King and Eleanor, Lady Butler, old Shrewsbury's daughter, when nobody was present but the couple and himself. The Bishop apparently claimed that, because his prosperity depended on royal favor, he never spoke of it and persuaded the lady herself to conceal it, which she did."

Elizabeth felt sick. The foundations of her world seemed to be crumbling beneath her. This could not be true! Just weeks ago, Father had been alive and reigning and she had been England's foremost princess, anticipating a glorious future. Now, with everything else taken from her, she might well lose her birthright, without which she would be nothing.

The Abbot's face was a picture of distaste. "Any bishop worth his salt should have known that a ceremony of marriage conducted without any witnesses present was invalid."

"It seems strange that it took him twenty years to speak out, especially if my lord was already married when he wed me," Mother said tartly. "And I recall that, some ten years back, he was among those who swore allegiance to my son as his father's undoubted heir—an odd thing to do if he knew he was not legitimate. But this Eleanor Butler—I knew her slightly. She was wed to Lord Sudeley's heir. She died years ago in a nunnery in Norwich. She was a strong-featured woman, not beautiful—and not my husband's type, I would have thought. I don't believe for one minute that he ever went through any ceremony of marriage with her. And why did she or her kinsfolk not speak out when he married me? There were many who protested against my marriage, as I well remember! Warwick would gladly have supported her, if only to be rid of me! And, if she was as pious as I remember, she would not have put her immortal soul in danger by staying silent. No, it is a nonsense, and my lord of Gloucester is a fool to think he can claim the throne on the strength of it!" She rounded on the Abbot. "Do you believe it?"

"No, Madam, I do not," he declared. "It seems suspicious that the story has only emerged at this time—very conveniently for Gloucester, since it provides him with a pretext for seizing the throne. I am sure there are many who do not give it credence and still regard your children as the rightful heirs of the House of York. And, of course, both King Edward and Lady Eleanor are dead, and cannot confirm or deny the allegations."

Elizabeth could keep silent no longer. "So we are not bastards?"

"By no means," the Abbot said. "The matter must be laid before an ecclesiastical court, which will expect to see proofs of this secret marriage. I suspect there are none."

"But Gloucester is to give his answer tomorrow. How can he accept the crown when his claim is not even properly established?"

"How indeed!" the Abbot replied. "I'll wager that the matter will never be laid before a church court."

"It is all lies!" Mother cried. "And, if he is prepared to go this far, why should he balk at killing my sons? While they live, they are a threat to him. You said that men wept at the mention of them, yet it seems they are prepared to stand by and let them be overthrown—and worse, I fear! I must act. I must get word to Dorset. If he can cross the sea, he can raise an army."

"Madam, how will you contact him? Do you know where he is?"

"No, I do not." Mother ceased her pacing and sat down. "Dear God, I am so alone, so frightened. When I think of those poor innocents in the Tower . . . They must know that something is badly wrong. Ned will be wondering why he has not been crowned. He has done nothing to deserve this. Kings have been deposed because they were bad or incompetent, but he has been given no chance to show his mettle."

It was horrifying. And it was happening. Elizabeth found herself staring bleakly into a future in which she had no status and the walls of sanctuary were closing ever more oppressively around her.

The next day, having endured a sleepless night, they waited in trepidation for news. The Abbot had gone to Baynard's Castle with the lords and other senior clergy. A pall of despondency hung over the sanctuary.

It was as they had feared. The Abbot's face told them everything.

"My lord of Gloucester was entreated to bow to the lords' petition. He made a show of reluctance, but he agreed, and was immediately proclaimed king as Richard the Third."

"And what of my boy, the rightful King?" Mother cried.

"I do not know, Madam."

Her son had been deposed, her marriage called invalid, and her children branded bastards, but there was no word from Richard, no attempt made to inform the Queen of what had happened. And now he was king, and they were all at his mercy.

Around them, as if in mockery, the abbey came to life. They were horribly aware of preparations for Richard's coronation, which was to take place on 6 July. The Abbot came less frequently, being distracted by the many calls on his time, yet his kindness and compassion never failed. He told them that the northern troops were still in the City. "I suspect the King fears some demonstration or coup against him."

"I pray there is!" Mother hissed. She would not call Richard "king." To her, he was the Usurper, which was tantamount to being the Antichrist in her eyes.

Elizabeth often took refuge in the quiet courtyard, where she did not have to endure the Queen's tears or tirades. From there, one morning, she heard the monks singing the *Te Deum*, rehearsing for the coronation no doubt. It made her cry, but she was distracted by the arrival of Cecily, who looked distraught.

"Bessy, you've got to come! Mother is in a terrible state."

Elizabeth picked up her skirts and hurried up the stairs. She could hear the Queen wailing piteously. "Oh God, oh God!" she was crying.

The Abbot was with her. It was not in his calling to have human contact, but he was patting her shoulder and exhorting her to accept the will of God. He stood upright when he saw Elizabeth. "My child, I am grieved to tell you that my Lord Rivers and Sir Richard Grey are dead. I have just received news that they were beheaded at Pontefract late last month by order of the King when he was Lord Protector."

Uncle Rivers, that brilliant knight, dead? And her brother Dickon? Anger kindled and burned in her. Gloucester had ordered this! She would not call him uncle anymore; he had forfeited all claim to that.

"But why?" She was in torment.

Abbot Eastney was shaking his head, perplexed. "Richard charged them with having plotted his assassination. My lady, there was more of will than justice involved, for they were beheaded without any form of trial. It was another act of tyranny, more innocent blood shed to further Richard's ambitions."

Was there any end to his wickedness? Had he any idea what he had done to them all? How could he be so cruel?

She knelt by her mother, trying to stem her grief and her fears for the future. But it was a vain effort.

They heard the bells ringing out for the coronation. Elizabeth stayed indoors. She would not go out to the courtyard where she might hear the crowds cheering for the Usurper. She could not bear to. She sat silently with her mother and sisters, knowing that they were suffering as she was, remembering that this day of triumph should have been Ned's. Those bells were a bitter reminder of all they had lost, one more trial coming fast upon all the others they had endured. Ned, in the Tower, would be hearing the chimes from the myriad steeples of the City. How must he be feeling?

* * *

A week later, the Abbot brought the news that Lord Stanley had been restored to the Council and granted lands and offices.

"It is encouraging news," he said. "It means that the King wishes to come to terms with his opponents."

"You mean, he has bought Stanley's loyalty," Mother sniffed.

"I imagine that Stanley is too rich and influential to be alienated."

"What of Bishop Morton, who was arrested with him?" Elizabeth asked.

"As far as I know, he is still Buckingham's prisoner in Wales," the Abbot said.

"And Archbishop Rotherham?"

"He is in the Tower. The word at court is that he will be freed after the coronation."

"Well, I will never come to terms with the Usurper!" Mother declared.

"And I am disappointed in Father Stanley, who promised Father he would look out for me," Elizabeth said. "It seems he has abandoned me."

"He is a wily fox and not to be trusted," Mother replied. "He has turned his coat before."

"Let us be charitable, Madam," the Abbot urged. "Lord Stanley may yet use his influence on your behalf."

"I wouldn't count on it!" she retorted.

That summer, Westminster was quiet. Richard had departed on a progress through the kingdom, leaving the palace slumbering in the sun. The abbey had reverted to its unending cycle of work and prayer.

Mother was fretting all the time about Ned and York. The Abbot had heard no news of them. Elizabeth kept wondering if they were even alive.

Travelers brought to the abbey reports of unrest and confederacies in the south and the west.

"It seems that the people there wish to liberate your son,

Madam," the Abbot related. "If my information is correct, they are in an uproar and forming assemblies."

Elizabeth was praying this was true. Mother was still convinced that loyal Englishmen would rise against the Usurper and restore Ned to his throne. Fired by hope, she shooed the children into the bedchamber and bade Elizabeth and Cecily sit close to her. "Listen and pay heed. I am going to try and get you girls out of here. The Abbot says there are men in the sanctuary who oppose the Usurper and have fled there through fear. They might help you to flee overseas. Then, if any fatal mishap befalls your brothers, this kingdom might still someday fall again into the hands of the rightful heirs. Never forget that you are next in line to the throne."

Elizabeth's heart leaped at the prospect of leaving sanctuary, but she knew that escaping would be fraught with dangers. There were no soldiers outside now, but men were constantly watching the abbey to see who came in or out. It seemed an impossible undertaking, and Cecily was looking nervous.

"How could it be done?" she asked.

"We could disguise you both in monks' habits, with the cowls hanging over your faces," Mother said. "The monks go in and out all the time. Then you could take a boat up the Thames to Queenhithe and get a ship there. We should act now while the court is away. I'm sure the Abbot will arrange for someone in the sanctuary to help us. He will know the right persons to approach, and I will offer the inducement of a reward when Ned is restored to his throne."

"If those men sought sanctuary for fear of the Usurper, they might not want to help," Cecily put in. "And they might want gold now, not just a promise for the future."

"Well, they can say no, but it is worth asking. We have a sacred trust to preserve the rightful bloodline. We must do something!"

"Maybe we should wait to see if the people in the south and west rise up," Elizabeth said.

Mother was adamant. "There is no certainty of that. We should look closer to home. And there is no time to lose. You must escape! The Usurper has already murdered one of my sons and has

my other boys in the Tower. I so fear for their safety that I think it
worth taking the risks involved in sending you away."

Elizabeth caught Cecily's eye. They both nodded. The lure of
freedom was too great to resist.

Abbot Eastney was willing to take a message to the sanctuary. He
could not say whether those in hiding there would agree to assist,
for there was great peril involved.

"They are thinking it over," he said, when he returned. "It is
not a question of willingness, but of how the matter is to be
achieved."

They waited . . . and waited. Elizabeth was nearly climbing the
walls with frustration. Why couldn't they just disguise themselves as monks and walk out of here?

The Abbot had brought no news for several days when he appeared in the Jerusalem Chamber one morning in late July, looking worried. "Soldiers have surrounded the abbey," he informed
Mother. "We are under siege again!"

"Do you think our plan has been discovered?" she faltered. Elizabeth felt her heart plummet like a stone. She had been so longing
to get away. Cecily's face said it all.

"Undoubtedly," the Abbot said. "My guess is that someone in
sanctuary talked in exchange for a pardon. Two fellows walked out
yesterday. Merciful Lord, this house of God is now like a fortress,
with all these troops guarding it. I must go and speak to their
captain."

He hurried out, leaving them near to tears.

It was dusk when he returned, in the company of a cold-faced
man with fine features, black hair, and a military bearing.

"Your Grace, this is Captain Nesfield," he said. The soldier
bowed, then fixed Mother with a steely gaze.

"Madam, it is best if I make my position clear now. King Richard has appointed me and my men to keep strict guard over you
and your daughters. I have been charged to set a watch on all the

entrances and exits of the abbey. From now on, no one shall go
forth or enter without my permission."

Mother regarded him coolly. "So many men to guard defenseless women and little girls."

"Some might regard you all as a threat to the King's peace." His
glare was implacable. "You are now under my command. Cooperate with me, Madam, and you will have nothing to fear."

Mother returned his gaze. "I've heard your name, Captain Nesfield. I believe the King my husband spoke of you."

Nesfield looked momentarily nonplussed. "King Edward appointed me riding forester in Yorkshire, where I pursued Lancastrians on his behalf. I later saw service in Calais, where I helped to
recapture an English ship seized by the French. I served his Grace
loyally, as I now serve his brother."

"I hope that loyalty will extend to his poor widow and children." Mother's voice was deceptively gentle.

"Madam, be under no illusions. I know that you and your
daughters have been plotting against the King. That must cease!
Then we will all get along very well."

Mother opened her mouth to protest, but he saluted her and
turned on his heel. "I will see myself out, Father Abbot."

She turned to the Abbot, who was looking distressed and somehow diminished, his authority usurped by this interloper.

"I am so sorry, Father, that our presence here has led to this. We
have made a great deal of trouble for you. They may know that
you helped us."

He managed a smile. "I doubt it, for Captain Nesfield said that
I am still free to come and go. It is you they fear." He lowered his
voice. "This all suggests to me that the King feels insecure on his
throne. He must know that his title is unsafe and can be challenged."

"Yes," Mother said, looking anguished, "and he might well decide to remove anyone who poses a threat to him. Pray for my
boys, I beg of you, Father Abbot, and pray that God turns the
Usurper's heart away from violence."

* * *

A week later, as they were having supper, Abbot Eastney joined them at table.

"I've just been talking to two merchants who have lately been in the West Country. They told me that there were indeed conspiracies there, and in the south, aimed at restoring your son to the throne, but that they have been vigorously suppressed."

Mother looked as if she had been punched. "I have prayed that they would succeed. It was our only hope. And now it has been cruelly dashed." A tear streaked down her cheek. "This bodes ill for all of us. The Usurper will never be secure on his throne while my sons live, and time is not on his side. In just over three years, Ned will be sixteen, the same age as Henry of Lancaster was when he assumed personal rule. He will then be old enough to fight for his rights, and he will not lack for supporters; his father was popular, and he is loved for his own sake. Do you think the Usurper will let him live that long?"

The Abbot regarded her gravely. "Alas, Madam, I wish I could answer yes to that question. But I must confess that I too am concerned."

They were in low spirits all through July and August. The children were fretful and bored, and Elizabeth and Cecily had all to do to keep them amused and prevent them from bothering the Queen, who could not bear loud noises or boisterous games.

The court was still away on progress; Westminster remained quiet, although news filtered through of how Richard rewarded loyalty—Buckingham had been appointed constable of England and governor of Wales and the Marches. Few subjects, Elizabeth thought drily, had ever been so honored. Yet travelers and tradesmen from all parts came to the abbey and spoke of rising anger at Richard's usurpation of the throne, and the Abbot faithfully relayed their words, no doubt wishing to raise Mother's spirits. Then, early in September, he brought momentous news.

"Buckingham has abandoned the King!" he announced, joining them at table.

"But he is his closest ally!" the Queen cried.

"Nevertheless, he has turned on him." The Abbot took the chair she indicated and mopped his brow, for it was a hot day, even within these stone walls. "It does seem strange that a man who has recently received such spectacular rewards for his support should suddenly have defected, especially as he has so much to lose. He must have had a compelling reason for turning his coat."

"How do you know this, Father?" Mother probed.

"From the Lord Chancellor, my friend Bishop Russell, who is with the court. He wrote that Buckingham left the progress and rode to his castle at Brecknock in Wales, where Bishop Morton is being held. Bishop Russell thinks there was a falling-out between Buckingham and the King. The councillors have speculated that the Duke was angry because the King had failed to give him lands he had promised him, but the Bishop says he was actually granted them in July. So it is a mystery."

"Buckingham's defection can only weaken the Usurper's position, which is a good thing," Mother observed. "Maybe the Duke has realized his great error in promoting that villain's false claim and helping him to a crown that does not belong to him."

"Yes, but why now, after he has been so lavishly rewarded?" wondered Elizabeth, toying with her roast pork.

The Abbot shook his head. "Maybe his conscience was pricking him. We can only wonder. Who can fathom the minds of men?"

There was no more news until late September. The Abbot had deputed two lay brothers to clean Cheyneygates. They came twice a week and did whatever was needful. On what was to prove the last warm day of the year, Elizabeth decided to make the most of the autumn sunshine and took her book down to the courtyard. As she approached the archway, she heard the lay brothers sweeping the flagstones and chatting to each other.

"I slipped into an alehouse when I took the cart to pick up fruit from the Convent Garden," one was saying. "Heard people talking."

Elizabeth stayed out of sight, intrigued to hear their gossip, thinking she might learn something.

"The common fame," the man continued, "is that King Richard has put to death the two princes in the Tower."

Elizabeth froze. *No. No! It was just a rumor. Please, God, don't let it be true!*

"I heard that, too, in Smithfield," the other replied. "People were saying that they died a violent death, but no one knew how."

Elizabeth thought her legs would give way. She was shaking so badly that she dropped her book. Stumbling back into the Abbot's house, she sat on the stairs and tried to master herself. It was gossip, just gossip. It must never reach Mother's ears. It would kill her to hear it.

"Oh, my poor brothers," she whispered. "What has become of you? Please, God, let me know somehow that they are safe. Let these rumors be false. Please, *please* . . ."

When the men had gone, she sat in the courtyard and tried to make sense of her teeming thoughts. Had Buckingham heard similar rumors and been shamed into abandoning the Usurper? Unlawfully seizing a throne was one thing; child murder quite another. But she was running ahead of herself. There was no certainty that her brothers were dead. She had to go on hoping and praying that they were alive.

The Abbot leaned out of his window as she sat there, weeping and murmuring prayers.

"Is something wrong, my Lady Bessy?" he asked kindly.

"Oh, Father," she said, rising and going over to him, "I heard the lay brothers talking. They had heard rumors that the Usurper has had my brothers killed in the Tower."

One look at his face told her that this was not news to him.

"Oh, Father, you don't think it's true, do you?" she cried.

"I pray not," he said, "but I gather that these stories are costing King Richard the hearts of the people, who fear he has slaughtered those innocents. The Bishop of London visited me yesterday. He had heard that some gentlemen were so horrified that they were intending the King's destruction."

"Do you think this has anything to do with Buckingham?"

"Do I think he spread the rumors? It's possible. But why?"

"What if the Usurper, counting on his support, had confided to him that he had had my brothers murdered?"

The old gray eyes met hers. In them, she read infinite pity and sadness. "That would certainly explain Buckingham's sudden defection. Yet we must not speculate too far. The King has other enemies. Anyone could have put about these bruits to undermine him. They could be just tavern gossip."

"I pray that is the case," Elizabeth breathed. "Please, Father Abbot, not a word to my mother. Poor lady, she has enough sorrows to bear."

It was true. Every day, Mother broke down each time she remembered the cruel ends of her son Dickon and her brother Rivers. She was white with exhaustion. Elizabeth had to suppress her own feelings, being unable to cope with all the emotion. She did her best to convince herself that the rumors of her brothers' deaths were unfounded, but they were all worrying about them.

"I have no intention of alarming her," the Abbot replied. "We are not the only ones worried about her health. Lady Stanley expressed to me her concern for the Queen only last week."

It was comforting to hear that wise, capable Lady Stanley cared about them. And then, only the next day, when Elizabeth was watching her mother staring into space, her embroidery forgotten on her lap, the Abbot announced that they had a visitor. "Lady Stanley is concerned about your plight, Madam, and has sent her physician to comfort you."

Mother raised her head. "Dr. Lewis Caerleon, the Welshman? He is very learned and experienced. Lady Stanley used to say what a support he was to her during times of adversity. How very kind of her to send him. But I'm surprised that he got past the soldiers."

"Even Captain Nesfield cannot refuse admittance to a doctor," the Abbot smiled. "And I told him that the consultation was a necessary one. Shall I send Dr. Lewis up?"

"Please do, Father."

The Abbot departed and presently the doctor appeared and bowed to the Queen, who extended her hand to him gratefully.

He was a small, soft-spoken man with a grave manner. He asked them all about their health and frowned at Mother's pallor. "Make sure you take the air daily, Madam, and that you maintain a good diet."

"I will try."

He hesitated, regarding the Queen with great compassion. "Actually, Madam, my primary reason for coming was not to inquire after your health. My Lady Stanley has agonized over whether to tell you, but she fears that the overwhelming likelihood is that the princes in the Tower have been murdered on the King's orders."

Mother's mouth fell open, but no words came. Her face was a mask of horror. Then she slumped in the chair.

"She has fainted," the doctor said. "Fetch a damp cloth and some wine."

Elizabeth was clinging to Cecily, both trembling at what they had just heard, which seemed to confirm the rumors, but they jumped to do his bidding. No, *no*, Elizabeth was saying to herself as she wrung out a holland cloth over the bowl in the bedchamber. It could not be! Not her brothers, gentle Ned and young York, who was so full of life . . .

It took them a while to revive the Queen. Elizabeth's heart went out to her when she came to herself again and wept pitifully, crying aloud in increasing desperation, until her shrieks must have been heard in the abbey. In her agony, she struck her breast, then pulled and tore out her hair, rocking back and forth.

"Oh, my sweet babes, my darling boys! Is it true? How will I bear it? I wish I could die and be with you. I must have been mad to let myself be deceived by false promises and to have delivered York out of sanctuary. If I had kept him, they would both be alive." On and on she railed, then fell to her knees, wild-eyed, begging God to take vengeance. "He will not let this pass unpunished!" she wailed, as Dr. Lewis tried ineffectually to soothe her.

"Is it really true?" Elizabeth asked, holding her shocked little sisters tightly. "How did they die?"

"Alas, I do not know, my lady Princess," the doctor said, giving her her rightful title. "But my Lady Stanley had it from the Duke of Buckingham that, after the late conspiracies, King Richard told him he had no choice but to remove the princes, since they would always pose a threat to him. His meaning was unmistakable. For Buckingham, that was a step too far. He would not condone the slaying of children. So he left court and went to Wales. That was last month. Almost certainly, the King has carried out his threat."

Mother began wailing again. "No, no! My poor boys, my dear lambs. Christ have mercy on us!"

Elizabeth was reeling. The likelihood that her brothers had been killed was devastating enough, but not knowing exactly what had happened to them, and not being able to lay them decently to rest, left her in anguish. Already she was torturing herself, imagining their suffering, and hoping against hope that they were not really dead. Yet her heart told her that they were.

Dr. Lewis stood patiently waiting until the Queen quietened a little. "Madam, Lady Stanley sent me to succor you in your loss. She also bade me tell you that my lord of Buckingham is resolved to rise against King Richard and overthrow him, avenging your sons."

"Hell would be too good for that monster!" Mother hissed. "I pray that God sends my lord of Buckingham a happy victory! But it will be too late for my boys . . ."

"Madam," said Dr. Lewis firmly, "Lady Stanley said to say to you that the time is now come for your eldest daughter, the Princess Elizabeth, to be given in marriage to her son, the Earl of Richmond. Together, they can unite the houses of York and Lancaster, and Richmond can claim the crown of England in her right. Heed me, Madam: it will bring an end to these wars of the two roses, for your daughter is now the rightful inheritor of the realm, the true heiress of the House of York."

And the true Queen of England! The realization hit Elizabeth like a hammer. The Usurper's title was based on lies. If her brothers were dead, the crown was rightfully hers, and Richard must know it. That was why he prevented her escape from sanctuary. Anger rose in her. He had destroyed their lives and stolen her birthright, consigning his rightful sovereign to penury, obscurity, and the ignominy of bastardy. He was unspeakable!

Through her grief, she tried to think logically about what marrying Richmond would mean. She had never thought him worthy of her, or able to bring her any great advantage. And yet . . . Oh, if only she could think straight. It did seem that he was her best—her only—option now. She wished she knew more about him . . . Could he be a refuge to her at this time when she so badly needed him?

Mother was looking doubtful. "But Richmond is a penniless exile."

"The Duke of Buckingham can provide all the resources he needs. They are in touch through Lady Stanley and Bishop Morton. Madam, they are confident of success."

Elizabeth made her decision, hoping that it was the right one in the long term, and that she was in a fit state to decide her marital future. But there was one point on which she was certain. She stood up, holding herself regally, as if she reigned already. "If God has decreed that I be queen, then so be it. I will fight for my right. But I do not see how a woman can rule. We are not fitted by Nature to wield dominion over men."

"Your husband would rule in your name," the doctor said. "But there is no reason why you should not share power. Look at the Spanish sovereigns, Ferdinand and Isabella. They are equal in their authority. And France has been ruled by a woman regent since King Louis died. It is clear that some women have it in them to be great rulers."

"But not in England, I think. Since the Empress Matilda was overthrown for her arrogance and stupidity centuries ago, the English have been averse to female sovereigns. No, Dr. Lewis, if it is my fortune and grace to be queen, I need a husband, and my lord of Richmond represents my best chance of ridding myself of the stain of bastardy and attaining the crown that is rightfully mine." She realized, as she said it, that she was acting as if her brothers were dead. And probably they were, although she wished desperately that it could be otherwise. But she must be strong now, if these plans were to succeed.

Cecily was staring at her in awe, the tears still wet on her cheeks. Dr. Lewis smiled. "This is a decision you will not regret," he said. "Richmond is a fine, upstanding young man, versed in courtesy and courtly graces, virtuous and imbued with all the qualities of nobility and knighthood."

Elizabeth could hear Lady Stanley saying those very words. Dr. Lewis had been well primed.

"You forget," Mother's voice was faltering, "that Richmond is no match for the Queen of England. He is not even entitled to call himself earl of Richmond, for the late King deprived him of that title; he is merely a landless exile."

"But, my lady, he is our only hope," Elizabeth declared. "He can help me to gain my throne. He can avenge the murder of my brothers. He is our way out of here!"

"The Princess is right," Dr. Lewis declared. "And my lord of Richmond is ready to do all those things."

Mother nodded. There was no fight in her, but there was a dawning light in her reddened eyes. "Very well, Dr. Lewis. Please tell the Countess that I agree to this venture and that I will do all in my power to persuade the late King's friends to support Richmond." She fixed her gaze on the doctor. "I am aware, of course, that we are all taking considerable risks, but it is necessary. My sons must be avenged—and Edward's blood must wear the crown."

Mother rallied, galvanized by the prospect of action. She did not take the Abbot into her confidence. She felt he was compromised enough by sheltering them in his house. But she wrote letter after letter to those friends of Father's whom she felt she could trust, urging them to abandon the Usurper and support Richmond. These she gave to Dr. Lewis, who came regularly, ostensibly to check on his patient and lift her spirits. By virtue of his calling, he could act as a messenger without incurring any suspicion. Mother was indeed suffering palpitations, digestive congestion, and nightmares, all brought on by grief and anxiety, and Abbot Eastney had firmly informed Captain Nesfield that she was in need of Dr. Lewis's ministrations. If he guessed that there was more to these consultations, he gave no sign of it.

Elizabeth felt guilty about deceiving the Abbot, but they were causing him enough headaches by remaining under his roof and trespassing on his charity, and it was safer for him if he was left in ignorance. He was sympathetic and had shown true kindness to Mother in her great grief, but she had sensed, since the abbey had been placed under siege, that he was very uncomfortable with the situation. She could understand it: she was uncomfortable, too. Yet to leave the protection of sanctuary might put them in grave danger. The Usurper must regard the very existence of the true Yorkist heiress as a threat to his crown.

Elizabeth helped to make copies of the letters for Mother to address and sign. Keeping busy took their minds off the tragedies that had engulfed them, but she couldn't help fearing that they would be discovered. Richard might well see treason as sufficient grounds for breaking sanctuary. But it wasn't really treason, was it? He was the traitor.

Dr. Lewis regularly informed them how matters were progressing. Fired up by Lady Stanley's zeal, his personal mission was to ensure that their plans succeeded. One morning, he had momentous news for them.

"Things are moving, your Grace! My lord of Buckingham has sent word to Richmond, inviting him to hasten to England as fast as he can to take possession of the kingdom and marry my lady Princess as soon as possible. On St. Luke's Day, the eighteenth of October, Buckingham will raise the men of Wales in rebellion. And there is news from Brittany. Duke Francis had offered Richmond the hand of his daughter and heiress, who could have brought him the duchy, but Richmond has rejected her, for he is resolved to wed you, my lady Princess, and gain a kingdom."

"But he does mean for us to reign jointly?" Elizabeth stipulated.

"Assuredly he does! He knows that he will reign in your right."

Things were moving quickly. All Elizabeth's prayers were directed to one end, that Richmond—or Henry, as she now privately called this man who would soon, God willing, be her husband—would be victorious.

"He is planning to join Buckingham in Wales," Dr. Lewis reported. "His mother has sent him a goodly sum of money to raise men for his cause, and many Yorkists have joined him, for they are outraged at the disinheriting of the late King's children, and rejoice at the prospect of the marriage of York and Lancaster."

Elizabeth and her mother smiled at each other. All that letter-writing had not been in vain.

The doctor had brought Elizabeth a book. "A gift from Lady Stanley," he told her. "She thinks you will find it uplifting."

After he had gone, she sat in the window with a goblet of wine and read avidly. The book was a romance, and related how Prince Blanchardin had fallen in love with Princess Eglantine. While he was fighting the Infidel, she devoutly said her prayers, had the city garrisoned, and planned their wedding, which was her heart's desire. Elizabeth was relieved to read that Blanchardin passed unscathed through a series of adventures, disasters, and escapes, and was finally able to claim Eglantine as his wife. The parallels between their story and her own situation were remarkable, and she was grateful to Lady Stanley for trying to raise her morale and help her to while away the tedious, tense hours in sanctuary.

Mother was still beset by doubts that she was doing the right thing. "What if this whole scheme is just a color for Buckingham to seize the throne for himself?" she asked anxiously. "He has royal blood; he is descended from Edward the Third."

"Yes, but from that King's youngest son," Elizabeth pointed out. "It is a weak claim. And, if Buckingham really intended that, why involve Henry?"

"To lure him to Wales and kill him?" Mother suggested.

Elizabeth shook her head. "I don't believe it."

When Dr. Lewis next came, Mother asked him bluntly if it could be true.

"Madam," he declared, "if I thought it was, I would not be supporting the rebellion, and I would warn off Lady Stanley." He checked her pulse.

"Yet I cannot help but wonder what Buckingham hopes to gain

from supporting Richmond. It is not as if he needs rewards. He has profited enough under the Usurper."

"Power and influence, Madam, that is what all men want," the doctor said sagely, feeling her brow. "At first, Buckingham's plan was to restore the young King, so I believe him to be sincere in your cause."

A look of pain laced the Queen's pale features. "We shall see," was all she would say, and she was still looking uneasy when Father Abbot joined them for dinner.

"I have received an intriguing letter from Bishop Russell," he said, as soon as the lay brothers had served the food and departed. "He tells me that Sir James Tyrell, the King's Master of Horse, left the court at York and rode south to the Tower to fetch necessities from the Royal Wardrobe for the investiture of King Richard's son as Prince of Wales, which took place at York Minster earlier this month. It seems strange that he should mention such an inconsequential detail."

Mother's lip trembled. "Do you think he was trying to suggest that Tyrell was somehow connected with the murder of my sons?"

"I did wonder."

Mother leaned forward. "Father, do you think there is any chance that they are still alive?"

Abbot Eastney looked at her with sadness. "Alas, Madam, I fear not."

"But there is no proof that they are dead," Elizabeth said. "When you boil it down, it is all just speculation." She could not share Dr. Lewis's report of what the Usurper had said to Buckingham, but there remained no evidence that he had carried out his threat to remove her brothers. She had thought about this endlessly. Was there still room for hope?

On his next visit, Dr. Lewis informed them that more disaffected Yorkists had joined the conspirators. "And Lord Stanley commands a private army, which he is placing at Richmond's disposal." So Father Stanley had kept his word. He had not let them down. "Buckingham has allowed Bishop Morton to escape from Brecknock, and the Bishop has gone to Ely to raise men in his diocese. Your Grace's kinsmen, the Hautes, are planning a rising in Kent."

Elizabeth was becoming increasingly confident that the uprising would succeed and she would soon be queen. She thought a lot about Henry Tudor, that unknown Welshman. What was he like, this man who had spent most of his life either as a fugitive or in exile? He was clearly ambitious, and had a dogged determination. But what did he look like? What character did he have? If only she could have some word from him, some indication that he saw her as a person rather than just a woman with a crown.

Dr. Lewis brought more news, all of it encouraging. Mother was overjoyed to hear that Dorset had emerged from hiding and was planning to rouse the men of Exeter. Uncle Lionel was planning to stir the men of Salisbury, his diocese. The Queen's other brothers, Sir Edward and Sir Richard Wydeville, were poised to play their parts, and risings were to take place in Guildford and Newbury, while Buckingham was to raise Brecon and all south Wales. Shocked at the rumors about the princes, many members of the late King's household had joined the conspirators. The net was spread far and wide. And soon, Dr. Lewis assured them, Henry would set sail from Brittany. Elizabeth felt a thrill just hearing it. Their champion and savior was coming!

As the days wore on, the news came to them little by little. The Hautes had risen in Maidstone, but had been crushed by the Duke of Norfolk.

"Do not be alarmed," Dr. Lewis told them. "In a few days, Buckingham will move and all our friends will rise with him."

Then the rain began. It poured and poured, and the Abbot told them there had been reports of flooding in some parts of the kingdom.

Elizabeth began praying that the awful weather would not impede Buckingham's plans. The day of the rising would soon be upon them. They were all in a fever of agitation. There were so many involved now in the conspiracy; was it still possible that the Usurper was unaware of what was going on?

* * *

"This must be my last visit," Dr. Lewis said, looking unusually nervous. "All is lost."

"No!" Mother cried.

"What has happened?" Elizabeth asked sharply.

"I must be brief," the doctor said. "I am known to serve Lady Stanley, and it will go ill for me if I attract suspicion. It seems that, by means of spies, the whole design of this plot became known to King Richard. Even before the day set for the rising, he had Buckingham proclaimed a rebel and offered free pardons to any who surrendered. In Wales, he set armed men in readiness to take the Duke. Buckingham left Brecon as planned, making for Hereford, but the storms and floods wrecked his plans. His army deserted him, and he was forced to flee to Shropshire, where he sought shelter in the cottage of one of his tenants, who betrayed him for a handsome reward."

"Dear God, no," Elizabeth faltered.

"Does the Usurper know of our involvement?" Mother demanded.

"In faith, Madam, I do not think so. I will not betray you, and I'm sure Lady Stanley will not either. As for my lord of Buckingham, he can say nothing. He was brought to Salisbury, where the Usurper had come with a great army, and, on All Souls' Day, notwithstanding the fact that it was a Sunday, he was beheaded in the marketplace."

There was a shocked silence. Mother crossed herself. She looked tragic, drained of hope, all her beauty gone. "God rest him."

"What of Lady Stanley?" Elizabeth asked.

"The King has been merciful, given that she has committed treason." Dr. Lewis's voice shook. "She has been deprived of her title and placed under house arrest in the custody of her husband, who has been given her estates. When it came to it, Lord Stanley rallied to the King."

"He was ever a weathercock," Mother said bitterly. "The Stanleys have always blown with the prevailing wind."

Elizabeth bit back tears. She had placed much reliance on Lord Stanley.

"My lady is being held in some secret place apart from her household," Dr. Lewis said. "I dare not go near her."

"What of my son Dorset and my brothers, and Bishop Morton?" Mother asked.

"The Usurper also extended clemency to them, and the offer of a pardon, but they have fled the kingdom to join Richmond."

"Is he yet in Brittany?" Elizabeth asked. She was hoping that, somehow, he would still descend on England with an army and topple Richard.

"There is no news of him," the doctor said. "And now I must leave you. It is dangerous for me to be seen here." With a quick bow, he hastened away.

"Well," Mother said flatly, "that's put paid to our hopes."

Elizabeth felt sick and frightened. From the Usurper's point of view, they had committed treason. Would he move against them?

Chapter 9

1483–1484

They spent the next week or so in an agony of trepidation, expecting Captain Nesfield and his men to burst through the door at any moment. Elizabeth felt trapped. What did they do to women who committed treason? She did not know and did not want to find out.

They heard from the Abbot that Henry had attempted an invasion, but had been blown off course by the foul weather. "He got as far as Plymouth, but was driven back to Brittany. He must have heard of the collapse of the late rebellion." The Abbot's piercing gaze swept them all. He knows, Elizabeth realized. Yet she knew he would not betray them. He was on their side, after all.

She sought refuge in the prayers in her Book of Hours, but even there she found a reminder of her confounded hopes. Just three weeks ago, beneath where she had written "Elizabeth Plantagenet" on the flyleaf, she had added the name "Henry," being so sure that she would soon be wed. Taking a quill pen, she scratched it out. No one should ever know that she had entertained sentimental thoughts about Henry.

* * *

Christmas was dismal. There were so many loved faces missing from the table. Father, Ned, York, Uncle Rivers, Dickon, Buckingham . . . all dead or disappeared. And Dorset, the other Wydeville uncles, Lady Stanley . . . all in custody or exile.

The Abbot did his best to cheer them. He provided a goose and a great plum pudding. He brought the choristers from the abbey to entertain them in the Jerusalem Chamber. They thanked him profusely, but it was hard to enter into the spirit of the season.

"We have been here eight months now, and I fear we shall never leave," Elizabeth grumbled to Cecily as they watched their sisters playing with their poppets.

"At least the Usurper hasn't dragged us out," Cecily replied. "But, at this rate, I shall die an old maid."

"Life is passing us by," Elizabeth lamented. "When I think how it was this time last year—that splendid court Father held."

"Don't! I can't bear to think about it."

"If he knew what has happened to us all since his death, he would be horrified. He would never have placed his trust in Richard."

"Do you think Henry will ever attempt to take the throne again?" Cecily asked.

"I pray he does. I have not given up hope."

One cold day in January, as they huddled around the fire, the Abbot brought the Queen a letter. "This was enclosed in one addressed to me, your Grace." He smiled and left her to read it.

"It's from Dorset!" she cried, reading it avidly. "Oh, merciful God—some good news at last. Listen to this! On Christmas Day, Henry went to Rennes Cathedral and publicly, upon his oath, vowed that he would take the crown of England and marry you, Bessy, and unite the houses of Lancaster and York." There were tears in her eyes.

Elizabeth thrilled to hear her words. They gave her such hope for the future.

"He writes also that four hundred Yorkists have now fled England and joined Henry in Brittany. This is tremendous news—it is a measure of the support the Usurper has lost because of those rumors about my sons. People will not tolerate the murder of innocents."

Something struck Elizabeth. "Richard must have heard the rumors. Why has he never denied them?"

"Indeed!" Mother said grimly. "When Henry of Lancaster died, his body was put on public display."

"But how would the Usurper explain the bodies of two children?" Cecily asked.

"He could have given out that they died of natural causes," Elizabeth said. "But no one would believe it."

"Maybe he does not want the people making a shrine to them," Mother suggested. "Think of how Henry of Lancaster has become revered as a saint. The Usurper won't have martyrs made of my sons. It would spark too many questions. No, he wants them dead and buried and forgotten."

"But they won't be," Cecily declared. "Henry will come and avenge them. And then we will discover the truth."

"I think the Usurper will find Henry a force to contend with," Mother said. "By his oath, he has achieved the near-impossible—he has united Lancastrians and Yorkists in a common cause. Dorset writes that many Yorkists swore homage to him in Rennes Cathedral as though he was king already."

"It's strange," Elizabeth mused, "but until recently, no one took his claim seriously."

"It is his vow to wed you, Bessy, that has changed things," Mother said. "People want an end to warring factions. They want peace, and this marriage will bring that."

They were aware that Parliament was sitting that January. The Abbot, as one of the lords spiritual, was attending daily.

Dusk was falling on a bitterly cold afternoon, and they were lighting the candles when he opened the door and bowed. It was obvious that he brought bad news.

"What is it?" Mother asked in alarm.

He hesitated momentarily. "Your Grace, Parliament has passed an Act confirming King Richard's title to the throne and setting forth the grounds of his claim. Your marriage to the late King has been formally declared invalid and its issue bastards. I am very sorry to have to tell you this."

Bastards. The shameful word reverberated in Elizabeth's head. She had known that Richard had dreamed up this lie, but to have it proclaimed to the whole kingdom made rage, rare, hot, and vengeful, rise in her. How dare that villain do this to them? How dare he do it to *her*, whom he knew at heart to be his rightful Queen?

Mother shivered and sank down on a stool. "How will I bear the humiliation?"

"You will bear it because you know the truth," Abbot Eastney told her. "Until proofs of this secret marriage King Edward is supposed to have made are laid before an ecclesiastical court, your marriage stands. Parliament is a lay court. It has no jurisdiction to pronounce on the validity of any union. I can only assume that it presumed to do so because of the great fear of King Richard that has struck the hearts of even the most resolute—and because Richard fears Richmond's intentions. In declaring your daughters bastards, he thinks to scupper Richmond's ambitions and protect himself."

"But, in law, according to this Act, we are bastards." Elizabeth found her voice. "We are stripped of our titles and barred from inheriting anything from our parents." She burned with the shame of it.

"I fear it is so, my lady Princess," the Abbot confirmed. He turned to Mother. "And I regret to inform you, Madam, that Parliament has deprived you of the income and property you held as queen."

She looked aghast. "So we are paupers then? Does he seek to take everything from us?"

"You will want for nothing while you are under my roof," he assured her. "And there are many who still regard the Lady Bessy as the late King's true daughter and the rightful heiress to the throne. King Richard is unpopular. Many have deserted him. This Parliament is passing some good and beneficial legislation, but I suspect that its chief purpose is to win support for his rule. Take heart, my ladies. You have many friends who will not let this insult pass, although . . ." He hesitated.

"What?" Mother asked shrilly.

"Parliament has attainted Richmond as a traitor, so you can no longer look for help from that quarter. If he returns to England, he will be arrested and summarily executed. Therefore, I must warn you, Madam, that anyone declaring for the mooted marriage between Richmond and the Lady Bessy could be deemed guilty of misprision of treason."

Elizabeth saw her hopes crashing into dust.

"The Usurper has well and truly outmaneuvered us." Mother's tone was bitter. "And there is nothing we can do about it."

They celebrated Elizabeth's eighteenth birthday with some early spring lamb from the abbey's farms and a flagon of good Burgundy wine. The Abbot and the Prior joined them, and they tried to put on brave faces and make it a merry occasion, for all that the children's clothes had been let out and down several times and Elizabeth's velvet gown looked worn and rubbed. But that was as nothing compared to the troubles that beset them. She did her best to smile, but she could not rid herself of the sadness of loss, or the feeling that time was passing her by. Was there a future for her? Would Henry defy Parliament and come to fulfill his vow? She was thinking gloomily that the prospect seemed remote when the Abbot turned to her.

"I was at Westminster today," he said. "I saw Bishop Russell. He told me that my lord of Richmond is now styling himself king of England and has applied for a Papal dispensation to marry you."

Elizabeth felt uplifted. "That is the best news you could have brought me. He really does intend to seize the kingdom."

"I pray for the day!" the Queen said fervently.

"King Richard is furious, as you can imagine," Abbot Eastney said. "He has just learned that the Chancellor of France has publicly accused him of murdering his nephews. Those rumors are spreading throughout Christendom."

"Then all he has to do to refute them and restore his reputation is produce my sons alive!" Mother said tartly.

"Which I suspect he cannot do," the Abbot said sadly. "But I fear he will try to get your daughters into his power. He knows that his growing number of enemies regard them as the true heirs of York."

"He shall not have them!" the Queen cried.

"He cannot make us leave here," Elizabeth said, giving up all pretense of eating. "And I will not go."

"Rest assured that you are safe in sanctuary," Eastney told them.

Mother shook her head. "You forget, Father Abbot, that they took my son from here. They said there was no need for a child to claim sanctuary, and they could very well say the same about my daughters. We would be defenseless against the might of those soldiers outside."

"They will have me to contend with!" the Abbot said fiercely. "This is a sacred place and I will not have it violated."

That was some small comfort. Yet, were Abbot Eastney to be pitched against a determined Captain Nesfield, who would be the victor?

It soon looked as if it would not come to that. The Usurper sent a deputation of councillors to the Queen. They stood before her, wearing furred robes and grave faces, looking uncomfortable. Among them were Archbishop Bourchier and Bishop Russell. They had known her and her daughters in another life and clearly felt awkward in her presence.

"Lady Grey," they addressed her, having omitted to bow.

She cut them short. "Who is Lady Grey? There is no person by that name here."

"Madam," the Lord President said, "our orders are not to address you as queen, for that title has been taken from you. But King Richard acknowledges that that was through no fault of your own and wishes to make amends. He has sent us to tell you that, if you will leave sanctuary and bring your daughters to court, you will be treated with every honor and his Grace will find suitable husbands for the young ladies and give them marriage portions."

"No," Mother said. "You may tell him that we feel safer here and do not want his charity."

"Madam, he promises you a comfortable future with a generous income."

"No."

"He would treat you as his honored and beloved sister and your daughters as his true nieces. You would be very great ladies."

"We *are* very great ladies," the Queen said. "I am a queen, and my daughters are princesses of the realm. This tale of a secret marriage is nonsense."

The Lord President pursed his lips. "I have not come to discuss contentious matters, Madam, but to extend the King's hand of friendship."

Mother glared at him. "If he wishes to show me true friendship, then let him send my sons to me."

The lords shifted uneasily.

"Alas, Madam, I am not authorized to discuss matters of high policy. But King Richard is concerned about his nieces remaining in sanctuary. They are not felons and have done nothing to justify claiming the right."

Mother was as fierce as a lioness. "You forget that Richard has committed acts of hostility toward me and mine. He has given abundant proof of his hatred for my blood."

"And you forget, Madam, that your family have shown themselves ready to destroy him," the Lord President responded angrily.

"He had my sons murdered!" Mother hissed. Elizabeth suppressed a gasp.

"He did not!" The lords looked at one another.

"Then where are they?"

"That, Madam, is a matter of state security."

"You cannot deny that he ordered the unlawful killing of my son Dickon."

The man lost patience. "Madam, if you continue to slander

King Richard, I must not listen. You are placing yourself in a very vulnerable position. This abbey is ringed by soldiers."

"Are you threatening me?" Mother challenged, her tone icy. "Does Richard intend to remove us by force?"

"That is not his intention at all. He wishes simply to make peace with you."

"And how do I know that, once we have left sanctuary, we will not be shut up in the Tower and made to disappear, as my sons were?"

"You will have the King's oath on it."

Her eyes narrowed. "And what is that worth?"

Another councillor spoke. "Madam, this wrangling is getting us nowhere. I can assure you that his Grace is sincere. There has even been talk of his marrying the Lady Elizabeth to his son, the Prince of Wales."

Elizabeth was taken aback. Edward of Middleham was just seven years old. Over my dead body, she told herself. Besides, she was promised to Henry.

Mother looked doubtful.

"King Richard will publicly guarantee your safety if you leave here," the Lord President assured her. "We strongly solicit you to do so."

"I will think on the matter," she conceded at length, to Elizabeth's astonishment. "If you return tomorrow, I will give you my answer then."

"I just wanted rid of them!" she said, when they had gone. She retired to the prayer desk in her bedchamber, as Elizabeth sat and thought about their predicament. Beyond the window, the sky was azure blue. Outside in the world, spring would be stirring, with all its promise of renewal and new life. She longed to be a part of it. And she could be, if Mother would agree to let her and her sisters leave sanctuary. But how could she bring herself to look upon the face of the man who had probably murdered her brothers and treated her family so cruelly, let alone be civil to him?

And yet, during these past long months, she had been given the courage and strength to endure isolation and deprivation, to weather tragedy and to think of others. And she was thinking now of her mother and sisters. If she went to court, made peace with Richard and dissembled, showing him that she was not a threat, she might do her family some good. In sanctuary, they had no future. In leaving here, she might salvage something from the wreckage of their lives. The more she thought about it, the more she felt that it was the right thing to do.

Only one thing held her back—the knowledge that Henry might come and claim her. That would be the best solution for them all. But since the support he had built in England had collapsed with the rebellion, it might be years before he could invade.

There were other considerations, too. She tried to enumerate them in her mind, marshaling the arguments for and against leaving. Oh, what should she do?

As soon as the younger children were in bed, Mother seated herself at the supper table. Elizabeth thought sadly that she had aged in these past months. That famous beauty had vanished, leaving a drawn-looking woman with sharp features and haunted eyes.

"I have made my decision," she said, when they finished grace. "It will be safer if we all stay here. I trust nothing that monster says."

Elizabeth drew in her breath. "I don't think we have a choice."

The Queen dropped her napkin and looked up in surprise. "Why?"

"If you don't agree, I think they will remove us by force. It does the Usurper's reputation no good to have a widow and orphans hiding in fear from him. It is tarnished enough as it is."

Mother poured herself some wine, frowning. She seemed to be collecting her thoughts.

"You think he will go that far?" Cecily asked. "Father Abbot said he would not allow it."

"What weight has Father Abbot against the might of those soldiers?" Mother replied bitterly. "And it is true: in law, you have no need of sanctuary. I cannot justify keeping you here."

"But we won't leave without you, Mother," Cecily protested.

"You may not have a choice."

"But, if all is done publicly," Elizabeth said, "and the Usurper makes it clear to everyone that his intentions are honorable and that we will be in no danger, then we will probably be safe."

"I really don't want you to go to court," Mother said. "I don't want you to have to be friendly to him after everything he has done, or address him as king. And I don't want him marrying you to his son—or anyone else of his choosing. He just wants to prevent you from marrying Henry."

"I know. He seeks to preempt anyone seizing the throne in my name. But I cannot invest all my hopes in Henry. Taking this kingdom will be no easy venture, and I doubt he now has the wherewithal to do so; he may never have it. Richard is thirty-one; he might be in power for a very long time. We cannot stay in sanctuary forever, especially if he gives us guarantees." She laid her hand on the Queen's. "Mother, you well know that our continuing presence here has placed a burden on the Abbot. We have been living on his charity for nearly a year and imposing on his kindness. The abbey is under siege because of us. Our staying here in the face of the Usurper's promises will place him in a very difficult position. And, if you refuse to let us leave, I have no doubt that Richard will take us away, as he did our sweet York."

Mother looked distressed. "I cannot surrender you girls to the man who murdered your brothers."

"My lady, I want to do what is best for us all. The Usurper rules here, and we have to come to terms with him. You could keep us here and defy him, but I fear it will do us no good. No, going to court offers us the best—the only—chance of a good life. I am willing to do it."

Mother still looked dubious. "You are a good girl, Bessy, and a brave one. It is a great sacrifice that you are making. You may not be safe, you realize that?"

"My lady, I think the worst he can do is marry me to his son. Then, God willing, I will be queen one day after all."

Mother looked at her. "Do you realize that his doing that would be tantamount to an admission that you are true-born? No king takes a bastard for his queen."

"Maybe he sees it as a way of strengthening his hold on the throne."

"And will you be complicit in that?"

Elizabeth shrugged. "Do I have a choice?"

Mother received the councillors, looking gaunt and regal in her black gown and widow's wimple. "Good my lords," she said, "I am willing to let the princesses leave sanctuary on condition that my brother-in-law"—and she would not give him his title—"publicly guarantees their safety."

The Lord President looked satisfied. "His Grace is willing to do that," he replied.

"He will keep my daughters safe and ensure that no harm befalls them?" Mother demanded.

"He will, you have my word on it."

On the first day of March, the lords returned and handed Mother a document.

"This morning, Madam, his Grace met with the Council and the Lord Mayor and aldermen of London and swore on the word of a king, with his hand on the Holy Gospels, that, since you have agreed to your daughters leaving sanctuary, he will offer them all his protection. This he has confirmed in writing."

The Queen read the document, then handed it to Elizabeth. She could sense her mother bristling because the Usurper had referred to her as "Dame Elizabeth Grey, late calling herself Queen of England," yet she had not protested. This was not the time to anger him.

Elizabeth read carefully. Richard had promised that if she and her sisters would come to him out of the sanctuary of Westminster, to be guided and ruled by him, he would ensure that they would be safe. They would not suffer any hurt or be ravished or defiled against their will. They would not be imprisoned in the Tower of London or any other prison, but would be housed safely and comfortably. He would ensure that they were treated honestly and courteously and had everything they needed to wear, as befitted their station, and a household fit for his kinswomen. Furthermore, he would marry those who were of age to gentlemen born, and dower each with lands worth two hundred marks yearly.

That was paltry compared with the ten thousand marks her father had willed her for her dowry, and it was a cruel reminder of her reduced status, but there was nothing she could do about it.

She read on as they all stood silent, waiting. Richard had promised to charge their husbands to love them and treat them well, if they wished to avoid his displeasure. And if anyone made an evil report of them to him, he vowed he would not give credence to it or punish them before they had a chance to speak in their defense.

She raised her eyes to the Queen's and nodded.

"Very well," Mother said, "I agree to my daughters leaving."

The Lord President smiled at last. "It is a wise decision, Madam. There is one more thing. Parliament has assigned you a life annuity of seven hundred marks, which the King has publicly confirmed. It will be paid to Captain Nesfield for your maintenance. He will continue here as your attendant."

Mother looked furious. "My jailer, more like! And I can manage my own income, thank you!"

The Lord President gave her a hard look. "You must be very naïve, Madam, to think that the King will place in your hands funds that could be used against him."

"And do *you* think that I would do anything to jeopardize his goodwill toward my daughters or their safety?" she retorted.

"The King will be glad to hear that you are being so amenable, Madam. Arrangements will be made for your daughters to be escorted to the palace this afternoon. Pray have them pack their belongings."

Mother broke down when the lords had gone, and drew them all to her. "I cannot bear to see you go," she wept. "You are all most precious to me. Bessy and Cis, you must look after your sisters."

Elizabeth knelt and embraced Anne, Katherine, and Bridget. "You are going to court, to live in the palace again. You'll like that, won't you?"

They eyed her doubtfully. "I want to stay with Mother," said Katherine.

"But you are a princess—your place is at court. And you will see Mother soon."

How true that was she did not know. The Queen might be here for some time to come. The Usurper had no quarrel with her daughters, but he knew her for his enemy, and had given no guarantees for her safety.

And there was something else missing from that document. He had given no guarantee for the princes' safety either. Did that mean that they really were dead?

It was a difficult parting. Mother clung to them, one by one, as if she would never see them again, and covered their faces with kisses.

"May God be with you, my sweet children!" she cried. "Keep them safe, Bessy, keep them safe!"

"I will, my lady, I promise!"

Elizabeth felt choked as she relinquished her mother's arms and the Abbot escorted the five of them from Cheyneygates and out into the world. A deputation of lords awaited them, and grooms hastened to take their traveling chests from the lay brothers who had carried them downstairs.

They walked the short distance from the abbey to the palace, where the guards stood to attention as they entered. It was good to be out of the confines of sanctuary and to see the old, familiar sights around them, but Elizabeth felt torn. Resentment against the Usurper and anxiety about Mother jarred with her pleasure and relief at being out of sanctuary. And it was a bittersweet experience to be returning to the place where, just a year before, they had been honored as royal princesses. But, above all, she felt nervous. Soon, she would come face-to-face with the Usurper. How would it be between them? She must dissemble and hide her feelings. Could she do it? And how could she bear to address him as king? Yet, as Mother had reluctantly agreed, she must do it, for all their sakes.

She was thankful that she had taken her best apparel into sanctuary. She knew she looked every inch the princess in her black velvet gown with the high waist and sweeping train. But her sisters had grown and their clothes were too short, although that could soon be rectified.

"The King will receive you in the White Hall," they were informed. So it was to be a public reception. She drew in her breath, trying to compose herself and forget the things her uncle had done. She reached for Cecily's hand and squeezed it. Cecily looked as nervous as Elizabeth felt.

When they entered the White Hall, she was shocked to see so many courtiers gathered there. She recognized many of them from the days when her father reigned, and it was humiliating to face them with the shame of bastardy hanging over her. It did not help being announced as the daughters of the late King Edward and Dame Elizabeth Grey.

Head high, she walked with her sisters the length of the hall to where the Usurper sat on his throne next to Aunt Anne. She could not bear to look at him, so she fixed her gaze on Anne, who smiled at her. As they sank into curtseys, Richard stood up and stepped down from the dais.

"Bessy, Cecily, my good nieces, welcome back to court. Please rise."

Elizabeth looked up, and there he was, the uncle she had known and loved, looking at her searchingly, with a slight flush on his cheeks. There was a new wariness in his gaze. She looked away, fearing that he would read accusation in her eyes.

"We are right glad to see you all," he said, then hesitated. "I know the past months have been a difficult time for you, but this is a new beginning. My lords and ladies, will you welcome my nieces?"

There were resounding cheers and everyone clapped. Elizabeth turned around and curtseyed, seeing Lord Stanley's beaming face and Bishop Russell's compassionate expression. She was deeply touched at these demonstrations of affection. Maybe coming to court was not going to be so humiliating after all. But if Richard thought that being so well received would make her forget the injuries he had done her and her family, he was mistaken.

* * *

She had resolved to brave it and probe Richard about his title to the throne and press him to tell her where her brothers were— how could she let those matters pass?—but there was no opportunity for a private conversation, for Aunt Anne had risen and led her and her sisters to the Queen's apartments, where she embraced and kissed them. She was as beautiful and pale as ever, her forehead shaven and her fair hair concealed under her fashionable butterfly headdress. She had lost weight: her gorgeous damask gown hung loose on her.

"You are to lodge with me for the time being," she told them. "When your lady mother can be persuaded to leave sanctuary, the King will appoint her some suitable place to live and you can join her there. In the meantime, you will live at court under my protection. Follow me, my ladies."

She led them into a luxuriously appointed chamber furnished with two large tester beds with embroidered curtains and counterpanes. One was for Elizabeth and Cecily, the other for Anne, Katherine, and Bridget. On the counterpanes lay some of the court gowns they had left behind and in the corner stood an open chest containing the little girls' toys.

"Is the Prince here?" Anne asked. "Can we play with him?"

"Alas, we have left him at Middleham," the Queen said. "He is delicate and the air in Yorkshire is much better for him."

"Is it true that the King plans to marry me to him?" Elizabeth asked, thinking that a frail boy of seven was not much of a prospect as a husband.

"I do not know," her aunt replied. "Where did you hear that?"

"The Abbot of Westminster told me. He had heard it at court."

"I am sure that the King will give due thought to your marriage, in time," the Queen told her. "Now, would you like to take advantage of this fine weather and take the little ones to play in my privy garden?"

Life at court soon fell into a routine, much as before, except that it was a relief to be attended by servants again, and they did not live in the Maidens' Hall, and the Queen who supervised them was not Mother. In fact, Aunt Anne left the supervising to her ladies-in-waiting and the Mother of the Maids, for she was not strong and spent much of her time resting, only gracing the court on ceremonial occasions.

Elizabeth had missed seeing Grandmother York while she was in sanctuary, but looked in vain for her, for it soon became clear that she was not at court. That did not surprise her, for the stately old lady must have been appalled at the things Richard had said about her. Elizabeth would have liked to visit her at Baynard's Castle, but was told that her grandmother was at Berkhamsted. She wondered if Richard felt guilty about the way he had treated his mother.

Meals were usually served in Anne's privy chamber and sometimes Richard joined them. These were awkward occasions during which the conversation often lapsed and the air was pregnant with so much that could not be said in company. Elizabeth found she could barely bring herself to speak to her uncle and confined herself to answering his questions as briefly as possible without being rude.

There were no opportunities to talk to him alone until the day came when he found her sitting by herself on a grass seat in the Queen's garden.

He bowed. "I am sorry to disturb you, Bessy."

She forced herself to rise and curtsey. "Her Grace is in the chapel," she said, and she would not address him as king.

"It is not the Queen whom I came to see," he said, sitting down beside her. "It is you. I know that you are bitter toward me, and I want to assure you that I mean you no ill."

"Like you meant my brothers and my uncle Rivers and the rest of us no ill!" The words tumbled out before she could stop herself. Nervously, she watched his face, and saw the pained look that crossed it.

"Bessy, Bessy," he said, "do not think the worst of me. I have done the best I could in a fraught situation. When I brought your brother to London, we found weapons that your kinsmen had stashed away to use against me. Your father, God rest him, had appointed me Lord Protector. He trusted me to do right by you all. But your mother and her relatives were determined to seize power."

"Those weapons were for use against the Scots," Elizabeth protested.

Richard shook his head. "Is that what you were told? No, they planned to prevent me from ever ruling as regent. That is why I had Lord Rivers and Sir Richard Grey imprisoned."

"You had them executed."

"They plotted my death!"

She stared at him. "I don't believe it. Uncle Rivers was an honorable and chivalrous man."

His dark eyes narrowed. "Despite that, he was determined to oust me, by whatever means—as was Lord Hastings. I had no choice but to order their executions, for my own safety and the stability of the realm."

She was not convinced. "Because of you, I lost a year of my youth shut up in sanctuary."

He shifted, suddenly looking angry. "That was not my doing. It was your mother's decision to go there."

"She was in fear of you!"

"*I* was in fear of *her*. She plotted against me, too. She sent Dorset from sanctuary to compass my ruin."

"She feared that you had set your mark at the crown from the first. She was desperately worried about my brothers, especially after you took York from us. And then you had us declared bastards!"

"Look at me, Bessy," Richard said. Reluctantly, she raised her eyes to his. "I did not have designs on young Ned's throne. But the Bishop of Bath laid proofs before me that your father was already married when he wed your mother. He had himself performed the first ceremony."

"Bishop Stillington?" Elizabeth echoed scornfully. She had heard plenty about this vile creature when her mother thought she was otherwise occupied. "I wonder that you would take anything that man says for truth. He is a knave. He never visits his diocese and he has baseborn children. And, knowing what he claims to know, he still swore allegiance to my brother Ned as our father's undoubted heir, when Ned was very young. Is he a reliable witness?"

Richard frowned. "He produced legal evidence and the depositions of several witnesses."

"May I see them? The matter affects me so nearly. At least grant me that."

Did he hesitate? She could not be sure. "I will show them to you."

She took a deep breath. "And what of my brothers? Where are they?"

"They have disappeared," he said heavily. "I do not know where they are."

For a moment, she could not speak. "Disappeared? What do you mean?"

"I mean that they were secretly removed from the Tower last autumn. I am convinced that Buckingham ordered it. He was Constable of England and had the means to get access. Not even Sir Robert Brackenbury, the Constable of the Tower, could say what had happened, and he's a vigilant officer. They were there one day—and the next, gone."

Richard got up and began pacing the gravel path. "I know what people are saying, that I had them killed. I've heard the rumors. But how can I refute them? Am I to announce that the princes have disappeared? I cannot produce them to show that they still live. Think what my enemies would make of it! We'd have all sorts coming forward to claim that they were the rightful heirs of York. And I would not have people think me a negligent guardian."

"It is better than their thinking that you are a murderer!" Elizabeth burst out, still aghast that her brothers had vanished, yet brimming with new hope that they were still alive.

"But I cannot counter that," he said, sitting down and burying his face in his hands. "And until I can, people will go on thinking the worst of me. I can never be safe on my throne while these calumnies persist. I am no tyrant, no child killer!" He sat up and looked at her. "You do believe me, don't you, Bessy?"

She wanted to believe him, wanted things to be as they had
been between them. She had lived so long in suspicion, thinking
the worst of him. Yet, sitting beside him now, she found it hard
to credit that he was really the monster she had thought him to
be. There had been tragic misunderstandings on both sides, as she
had believed right at the start. And there was no doubt that
Mother would have done everything in her power to unseat Richard, given the chance.

If he would just show her the proofs of her father's marriage to
Eleanor Butler, she might be able to accept what he had said. He
could still, even now, be the Uncle Richard she had loved.

He was tense, waiting for her response.

"I need to think," she said.

His face darkened. "I'm not lying to you, Bessy. But I fear your
mind has been poisoned against me."

"How could you blame us for thinking the worst?" she cried.
"We thought you had killed my brothers. My mother is in grief
because of that. You took everything from us. My life has been a
misery ever since my father died."

"But that was not all my fault, Bessy." He laid his hand on hers,
but she drew it away.

"I don't know what to think," she told him. "I need to clear my
thoughts. Have you searched for my brothers? Could they have
been hidden in one of Buckingham's castles?"

Richard sighed. "My officers have searched. There is no trace of
them. They have been spirited abroad—or done away with. And
I'm sorry to say this, Bessy, but I think the latter is the likeliest
possibility. Buckingham's aim was not to put Henry Tudor on the
throne, but himself."

She clung to her hopes. "But they could still be alive somewhere?"

"Why would he let them live? They would remain a threat to
him."

"As they were to you." She watched his reaction.

He shook his head wearily. "I told you, Bessy—I did not kill
them." Did it ring like the truth? Holy Mother, was she to tor-

ment herself with doubts all her life? Would she ever learn what had happened to her brothers?

Richard was still waiting for her answer, but she could not say what he wanted to hear.

"I will leave you in peace to think," he said, rising.

If only Mother was with her to give her advice. Elizabeth worried about the Queen being all alone in sanctuary with her griefs and her anxieties. She wished she could write and tell her Richard's version of events, but it was too dangerous to commit that to paper and, anyway, Mother would probably not believe it. But supposing she told her that she believed him and that, if Mother would consent to leave sanctuary, they could all be together again, away from the court. Maybe Mother would see the sense in it.

She had to get a message to her. But how?

She knew that Abbot Eastney was often at court and wondered if she could speak to him. It would not be easy. She was confined to the Queen's apartments and could not go running about the palace at will as she used to. When she went to the chapel or the White Hall, a lady-in-waiting was always in attendance.

But there was a way. She had learned all about subterfuge from the secret dealings in the late rebellion.

"When I was in sanctuary," she told Aunt Anne, "the Abbot was a great comfort to me. I miss that spiritual consolation. Your confessor is very kind, but it is not the same. Would it be possible for the Abbot to visit me?"

Anne smiled at her. "Of course. I will send to Westminster Abbey."

The Abbot came to her as she waited in the Queen's chapel.

"Father, I am so pleased to see you," she welcomed him. "How is my mother?"

"She is in health, but she misses you all," he said.

Elizabeth looked around, checking that they were alone. "I

asked for you to come because my uncle has told me things that will be of great import to her and I cannot confide them to a letter." She related what Richard had said and he listened gravely.

"If this is all true, then I agree, it is unlikely that the princes are still alive," he observed. "Have you been shown the proofs of the secret marriage yet?"

"Not yet. I have not seen my uncle since we spoke two days ago. Tell me, Father, what do you make of it all? Do you believe what he says?"

"I try to keep an open mind," he told her. "It may be true—it is a plausible version of events. Rest assured, I will tell the Queen what you have said. It may be what she needs to hear in order to make the decision to leave sanctuary." He smiled at her. "Now, shall I hear your confession?"

Chapter 10

1484–1485

Elizabeth and her sisters had been at court for barely a month when they learned that Mother was leaving sanctuary. She had sent the Abbot to convey her decision to Richard.

"You are to reside at Heytesbury in Wiltshire," Aunt Anne told them.

So far from the court! Elizabeth had never heard of Heytesbury. "Is it a royal house?" she asked.

"The King recently granted it to Captain Nesfield in gratitude for his assistance in suppressing Buckingham's rebellion. Captain Nesfield has placed it at your mother's disposal and will attend on you there."

Captain Nesfield! So Mother was to remain under surveillance. Elizabeth's spirits plummeted. They might have fewer freedoms at Heytesbury than in sanctuary, and they would be watched all the time by that horrible man. Miserably, she helped the Queen's maids to pack her sisters' belongings.

Richard dined with them that evening and bade them farewell. He had not brought the promised proofs and Elizabeth had not given him any assurance that she believed his story. There was no opportunity for a private word anyway. She doubted that the proofs would ever be forthcoming, especially now that Mother needed no more inducements to leave sanctuary.

Elizabeth and her sisters were lined up on the steps of Westminster Hall when the Queen Dowager arrived the next morning, escorted by Captain Nesfield. Their baggage carts were laden and two litters stood ready.

Mother embraced them all, weeping with joy to be reunited with them.

"We must make haste," the Captain said, mounting his horse. "We have a long journey ahead." His manner was as aloof and cold as ever.

The journey took four days. It was good to see the countryside again, drowsing in the summer sunshine, good to hear birdsong and feel the soft breeze through the windows of the litter. They stayed overnight in abbey guest houses and inns. Captain Nesfield made his own arrangements, but a member of their escort was never far away. At night, he would be stationed outside the door to their lodgings; at meals, he was at another table.

At long last, they came to Heytesbury. It was a pretty little town on the banks of the River Wylye with broad hills surrounding it. East Court, Captain Nesfield's house, lay to the north in a vast hunting park. Their little procession entered through a fortified gatehouse and halted in a spacious courtyard. Ahead stood the imposing stone house, while on the other three sides of the quadrangle were offices, stables, and, Elizabeth guessed, servants' quarters.

Captain Nesfield led them into the house, through a timber-beamed hall and up a spiral stair to their lodging, which comprised an old-fashioned solar and two bedchambers. Maids in white aprons and coifs were waiting to attend on them. The furnishings were of solid oak, the beds hung with red worsted curtains, and the floors covered with rush matting. Bowls and ewers of water had been set out on a chest for them, and there was a pleasant view of the gardens and park from the windows. Elizabeth thought it rather charming, but Mother sank down on the bed, looking around dubiously.

"I hope you will be comfortable," the Captain said stiffly. "If you need anything, my steward will supply it."

"Are we prisoners here?" Mother asked.

"You are my guests," he replied, his face impassive. "You may walk in the gardens and ride in the park. You can visit the village on market day and the fair that is held in September. But the King wishes you to be attended by an escort at all times, for your own security."

Elizabeth watched the Queen bite back a tart retort. Of course, it was more for Richard's security than their own that they were to be kept under supervision. Clearly, he still did not trust Mother.

"Before I leave you to settle in, Madam," Nesfield said, "there is one thing I require of you. The King wishes you to write to your son Dorset in Brittany and urge him to abandon Henry Tudor."

Mother looked as if she was about to protest, but pursed her lips. "Very well," she said, and turned to Elizabeth. "I promised to do that before I left sanctuary. My writing chest is in that coffer." Cecily fetched it and Mother wrote the letter. Watching her, Elizabeth knew that it would strike a blow to Henry's hopes, for Dorset was one of his most influential supporters. But she knew that Mother had no choice in the matter.

Daily life at Heytesbury was lived at a tranquil pace. Captain Nesfield did not trouble them much, for his rooms were at the other end of the house. He kept to himself and did not appear at meals, which were served to them in the solar. Yet they were aware of a household running like clockwork on his orders, and of the guards who kept watch at all the doors. When they rode out in the park—a pleasure in which they reveled after being cooped up for so long—men-at-arms followed them at a discreet distance.

They had not been at Heytesbury for long when Captain Nesfield informed them of the death of the Prince of Wales, Richard's only legitimate child. Looking unusually moved, he told them how Edward of Middleham had departed this life at Middleham Castle after a short illness. "He was the hope of his line. The councillors say that, when the news came, his father and mother were in a state almost bordering on madness by reason of their sudden grief."

Mother crossed herself. "God rest him," she murmured. More than that, she would not give.

Poor little boy, Elizabeth thought. He had been just eight years old. "We will pray for his soul," she said. Nesfield nodded and left.

Mother waited until his footsteps had receded down the stairs. "Now we see how vain are the ambitions of a man who desires to establish his interests without the aid of God. What good is all his worldly status and wealth when he has no son to inherit? Truly, I see the hand of divine vengeance in this. An eye for an eye, it is written . . . Fate has decreed that he suffers such a loss as we have. And he has no heir of his body left to succeed him." She sniffed. "Of course, he has his bastards. I expect he has brought John of Gloucester to court, and I've heard that he has married his daughter to the Earl of Huntingdon. But he is nothing without an heir!"

Elizabeth went to the chapel to pray, out of charity, for the Prince's soul. She could not help wondering if his death would strengthen her own position as the rightful heir of York. But that hope was soon dashed when Captain Nesfield informed them that Richard had named his nephew, John de la Pole, Earl of Lincoln, Aunt Suffolk's son, as his heir.

In the summer, the Captain was sent north to repel French and Scottish ships off Scarborough. They learned later that he had been captured and that Richard had had to ransom him.

While he was away, his sergeant, a big, burly bull of a man with a temper to match, kept watch on them. But the fight had gone out of Mother. She seemed content with their peaceful domestic round, although she still speculated endlessly on what might have become of her sons. The only time she erupted in anger was after Sergeant Smith said he had heard from a friend at court that the

King intended to wed Elizabeth to Bishop Stillington's bastard son, William.

"What an insult!" she raged, as soon as they were alone. "Never will I allow you to demean yourself by wedding such a low-born knave. And to suggest that we ally ourselves to that lying creature Stillington, who has brought our house to ruin! It beggars belief!"

"I shall refuse," Elizabeth declared, more bravely than she felt. The thought of marrying the Bishop's bastard chilled her to the bone. She would never submit to such an indignity. But would Richard force her to accept? She honestly did not know.

To their relief, they heard no more of it, even when letters began flying back and forth between Heytesbury and the court, for Richard had turned his attention to marrying off her sisters. Nine-year-old Anne, who had once been destined to be duchess of Burgundy, was betrothed in her absence to Lord Thomas Howard, grandson of the Duke of Norfolk.

"It is a good match, in the circumstances," Mother conceded. "You will be a duchess one day, my child."

Anne, interrupted as she played with her dolls, looked uncertain.

"Don't worry, it will be a long time before you are wed," Elizabeth smiled. She turned to the Queen. "In the light of this, I think that nonsense about my marrying Stillington's son was just a bruit."

"One I could have done without," Mother said acidly. "No doubt Sergeant Smith relished relaying it to us." She looked down at Richard's letter. "Oh! Aunt Suffolk's daughter, Anne de la Pole, is to be married to Prince James of Scotland."

"But *I* was to be queen of Scots!" Cecily protested.

Mother looked at her sadly. "Not anymore, my child. There will be another match for you, I am sure. Anne's betrothal gives us hope that the Usurper will do right by us."

"It seems odd that Cecily and I, the two eldest, have not been found husbands before our younger sister," Elizabeth pondered.

"Maybe our uncle has other plans that we don't know about," Cecily suggested.

"He ought to!" Mother declared. "He knows that you are the true Queen of England, Bessy. Let us hope that he will marry you appropriately."

"To whom?" Elizabeth rose and opened the casement, breathing in the heady scent of the flowers in the garden below. "There is only Henry who is worthy. It seems odd to me that Richard has not married me off to put me beyond Henry's reach."

"I'll wager he won't leave you unwed for much longer," Mother said. "He'll be negotiating a match as we speak, mark my words."

"Oh, if only Henry would come," Elizabeth sighed.

"Don't waste your hopes in that direction," Mother warned.

In September, Elizabeth and Cecily went to the fair, with two men-at-arms and two of the Heytesbury maids in attendance. They wandered around the stalls, spending pennies on ribbons, buttons, and other fripperies, and made their way to the hog roast to eat hot pork served on thick trenchers of bread, then watched some tumblers performing marvelous feats. No one recognized them, for they wore simple gowns and headrails and could have been taken for the daughters of a well-to-do yeoman.

As they stood drinking cider afterward, they became aware of a group of people gossiping nearby. "There's no doubt about it," a man was saying, "King Richard had the children of King Edward put to death."

"Well, God has spoken," a fat woman said. "He took his son."

Elizabeth and Cecily exchanged glances.

"I've heard tell that Richmond will come again," another man said. "He's sworn to marry King Edward's daughter."

"Nah," said his fellow, "he had his wings clipped last year. King Richard'll be ready for him. He won't come now."

Elizabeth had been holding her breath. Suddenly, she didn't want to hear any more.

"Come, Cecily, let's go and watch the fire-eater," she said.

At the beginning of December, a royal messenger arrived at East Court and Captain Nesfield summoned them all down to the hall to receive him.

The man was wearing Richard's livery of murrey and blue and

his white boar badge. He bowed to Mother and handed her a letter. "Madam, the King's Grace requests that you send your daughters to Westminster to attend on the Queen for the Yuletide season."

Elizabeth's heart leaped. After the humdrum months at Heytesbury, going to court would be wonderful, and she could see that her sisters thought so, too, even four-year-old Bridget. They were all looking hopefully at their mother, praying that she would not turn down the invitation.

The Queen hesitated, her eyes scanning the letter, and frowned. Elizabeth guessed that she was wondering if it was safe to deliver her remaining children into the King's hands.

"Please, my lady, may we go?" she asked.

"It is a high honor," Captain Nesfield said, in a tone that conveyed just how high an honor he thought it for unworthy bastards.

Mother seemed about to protest, but said nothing. She folded the letter and put it in her pocket. Elizabeth wondered what was in it. More assurances, she assumed.

"I need time to think about this," she said. "I will give my answer after I have sought guidance from God."

"Oh, my lady . . ." Elizabeth, Cecily, and Anne cried in unison.

"You must be patient," she said firmly. "Captain Nesfield, would you kindly arrange for this messenger to be given some dinner?" With that, she rose and withdrew into the chapel.

The sisters were on edge. They could settle to nothing, so much did they want to hear that they would be allowed to go to court. It seemed hours before the Queen returned.

"I have decided," she said. "You may all go."

"Thank you!" they chorused, almost jumping up and down in their excitement.

There followed a flurry of packing. Amidst all the excitement, Elizabeth spared a thought for her mother, who would be left all alone with only the maids and Captain Nesfield for company. Christmas would be bleak indeed for her.

"Are you sure you will be all right?" she asked her.

"I will," Mother assured her. "You are not to worry. Captain

Nesfield has given permission for your aunt Mary, Lady Rivers, to visit me. We two widows can commiserate together."

Elizabeth was pleased to hear that. It meant that she could go to court with a clear conscience.

Queen Anne looked ill, and much older than her twenty-eight years. Elizabeth could not credit the change six months had wrought. Her aunt was thin and gaunt, a travesty of her former self, and her pale features were ravaged by grief. Yet she received them with kind courtesy, and made much of Elizabeth, singling her out for special favor and treating her like a sister. But her sadness kept surfacing. Neither good company nor the pomp and festivity of the season could heal the wound in her heart caused by the loss of her son.

Elizabeth soon heard the gossip among the Queen's ladies. They would shake their heads sadly and whisper that Anne was not long for this world. She was fond of her aunt and sorry to see her so overcast by tragedy—and so bravely striving to carry on as normal.

Profound sorrow had affected Richard, too. He looked drawn and tense. She remembered that, in addition to coping with the agony of loss, and worrying about Anne's health, he must always be looking over his shoulder in case his enemies were stealing a march on him. Yet he welcomed Elizabeth gladly and with a warm embrace. Almost, she felt affection for him. This was the uncle she had known. If only she could believe he had not lied to her.

Christmas was kept with great state. There was much feasting, singing and dancing. It was as if Richard was determined to display to the world what a magnificent and mighty king he was. Elizabeth and her sisters entered enthusiastically into the revelry, aware of poor Anne sitting sadly on her throne, and Richard brooding beside her. After a while, she noticed that his eyes were resting on her as she twirled and skipped in the dance.

At the gift-giving ceremony on New Year's Day 1485, Richard presented her with two beautifully illuminated books. One was a

French translation of Boethius's *The Consolation of Philosophy*, the other *The Romance of Tristram de Lyonesse*, written by Sir Thomas Malory, the author of the famous *Morte d'Arthur*, one of her best-loved books.

"These are two of my favorites, Bessy," he said. "I want you to have them. Cherish them as I have."

She was touched by the gift and thanked him warmly. She was even more delighted when, on the morning of Twelfth Night, a page appeared in the Queen's apartments with a heavy parcel for her wrapped in damask. After he had laid it on her bed and departed, she read the note that came with it. *It would please me to see you wearing this for the feast tonight. Richard R.*

Cecily had followed her into the room and watched as she pulled aside the damask, revealing a glorious gown of purple velvet trimmed with ermine at the wide collar and tight cuffs.

"Oh!" she gasped. "It's exquisite!" Cecily was gaping at it, awestruck.

Then the significance of the gift occurred to Elizabeth. "Do you realize, Cis, that purple is reserved only for royalty? Does this mean that Richard regards me as true-born?"

"How can he? If he acknowledges you as legitimate, he admits himself a usurper."

"Even so, if I appear tonight in this gown, people will wonder."

"Let them! Just enjoy the admiration. You'll look beautiful in it. I wish I had a gown like it."

"You can borrow my silver tissue one," Elizabeth offered.

Cecily was right. She did look good in the gown. Its high waist was cinched in by a wide white satin belt, and its train flared out gracefully behind her. She had no jewel to wear at her neck, so she left it bare, and the simplicity became her. Her long copper hair she wore loose, as befitted a maiden.

When she entered Westminster Hall, her sisters walking two by two behind her, everyone's heads turned. She walked past a sea of faces, some admiring, some envious, some just staring, and held her head high like the queen she ought to be. It wasn't until she

began to ascend the steps to the high table that she looked at
Queen Anne and realized that she was wearing exactly the same
gown. She was so shocked that she froze for a moment, before
sinking in a curtsey to hide her confusion. When she dared to
raise her eyes, she saw that Anne was smiling graciously, although
there was that familiar sad look in her eyes. Next to her, Richard
beamed approvingly at Elizabeth and indicated that she should sit
in the chair beside his. It was where she would have sat at one of
her father's feasts.

No wonder people had been staring! As she took her seat, her
heart was pounding. No one should be wearing the same gown as
the Queen. It was just not done. In her father's time, she and her
sisters had worn attire of the same color as their mother's, but
simpler in design and never as sumptuous. Why had Richard sent
her the same gown as he must have given his wife? He must have
known what he was doing. What had possessed him?

"You look beautiful," he said in her ear.

She looked down at her plate. "I feel so embarrassed," she muttered. "The Queen is wearing the same gown."

"She is pleased for the world to see how greatly she esteems you,
Bessy."

It was flattering to hear that, but Elizabeth was aware that the
lords and clergy were still scrutinizing her and murmuring among
themselves. She felt exposed and aggrieved. As if she would have
chosen such a gown herself!

All her pleasure in the evening was gone. To join in the dancing
would be to lay herself open to more unwelcome attention, so she
remained at table, even though Cecily tried to pull her to her feet.
And when the King of the Bean asked everyone to kiss their
neighbor, she turned her back on Richard and allowed the Duke
of Norfolk to peck her cheek. As soon as she decently could, she
pleaded a headache and asked for permission to retire.

"I am sorry to hear that," Richard said. "I will send to ask after
you tomorrow."

"I wish you a good night," Anne said kindly.

* * *

There was no headache, of course, but Elizabeth could not have felt worse. Never before had she been the object of such curiosity and—she feared—censure. As soon as she reached her bedchamber, she struggled out of the gown and left it lying on the floor. She would not wear it again.

The next morning, the Queen had a bad coughing fit that left her drained, and stayed in bed. Elizabeth sat with her until she slept, dying to probe her thoughts about the matching gowns, but fearing to agitate her further, lest she bring on another bout of coughing. There had been blood on Anne's kerchief.

Left to herself, with Cecily playing skittles with their sisters, she found a window seat in a gallery and began leafing through the tale of Tristram of Lyonesse. She knew the story of old, but Malory's version was different. In it, Tristram fell in love with the lovely Isolde, having killed her uncle.

She paused at that. Was there a parallel to be drawn with her own story? For Richard had had *her* uncle, Lord Rivers, killed. Was there a message here? No, surely it was pure coincidence. Richard too was her uncle, for Heaven's sake!

The words danced before her eyes as she struggled to make sense of his behavior. At length, she rose and returned to the Queen's lodging. The antechamber was empty, but she could hear men and women talking in the great chamber, the door being ajar. Hesitating, she hovered outside, hearing the voices rise and fall, until suddenly she heard her name mentioned. She recognized the voice of the Duke of Norfolk.

"The King is bent on contracting a marriage with the Lady Elizabeth," he was saying.

She froze in shock. A marriage? How? Richard had a wife already.

"The Queen is not long for this world," the Duke continued, as if in response to her unspoken question. "Or he will seek an annulment, for which he supposes he has quite sufficient grounds. He has come to the conclusion that there is no other way to establish his kingly power and put an end to Richmond's hopes. He knows that his throne is built on shaky foundations and that many believe Elizabeth to be King Edward's true heir. If he marries her, he can unite their two claims and satisfy his critics."

"I can't believe what I'm hearing," a woman's voice said. "She is his niece!"

"It's the talk of the court," Norfolk said.

Elizabeth's cheeks flamed as indignation flared. It was outrageous that she, the object of all this scandalous talk, was the last to know about it. How could they sit there speculating when the Queen lay ill in the next room? And should not Richard have approached her mother before he made his intentions public?

"It's disgraceful, if you ask me," another lady opined. "Appearing in that gown before the Queen . . ."

"And yet," the Duke countered, "the Queen did not seem at all discomposed. She thinks highly of the Lady Elizabeth. Maybe she knows she is dying and has appointed her successor. Who can say? All I know is that, since November, the King has been applying his mind in every way to contracting a marriage with Elizabeth."

Elizabeth did not want to hear any more. It was horrible, knowing that people thought her complicit in such a scheme. Even if Anne was decently dead, she would have expected Richard to leave a proper interval before broaching the idea; and if he were not her uncle . . .

She returned along the gallery, feeling the weight of the book in her hands, tangible evidence of his intentions, a gift to the woman he intended to marry.

After a brisk walk in the frost-covered privy garden, Elizabeth reluctantly returned to the Queen's apartments, taking care to avoid the speculative eyes of the ladies-in-waiting, for she could not bear to see accusation or disapproval in them. Gratefully, she shut herself in her bedchamber, thrust the book in her chest and lay down on the bed, her thoughts in turmoil.

What would Mother say? Would she be horrified at the prospect of her daughter marrying the man she believed had killed her sons? Or would she rejoice in the knowledge that Elizabeth would be queen?

That thought led inexorably to another. This could be a Heaven-sent opportunity. What had she come to court for? To help her mother and her sisters. As yet, she had done nothing for them. But as queen, she would be in a position of influence. She could ensure that her sisters made brilliant marriages, for princes would be eager to wed the Queen of England's close kin. She could provide her mother with an honorable and comfortable widowhood. She could do good to many through charitable works and patronage; she could use her influence to create a peaceful, prosperous and—above all—united England. And she would have a husband who was familiar to her and thought warmly of her; and they would have children, something she longed for. In fact, she was beginning to think that God was calling her to this destiny, however strange His means, and that it would be wrong of her to resist.

When Cecily came looking for her, some hours later, Elizabeth had convinced herself that marrying Richard was her best way of helping and advancing all who were dear to her. She would be a unifier and a peacemaker, and take her proper place as the heiress of York. All this she laid before Cecily, asking for her opinion.

"He is not a murderer," she insisted. "He had his reasons for doing what he did. And he is grieved that our brothers have disappeared. He has searched in vain for them."

"And what if they turn up and challenge his throne?" Cecily's pretty face was looking ever more doubtful.

"I don't think that will happen," Elizabeth said, "and neither does Richard. It stands to reason that Buckingham had them killed. But if they ever appear, I will gladly stand aside."

"But will Richard?"

Elizabeth fell silent.

"And will he ever be secure as king?" Cecily persisted. "Henry might yet invade."

"I fear the likelihood of that lessens with each day," Elizabeth said. "Fine words and promises are all very well, but they need to be backed by force, and Henry's allies here have been crushed."

"I wouldn't be too sure of that. My lady of Norfolk told me that he has fled from Brittany, having got wind that the Breton chan-

cellor was plotting with Richard to seize him. Now he is in France
and King Charles has made him very welcome. The Duchess said
her lord thinks he might furnish him with an army."

Elizabeth reflected that she would have been married to Charles
if her father's plans had come to fruition. Now, even this late in
the day, he might prove her savior and send Henry on his way. No
wonder Richard wanted to marry her!

And yet, would it not be better to wed a king who actually had
a crown on his head rather than waiting for one who only had
hopes of one?

Cecily had apparently had the same thought. "Maybe you're
right," she said. "Maybe you should marry Richard. At least then
I might get a decent husband."

"Am I to sacrifice myself just for that?" Elizabeth smiled.

Cecily hugged her. "No one wants you to sacrifice yourself. But
you are loved by the people and if you marry Richard, it will go a
long way to stilling those horrible rumors. No wonder he is eager
for it, as it will restore his reputation and win back the loyalty of
those who have deserted him."

"And if we have children, no one can say they have no right to
inherit the throne."

"And you'll be a queen!"

"That is the least of it, in terms of seeking glory for myself. But
it is my right by inheritance. Yet there is the major problem of
Richard being my uncle. Many will think the union incestuous. I
do not feel comfortable about it myself, to be honest."

"Popes issue dispensations all the time," Cecily shrugged.
"What kings want, they get. There is no impediment that cannot
be overcome with money."

Elizabeth raised her eyebrows. How cynical her little sister had
become! "I would want my marriage to be lawful!"

"It would be if it was dispensed with."

"I should hope so!" She paused. "Am I being wicked, talking of
this when poor Aunt Anne yet lives?"

"There is nothing wrong in planning for the future. After all,
nothing can happen until she dies. And Richard needs an heir. He
will be much stronger with a son to succeed him."

"Well, I can only pray that this matter does not come to Anne's ears. It can only cause her grief when she is so ill."

"She won't hear it from me. But, as for those gossiping ladies of hers . . ."

"I know. Let's pray they have the grace to spare her."

After Cecily had gone, Elizabeth sat there for a while, thinking that it was a far leap from just coming to court to marrying the man who, until recently, she had seen as a wicked child-murderer—and of whose innocence she was not, as yet, entirely convinced. She tried to imagine what it would be like to go to bed with him. Now that she was nearly nineteen, the fourteen-year age gap did not seem so great. She had always felt a special affection for Richard. There was an indefinable charm to him, an enigmatic quality that drew you in. She was not attracted to him physically, but then she had never felt the stirring of desire for any man. But her old love for him, long suppressed and then replaced by hatred, still bubbled beneath the surface. She realized she was longing to forget her suspicions of him and acknowledge her feelings.

No, the marriage act with Richard would hold no terrors for her. So what if he had a twisted back? It was not evident through his clothes and, anyway, it was the man who counted, not the body. She knew he would be kind and anticipated that, as time went on, she would come to love him as a wife should.

It was all very well deciding that she would marry Richard, but the fact remained that he hadn't asked her yet. But that very afternoon, when she felt the need to be on her own and had escaped to the garden once again, with a book, he appeared, wearing a fur-lined cloak and hat.

"I'm glad I found you here, Bessy," he said, as she rose and curtseyed, watching him warily. "There is something I need to discuss with you, and we can be private away from prying eyes. You may have heard talk; alas, the court is full of it."

"I have," she said, "and I was wondering when you were going to come and explain it to me."

He shot a sideways glance at her. "It is true, Bessy. Anne is dying and I must remarry as soon as possible to secure the succession." He took her hand in his gloved one and turned her around to face him. They were of the same height, for he was not a tall man. She saw in his troubled eyes that innate kindness that had always drawn her toward him—and something else, something new. "Bessy, when Anne dies, which cannot be long now, I want you to be my Queen."

This was the old, familiar Richard, but she could now see him as a man, with a man's needs. Instinctively, she knew that this was more than a matter of politics. She realized that he desired her, not just as a good match, but as a woman.

They sat together on the stone bench.

"Say you will marry me when the time comes," he urged, his face close to hers, his eyes dark and full of intent. Something moved in her, yet still she held back.

"We are uncle and niece," she said. "How can it be possible?"

"I shall apply for a dispensation," he told her. "I have taken advice and been told that one could be granted if there were pressing reasons."

"But I have heard people talking," she said. "They are scandalized."

"I know," he told her. "You should hear my councillors. Even my most trusted advisrs have told me that the idea is ill-judged, inept, unrealistic, and foolish." He gave her a wry smile. "They say that my subjects want no such thing. I know our marriage would be controversial, but there are compelling reasons for it and, if we can get over this initial hostility, people will come to see the benefits. A solid monarchy, my critics silenced—and the hope of heirs." He took her other hand and drew her to him. "And, for me, the comeliest bride in Christendom."

She thought he was going to kiss her and drew back. She would not be a party to any betrayal of Anne, however much she wanted to be queen.

He had sensed her scruples. "Do not fear, Bessy. I would give the lie to those who say I am only pursuing this marriage to gratify an incestuous passion for my niece. While Anne lives, I will not dishonor her. And my intentions toward you are honorable, too."

Again, her emotions stirred. She sat there, looking down at the book in her lap, not knowing how to answer him.

"You have my Boethius," he said. It was one of the books he had given her.

"I've just made a start on it."

He took it from her. "Normally, I write my motto in my books, but I seem to have omitted to do that in this one."

"'Loyalty binds me.'"

"Yes." His eyes caught hers and held them. "The words are most apt."

She removed the book from his hands, her heart pounding. "Then let me write them for you, for they can apply to both of us." She caught her breath, realizing she had more or less agreed to what he proposed.

"Do that for me," he murmured, and kissed her hand.

But it was never going to be accomplished as easily as that. She sat there, wondering if she had been too hasty, and if he had an ulterior motive.

"If I may be so bold," she said at last, "this is not just a ploy to discountenance Richmond and deflect him from his plans?"

He let out a brief laugh. "Bessy, if that were my sole intention, I would have married you to someone else long since."

"But I am branded a bastard," she said bitterly. "Kings aren't supposed to marry bastards."

"I am aware," Richard said slowly, dropping her hands, "that there are those who still hold that you are my brother's lawful issue. For them, you can supply all that is lacking in my title to the throne."

"Then you will have Parliament declare me legitimate?"

"And have men say that I hold my crown in right of my wife? It will make me a liar. It will be said that I gained the throne on a false pretext."

She turned to him. "You still haven't shown me those proofs Bishop Stillington gave you."

He did not flinch. "I will. The Bishop has them in safe keeping."

She stood up, feeling troubled. "I am not sure about this. Every time I look at the Queen, I feel guilty, even though I have done nothing to deserve it. I do not like the idea of waiting to fill a dead woman's shoes."

"All I want, Bessy, is your consent to our eventual marriage," Richard said, taking her arm and strolling along the graveled path. "Besides, it's not really a question of waiting for Anne to die. I have been told that the dispensation I obtained when we wed was insufficient and that our marriage could easily be dissolved. Yet Anne knows she is dying. She wants me to remarry. She understands that I need an heir, and that there is no time to waste. Kings cannot always afford the luxury of observing long periods of mourning."

It was growing cold and they had reached the door to the spiral stair that led up to the Queen's lodgings.

"There is something else, Bessy. Your mother knew of my intentions before she sent you to court."

"What?" She stared at him. "She never said anything."

"I asked her not to, in case there proved to be insuperable obstacles to the plan. She wrote to signify her consent."

And she had anticipated that her mother would oppose the very notion! The dangling prospect of a crown for her daughter had proved persuasive after all.

"I suspect she sees this marriage as a means of restoring your status and believes it will be much to her advantage, too," Richard said. "She understands the need for discretion. She agreed to send your sisters with you, so that your appearance at court would not give rise to comment."

"But you gave me that gown—the same one as the Queen's! That certainly gave rise to comment. I was shocked myself."

"That was not my intention, Bessy. It was a misjudgment. I wanted people to see that I regard you as being of royal status, to prepare them for the announcement when the time comes. I am sorry it rebounded on you." He paused. "You are cold. You should go in. I will look to see you at the Epiphany feast tonight."

She had been dreading it, fearing all those stares and the whispered innuendos.

"Do not single me out, please," she begged.

"Of course not. But you will do me the courtesy of sitting at the high table as an honored guest?"

"I will," she agreed reluctantly.

"And you will think over what I have said."

"Do I have a choice?" she asked.

"I would not force you," he said. "I am asking you not just as a king, but also as a man, a man who loves you." His gray eyes were serious, beseeching.

"I will think about it." She needed time to gain a perspective on the matter and make sense of her teeming thoughts.

"Bless you," Richard said, and kissed her hand.

As soon as she had shut the door on her chamber, she inscribed the book as she had promised. And then—because it would be too much of a giveaway to write it in the Boethius—she took the Tristram and wrote her own motto, the one she had chosen for herself: "Without changing, Elizabeth." The past was behind her. She would make her decision and keep to it.

She wore a gown of dove-gray velvet, nothing too showy, for she did not want to draw attention to herself. Everyone stood as the King entered, hand in hand with Queen Anne, both of them resplendent in their crowns and royal robes, for this was a solemn feast day. They took their places beneath the canopy of estate and Elizabeth was pleased to find that she was seated next to her aunt.

The feasting was well under way when a messenger approached Richard, bent down and murmured in his ear. The King nodded and dismissed him, then rapped on the table.

"Good tidings!" he announced to the court. "My lookouts on the coast have information that the pretender Richmond will without doubt invade this kingdom early in the summer."

There was some clapping and cheering. Despite all that had passed between them, Elizabeth could not help the upsurge of excitement in her breast. But she must forget Henry now. She could be queen of England anyway. And why would she not prefer a man she knew and loved to a stranger?

"This is excellent news," Richard was saying, as his fellow diners leaned forward, listening avidly. "We will be ready for him. I welcome the chance to vanquish that traitor and put an end to the doubt and misfortune of the past months."

Lord Lovell, who was seated on the King's right, leaned toward him, looking uncertain. "Sire, the treasury is low in funds," he muttered. "We cannot afford a war."

"That can be remedied by loans," Richard said.

"Forced loans?" Anne asked sharply. "Did you not condemn that practice in Parliament?"

His face darkened. "Needs must when the Devil drives, Madam! I must do what Fate compels me to. I have to crush Henry Tudor's ambitions, once and for all."

Two days after Epiphany, Anne summoned Elizabeth and Cecily to her privy chamber.

"Sit down, both of you," she invited, her eyes dark blue pools in her thin face. "I have some news for you, Cecily. You are to be married."

Cecily's own eyes widened.

Elizabeth watched the Queen nervously. Did Anne not think it odd that the younger sister was to be wed before the elder? But there was nothing in her manner to suggest that she saw anything amiss. Hopefully she knew who Richard's chosen bride would be and had given him her blessing.

"You may know that Henry Tudor has vowed to marry you, Cecily, if he cannot have Bessy here." Her eyes met Elizabeth's. She knew. It was glaringly obvious why Henry could not marry Elizabeth. But Anne's gaze was calm; there was no hostility in it, only sadness.

It made things a lot easier, having the first wife's permission, but Elizabeth still felt guilty, and knew a deep sorrow for her aunt, who was being incredibly brave and so generous-hearted.

"Cecily, it is imperative that you be married soon, to disabuse Henry Tudor of his ambitions," Anne said. "The husband the King has chosen for you is Ralph Scrope, the second son of Lord Scrope of Masham."

Cecily could not hide her dismay. A deep flush spread across her fair cheeks. "A second son?" she echoed.

Elizabeth felt her humiliation keenly. Ralph Scrope was of the lowest rank of the peerage, a nobody—hardly a suitable match for Cecily.

"No, I will not marry him," Cecily declared.

"But you must, my dear." Anne looked troubled. "It is the King's wish."

Cecily burst into tears. "I am worthy of better!"

Elizabeth took her hand. "At least meet him before you decide."

"I can arrange that," Anne said, "but there is no room for negotiation. The matter is settled. I am very sorry."

Cecily cried all night. When Ralph Scrope came at the Queen's summons the next day, his bride's face was puffy and tearstained, and the young man was clearly taken aback. He had obviously taken care with his appearance, and was pleasant-looking, with dark hair and blue eyes. "Are you unwell, my lady?" he asked Cecily, as soon as he had risen from his bow. His voice, with its northern burr, was gentle.

"No, Sir, I just do not wish to be married," she blurted out, as Anne raised her eyebrows.

"I understand," Ralph said kindly. "It was a surprise for me, too. But let us help each other. I know I am more than fortunate in being given such a bride—and that I am unworthy. But I swear that I will be a good husband to you and that I will cherish you always."

Elizabeth was touched, for he was clearly sincere. Already, she had warmed to him. And she suspected that Cecily was thawing.

"Then it is settled," Anne said briskly.

"Yes," Cecily whispered. "I shall try to be a good wife, Sir."

They were married three days later in St. Stephen's Chapel, in the presence of the King and Queen. Cecily looked beautiful in a gown of white cloth of gold lent to her by Anne, and Elizabeth and her sisters were bridesmaids. Elizabeth was sad that her mother had not been invited, and she had a great lump in her throat at the imminent prospect of being parted from Cecily, to whom she had been close since Mary's death; Anne, her next sister, was not yet ten, and could never replace her. And Cecily herself had wept again when she understood that, after the wedding, Ralph would carry her north to Upsall Castle, the Scrope family seat in Yorkshire.

"It is so far away," she'd sobbed. "I shall never see you again."

"You will be able to come to court," Elizabeth soothed her, "and maybe I will visit you. I should like to see Yorkshire. And in the meantime, we will write to each other."

For all her brave words, she had to keep a grip on her emotions when it came to bidding Cecily a final farewell. "God bless you!" she called after her, as the litter trundled away, leaving her feeling bleak and cast adrift.

Queen Anne had looked very frail at the wedding and now took to spending the afternoons resting on her bed. One day, Elizabeth found her there, weeping.

"Your Grace, what is wrong?" she asked gently. "Shall I send for your physicians?"

Anne turned a tear-streaked face to her. She looked anguished. "Where is Richard? He has not come to see me these three days, and he has not visited my bed for weeks. He said the doctors warned him that my illness might be contagious. But, Bessy, there is more to marriage than bed sport. I miss the closeness and the kindness we had when we lay together, the knowing that I could reach out and touch him."

Elizabeth did not know what to say. She could feel her cheeks burning and guilt washing over her. How could she be entertaining thoughts of marriage and queenship when Anne was lying here suffering? And why was Richard shunning his wife's company when she most needed him? What sort of man did that?

"Shall I ask him to come?" she asked.

"No. I think he is glad to have an excuse not to visit me. I am no longer of any use to him. Whatever was once between us is dead." A sob escaped Anne. "Well, he will soon be free of me."

Elizabeth took her hand. It was ice-cold. "Oh, Madam, do not say such things. He is probably much occupied with state matters. I will tell him that you were asking for him—"

"No!" Anne cried. "I do not want him to feel obliged to come. That would mean nothing. Bessy, do not mention me to him, I command it."

"I won't," she promised. But she had not spoken to Richard herself since Epiphany.

Soon afterward, Anne took to her bed for good. Looking at her lying there, her thin form hardly raising the covers, her coughing more violent and bloody now, Elizabeth knew, with dread certainty, that she would never rise again.

Anne lay exhausted as her ladies and maids hovered around her, doing their best to keep her comfortable, and exchanging worried glances. Elizabeth sometimes sat reading to her, but the doctors all shook their heads and warned her that she should limit the time she spent with the Queen because her malady could be contagious.

Richard did come, several times, and stood staring down darkly at Anne's sleeping form. Once, she opened her eyes and knew him, and there was a brief glimmer of joy. When Elizabeth glanced at him, she saw that there were tears in his eyes. But he would not take his wife in his arms, or even grasp her hand, even though she was reaching feebly for him.

"Oh, Anne," he said helplessly. "Oh, my dearest." He left without saying a word to Elizabeth, but she would not have expected him to in the circumstances.

All through February, Anne clung on to life. Her suffering was pitiful to see. She lay feverish, racked by coughing and gasping for breath. She sounded as if she was drowning. By rights, God should have taken her by now, but He let her linger. Elizabeth could not bear to see her gentle aunt dying by inches and prayed fervently that she would soon be released from this living hell.

Richard still came, but kept his distance. No one was allowed to be near Anne for long. The doctors were too afraid of the consequences—and Richard was the King, a king without an heir. He dared not risk his health.

Each time he visited his wife, he paid Elizabeth only the briefest of courtesies, doubtless aware that they were both objects of scrutiny on the part of Anne's ladies. He had made no attempt to see her or ask for an answer to his proposal. With each day that passed, her fear increased that he would think better of embarking on such a controversial marriage and look elsewhere for a bride. Then where would her hopes of a crown be? There was no certainty that Henry would come, still less that he would be victorious. All she could hope for was that when Anne died, Richard would press her to wed him.

By the end of February, she was going mad with frustration. There were few people she could confide in, apart from her sisters. She would not approach Richard directly—she had too much pride for that. But it occurred to her that she could use an intermediary. Yet who? She did not know his chief councillors well enough. She thought of Lord Stanley, but was aware that in abandoning Henry for Richard, she had somehow betrayed Lady Stanley.

In the end, she resolved to write to the Duke of Norfolk. She trusted him because the King her father had loved him, and Norfolk had been a faithful servant to him and to King Richard. He had long shown himself friendly toward her and must be aware of Richard's plan to marry her.

It was a hard letter to write. She had to strike the right note, convey that she was greatly desirous to be married, and ask Norfolk to do everything in his power to help her. *I pray you*, she wrote, *be a mediator for me in the cause of the marriage to the King, for his Grace is my only joy and maker in this world, and I am his in heart and in thoughts, in body and in all*. She had thought long and hard about this sentence, choosing her words with care. It was important to show Richard that she was ready to dedicate her whole self to him. He would know that this was her answer. She added that the better part of February was already passed, and said she feared the Queen would never die. Only later, after she had dispatched a messenger with the letter, did she realize that this sounded somewhat callous, when in fact she had only meant to convey her distress at Anne's prolonged suffering and her wish that God would take her to Himself. She hoped that Norfolk would not think ill of her, but would realize that she was only trying to safeguard her future, and act tactfully on her behalf.

In the early afternoon of 16 March, there was a great eclipse of the sun, which disappeared for five minutes, plunging the world into total blackness. Anne, Katherine, and Bridget were frightened, burying their faces in Elizabeth's skirts as she stood at the window, and she began to wonder if the eclipse was a portent, and shivered. It was a relief when the light returned.

But Queen Anne's light had gone out forever. She slipped away quietly while her household were agog at what was happening in the heavens.

Elizabeth wept, looking down at the still, skeletal form in the bed. The bloodstained pillows bore testimony to the Queen's last hemorrhage, and Elizabeth could only feel relieved and thankful that her torments were over. She knelt for a short while, praying for her soul, then retired to her bedchamber to weep. She did not see Richard, but she learned later that he had come to pay his respects. She had not expected him to seek her out at such a time, but she hoped that he would approach her after the funeral. He must know by now what she had written to Norfolk. It was frustrating not to have received any response, yet she knew that she could not hope for one yet.

She joined the other ladies in keeping vigil over the Queen's coffin in St. Stephen's Chapel, wearing deepest mourning. On the doctors' advice, the burial took place quickly, but Richard sent to forbid Elizabeth to join the procession that followed Anne to her grave in Westminster Abbey. Clearly, he did not want her appearing in public with all the rumors flying about.

The next day, the Lord Chamberlain broke up the Queen's household and sent everyone home. Elizabeth and her sisters were

commanded to return to Heytesbury. There was no place now for
women at court. But there soon would be, wouldn't there?

Elizabeth knew that she could not stay at Westminster, but
being ordered back to Heytesbury filled her with concern. She had
had no word from Richard. Courtesy alone demanded that he offer
her some explanation for his silence. Was he staying away from
her on purpose, wishing to distance himself from a situation he
now regretted? Or was he simply mourning Anne? Yet he had
said that kings did not have time to grieve.

Arrangements had been made for the sisters to travel to Wiltshire in a week's time. Elizabeth prayed that Richard would speak
to her before then. She was desperate not to depart before she
knew what her future would hold.

Restless with anxiety, she grabbed her cloak and hurried down
the spiral stair to the gardens, hoping to walk off some of her frustration.

Voices were echoing up the stairwell. It was a moment before
she realized that it was the guards on watch at the door below—
and then she froze on the spot, for they were saying that King
Richard had poisoned the Queen, that he might then marry the
Lady Elizabeth.

"It's not true!" she wanted to shout, but dared not reveal her
presence because she feared a derisory reaction. Was this the common bruit? She was horrified to think that people might believe
she was an accessory to murder.

She retreated upstairs and spent the afternoon amusing her sisters, trying to quell her unease. During her remaining days at
court, she saw people turn and whisper at her approach, or give
her hostile stares. It was horrible, especially after she had known
nothing but good opinions all her life.

She had still not seen Richard when the time came for her to
depart. She left court with a heavy heart, fearing that she had been
rejected. Yet hope had not died in her. Anne had been dead only a
week. It was still early days. And it was proper for her to be going
home to her mother. Things must be done formally.

Mother welcomed them with joy, embracing them warmly. She
had heard from Cecily, she said, who was settling happily into

married life and had written of the kindness of her husband and the wild beauty of the countryside around Upsall Castle.

As soon as they were alone, she turned to Elizabeth. "Well? Have you anything to tell me?"

"Nothing," Elizabeth admitted miserably. She related what had passed between her and Richard and described the letter she had sent. "And I've not heard from him since."

Mother looked pained. "There is talk about this marriage even here," she said. "But the people do not approve."

"But there are so many good reasons for it," Elizabeth protested. "It will bring me the crown that is rightfully mine and enable us all to live in honor and comfort."

"Then we must hope that the plan comes to fruition. Do not despair, Bessy. You cannot expect a newly bereaved husband to come a-courting. Just be patient. All will turn out well, you'll see. This marriage is as important to Richard as it is to you."

Elizabeth was surprised to find that her mother had struck up some sort of rapport with Captain Nesfield. At Christmas, mellowed with Yuletide spirit, he had invited her and Aunt Mary to dine at table in the hall, and had been almost jovial. He clearly knew that the Queen supported Richard's plan to marry Elizabeth and believed her no longer a security risk. He was now quite relaxed with her and much more courteous. Of course, it was wise to keep in with the mother of the future Queen; but if that made their lives at Heytesbury easier, that was all to the good.

At Easter, however, there was a noticeable cooling in Captain Nesfield's attitude when he presented himself in Mother's chamber.

"I have news for you, my ladies," he announced, and Elizabeth somehow knew that it would not be good. She laid down her embroidery tambour.

"My Lady Elizabeth, the King has publicly denied, before the Mayor and commons of the City of London, that he ever intended to marry you. His speech is being circulated to the chief towns and cities of the realm to counter any bruits or slanders."

She was struck dumb, unable to grasp the fact that, for the second time in her life, she had been publicly jilted—this time, by a man who was supposed to love her and had pressed his suit. And—oh, the humiliation—she had shown herself eager for the match!

"I am to inform you," the Captain continued, "that his Grace is pursuing a double marriage alliance with Portugal. He himself hopes to wed the Infanta Joana, and he has offered your hand, my lady, to Manuel, Duke of Beja, the nephew of the late King Alfonso."

"How dare he!" Mother spluttered. "He promises my daughter a crown, then has the gall to reject her and offer her a mere duke with no hopes of the Portuguese throne. I knew it was wrong to trust him!"

"Madam, you must not speak of the King thus," reproved Captain Nesfield. "I dare say there are many good reasons for his decision. The marriage *was* controversial and unpopular. I warn you not to give credence to any gossip you hear. People are saying that the King poisoned the Queen his wife, which is a gross calumny."

"It may be untrue, but his own conduct has spawned such rumors," Mother said coldly.

Elizabeth's cheeks were burning. How could Richard shame her like this? He had said he loved her. Where was his honor? He had dangled the crown before her—the crown that was rightfully hers—and now he had cruelly deprived her of the chance to wear it. How, now, would she bring honor, prosperity, and security to her family? Anger surged in her.

She would not give up hope. She would fight for her right. She would refuse to go to Portugal. Her place was here in England, as its rightful Queen. And if these vile rumors lost Richard the hearts of the people, it was no more than he deserved.

Why had she been such a fool as to trust him? This was the man who had ruthlessly maneuvered his way to the throne, impugned her legitimacy—and his mother's honor in the process—and committed acts of tyranny, justified by what many still regarded to be lies. The man who was widely reputed to have murdered his nephews—and she still had not managed to convince herself of his innocence, whatever he had told her and she had tried to tell herself.

Hopefully, time was on her side. Marriage negotiations could take months, even years. And Henry was planning to invade this year.

It was time, once again, to place all her hopes in Henry. She would not sit by passively, waiting for him to arrive. She would do everything in her power to speed him on his way—and be revenged on Richard.

Chapter 11

1485

Mother offered her unconditional support. "The sooner that villain is overthrown, the better," she seethed.

"I must make contact with Henry," Elizabeth declared. "But how?"

Mother was pensive. "His mother is still under house arrest."

"Lord Stanley might help," Elizabeth suggested hopefully.

"I wouldn't count on it." The Queen made a face.

"He said he would always be at my service."

"He bends with the wind. And do you think Richard would let you visit him?"

"It's worth a try, my lady."

"Very well. But I would not trust him."

Elizabeth wrote at once to Lord Stanley, saying that she was finding life in the country tedious and asking if he would obtain the King's permission for her to visit him in London. If his loyalties did lie with his stepson Henry, then he would use every persuasion. And Richard would not want to antagonize so great and powerful a noble. He could not afford to lose the support of the likes of Stanley.

She waited for a reply in trepidation, wondering if she should have sent the letter to Lathom, Stanley's country seat in Lancashire. She was itching to be on her way, sure that he would be willing to help her, hoping that he would have read between the lines. He must know that Richard had abandoned her, and he could surely guess how she felt. But how far would he go on her behalf? Would he be ready to commit treason?

Just when she was beginning to give up hope, a letter came. Lord Stanley would be honored to receive her, and the King had given his permission and had written to Captain Nesfield, requiring him to make the necessary arrangements. "Richard owes me this, at the very least," Elizabeth observed scathingly.

The Captain had the litter made ready and provided an escort of men-at-arms. With Elizabeth went two of her mother's maids to attend to her personal needs.

"Good luck, my brave Bessy," Mother said, as she bade her farewell. "You will be a queen one day—I feel it in my bones."

Elizabeth could not get to London fast enough. She was still smarting from Richard's public rejection, still deeply distressed. When she arrived, and saw the broad, reassuring figure of Lord Stanley, she could not help breaking down.

"Why, Lady Bessy, what's all this about?" he asked kindly.

"Oh, Father Stanley, I am so pleased to see you," she wept.

"Come to the fireside and tell me all about it," he invited.

They sat down by the great hearth in the parlor and the steward placed in Elizabeth's hands a steaming goblet of spiced ale. Then Lord Stanley waved the servants away and sat quietly until she had composed herself.

"Help me, Father Stanley, I pray you!" she cried.

"Is this about the King changing his mind about marrying you?" he asked.

"Yes, it is! He told the world he never intended it, but he did! He proposed to me and led me on. He said he would have put away his Queen to have me. And I wrote this letter . . ." She could not, for shame, go on. "He said he would show me proofs of my father's so-called secret marriage, but he never did. He told me that my brothers had disappeared while they were in the Tower, but now I fear he was lying and that he had them put to death."

She wrung her hands. "I beg of you, Father Stanley, help me to unseat him, lest more royal blood be spilled. I want my revenge on that traitor! I want to help Henry to win the crown. For if he becomes king, I shall be queen. In God's eyes, it is my right to succeed my father, and England deserves a legitimate monarchy. Even though I have never seen Henry, I love him for what he can offer me and my realm."

She paused, suddenly realizing that she had spoken rashly and treasonously, and that Stanley might not approve, having escaped Richard's displeasure after Buckingham's rebellion. Seeing him regarding her sternly, her blood ran cold.

"You will not help me!" she cried, tearing at her hair in panic, and then, suddenly, the world went black.

When she came to, she was lying on the floor, her head in Lord Stanley's lap, and he was mopping her brow with a cloth. A servant was standing by with a bowl of water.

"You fainted, Bessy," he said kindly, nodding to the servant to leave.

She struggled to a sitting position, her head muzzy, and burst into tears. "I will never be queen unless I marry Henry. I had thought you would help me."

She paused, seeing him regarding her sympathetically and nodding sagely.

"Of course I will," he said at length. "Whatever made you think that I would not? My sword is at your service, and not yours alone. My good wife's dearest wish is that her son will be king. Alas, she is at Lathom, where Richard wishes her to remain for now. I wish she were here, for she would rejoice to hear your words. She had thought you lost to Henry. He too was dismayed to hear that Richard was minded to marry you."

"You are in touch with him?" she asked, astonished. This was more than she could ever have hoped for.

"Yes, I and my wife have our chain of contacts," he smiled. "I can tell you that he is busy preparing ships for his invasion. But he was pinched to the very stomach when he thought he had lost you and feared that his friends would forsake him, for no other bride could bring him the crown of England. He was even contemplating a marriage to Maud Herbert, the Earl of Pembroke's daughter, thinking that might rally the Welsh to his cause."

Elizabeth could not hide her dismay. "But—"

"But when Richard announced that he did not intend to marry you, my wife wrote to Henry, urging him to make good his vow to take you to wife, for it is crucial to his success in winning the crown. Now the King of France has recognized Henry as king of England. He has given him money, ships, and men for an invasion, with the just aim of depriving that homicidal and unnatural tyrant of the crown to which he has no right. And, Bessy, many Englishmen are hastening to France to join him."

Elizabeth was thrilled to hear of these stirring developments. "I had not realized, Father Stanley, that you are so staunch in Henry's cause."

He gave her a wry smile. "Any man married to the Lady Margaret would support him, too, if not out of loyalty, then out of fear! But, Bessy, I will not show my hand until it is safe to do so, and my wife must be doubly careful. She got off lightly after supporting Buckingham in the late rebellion. You must know the penalty for women who commit treason."

"Are they beheaded?" she asked.

"No. They are burned at the stake. The Lady Margaret dare not count on Richard's leniency a second time. She takes pains to keep her dealings with her son as secret as possible."

Elizabeth nodded, appalled to learn what a narrow escape Lady Stanley had had.

"And I should warn you," Stanley continued, as he rose and stoked the fire, "that you too will be placing yourself in peril if you actively support Henry. No one will think the worse of you if you decide that you would rather not get involved, for you are very precious to all who love him."

She did not hesitate. "I will not flinch from doing what I believe is right. I am fighting for my crown, too. And I wish to redeem myself in Henry's eyes and make amends for what he must have seen as a betrayal. I hope he realizes that I felt it was the only choice for me at the time."

"I am sure he does," Stanley said, draining his goblet.

"I'm so glad I came to you," she told him. "I remembered how my father, on his deathbed, asked you to govern and guide me."

"And so I will," he declared.

"I have been thinking of ways to overthrow Richard. How many men can you raise?"

He raised his eyebrows. "I never thought to see so fair a maiden become a general!"

She laughed. "I have read my histories and heard many tales of the late wars of York and Lancaster. I know that victory lies not just in numbers, but in strategy—and luck. But it would help to have a strong army, ready for when Henry comes."

"My aim exactly. My brother, Sir William, can summon up five hundred men. My eldest son, Lord Strange, could support a thousand men for three months, and my younger sons could send soldiers, too. I know for a fact that my nephew, Sir John Savage, can raise fifteen hundred, and that old Shrewsbury's son, Gilbert Talbot, could send a thousand. I can provide another thousand."

Elizabeth was doing a quick reckoning. "That's five thousand men at least!"

"Fifteen hundred more than we had when we were victorious at Tewkesbury," Stanley said, grinning.

"Then you and your affinity can bring Henry over the sea!"

Stanley nodded slowly, his expression now serious. "I understand your enthusiasm, but, again, I must caution you. If Richard discovers what we are plotting, we will be undone, both of us, for he will see it as high treason. If anything goes wrong, he could send you to the fire, while I will lose my head and my lands. You do understand that?"

"I do," she said, feeling tremulous, but still determined. At heart, she did not believe that Richard would ever go so far. Too many people regarded her as the rightful heir, and there would be an outcry. "I *will* be queen of England! I care not whether I hang, burn, or drown in the attempt, for otherwise my life is not worth living."

She was surprised to see tears in Stanley's eyes. "Then," he said, "let us proceed, good Bessy—and carefully. Here in this room, there is no one but you and me, but be wary, for you can never tell who is listening, so say nothing of our plans to anyone until you are sure it is safe to do so. Now, I pray you, go to the bower I have prepared for you. Send away your maids, and I will come to you at nine o'clock tonight, when we will talk more of this matter. Ask the servants to bring you wine and spices, pens, ink, and paper."

She was ready when he arrived. Paper, ink, and quill pens were arranged on the table below the latticed window, which looked out on the verdant greenery of the garden. Beside them, she had set out a ewer of wine and the two goblets of precious Venetian glass she had found in her bedchamber. Every sense alert, she had been pacing the floor, knowing that she had crossed a line and was doing a momentous thing, and that many a guiltless man might die in her cause.

It was not too late to back out. But she could never let might triumph over right. She owed it to her house, to the people of England. Richard was a usurper, a man of no honor—and a tyrant. He might well have murdered her brothers—he had certainly murdered her half-brother. She had always had reservations about his version of events, even when she felt at her warmest toward him. It was only the prospect of the crown that had drawn her in. She saw that now. What a fool she had been to trust in him! Even now, she felt the sting of humiliation.

When Stanley arrived, she quickly brushed the tears from her eyes and invited him to be seated. Then she poured the wine.

"Drink to me, Father Stanley," she said, raising her glass. He did so, looking quite emotional himself.

"Ask me now, Bessy, whatever you wish, and I will grant it, if it is in my power," he said.

"I want neither of gold nor money, but Henry," she told him. "I wish to write a letter to him."

"I would grant that, but there is no clerk I can trust to write to him on your behalf."

"Father, there is no need," she assured him. "I can be my own clerk."

"Excellent!" He looked at her admiringly. "So, down to business. Will you first write to my brother, Sir William, at Holt Castle in Wales?"

"Of course."

"Bid him join me here and bring seven yeomen with him. Ask him to stay in different inns from those he normally uses when he visits London, and to make sure that he sits facing away from other guests."

When the letter was finished, Elizabeth wrote others, to Stanley's three sons, Sir John Savage, and Gilbert Talbot, all with the same instructions. They, and Sir William, were to be with Stanley by 3 May.

Stanley affixed his seal, then paused. "Now who might be a trustworthy messenger?"

Elizabeth thought for a moment. "Isn't Humphrey Brereton in your employ? He served my father loyally and I know he will be true to me. Let him take the letters."

Stanley looked doubtful. "My squire? He seems a good man, but I have never put his loyalty to the test."

"Why do you think he came to you and did not stay to serve the Usurper? Go to bed, Father, and sleep, and I shall work for us both. Tomorrow, by the rising of the sun, Humphrey Brereton shall be waiting here."

After Stanley had gone, Elizabeth stayed up through the night, so fired up with plans that she could not sleep. Instead, she sat at the table, writing letters to all those she believed she could count on to give their allegiance to herself and Henry. It occurred to her that her letters could be used against her as incriminating evidence, but she would not think about that. Being able to take action at last had given her a new sense of courage.

Early the next morning, she emerged from her room before dawn, washed and wearing a fresh gown, and asked a servant where Humphrey Brereton lodged. His room was up a turret stair and she called his name through the door.

"Lady, who are you?" came a voice.

"King Edward's daughter," she told him. "You must come with all the haste you can to speak with Lord Stanley."

"Of course, my lady!" came the startled reply. She waited a few

moments and then Humphrey appeared in a night robe and slippers. He was just as she remembered, still the freckled-faced usher
who had served her father so well. She had heard at court how he
had been so grieved at the King's death and Richard's coup that
he had left royal service and gone to Lady Stanley, begging for a
position. Yes, she knew she could trust him.

He bowed to her, looking awestruck, then followed her to the
chamber where Lord Stanley slept and received visitors. She knew
he would forgive this intrusion on his rest.

He woke instantly and sat up.

"Brereton, you served King Edward," he said, "and I am assured by the Lady Bessy that you are loyal to the rightful heirs of
York."

Brereton went down on one knee before Elizabeth. "My lord,
my loyalty lies with our true Queen and those who love her."

As Elizabeth smiled down at his earnest, honest face, Stanley
regarded him shrewdly. "How far would you be prepared to go on
her behalf?"

Brereton did not hesitate. "I would lay down my life for the
Lady Bessy."

"Then you will help her to her rightful crown?"

"It will be an honor, my lord." There was no doubting the sin-
cerity in him.

"Richmond will be invading this year," Stanley said. "The Lady
Bessy and I are raising support for him. We need a messenger we
can trust."

"I am your man, sir," Brereton declared.

"Know this," Stanley said sternly, "my trust, my life, my lands—
all these, Humphrey, lie in you. You can make, and you can mar; if
you are not careful, you can undo the Lady Bessy and me."

"You can count on me," Brereton declared.

Stanley nodded, satisfied. "Good man. Now, I wish you to deliver these letters to the people whose names are written on them."
He gave him those that Elizabeth had written the previous evening, and she handed him the ones she had dashed off in the night.

"They are for our friends," she said. "People I trust, who served
my father."

Brereton was poised to depart, but she stopped him. "Wait, Humphrey. I have only a poor reward for you." She put three gold coins in his palm. "If I become queen, you will be better repaid."

"My lady, I look for no recompense but our success," he replied.

"Take with you only those you can trust," she warned. "Do not sit too long in inns, drinking wine, lest you get merry and become indiscreet. Here are nine nobles to cover your expenses. God speed you!"

He was back after two tense weeks, having ridden to Wales, Manchester, and Sheffield, a journey of five hundred miles. Elizabeth leaped up when he and Stanley appeared at the door to her bower. She was so pleased and relieved to see Brereton that she kissed him on the cheek three times, much to his embarrassment, while his master looked on grinning.

"Welcome home!" she cried. "How did you fare?"

"Very well!" said Stanley. "But they told him here that I was at court and he found me there with Richard, walking in the privy garden. It was a tricky moment."

"My lord welcomed me warmly as I knelt to the King," Brereton related. "I pretended I had been visiting the place where I was born and bred and, so that he would not suspect me of duplicity, I told Richard that support for him is strong there and that the people will fight for him if the pretender comes. I could tell that pleased him, for he thanked me courteously. Then he told Lord Stanley that he was dear to him and, in return for his support, half of England would be his."

"He is desperate to secure my loyalty," said Stanley.

Elizabeth could easily imagine Richard making such extravagant promises. He could not afford to lose the backing of such a powerful lord.

"I must go and change for supper," Stanley said. "I will leave Humphrey to tell you about his journey."

"I am eager to hear it," she smiled.

"The lords are all on their way," Brereton reported. "The Stanley brothers praised your Grace for your good advice and said they trusted in Almighty God to bring your lord over the sea. Sir John Savage said that women's wit is a wonder to hear." Elizabeth smiled at that. "And the Lord Gilbert Talbot asked to be commended to you and commanded me to tell you that he too trusts in God to bring your love over the sea."

It was the best response she could have hoped for, yet, even as she rejoiced, she remembered that their plans were dangerous and fraught with difficulties.

"Fear not, my lady," Brereton soothed, reading her expression. "Lord Stanley's kinsmen and allies are ready to overthrow King Richard. By the third day of May, they will be in London. They have vowed that you shall be queen of England—or else they are ready to die in your cause."

It was too dangerous to meet up with their friends at Stanley's London house, so he arranged to rendezvous with them at an old inn outside the City walls. When he, Brereton, and Elizabeth arrived there, dressed as merchant folk, he pinned a drawing of an eagle to the sign above the doorway.

"It is from my cognizance of an eagle and child," he explained, "and the men who are coming have been told to look for it."

They went inside and Stanley ordered flagons of wine. Elizabeth kept glancing around furtively, but, apart from a few initial stares from the locals, no one seemed to be interested in them. Money changed hands and the innkeeper showed them to a private room, dark and paneled with oak.

"Will you take the shilling ordinary, Sir?" he asked.

"No thank you," Stanley said. "If anyone asks for Tom, please send them in."

"Very good, Sir," the host said, and left them alone.

Brereton spoke of his plans to travel to France to take news of their plans to Henry. Elizabeth showed Stanley a letter she had brought with her, to be delivered to her intended husband. It had not been an easy letter to write, for normally it would have been the suitor who initiated contact, but she was the rightful Queen and of higher rank. It was for her to make the first move.

My lord, she had written, *I know that you have vowed to take the throne of England and marry me. I gladly give my consent and wish you Godspeed and success in your enterprise, which I have done all in my little power to advance. Yours as long as life endures, Elizabeth Plantagenet.*

"It's a good letter, Bessy," Stanley complimented her.

But it sounded so formal, so stilted. Never having met Henry, it was impossible to write the words she wanted to write. She longed to assure him of her love and loyalty, for she believed that love *would* flower between them—how could it not, with such a great cause to unite them? But she still felt that it was for the man to speak first of love.

Presently, Lord Strange arrived, a dignified young man in his mid-twenties with a martial bearing, who greeted his father warmly and gave Elizabeth a discreet, respectful nod. She smiled at him, having seen him often at court. Stanley's two other sons, Savage and Talbot soon followed. They all looked pleased to see her and greeted her with great courtesy. There was no bowing— they could not risk anyone seeing—but she felt as if, to them, she was already wearing a crown.

"My lords," she asked, "will you help me? Will you relieve our Prince who is exiled beyond the sea?"

They nodded eagerly.

"I will supply twenty thousand men to make you queen," Stanley said.

"I have raised a thousand men, who will be ready at an hour's warning," Sir William told her. "Remember, Lady Bessy, who is doing their best for you."

"Aye," said Stanley's son Edward. "As a younger son, I have no men or gold to give you. But I will march under my father's banner, to live or die in your cause."

"How could I forget your great kindness or your stout hearts?" Elizabeth said. It was only just that they would expect to be rewarded once she was queen, and they would be, she would make sure of it.

"I am sending a thousand marks to your beloved beyond the sea," Sir John Savage offered.

"It might be hazardous to send gold abroad," Gilbert Talbot warned.

Elizabeth drew off her ring, a great diamond in a gold setting. "I will also send this to my love. It is worth ten thousand pounds."

Brereton looked at her aghast. "My lady, I dare not take the gold over the sea lest I be robbed or drowned."

"Hold your peace, Humphrey," she smiled. "You can carry it without jeopardy if you take three mules with side-skirted saddles to cover the bags of gold beneath. Take any good vessel, and if any man asks on whose ship you are sailing, tell them it is the Lord Lisle's, because he is beloved both in England and France—and by Richard." But not any more by her mother, she thought, for Lisle was one of those who had failed to respond to her pleas for help when they were in sanctuary.

Stanley shook his head. "No, Bessy. I have a good ship of my own and I will send it across the sea with my eagle flying from the topmast. If anyone asks whose ship it is, the crew can openly say it is mine. None will dare attack it. I too ride high with Richard."

The others nodded their approval. Brereton still looked uneasy, but he took the ring and Elizabeth's letter and tucked them inside his jerkin.

The others rose. Money bags were handed over and stowed in a small chest that Brereton had brought with him.

"God speed you, Humphrey," Stanley said.

"May He have you in His keeping," Elizabeth added, and gave Brereton her hand to kiss.

She could barely contain herself as she waited for his return. Stanley did his best to keep her spirits up and she was grateful for his calm confidence that their plans would succeed. She missed him when he went to court, and felt her courage falter when he told her that Richard was busy preparing for war.

"He has all the resources of the kingdom at his disposal," she fretted.

"Yes, but he does not have the hearts of the people. Many will rise against him when the time comes, mark my words."

The days, and then the weeks, passed all too slowly. When Elizabeth wrote to her mother, as she did regularly, she said nothing of what was happening, for it was too dangerous to commit it to a letter that Captain Nesfield might read. Yet she longed to tell the Queen how zealously she was furthering Henry's cause. She would have liked to write to Cecily, too, in the hope that she could persuade Ralph Scrope to declare for Henry when the time came, but dared not compromise her sister. No, it was best for her to confine her dealings to Lord Stanley, who had sworn to care for her, and those with whom she had no known connection.

At the beginning of June, Brereton returned. Elizabeth leaped up from her seat in the window when Lord Stanley brought him into the parlor; how she rejoiced to see him, and to see that he had brought letters from Henry, one for her and one for his stepfather. It was her first communication from her intended, and she could not wait to be alone so that she could read it in private.

"You have seen Richmond, then?" she breathed.

"I have, my lady," Brereton replied. "I found him at the abbey of Bec, near Rouen, where he is assembling an army of mercenaries, and then I traveled with him to Harfleur, whence he plans to sail to England."

"Did you give him my ring? Tell me how he received my letter."

"My lady, when I came before him at Bec, I knelt and delivered both. My lord of Richmond was so gladdened at the gift of your ring that he kissed it three times. But then, to my surprise, he stayed silent for a time. In the end, I got to my feet and asked him why he stood so still. I said I was come from the Stanleys to help make him king of England and take the fair Lady Bessy to wife." He smiled at Elizabeth. "Pardon, my lady, but I told him there was none more lovely in Christendom. Yet still he said nothing, so I told him that, since he would not speak to me, I must return home with a heavy heart, and I asked him what I should say to his friends in England."

Elizabeth's own heart was sinking. Had her letter struck the wrong note? But then she remembered that Brereton had seemed quite jubilant when he arrived—and Henry probably hadn't yet read it at that point. "What did he say?" she asked.

"He turned to the Earl of Oxford and Lord Lisle, who were standing by, and conferred with them," Brereton continued. "Then he told me that he could not give me an answer straight away. The next day, he rode off with his lords to Paris to ask the King of France to lend him ships and arms. So I waited for him at Bec. After three weeks, he returned and gave me a hundred marks for my pains and promised that I would be better rewarded in time to come."

"Did he speak of me?" Elizabeth cried, unable to contain herself.

"He did," Brereton told her warmly. "He asked to be commended to you, and said he trusted in God that you will be his Queen. He said that for you, he would travel across the sea." He turned to Lord Stanley, whose frown had lifted. "He asked to be commended to you too, my lord, and Sir William, and gave me these letters for you and Lady Bessy. He said that he trusts to be in England come Michaelmas."

Just over three months away! Elizabeth did not have long now to contain herself in patience.

"Excellent!" Stanley said, rubbing his hands together. "I must go to Lathom to tell the Lady Margaret the good news, and I will get word to our friends and bid them raise their levies."

It was happening at last. Henry really was coming. Elizabeth sent up a silent prayer of thankfulness.

Back in her chamber, she broke the seal on the letter.

To the illustrious Princess Elizabeth, Henry had written, giving her proper title. *It was a great comfort to me to receive your kind letter and to know that you long for this victory and our marriage as greatly as I do. God will favor the righteous and, if He wills it, we shall see each other very soon. By the hand of him who will make you queen, Henry R.* He had signed himself as if he were already king.

She clasped it to her breast. "Not long, my love, not long now," she whispered.

* * *

"Richard has made a proclamation," Stanley announced a few days later, casting off his doublet and sitting down in his shirtsleeves on the settle next to Elizabeth. "I heard the herald in Cheapside. He obviously fears that Henry will invade soon, for he has called upon all true Englishmen to rally to him, calling Henry a pretender who is descended of bastard blood both on the father's side and the mother's side."

"But that's not entirely true," Elizabeth observed. "There is no bastardy on the father's side."

"According to Richard, Owen Tudor, Henry's grandfather, was baseborn, which is nonsense," Stanley snorted.

"And the Beauforts were declared legitimate when John of Gaunt wed Katherine Swynford," she added. "Where does truth come into this?"

"It just proves that Richard is a liar."

"He is trying to ram home the message that Henry has no title to the throne to justify his entering this realm purposing a conquest," Stanley concluded. "I am for Lathom, Bessy, with my son Strange. I must tell my wife to expect Henry imminently and then await events."

"Take me with you, Father Stanley!" she begged. "I would see her, too, and tell her of my efforts on Henry's behalf, and I can wait there for him with you both."

Stanley nodded. "That would be fitting. You have been permitted to stay with me this summer, and no one has said that you cannot accompany me to Lathom. But, given that Richard is probably counting on me and my son to support him against Henry, I should ask his permission to visit Lathom. I will tell him that I have to raise my tenantry there. I'll seek him out on the way north, as I learned at court that he is to be at Kenilworth this week, raising men. But I won't tell him that you are with me. If he finds out that you are going to visit my wife, he will surely smell a rat."

Stanley installed Elizabeth in the nuns' guest house at Pinley Priory before he and his son rode to meet Richard at Kenilworth

Castle. She had donned a plain gown and wimple and gave her name as Catherine Cooper, widow, saying that her cousin was conducting her to the north, where she was to live with him and his wife, and asking if she could rest awhile at the priory while he went into Kenilworth to buy provisions for the long journey. The guest-mistress smiled and showed her to a sparsely furnished but clean chamber. She also brought Elizabeth some dinner—a simple stew of mutton and vegetables, with bread, ale, and a hard apple.

Stanley reappeared later, without Lord Strange, and they resumed their journey, riding ahead side by side, with the empty litter trundling behind with their escort. He seemed troubled.

"Richard has given me permission to visit Lathom," he said, as soon as they were through the priory gates, "but I have had to leave my son with him as a condition of my going there. Evidently, he does not trust me. He probably fears that the Lady Margaret will induce me to go over to her son."

"Look, Father Stanley," Elizabeth said, "if you are worried about Lord Strange, I will go back to Heytesbury and wait for Henry there."

"No, Bessy," he said firmly. "Having brought you so far, I feel responsible for you. I promised your father I would look after you."

She was aware of a certain reluctance in his voice. It was only natural that the safety of his son would come first with him. Until now, he had been bullish in her cause; now he might, understandably, be wavering.

She brooded on this new situation all the way to Leicester. Stanley was his usual kindly self, but he was preoccupied. How could he be enthusiastic about Henry's coming when it might mean his son's death?

They lodged at the White Boar, a large new timbered inn on the high street. Having given his real name and introduced Elizabeth as his niece, Stanley commandeered a private room, where they were served succulent roast beef and mustard.

"We have made good time," he said.

"How much further?" Elizabeth asked.

"Just over a hundred miles. We might do it in four days." He

fell silent, thinking no doubt that each mile was taking him further from his son.

The innkeeper's wife bustled in with bowls of quince jelly and
removed their trenchers. No sooner had she gone than the captain
of Stanley's escort entered.

"My lord, a royal messenger has delivered this letter for you." It
bore the King's seal.

Stanley dismissed the captain and read it. Then he looked up,
frowning. "Richard has summoned me to join him at Nottingham to aid him against Henry. I am to bring as many men as I can
muster."

"What will you do?" Elizabeth asked. She would not ask him to
fight for her now.

"I will go on to Lathom and raise men," he said. "It will be to
my advantage to have an army at my back when Richard faces
Henry in battle, and it is only what he has commanded. But I cannot take you with me, Bessy. It is too dangerous. The King already doubts my loyalty and may have sent men to watch my
movements. If he knew you were here, he would assuredly suspect
treason."

"Are you abandoning me?" she cried, clutching his sleeve.

"No, Bessy, I will find you somewhere to stay in Leicester, where
you can hide until I come for you."

"No, don't leave me!" She was nervous of being by herself
among strangers in a place she did not know. She wanted the security of Stanley's protection and stalwart presence.

"Bessy, don't you understand?" His tone was urgent. "If the
King's men find you here, you could go to the fire. How would
you explain your presence in Leicester?"

"I could the more easily explain that I am traveling to Lathom
with you for safety, and that you are taking me beyond Henry's
reach."

"To his mother?" Stanley shook his head, adamant. "No, you
must wait here. It cannot be for long. Henry will be sailing soon."

She summoned her courage. "Where will I hide?"

"I will take you to Langley Priory tomorrow. It is on the road
north from here. You can stay with the nuns. You will be quite

safe there, and I will know where to find you when the time comes."

When they had finished supper, they left the dining room and walked through the inn to the staircase that led to their chambers. Elizabeth kept her eyes down, but could not help glancing sideways, and when she glimpsed a familiar figure by the hearth, she froze. Although he wore no livery or badge, she was sure that she recognized one of the royal guards. He was looking her way. She turned from him, trembling, and hurried after Stanley. At the top of the stairs, she stayed him.

"I think we are being followed," she whispered, and told him about the man downstairs.

"Then we leave tonight," he said grimly. "Get your things. I'll alert the escort."

Ten minutes later, they stole out of a side door and Elizabeth climbed into the litter, closing the curtains. At once, they were moving out of the inn yard and making for the road north.

The priory was a poor house, inhabited only by the Prioress and eight nuns. They clearly did not want a boarder, but were too in awe of Lord Stanley to refuse his "niece" accommodation. The Prioress visibly thawed when he handed over a handsome sum for her keep.

When he had bidden Elizabeth farewell, she was shown to the guest house, an ill-kept building by the gatehouse. Her room was like a cell, with just a narrow cot, a stool, and a peg on the wall. Meals, she was informed, would be served to her in the small refectory below. They proved to be almost inedible, the daily fare consisting of thin pottage or tough fatty pork. But if this was the price she must pay for her safety, then so be it.

The nuns left her to her own devices. If they wondered why Lord Stanley had deposited her with them, they showed no outward curiosity. The hours were long and tedious, the night full of terrors. What if that man came after her and she was discovered? How would she explain her presence here? It occurred to her that Stanley might have abandoned her. She would not blame him if he felt that the safest course was to disassociate himself from her. But she felt so vulnerable that she even contemplated trying to make her own way south, or at least get away from the vicinity of Leicester. She had money on her, but she did not know this country. It felt as if she was in the middle of nowhere. And, more to the point, she had no horse. She would just have to stay here until a suitable opportunity to leave presented itself.

She had been at Langley for two days when a nun appeared and told her that a gentleman was in the visitors' parlor, asking if Lord Stanley had left a young lady at Langley Priory.

"I told him that you were here, and he is asking to see you, mistress," she murmured.

Elizabeth's spine tingled. Would it be the man she had seen in the White Boar? Had he come to arrest her? She shuddered to think what that might mean. But surely he would not drag her from a convent?

She forced herself to walk calmly to the parlor, consumed with dread. Had Richard discovered that she had been plotting against him? Was there an armed escort waiting outside? By the time she opened the door, her knees were about to give way.

She recognized the man at once, though today he was wearing the royal livery. Her heart sank like a stone. But he bowed to her. "My Lady Elizabeth?"

There was no point in lying. "Yes," she said, her voice faltering.

"You are to come with me. The King orders that you be escorted to Sheriff Hutton Castle to join the household he has set up for my lord of Warwick, the Lady Margaret of Clarence, and my Lord John of Gloucester, in the charge of the Earl of Lincoln."

She was taken aback, but overwhelmingly relieved that all she was to suffer was to be sent north and relegated to the company of her young cousins. If Richard did know of her plotting, he was being remarkably lenient; but then he had been lenient with Lady Stanley. Or perhaps he did not know.

"Can you tell me why I am being sent there?" she asked.

"His Grace wishes to be assured of your safety in the event of an invasion," she was told.

That made sense. All the same, she did not want to be sent so far north, to the wilds of Yorkshire. But it would be fruitless to protest.

"When am I to leave?" she asked.

"Now, my lady," the messenger said. "Make ready. You will travel in a closed litter."

Wonderful! she thought bitterly.

She wondered why she had not been asked to explain what she was doing at Langley Priory. Maybe that was to come, for Richard had enough on his hands for the present. This might not, after all, be the end of the matter. Resolutely, she stifled her fears. She might be worrying for nothing. Henry would soon be here, please God.

Packing her traveling chest, she told herself that Richard was probably shutting her up in Sheriff Hutton Castle because he feared that she might attempt to join Henry. Clearly, he was taking no chances. He knew that many regarded her as the rightful heiress to York, and it followed that she was vulnerable to being captured by his enemies. Surely if he knew how deeply she had been involved with them, she would be on her way to the Tower. Even if he didn't, she was going to have a hard task explaining her way out of this pretty pass.

As the armed escort conveyed her northward, trapped in the stuffy, juddering closed litter, she felt utterly helpless. She did not want to go to Sheriff Hutton, of all places, for it was there that Uncle Rivers and Dickon had been imprisoned before being executed at Pontefract. It was a long way away from her mother and sisters, and London and all the places she knew. But she would not be there for long, she comforted herself. By the time she arrived, Henry would hopefully be on his way—and then, God willing, her trials would be over.

* * *

It was six days before they arrived at Sheriff Hutton, a quiet village ten miles northeast of York. The castle had been a Neville stronghold before it had passed into Richard's hands. When she peeked through the litter's leather curtains, she saw it immediately ahead of her, standing on a rising bank in a hunting park. It was indeed a mighty fortress. It had two moats and stout walls, and she counted nine towers that all looked to be over a hundred feet high. She felt nervous as they passed through the gatehouse into a large courtyard.

She had expected to see her cousin Lincoln waiting to receive her, but it was the constable who was standing in front of what she later discovered was the Warden's Tower. He was a dapper man with dark hair and a beard, and he greeted her courteously.

"My Lady Elizabeth, welcome." He bowed. "My name is Walter Stable. I am sorry that my lord of Lincoln cannot be here to receive you, but he is in Nottingham with the King and we do not expect to see him until after the pretender has been defeated."

"Greetings, Master Stable," Elizabeth said, nettled at the assumption that Henry would be vanquished, but knowing she must not show it. "Am I a prisoner here?"

"No, Madam. You are merely being held in safe custody, as a precaution." Against what? she wondered. Against Henry seizing her—or her plotting with Lord Stanley?

"Shall we go indoors?" the constable invited. "The men will bring your chest."

He led her through a series of narrow, vaulted chambers set into the walls until they ascended a stately staircase and entered a magnificent hall. It was like a princely lodging, and the two chambers she was assigned, which were above it and accessed by a spiral stair, were equally impressive, with arched ceilings and murals painted in brilliant colors. The views from the windows over the Forest of Galtres were breathtaking.

She began to relax a little. Surely, surely, Richard would not have sent her here and had her lodged in such splendor if he suspected her of treason?

A maid entered, a local girl whose Yorkshire accent was so broad that Elizabeth could barely understand half of what she was saying. She remembered hearing that northern folk had tails,

which several people she knew believed, and she had heard south-
erners asserting that they were all savages, an impression that had
been fueled by the brutality of Queen Margaret's troops in the late
wars. But this girl seemed docile and willing, and after a surrepti-
tious glance, Elizabeth was certain that she had no tail.

As the maid stowed away her belongings and fetched a ewer of
water so that she could freshen up before supper, Elizabeth stood at
the window gazing out over the glorious landscape. She felt like the
Arthurian heroine Elaine, who was shut up in a tower, and prayed
that Henry, like another Sir Lancelot, would come to rescue her.

In the meantime, though, this was no bad place to be waiting
for him. Maybe it was as well that her cousin Lincoln had not been
here to welcome her. He was the King's Lieutenant in the North,
President of the Council of the North and heir presumptive to the
throne, and had every reason to be loyal to Richard, for he stood
to lose much if Henry was victorious. She would have found it
hard to keep up a pretense in his company, whereas Walter Stable
seemed an amiable fellow. Already, she was warming to him.

When the maid led her down to the dining hall, she was delighted to see her cousins, ten-year-old Warwick, and Margaret,
who must be nearly twelve now. When they embraced, Warwick
clung to Elizabeth.

"I am so pleased to see you, Bessy," he lisped. He was an enchanting child with a cherubic face and a cloud of fair hair. He reminded
her so much of her brothers that she felt a lump rise in her throat.

There were two youths in the room, hanging back while the
cousins were greeting each other. John of Gloucester, Richard's
bastard, who looked so like him, introduced himself and presented
Lord Morley. The two boys appeared to be great friends.

They all sat down to a lavish meal, with serving dishes piled
high with delicious food and flagons brimful of ale and wine. Margaret, with her pale face and thin features—she was no beauty—
assumed the role of hostess, dismissing the servants so that they
could all talk freely.

"It is so good to see you," she said to Elizabeth, who smiled at
her and squeezed her hand.

"It's been far too long. Tell me, are you all happy here?"

"We lead a quiet life," John told her. "But Morley and I get to do some military training and sports. The sergeant is a good man. He fought at Tewkesbury."

"My Lady Elizabeth, they say you're here because the King fears Henry Tudor getting you into his clutches," Morley grinned.

"Something like that," she replied, not wanting to be drawn on the matter.

The talk grew lively. Sheriff Hutton might be congenial lodging after all. She liked being with her cousins. If only her sisters could be here; she did miss them. She wondered if she would be allowed to write to her mother.

She noticed that young Warwick had little to say for himself. There was a vacant look in his eyes that worried her. He laughed excessively, and his table manners left much to be desired. She saw that Margaret watched over him closely and cut his meat for him. Once or twice, she gently reproved him. There were only two years between them, yet he seemed so much younger, and he was far slower than Elizabeth's sister Anne, who was the same age. Yet he was a sweet, engaging boy, and kind, too, as he kept offering her a plate of sweetmeats and repeatedly asked how she was. Her heart warmed to him, and she felt a rush of protectiveness.

The lazy August days passed in a haze of heat. Elizabeth was delighted to be allowed to go hawking in the forest with John and Morley, although there were always two men-at-arms shadowing them. In the afternoons, she sat in the courtyard with Margaret and Warwick, the girls doing embroidery while he played with his skittles or his hoop. She was permitted to write to her mother, although Walter Stable had to see the letters before they were sent. In the evenings, after supper, they all played cards or dice. It was a pleasant existence, but Elizabeth was always anxiously on the alert for news, always expecting a horseman to come galloping through the gatehouse. What was happening in the outside world? Had Henry invaded? Had there been a battle? And who would come for her? She prayed and prayed that it would be Henry, bringing a crown.

Chapter 12

1485–1486

In the third week of August, a company of riders cantered into the courtyard in a cloud of dust. Elizabeth and Margaret, seated in the shade of one of the towers, dropped their tambours and rose, just as Walter Stable and his sergeant emerged from the Warden's Tower.

The newcomers reined in their horses and the two leaders dismounted. They were wearing no recognizable livery. Walter hastened over to them.

"Good sirs, welcome. Can I help you?"

"Sir Robert Willoughby and Sir John Halliwell at your service," one said. "We seek the Princess Elizabeth."

Princess? Elizabeth's heart leaped. There could be only one reason for them to dare to call her by her true title.

"I am here," she said calmly, although inside she felt wildly elated. Holding herself like a queen, she walked across the courtyard. Seeing her, the newcomers fell to their knees.

"Your Grace!" they saluted her.

"Please rise, good sirs." She smiled, extending her hand to be kissed.

"Madam, we are come from Leicester," Willoughby said, as a

small crowd of castle staff gathered around them, all looking at her with new respect. "There has been a great battle, at Bosworth. King Richard has been slain. The crown was found on the battle-field and brought to Richmond by Lord Stanley, who placed it on his head and proclaimed him King Henry the Seventh."

Elizabeth fell to her knees. This was the moment she had longed for. God had shown His hand. Right had prevailed. All her dreams were about to come true. Her heart glad and full of thanksgiving, she clasped her hands in prayer and raised her eyes heavenward. "So even at last, thou, O God, hast regarded the humble and not despised their prayers," she breathed. "And now we thank thee and praise thy glorious name."

Richard was dead. She spared a thought for him, for he had been dear to her once, and she would pray for him. But Henry— King Henry VII, as she must now think of him—now ruled England. It was nothing short of a miracle.

"Let us go within," she said, rising. "You must tell me everything."

Once they were seated in the hall and Walter had hastened in with wine, Sir Robert recounted the recent events. "His Grace's forces landed with a fair wind at Milford Haven, near Pembroke, a week ago. When he disembarked, we saw him fall to his knees and cry, 'Judge me, O God, and plead my cause against an unworthy nation.' Then he kissed the ground. It was a moving moment."

Sir John took up the tale. "Calling on the aid of St. George, he urged us onwards, marching under a banner bearing the red dragon of the Welsh prince, Cadwaladr. At every place we passed, it was announced that he came to reconcile the warring factions of Lancaster and York."

"His army met Richard's in Leicestershire, near Market Bosworth," Sir Robert went on. "The battle lasted two hours; it was savage. His Grace did not engage in the fighting, but remained under his standard behind the lines, leaving the Earl of Oxford in command."

Thrilling at the tale, Elizabeth interrupted. "What of Lord Stanley?"

"He and Sir William were there with their forces. We heard that Richard had commanded his attendance, but that Stanley had sent word that he was ill. On the day, he and Sir William positioned themselves some way off and did not immediately engage in the fighting."

Waiting, no doubt, to see which way the battle was going before committing themselves.

Sir Robert was watching her. "I know what you are thinking, my lady—that they thought only of themselves. But you should know that, on the morning of the battle, Richard again ordered Stanley to join him, if he wanted to see his son alive again—and Stanley sent back word that he did not feel like joining him, and that he had other sons. Richard was furious and ordered his captains to put Lord Strange to death. But they refused and, with the battle imminent, all he could do was tell them to keep him under close guard until he could deal with him afterward."

"Stanley took a terrible gamble," Elizabeth observed, regretting that she had doubted his loyalty.

Sir John drained his goblet. "The battle was fierce. We were lucky, Robert and I, to escape without a scratch. Men were fighting like demons. When it appeared that Richard's side was losing the day, we feared that the Earl of Northumberland would come to his aid, but, although he was nearby with his men, he did nothing. And then Richard did a mad thing. He must have realized that he had been deserted by those in whom he had trusted, for he made one final, desperate charge toward the red dragon banner beneath which Richmond was standing. He killed the standard bearer, and was about to cut down Richmond himself, but the Stanleys now bore down on him, which turned the tide of the battle, and Heaven granted a glorious victory to Richmond."

Stanley had been true after all! She owed him so much. As did Henry and all England. She was trembling with the realization of how close things had been.

"What happened to Richard?" she asked.

"Let me say the truth to his credit," Sir Robert answered. "He bore himself like a noble soldier and honorably defended himself to his last breath, shouting again and again that he was betrayed, and crying, 'Treason! Treason! Treason!' "

"Aye," Sir John agreed. "I'll give him that, tyrant though he was. He was killed fighting manfully in the thickest press of his enemies."

"The crown fell from his helmet and rolled under a hawthorn bush," Sir Robert related. "Lord Stanley retrieved it. As he placed it on Richmond's head, the soldiers were crying out, 'God save King Henry!' As you may imagine, my lady, his Grace was filled with incredible joy. Everyone was praising him, as though he was an angel sent down from Heaven to deliver his people from the evils with which they have been afflicted."

"The children of King Edward have been avenged at last," Sir John said quietly, and, in that moment, Elizabeth realized just how strong public sentiment had been against Richard.

"And now we have a new dynasty to reign over us," Sir Robert said. "To avenge the white rose, the red rose has bloomed. And, my lady, we look to a happy union between the two illustrious houses of Lancaster and York."

Walter Stable and the crowd who had gathered in the hall all raised their glasses. "To King Henry and Queen Elizabeth!"

Elizabeth rose and curtseyed, and everyone cheered. All she could think of was how proud her mother would be if she were here! And then she spared a thought for those who had died in the field to bring her to this place.

"Tell me who fell at Bosworth," she said to the knights.

"The Duke of Norfolk, Madam," Sir John told her. "Sir Robert Brackenbury, the Constable of the Tower, and Sir Richard Ratcliffe, the Usurper's close adviser. And a thousand men who fought for Richard."

"How many were lost on the new King's side?"

"About two hundred, it is reckoned."

Elizabeth crossed herself. "It is very sad that so many had to die to ensure that right triumphed over might. I will order a Mass to be said for their souls." She blinked away the tears that were threatening.

Sir Robert spoke gently to her. "Madam, it is time to look to the future. We have been sent by his Grace to escort you and my lord of Warwick to London with all convenient speed. There, you are to lodge with the Queen your mother. Until then, you will be under my protection and served with the honor due to the future Queen of England."

"Is Warwick to travel with me?" she asked.

He looked momentarily uncomfortable. "No, my lady. Sir John will convey him separately. The Lady Margaret may accompany you. If your Grace would make ready with all speed, we can be on our way. We will lodge in York tonight and then take the Great North Road south."

Elizabeth hastened to her chamber and set her maid to work packing the stuff she had so recently unpacked. Leaving the girl to her task, she went to the chapel and knelt down, trying to still the turmoil and excitement in her breast, and gave thanks for King Henry's victory.

"Let nothing prevent this marriage," she prayed. She had just had the unsettling notion that, now that the crown was his, Henry might take a wife from foreign parts, whose beauty, age, and fortune would please him more than hers. The more she dwelled on this, kneeling there on the hard floor, the more anxious she became. She was the rightful Queen of England and the whole world was expecting Henry to marry her to validate his conquest of the crown. Pull yourself together! she admonished herself. *Why dream up a problem, when you have every cause to rejoice?* It was just that so many bad things had happened in the past two years that she had almost come to expect ill fortune. She must stop being negative and look to the future, which had every expectation of being a glorious one.

When she rose to her feet, her prayers done, she made her way resolutely downstairs to where her escort was waiting and smiled upon those who had come to wish her happiness and wave her on her way. All would be well, she told herself. When she met Henry, she would know that for certain. God always succored those who trusted in Him, therefore she would cease fretting and repose her whole hope in Him.

* * *

In York that evening, over a private dinner hosted by the Prior of the Franciscans, the men spoke of Bosworth and how Almighty God had shown His hand.

"A tyrant never prospers in the long run," the Prior declared. "God always judges the secrets of man."

Sitting next to a rather subdued Margaret, who was fretting about her brother, Elizabeth pressed her cousin's hand reassuringly. All would be well, she was sure, especially when Henry found out that Warwick was not like other children.

She was preoccupied herself, wondering just what secrets Richard had been keeping. Had he lied to her about her own brothers? She was painfully aware that it should have been Edward V who was now sitting on the throne that Richard had stolen from him. That in itself had been crime enough. But God had now exacted vengeance.

"What happened to the Usurper's body?" she asked.

The knights exchanged glances, looking uncomfortable.

"He was buried in the church of the Grey Friars in Leicester," Sir Robert said.

"There's something you're not telling me," she challenged.

"Alas, your Grace, his body was subjected to insults, but the details are not suitable for a lady's ears."

"Insults? What do you mean? I insist you tell me."

Sir Robert hesitated. "The soldiers stripped it and slung it over a horse's saddle with a felon's halter around the neck, and it was borne thus, spattered with mire and filth, to Leicester, where it was put on display for two days in the collegiate church in Newark before it was buried."

She suspected that there were worse details he wasn't telling her, but did not press the point. The soldiers' behavior had been unforgivable, but who could blame them? Richard had brought this on himself. Some would say it was a just retribution for his crimes.

By the time she reached London, many lords and ladies had joined her, and it was a joyful cavalcade that wended its way into the capital. From her litter, Elizabeth acknowledged the welcome of citizens who recognized and cheered her, touched by their demonstrations of love. It was reassuring, especially since, as her meeting with Henry loomed ever nearer, she felt her heart faltering.

Clearly, he did intend to marry her, but now another concern had reared its hydra-like head. In the night, it had come to her that, until she was safely wed to him, she was essentially a rival claimant to his throne, for all that she was a woman; and he must know that she could transmit her claim to any man she married. But the sole letter he had sent her had betrayed no suspicion on his part; rather the contrary. And their union was popular, so it was hardly likely that he saw her as an enemy, or that he would renege on a promise that had won over so many Yorkists to his cause. The courtesy, honor, and acclaim just accorded her gave her cause to believe that she *would* soon be queen.

Yet something fundamental was also troubling her and had been gnawing away since she had learned of that crowning on the battlefield and heard Henry referred to as king. It seemed he had assumed the royal dignity in his own name, when, in fact, he would only have the right to it when he married her, which would give legitimacy to his title. She had found it strange that no state welcome had been arranged for her in London, nor any celebrations to mark her arrival, as was usual for a royal bride. Of course, that might have to wait until Henry himself got to the capital. Or, she fretted, he might not want it to appear that he owed his kingship to her. Had he deliberately intended that she should not enter the City in triumph, lest it look as if she herself was the rightful sovereign? Was he claiming to be king in his own right? But how . . . ?

Her litter drew up on Thames Street, outside Coldharbour, the tall and imposing London residence of Lady Stanley, which fronted the river. And there, standing in the great hall, waiting to receive her, was the lady herself and—glory be to God, her own mother and sisters. They all sank into deep curtseys, but then the Queen held out her arms and Elizabeth went into them, realizing how much she had missed her. After that, it was the turn of her sisters, as their hostess looked on, smiling. Only Cecily was missing to make her happiness complete.

"Lady Stanley," Elizabeth said, kissing her. "You must be so proud."

"I have longed for this day," the older woman exulted. "Yet I had faith that God would prosper the righteous. He has prevailed and we can all rejoice, for we have my own sweet and most dear King to reign over us." She smiled beatifically. "He is all my worldly joy, as he will be yours, my dear. And you will see him soon, for he is making his way south as fast as he can, but, of course, everyone wants to see him and congratulate him. I long to see his face! I have decided—and he agrees—that I wish henceforth to be known as my Lady Margaret, the King's mother."

"That is very fitting," Elizabeth replied.

As they conversed, Margaret's passion for her son shone forth. It seemed hard to believe that she had not seen him for fourteen years. There seemed to be as close a bond between them—at least on her side—as if they had never been apart. Margaret would surely see a huge change in Henry. When he had last left England, he had been a boy of fourteen. Now, he was a man of twenty-eight, and might seem like a stranger. Elizabeth fervently hoped that the long years of separation would be easily bridged, for both their sakes.

After refreshments had been served amid a lot of excited chatter, the Lady Margaret personally showed Elizabeth to the apartments that Henry had commanded to be made ready for her, which were next to those assigned to her mother and sisters.

"You have been entrusted to my care, Bessy," the Queen told her as they ascended the stairs. "It is proper for a bride-to-be. But the Lady Margaret will have the keeping and guiding of your sisters, and of your cousins, Warwick and the Lady Margaret of Clarence, and the young Duke of Buckingham, who has also been brought to London."

"Is Warwick here?" she asked.

"He is," Margaret replied. "But he is indisposed after the long journey, so you will not see him today."

"I will look forward to seeing him later then. I am praying that my brother Dorset has returned with the King. We have all missed him so much. He is the only son my mother has left to her."

Margaret looked uncomfortable. "Alas, my dear, his Grace had to leave him behind in France, as a hostage for his debts."

That was a blow. "But he will come home?"

"Of course. As soon as the debts are paid."

She opened the door to the apartment. It was so beautifully furnished, fit for a queen, that Elizabeth felt reassured. Everything would turn out well. The wheel of Fortune had righted itself at last.

After she had washed off the stains of travel and changed, she spent time in the parlor talking to her sisters, marveling how Bridget had grown and how speedily Katherine had made progress with her letters. Anne, rising ten, was already a delicate beauty with her corn-gold hair and blue eyes. Then Margaret of Clarence joined them and there was much merriment.

Back in her chamber, while the maids assigned to her dressed her for supper, Elizabeth felt a little sad that there had been no word or token from Henry to welcome her. But the Lady Margaret had said that he was still on his way south from Bosworth. He would soon be here, and then all—please God—would be well.

Warwick did not appear the next day or the day after. On the third day, Mother entered Elizabeth's bedchamber, just before early Mass.

"Warwick has been taken to the Tower. The Lady Margaret told me it was just a security precaution and that she trusted it would not be for long."

"I should hope not! Warwick wouldn't hurt a fly." Elizabeth fastened her girdle. "He's a sweet boy, if a little slow."

"I don't think King Henry sees him that way. But for the attainder against Clarence, Warwick would be the rightful male heir of the House of York. Your claim is better, but you are a woman. Maybe Henry fears that some Yorkists might now look to Warwick in preference to you and stir up discord."

"So, through no fault of his own, since he cannot help his birth, he is imprisoned?" Elizabeth was appalled.

"As your poor brothers were," her mother reminded her. "Innocence is no armor against men's plotting. Once things settle down and the King is crowned, he may be released. Let us hope so. But let us not dwell on sad things. We must be grateful for our great good fortune. This marriage is what your father wanted; had he not died, he would have betrothed you to Henry. Better times are ahead, Bessy."

"They are!" Elizabeth took her mother's hands and squeezed them, wondering how long it would be before Henry came to make her his Queen.

The new King made his triumphal entry into London on the third day of September. The cheering could be heard at Coldharbour. The Lady Margaret, regal in her ermine-trimmed robes, had gone to St. Paul's Cathedral to see him give thanks for his victory and his crown. Elizabeth wished she could be there herself.

When Margaret returned, she was full of the day's ceremonies and the acclaim her son had received. Then, when she had seated herself by the hearth in her great chamber, she invited Elizabeth and the Queen to take the chairs opposite and beamed at them.

"Bessy, when his Grace retired to the Bishop's Palace to hold his first Privy Council, I stayed to watch the proceedings. And the first thing he did was declare his intention of marrying you."

Elizabeth felt her spirits soar. It was as if a weight had been lifted from her. Mother was almost preening.

"The matter was discussed at length," Margaret said, "but there are two obstacles that must be overcome before the wedding can go ahead. Parliament has to repeal the Act that confirmed the Usurper's title and deemed you illegitimate. Your royal status must be restored, for it is unthinkable that the King should found his dynasty by marrying one tainted with bastardy. Then a dispensation has to be obtained, for you are related in the fourth degree of kinship."

Elizabeth plucked at her skirts, a little dismayed to hear all this.

"Don't look so worried, child. These are mere formalities. You must hold yourself in patience for a little longer. But first, you will be pleased to know, his Grace wishes to meet you. In two days, he will be at the Tower and has asked that you be brought there."

At last! The moment she had thought might never come. Soon, she would see her destiny in the flesh.

Elizabeth peered in her mirror. It was not the old-fashioned kind of burnished silver, but of Venetian glass. She was pleased with what she saw. Her long red hair fell like a silken cape over her shoulders. She had pinched her pale cheeks to bring some warmth to them. Her eyes were clear and beautiful, her lips cherry red. Her virginal gown of white damask had the newly fashionable square neck and ermine cuffs, and she had donned a rich collar of gold and precious stones.

The Queen and the Lady Margaret beamed when they saw her.

"You're a sight to dazzle any bridegroom," Margaret said.

"The King is a lucky man indeed!" Mother smiled.

"They are lucky to have each other," Margaret corrected her.

The royal barge bore Elizabeth down the Thames to the Tower, where she alighted at the Court Gate and was escorted up the Queen's Stairs to the Byward Tower. It was the first time she had visited the Tower since her brothers had been held there, and it pained her to think that they—or their bodies—might still be somewhere within these walls. Fleetingly, she thought of that long-ago time she had been in the fortress when it was under bombardment, and shivered again. Yet times would be different now. The struggle between York and Lancaster was over.

The Earl of Oxford, the newly appointed constable, greeted her and escorted her to the royal palace, where she was shown into a room with a vast hooded fireplace in the French style and vivid wall paintings of angels in green and vermilion.

That was all she could take in, because there, by the hearth, stood a tall, slender man in a gown of crimson cloth of gold and a black velvet cap with a large ruby brooch. He had a fair complexion, chin-length hair like burnished gold, a jutting jaw, high cheekbones and winged eyebrows, and his heavy-lidded gray eyes were regarding her intently. Not a handsome man, exactly, but an arresting one, exuding authority.

The smile he gave her transformed his face. "My lady," he said, holding out his hands before she could curtsey. "I have longed for this moment."

"As I have, too, your Grace," she said, surrendering to his grasp. He bent and kissed each hand in turn.

"They told me you were beautiful, and they spoke truth," he said. He had a French accent, with a hint of Welsh. He really was most charming, yet she could sense the steel beneath and that he was assessing her, which was only natural, of course, for he would be acutely aware that her house had been his enemy.

"Some wine?" he asked.

"That would be most welcome, Sir," she told him, and watched him pour it.

"Do sit down," he invited. "I must thank you, my lady, for all your efforts on my behalf, which prospered my fortunes beyond measure. Had it not been for you, Lord Stanley, and his friends, I might not be here now."

"I was determined to do whatever I could to support your righteous cause," she told him. "I and mine had been cruelly wronged by the Usurper. You offered us hope of salvation and redress."

"I offer you much more, Elizabeth," he said. "I hope I may call you that, as we are going to be married?"

"Of course," she smiled, beginning to relax in his company.

"Then you must call me Henry. No ceremony between us, eh?" Suddenly, his gaze was compassionate. "You have had a difficult time."

"You too—Henry," she replied. "Your long exile cannot have been easy."

"No, it wasn't. Since I was five, I've been either a captive or a fugitive. Never did I think I would be king of England."

"Your lady mother cannot stop thanking God," she told him.

"I owe her so much. She never lost faith in me."

"She has worked indefatigably on your behalf, even risking her life."

"She is a great lady. I trust that you and she will be friends."

"Oh, we have long been that—and of late I have become closer to her."

He gave her that dazzling smile again. "I think you and I are going to accord well together. I shall count the days until we can be wed. And I shall be staying at Coldharbour for the next fortnight so that we can have some time to get to know each other. My mother has explained to you why our marriage has to be a little delayed?"

"She did." She was pleased to hear that he wanted to spend time with her, for she was finding his company stimulating. They had so much to talk about that she didn't know where to begin. But it could all wait. What was important was that they liked each other and had shared aims. And she did like him. She had the strong impression that the feeling was mutual.

Henry seemed to have a thousand things to attend to during his stay at Coldharbour, and his mother always seemed to be hovering somewhere nearby. He and Elizabeth had to dine and sup together with their mothers and the princesses, of whom Henry was becoming fond, but they managed to spend a fair amount of precious time alone together. There were no gardens, so they sat in the courtyard while the early autumn weather remained fine, or played chess or cards in the parlor. Often, they just talked. They found that they had much in common, especially a love of music and the tales of King Arthur and Camelot.

"I am descended from him, you know, and from the ancient kings of Britain," Henry told her. "One of my forebears was the great Welsh prince Cadwaladr, King of Gwynedd. That is why I had his red dragon emblazoned on my standard and am using it on my arms as king." He had a dreamy look in his eyes. "On his deathbed, Cadwaladr foretold that a Welsh king would restore the ancient royal line of Britain, and that his descendants would rule the whole island. I fully believe that prophecy has been fulfilled in me."

Elizabeth stiffened. The message was clear: Henry Tudor regarded himself as the true successor of those ancient rulers; it was those who had come since—Saxons, Normans, and Plantagenets—who were the real usurpers.

"My father too was proud of his descent from Cadwaladr," she hastened to say, for she would not allow any suggestion that King Edward had had no right to his throne. "And I am descended from the ancient princes of Wales through my ancestor Roger Mortimer, who married Gwladys Ddu, the daughter of Prince Llywelyn ap Iorwerth."

"Then you are an eminently suitable wife for a Welsh-born king," Henry declared, taking her hand and kissing it. He had still not kissed her on the lips. "But I must bear in mind English sensibilities. They distrust foreigners, even the Welsh. I do not want my subjects thinking me one, so I intend to make known my devotion to their patron saint and mine, St. George."

She was aware that awkward matters lay between her and Henry, and that they must be broached. She wanted to remind him that without her, his claim to the throne was weak and open to challenge. Every one of her Yorkist kinsmen had a better claim. Until they married, Henry would be vulnerable. He was clearly aware of that, for the Queen had told her that he had dated his reign from the day before Bosworth, effectively branding as traitors Richard and all who had fought for him. Mother had been shocked.

"What security will kings have in future, that, on the day of battle, they will not be deserted by their subjects for fear of being branded traitors?" she had cried. "I'm sorry, Bessy, I shouldn't criticize your future husband to you, but this is a step too far."

Yet Henry *had* issued a general pardon to those commoners who had fought at Bosworth. Richard's supporters were either scattered or in prison. Norfolk had fallen in the field, but his son, the Earl of Surrey, was in the Tower, as was the Earl of Northumberland. Henry had told Elizabeth that he intended, after an in-

terval, to pardon them and set them free. Some had prudently
changed sides, while others had disappeared. Her cousin Lincoln
had made his peace with Henry and had not only obtained a pardon, but been given a seat on the Council. She hoped that would
be enough to win his enduring loyalty, given that he had been
Richard's designated successor. Even Grandmother York sent her
felicitations to Henry, although Mother said it must have stuck in
her craw to do so, given that her son was dead because of him. But
Elizabeth knew that she would always do what was right and politic.

The only member of the House of York who did not send con-
gratulations was Aunt Margaret. There was a distinctly chill wind
blowing from Burgundy.

"It's patently clear that Margaret hates Henry because he slew
her brother and toppled the House of York from the throne,"
Mother said. "She's beyond his reach and does not fear to show her
hostility. He should be wary of her; she's a forceful woman and a
great meddler."

Elizabeth dismissed the threat from Aunt Margaret from her
mind. There was a more contentious matter that she dared not
raise with Henry, who must be aware that Richard had planned to
marry her. Did he wonder how willing she had been? Did he know
of that letter she had sent to Norfolk? She fervently hoped not,
because it suggested that she had been eager for the marriage for
personal reasons. In Henry's eyes, that might look like betrayal,
after he had publicly vowed to take her as his wife.

There came the day when he arrived in a strange mood. He
seemed preoccupied, and there was a coldness in his manner that
unnerved her. They played chess, and his king took her queen.
The irony of this did not escape her, or him, for he looked at her
quizzically.

"It seems strange to think that you were once my enemy," he
observed.

"I was hardly that," she retorted. "It was my father who feared
you. And that enmity has ended in peace."

He paused, his eyes narrowing. "And yet, you schemed to marry
the Usurper, who would have destroyed me and brought your

house to ruin. It was the most wicked and unspeakable plan—the foulest that ever was heard of." His anger was all the more vehement for being expressed in such quiet, clipped tones.

A silence fell, as she sought for the right words to defend her actions. "I felt I had no choice. It was the only way to secure the crown that was rightfully mine and a future for my mother and sisters. Buckingham's rebellion had been crushed. I thought your cause lost and that you would never come."

He regarded her shrewdly. "And how did you reconcile yourself to marrying the man who had done away with your brothers?"

"It was a question of priorities!" she said sharply. "I had to sacrifice myself and my scruples for a higher good. And Richard assured me that he had not had my brothers killed. He said they had disappeared from the Tower, and blamed Buckingham. I so wanted them to be alive that I believed him."

He nodded. "I hear what you say. But it seems to me that Richard was more to you than you would have me believe. What do you have to say of this?" He took a piece of paper from his doublet and laid it on the table. She saw, with dismay, that it was her letter to Norfolk. There were the words she had hoped that Henry would never read. *His Grace is my only joy and maker in this world, and I am his in heart and in thoughts, in body and in all*. No wonder he was angry.

"I was desperate," she said. "Desperate to have the stain of bastardy removed, to regain the crown that should have been mine. I wanted to spare myself and my sisters from making ignominious marriages. The words I wrote were intended to assure Richard of my loyalty. I was offering my whole being to him. There was no true love between us, only that of uncle and niece, for there had always been affection there. You should know, Henry, that if I had thought you would be coming to rescue me, I would never have entertained any idea of marrying him, and that letter would never have been sent. It was you I wished to wed—all along. But I believed you were lost to me. I had to live!" Tears welled up in her eyes.

At once, Henry's expression softened, and he took her hand. "I'm sorry, cariad. I should not have spoken so harshly to you. But when I read that letter, which was found when Norfolk's house was searched, it gave me a nasty jolt. I was, I do confess, jealous. And I could not believe that you had entertained feelings for that monster. But now that you have explained everything, and I understand why you acted as you did, I cannot blame you for it."

He leaned in closer as relief swept over her, and tilted her chin up toward him. Then he kissed her gently on the lips. It was the first time a man had ever kissed her, and she melted. It was sweeter than she could ever have dreamed, and all the more so for feeling like a benediction, drawing a line under all that had gone before. And then he kissed her again, and they were in each other's arms, and life had just become infinitely better.

After that, a deeper understanding and intimacy blossomed between them, and love flowered. Lord Stanley, back from Lancashire, smiled at them as they sat, heads together, making wedding plans.

"It is good to see you so joyful together," he said. "I prayed for a happy outcome, but I never thought it would be crowned with such bliss."

Henry beamed at his stepfather. "And I never looked to find such joy in a marriage made for policy!" He kissed Elizabeth's hand. She was learning that the Welshman in him had a romantic side.

"And you, Bessy?" Stanley asked.

"I could not have asked for better, Father Stanley."

She had become conscious of the fact that some of her clothes were showing signs of wear. Her best gowns were of cloth of gold, but were too grand for everyday use.

"My Queen should have new apparel," Henry said. "I will order the Wardrobe to send you some materials." She was thrilled when several large packages were delivered to Coldharbour. Her mother and the Lady Margaret watched as she unwrapped yards and yards of crimson velvet and russet damask, and numerous pieces of ermine. Immediately, Margaret sent for her tailor to have them made up.

Mother had been suspicious of Henry delaying his marriage, but she was thawing. She could not fault his courtesy to her, or his tenderness toward her daughter. But she was forever urging Elizabeth to press him to have the Tower searched. "I must know what happened to my sweet boys," she kept saying.

Reluctantly, Elizabeth brought up the subject. It was her last opportunity, for their idyllic fortnight was up and Henry was departing for Woking Palace tomorrow.

She asked if she might sup alone with him the evening before, and Margaret, seeing her so sad about his leaving, readily agreed and ordered her cooks to serve them special fare.

After they had feasted on succulent guinea fowl in ale broth, creamed fish, and warden pears in red wine, she passed Henry the loving cup.

"My dearest, you remember me saying that Richard told me that my brothers had just disappeared? Do you think they could still be alive?"

He frowned. "It is possible. But I am sorry to say I think it more likely that they are dead."

"I think so, too," she said. "I don't believe they ever left the Tower. Henry—would it be possible to have a search made there?"

"I already have," he told her. "Nothing was found, even though my men were thorough. Either the princes were buried so obscurely that no trace remains, or they were taken away, dead or alive."

"So Richard could have been telling the truth?"

"I suppose so," he said reluctantly. "But Buckingham informed me that Richard had confided to him that he intended to have them killed, and it followed that he had done so. I believed then that they were dead, as did my mother, Buckingham, and even your mother. I would not have sworn to take England and marry you if I had thought they were still alive."

She had a sudden, treacherous thought. If it was possible that Richard had spoken the truth, and Buckingham had arranged for her brothers to disappear, then it was also possible that Henry or his mother had colluded. Henry had had more to gain than anyone except Richard. But he had been overseas at the time, and Buckingham had been in Wales. She did not see how either of them could have breached the Tower's defenses and had her brothers murdered, unless they had had accomplices within the fortress. But who?

It seemed strange now that Richard had never publicly accused Buckingham of spiriting them away, even after his arrest. It would have been in his interests to do so, given how rumor was damning him. But maybe they had never been spirited away at all.

She looked at Henry as he sat opposite, drinking the remains of his wine. She did not have the measure of him yet. Could he be ruthless enough to take out two children who stood in his way? Was it because he had known for certain that they were dead that he had made that vow to take England and marry her? And had that search of the Tower been undertaken to cover up any traces that might have been left, rather than to find her brothers? It seemed odd that he had not told her, the other person most crucially interested, about it being made. Would he have said anything if she had not asked?

She must not think like this. He was her future husband and she had to learn to trust him. But the thought persisted, like an itch that needed scratching. And there was no one to whom she dared confide such disloyal thoughts.

In the morning, Henry said an affectionate farewell, kissed her, and then departed for Woking. By then, she had convinced herself that her fears of the night before had been irrational, and that the likeliest culprit was Richard.

She sent for the tailor to discuss her new gowns. Then she filled the time with reading, helping her sisters with their lessons, and spending the afternoons embroidering with her mother and the Lady Margaret.

The following week, as they dined together, Margaret had some news.

"The King my son is planning a joint coronation, and the heralds are drawing up plans for it," she announced.

"Then he expects Parliament and the Pope to move quickly," Mother said.

"It does seem so," Margaret replied, and turned to Elizabeth. "My dear, you should start thinking about your attire for the wedding and the coronation."

Elizabeth was elated. But as the days went by and she heard no more, she became increasingly despondent. Then Margaret, looking embarrassed, informed her that she and Henry could not have a joint coronation after all, since he could not summon Parliament until he was crowned, and its business must not be further delayed. Therefore, he was to be crowned alone. "You will be crowned after your marriage, my dear," she concluded.

It was a crushing disappointment, and did not seem right, but Elizabeth managed to keep smiling and meekly agreed that it was for the best.

Her mother was suspicious, though.

"I've said it all along," she seethed as soon as they were alone in Elizabeth's bedchamber. "He is making it clear that he does not owe his crown to you. A joint ceremony would have made people think you equal sovereigns."

Elizabeth was near to tears. "I am not even to attend the coronation. It is as if I am of no importance."

"Child, it is precisely because you are vitally important to Henry that he seeks to exclude you. He will not have it said that he owes his crown to you."

"But he does!"

"Indeed. And many will remember the oath he swore; many know who is the true sovereign of England."

"Would that I had been born a boy," Elizabeth sighed. "Although, if I had, I would likely be dead!"

At the end of October, the Lady Margaret, decked out in purple and ermine, went to her son's coronation.

"In all that great triumph and glory, I just wept, I was so overcome," she related two days later, after she had returned from court. "It was the most moving, uplifting occasion I have ever been blessed to witness."

Elizabeth listened as she described the ceremony in detail, and the banquet and festivities that had followed. I should have been there, she kept thinking. *All these triumphs should have been mine, too.*

But it was too late to remedy the matter. She would have her moment of glory soon, God willing. And Parliament would be meeting this week.

Lord Stanley had been rewarded by his grateful sovereign with the earldom of Derby and the offices of Constable of England and Chief Steward of the Duchy of Lancaster; he was now one of the foremost men of the kingdom, and he attended Parliament daily, regaling them all at supper with its proceedings.

It had opened with all due ceremony.

"His Grace was hailed as a second Joshua who had rescued his people from tyranny. And the sovereignty was confirmed to him as being his due, not by one but by many titles; he rules rightfully over the English people, not so much by right of blood as of conquest. He himself declared that it was the true judgment of God, expressed in his victory at Bosworth, that gave him the crown by divine right."

Elizabeth drew in her breath. So that was how he defined his title. No mention of her! She dared not catch her mother's eye.

"The Act confirming the throne to the Usurper has been repealed and your Grace's legitimacy confirmed," Derby (as she must now call him) told her, bringing tears to her eyes.

"Then my marriage to Edward was lawful, and all my children, too," Mother declared, with some emotion.

"Indeed, Madam. The King has ordered the Act to be suppressed, so that no slur of bastardy remain. I should tell you that the judges deemed it too scandalous even to be read out in Parliament, lest its shameful falsehoods be perpetuated. His Grace said it deserved utter oblivion, and he has ordered the Parliament roll on which it was written to be burned by the public hangman. Every copy is to be surrendered to the Lord Chancellor before Easter, on pain of imprisonment or a heavy fine."

"I am most reassured to hear that," Mother said.

"And Richard has been attainted for treason."

"For murdering my sons?" she asked sharply.

"For seizing a throne that was not rightfully his," he answered. "The princes are not specifically mentioned in the Act of Attainder, but it does convict him of homicides, murders, and the shedding of infants' blood."

"That seems very strange," the Queen declared, her face pale. "Given that my sons have now been declared legitimate, one would have expected Parliament to make public their deaths in order to show the world that Elizabeth is the undoubted heir of York."

There was a long pause.

"Madam," said the Lady Margaret, "there is no proof that they were murdered, and while that is lacking, it is best not to draw attention to their disappearance. Surely you do see that?"

"Then where are they?" Mother shrilled.

"That is what the King is trying to establish," Margaret said evenly. "He has had the Tower searched. They are not there. Our belief is that Buckingham, not Richard, spirited them away or had them killed."

Mother looked distressed. "The King will keep searching for them?"

"He will. It is in everyone's interests."

"Then they might still be alive?"

"I would not raise your hopes," Margaret said kindly, laying her hand on the Queen's arm. Elizabeth lowered her eyes. Margaret was the one person, apart from Henry, who would not want her brothers to be found.

"I told you!" Mother said later. "He does not mean to wear his crown in right of his wife. He is quite content to usurp it!"

"Hush, Mother! That is treason!"

"And who is the real traitor here?"

Elizabeth shook her head. "Please don't make matters worse." But nothing she could say would allay her mother's anger and, in truth, she agreed with her. But what could she do?

One evening, later that week, Derby signaled to Elizabeth to stay behind when the others rose to go to bed.

"I think I will stay down here and read," she said. "I am not tired."

"And I will have a nightcap," he said. "Do you mind if I join you?" He kissed Margaret good night and closed the door behind her.

"I just wanted to draw your attention to a clause in the Act repealing Richard's title," he said, sitting by the fireside opposite Elizabeth. "It provides that nothing in the reversal should prejudice the Act establishing the crown to the King and the heirs of his body."

"What does that mean?" she asked, confused.

"It means that even if your brothers are found alive, they cannot challenge the crown."

Understanding dawned. Henry was covering all contingencies— and it could mean only one thing: that he truly did not know for certain if the princes were dead.

"Thank you for telling me that," she said, feeling hugely relieved that she was not about to marry her brothers' murderer. "Although if Ned is alive, it would be sad for him to be deprived of the crown that is rightfully his."

Derby nodded. "But the realm needs stability, Bessy. You must also realize that it is a matter of concern to the King that he does not know what happened to the princes or where they are. The uncertainty undermines your own title, and he wishes me to tell you that that is why Parliament has confirmed him as king by right of conquest."

It sounded so reasonable, and yet Elizabeth felt a spurt of anger that Henry had claimed as a conqueror what was, after all, her throne. She had been the rightful queen all along. He would not have done this if she had been a man.

Derby was watching her thoughtfully. "Marrying you will consolidate and confirm the King's title," he said, and she knew he was trying to placate her. "He knows there are many who believe he must do so to make good his claim. That is why he was concerned to establish that your legitimacy is beyond dispute."

"I will not say anything against the man who is to be my husband," she said.

"Your words speak volumes," he smiled. "I understand. But there is something else you should know. Immediately after Bosworth, his Grace ordered Bishop Stillington's arrest and he was imprisoned. Yet, in Parliament, on the grounds of the Bishop's age and infirmity, the King has just pardoned him for what were described only as horrible and heinous offenses imagined and done by him to his Grace. I think we both know what those offenses were."

"Lying about my father being married to Eleanor Butler," Elizabeth said, tart. "And helping Richard to the throne. Richard never did show me any of the promised proofs."

"Because they did not exist," Derby said. "If they had, why hold them back?"

"He said the Bishop had them."

"A convenient excuse." He yawned. "I am for my bed, Bessy. Do not fret about any of this. All will come well in the end."

She knew that legislation and dispensations took time, but as the weeks passed, she gained the impression—rightly or wrongly—that Henry was in no hurry to marry her. It did not help that he had paid a secret visit to his mother. Anne had come upon them when they were talking in the library, and had made a swift curtsey and exit, but, her curiosity piqued, had then stayed listening outside the door to hear Margaret declare, "None shall ever say that you owe your crown to your Queen."

"And then the King replied that many would," Anne related,

"and he said he would not be his wife's gentleman usher. If he relied on your title, Bessy, he would be but a king by courtesy." She
had not risked waiting to hear more, but what she reported was
worrying. Elizabeth knew now that her own concerns, and her
mother's, had been justified. She knew too that Henry's delay in
marrying her suited him well, but must seem like a betrayal to
many.

She was a mere woman. There was no law (unlike in France) to
prevent her from ruling in England, but she knew that it was
against the laws of God and Nature. No woman could wield dominion over men, lead armies in battle, or fully comprehend affairs of state. People might make protests, but no one would
seriously think of taking up arms in her cause, even if she wanted
them to, which she didn't, for there must be an end to this dynas-
tic warfare—that was what her marriage to Henry was for.

Derby took evident pleasure in informing Mother that Parliament
had repealed the Usurper's Act confiscating her property.

Her smile was radiant. "God has at last heard my prayers. And
I am deeply grateful to our lord the King. Tell me, when will my
property be restored to me?"

"That property, Madam, was yours while your husband lived.
You are now to be assigned the widow's jointure he settled on you,
as well as the rights and privileges normally enjoyed by a queen
dowager. And you have been granted your jointure as a *femme sole*,
which gives you full control of your lands."

Elizabeth could see Mother doing mental calculations as to how
much better or worse off she would be, but it was clear that she
would have a fortune sufficient to maintain the state to which she
had once been accustomed. And, as queen dowager, she would
rank as second lady in the land after Elizabeth herself—and before
the Lady Margaret, which would please her, no doubt! Because it
was plain to everyone that Margaret was already enjoying great
influence and acting as an unofficial queen dowager. She always
put on her countess's coronet whenever she appeared in public,
which Elizabeth thought excessive because kings and queens only

wore their crowns on state occasions. But she liked Margaret
enough to overlook her little triumphs. It was only natural that
she should bask in the reflected glory of her adored son. Margaret
had always been kind to her, and Elizabeth knew that, as long as
she deferred to the older woman and was a loving helpmeet to
Henry, she would have nothing to fear from her.

Now that Parliament had spoken and Elizabeth had been legitimated, there was no cause for her marriage to be delayed further—
apart from waiting for the dispensation. She was thrilled when
Henry visited Coldharbour in November to show her a new-
minted coin stamped with a double rose symbolizing the union of
Lancaster and York. What better proof could there be of his firm
resolve to proceed to the marriage? But when he told her that he
had only just applied for a dispensation, she thought she would
scream. How long would it take for his envoys to get to Rome and
back, even without taking account of delays in the Vatican? But
Henry did not seem to feel any sense of urgency. Her feelings for
him had grown during the weeks since their meeting, but they
were tempered with frustration. Yet she knew in her bones that
the attraction that was burgeoning between them could grow into
passion, given the chance.

As Christmas drew nearer with no sign of any marriage preparations, she grew anxious, especially when her mother came into her
chamber one morning looking distraught.

"Bessy, you have to hear this! It is better coming from me than
anyone else. My lord of Derby says he has heard gossip at court
that the King is considering marrying the Duchess of Brittany."

"What?" Elizabeth jumped up, knocking the table sideways so
that the ink spilled from its well. "No! He can't be! He can't do
that to me! He needs me." Hysteria was rising in her.

"He also wants that great duchy of Brittany the French King
covets. And it is being said that he desires the Duchess, too. My
lord believes there is no substance to these reports, but I have long

doubted—and I know you and others, have too—that the King is fixed on your marriage, even though all England much desires it."

Elizabeth broke down, covering her face with her hands. All her instincts urged her to go to Henry and confront him, but she feared to hear his answer, and, anyway, it was not done for a princess to broach such matters.

She felt her mother's arms enfold her. "Hush now, Bessy. It is only gossip and we are both probably overreacting. I'm sorry, I should not have burst in on you like that, but, given the shocks and anxieties of these past years, I tend to make a catastrophe of everything."

"It's all right, Mother," Elizabeth soothed, hugging her. "This interminable waiting is impossible." She pulled away and moved to the window overlooking the Thames. "I long to marry the King, and I am so frustrated at being made to wait. But let's not dwell on rumors. People love to create dramas. Hopefully, the only thing holding up my marriage is the dispensation."

She wished that Henry would come. His presence enlivened her, made the world seem a brighter place. Without it, she found herself moping, or embroidering his name in silken threads on canvas, or praying to the saints to send him to her. He would come, she was sure of it, and all would be well. Yet still she waited.

Derby arrived during dinner one day in the middle of December. "My apologies, ladies. I was kept late waiting for Parliament to be prorogued. Bessy, the lords and commons have told the King that he must honor his vow to wed you. They are not impressed by his claim to rule by right of conquest. They declared that only you can make good his royal title. His Grace was moved to consent. As he sat enthroned in the Parliament chamber, it was announced that he wished to make you his wife and consort. The lords and commons expressed their hope that from this marriage there would come offspring for the comfort of the whole realm."

Elizabeth listened with mounting excitement. Her fears had been for nothing. And yet she was not pleased to hear that Henry was calling her his consort; she should be his queen and his equal.

"All the lords rose to their feet," Derby continued, as Margaret looked on with a radiant smile on her face. "They urged the King to proceed to the union, and he replied that he was very willing to do so and that it would give him pleasure to comply with their request. And so it was decreed by harmonious consent that two families that had once striven in mortal hatred should be united, to put an end to civil war. The wedding is set for the eighteenth of January. Bessy, the King said afterward that he was marrying you not just for the sake of the peace and tranquility of his realm, but also for your beauty and virtue, and on account of the love he bears to you."

She blushed. Mother squeezed her hand, delighted.

"I took the liberty of telling his Grace," Derby said, beaming, "that, out of love and affection, you desire to marry him."

"I do," she replied. "I believe we are of one mind."

"This calls for a toast," Margaret said, signaling to her steward to pour more wine. "The whole realm will soon be rejoicing in the surety that your marriage will now put an end to war. To Elizabeth, our future Queen!"

"To Elizabeth, our Queen," Mother said firmly.

Everyone raised their goblets.

From that day, Elizabeth found herself being deferred to as if she were queen of England already. It brought back memories of that long-ago time when she had been treated as the future Dauphine of France. But a far more glorious future beckoned.

Everyone threw themselves into preparations for the wedding, which was to take place in the soaring beauty of St. Stephen's Chapel. That brought a pang, as she recalled her brother York's wedding there nearly eight years ago. As she watched her sisters being fitted for their gowns, she thought how wonderful it would be if her brothers could be there to see her wed.

Henry visited Coldharbour several times. On the first occasion, he commanded that he and Elizabeth be left alone, and then embraced and kissed her like a lover.

"It will not be long now, cariad," he said. "I have ordered tour-

naments to celebrate our wedding, and a new bed." Elizabeth felt
herself flush; soon she would know Henry in every sense, and the
thought set her tingling. He grinned at her, then kissed her again.
"Once the Christmas evergreens are down, we can have the palace
decorated for the wedding. I trust you have everything you need?"

"What I need, Henry, is only you," she answered, and entwined
her hand in his.

Christmas was very merry, like one long celebration. The Lady
Margaret kept a laden table, and there were games of blind man's
buff and hide-and-seek, and disguisings and forfeits, while the
wine flowed plenteously and Elizabeth's fool, Patch, had the company splitting its sides with laughter. Henry and Elizabeth led the
guests in the dancing, and it was good to see her mother and sisters joining in the fun. And she herself was at the center of it, the
bride-to-be, the hope of England. She was young and glowing
with happiness. Henry kept telling her how much he loved her.
She had much to thank God for.

After Epiphany, the King came again, and she served him claret
in her mother's chamber.

"God willing, the dispensation will be granted soon," he told
her. "I instructed my envoy to the Vatican to praise your beauty
and virtue in a formal oration to his Holiness, who cannot but approve our marriage. But, Bessy, the Papal Legate here has told me
that, if we petition him, he can grant the dispensation on the
Pope's behalf, which will save us from waiting for it to arrive from
Rome. What do you say? Shall we do it?"

"Yes!" she answered, thrilled to hear him so eager, and went to
fetch her writing chest. Seated at the table, their heads almost
touching—burnished gold and copper red—they drew up their
petition.

A week later, Henry arrived at Coldharbour and burst into the
hall without waiting to be announced, waving a document.

"We have our dispensation, Bessy! In two days, we can be wed
as planned."

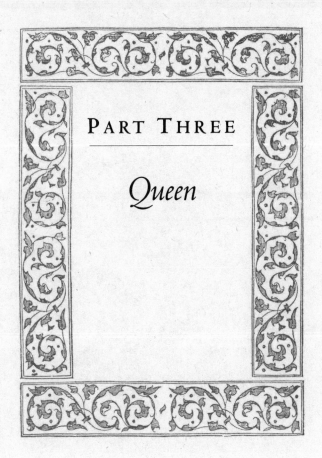

PART THREE

Queen

Chapter 13

1486

The chapel looked magnificent, hung with cloth of gold and costly tapestries, its tall windows soaring heavenward.

The purple silk damask and crimson satin gown felt heavy over the kirtle of white cloth of gold as Elizabeth stood with Henry before the altar, wearing a mantle furred with ermine against the January chill. Her hair was loose beneath her circlet of sparkling jewels and threaded with gems, which gave a pleasing effect. Around her neck hung a necklace of gold studded with sapphires, emeralds, and rosy carbuncles. Henry, who was gorgeously attired in cloth of gold, could not take his eyes off her.

The ceremony was conducted by Cardinal Bourchier, the aged Archbishop of Canterbury. Praying that the King and Queen might have a prosperous and happy issue, he conjured up the image of a sweet posy in which the white and red roses were happily tied together. At last, the ring was on Elizabeth's finger and she was queen of England in fact, as well as by right. Jubilantly, she and Henry processed out of the chapel, hand in hand.

The wedding feast in Westminster Hall was lavish. The royal couple and their guests were served roasted peacocks, swans, larks, and quails, followed by sugared almonds and fruit tarts. Gifts were showered on everyone. There was jousting and dancing to mark the joyful occasion.

Derby stood up and raised his goblet. "A toast, my lords and ladies, to the union of the white rose of York and the red rose of Lancaster, which has put an end to the conflict between the two royal houses. Because of this marriage, peace has descended out of Heaven into England, for the lines of Lancaster and York are now brought into one knot, from which one true heir might succeed and peaceably rule! So let us salute two bloods all made in one, now that the red rose has taken the white in marriage! To the union of the two roses!"

"The two roses!" roared the company, raising their glasses amid loud acclamation.

Henry rose. "I thank you, my lord of Derby, and you, my lords and ladies! Victory gave me a kingdom and the knee of submission, but my marriage with the Lady Elizabeth gave me its heart, so that both knee and heart may truly bow before me." He raised Elizabeth's hand and kissed it, to more cheers.

The revelry went on late into the night until Elizabeth was almost dizzy from twirling around the floor and the goblets of fine wine she had drunk. When Henry led her back to the high table, she sank gratefully into her chair.

"Time for bed, I think," he smiled, and nodded at the Lord Chamberlain, who called for silence as hippocras and wafers were served and largesse was proclaimed. When the spiced wine had been drained, Henry and Elizabeth rose, and everyone stood and made obeisance to them. Then the Queen Dowager—as Mother now was—and the Lady Margaret led Elizabeth away to prepare her for bed.

Clad in a night-rail of lawn with beautiful embroidery around the square neckline and gathered cuffs, with a velvet nightgown on top, Elizabeth was escorted by the ladies to the King's vast bedchamber, the fabulous Painted Chamber. Mellowed with wine, she did not feel nervous of what lay ahead, but filled with a sense of destiny—and rightness. Her mother and mother-in-law helped her into the bed, which stood beneath an ancient mural depicting the coronation of St. Edward the Confessor. Around her, the walls were decorated with huge paintings of biblical battles. In the fireplace, a great fire crackled, but the room was cold. She noticed that the headboard's carvings of Adam and Eve bore strong resemblances to herself and Henry. They were surrounded by the fruits of paradise, symbolizing fertility and the royal heirs that would—God willing—be conceived in this bed. She shivered and drew the bedclothes up to her chin, glad of the crisp white linen and the warm furred counterpane.

Male voices approaching. Laughter. Henry was coming. The door opened, and there he was, wearing a crimson night robe and a matching nightcap. His eyes lighted on her and she saw the desire in them. The courtiers gathered around the bed as he divested himself of his robe and, clad in a nightshirt, climbed in and laid his hand on Elizabeth's. Then the Archbishop entered and censed and blessed the bed, praying that God would make it fruitful.

"Thank you, my lords and ladies," the King said, when he had finished. "I and my wife would be alone now."

Rapidly, the chamber emptied in a flurry of bows and curtseys. At last, the door closed, and Henry turned to Elizabeth, taking her in his arms.

"You're shivering, cariad," he murmured. "It's freezing in here. That fireplace is completely inadequate. They should have brought in braziers." He got up, raked the fire and piled on more logs, then returned to her and closed the bed curtains.

"Come," he said smiling, drawing her to him, "let's keep each other warm." She had never heard him speak so tenderly before and her heart melted in her. She allowed herself to be gathered up as he began kissing her and pulling at her night-rail. "At last, we can engage in some sweet combat," he breathed. "This will be a greater victory than Bosworth! Come, Bessy, let's make ourselves a son!" And then he proceeded, very vigorously, to do just that, and the world exploded in a profusion of stars.

* * *

In the morning, Elizabeth woke to the memory of the night before and lay there smiling. She had not expected Henry to be so accomplished a lover. Yet she could hardly have expected him to have reached the age of twenty-nine without gaining some sexual experience. He must have been discreet, for she had heard no word of scandal about him.

But he was hers now. It had been a heady and sweet surrender for both of them and now she was content to lie there watching him sleep, his angular features relaxed against the pillow. The bed was warm, even if the air was cold. She wondered where her night-rail was. He had pulled it off in the heat of their loving. She found it hanging off the side of the mattress.

Henry stirred as she put it on, then wrapped an arm around her. "Good morning, Bessy!" He gave her a sleepy, knowing smile, making her blush. "It is customary for a husband to give his bride a morning gift, and I have something for you. It is not jewels or riches—you will have those in plenty now—but a poem I commissioned from Giovanni de' Gigli, that Italian prebendary of St. Paul's who writes wonderful verse. It is an epithalamium—a hymn to our marriage." He reached over to the table by the bed and handed her a scroll of parchment bound with ribbon.

She could hardly take in the words. To see herself described as "the most illustrious maid of York, most beautiful in form," and a lady "whose matchless face adorned with most enchanting sweetness shines," knowing that Henry had commissioned the piece, moved her deeply. Gigli had even described how she had longed to marry her King, and how frustrated he had been at having to wait; and he had lauded their wedding as an "ever-honored and auspicious day, when in blest wedlock to a mighty king, bright Elizabeth is joined." A child, he predicted, would soon gambol in the royal halls, and grow up a worthy son of the King, emulating the noble qualities of his parents and perpetuating their name in his illustrious descendants forever. It brought tears to her eyes.

When Henry had disappeared into his dressing closet with his gentlemen, Elizabeth's newly appointed ladies-in-waiting, all thirty-two of them, came to attend her for her uprising on her first morning as a new wife. They bound up her hair, which, henceforth, as a married woman, she would normally be expected to keep covered, and placed on her head one of the new-fashioned gable headdresses with long velvet lappets and a black veil hanging down behind. Her mother had explained, though, that as queen, as the living mirror of the Virgin Mary in chastity, humility, motherhood, and acts of mercy, she would be invested with symbolic virginity and could wear her hair loose on ceremonial occasions.

Looking at her reflection in the mirror, Elizabeth found it hard to believe that she was the first lady in the land. It was now down to her to bear the heirs who would embody the union of York and Lancaster and ensure the continuance of the new Tudor dynasty. It was a heavy responsibility, but she trusted that God would make her fruitful.

"You must choose a new motto and an emblem for yourself," Henry said, returning to the bedchamber fully dressed and looking admiringly at the becoming headdress.

As princess, she had used the motto *Sans removir* which meant "Without changing," but she felt it was time to put the unhappy past behind her.

"I thought I might take 'Humble and reverent' for my motto," she said, "if it pleases you."

"It does," Henry smiled. "It's very fitting."

"And as you have adopted the red-and-white rose as your emblem, I would like the white rose of York as mine," she added.

"Of course. And your servants should wear the murrey-and-blue livery of the House of York."

That pleased her. It was good to see some continuity in this new world she inhabited.

Later that day, she and Henry were told that the people of London, to show their gladness, had celebrated their wedding with bonfires, dancing, songs, and banquets, beseeching God to bless the King and Queen and grant them numerous children. It was said that the people's joy and gladness were greater than when the King had entered London or been crowned. Henry frowned a little at that, but the cloud soon passed. Nothing could detract from the sense of unity and reconciliation that the wedding had generated.

* * *

Marriage, Elizabeth found, was an adjustment. Henry was loving, but he was complex—a dark prince and infinitely suspicious, which was not surprising, considering that, from childhood, his life had been overshadowed by war and intrigue. He was always imagining secret conspiracies. It was clear that he did not feel safe on his throne.

Much that was unspoken lay between them. She guessed that he regarded her relatives with mistrust, fearing that they coveted his crown. Her brothers were rarely mentioned. When she asked after Warwick, and how long he would be kept in the Tower, Henry became abrupt.

"I have not decided yet. The lad is well cared for. Do not fret about him." She took that as her cue to keep her mouth shut.

But there were other sides to him. She discovered that he knew four languages, was well read, brilliant with money and cultured. Able, clever, hardworking, and shrewd, he was a good husband and son, caring toward his family. She loved him for that, and his dry humor. And she applauded his determination to bring stability to England.

"I want a secure throne bolstered by wealth," he told her, during the first week of their marriage, as they sat alone at dinner. "I mean to impose and maintain strong government, law, order, and peace, and work for the prosperity of my house. I will make this realm a power to be reckoned with and respected throughout Christendom." Elizabeth was impressed by his plans to boost foreign trade and commerce and bring economic prosperity to English merchants.

"Above all, I have to survive as king," he said, and she suspected he was thinking of her kinsfolk. "I am haunted by the knowledge that I was able to defeat the Usurper at Bosworth with only a small army, and how easy it would be to overthrow me. All the great lords keep private armies, which is what made the recent wars of Lancaster and York possible. I mean to ban such armies. And I hope to promote men who are qualified by their abilities, rather than their noble blood, for royal service." His eyes were shining at his vision of the new England he was resolved to create.

Elizabeth marveled to see him painstakingly checking his accounts and initialing every item. She was learning that he was a man who liked to keep an eye on details that other kings—her father among them—normally left to others. He was constantly writing himself notes and recording his thoughts in a journal. But she had to laugh when, entering his study one day, she found him sternly rebuking his pet monkey, which had torn his notebook to pieces. The story got around and the court rocked with laughter. Henry's meticulousness was not liked, nor was his growing reputation for parsimony, which was not wholly undeserved.

Yet he was not mean. He knew when to spend lavishly in order to show himself a magnificent monarch.

"It is essential," he told her, as he was being fitted for a violet-colored gown lined with cloth of gold. "A king who wears his greatness outwardly commands respect and awe."

In those early weeks of their marriage, Elizabeth found Henry, above all, to be cheerful and companionable. They shared a love of music and played many games of cards and dice. He laid on dancing and plays for their entertainment, and there came a wonderful evening when they thrilled to the feats of tumblers, jugglers, acrobats, and fire-eaters. Another time, Morris dancers performed for them. And, as always, Patch and the other royal fools made them laugh. But there were quieter pleasures, too. She was glad that Henry loved learning for its own sake and was an avid reader, like herself.

She was impressed to learn of his numerous kindnesses, the money he gave to a man wrongfully arrested, to a needy pregnant woman, to children who sang for his pleasure, to a poor maiden who lacked a marriage portion, and to a little girl who danced for him. Rarely was a petitioner turned away empty-handed. A man whose heart was touched by cases like these must possess true goodness and warmth.

She was in no doubt now that Henry loved her. In their bed, she saw the passionate and romantic side of him that was never revealed to anyone else; with her, he let go. But there were also public manifestations of his love. Even in official documents, he referred to her as his most dear bedfellow or his dearest wife. His care for her showed itself in his concern for her well-being and happiness, and in his dependability. And his mother was just as solicitous—so much so that Elizabeth understood that she too loved her.

Yet, beyond telling Elizabeth of his ambitions and aims, Henry would not discuss politics with her. He made it clear that even her high lineage did not qualify her to have views on state affairs. She learned that he loved his own will and his own way, and that he kept most people at a distance. He would be governed by none. It was actually a relief not to be involved in political intrigues any more. She was happy in her new life and quite content just to be a wife, a companion, and—God willing—a mother of princes. And if that rid Henry of any lingering suspicions about where her loyalties lay, so much the better.

It was her constant prayer that their marriage become a true partnership based on love, co-operation, fidelity, and trust. She was resolved to devote herself to supporting Henry's interests and prove herself a true helpmeet. This, she was sure, was the way to enjoy a successful and stable union.

They had not been wed a month when the Lady Margaret suggested that she and Elizabeth jointly found a chantry chapel in the parish church of Holy Trinity, Guildford. Henry, delighted to see them happily working together, gladly granted them a license. Elizabeth was pleased to find that Margaret was willing to listen to her ideas and full of creative ones herself. She had feared that her mother-in-law might be overbearing, but there was an innate sweetness about her that drew you in. It was not reserved for everyone—she could be quite strident when moved to it, and most people went in awe of her, for she did not suffer fools gladly and was vigorous in defending her rights. But she was wise and she was sensible, and universally admired for her holiness of life. People praised her generosity, her chastity, and her scholarship. Elizabeth now understood why those who knew her well loved her.

Henry would not hear a word said against his mother. Lying in bed one night, he told Elizabeth how pleased he was that the long years of separation had seemed as nothing when he and Margaret had been reunited.

"I owe her so much," he said. "I am as bounden to her as to any creature living, for the great love and affection that she has always borne me, often at great cost to herself."

"She never gave up hope that you would conquer England," Elizabeth said, cuddling up to him. "But the great anxiety she suffered took its toll. Either she was in sorrow due to adversity, or, when all was going well, she was in dread of adversity to come. I too owe a debt of gratitude to her. It was she who first suggested our marriage."

Henry turned and kissed her. "Then I have even more cause to love her!"

Margaret often spoke of her hopes of founding a college in Cambridge. "I want to use my wealth for the benefit of others and education," she told Elizabeth as they walked in the frost-rimed gardens at Westminster. "Do you not think those worthy causes, my dear?"

Elizabeth agreed that they were. She was growing closer to Margaret every day, trying not to mind that her mother-in-law lived in as much royal state as she did and exercised patronage like a queen. Whenever she attended divine service with Henry and Elizabeth, she sat beneath her own cloth of estate. After Vespers, wine and spices were served to her as well as to the King, and Elizabeth was not served any. When Elizabeth went in procession through the court, Margaret walked only a little way behind her. But it was only natural that she should wish to bask in her son's reflected glory.

Elizabeth was learning to accept the fact that Margaret was always present, or never very far away. Wherever the King was, there she would be, and Henry made it quite clear that he intended to take her with them on their travels and progresses around the kingdom. He arranged for lodgings to be kept for her at all the royal residences, often next to his private apartments. Royal officials already knew to include her when making arrangements for the King and Queen. Elizabeth found it a little stifling.

But then Margaret would disarm her by random acts of kindness and warm companionship, and she found that she could not
resent her. And it would be foolish to disrupt the peaceable har-
mony between them. She was grateful for the support that Margaret so readily gave her and genuinely happy to cooperate with her.

It was wonderful to be once again at the center of the English court,
lauded and honored as queen. Henry was resolved to keep a splendid court, as magnificent as her father's, and Elizabeth was pleased
when he asked for her help and listened avidly when she described
how it had been modeled on the fashionable court of Burgundy.

"Whatever I outlay, I mean to make mine as splendid, one that
will become renowned throughout Christendom," he enthused, as
they sat before the roaring fire in her chamber drawing up a list of
all the things he planned to do. "I want to rebuild my palaces and
furnish them with the best plate, tapestries, and decoration. We
will make our court a fitting setting for feasts, tournaments, and
pageants."

"And there must be sports," Elizabeth added. "Hunting, hawking, and archery." She enjoyed all three.

"I could build bowling alleys and tennis plays to keep my
courtiers diverted."

"Don't forget musical entertainments. And it is important to
encourage men of learning and piety."

"Yes, I must set a good moral tone," Henry agreed. "I really am
grateful for your ideas, my Bessy."

She smiled at him, stifling a yawn. For the past two days, she
had felt tired, and put it down to being kept awake into the small
hours by her amorous husband. Today, she could have slept standing up, which was not like her. But it was worth it!

One evening, Henry hosted a great feast for hundreds of guests,
wishing to proclaim his magnificence and counteract accusations
of parsimony. Although personally frugal, he kept a sumptuous
table and dish after dish of rich and tasty food was served. Elizabeth took one look at the venison in red wine and felt nauseous,
yet she almost fell on the fish and devoured it. Strange!

But the sick feeling persisted. She sat there, smiling, as the musicians played, praying that she would not vomit. The evening, which she had been enjoying, suddenly seemed interminable.

The Lady Margaret leaned across. "Are you all right, my dear?"

"A little indisposed, I think," Elizabeth admitted.

"Then you must retire and get some rest," Margaret said, and turned to Henry. "The Queen is unwell. Pray excuse her."

"Of course," he replied, looking concerned. "Shall I have the physicians attend you, cariad?"

"No, I'd rather not make a fuss. I'm just tired, that is all."

Gratefully, she slipped away, her ladies following. It was bliss to lay her head on the pillow. She picked up her beautiful, colorful Book of Hours, but was asleep within seconds and did not stir when Henry joined her in bed.

The morning brought a fresh attack of nausea.

"You ought to see a doctor, cariad," Henry urged.

"It is nothing," she told him.

"But I insist," he said.

Dr. Lewis was summoned; Elizabeth had made him her physician in gratitude for his support in the dark days of Buckingham's rebellion. He asked her lots of questions and tested her urine. "Well, your Grace," he said, smiling, "I have some very good news for you. The signs are that you are with child."

With child, already? She was seized with an all-consuming joy. She could not wait to tell Henry. "Where is the King?" she asked.

"He is waiting without, Madam. I will fetch him."

Henry's face was a picture of jubilation. "My sweet Bessy, this is the most wonderful news! An heir to crown our marriage. Truly, God has smiled on us and endorsed my victory at Bosworth." He kissed her tenderly and squeezed her hand. "You must rest, my love, and take care of that precious burden you carry."

"But I feel better now." It was true: the nausea had passed, and she could not wait to be up and telling her mother and sisters the glad tidings. But Henry made her promise to stay in bed an hour longer.

His mother came to see her and embraced her warmly. "I had an idea when I saw you flagging last night," she said happily. "Oh, joy! I have prayed for this. Now, my dear, you must take great care. All England is depending on you."

"Then I must not disappoint them!" Elizabeth laughed.

Mother was thrilled to hear the news, and the princesses were dancing around with excitement.

"You've done better than I did, Bessy," the Queen said. "I had been married for eighteen months when you came along."

"Ah, but you had ten children," Elizabeth reminded her.

"Indeed, and I pray that you are similarly blessed. By my reckoning, the child must be due in October."

"So the doctor says." It seemed so far ahead, so long to wait. She longed to hold her babe. Let it be a son, she prayed. She knew how much Henry wanted an heir.

He came to her bed that night and took her in his arms, to her surprise.

"Should we . . . ?"

"I'm afraid not, cariad," he murmured against her hair. "The doctors say it would not be wise. But there is nothing to stop us from taking comfort in lying together." He kissed her. "I have a gift for you, to express my appreciation." He relinquished her and turned to his night table, then placed a manuscript in her hands. It was exquisitely illuminated and bore their joint arms. She turned a page and saw that it contained the poems of Charles, Duke of Orléans.

"He was a French prince who married a queen of England, although she died tragically young," Henry said, putting his arm around her. "Later, he was captured at Agincourt, and wrote poems to while away the time when he was a prisoner in the Tower of London. I think you will like them. I specially wanted you to read this one." He found the page, then indicated a verse. "Strengthen, my Love, this castle of my heart," she read. He showed her another in which the lover described his lady as "the fairest thing to mortal eyes." Then she could read no more for the tears that flowed. To be so blessed, to have this man to love her, and to be bearing his child . . . Happiness engulfed her.

* * *

Elizabeth was well aware that maintaining two queens and his mother placed a heavy financial burden on the King. He had granted her a dower on marriage, but it was not as substantial as he would have liked, he said ruefully, from his perch on the window seat.

"Your own mother received much more in her day. I support her as well as I can, and your grandmother of York, but there is just not enough for your sisters."

"Not even dowries?" she asked, looking up from her embroidery.

"I fear not. From the income I have allocated you, you need to pay them allowances and cover their expenses. But I will ensure that you are assigned lucrative privileges and I am granting you the use of some of Warwick's properties until he is of age. The income from those should help."

She hoped that it would be enough. A queen had to maintain a certain state and already she was finding it hard to make ends meet. Her councillors wanted to raise as much income as they could from her tenants, but she did not want to provoke resentment. Having begun her reign on a tide of love and popularity, she feared to lose it.

When she told Mother about her reduced settlement, the old Queen snorted. "You brought him England itself, but he keeps you short of money. I tell you, Bessy, he wants to make you dependent on him."

"I'm not sure about that, but my funds will be so stretched that I fear I shall have to ask him for a loan."

"When your son is born, you must seize your advantage and demand a better settlement," Mother urged. "The Queen of England cannot live in penury!"

It was hardly that, Elizabeth thought, looking at the sumptuous tapestries and gold plate that graced her chamber. She lacked for nothing materially, but maybe she should take her mother's advice. With his heir in her arms, Henry would surely grant her anything.

To give him his due, he gave her the money she asked for. "Take it as a gift," he said. But it soon ran out and, because she did not like to ask for more, she took to borrowing small sums from her ladies, her sisters (although they were poor as an honest lawyer), and even her servants. She began to fear that she would never be able to settle the debts that were already mounting.

She tried not to be extravagant. She practiced economies in her household. She was never profligate in her personal expenditure. The most costly items she bought for herself, apart from the rich apparel a queen was required to wear, were two clavichords and a popinjay. But she loved to help others, and it grieved her that Henry gave her only a small allowance for the charity she was expected to dispense, so she had to make sacrifices in order to give to the poor and make gifts to churches and religious houses. She might live in great state and luxury, but the Queen of England was juggling her finances as carefully as any farmer's wife.

Elizabeth had expected to be crowned immediately after her marriage, and Henry had commanded the purchase of items for her coronation. Ermines and miniver for her robes had already been delivered. But then he called a halt to the plans.

"Cariad, the ceremony is long and arduous, and I will not have you endure it in your condition," he told her. "Let us wait until the child is born."

It was disappointing, but she saw it as further evidence of his care for her and was content to wait.

Her pregnancy was announced during Lent. There was widespread rejoicing and great excitement gripped the court, for the swift arrival of an heir would ensure the stability and continuance of the Tudor dynasty. People began congratulating Elizabeth and wishing her a happy hour.

Yet not everyone was delighted at the news. Her marriage should have brought an end to strife, but it seemed that it was insufficient to stifle treason. Some diehard Yorkists just would not accept Henry as king, and they were making their opposition plain.

"I must go north to Lincolnshire and Yorkshire," Henry said

one evening, as he joined Elizabeth for dinner. "I need to be seen by my subjects in those parts, and it is necessary to root out traitors."

She was not surprised. Richard had been popular in the north.

"Am I to accompany you?" she asked.

"No, cariad. You should not travel that far in your condition. You can stay at the palace of Placentia at Greenwich with your lady mother and sisters while I am away. Besides, I will be visiting places where there might be unrest, and I cannot have you exposed to any risks."

He left before Easter. He was planning to be gone for three months, taking the opportunity of visiting various parts of his kingdom on his way to and from the north.

Elizabeth had loved the palace of Placentia since childhood. It certainly was a pleasant place, though throughout there were reminders of the pretended Queen Margaret. The terra-cotta floor tiles bore her monogram, and her marguerite badge was emblazoned on the windows and the cloister that surrounded the grassed courtyard. It seemed incongruous to Elizabeth that she should love a place made beautiful by the woman who had striven to overthrow her house.

It was too cold to sit for long in the ladies' arbor in the gardens, and Henry had forbidden Elizabeth to ride, but, each day, she walked with her mother and sisters in the great park, taking in the fresh air.

"This will do you good," Mother said, striving to keep up with her. "But slow down, Bessy, it's not a race." Anne, Katherine, and Bridget had gone running ahead, loving the freedom Placentia afforded.

Henry wrote frequently. He was well, he kept assuring her, and he had emerged unscathed after suppressing risings by Yorkist adherents. It pained Elizabeth to realize that those whose loyalties lay with her house were Henry's enemies, and she experienced what was beginning to be a familiar conflict of fealties; but mostly she worried about her husband and prayed fervently that he would return safely to her. It heartened her to hear that he had been well received in York, where the city fathers had once supported Richard.

At Placentia, she set about doing charitable works, taking orphaned children under her wing and arranging for them to be brought up on one of her dower manors. She freed debtors from prison. She gave money to the needy, to pay for the burial of pirates who had been hanged at Execution Dock on the Thames at Wapping, and to the clerk of the King's works at Richmond, whose house had burned down.

Petitioners soon learned that they could come to her, among them the destitute son of a madman, who had no money for food or a decent gown. And then there was a little girl, Anne Loveday, whose mother brought her before the Queen.

"She wants to be a nun, your Grace," she said, "but I can't afford the dowry."

Elizabeth looked at the girl, who seemed to radiate a spiritual beauty.

"You have a true vocation?"

"I desire to serve God, by prayer and labor," Anne Loveday said, with feeling.

Elizabeth smiled at her mother. "I will pay her dowry," she told her.

The woman threw herself to her knees. "Oh, my lady, I cannot thank you enough! Now I know why they call you the Good Queen."

Elizabeth was touched. As she watched the happy pair leave, she too felt emotional. Ahead of them lay a parting; the mother was clearly sacrificing her need to have her daughter with her so that Anne could follow her chosen path. Such a parting lay ahead for her, too. She could never forget that Bridget was promised to God. Bridget was only five now, and seemed quite happy about her fate, but she was too young to know what she would be giving up—her life at court, her family, her freedom. And she would never know the love of a man, never have children. Thank God that she would not enter a nunnery for some years. Maybe, when the time came, she would have a different view of it, and Mother might be persuaded to abandon the idea.

* * *

When Henry returned to Elizabeth at Placentia at the beginning of June, she had a high belly and had loosened the front laces of her bodice. His face lit up as he looked her up and down.

"Bessy, you are beautiful!" he exclaimed, and embraced her tenderly. "You look so well."

"I am, my lord," she said, holding on to him as if she would never let him go. The sight of him had brought her such joy.

After London had officially welcomed back its King, he and Elizabeth retired to Windsor Castle.

"Shall we stay here for the birth?" she asked, as they strolled around the gardens in the Upper Ward.

"No, cariad," he replied. "I want my heir to be born at Winchester. It is the site of Camelot, the seat of my ancestor, King Arthur, and a fitting birthplace for my son. I pray that he will be a second Arthur, who will bring a new golden age to England."

His words sent a thrill coursing through her. This prince—pray God it was a prince—was to be born to greatness and high expectations. In him would be united the royal blood of York and Lancaster. He would be a living symbol of the peace between those rival houses.

Mother had not accompanied them to Windsor.

"I need a house of my own," she had told Elizabeth, while they were at Placentia. "I have no place at court."

"But I want you with me!" Elizabeth had cried. "And you know you are welcome here."

Mother had embraced her. "There is not room for two queens in one court, Bessy. If your brother had lived to his majority, I would have retired to one of my dower properties, as dowager queens do. I have taken a forty-year lease on Cheyneygates—you remember, the abbot's house at Westminster Abbey?"

Elizabeth had stared at her, astonished. "But why there? It has such unhappy associations."

"That was in the past. Now, it seems like a haven of peace. You are happily settled as queen, and there is room at Cheyneygates for your sisters. So I can please myself. Abbot Eastney has been most accommodating; he is to keep one half of the house and I shall have the other. Don't look so dismayed. I won't be cloistering myself away from the world. I'll only be at Westminster and we will visit each other."

"If it's what you want . . ."

"It is. I'm nearing fifty and a quiet life appeals to me."

"Then I am happy for you." Elizabeth had hugged her sadly.

But Mother had no sooner moved into her new abode than Henry negotiated a truce with the Scots and offered her as a bride for the widowed King James III.

Elizabeth could not contain herself. "But she has only just taken the lease on Cheyneygates! She loves it there. And he's about twenty years younger."

Henry looked—yes—shifty. "My priority is to seal this peace with Scotland. Other considerations come secondary to that."

"But she is no fitting bride! He can expect no children from her."

"Enough, Elizabeth. I have decided." He had never been so abrupt with her. It was a warning not to interfere in politics.

"Very well," she said sharply, and left him alone.

It dawned on her that he had more than one compelling motive for marrying his mother-in-law to the King of Scots. Not only would it bring peace between two nations that had long been enemies, but it would also relieve him of the burden of providing for two queens, for Mother would become King James's responsibility.

At supper that night, Henry was again his usual congenial self. He almost apologized.

"Do not fret about your mother, Bessy. Nothing is decided. Anne and Katherine have been proposed as brides for King James's sons, which rather complicates matters. It may be that the King will prefer to wed one of them himself."

Elizabeth relaxed. "That would be more fitting, I think." She wondered how Cecily would react to the news that one of her younger sisters might be queen of Scots, a position that she herself had one day hoped to occupy. But, during her brief visit to court for the wedding, Cecily had said how happy she was with Ralph Scrope at Upsall.

"As I said, nothing is settled," Henry replied.

* * *

They traveled to Winchester at the end of August. Henry wanted Elizabeth to be settled there in good time for the birth. She reckoned she had only six or seven more weeks to wait.

She had been fully anticipating moving into the castle.

"There has been a change of plan," Henry told her, as they dined in the private parlor of an inn in the village of Bracknell. "My surveyors have warned me that the castle is not in a good state of repair, and certainly not a suitable place for the birth of my heir."

"Then where shall I be confined?" she asked.

"In St. Swithun's Priory." The priory was attached to Winchester Cathedral. "Prior Hunton has a luxurious house, which he is delighted to place at your disposal. It's in the Great Cloister."

"But I should like to visit the castle first," she said. "There is something there I want to show you."

They went to the castle as soon as they arrived in Winchester. Leading Henry into the great hall, Elizabeth told him to look up at the massive round table hanging high on the wall.

"It was King Arthur's," she told him as they stood gazing at it. "It's quite ancient."

"It is talked of even in Brittany," he said. "It is a marvel! But it looks shabby. We must have it repainted."

"You might ask them to make the figure of Arthur look like you!" she smiled. "It would underline your descent."

"A capital idea!" he agreed, and kissed her, prompting smiles among their retinue.

The Prior's house was quite palatial. Its great hall, with its magnificent timber roof, was to be the chamber where she would hold court with her mother, her sisters, and the Lady Margaret in attendance. The bedchambers were sumptuously appointed, and there was a little jewel of a chapel for their use.

Henry was staying in the castle, where a suite of rooms had been hastily refurbished for him.

"It is not fitting that he lodges with you while you are in seclusion awaiting the birth," the Lady Margaret said, and Mother agreed. But he was a frequent visitor, often arriving for supper after a good day's hunting in the New Forest.

Elizabeth took everyone's advice and rested, sitting with her feet up in the hall or enjoying the sunshine in the Prior's garden. When the summer drew to an end, she stayed warm and cozy indoors as torrential rains swept the land.

Henry was anxious that all due ceremonial be observed before and after the birth of his heir. He had two fine beds delivered for Elizabeth, along with pillows of down and scarlet counterpanes bordered with ermine. He bought her bolts of velvet, damask and other fabrics, and pieces of ermine and miniver, to wear for the ceremonies that would follow the child's arrival. Her tailor was kept very busy.

She sat for hours, happily making clothes for the baby. To her delight, Cecily arrived from Upsall to join them, very excited about the coming birth, for she as yet had no babes of her own, much to her regret. The days passed easily. Elizabeth was not frightened. A pleasant euphoria had overtaken her, and she was looking forward to the birth with equanimity. She knew that many mothers and babies were lost in childbed, but she had great trust in Alice Massey, the experienced midwife she had appointed. She, her mother, and the Lady Margaret had interviewed the woman, who had come highly recommended by several ladies-in-waiting. And she would have Mother and Margaret as her gossips, to cheer and divert her as she labored.

Mother Massey was very forward-thinking, prescribing herbal baths to relax her patient. Elizabeth gave herself up to the daily luxury of a fragrant soak in her oak tub, seated on sponges beneath a linen canopy.

"My mothers always learn breathing exercises, Madam," the midwife told her. "It helps you to manage the pains during your travail."

"Will it be very painful?" Elizabeth asked nervously.

"It will be easier if you do the breathing exercises. If you need it, I will give you some poppy seeds or make an infusion of herbs."

"I have heard that some saints' relics offer protection for women in labor."

"Indeed, they do," Mother Massey agreed, "and you could write a prayer on a long scroll of parchment to wrap around you as a birth girdle. Don't worry, Madam, I will do all I can to make it as easy as possible for you."

One bright morning, nearly three weeks into September, Elizabeth got up from the breakfast table and felt a slight clenching pain deep down in her belly, radiating toward the small of her back.

"Oh! What was that?" she exclaimed, and sat back down again.

Both Mother and Margaret were instantly alert.

"It can't be," Elizabeth said quickly. "By my reckoning, I am only eight months gone. It is too early."

"Wait and see if it comes again," Mother advised.

Elizabeth sat there and buttered some more bread, lathering it with quince jelly.

Ten minutes later, the pain came again. "Oh no," she muttered, rubbing her back, waiting until the feeling passed.

Mother looked concerned. "I think we should send for the midwife."

"That would be wise," Margaret agreed.

When Mother Massey arrived, Elizabeth had another contraction. An hour later, her travail was well established, and she was wondering how she would bear the pain if it got any worse. All that day, she labored, feeling as if she was getting nowhere, and becoming increasingly distressed, and worried because the babe would be premature and might not survive.

The Queen wanted her to lie down, but Mother Massey shook her head. "It is better if her Grace keeps moving. Walking will help."

So Elizabeth walked up and down her bedchamber, pausing to brace herself on the table when the pains became intolerable, and wishing that Henry could be with her—but it was out of the question.

"Men have no place in birthing chambers," Mother Massey said firmly. "His Grace has been told that the child is on its way and has asked to be kept informed."

"He sends you every good wish and his prayers for a happy hour," the Lady Margaret said.

In the evening, Elizabeth's women began opening doors and chests and untying knots to unlock the womb, as Mother Massey looked on, shaking her head at their silliness. But still the pains came relentlessly.

Soon after midnight, just when Elizabeth felt that she could take no more, the midwife cried, "The head is crowning!"

And there he was, her son, a tiny, bloodstained stranger, laid in the crook of her arm. Mother and Margaret were weeping with gladness.

"An heir, an heir for England!" Margaret exulted.

"Thanks be to God!" Mother cried. Pulling aside the curtain that hung across the door, she summoned an usher. "Kindly inform our lord the King that he has a son and heir."

"We'll go and tell him ourselves," Margaret said, hastening the Queen from the room.

Mother Massey took the child to clean and swaddle. Exhausted as she was, Elizabeth was aware that the midwife was not exulting as she should have been.

"Is anything wrong?" she asked anxiously, as her maids tended to her.

Mother Massey laid the infant in the great gold-painted cradle that had been made for him. "He is small because he is premature, Madam, and I fear he is not strong. I would have expected to hear a pair of lusty lungs, but this little one is quiet." She turned to the ladies-in-waiting. "I want the wet nurse here now, so that we can get him to take suck."

Despite feeling weak after her ordeal, Elizabeth raised herself up in the bed. "Is he going to be all right?"

"With careful nursing and prayer, he should do well," Mother Massey smiled, but Elizabeth feared she was putting on a bright front. "I advise your Grace not to move him too often from house to house. Settle his household in one place until he is stronger."

She handed him back and Elizabeth gazed down at him. He was auburn-haired, with delicate features, and favored his father. The resemblance brought forcefully home to her that this tiny babe was destined to shoulder the heavy responsibilities of kingship. Her heart contracted. Her son was to usher in a new era in

England and live up to the high expectations of his subjects. He would be hers for such a short time; he would be taken from her to be versed in becoming the great king his father envisaged.

Was it because she knew this that she felt a disturbing sense of detachment? She had expected to be suffused with joy and overwhelmed with love for her child, but was horrified to find in herself only a strange numbness. Probably she was too drained after her ordeal to feel anything. With that comforting thought, she let sleep claim her.

Chapter 14

1486–1487

When she awoke, the sun was shining through the casements and she could hear the cathedral bells ringing. Henry was sitting beside her. He smiled and squeezed her hand.

"We have a fine boy," he declared. "An heir to unite Lancaster and York. Bessy, I can never thank you enough. Everywhere, people are rejoicing!"

"He is all right?" she asked, feeling muzzy-headed and sore down below.

"He is. I spoke with the midwife, who said he is very small, so I had my physicians look at him. They say he is healthy and feeding well, and that he will grow stronger. You must not worry, Bessy."

"Oh, thank God," she murmured.

"Just concentrate on recovering your strength, cariad." He patted her hand. "I hear that you bore your travail bravely."

"By the end, I did not know what to do with myself. But it was worth it."

Henry bent over the cradle and picked up his son, now sweet-smelling and wrapped in a velvet robe, his little head in its embroidered bonnet peeking out at the top. "He is beautiful," he said, in awe. "I am calling him Arthur, after his illustrious ancestor. I hope you like it."

She had anticipated all along what his choice would be. "It suits him. I like it very much."

"Englishmen rejoice over that name, and foreign princes quake at it, for it is terrible and formidable to all nations. We shall usher in a new Arthurian age, Bessy. England will be great again."

She smiled at him. "God has indeed been good to us." She was elated, but she was yet to be filled with love for her child, which was something she could not tell Henry.

"Arthur will be known henceforth as the Duke of Cornwall. When he is a little older, I will create him prince of Wales."

"The high and mighty Prince Arthur, Duke of Cornwall. A grand title for such a tiny boy." She shifted in the bed. "Oh, Henry, I don't feel very well. Could you please send for Mother Massey?"

He looked faintly alarmed and felt her forehead. "You are hot," he said. "I will fetch her." He laid Arthur back in his cradle and hastened away.

It was an ague and she had a high fever for two days, during which Mother Massey repeatedly sponged her down and made her drink plenty of cordial. Henry visited frequently and brought fruit and comfits to tempt her appetite.

As was her privilege as queen, she dispatched the yeomen of her chamber to carry the good tidings of the birth to all the lords and cities of the realm. She had expected to send them out with pride and excitement, but fever made her weak, and still she could not rejoice in the child as she should.

Henry ordered that church bells be rung throughout the land and that the *Te Deum* be sung in churches in thanksgiving for God's precious gift of a Tudor heir.

"In London, the people have lit bonfires in praise and rejoicing," he reported. "Every true Englishman is celebrating."

Elizabeth was still unwell when, on a cold, wet Sunday, three-day-old Arthur was made ready for his christening in Winchester Cathedral. The silver font had been brought specially from Canterbury Cathedral. By tradition, she and Henry were not to attend. He would remain with her, seated by the bed of state on which she lay in her rich robes. It was the godparents who would take center stage at the ceremony.

Henry was fussing because the Earl of Oxford, one of the god-fathers, was late, delayed no doubt by the weather. After three hours, he gave the order for the procession to form in the Queen's great chamber. Cecily carried the Prince, who was wrapped in a mantle of crimson cloth of gold furred with ermine, and his long train was borne by the Earl of Lincoln. Watching Lincoln, Elizabeth wondered if he was resentful at being displaced in the succession first by Henry, and now by Arthur, but he appeared to be enjoying himself, chatting to Anne and Dorset, who, to Mother's delight, had recently returned to England after Henry had paid his debt to the French King. Still feeling shivery, she watched as Arthur was borne away, preceded by two hundred esquires and yeomen carrying unlit torches, and attended by a great company of lord and ladies. Mother, looking every inch the Queen, had gone ahead to receive her grandson in the cathedral.

Elizabeth was touched that Henry had assigned prominent roles to her kinsfolk. It was a measure of his gratitude toward her—and no doubt he wished his subjects to see her Yorkist relations publicly acknowledging Arthur as the heir to England, thus demonstrating their loyalty to the new dynasty. And it showed them that, in return, Henry was ready to treat them with the honor their blood deserved.

The only person who was absent was the Lady Margaret. She had pleaded a megrim, but Elizabeth had wondered if she did not wish to be seen to be taking second place to the Prince's other grandmother, who outranked her. But maybe she was misjudging Margaret, and she really was unwell.

Elizabeth wished she could be there in the cathedral, watching her son being christened. But she would not have felt up to it even if she had been permitted. Instead, she and Henry sat companionably together, sharing a ewer of wine and congratulating each other. Beside the bed stood the state cradle with its cloth-of-gold canopy and royal arms. It was enormous, and quite magnificent, made up with luxurious bedding of crimson cloth of gold, scarlet, ermine, and blue velvet.

"I've had two pipes of wine set up outside the cathedral, so that every man might toast the Prince," Henry told her. "I want my subjects to share in my joy."

"They will love you for that," Elizabeth smiled.

Soon, the trumpets sounded again and the great procession returned, with many rich gifts being borne aloft by the lords. Minstrels played as Cecily laid Arthur in Elizabeth's arms. Ancient custom decreed that his mother should be the person who first called him by his Christian name.

"Welcome, Arthur, my sweeting," she said, and kissed him. "May God bless you all the days of your life."

Then Henry gave him his blessing, too, in the name of Almighty God, Our Lady, and St. George. Arthur was laid in his cradle, in which the poor little mite looked lost, and the christening gifts were presented and admired by the royal parents. Then it was time for the Prince to be taken to the nursery that had been prepared for him, and for Elizabeth to get some much-needed sleep.

Days of celebrations followed, as England rejoiced. Arthur's birth was hailed as the beginning of a new golden age. Henry proudly showed Elizabeth ballads that had been written in honor of the Prince, on parchments decorated with red-and-white roses, and her heart swelled with pride.

"Did you know, cariad, that Merlin himself foretold the birth of a new Arthur?" he asked, as they sat together reading these offerings. Although she still had a low fever, Elizabeth had healed quickly after the birth and was now up and sitting in a chair; she was not yet well enough to resume normal life and Dr. Lewis had been called in to prescribe some physick.

"I like my mothers to lie in for as long as possible," Mother Massey had told her, but she was so pleased with her patient's progress that she had approved her getting up.

Soon afterward, she pronounced her completely recovered, and after Michaelmas, Elizabeth presented herself at the door of the Abbot's chapel and was churched and purified, wearing a new gown of crimson velvet and russet damask. She was still suffering the after-effects of the ague, however, and her knees trembled as she knelt before the altar.

Fervently, she gave thanks for her child, for the blessing of motherhood, and for surviving the perils of childbed. She prayed too that she might come to love Arthur as he deserved; already she felt fiercely protective toward him, so love would surely follow.

When the ceremony was over, she sat enthroned in her great chamber under her canopy of estate, and distributed alms for the poor. Now she was ready to resume everyday life, and Henry returned to her bed. It was a joyful coupling, and he was gentle, but she prayed that God would give her a little respite before she fell pregnant again. The thought of going through another painful delivery was daunting.

Her feverish malaise lingered into October. Only then did she begin to feel strong again. Before the court left Winchester, she made a generous offering to the cathedral in thanksgiving for her return to health. Prior Hunton was delighted.

"Madam, we shall use your bounty to enlarge the Lady Chapel where Prince Arthur was christened. I have long wanted to install larger windows with beautiful glass, and I hope also to commission wall paintings of the life of Our Lady. Your arms will have pride of place, in gratitude for your wonderfully generous gift."

"It is the least I can do, Father Prior, in return for the kindness and hospitality you have extended to me," she said, and knelt for his blessing.

They moved eastward to Farnham Castle, where Arthur's nursery was to be established. It was the palace of the bishops of Winchester, and Bishop Courtenay had suggested to Henry that it would be a perfect residence for the Prince, for the air was clean and healthy and the location convenient for visits from the royal palaces near London. Henry had leaped at the idea, for Courtenay had abandoned the Usurper to join him in Brittany, and Elizabeth was happy to entrust her son to him, as she had known him in childhood, when he had served her father. He was now Keeper of the Privy Seal and utterly dependable. He would be a careful and diligent guardian.

Henry had laid down rules for the management of Arthur's nursery, but it was Elizabeth who interviewed and appointed the lady governor, the nurse, the rockers, and the chamber servants. As lady governor, she chose the amiable and capable Lady Darcy, who had been in charge of Ned's nursery and could be relied on to vouchsafe Arthur all the love and care he needed and which, she thought guiltily, she herself still seemed unable to give him.

As they walked around the spacious nursery apartments at Farnham, Lady Darcy admired the rich hangings and cushions of crimson damask, the carpets, and the fine but practical warming dish and laundry basins of brass and pewter.

"His Grace has thought of everything," she said approvingly.

"Our son is not strong, and he needs careful nursing," Elizabeth told her, "but the world does not know that. We are relying on your discretion, Lady Darcy."

"Of course, Madam."

"We worry that he is vulnerable to infection. My lord the King does not wish him to be weaned until he is two, and we are content for him to remain at Farnham until then. Also, he requires that the wet nurse's meat and drink be essayed for poison every day. We cannot take any risks with our precious jewel."

"Of course, Madam. I will see that his Grace's orders are carried out to the letter."

It was with a guilty sense of relief that Elizabeth departed for Placentia to rejoin Henry. She told herself she should not feel blameworthy, for she had discharged her chief responsibility of appointing trustworthy attendants to care for Arthur. And she could not have chosen anyone better than Lady Darcy. It was not necessary for her, his mother, to be with him, and it was impractical, for queens had duties to perform. She herself and her siblings had been raised by their lady mistresses; it was the way of the world. Arthur was in the finest place. She had done her best for him.

Yet her conscience kept telling her that she should feel some pang at being parted from her baby. Arthur was deeply important to her, but still she could not feel for him that all-encompassing love that other mothers clearly felt for their children. She prayed constantly that, one day, it would come; and she told herself that a good mother, after all, was one who cared for her children, looked to their advancement, supervised their upbringing and education and, later, ensured that they made advantageous marriages. She had made a creditable beginning with all that and knew that she always would continue to look to Arthur's best interests.

Lying next to Henry the night after she arrived at Placentia, the bedclothes rumpled with their lovemaking, she thought she might go mad if she could not rid herself of this guilt. It occurred to her that she might be armoring herself in case Arthur was taken from her. Because once you loved, you laid yourself open to loss— and what could be worse than the loss of a child?

"We must see to your crowning, Bessy," Henry said, rising from bed and stretching the next morning. "I thought not to tire you while you were pregnant, but now I will order that preparations be made."

"That would be wonderful," she said, admiring his lean and muscular body, and wishing that he would climb back between the sheets and take her in his arms. But his mind was now on coronations and state affairs, and she had lost him for the present.

There was no point in lying abed now. She got up and summoned her women to dress her, then went to her chapel for Mass. There, she was astounded to find Cecily in tears, sitting in the royal pew.

"Whatever is wrong?" she asked, hastening to her. "Cis?"

Her sister turned a tear-streaked face to her. "It's the King!" she sobbed. "He is having my marriage to Ralph annulled. I am not to go back to Upsall or ever see him again."

Elizabeth was speechless for a moment. "What? He hasn't said a word of this to me."

Cecily dabbed at her eyes. "He summoned me to his closet this morning and said that Ralph is not a fitting husband for me because his father supported King Richard."

"But Lord Scrope was one of those pardoned after Bosworth."

"The King still suspects his loyalty. But Ralph is no enemy to him, I swear it. Bessy, can't you speak to his Grace and plead for us to be allowed to stay together? I love Ralph. I cannot bear the thought of being parted from him." Cecily broke down in tears again, her shoulders heaving.

"I certainly will," Elizabeth said. "Wait here."

The King, she was informed, was at breakfast.

"Let me pass," she commanded the guards, and swept past them into Henry's lodgings. He looked up in surprise as she burst into his dining parlor and gestured to his servants to leave them.

"Cariad, to what do I owe the pleasure? You seem agitated."

"Indeed, I am!" she retorted. "I have just heard the most appalling news. My sister is in grief because her marriage is to be annulled. It was the first I'd heard of it. I found her in my chapel, just now, crying her heart out. Tell me it isn't true."

"Elizabeth, sit down," Henry bade her, with the air of someone about to explain something to a child. "It is true. I have my doubts about the loyalty of the Scropes, and Ralph is not a fitting husband for Cecily. I have a far better match in mind, for I would see your sisters well married."

"And who might that be?" She was not prepared to be mollified.

"Lord Welles, my uncle. He is my mother's half-brother."

"I see." She did. Margaret had probably had a hand in brokering the marriage.

She knew Lord Welles. He had been in high favor with her father and one of those prominent Yorkists who had opposed the Usurper and joined Henry in Brittany. For that, he had received his peerage. He was a likable man, but twice Cecily's age, although that was not an argument that would wear with her husband.

She opened her mouth to protest, but what was the point? She would not win. That was as certain as the Last Judgment. When Henry had made his mind up, he was immovable.

The fight suddenly went out of her. She saw why the match appealed to him, for he must regard her sisters—or the men they would wed—as potential threats to his throne. It would benefit him to marry them off to his loyal supporters. She could not argue with that. But it was hard on Cecily, being forced to leave the amiable Ralph.

She comforted her as best she could, even as she guessed that Cecily thought she had let her down.

"I did my best," she told her, knowing that all the protests in the world would not have moved Henry.

Cecily shook her head. "Was ever princess so unfortunate? We are but pawns, Bessy, to be moved at a king's whim. And he will not listen, even to you."

The annulment was speedily granted, and, late in November, Elizabeth found herself standing with Henry in St. Stephen's Chapel, witnessing Cecily's wedding. The bride wore cloth of gold and a tragic countenance; the groom was attentive, coaxing—charming, in fact—and before the feast was finished, he had won from Cecily a poignant smile. Elizabeth allowed herself to relax a little. It would be all right. Welles would make her sister a good husband.

Henry and Elizabeth spent many hours together that autumn and over Christmas, making plans for her crowning and drawing up lists of the ladies who were to attend her, the rich apparel she would need, and the guests they wished to invite. But, over the festive season, Henry seemed troubled.

"There is a rumor gaining currency that more will be heard of the Earl of Warwick before long," he said, sitting down beside her to listen to a performance by the choristers of the Chapel Royal. "Some of my councillors have heard it, in taverns and churches, but no one knows where it originated. There are other rumors, too, that Warwick has escaped, or been murdered in the Tower, but he was there today, and very much alive and well."

She was pleased to hear that, for she had been worrying about her young cousin. But the rumors were troubling.

"Do you take these bruits seriously?" she asked.

"I think we need to stay alert," he said. "I can risk no threat to my security."

The choristers were waiting. Henry nodded, and their voices soared.

On a cold January day, Elizabeth was playing backgammon with Anne when Henry arrived and sent her sister away. She could tell from his face that he was agitated about something.

"Cariad," he said, joining her at the table, "I am very sorry, but your coronation must be postponed again. News has just reached me that a pretender to my throne has appeared in Ireland, claiming to be Warwick."

She was shocked. "But Warwick is in the Tower!"

"He is indeed—we've checked. But this Lambert Simnel— that may not be his real name—claims to have escaped from his prison there."

"And who *is* Lambert Simnel?"

"A mere boy; the tool—I fear—of some chance opportunist. It's an odd name. One of my agents told me that his name is John, so it may be made up. The frustrating thing is that we're very much in the dark about this conspiracy, and what worries me is that people are being taken in by this imposter. One, I might add, is Lord Scrope." He looked at her as if to say *I told you so*, which she tried to ignore. "By all reports, the boy is well spoken, handsome, and gracious, and he apparently gives an accurate and convincing account of his past. Some think he really is Warwick. And he is bragging that he means to overthrow the Welsh milksop who has seized his crown." He snorted contemptuously.

"Someone must be coaching him," Elizabeth said, clenching her fists in outrage. Anyone who moved against Henry threatened Arthur, too.

"Exactly my thoughts," Henry agreed. "I think it is some prominent Yorkist with a close knowledge of the court and the royal family."

"But prominent Yorkists will know that Warwick is in the Tower!"

"Ah, but they might believe that he *has* been spirited away." Henry hesitated. "They may even want to believe it, just to dis-

countenance me. This lad may be a front for one who has pretensions to the crown but dare not come out in the open. And, Bessy,
I have reason to fear it may be your cousin Lincoln."

She was about to protest, but realized that he could well be
right. Henry's victory at Bosworth had put paid to Lincoln's hopes
of a crown. Those who wanted a Yorkist king on the throne would
readily back his claim. It was certainly possible that Lincoln had
secretly groomed Simnel as a pretender to mask his own intentions.

"He pledged his allegiance at my accession," Henry said, "but
I've always found it hard to trust him. He was Lord Lieutenant of
Ireland under the Usurper. Do you not think it significant that
this pretender has emerged in Ireland?"

"You may be right." Still she was reluctant to accept that a
member of her house was a traitor. "What will you do? Arrest
him?"

"No." Henry's smile was grim. "I'm having him watched and
my Council is trying to find out more about Simnel. I've tight-
ened security at the ports and am ready to act swiftly if need be.
Do not worry, cariad. We will deal with this pretender." He made
to stand up, then paused. "What do you know of Sir James Tyrell?"

The question startled her. "Why do you ask?"

"The Usurper made him governor of Guisnes in the Calais Pale.
He's still there, and I am pondering on whether I should confirm
his appointment."

"All I know of him is that he was sent to the Tower to collect
items from the Wardrobe for the investiture of the Usurper's son,
and he was there at the time my brothers disappeared."

Henry frowned. "You think he was involved?"

"I don't know. I have often wondered. Probably it was just a
coincidence."

"Hmm. According to my clerks, he received several high offices
from Richard in the months afterward. Yet he did not fight at
Bosworth and so escaped being attainted for treason. I've sounded
out others on his worthiness, and he's served me well in Guisnes
so far, so I will confirm him in the post."

He kissed her and left. She sat there, wondering why Richard had given Tyrell those high offices. Had his service and abilities really merited them? Or were they rewards for a deed secretly done?

She must not think that way. She must rely on Henry's judgment, which was more objective than hers.

There was no more news for a while. As she traveled to Farnham in February to visit Arthur, Elizabeth felt uneasy, as if a storm was about to break. The threat from Simnel, she feared, would not go away.

At four months, Arthur had put on weight, although he still looked delicate. When she held out her arms to him, he shrank back against Lady Darcy's ample bosom and regarded her warily.

"That's no way to greet your lady mother, my lord Prince," the lady governess chided him. "Come now." She handed him to Elizabeth, who kissed his downy head and tried to feel maternal. Her inability to do so made her panicky. Even a sweet gummy smile failed to tug at her heartstrings. What she did feel was an overwhelming pity for this frail little boy who lacked for nothing materially, but whose mother could not love him. And yet, she would have died to protect him, for he was of her blood and he was vulnerable. Maybe that was a kind of loving.

She returned to Westminster feeling miserable. What a sorry mother she was. She made up her mind to visit Arthur more often.

"How is our son?" Henry asked, when he arrived in her chamber for supper.

"He is doing well," she said. "He's certainly heavier, and he is smiling and taking notice."

"Good. That's reassuring. I will go to see him myself soon." He smiled at her, but there was a look in his eyes that perturbed her.

"Is something wrong?" she asked, laying down her knife.

There was that shifty expression again. He had done something she wasn't going to like.

"Bessy, I have some concerns about your mother."

"What?" He had always been courteous to Mother, had chosen her to be Arthur's godmother. "What concerns?"

He swallowed. "I cannot forget that she imperiled my cause when the Usurper was reigning."

"She aided it!" Elizabeth was quick to spring to her mother's defense.

"But she made her peace with him and voluntarily submitted herself, you, and her other daughters into his hands."

"She had no choice!"

"Didn't she? Had she remained in sanctuary, he could not have schemed to wed you." So there it was, still festering, his anger at Richard trying to take her from him.

"By leaving, she betrayed those who had, at her most urgent entreaty, forsaken their lands and fled to me in Brittany, on the understanding that I would pledge myself to marry you."

Elizabeth's cheeks were hot with anger. "Henry, listen to me, once and for all, please! We could not stay in sanctuary. Leaving seemed, as I have explained before, to be the only course open to us. If Mother had not let us go, Richard would probably have taken us away by force, as he did my brother York. Our remaining there was causing embarrassment and inconvenience to the Abbot; Westminster Abbey was under siege. It was a terrible time, and we thought your cause lost."

He did not look convinced. "But she must have known that I would try again. I had sworn to marry you, and I meant to keep my vow. She schemed to wed you to the Usurper, and if the marriage had taken place, you would have been lost to me, and those loyal noblemen who, at her urging, took my part could never have returned to England without danger to their lives."

She was shocked to realize how deeply his resentment went, how savage a blow her mother's actions—and her own—had dealt him. She had hoped they had been forgiven. She'd believed Henry had understood why she had acted as she had.

Evidently that understanding did not extend to her mother.

It did not make sense. She reached across the table and laid her hand on his. "Henry, this is history; none of it is news to you, so why grieve about it now? You have never shown any resentment toward my mother. On the contrary, you restored her royal status and you have always treated her honorably. You chose her above your own mother as godmother to our firstborn. You are even thinking of making her queen of Scots."

Henry withdrew his hand. "I have never trusted her. I have been keeping a watchful eye on her. Now that we are threatened by the pretender Simnel, my Council has advised me to deprive her of the wherewithal to make any more mischief."

She could not credit that he had it in him to be so two-faced. "What have you done?"

"The Council has issued a decree depriving her of all her possessions. I have taken her property into my hands, and Parliament will allocate her a pension."

She was momentarily speechless. "And you waited until I was away to do this!"

"Elizabeth, calm down. This is a matter of security."

"You really think that my mother would plot to overthrow us—and her grandson—in favor of some upstart who has the idiocy to claim he is Warwick? She would not do that for the real Warwick! This is madness."

Henry's expression darkened. "You forget yourself, Madam. None could hold the book so well to prompt and instruct this stage play as she could."

"I can't believe you said that!" She was horrified, unable to grasp that he had dissembled for so long. "How much is the pension to be?"

"Four hundred marks."

"That is less than Richard assigned her."

"It is more than she deserves. She will be an example to others to keep faith."

"Henry . . ." she began, but suddenly her vision cleared. "I know why you are doing this. You're making an excuse to relieve yourself of the responsibility of providing for her."

He banged the table, anger flaring. "You have me all wrong, Elizabeth! Your mother is a busy, negotiating woman, and it was she who hatched the conspiracy against the Usurper."

"No, it was your own mother."

"Whoever it was, yours was in the thick of it, and she might well decide to plot against me, too."

"But why?"

He paused. "I think she anticipated that you would enjoy more influence as queen, the kind of influence she enjoyed in her day, and I believe she is extremely discontented with me, thinking you not advanced, but oppressed."

"That's not true. I am contented with my life and she knows it. She has never made any complaint against you. You are not making sense, Henry. Why would my mother plot against you when it could only be to the detriment and ruin of her own daughter and grandson? She worked indefatigably to bring about our marriage. And even if she did resent my having too little power, she would know that I'd have even less if you were deposed."

Henry's eyes were like steel. "But what if she believes her sons to be still living?"

"Then she has even less cause to support someone who claims to be Warwick!"

His mouth set stubbornly. "I still don't trust her, and I cannot afford to take any chances at this time. Forgive me if I am being overcautious. Your mother is to retire to Bermondsey Abbey tonight, and her son Dorset is to be kept in the Tower until the threat from the pretender is past."

"Bermondsey Abbey? But what of her lease on Cheyneygates?"

"That can be broken."

"Henry, please . . ." She was beside herself now. "My mother is no traitor. She leased Cheyneygates because she wanted a quiet life. Don't look at me like that."

But there was no reasoning with him, and no point in arguing further, for she could only lose. "May I at least visit her?" she asked.

"Of course."

"And what of my sisters? Where are they to go?"

"They can join your household. Bridget remains with your mother. As she is promised to God, Bermondsey is a fitting abode for her. Remember, it has long enjoyed the patronage of royalty. My own grandmother, Queen Katherine, the widow of Henry the Fifth, died there fifty years ago."

She knew her history, and that he had omitted to mention that

Katherine de Valois had been sent to Bermondsey in disgrace after her secret marriage with Owen Tudor was discovered, and had perished bearing a child.

She had lost her appetite. Her supper lay before her, untouched, the sauce congealing.

"If you will excuse me," she said, "I will go and see my sisters."

"Of course," Henry said, his tone cool. But it was not as frigid as the icy rage she was feeling toward him.

She found Anne and Katherine tearful, bewildered at the change in their lives. They were only eleven and seven, and they were missing their mother and sister already.

"I will take you to see them," Elizabeth promised, inwardly cursing Henry for what he was doing to her loved ones.

They went to Bermondsey the very next day. The great abbey stood by the Thames, opposite the Tower—not a happy outlook for Mother, given that her sons had probably perished there. It might be an important house, but as Elizabeth and her sisters were escorted by the guest-master to the boarders' lodgings, she noticed that it was poorly kept and showing signs of neglect.

Mother's drawn face lit up when she saw them, but then she collapsed, weeping, into Elizabeth's arms.

"Say you have come to take me away from here," she begged. "This is a horrible place."

Elizabeth felt tears stinging her own eyes. "Alas, my lady, would that I could! I have done my utmost to persuade the King to let you leave, but he is adamant. He is obsessed with security, with this pretender in Ireland."

"The councillors accused me of supporting him!" Mother wept. "As if I would do anything to harm you, or sweet Arthur."

"I know that," Elizabeth reassured her, guiding her to a chair. Her sisters were weeping and six-year-old Bridget was clinging to her skirts. Another girl stood quietly in attendance. Elizabeth recognized Grace, one of her father's bastards, of whom Mother was fond.

"This is so unjust," the old Queen sobbed. "I just want to go home to Cheyneygates. *Please*, will you speak again to the King for me?"

"I will," Elizabeth promised, looking around her and shivering. This lodging might have been fine hundreds of years ago, when it was built, but it was cold and damp, and smelled of river water.

"The earls of Gloucester built these apartments," Mother told her, following her gaze. "They were benefactors of the abbey in the thirteenth century. They are now used for boarders, and the monks don't charge, which is why the rooms aren't very comfortable. But they are obliged to keep a permanent residence for the use of the King. Not that any king would want to stay here." She reached for her shawl and wrapped it around herself.

Elizabeth now saw why Henry had chosen Bermondsey. Mother could lodge here at no charge to him. She was disgusted at his parsimony and his stubborn refusal to see how unjust he was being.

"I will speak to him again," she said. "I will tell him that you cannot stay here."

"Oh, thank you!" Mother breathed, wringing her hands.

They stayed for dinner—simple fare of bread, pottage, and tough chicken wings, served by the unobtrusive Grace—and spent the afternoon with the Queen, before bidding her a reluctant, emotional farewell.

"I will come as often as I can," Elizabeth promised, hating having to leave her mother in this depressing place.

She returned to Westminster, determined to see Henry, but was informed that his Grace was in council. He would try to see her later. She could settle to nothing in the meantime, envying her sisters their ability to enjoy a game of dice.

When Henry did come, they had gone to bed, for it was late in the evening. He looked drawn and was in no very good mood, regarding her warily.

"You wanted to see me, Elizabeth," he said.

Resentment had been churning in her since their quarrel the evening before and had been fueled by her visit to Bermondsey. "I did."

"I suppose it's about your mother. Well, it must wait. I have far more pressing matters to deal with now."

"No, it cannot wait!" she retorted, her fists clenched. "She is in grief, immured in that horrible, dank place."

"You exaggerate, Madam. She is lodged in the royal apartments, by my order."

"Royal? They might have been in the thirteenth century, but they are dismal now. You should try lodging in them yourself!"

Henry sat down and rested his head against the back of the chair. "Elizabeth, I am weary and beset by problems. I don't need this now."

"Then say the word and let my mother go back to Cheyneygates. That is all you have to do. She is no threat to you, I assure you. Henry, please!" She slid to her knees before him and raised her hands in supplication, her eyes swimming with tears.

He gazed down at her and she saw him hesitate.

"If you care for me, my lord, and do not wish to condemn me to a life of worrying about my mother, then I beg of you, grant me this favor. I myself will stand surety for her, although I assure you it is not needful."

"Bessy," he said, in a kinder voice, and his use of her familiar name gave her hope—soon to be dashed. "Bessy, I cannot let her leave Bermondsey. You shall have money to make her lodging more comfortable, but she must stay there. There have been new developments today."

She did not want to hear about them. She could only think desperately of how she was going to explain his cruel intransigence to Mother.

"Bessy," he said again, taking her hands. "My priority has to be the safety of the realm. I am learning that kings have to make unpalatable decisions. While there is any suspicion attached to your mother—and I am not the only one who doubts her loyalty, I assure you—she must remain where she is. It is not what I want; it is a necessity."

Dejected, she rose to her feet and took the other chair. "I cannot agree with you, and I know her better than anyone, but what does my opinion count for?" Her tone was bitter.

Henry sighed. "There are powerful people behind this Simnel conspiracy. We now know that he's the bastard son of an organmaker in Oxford, and he's twelve years old, the same age as Warwick. My intelligence reports state that he was coached in his role by a priest, Father Symonds, who supposedly had a dream that he would be tutor to a king. All quite innocuous, you might think, a plot thought up by fools. But the likelihood is that Symonds has been acting on behalf of Yorkist interests."

"But who?" Reluctantly, she could see the danger.

"Do you not think it significant that this conspiracy originated in Oxford, not far from my lord of Lincoln's house at Ewelme? And that meddling Bishop Stillington has been living in retirement at the University of Oxford since soon after Bosworth. I'm in no doubt that he is involved and I've ordered that he be summoned before the Council."

"Him again! It was thanks to him that I was declared a bastard and Richard was able to take the throne."

"Well, he shall answer for himself once more. I've pardoned him before, and I won't be pardoning him again." Henry looked pained. "I hope you see, Bessy, why I cannot free your mother. I do not wish this to lie like a sword between us."

She shook her head. "The thing is, Henry, I don't see. But I have no choice but to bow to your will, however much it grieves me. Just imagine how you would feel if it was your mother who had been incarcerated in such a place as punishment for something she had not done."

He stood up abruptly. "I am for my bed. I am sorry that you are so upset." It was no apology at all. As the door closed behind him, Elizabeth dissolved in floods of tears.

The next day, she went alone to Bermondsey.

"I tried, God help me, I tried!" she wailed to her mother. "He is made of stone, and so suspicious. But, once this pretender is dealt with, I will press him again and make him listen, I swear it."

"Do not fret, Bessy," Mother said sadly. "You are a good, kind girl, and I know you have done your best. Don't worry about me. I will learn to like it here."

"He said he would give me money to make it comfortable," she told her. "I will bring furnishings, rugs, and hangings to cheer you—and toys for Bridget."

Bridget looked up at that. She was a stolid child, still a little slow, but winning.

"We are both grateful, aren't we, Bridget?" Mother said. "Now, Bessy, tell me more about this pretender."

A week after Mother retired to Bermondsey, Henry had Warwick paraded in procession through London to St. Paul's Cathedral, where he attended Mass.

"With rumors about the pretender flying thick and fast, I want the people to see that the real Warwick is here in London, alive and well," Henry said, as he stood with Elizabeth in the porch at Sheen Palace, adjusting his robes before departing by barge for the City and the Bishop's palace, where there was to be a reception after the procession. "I've invited Lincoln to attend. It's best to keep him under my eye, and Warwick knows him. You will see your cousins later today when I bring them back here."

Elizabeth felt tense as she watched him leave. She had not seen Warwick for nearly two years and had often worried about how his imprisonment was affecting him. And she too was suspicious of her cousin Lincoln.

Late that afternoon, a colorful procession arrived at Sheen, the King at its head. She saw it from her window. Henry himself brought Warwick and Lincoln to her chamber, and she rose and extended her hands to her younger cousin, who looked older but thinner than she remembered.

"My lord of Warwick, it does me good to see you," she said.

He regarded her dully. "Thank you, my lady," he said, staring around the room at the sumptuous tapestries and the lords and ladies gathered there.

"Edward?" she prompted. "Are you well?"

He did not answer.

"Here is Margaret," she said, beckoning forward his thirteen-

year-old sister. Margaret embraced her brother, visibly moved to
see him. He let her do it, standing there stiffly, but did not respond. The girl looked distressed and bewildered.

Elizabeth welcomed Lincoln, noticing that the tall, dark young
man before her was more reserved than she remembered. But he
too was looking at Warwick with some dismay, so perhaps he was
as concerned as she was to see him so unresponsive. As Margaret
tried to coax some sense out of the boy, Lincoln leaned forward.

"I spoke with our cousin earlier, or tried to," he said in a low
voice. "He's as innocent as a year-old child. He can't tell a goose
from a capon."

"I am deeply saddened to hear it," Elizabeth replied.

"Being shut up in the Tower does not help," Lincoln muttered.

"The King has his reasons," she said coldly. It was not Lincoln's
place to criticize his sovereign. Warwick was of unsound mind, it
was true, and harmless in himself, but merely by existing, he
posed a threat to Henry and might always be a focus for malcontents. Nevertheless, she felt sad for him when, at the end of what
must have been a bewildering day, he was returned to his dismal
existence in the Tower.

Henry now summoned Bishop Stillington before the Council.
"I want the truth about these damnable conspiracies, and I'm sure
he's behind them," he told Elizabeth. He was furious when Stillington refused to obey the summons, claiming the protection of
the university, where he stayed entrenched throughout March. In
the end, a fuming Henry was forced to issue a safe conduct.

"It's the only way he will agree to meet me," he growled. "And
I have no choice, for I needs must examine him. He wants it to be
in private. By God, that he should dictate terms to me!"

He saw the Bishop at Windsor. Elizabeth was not present, but
Henry came to her chamber afterward, and he was not a happy
man.

"He will say nothing," he sighed, as he slumped in the chair by
her fireside. "Well, I'm going to keep him here under house arrest
until he decides to talk. And if he doesn't, he can stay here. It'll be
one troublemaker out of the way."

Elizabeth poured him some wine, wondering if his real reason for incarcerating Stillington was his fear that the Bishop would say something indiscreet about that old precontract story. It might be nonsense, yet its consequences had had such a profound impact on her life that she lived in dread of it being resurrected by Henry's enemies. She was glad that Stillington was being silenced.

The next day, Henry hurtled into her privy garden, white-faced. "Lincoln has gone!"

"Gone?"

"Disappeared, fled in the night. If that doesn't proclaim his guilt in this pretender business, pigs will fly! He means to be king, Bessy. I've suspected it all along."

It was all too believable.

People were shocked at Lincoln's treachery, and even more so at the news that he had surfaced in Flanders, where Aunt Margaret, the Dowager Duchess of Burgundy, had welcomed him.

"We can say goodbye now to all hope of a peaceful solution," Henry growled, pacing up and down the garden. "Margaret has declared herself my enemy. She'd give anything to undermine my crown." He paused, absentmindedly breaking off a leaf and crushing it in his fingers. "She does not care that our marriage united York and Lancaster. My agents warn that she means to pursue me with insatiable hatred. And Fate has just dealt her a powerful weapon in Lincoln."

"I fear so," Elizabeth said, drawing her mantle closer about her against the April chill—and the chill in her heart. "She must hate me, too, for being the means of your gaining the crown."

Henry gave her a sharp look. She had spoken without thinking and, too late, she remembered that he did not like it to be thought that he owed his throne to her. "I think not," he said. "More likely, she resented your displacing her as the eldest daughter of York, and then outranking her as queen of England. She is a silly and shameless woman, but dangerous, too and, given this chance, could prove a serious threat to us."

"She should be pleased to see her niece reigning in honor and with such a fine son, in whom runs the blood of her house."

Again, Henry gave her that look, and she realized she had referred to herself as reigning. Well, she *was* reigning, even though she might not rule.

When he had gone to meet with his Council, she remained on the bench, heedless of the cold breeze, feeling somehow guilty because one of her blood had come out in open rebellion against the King. She feared it might set Henry against the House of York and make him doubt the loyalty of anyone with Plantagenet blood. He had, after all, been suspicious of her mother, with no justification whatsoever. Maybe he was even entertaining doubts about her own fidelity. The very idea depressed her.

That evening, making an effort to demonstrate her support, she invited him to a private supper.

"I am so worried about this situation," she said, as they sat down to spring lamb with prunes. "What measures will you take against that traitor Lincoln?"

Henry's eyes narrowed. "I have not decided yet."

"But you must move against him—"

"I said, Elizabeth, that I have not decided."

It dawned on her that he would not tell her because he did not trust her. She sat there for a moment, feeling like crying.

"I hope you don't really believe that I too would turn traitor and betray your plans," she said scathingly.

Henry had the grace to look embarrassed. "Not for a moment," he said hastily. "I am sorry you should think that."

"I will not meddle in your affairs again," she told him, hurt.

"Bessy, please. Let us not quarrel."

"I was only trying to support you," she declared.

"I'm sorry, it has been a trying day." He reached across the table and took her hand. "I'd rather just put it all to one side."

She smiled at him, still unsure whether he had entertained any doubts of her, and led the conversation in a different direction. Then she made the mistake of saying that she intended to visit her mother on the morrow.

"No," Henry replied firmly. "Not at this time."

"She has nothing to do with this conspiracy," she insisted.

"We don't know that, Bessy."

Exasperated, she threw down her napkin. "Henry, please get it out of your head that my mother is a traitor."

"Let me remind you that if her plans had come to fruition, you would now be Richard's queen and I a penniless exile." His tone was cold.

"That was not her plan. It was his, and she endorsed it when she saw that I was willing to make the sacrifice—and when we had abandoned all hope of you. It was not what we wanted, Henry, but it was the only way to ensure a future for us. How many times do I have to keep saying this?"

Again, he looked chastened. "I cannot help it, Bessy. I have learned to trust no one."

"But you can trust me—and my mother."

He gave her a wary smile.

"You can!" she cried. "And I *am* going to visit her tomorrow."

The smile vanished. "No, Bessy."

"Is it now so dangerous to visit an aging woman in a monastery?" she erupted.

"I wish I could answer that. And you will obey me."

"Oh, I am ever the dutiful wife!" she returned. "But at some cost to myself." She rose. "Have I your leave to retire?"

He stood up. "Don't think the worst of me, Bessy. I have to consider the security of my kingdom and the views of my Council. Just be patient. Once we have dealt with this pretender, and all is well, you may see your mother."

And with that, she had to be content.

Henry was riding north to deal with Simnel. An invasion was expected at any time.

As he and Elizabeth walked down the stairs to the courtyard where his retinue was waiting, he took her hand. "I will miss you, cariad." She knew he was trying to say more, for matters had been tense between them since their quarrel three weeks earlier.

"I will pray for your safe return," she said. She was dreading the separation, fearful that he might never come back—in which case, she could only hope that Lincoln would deal kindly with her and

Arthur. And yet, what king would tolerate a rival? Look how
Henry had treated Warwick. She shivered. "God send you a great
victory," she continued, with feeling—and then, knowing she
dared not let him go into the unknown without making things
right between them, she pulled him to her, there on the stairs, and
held him so tightly that she could feel their two hearts beating
together. "Stay safe!" she enjoined him. "Come back to me!"

Below, the lords and ladies were smiling up indulgently at
them. Some looked as emotional as Elizabeth felt.

"You can count on it," Henry said, gazing down at her tenderly.
"Come, I must be on my way." He took her hand and led her
through the door. Outside, the sun was shining. "See how God
smiles on our righteous cause?" he said, indicating the glorious
weather.

He mounted his horse, then waited as she handed him the stir-
rup cup. "On Easter Day," he told her, "you will receive your full
dower at last. I know you have found it hard to live on the settlement I made on our marriage, but this should make a great difference."

"I thank you, my lord," she said, curtseying, as he dug in his
spurs. "God speed you and bring you safely home."

"Bless you, my lady," Henry said, and then he was gone from
her, riding away through the great gate, his lords following, all
looking splendid in battle array.

It was as she had suspected. At Easter, when she received the grant
of her dower, she read that the King's officers of the Exchequer
were to pay her all the dues from the estates and properties that
had been seized from the Dowager Queen Elizabeth. So she was to
profit from her mother's misfortune. It did not seem right. But
what could she do?

She contemplated disobeying Henry and visiting her mother at
Bermondsey. She needed to explain that this was none of her
doing. But she felt impossibly torn. It would be rash to defy her
husband, and she did not want to compromise the new tenderness
between them. Poor Mother would have to wait.

* * *

Elizabeth was staying with the Lady Margaret at Chertsey Abbey when, in May, her chamberlain came to inform her that the King had summoned them both to Kenilworth Castle.

"His Grace has received news of an imminent invasion and has commanded me to escort you both there to join him," he told her.

"At last, Henry will be able to settle this matter once and for all," Margaret said.

"I pray it will be settled soon," Elizabeth replied, her heart thudding in fear. "I cannot bear to think of him in danger."

Her first concern was for her child. Accompanied by Arthur's host, Bishop Courtenay, she hastened to Farnham Castle to collect her son, while Margaret made her way north separately.

"If the traitors invade now, we can claim sanctuary at Romsey Abbey, which is convenient for the coast," the Bishop informed her, as they set off from Chertsey. "From there, we can escape across the sea to safety."

Elizabeth prayed that would prove unnecessary, but, at all costs, she must keep Arthur safe. She was struck by the change in him. He was eight months old now, and a solemn little fellow, but he had gained weight and was stronger. Still, she was dismayed when holding him in her arms in the litter carrying them northward, she felt again that disconcerting sense of detachment.

Kenilworth Castle loomed ahead, a strongly built fortress on a great lake. They would be safe behind its mighty walls. Henry welcomed her warmly, but he could not spend much time with her as he was busy setting up his headquarters and planning strategies. That night, he fell wearily into bed beside her, content just to hold her in his arms.

"It seems that there is much support in Ireland for Simnel," he muttered. "Only Waterford has declared itself loyal. That scoundrel the Earl of Kildare and other rebel lords have had the lad crowned as Edward the Sixth in Dublin Cathedral. By God, they will crown apes next!"

"It cannot have any legal force," she said sleepily, remembering how popular the House of York had always been in Ireland. "And they are fools if they believe Simnel to be Warwick."

"Well, soon, God willing, we will teach them a lesson. If I wasn't concerned about Lincoln invading, I'd have gone to Ireland myself and dealt with them."

Early in June, an army headed by Lincoln landed in Lancashire.

"We march to defend my kingdom," Henry announced, and everyone moved quickly. Elizabeth felt a tightness in her throat as, with Arthur in her arms, she stood with Margaret before the gatehouse at Kenilworth, watching her husband and his great company march off toward Coventry.

Then began the long, tense wait for news. Over the next three weeks, messengers informed them that the armies had moved south, then swung east, in some grim game of chase. Then, just as she and Margaret thought they might go mad with anxiety, another emissary, caked in mud, was brought to the Queen and threw himself at her feet.

"Your Grace, the King has won a great victory at Stoke, near Newark. The Earl of Lincoln is slain and the pretender Simnel taken prisoner."

Elizabeth turned to Margaret and hugged her. "He is safe! Henry is safe! And God has granted him another great victory!"

Margaret's eyes glistened with tears of exultation. "He has triumphed again. This battle, truly, has put an end to the wars of Lancaster and York. The dynasty is safe."

They dined that night, at Elizabeth's insistence, in the oriel window of the magnificent great hall, where a table was set up and they could celebrate in royal style, toasting the King and his marvelous victory.

Chapter 15

1487–1490

Elizabeth settled herself with her embroidery on a window seat high in the keep. It had become her favorite perch, affording her a view of the gatehouse and the long approach to the castle. She had sat there every day, watching for any sign of someone arriving. And today her barely suppressed impatience was rewarded, for she could see a column of horsemen in the distance, their banners flying. And there, at the front, was the royal standard!

She flew down the spiral stair, nearly tripping in her eagerness, calling out to anyone who was listening that the King was coming. She sped across the courtyard to the royal apartments where Margaret and Arthur lodged, and rallied them, sweeping Arthur up in her arms. By the time Henry came clattering through the gatehouse, she was waiting with them in the bailey. At the sight of her, he swung himself out of the saddle and embraced and kissed her heartily in front of his men and the household, who had come running at his approach. Elizabeth feasted her eyes on him, drinking him in, as he greeted his wide-eyed son.

"Welcome, my hero!" she cried, as cheers erupted around them. Then it was Margaret's turn, and she hugged Henry, weeping with joy.

"Well done! Well done!" she kept saying.

Elizabeth had supper served again in the great hall, with the trumpets sounding and the King's captains seated as guests of honor.

"Thanks be to God, I have triumphed over my enemies," Henry declared, "and, with our fair son thriving, my throne is more secure than it ever was."

"And Lincoln has paid the price for his treachery," Margaret said, daintily cutting up her meat.

"We are well rid of that perfidious dark Earl," Henry replied. "My only regret is that he cheated the hangman and deprived me of the chance to make a public example of him."

"His infamy is surely notorious by now," the Earl of Oxford observed. He had been Henry's commander-in-chief at Stoke Field.

"What of Simnel?" Elizabeth asked. "What will you do with him?"

"He is but twelve years old," Henry said, draining his goblet. "I do not make war on children. Besides, he was the tool of others. I shall set him to menial work in my kitchens. That should disabuse him of any notions of his importance."

"That is a meet reward for him. And he may make good in your service."

"He is young enough to be molded," Henry said. "If he gives satisfaction, I will look favorably on him." He laid down his knife. "And now, cariad, we can think of happier things. I will free your brother Dorset; I know now that he is no threat to me. And we must start planning your coronation. And next month, I think, we can make a progress into East Anglia. Sir Edmund Bedingfield has long been pressing me to stay with him at Oxburgh Hall. The shrine of Our Lady of Walsingham is not far from there, if you wish to make a pilgrimage."

It crossed her mind that he wanted her to. Our Lady of Walsingham was known to aid those who wished for a child, and Elizabeth had not conceived again since Arthur's birth. She would go to the shrine; it would do her good in many ways.

"Can I see my mother now?" she asked, helping herself to some strawberries.

"You may," Henry smiled. "If she wishes, she may visit you at court, too. I will make sure she has enough money for her personal expenses, and order the Royal Wardrobe to send furnishings to make her lodging more luxurious."

"Must she stay at Bermondsey?"

"I think it best. I cannot maintain two queens in my kingdom. And I imagine that she has acclimatized to it now."

It was useless to argue. Henry had made his position plain. He had not really suspected her mother of treason. This was all about money.

After the court returned south, Elizabeth hastened to Bermondsey. Henry had been true to his word, for she found the Queen Dowager much better housed. Tapestries graced the stone walls, cushions were plumped on the chairs, and there was a carpet on the floor and silver candlesticks on the table.

Mother was overjoyed to see her, and the talk was all of Stoke and Arthur and the progress in Norfolk. Then, after a much better dinner than Elizabeth had been served before, Mother showed her Bridget's school books, while the child played unheeding with her dolls.

"She is going to Dartford Priory, where the standard of education is high," she said, looking concerned. "I have been tutoring her myself. Do you think she has made progress?"

Elizabeth looked at the primers in dismay. Bridget was rising seven, but her script was untidy and clumsily formed. She was reminded of Warwick's backwardness. Could it be that Bridget was similarly afflicted? She had always been slow, and her speech and deportment left something to be desired.

"I think so," she said tactfully. "But it's a long time since I've seen her work."

"She finds learning challenging," Mother said unhappily. "I don't think she is making any progress. Marriage is not an option, for your father and I vowed her to God, and I so want her to go to Dartford. It's one of the richest convents in the land and has a wonderful reputation for prayer and learning. But will they take her?"

"My lady," Elizabeth said, grasping her hand, "Dartford enjoys royal patronage. She will be welcome for her royal birth alone."

"If I had my freedom, I would go and visit the Prioress and explain my concerns."

"The King has said that you may visit the court when you wish. I am sure he would let you go to Dartford, especially for this purpose."

"Would you ask him for me? You see, Bridget can enter the priory as a boarder before entering the novitiate, and be tutored in the school there. It would be of great advantage to her—Dartford offers the best education a girl could have."

"I will speak to him. But—I must ask this—is Bridget fitted for the religious life? Will she be happy at Dartford? I fear it might be too demanding for her."

"We can at least try her there. I am sure they will let me know if she is not suited to the life. But there is one huge favor I must ask, Bessy. Could you fund her dowry?"

"Of course," Elizabeth agreed, thinking that at least some of the money wrested from her mother would be put to a use that benefited her. But she still felt guilty for having profited from Mother's misfortune.

Elizabeth was aware of public anger about her coronation being delayed. Her women gossiped, and even at Bermondsey her mother heard talk, especially among the other boarders.

"I'll wager the root of it is Henry's determination to suppress the House of York," Mother said tartly when Elizabeth next visited her. "Yet the people love you. If he is not careful, he will lose the hearts of his subjects, who are already angry that he has not treated you as England's rightful Queen."

Henry seemed to be aware of public feeling, for he was now planning a coronation that would exceed even his own in splendor.

"Mark me, it is an act against his stomach and put upon him by necessity and reasons of state," Mother seethed, yet Elizabeth felt that was unfair.

"He has risen magnificently to the occasion," she countered. "There are to be jousts and feasts. The guest list is endless. It all sounds wonderful. Henry means to use my coronation to proclaim the legitimacy of the Tudor dynasty to the world, but I also believe it will be an expression of his love for me. He has just written to the Pope, saying he feels he has come to a safe haven after all his troubles. He said to me that I am that haven."

As soon as she had spoken, she felt guilty. Mother had no safe haven in life, no husband to cherish her, and likely never would, for she was fifty now. And she would not be a part of the coronation. None of this was her fault, but Elizabeth's conscience troubled her because, while she herself was enjoying a full life lived in luxury and great state, her mother was mostly confined to these rooms, her freedom limited, her triumphs past. She was always painfully aware of that.

But Henry gave permission for Mother to visit Dartford and speak to the Prioress. All went satisfactorily, and it was decided that Bridget would enter Dartford Priory as a boarder after Christmas. Again, Elizabeth felt a pang for her sister. How sad to be confined to a cloister at seven. Surely, if Bridget wasn't fitted for the life, the Prioress would say so. But what if she looked more to the prestige of her house than to a little girl's happiness? Would she—knowing that the girl had been vowed to God—let Bridget go?

Royally gowned, Elizabeth and the Lady Margaret sat in a window of the hospital of St. Mary Spital in Bishopsgate, with lords and ladies crowding around, to watch the King, the victor of Stoke, making his triumphal entry into a capital city packed with cheering crowds. All resentments set aside, they roared their approval as, cutting a splendid figure on his horse, his armor gleaming, he was escorted in procession by the Lord Mayor to St. Paul's Cathedral, where the *Te Deum* was to be sung in honor of his victory.

And then it was Elizabeth's turn.

On a chilly Friday in November, decked out in robes of velvet and ermine, she left Greenwich with Margaret to make her state entry into London, attended by a great train of lords and ladies. At the landing stage, she boarded the richly decorated royal barge that was to convey her to the Tower. The citizens had planned a spectacular water pageant, and the banks of the Thames were crowded with spectators, come to see their Queen and the marvels that were to be performed. When her barge glided out on the river, they roared their acclaim, bringing tears to her eyes.

"Truly, they do love you, my dear," Margaret smiled, as Elizabeth waved through the window of the gilded state-house. As the oarsmen gathered speed, they were joined by a flotilla of craft, come to escort the Queen to the Tower. There was the Mayor in his barge, with the sheriffs and aldermen, and numerous boats filled with the guildsmen of London. Every vessel was festooned with banners, silk streamers, coats of arms, and badges.

The barge of the bachelors of Lincoln's Inn sailed alongside Elizabeth's, making her start, because it contained a huge model of the red dragon of Cadwaladr, which, by a clever device, spouted flames of fire into the Thames. Manning it were the handsomest legal graduates she had ever seen, who hailed her as they kept pace with her barge and played sweet music. The crowds loved them, yelling and whistling their acclaim.

In the craft that followed, there were other pageants for Elizabeth's pleasure, and the sound of trumpets, clarions, and other minstrelsy filled the air. She was so stirred by the pageantry that she never wanted the journey to end. All too soon, however, they were approaching the Tower, and there was Henry, waiting on Tower Wharf to welcome her. The entire court looked on as he embraced her lovingly and kissed her.

"You look wonderful," he said, and led her across the draw-bridge to the royal apartments in the Lanthorn Tower, where, that night, he created fourteen new Knights of the Bath and Elizabeth joined him for a reception in their honor.

* * *

The next day, she could not eat her dinner for excitement, because immediately afterward she was to ride in state into London. Abandoning her meal, she hastened to her apartments, where her sisters were waiting for her. Cecily was eighteen now and her red-gold beauty had blossomed. She looked radiant, for, against all expectations, she had found happiness with Lord Welles. Anne and Katherine were looking after Bridget, who had been enjoined by Mother to be on her best behavior. How pretty they looked, the daughters of York, all together again at last.

They dressed Elizabeth in a kirtle of cloth-of-gold damask in white, symbolizing chastity, and a matching mantle furred with ermine and fastened with silken tassels. They brushed her long hair until it shone and placed on her head a coif of netted gold cords, the very latest fashion in France. On top, they set a circlet of gold garnished with precious stones. It was a gift from Henry to mark her crowning, and exquisitely wrought.

As she emerged from the Tower, with Cecily carrying her train, she found the great procession assembled and waiting, and a sea of faces acclaiming her. She climbed into an open litter richly hung with white cloth-of-gold damask and upholstered with matching cushions, wishing that her mother could see her. Above her head was a canopy on gilt staves borne by four of the new Knights of the Bath. Eight white horses drew the litter up Tower Hill, preceded by Jasper Tudor and followed by the Queen's Master of Horse, leading her steed, and several chariots bearing the great ladies of the realm. Then marched the lords, and she was pleased to see Lord Stanley prominent among them, for he had been such a support to her when she'd needed it most. It was a magnificent procession, devised to impress the people, enhance the reputation of Henry's dynasty, and court universal approval of his Queen.

In the City, Elizabeth was overwhelmed by the sight of the huge crowds that had come to cheer her through the capital. She passed through streets hung with tapestries or hangings of cloth of gold. Children dressed as angels, saints, and virgins sang sweet songs to greet her. Her heart was full when, finally, the litter trundled into the precincts of the palace of Westminster. But the greatest triumph was still to come.

On St. Katherine's Day, Elizabeth went to her coronation gloriously attired in purple velvet and ermine, and the circlet Henry had given her. Again, Cecily bore her train as she entered Westminster Hall beneath a purple silk canopy of estate supported by the barons of the Cinque Ports. Attending her were the Lady Margaret, Aunt Suffolk, and Margaret of Clarence. A striped runner had been laid between the palace and the abbey, and she walked in procession along it, with the people surging forward behind her, everyone eager to snip off a piece of the stuff on which she had trodden. But the crowd was too boisterous; she kept looking over her shoulder nervously and soon realized, to her horror, that it was out of control. People were lying in the street, being trampled, and her ladies were scattering in fright. No! Someone must do something! This day could not be blighted by the spilling of blood; it was too auspicious an occasion.

Too late, the guards and marshals stepped in to break up the fray. The mob was pushed back and the wounded carried away; one or two looked dead. There was blood on the runner. It took an immense effort for Elizabeth to compose herself and wait for her ladies to regroup and walk on into the abbey. She was praying that no one was hurt too badly. Tomorrow, she would make inquiries.

In the hushed calm of the church, she moved slowly along the nave, supported on either side by the bishops of Ely and Winchester. Her uncle, the Duke of Suffolk, carrying a gilt scepter, went before with the Earl of Arundel, who bore the rod with the dove, and Jasper Tudor, bearing her crown. The abbey was packed with the nobility of England and the princes of the Church, and they were all craning their necks to catch a glimpse of her, the living symbol of the union of York and Lancaster.

Henry was nowhere to be seen. "The day is to be yours alone," he had told her. But she knew that he was watching the ceremony from behind a latticed screen covered with tapestry, which stood between the altar and the pulpit.

John Morton, who, on Cardinal Bourchier's death, had been made archbishop of Canterbury in reward for his loyalty to Henry, was waiting to receive her. She prostrated herself full-length before him as he prayed over her, exhorting her to be virtuous. She knelt for her sacred anointing with holy oil on the forehead and breast; it was an exalting, precious moment. The coronation ring, symbolizing her faithfulness, was blessed and put on her finger, and she received the scepter and rod. Then, with great solemnity, the Archbishop raised the crown and reverently placed it on her head.

The sense of elation lingered as, still wearing her crown, she presided alone over the coronation banquet in Westminster Hall. Henry and his mother were watching the proceedings behind another lattice, in a window embrasure to the left of the high table. Archbishop Morton, seated on Elizabeth's right, was the guest of honor. When all were assembled, the trumpeters and minstrels began playing and a procession of knights entered the hall, carrying a vast array of dishes up to the high table, where the Queen would make her choices before they were offered to others.

The royal cooks had excelled themselves. Elizabeth was not hungry—who could be, on such an exciting day?—but she stared in wonder at the two dozen offerings that comprised the first course, and helped herself to small portions of brawn, venison with spices and dried fruits, spiced swan, and perch in jelly, most of which she only picked at. She did better with the custard royal and fruit confections that followed. And then the trumpets sounded again and—unbelievably—another course was borne in. There were twenty-seven choices this time, of which she could eat only morsels of roast peacock and crayfish. Beside her, the Archbishop was tucking heartily into venison in pastry. Elizabeth only had room left for a baked quince and a spoonful of a jelly formed like a castle. Tomorrow, she knew, she would be hungry again and regret not having sampled more of this wonderful food.

After the feast, she distributed largesse and the Kings of Arms formally thanked her on behalf of the lucky recipients. Then, after another fanfare, fruit and wafers were served to her, and the Lord Mayor came forward and offered her the traditional golden goblet of hippocras. As she departed, the guests called down God's blessings on her.

"You have caused many a true Englishman's heart to rejoice today," Henry said, as he took her in his arms in the Painted Chamber, where he had been waiting for her. Flushed with wine and triumph, she surrendered herself eagerly to his kisses as his hands moved busily with her laces and the purple velvet gown slid in a rich heap to the floor.

The next morning, they went in procession with the Lady Margaret and the princesses to hear Mass in St. Stephen's Chapel, attended by eighty peeresses, ladies, and gentlewomen. Then Elizabeth sat enthroned in the Parliament chamber and received her guests, with the Lady Margaret seated firmly at her right hand, and Cecily and their aunt, Katherine Wydeville, the Dowager Duchess of Buckingham, who had married Jasper Tudor, now Duke of Bedford, on her left. After the state dinner that followed, Elizabeth led the dancing with her ladies.

Now she was truly a queen.

In March 1488, although Arthur was only eighteen months old, Henry began looking for a bride for him. Nothing but the best would do for his heir, but he ventured into the royal marriage market cautiously, for, he had confided to Elizabeth, he feared that the other ruling houses of Europe regarded him as a usurper. He was jubilant, therefore, when the prospect of a marriage alliance with mighty Spain opened up, and came hastening to her chamber to tell her the good news.

"The Spanish sovereigns are ready to commence negotiations," he told her, embracing her warmly. "I never thought to see it. They are the most renowned and respected monarchs in Christendom."

"What marvelous news!" she cried, kissing him. She had long admired King Ferdinand of Aragon and Queen Isabella of Castile, who had not only united Spain by their marriage, but were now winning a centuries-long Christian war to recapture the kingdom from the occupying Moors. How could she not applaud a queen who actually ruled her kingdom and even led her armies in battle?

"An alliance with Spain will assuredly bolster England's standing both at home and abroad," Henry said. "It will be a sterling endorsement of my crown."

"They have several daughters, I believe."

"Five. The Infanta Catalina is the youngest. She is two years old. Her sisters are earmarked for great marriages, so this alliance will bring us valuable political connections."

It was Elizabeth's duty, as a queen and a mother, to ensure that her children married well, and she was present when the new Spanish ambassador, Dr. Rodrigo de Puebla, arrived in England and was received by Henry. He was a portly, swarthy, fussy little man, and his first request was to see Prince Arthur.

Arthur was duly brought from his nursery by Lady Darcy, who set him down on the floor so that he could make a wobbly bow to his parents. He was a pretty child with his auburn hair and fair skin, and looked delightfully engaging in his cloth-of-gold finery as he toddled over to his father and held up his arms, wanting to be picked up. Henry swooped down and lifted him high, to his evident delight, and he nestled there, crowing to himself.

"A fine prince, your Majesty," Puebla beamed. "He is tall for his age."

Henry inclined his head graciously.

"I wonder," the ambassador continued, "if your Majesty would allow me to see him, er, stripped."

It was not an unreasonable request. The sovereigns must be assured that they were not buying a deformed or sickly bridegroom for their daughter.

Henry smiled and put Arthur down, patting his head. "Of course. Lady Darcy, will you undress his Highness?"

The lady governess led her charge to the fireside and proceeded to remove his clothes. When he was naked, she twirled him around, as if it was a game. Elizabeth sent up silent thanks that Arthur had put on weight and looked healthy.

Dr. de Puebla nodded. "Your Majesties have cause to be proud. The Prince is a child of remarkable beauty and grace. I see in him so many excellent qualities. In looks, of course, he favors his beautiful mother." He bowed to Elizabeth. "I will report all this to my sovereigns."

Henry bestowed another gracious smile on him, then signaled to Lady Darcy to dress Arthur and take him back to the nursery. "Let us proceed to business then," he said.

Elizabeth took that as her cue to retire. But after dinner, Henry came to her apartments frowning. "Dr. de Puebla clearly has reservations about the marriage. He had the effrontery to say that, bearing in mind what happens every day to the kings of England, it is surprising that Ferdinand and Isabella should dare to give their daughter at all. And that when I have striven to maintain the peace these past three years. But I suspect this is his own view, rather than that of the sovereigns."

Elizabeth felt affronted as well. The wars of Lancaster and York were past history now, and in Arthur the rival claims were united. After a tense few weeks, she and Henry were relieved when, in April, on the instructions of Ferdinand and Isabella, Dr. de Puebla was authorized to conclude the treaty of marriage between the Infanta and Prince Arthur.

The sumptuous red gown furred with miniver was tight. Elizabeth stood looking at herself in the mirror as her maids laced it up. She hoped she was not running to fat like her father; but he had been in his thirties when he put on weight, and he had loved gorging on rich food. She was just twenty-three, still in the bloom of her youth. She really must watch her diet.

A lady-in-waiting arranged the blue garter ribbon over her shoulder. It was St. George's Day 1489, and the feast of the Order of the Garter. Elizabeth and the Lady Margaret were to join the King for the annual ceremonies in St. George's Chapel, the glorious—and still unfinished—church built by her father at Windsor. She always felt a pang when she worshipped there, for it contained his tomb. He had been gone six years now, and she still missed him greatly.

But there was much to celebrate. Last month had seen the signing of the Treaty of Medina del Campo, which concluded the negotiations for Arthur's betrothal. Henry had been almost rubbing his hands in glee, for the Infanta was to bring to England a dowry of two hundred thousand crowns. It was a triumph of his foreign policy; Spain's recognition had established the Tudors in the top rank of European monarchies.

It would be many years, however, before the marriage could take place. Arthur was not yet three and Catalina only nine months older. Elizabeth knew from bitter experience that betrothals could be broken; she could only pray that this great marriage would come to fruition.

After the Garter celebrations, Henry rode north to York. The Earl of Northumberland had been murdered when the citizens rioted in protest against high taxation, and he was going to preside over the trials and teach them a lesson.

It was a joyous homecoming for, when he returned to Windsor, Elizabeth was able to tell him that she was again with child.

"That is the best news you could have given me, Bessy," he said, kissing her heartily. "Now, you must take great care of yourself and your precious burden."

He spent the long months of her pregnancy fussing over her. He lavished gifts on her—bolts of black velvet, russet cloth and soft linen, a carpet, feather beds filled with down, and sheets of Holland cloth. He laid down new rules for the confinement of a queen, for which his mother gave him detailed advice. He spoke often of the son who would soon join Arthur in the royal nursery. No husband could have been more attentive.

Elizabeth was content to be cosseted, spoiled, and indulged. The Lady Margaret was a constant, hovering presence, making sure that her daughter-in-law lacked for nothing. Mother Massey had once more been engaged and encouraged the Queen to practice her breathing exercises. Elizabeth spent a lovely, restful summer walking or sunning herself in the gardens, taking pleasure trips along the Thames, gossiping with her ladies, and visiting her mother at Bermondsey. She even made a trip to Berkhamsted to see Grandmother York, who sadly had aged a lot, but who took great pleasure in hearing about Arthur and life at court, and gave the Queen her hearty blessing when she departed.

On All Hallows Eve, Elizabeth took to her chamber at Westminster. Before she retired from public life, she went in procession to Mass in St. Stephen's Chapel, which was lit by torches against the autumn grayness. After the *Agnus Dei* was sung, she was led to her great chamber, where she stood beneath her cloth of estate and was served spices and sweet wine. Then her chamberlain's voice rang out: "My lords and ladies, I desire you, in the Queen's name, that you and all her people here present pray to God to send her a good hour."

That was the sign for Elizabeth to depart to her bedchamber, the ceilings and walls of which had been newly lined with blue hangings stamped with fleurs-de-lis of gold and hung with glorious tapestries. Dominating the room was a rich bed of estate, beside which was a smaller bed with a canopy of gold hung with velvet embroidered with bright red roses and covered with an ermine-trimmed counterpane. There was an altar on which were displayed several religious relics, and a great court cupboard laden with food.

Elizabeth turned to Margaret. "I know you had a hand in this, dear Mother, and I cannot sufficiently express my gratitude. These tapestries are exquisite."

"We thought it best to have ones woven with flowers and pastoral scenes, rather than people," Margaret explained. "We don't want the infant frightened by gloomy, staring figures!"

Elizabeth moved to the door and thanked the lords waiting outside; then her chamberlain drew the curtain over the door and closed it. From now on, no men, apart from the King and her chaplain, would be permitted to enter. For the period of her confinement, her ladies were taking on the roles of the officers of her household.

That afternoon, she was delighted to see Mother, who had come to visit her and stay for the birth. She was even more pleased when Henry, breaking his own rules, asked them jointly to receive the new French ambassador, who was related to the Queen Dowager. Of course, the Lady Margaret was present, ever amiable, ever attentive. Clearly, Henry no longer thought Mother a threat. Yet still—and Elizabeth had asked him again—he would not let her move from Bermondsey.

The last month of her pregnancy dragged, with little to divert her. Her bedchamber felt oppressive, with the hangings covering all but one of the windows. She wished she could have been present when Arthur was brought to Westminster to be dubbed a Knight of the Bath, but, even had protocol allowed it, she could not have been, for her pains began while the ceremony was taking place. Mercifully, her labor was quicker this time. At nine that night, Mother Massey laid her daughter in her arms, an angry, kicking little soul with a fuzz of auburn hair. Elizabeth felt a rush of love.

Henry came hurrying to see her. "A fair maid! Cariad, what a precious gift." He bent down to embrace her, then lifted the child from her arms.

"Margaret," he said, beaming at his mother. "She shall be called Margaret, after you, my lady mother." The baby gave him a grumpy stare and waved her tiny fists. "She's certainly healthy."

"You are not sad that she is not a son?"

"Not at all," he smiled. "We are young yet, Bessy, and there is plenty of time. For now, I am happy with this lusty girl. Princesses are the key to great alliances. We shall have to find you a great prince, won't we, sweetheart!" Little Margaret made her disapproval plain by yelling.

After Arthur had been brought in to see his sister and had stroked her head and said "Baby!" in an awed voice, Elizabeth was left to rest. She slept soundly after her travail, happy and contented, with her mother sitting sewing by her side.

The next day, the newborn Princess was carried to St. Stephen's Chapel in great state for her baptism. As before, Henry waited with Elizabeth until she was brought back to them for their blessing and laid in an oak cradle lined with ermine and covered with a cloth-of-gold canopy.

Later that day, in the Parliament Chamber, Arthur was created Prince of Wales. In the evening, Henry brought him to see Elizabeth and told her how well behaved he had been as he sat on the throne beneath the cloth of estate and presided over the feast held to celebrate the occasion.

"You'll make a fine king one day," he told his son.

"But not for a long time, I hope," Elizabeth said, stretching out her hand to her husband, as Arthur crawled across the bed to her.

She was still lying in when she received a personal letter from King Ferdinand, informing her that he had conquered the town of Baca in the kingdom of Granada, and had made great progress in the war against the Moors. *As our victory must interest all the Christian world*, he had written, *we thought it our duty to inform the Queen of England of it*. She liked that. He could easily have written only to Henry, or jointly to them both, but he had recognized her status as the rightful Queen of England.

She was thinking how she might respond when the Lady Margaret appeared. "I don't want to worry you, Bessy, but some of your ladies have caught measles."

Elizabeth instinctively bent over the cradle beside her. "Have they been in here?"

"No, thanks be to God. But I think you should remain in confinement until the danger is past."

"What of Arthur?" She was suddenly in terror. If he caught measles, he might not have the strength to withstand it.

"Henry is sending him to Richmond today. He thinks it is safer there. Shall I bring him to say farewell?"

"No. I don't want to put him at any risk." It came to her, forcibly, that only a mother who loved her son would deny herself the sight of him for the sake of his safety. Fearful as she was, a great sense of relief filled her heart. She did love Arthur! She wasn't an unnatural mother.

The measles outbreak persisted. Several ladies of the court died. Although Elizabeth had made a good recovery from Margaret's birth and was out of bed and sitting in a chair, she remained in her chamber, keeping the baby with her. She was not churched until the feast of St. John, the third day of Christmastide, and then only in private. Two days later, Henry moved the court to Greenwich to escape the contagion. There were no disguisings and fewer plays and entertainments, but he did sanction the appointment of a lord of misrule, who made much sport and good cheer.

By Candlemas, the measles outbreak had died away and the

court was back at Westminster, where Henry and Elizabeth went in procession to Westminster Hall, and thence to Mass. Afterward, they watched a play in the White Hall. That night, in the Paradise Bed, he took her in his arms and reclaimed her after the long months of abstinence. It was life-affirming to be one with him again. Afterward, as they lay drowsily, her head in the crook of his shoulder, he told her that he was increasing her mother's allowance. Silently she rejoiced, very sure that soon he would grant Mother the freedom to return to Cheyneygates.

Chapter 16

1491–1492

On a rainy day at the end of June 1491, Elizabeth's second son was born at Greenwich Palace. When he was placed in her arms, she fell instantly in love. Red-haired and sturdy, he was a true Plantagenet, the image of her father, and he could easily have passed for a child of two months.

Henry, gazing down on the lusty infant, was inordinately proud. "This little one's birth makes my dynasty doubly secure. We shall call him after King Henry VI, who, I am sure, will soon be made a saint—if all the gold I am spending in Rome is sufficient to stir the Pope! And it's my name, too, so a fitting one."

Elizabeth fleetingly recalled poor, confused Henry of Lancaster quavering in the Tower. He had been a gentle soul, unfortunate to find himself at the center of a civil war. God willing, his young namesake would enjoy a happier life.

Wrapped in a mantle of gold and ermine, and escorted by two hundred men bearing torches, the new Prince was baptized in the nearby church of the Observant Friars, in the same silver font used for Arthur.

He thrived. Elizabeth could barely let him out of her sight. This was what she had wanted to feel—but had never felt—for

Arthur; it transcended even her love for Margaret. Henry—or Harry, as they called him—was so much the image of her father that he won all hearts. She could not help but wish that he had been the firstborn son, rather than Arthur; he was infinitely stronger and there was something innately special about him, as if God had showered him with gifts and talents. Look at those plump little hands, stretching out to grab everything in reach! Beside him, poor Arthur was a weakling. At nearly five, he was a serious little boy, diligent at his lessons and striving to live up to his father's expectations. Harry, she knew, would never have to make an effort.

Alas, the maternal idyll could not last. Soon after Elizabeth had been churched, Henry established a household for their children at Eltham Palace, east of London. It stood in a bracing location on a high hill with commanding views over the City, and Elizabeth knew it well, for it had been one of her father's favorite houses. It was he who had built the soaring great hall.

When Henry told her, over dinner, that Harry was to be sent away with Arthur and Margaret, she burst into tears.

He squeezed her hand. "Eltham is not far from London. You will be able to visit the children whenever you wish. Lady Darcy will be in charge and Mistress Oxenbridge comes highly recommended as a nurse for Harry."

"I know. I appointed her myself. But I cannot bear to miss out on Harry's babyhood. It pains me to think he might grow fonder of his nurse than of me."

Henry smiled at her. "I'm sure that won't happen, especially if you visit him frequently."

"Oh, I shall. With your leave, I will stay there regularly."

"Of course. And when Eltham needs cleansing, we can send the children to Sheen or Greenwich. Both are well away from the unhealthy air of London. But your place is here with me, Bessy. You have your duties as queen. The children will be well cared for and, in time, you will interest yourself in their education and their marriages. That's what good mothers do."

She appreciated Henry's efforts to cheer her, but leaving her little ones, especially Harry, at Eltham was heartbreaking, all the more so when the baby gave Anne Oxenbridge a gummy smile as she took his swaddled form in her arms.

Lady Darcy smiled. "I know it's not easy leaving them for the first time, Madam. But young Prince Henry looks more than capable of taking change in his stride. We will keep him in good remembrance of you."

"Thank you," Elizabeth said, blinking back tears. "And I will come next week."

With her ladies following her, she made her way back through the palace. On the great hammerbeam roof of the hall, her father's gilded badges of the white rose and the sun in splendor still gleamed. If she closed her eyes for a moment, she could imagine that time had rolled back to when the vast empty space was filled with the Yorkist court, and that she was there, at the center of it, with her tall, magnificent sire, larger than life as she remembered. How proud he would have been of his grandchildren, especially Harry.

As her chariot bumped across the drawbridge, Elizabeth reflected that her children would be happy at Eltham. And next week, she would bring bolts of velvet, satin, and damask, to be made up into clothing for them. It was important that their royal state was observed from infancy.

She became a regular visitor to Eltham and was slowly growing accustomed to the separation. But life never seemed to go on smoothly. Always, there was something to worry about.

It was Anne, now sixteen, who told her about the gossip.

"I heard the other ladies talking," she said, as she prepared Elizabeth for bed. "There are new rumors that one or both of our brothers still live."

Elizabeth caught her breath. "There have been rumors before."

"I know. But where do they come from, Bessy? Is it just idle gossip or wishful thinking—or could there be any truth in them?" Anne flushed.

It was true that Henry's popularity had dwindled, for he had gained a reputation as a miser. But that was too simplistic a view.

He was building up the wealth that would bolster his dynasty, tightening the laws so that the great nobles could not rise up and make war as they had under Lancaster and York. Some of his measures were disliked, so it was no wonder that a few people harked back to the promising young Edward V.

"I wish I knew where these rumors originated," Elizabeth said, taking off her rings. "And I wish we knew for certain what happened to Ned and York."

Anne caught her eye. "Do you still think that they could be alive?"

"I have long wondered. But, in the absence of any news of them, I think, sadly, that we must assume they are dead."

Anne nodded. "I think so too."

The next morning, Henry arrived unexpectedly in Elizabeth's privy chamber as she sat among her women embroidering an altar cloth. His face was gray.

"Ladies, leave us," he ordered, and they disappeared into the great chamber in a rustle of silks.

Elizabeth had risen. Her first thought was for the children. Had something awful happened? "You look shaken, Henry. What is wrong?"

He sank down on the settle by the fire. "Another pretender has appeared in Ireland."

Her mind flew back to her recent conversation with Anne. Had this something to do with that fresh crop of rumors?

"A week ago, a Breton merchant ship docked in Cork. There was a youth on board, a fair young man magnificently attired, who bore himself with such dignity that the people were at once convinced that he must be of royal or noble blood. At first, there was talk that he was Warwick, escaped from the Tower. But then it was announced that he was your brother York. He's about the same age that York would be now, and he bears a strong resemblance to your father. My informants also report that he knows a lot about King Edward's court." Henry leaned back and sighed. "In truth, Bessy, I know not what to think."

She sank down beside him, trembling. Could this youth really be her brother? Had Richard been speaking the truth about the princes having just disappeared? Oh, if it was York . . .

Henry reached for her hand. "I know what you are hoping for. But, Bessy, if this young man really is your brother, many will say that he has a better claim to the throne, never mind the Act confirming my title."

"And we would be displaced—and our children. Oh, Henry . . ." She was wringing her hands. "You must understand how torn I feel. My brothers were robbed of their future; all these years my poor mother, my sisters, and I have been wondering what happened to them, always imagining the worst. Finding that York is alive would be the best news we could receive—and, for you and me, the worst." She was sobbing now.

Henry drew her into his arms. "I understand how you feel," he murmured against her hood. "But *you* must understand that I am King now; Parliament has named me so. If this lad is York . . . It all depends on what his intentions are, and who is helping him. And, Bessy, I fear he might be making a bid for the throne. The priority now is to find out if he is who he claims to be. So hold yourself in patience until we know what we are dealing with."

"I will," she said, knowing it would not be easy.

Anne and Katherine were agog when they heard the news.

"Do not mention this to anyone," Elizabeth cautioned. "We don't know anything for certain yet. The youth might be an imposter."

"And he might be our brother!"

"We'll meet that when we come to it," she countered, wondering how on earth Henry would deal with it. She was not optimistic, given his treatment of Warwick, who still languished in the Tower and looked to be there for good. York, if it truly was he, merely by existing could not be anything but her husband's enemy—and hers.

Within a few weeks, Henry had more information, which he relayed to Elizabeth as, wrapped in their cloaks, they walked in the autumnal gardens, the dead leaves crackling beneath their feet. "Four years ago, this boy was taken into the service of King Edward's godson, Sir Edward Brampton, who fled into exile in the Netherlands after Bosworth. He could have told the lad what he needed to know about your father's court."

"Yes, but do we know who he is?"

"Not yet. He might conceivably be King Edward's bastard; that would account for the resemblance. But, for all he claims to have been brought up at the English court until he was ten, he knows very little English."

Elizabeth felt torn between relief and sadness. "That's telling. No one would forget the mother tongue they had spoken for ten years. He must be an imposter."

"The brainchild of your aunt Margaret, no doubt," Henry said grimly.

"You think she's behind this?"

"Assuredly. She has doubtless been waiting for an opportunity to unseat me since Stoke. I'll wager that Brampton pushed the boy in her path and she took advantage of the situation. Probably she knows that the lad is not her nephew."

Elizabeth pulled her cloak tighter around her and thought back. "She never saw York. She might believe the boy's tale."

Henry looked dubious. "I think she's been looking out for a handsome youth to play the Plantagenet. She could have taught him all he needed to know to convince people that he was York—and arranged for him to go to Ireland to stir up the Yorkists there."

"She could have done, yes. But, Henry, this is all pure speculation. You don't know for certain if my aunt has ever met the boy."

"True," he conceded reluctantly, as they ascended the spiral stair to the Queen's lodgings. "But some conspiracy must have been formed before he appeared in Ireland. I'm still convinced it originated in Burgundy. That woman would do anything to overthrow us and replace me with any member of the House of York who is remotely suitable."

Elizabeth could not disagree, even though she hated the idea of any of her kin being actively hostile to Henry. It had been bad enough when Lincoln rose against him, but Lincoln had paid the price. Henry could not touch Aunt Margaret.

They had reached the door to her chamber and he raised her hand to kiss it. "I have accounts to check now, Bessy, but I will let you know if I hear any more about this feigned lad."

That warmed her heart a little. Even though she was sad that the pretender could not be her brother, she was pleased that Henry now trusted her enough to take her into his confidence.

He and she might believe that the young man in Ireland was a fraud, but they could not stem the tide of public opinion. The news of York's apparent survival seemed to have come blazing and thundering into England, arousing much excitement and speculation.

Henry showed Elizabeth the reports, exasperated. "There's no doubt now that this is all down to the magicking of the Duchess Margaret, who has raised up a ghost to vex me!" he fumed. "And a finer counterfeit than Simnel. This lad who calls himself Plantagenet seems to move people to pity and induce belief. It's as if they are gripped by a kind of fascination or enchantment."

He flung the papers on the table and joined her by the fireside. "He claims to have been spared by those who came to kill his brother. As if they would leave him alive!"

"We do not even know for certain that Ned is dead," Elizabeth reminded him. "Do you think this pretender will attempt an invasion of England?"

"At present, he appears to be doing his best to win over the Irish, no doubt in the hope of raising an army. But my agents tell me he is having little success. I am following a policy of watch and see. It may be that this imposture will fizzle out before any harm is done."

"Oh, I do hope so," Elizabeth said.

They heard little more of the pretender for some time. Christmas passed, and soon spring was dawning. It seemed that the Irish had thought better of supporting him.

And then, in March 1492, as Elizabeth, pregnant once more,

sat watching Henry receive foreign ambassadors, his uncle of Bedford came in and passed him a note. Henry frowned, but continued with the reception. As soon as it was over, he hurried Elizabeth away to his closet.

"The pretender is in France. King Charles sent a ship for him and has received him with royal honors as King Richard the Fourth."

Her hand flew to her mouth.

"We have good cause to worry," Henry muttered. "France is angered at my alliance with Spain, her enemy, and Charles will be glad of an opportunity to discountenance me. He could even set an army at the feigned lad's back. Would you believe he has assigned him royal apartments and a guard of honor? The young fool must think himself in Heaven." He got up and poured himself a goblet of wine, spilling some in his agitation. "What worries me is that he has already subverted the loyalty of some of my subjects—fools who are discontented with my rule and the taxes I have to impose, others who are ambitious, those who enjoy change and novelty, but most the simpletons who love to nourish these bruits. By God, I govern a nation of idiots! I bring them peace, and this is how they reward me."

Elizabeth knelt at his feet. "If only you could obtain proof of who the lad really is—then you could publicly confound his claim, and all this will go away."

Henry huffed. "I've had every agent abroad looking for proof, but they have as yet found none. Yet I will not desist. I'll have them keep searching until we get to the bottom of the pot!"

Two days later, Elizabeth went to Bermondsey. She was alarmed to find Mother still in bed at noon, and her dinner left congealing on the table. The sight of it made her feel queasy.

"You are not well," she said, bending to kiss her and noticing the older woman's pallor. Her mother had lost weight since she had last seen her a month ago. "Let me make you comfortable." As she plumped the pillows, Grace entered the room and hastily curtseyed.

"Your Highness, my lady won't eat anything," she said.

"Try, just for me," Elizabeth coaxed, offering her mother a spoonful of syllabub, which she normally loved. But it was pushed away.

"Has she seen a doctor?" she asked Grace.

"She will not, Madam. She says it is an ague and will pass."

Elizabeth felt her mother's brow. It was cool. "This is not a fever. I will send my own physician. She knows Dr. Lewis and I'm sure she will let him treat her."

"I'm not deaf," came Mother's acerbic voice from the bed. "I will see him, if it pleases you. But there is nothing he can do for me."

Elizabeth froze. "What do you mean?" she faltered.

Her mother reached for her hand. "I have a canker in my breast. I've had it for some time. Now it is painful, and I feel my strength weakening."

"Oh, no. Why didn't you tell me?" Elizabeth embraced her, weeping. "Dear Mother, you mean the world to me. I would have got help for you. I will now, for I have heard of a lozenge made of silk, ivory, emeralds, sapphires, gold, silver filings, and the bone from the heart of a deer, which is said to be efficacious in such cases. I will obtain it for you, whatever the cost."

"Don't listen to quacks," Mother said, patting her shoulder. "They are just out to make money. No, dear child, I will not see a doctor because they have but one remedy for my complaint, which is to remove the breast, a slow and agonizing process. I'd be dead before it was done. I could not face an ordeal like that. I am quite content to leave this vale of tears and be reunited with your father. My only regret is that I will be leaving you and all my other be- loved children."

It was not what Elizabeth wanted to hear. She was still trem- bling with shock. She had troubles enough—and now this, the worst of all. "But I cannot bear to lose you. There must be some- thing else the doctors can do."

"No, Bessy, there isn't. Now, let us put this unpleasant business aside, and enjoy our time together. How are my grandchildren?"

Elizabeth dried her tears and tried to marshal her thoughts. As she spoke of Arthur's progress at his lessons, Margaret's naughtiness, and Henry's forward speech, she could not banish from her mind the terrible knowledge that her mother was dying. But she must be strong for her. It was what Mother wanted.

"I am with child again," she told her.

"That is the most marvelous news! When is the babe due?"

"July, I think."

Mother's face grew wistful. "Then I pray I will be here to welcome him."

"So do I," Elizabeth said fervently, tears welling again.

"You must take care," her mother said, with some of her old briskness. "Put your needs before others. I know you, Bessy. You are unsparing in your care for everyone, and in your charities. Promise me you will rest when you can."

"I will," she replied.

The old Queen nodded. "Is there any more news of the pretender?" Elizabeth had kept her abreast of events. Much as Mother had hoped that he really was her son, she agreed with Henry and Elizabeth that that was unlikely. But Elizabeth did not tell her that the feigned lad was in France. There was no point in alarming her—not yet.

"Grace tells me all the lay brothers' gossip," Mother said. "They say that some support the pretender because they think the King has done you a great wrong in denying you your right to reign."

"It sounds as if you agree with them," Elizabeth said gently.

"I did not say that. But you can see why some might welcome this pretender."

"If I am contented with my lot, then others should be, too," Elizabeth said. "Have you ever heard me complain? Have the gossips?"

Mother gave her a wry smile. "They would say that you are subjugated."

"That's nonsense!"

Mother shifted in the bed and winced. "Give me some of that cordial." She indicated a vial on the table. "It's poppy syrup. The infirmarer mixed it for me. It deadens the pain, but it sends me to sleep."

"Would you rather I left?" Elizabeth asked, not wanting to be parted from her mother now that she knew each time she saw her might be the last.

"No, stay a while. I like having you near me. There is no face I'd rather see." Mother drank the syrup. "That's better. Now what was I saying?" Her voice faded. Soon, she was deep in slumber. Elizabeth sat watching over her, taking in every detail of that care-worn pale face.

She put off taking to her chamber for her confinement until the last possible moment, so that she could visit Bermondsey as often as possible. She was worried that Mother would die while she was in seclusion and that she would not be with her. But Dorset and her sisters all promised to hold themselves in readiness and told her she was not to fret.

When she could delay no longer, she hastened to her mother's bedside. She could not bring herself to say goodbye, lest it upset them both, but she knelt for her blessing and kissed her tenderly when she said farewell.

"God keep you, my lady," she said. "You know how much I cherish you. May He watch over you for me."

"And may He be with you when your hour comes," Mother said, squeezing her hand.

The messenger arrived one fine June morning as Elizabeth was taking breakfast.

Anne brought the note to her. It was from Grace. She was unhappy about the way Mother looked and thought that someone ought to come.

By great good fortune, Cecily had arrived at court to be with Elizabeth during her confinement. She, Anne, and Katherine sent for Dorset and they all took a barge to Bermondsey.

When her sisters returned in the afternoon, Elizabeth did not need to be told the news, for she could read it in their tearstained faces. For a long while, they sat and wept together, hugging each other for comfort. It would take time for their loss to sink in, but all she could think of now was that Mother was at peace and beyond suffering.

"When we arrived," Cecily related, "she was alone, for Grace had gone to make her more cordial, even though she had refused it earlier. She was sleeping. I saw her shoulder move and then—no more. We sent for the infirmarer, for we did not know for certain that she was dead, and he confirmed it and sent for the priest to say prayers over her. Fortunately, she was shriven yesterday."

"Where is she now?" Elizabeth asked.

"In the chapel, lying on a bier before the altar. The monks are watching over her, Grace too. She was quite overcome." She drew a document from her pocket. "I have Mother's will here. Grace said that, shortly before she died, she asked that her body be taken by barge to Windsor to be buried promptly, without worldly pomp, in our father's vault, as he had wished."

Elizabeth took the will and read it. Her mother had had no worldly goods to leave her dearest children, as she had wished from the heart to do, but she beseeched Almighty God to bless Elizabeth especially and all her children. It brought tears to Elizabeth's eyes, and she wished that she had cherished and appreciated her mother more. In these last years, Mother had no longer been as remote and haughty as when she was queen consort. It had been much easier to love her.

As soon as he heard the news, Henry came hurrying to comfort Elizabeth. He ordered the court into mourning and took control of the funeral arrangements. As Mother had wished, there was no fuss. She was laid to rest two days after her death, at eleven o'clock at night, in St. George's Chapel, without any bells being rung or a solemn dirge chanted. Elizabeth's sisters attended the requiem Mass later that week, and Bridget was brought from Dartford Priory to join them. They reported that she was pining for Mother, and indeed for them all, and that she found life at the priory demanding. Elizabeth wondered if, with Mother gone to her reward, she might be able to remove Bridget, and wrote to the Prioress, asking for an honest report on how her sister was faring. Back came the prompt reply. She was doing well; most girls took time to settle. The Prioress asked the Queen to remember that Bridget had been vowed to God. The message was clear.

Elizabeth inwardly retreated. She had done her best and must now leave Bridget to God's care. Instead, she bowed to the wish of her half-sister Grace, who desired to enter the cloister, and wrote to the Abbess of Barking, asking if she would accept her into the novitiate and promising a dowry. Barking was a wealthy house much favored by the nobility; she could not have secured for Grace a better reward for the girl's care of Mother.

Mother Massey, once more engaged as midwife, made a great fuss of Elizabeth. "Losing your mother is a grievous blow, Madam, especially when you are about to give birth." Lying on her bed in her blue mourning robe, Elizabeth often found herself weeping. If Mother Massey found her upset, she had delicacies and confections brought for her, and made sure that one of her sisters was always sitting with her. "Distractions, that's what your Grace needs," she pronounced, "and you get precious little of them shut up in here. But company helps."

"The King comes when he can, but I wish I could see my children," Elizabeth murmured.

"Don't you go fretting about them, Madam. They're well looked after, I'm sure. You'll see them soon enough."

"It will be weeks," she sighed.

Her child, born early in July, was an exceptionally beautiful daughter. Henry gazed down at her in wonder and readily agreed that she should be baptized Elizabeth in honor of her late grandmother as well as her mother. Mother and daughter spent a few precious weeks together until little Beth, as they called her, was borne away to join the nursery household at Eltham. As soon as she was churched, Elizabeth hastened down there and thankfully gathered all her little ones around her, kissing and hugging them. Oh, how blessed she was to have such happy, healthy, pretty children.

Cocooned away from the world as she had been, Elizabeth had not realized how badly England's relations with France had deteriorated, for Henry had not wanted to worry her. But in October, the situation became critical, and war loomed. The King departed for France at the head of an army, leaving Arthur at Westminster to act as nominal regent in his absence, and Elizabeth at Eltham with their younger children.

She felt Henry's absence keenly. When she heard that he had laid siege to Boulogne, she was frantic with worry, beseeching God on her knees to keep him safe. She bombarded her husband with loving letters, begging him to return to her. And he did. For her sake—and to her astonishment—he raised the siege and concluded a peace treaty with King Charles; it was the measure of his love for her. He was back in her arms in November. She marveled at how close they had become in almost seven years of marriage, and that Henry had felt the parting as keenly as she had.

He was in a bullish mood as they rode together in the park at Eltham. "The treaty has put an end to Charles's support of the pretender. He is no longer calling him Richard the Fourth! I had hoped that he would deliver the boy up to me, but he merely banished him from France. I suspect he has gone to Burgundy. We shall see." They were out hawking, and he held out his gloved hand so that his falcon could alight on it. Tying her jesses, he grinned at Elizabeth. "I wonder what mischief your aunt Margaret will make for us!"

They soon found out. One afternoon, when Henry was helping her to make sense of her household accounts, an usher brought him a sealed letter. He read it carefully, making grunting noises, then frowned. "As I thought. Your aunt Margaret is acting true to form. At first, she pretended to be dubious about the feigned lad's claims, but then she said she had questioned him and been persuaded that he was indeed her nephew, raised from the dead, and she publicly congratulated him on his preservation. He has now been taken under the protection of her step-grandson, the Archduke Philip. Philip, the arrant fool, is treating him like a king. My agent writes that he has given him a palatial house in Antwerp, where he has the effrontery to hold court seated beneath the royal arms of England. When he goes abroad in the streets, he is escorted by a guard of thirty archers wearing his white rose badge.

Soon, he is off to Vienna, where that fox the Emperor Maximilian will no doubt welcome him as the rightful King of England. Pshaw!" He flung down the letter on his desk.

Elizabeth picked it up and read it. "He is still claiming to have been spared by those who murdered Ned. He says they were stricken with remorse and took compassion on him, then delivered him to the gentleman who had sent them to kill him, who took pity on him and preserved his life on condition that he swear on the sacraments not to disclose his identity for several years."

"An unlikely tale," Henry snorted. "The assassins would have known that their remit was to do away with the Yorkist heirs who posed a threat to the Usurper. Why kill one and spare the other? With the older brother dead, York would have been the true King of England." He took the letter from Elizabeth. "It's telling that the feigned lad will not be drawn on the details of your brother's murder or his own deliverance from the Tower. He says it is best to stay silent on such matters, for they may concern some who are still alive and stain the memory of some who are dead. That's a neat way of forestalling all discussion of the anomalies in his story."

"But my aunt has clearly swallowed the tale. Your agent says she takes pleasure in hearing the boy repeat it."

"And now I suppose the Flemings believe that the pretender escaped the hand of Richard by divine intervention, to be brought safely to his aunt. What concerns me, Bessy, is that many people in England are convinced he is York and think his survival miraculous—not just ignorant common folk, but important men, too."

Even now, Elizabeth found herself wondering if there was substance to it after all. Was it just possible that the boy was her brother? But she must never voice such a fantasy to Henry. She must be his support and mainstay and not indulge in wishing for the impossible. Her brothers were dead; they must be dead.

"I just wish I could get a look at this youth," she said. "I, of all people, would know at once that he is an imposter."

"When I get my hands on him, you will see him," Henry said grimly.

* * *

Against Elizabeth's unvoiced expectations, Arthur was growing into a promising boy, blessed with such charm and goodness that all who knew him loved him. He was six now and shooting up in height, although he would never be as robust as Harry.

"Arthur is too old now to be brought up among women," Henry declared during a wintry visit to Eltham, as they stood at a window and watched their children playing in the snowbound garden. Arthur was staring at a robin perched on a branch, trying to coax it to eat a crumb from his hand, while Margaret and Harry were rolling in the snow, pummeling each other. Their nurses hastened to chide them, but Elizabeth could not stop herself smiling at their antics and Henry laughed out loud. "That's the spirit. They're true Tudors, the pair of them."

He turned to her. "Your father set a precedent in sending his heir to live at Ludlow Castle, so that he could learn how to govern his principality of Wales. It's an excellent apprenticeship for a future king, and I've decided to send Arthur there after Christmas. He can preside over the Council of the Marches and Wales—nominally, of course, for now."

"It's good to see the tradition living on," she said, realizing that she would see Arthur only intermittently in the future and that this was the parting of the ways she had anticipated when he was a newborn. The prospect was daunting. It was not so much that she would miss him—but that she worried how much she would miss him.

"I'm appointing my uncle of Bedford to head the council," Henry continued, walking over to the fireplace and warming his hands. "Among the Prince's councillors, I'm including Dorset and Sir William Stanley. I'm still considering who should be president."

"Bishop Alcock held the post in my father's day and served him well."

"He's a sound man. Very well, Bessy, we'll have him. And I think that Sir Richard Pole should be the chamberlain of Arthur's household."

Elizabeth had mixed feelings about Arthur going to Ludlow.

She saw that it was desirable, but how would his health hold up in the rural fastness of the Marcher country? "We ought to appoint a physician. Dr. John Argentine served my brothers well, and I would highly recommend him to serve Arthur."

"Yes, I remember him." Henry frowned. "He came to me in Brittany that summer after the Usurper was crowned. He said he had fled England because it had become too dangerous for him. You will know that he attended your brothers in the Tower."

"Yes." She shivered. "My poor brothers. How dreadful their last days must have been, cut off from everyone they loved and in great fear. Dr. Argentine was probably one of the last people to see them alive. I think he deserves some mark of royal favor for his loyalty."

"Then we'll have him. Dr. Rede will go with Arthur, too. The boy is making great progress under his tuition."

A horrible thought occurred to her. "You will not send the other children to Ludlow, will you?" The idea of being so far distant from them all was appalling.

"No, Bessy. I am following the precedent set by your father. It is fitting that the heir to the throne be educated for kingship, but Harry, Margaret, and Beth will stay at Eltham with Lady Darcy, where you can see them often and supervise their lessons."

Elizabeth relaxed. Yet the old familiar guilt washed over her again, for the prospect of being separated from Arthur was far less upsetting than the prospect of being parted from Harry.

Chapter 17

1493–1495

Arthur had gone to Ludlow in February and, by all reports, had settled happily and was adapting well to his new role. Henry was pleased, poring over Bedford's letters and nodding his head in satisfaction. Elizabeth was relieved to hear that Arthur's health was giving no cause for concern. He was prone, especially in winter, to catch every cold and ague going around.

That spring, she traveled down to Dartford to see Bridget take her final vows. Her sister was twelve now and eligible to become a professed nun. Elizabeth still felt sad to think of her devoting herself to God at such a young age, but Bridget had written that it was what she wanted. Even so, as she was clothed in the white tunic and scapular and the black mantle and veil of the Dominican order, and dedicated her life to a strict regime of prayer and contemplation, Elizabeth shed a tear.

"I will write regularly," she promised afterward, when she was allowed a few minutes to say farewell to her sister in the guest parlor. "And I will continue to pay Mother Prioress for your keep."

"Thank you, dear Bessy," Bridget replied, still looking exalted after her profession.

"May God keep you," Elizabeth said, taking her hands and leaning forward to kiss her. But Bridget freed herself and drew back. Nuns were not permitted human contact. It suddenly seemed to Elizabeth that a great gulf had opened up between them.

There was a knock on the door. "It's time for Vespers, Sister Bridget."

Bridget curtseyed. "Farewell, Bessy. May God be with you."

On a blazing July day, Elizabeth was seated in her barge, about to take a pleasure trip along the Thames with her sisters, when Henry came bounding aboard. As Anne and Katherine rose to leave the state-house, he stayed them. "No, ladies, I have news and you can all hear it." He sat down beside Elizabeth on the cushioned bench and gave the barge master the order to sail.

"I've received intelligence from Burgundy," he said, a gleam in his eyes. "I know for certain now that the feigned lad is an imposter. His name is Perkin Warbeck and he is the son of a boatman of Tournai. He has not a drop of royal blood!"

Elizabeth knew she should feel relieved, as jubilant as Henry, but she had clung on to the faint hope that the young man might be York, and it was hard to let go of that fantasy. She had let herself imagine a joyful reunion, and York saying it mattered not that Henry was king, because he had no intention of pressing his claim, for he would do nothing to injure her or her children. But— unless, by some miracle, the real York ever surfaced—that would never happen now. She detected a similar disappointment in her sisters' faces.

"I've made a formal protest to Philip and Maximilian against their harboring such a dangerous rebel," Henry was saying. "At least now we know what we are dealing with. No one will take this charlatan seriously now."

But his optimism was misplaced. Warbeck's story had spread far and wide, and too many people believed it—or wanted to believe it. One night, Henry came fuming into Elizabeth's bedchamber and flung himself into a chair.

"There are still reports of conspiracies—too vague, all of them, to merit action, but worrying nevertheless. I'm told that felons have broken out of the sanctuaries to join Warbeck in Burgundy. My council suspects that many among the nobility have turned secretly to conspiracy. I'm sorry to tell you this, Bessy, but one of your own yeomen—one Edwards—has defected to Warbeck."

She was shocked. "I had no idea. I hadn't even missed him." That there should be a traitor in her household was horrifying.

Henry rose. "I'm sorry, cariad, but I'm not in the mood for bed sport tonight. I'm too angry about these reports. I'll leave you to get some sleep." He kissed her, picked up his candle, and left. She heard his guards spring to attention beyond the door.

She lay down, her head sinking into the soft bolster. It was worrying that people still believed Warbeck's claims, or were bent on exploiting them to their own ends, but they could be countered now, couldn't they?

Then the most disconcerting thought struck her. Did Henry really believe those intelligence reports about Warbeck's true identity? Or had they surfaced all too conveniently? Had his behavior tonight suggested that he still entertained at least a grain of doubt? Yet, surely, her rational self countered, if Henry was going to manufacture false evidence to prove the young man a fraud, he'd have done it long ago and spared himself months of anxiety? No, she was being silly.

The rumors of conspiracies had been misleading. The land had lain quiet for months and Elizabeth had long dismissed her fears as irrational. Little more had been heard of Warbeck and she dared to hope that he would trouble them no more.

But Henry was ever on the alert for danger. He had not dismissed the threat from Burgundy. "Yes, Warbeck is quiet—too quiet," he said, as they competed with each other at the archery butts at Sheen on a mild autumn morning. "But God only knows what he is up to in secret. And don't forget, Bessy, that your aunt is still harboring him, and I doubt she would pass by an opportunity to ruin me."

"But most people now seem to accept that Warbeck is a fraud." Elizabeth let loose her arrow.

Henry nodded. "I hope so. A good shot," he observed. "Let's see if I can beat you." He drew his bow. The arrow zinged through the air and landed just outside of hers. "It seems that you are winning!"

Later, as they walked back to the palace, their attendants following at a discreet distance, Henry took her hand. "I mean to discountenance Warbeck once and for all. Calls himself York, does he? Well, I'll put paid to that. I'm creating Harry duke of York. It's his due as the second son of the King."

Elizabeth beamed at him. "Nothing could please me more!"

Henry grinned. "We'll make a big festival of it, thumb our noses at our enemies, so to speak!"

"That would be wonderful!" But she grew wistful. What Henry would be proclaiming to the world was that her brother, the previous duke, was dead. It did not matter whether he was or not in actuality; what mattered was that people believed he was. Yet she could not but rejoice that the title was going to Harry.

Toward the end of October 1494, Elizabeth, Henry, and the Lady Margaret took a barge from Sheen to Westminster. That afternoon, Harry was to be escorted through London prior to his ennoblement. Last week, his father had given him a new courser for the occasion. Elizabeth had thought it a large horse for a three-year-old, but seeing him sitting so confidently in the saddle, shouting, "Look at me!" her fears dissipated. She wished she could be in the City to watch him go by, escorted by the Lord Mayor, the aldermen, and the guildsmen. He had been so excited about the procession and the ceremonies that were to follow. He reveled in being the center of attention.

When, finally, the cavalcade arrived in the palace yard, Harry was still sitting proudly on his courser. Chubby-cheeked and shining-eyed, he looked so sweet and noble in his long gown and feathered hat. Henry lifted him down and kissed him.

"I was good, all the way!" the child crowed, as his parents took his hands and led him into Westminster Hall, where the assembled courtiers cheered.

Three days later, Harry was deputed to wait upon the King while he dined. He stood there with a towel over his arm, as stiff as one of his father's new yeomen of the guard. Elizabeth was impressed by his stately demeanor; he looked as if he had been born to greatness. Again, she hated herself for wishing that he had been her firstborn. But he would be far better suited to kingship than Arthur.

When dinner was over, Henry signed his son with a cross and Elizabeth gave him her blessing. Tomorrow, with twenty-two others, he was to be made a Knight of the Bath.

"You will go now to receive your ceremonial bath, and then keep vigil in St. Stephen's Chapel through the night," the King said. "Do you think you can stay awake for that, Harry?" It was a lot to ask of so young a child. But Harry nodded eagerly.

"Yes, Father. I'd like to stay up every night!" Elizabeth remembered Lady Darcy saying that they always had a hard time getting him to go to sleep. "I can't wait to wear my new suit of armor!" It had been specially made for his investiture.

The night passed without incident and, in the morning, Harry was dubbed a Knight of the Bath. The ceremony of ennoblement took place the following day, when he was formally created duke of York in the presence of the whole court, both houses of Parliament, and the Lord Mayor and aldermen of London. Afterward, Henry and Elizabeth, crowned and robed in ermine, with Harry, proudly wearing his armor, walking between them, processed to Westminster Abbey to attend Mass as the watching crowds cheered.

The celebrations went on for a fortnight. There were three days of jousts, which saw Harry jumping up and down in excitement in the royal stand. It took all Elizabeth's patience to keep her son seated on his golden cushion. Five-year-old Margaret was there, too, very excited to be presenting the prizes.

Watching their children, two copper heads together, waving to the spectators, Henry murmured to Elizabeth, "I made the right decision to create Harry a duke. I was thinking of a career in the Church with a view to his becoming archbishop of Canterbury. It's a glorious way of advancing a younger son, and it could be done at the Church's expense, but—"

"No!" Elizabeth interrupted. "Harry will never be a church-man. He has not the temperament."

"Exactly my view. I think his future lies in the world. We must find him a great heiress to marry."

As he spoke, Elizabeth's attention was distracted by a loud cry from the spectators. A knight had been unhorsed, and the victor, helm doffed, was riding toward the royal stand to claim his prize. Henry murmured, "That's Sir James Tyrell, cariad. He has given good service these past nine years."

Elizabeth made herself smile at the thickset knight bowing in his saddle, and wondered if she was showing a fair countenance to her brothers' murderer.

They spent a wonderful, glittering Christmas at Greenwich. Arthur came up from Ludlow and Henry made much of him. The Prince was eight now and knew how to carry himself like a future king. His father's pride shone forth, and the people loved him. Elizabeth loved him, too, but not enough, not in the way she loved Harry, who was already resentful of Arthur getting all the attention and praise he thought should be his. It was wearing trying to reassure him that he was important, too.

When Arthur departed after Twelfth Night, the court moved to the Tower. The previous month, Henry had been apprised of the capture of a traitor, Sir Robert Clifford, who had left England for Burgundy two years before and espoused the cause of Perkin Warbeck. To the surprise of many, he had granted Clifford a free pardon and invited him to return to England. He had now been summoned to the Tower.

"I mean to question him myself," Henry said, as he and Elizabeth supped in the royal apartments. "He knows of others who were in league with Warbeck. I'll let you into a secret. Clifford was working for me, while posing as a traitor."

Elizabeth was stunned. She had believed Clifford false, treacherous, like those others who had defected to Warbeck.

"I am astonished," she said at last, "and that you did not tell me the truth about him."

Henry regarded her gravely. "I'm sorry, but sometimes such things must be kept secret. I would trust you with my life, but I would not have you bearing the burden of keeping sensitive information to yourself."

She felt better, hearing that. "Thank you. But I would rather have known. If he had discovered something about my brother . . ."

"Then I would have told you. Alas, it seems certain that York is dead. Were he alive, with all this ado about the pretender, he would surely have come forward."

Elizabeth rather doubted that. What could York expect from Henry?

"We do know for certain who Warbeck is?" She was watching Henry closely.

"Of course we do." He was adamant.

After he had interviewed Clifford, Henry came to her immediately, looking ashen.

"What's wrong?" she asked, taking his hands.

"Treason!" he growled. "Sir William Stanley—would you believe it?—has abandoned me for that feigned lad. My own dear stepfather's brother! He, who came to my aid at Bosworth and helped to win me the crown. He's my chamberlain, for God's sake! And there are others, too, men who have enjoyed my confidence. They have turned their coats." He sat down heavily and covered his face with his hands. "Stanley told Clifford he would not fight against Warbeck if he was the true son of King Edward."

Elizabeth shuddered. "But why would he abandon you?"

Henry raised his face to her. "Clifford was plain with me. Stanley resents my rule, my taxes, and my treatment of you."

"Me? But you have always treated me well. I could not ask for better."

"Stanley thinks we should be ruling jointly, like Ferdinand and Isabella." Henry looked away. It was a conversation they had always avoided.

Elizabeth said nothing, but just sat there, staring into the fire.

"At first, I could not believe what Clifford told me," Henry

said, breaking the silence. "I trusted Stanley. He has grown rich in
my service. I see him daily; I must be a fool, for I never doubted
his loyalty. God, Bessy, what a mess. I don't want to offend Derby,
for it's clear that he isn't involved, but I must deal with Stanley
with due severity, and make an example of him that will deter
others from throwing in their lot with Warbeck. There can be no
mercy."

Elizabeth was shocked that Sir William, who had worked with
her to put Henry on the throne, had betrayed him. How would
dear Father Derby feel when he learned that his brother was a traitor? And the Lady Margaret, William's sister-in-law? This would
touch her closely, too.

She rose and put her arms around Henry. "Yes, you must be
firm with this Judas. I will not plead for his life. For your own
security, let everyone see what happens to those who conspire
against you."

Sir William Stanley and his associates were arrested and condemned to death for plotting the death and destruction of the
King and the overthrow of his kingdom. Derby left court and
rode north to Lathom. He was an old man now and bowed by his
brother's fall. Before he departed, however, he assured Henry of
his loyalty and told him he would never have cause to distrust a
Stanley again.

Elizabeth spent much time at prayer during the twelve days of
executions that followed the trials, on the last of which Stanley
was beheaded before dawn on Tower Hill.

"Warbeck's cause is now as stone without lime in England, and
he must know it," Henry told her on that dour February day. "Yet
my spies report that, in return for their continuing to supply him
with money, he has pledged part of my kingdom to Maximilian
and Philip and promised to give them all my possessions, even our
children's toys!" He snorted in disgust. "He is raising mercenaries
for an assault on England and is counting on the affections of the
common people toward the House of York. Let him dare! We'll
soon deal with him."

He was on edge, badly shaken by Stanley's treason and Warbeck's threatened invasion. He was suspicious of everyone.

"I would see your sisters married to men loyal to me," he announced one suppertime, having pushed his uneaten meal aside. "Any fool might seek to wed one of them and seize the throne. Remember that Warbeck has no wife as yet!"

Elizabeth drew in her breath. "I understand, Henry, but please, I beg of you, find husbands my sisters can love. Think how happy we have been."

"Anne has a fine future ahead of her. She has long been betrothed to Lord Thomas Howard, the Earl of Surrey's heir, and it's high time they wed. He is a loyal subject and a good match for her."

With a sinking feeling, she thought of Lord Thomas, with his long, thin face and martial temperament—and fair, delicate, sensitive Anne, who was just nineteen. At least he was only a year or two older than her. Doubtless Surrey—who had been imprisoned after Bosworth for fighting for Richard—was keen to ingratiate himself with the King and win royal favor through his son. He had spent three years in the Tower, on account of Henry dating his reign from the day before Bosworth. When the King asked why he had supported Richard, he'd replied: "If Parliament set the crown on a post, I would fight for it, as I will fight for you." He had continued to show himself an honorable, upright man, and Henry had pardoned and released him, and restored his earldom. Since then, Surrey had further proved his loyalty. It was only natural that he wanted to succeed to his father's dukedom of Norfolk, which had been declared forfeit after the Duke was killed at Bosworth. Who could blame him for pushing this marriage, which would bind the Howards to the royal house by kinship as well as loyalty? If only his son was as prepossessing as he was!

But Anne submitted to her marriage without complaint, and Elizabeth helped to arrange it, working with Surrey to finalize the marriage settlement. It was a far cry from the royal match Anne might once have expected, but it was an honorable one, and she was marrying into the highest ranks of the nobility. Even so, Elizabeth shed a tear as her sister entered the chapel at Greenwich on Henry's arm and he placed her hand in Thomas Howard's.

Surrey had driven a hard bargain. Henry had refused to advance the marriage portion willed to Anne by King Edward, so Elizabeth had to provide the couple with an annuity, to which the King had agreed to contribute a small sum, and allowances for the upkeep of their household and for food and drink.

"I even have to maintain their seven horses," she complained to Katherine, "and pay for Anne's clothes." She could see herself having to do the same for Katherine, too, and held her peace lest Katherine had foreseen that and felt she begrudged it. Henry had not yet said who he had in mind for her, but she was sure that Katherine would be married off soon. How she was going to meet the expense, she did not know.

She missed Anne, who had left court and gone to live in Surrey's mansion at Lambeth. Her sister was pregnant already and sickly with it, so she was obliged to rest at home and was unable to attend Katherine's wedding to Lord William Courtenay, whose father had supported Henry during Buckingham's rebellion, fought for him at Bosworth, and been rewarded with the earldom of Devon. The handsome William was a worthy match for a princess, a bridegroom of courage, manly bearing, and virtue. Elizabeth helped to arrange this marriage too and, trying not to think about the cost, had negotiated with the Earl of Devon a similar settlement to Anne's. Then Katherine also disappeared from Elizabeth's life, for Lord William bore her off to Devon, where his father had three castles. Not long afterward, Katherine wrote that she too was with child.

Elizabeth felt very lonely with her sisters gone; they had been such constant presences in her life. Cecily visited court but rarely, for she had two little girls now, and Bridget was lost to her. She was also panicking about her mounting debts. Sitting alone in her chamber, she felt a headache coming on as she tried to make her accounts balance. She had already had to pawn her plate and again borrow money from her chamberlain and her ladies; the buckles on her shoes were no longer of gold, but of tin, and there would be no money for new gowns until her next quarter's allowance was paid.

In the end, she poured out her woes to Henry and wished she

had done it sooner, for he was very kind, and gave her a loan to clear what she owed, as well as the town and castle of Fotheringhay, which had been the chief seat of her Yorkist forebears. It was deserted now, and it was hard to believe that it had been the scene of such splendor when her ancestors had been reburied there almost twenty years ago. So many who had been present on that day were gone now. Her grandmother of York still lived, but had retired to a nun-like existence at Berkhamsted Castle and was in poor health. Elizabeth felt guilty for not having visited her very often in recent years, but Grandmother was a forbidding figure and, on the few occasions she had seen her, Elizabeth had been made embarrassingly aware that she did not approve of Henry. It had not made for easy conversation.

Concern that an invasion by Warbeck was coming loomed over the time she spent with Henry. Trying to feel more positive about life, she sought solace in prayer and in the company of her children. She wrote frequently to Arthur, wincing a little at his formal replies, and traveled down to Eltham whenever she could. Margaret, now rising six, was growing into an imperious young lady who would surely lead some hapless prince a merry dance one day. Harry, now nearly four, was quite the budding knight, fascinated by the tales she told him of King Arthur and St. George, and confident in the saddle. Three-year-old Beth was pretty and graceful, never happier than when she was dancing or playing with her dolls, and happily oblivious to the fact that her father was negotiating a marriage for her with the future King of France. Elizabeth spent many a happy hour with her children, teaching the older ones to read and write, with Beth sitting on her lap, taking it all in.

In April, on the feast of St. George, Henry named Elizabeth chief Lady Companion of the Order of the Garter and made Harry a Knight of the Garter. Harry behaved very well at his investiture, looking very grown-up in his new crimson velvet gown and cap and his miniature Garter mantle.

At the end of May, Elizabeth learned that Grandmother York had died. It had been a peaceful end to a long life. She gave orders for the Duchess's body to be clothed in the black Benedictine habit she had worn for many years now and buried with her husband, the Duke of York, in the church at Fotheringhay. When the will was proved, she was touched to find that Grandmother had bequeathed to her a psalter and a relic of St. Christopher, and overwhelmed to learn that she was to inherit the Duchess's revenues, which helped to solve her financial problems. She also inherited Baynard's Castle, her grandmother's Thames-side London residence, which, with Fotheringhay—fittingly, she thought—made her the owner of the two great seats of the House of York.

"It's been a difficult year for you, cariad," Henry murmured one summer night, as she lay in his arms with a soft breeze from the open window playing on her skin. "But we have our progress coming up, and we'll be seeing Arthur. That will cheer you."

"I think you need cheering, too," she said, pressing herself closer to him. "But do you think you ought to be away just now, with Warbeck's invasion expected daily?"

"I have to be," he said. "We'll be ready if the feigned lad comes, and I can rely on my captains. But Stanley's execution has cost me much popularity in the northwest, where the Stanleys have a great affinity. In Lancashire, I think they command more respect than I do!"

"But Derby is loyal, surely?"

"Yes, but the loyalty of his brother's people hangs in the balance. It's necessary that I be seen in those parts, and with you, in order to regain the love of my subjects there. You'll know how to work your charm on them."

"I shall do you proud," she promised, and then Henry was kissing her and all thoughts of politics went winging out of the window.

Chipping Norton, Evesham, Tewkesbury, Worcester . . . Wherever they went that July, the people came hurrying to see and acclaim them. It was heartening, giving them hope that public opinion would form a bulwark in the face of Warbeck's pretensions. Every day, Elizabeth and Henry expected to hear news of the approach of his fleet, but there was none. Every night, she prayed there never would be.

Presently, they came to Tickenhill, Arthur's residence near Bewdley, Worcestershire. It was a fair manor house west of the town, standing on a hill in a wooded park. Elizabeth's father had had it enlarged for Ned, and Henry had transformed it into a beautiful palace for Arthur, who was standing in the porch waiting to receive them. At nearly nine, he had a new dignity about him and greeted them with formal courtesy. His tutors had done well; he was every inch the Prince of Wales and looked healthier than Elizabeth had ever seen him, thanks no doubt to the good air hereabouts. But she felt like a stranger to him, and it was not just on account of the long separation. The feeling persisted over the next days, when Arthur rode ahead to receive her and Henry at Ludlow and entertainments were laid on for them, As she sat watching him absorbed in a play staged for their pleasure in an amphitheater hewn into a quarry, or seated next to his father at a feast, she tried again to feel what she should feel for him, just as she had done when he was small. If only she could summon up the unbounded, joyous love she had for Harry—and her other children. It was so wrong of her to have a favorite, but she could not help it.

She did not think that either Henry or Arthur had any idea of her failings as a mother. She had striven so hard to hide them; she was openly affectionate to her son, admiring of his academic attainments, his princely bearing, his growing knowledge of statecraft— when all the time she was aware that she should feel more, more, more! It was a relief when she and Henry left for Shrewsbury.

From there, they rode northward to Chester, and thence, late in July, to Hawarden in Wales, where Derby and the Lady Margaret awaited them. Derby greeted them genially, which was a relief, as Elizabeth had feared that he might have been angered or alienated by his brother's execution. But Sir William Stanley was not mentioned. It was as if nothing had happened. And as the Earl escorted them to Lathom House, the palatial mansion in Lancashire she had never reached in that turbulent summer of 1485, she was touched when he told them that, to ease their journey, he had had a fine stone bridge built at Warrington. All along the route, crowds had gathered, some enthusiastic, others not so, but Elizabeth turned her smiles on them, nodding and waving graciously, and was heartened to hear them applaud her.

"Largesse for the people!" Henry cried, and as his attendants scattered gold coins among the throng, some began crying blessings on him. By the time they neared their journey's end, he was smiling.

Elizabeth gasped when she saw Lathom, and saw Henry's eyes narrow at the sight. It was magnificent, worthy of a king, and she could imagine him thinking that it was too splendid for a subject. As they approached through the deer park, she counted eighteen towers bisecting the mighty walls.

The Lady Margaret was waiting in the courtyard to greet them, avid for news of her grandchildren. She personally conducted them to their lodgings, where they were grateful to rest and refresh themselves after their journey.

"It was good to receive such a warm welcome from the local folk," Henry said, kicking off his riding boots and stretching out on the bed. "You charmed them, Bessy!"

"I think the largesse helped," she smiled.

"Come here," he said, and held out his arms.

At Lathom, they were royally entertained with good food, music, and dancing. On the second day, Derby showed them over the house and took them up to the leads to see the fine view of the countryside roundabouts. Elizabeth had a nasty moment when Henry walked to the unguarded edge of the roof and stood looking about him. She could not believe her ears when Derby's fool stepped toward his master and whispered in his ear, "Tom, remember Will." She froze, for he was referring, of course, to Sir William Stanley, and for a horrible few seconds, she thought that Derby might push Henry off the leads—it would have been so easy. Her heart was in her mouth. But Henry too had heard the aside and swung round.

"Let us go down now," he said. Derby made a furious face at the fool and led the way.

"That man should be hanged!" Elizabeth cried, as soon as she and Henry were alone.

"He is a fool; he has license to say what he likes," Henry replied.

"He was inciting your stepfather to treason. I really thought that they would make an end of you."

"It was in bad taste, but Derby is loyal—and he is married to my mother, surety enough for my safety. No, Bessy—least said, soonest mended. But I will have a word in Derby's ear about dismissing the wretch."

On their third day at Lathom, Henry and Elizabeth were at supper with their hosts when a fast messenger arrived with a dispatch for the King, who looked up, frowning. "Warbeck attempted an invasion. He had fourteen ships full of mercenaries and anchored off Deal. He sent soldiers ashore to reconnoiter, but the men of Kent were on the alert, and summoned the forces I had left standing ready. They cut the invaders to pieces, and Warbeck's fleet fled west to Ireland, where he tried to attack Waterford, but my deputy, Sir Edward Poynings, repelled him with ease. My councillors believe that Warbeck is now on his way to Scotland."

"And good riddance!" muttered Derby, as Elizabeth exhaled in relief.

"That remains to be seen," Henry said. "Everything depends on whether King James will receive him. Well, I refuse to lose sleep over it, and I see no reason to interrupt the progress just now. Maybe the Scots will repel Warbeck—or maybe James will take pleasure in stirring things up! Either way, we'll know soon enough."

"So you will be able to come with us to Knowsley?" his mother asked.

"We will, my lady," Henry replied.

The hunting lodge at Knowsley lay east of the village of Liverpool, and Henry and Elizabeth spent an afternoon enjoying the chase. Then it was farewell to Derby and the Lady Margaret, and on to the market town of Manchester and the south. As they passed through Macclesfield, Stafford, and Lichfield, Elizabeth began to feel increasingly tired and nauseous, and by the time they reached Woodstock, she knew she was with child again. Henry was delighted, but concerned, too, because she was so exhausted.

"We'll rest here a while," he said. "There's no business that can't wait."

Elizabeth was glad of the respite. When the nausea passed, she spent her mornings strolling in the park or visiting the animals in the menagerie, and her afternoons lying on her bed with a book. Her ladies diverted her with gossip and music, and Henry joined her for every meal. It was such a relief not to be on constant public display, especially when she often wanted to do nothing but sleep.

September started out as a beautiful, golden month, still warm and with a light breeze. But then it turned dull and gusty, and the leaves began to fall. When Elizabeth went abroad, she found she needed a cloak. It was during one of her solitary walks in the gardens that she heard running footsteps behind her. Swinging around, she saw that it was Henry, and that his face was working in distress.

"Bessy," he panted, coming to a halt and resting his hands on her shoulders. "Bessy, cariad, I have news. Sit down." He drew her to a stone bench, took her in his arms and seemed to be struggling to speak.

"What is it?" she cried in alarm.

"It's our sweet Beth." He swallowed. "God has taken her to Himself."

Her hands flew to her mouth. "No! No! Not Beth—not our little Beth!" She collapsed against him in a storm of weeping. To lose a child—it was terrible, something that happened to other people, but never to her and Henry, for God had smiled on their union, hadn't He? As she raged in his embrace and their tears mingled together, all she could see was the years stretching out ahead without Beth, the long, empty, grief-filled years . . .

"Why?" she asked eventually. "She was healthy. We had no warning—it must have been sudden."

Henry wiped his eyes. "It was a fever. You know how quickly small children can go down with it. The doctors could do nothing."

"It's dreadful. To have her life cut short like that. She was just three years old. Oh, I can't believe it. My baby, my little girl . . ."

"We must bear it patiently, Bessy, and not question God's will," Henry faltered, but then he too was weeping and they clung together, crying out their sorrow.

Ten days later, Elizabeth knelt in the chapel at Woodstock, thinking of what was happening in London. She could envisage the tiny coffin on the black-draped chariot, the horses drawing it past silent crowds to Westminster Abbey, the Prior waiting to receive it. Archbishop Morton, now a cardinal, had seen to the arrangements, and Henry had spared no outlay. A hundred poor men had been given black gowns for the occasion and were to walk in the procession behind the mourners. The ceremonial would be lavish, but she and Henry were not there, much to her distress. She was still too poorly to travel and the royal physicians, concerned about the impact of grief on her delicate condition, were adamant that she must rest.

Kneeling beside her, Henry reached across and laid his hand on hers. After a time, they looked at each other, genuflected and stood up.

"It must be over now," Elizabeth whispered, looking up at the gilded statue of the Virgin Mother and remembering that she too had known what it was like to lose a child.

Henry pulled her to him. "She is safe now, next to St. Edward's shrine and in God's keeping. We will raise a beautiful tomb for her. Something in marble, perhaps, with an effigy?"

"Yes," she breathed. "And an epitaph that tells how her life was cut tragically short and she was snatched away from us."

"To inherit eternal life in Heaven," Henry added.

"I keep thinking of the other children, how they must be feeling. I wish I could be there to comfort them."

"They are all in good hands," he reassured her. "Sir Richard Pole, Lady Darcy, and Mistress Oxenbridge can be depended on to support them. Alas, that they should have to confront the reality of death so young."

"My heart weeps for them," Elizabeth replied. She leaned on Henry's arm and they walked slowly out of the chapel and into the bleak landscape of their lives ahead, from which their little girl would be eternally absent.

Two days later, Elizabeth was ready to leave Woodstock. She was yearning to get to Windsor so that she would not have to endure more long days of traveling, but before that, she and Henry lodged at Ewelme in Oxfordshire with her cousin, Lincoln's brother Edmund de la Pole, Earl of Suffolk, who was most sympathetic to them in their loss. They then visited Bisham Priory, where Elizabeth paid her respects at the tombs of her Neville ancestors. She spent some time looking down on the effigy of her late godfather, Warwick the Kingmaker, thinking how the mighty were brought low and that his vast ambition had availed him nothing in the end—and wishing she could be standing before another burial place, where her heart lay interred.

At last, at long last, the walls and towers of Windsor were before them. Elizabeth's spirits rose a little. It had been a long progress, with a terrible ending, and now she needed to rest for a few days before taking a barge to Eltham to see Margaret and Harry. How she had missed them and yearned to be with them. In four months, they would have grown. And then she thought about the child who would grow no older, and wept again.

In November, bravely trying to come to terms with their grief, Henry and Elizabeth attended the traditional feast held by the newly appointed sergeants-at-law amid the splendors of Ely Place in Holborn. Elizabeth and her ladies dined in one room, and Henry and his retinue in another, as was customary. They were intrigued to see Ely Place, for, a century ago, it had been the London residence of their common ancestor, John of Gaunt, Duke of Lancaster, and his beautiful, but notorious, third wife, Katherine Swynford, the mother of his Beaufort children. Yet Elizabeth was finding it hard to take much interest in anything.

She knew that she must pull herself together. She owed it to Henry, to their children, to the little one as yet unborn—and to herself. Henry was hoping for a son, but—God forgive her—she was praying for another daughter. There could never be a replacement for Beth, but having a new child to love, whatever it was, would help to take the edge off her grief.

Physically, she was feeling better. The nausea and fatigue had gone. If she were not feeling dragged down by misery, she would be bounding. Seeking spiritual comfort and wishing to pray for a safe delivery, she journeyed again to Our Lady of Walsingham, who was renowned for bestowing calm and serenity on those beset by troubles. Hooded and cloaked, she removed her shoes at the Slipper Chapel and walked the remaining mile to the shrine barefoot with the other pilgrims. Reverently, she entered the holy sanctum, assailed by the scent of incense and candle-wax, and then fell to her knees before the gilded and bejeweled image of the Holy Mother. Nearby were displayed famous relics, including a vial of the Virgin's milk. In this sacred place, she prayed for her daughter's soul, and for the grace to accept her loss and to submit with a glad heart to God's will. Finally, she offered up a plea for a safe delivery and a healthy child.

When she rose to her feet, she made her offering and walked out into the wintry sunlight. And then it was as if a little hand had placed itself in hers. She looked down—and there was nothing. But it had been no illusion, she was certain. Our Lady of Walsingham had heard her, had understood her loss, and sent her child to comfort her. She felt blessed indeed.

When she returned to court, she found Henry seething.

"Warbeck has surfaced in Scotland, and King James has received him with royal honors!" he barked. "He's had him decked out in clothes befitting a king and settled on him a very generous pension, and he's taken him on a triumphal progress through his kingdom."

"Oh, no." This did not augur well. It was awful news.

"And just as I was hoping to negotiate a peace with Scotland and offer Margaret as a bride for James!"

Elizabeth's eyes widened. This was news to her. "But she's only six!"

"Come, Bessy, you know better than most that princesses are often betrothed in childhood. We wouldn't be sending her to Scotland for years yet—if at all, given James's behavior."

"I wish you had talked to me about it. I'm her mother."

"You were away when I had the idea, and I'm talking to you about it now," Henry said irritably. "But it's unlikely to happen. James seems determined to provoke me."

Elizabeth was relieved to hear that. "Does he really believe that Warbeck is my brother or is he just pretending to in order to make trouble for you?" she wondered, deciding to let the matter of the betrothal drop.

"I fear he believes it. He's given Warbeck his kinswoman, Lady Catherine Gordon, in marriage. He'd hardly do that if he thought him a fraud. What's worse is that Ferdinand and Isabella have heard and are stalling at concluding Arthur's marriage alliance; Dr. de Puebla says they won't do so while the pretender is at large. By God, what a mess!" He began pacing up and down. "But I'm doing my best to neutralize these threats. I'm working to seal a peace treaty with Maximilian, and I shall insist that we each undertake not to support the other's rebels."

"Will Maximilian agree?"

"He will. It's in both our interests. The treaty will effectively slam the door to Flanders in Warbeck's face, for Maximilian has already warned your aunt Margaret that she will lose her dower lands if she does not honor its terms. And now that I've made peace with the French, Warbeck is isolated in Scotland."

"You have done brilliantly," Elizabeth said, embracing him.

He kissed her. "Thank God you're back—and looking much better."

"Yes. My pilgrimage did me a power of good." She would tell him later about what had happened in the chapel.

He drew her close. "I'm sorry I was short with you. I'm over-burdened."

She touched his cheek. "I know. And I understand. But things will get better, I'm sure of it. And I think that James will come to regret befriending Warbeck."

"Let's just pray that England hasn't bowed the knee to the feigned lad before he does so," Henry said grimly.

Chapter 18

1496–1497

The baby was a girl, as Elizabeth had hoped. Henry was as thrilled as she was and gladly consented to her calling the child after her long-lost sister Mary. She was an exquisitely pretty infant, blue-eyed and golden-haired, with dainty features and rosebud lips.

"She is a paradise," Elizabeth breathed, looking down on her as she slumbered in her arms, and thanking God that she was healthy, unlike Anne's newborn son Thomas, who looked not long for this world.

"She looks like you," Henry smiled, squeezing her hand.

It was a wrench, having to give Mary to Alice Skern, her very capable nurse, to be taken to the nursery household at Eltham. Elizabeth longed for her churching to be over, so that she could visit her children, but her travail had taken a lot out of her, and she did need the rest. Mother Massey was insisting that she did not rise from her bed for at least thirty of her forty days of lying in.

When she did finally get to Eltham, she was not surprised to find Margaret exhibiting signs of jealousy toward her new sister— Margaret, who had never resented Beth. Mary was almost as beautiful as Beth had been and had naturally become the center of attention.

"My young lady's nose is somewhat out of joint," Lady Darcy murmured, as they sat watching the children playing with Harry's toy castle, "but she will get over it, Madam."

Harry, however, doted on the newcomer. Every so often, he would hasten over to her cradle to coo at her and check that she was all right. He was inordinately delighted when he got a broad smile for his pains. It was a joy to see how much he loved Mary. Elizabeth thought again of the child who would never again run into her arms, and also spared a thought for Arthur, who was far away from his siblings and missing out on the happy camaraderie of the nursery. It was a long time since she had seen him.

She was rather dreading the summer progress because, like last year's, it was going to be demanding. But she put on a brave show and was touched to see people running to see her, some bringing offerings of cherries, apples, pies, flowers, and even chickens. It was the same wherever she went, and she wondered what she had done to merit it. Had her charitable works and her intercessions on behalf of felons and others become common knowledge? Or was it her piety and her fruitfulness that had endeared her to Henry's subjects? Or the fact that she was her father's daughter and belonged to the old royal house? Whatever had moved them, it was humbling to see how much they loved her.

By slow stages, they traveled west through Chertsey, Guildford, Farnham, Porchester, and Southampton. They stayed at Beaulieu Abbey and crossed the Solent to the Isle of Wight, then moved on to Christchurch, Poole, and Corfe Castle. In August, at Elizabeth's request, they visited Heytesbury and stayed at the manor house as the guests of its chatelaine, Lady Hungerford. Her old jailer, Captain Nesfield, had been dead these eight years, but the house was full of memories of Mother, her sisters, and the anxious time they had spent there; and over it all hung the shadow of her scheming to marry Richard, which must never be mentioned to Henry. How differently things had turned out; but, looking back, she still could not see that there had been any other avenue open to her at the time. She could not help comparing those dark days with her settled life now.

They returned to Windsor in September, in time to watch

Harry perform his first public duty, witnessing a charter granted by the King to Glastonbury Abbey. She looked on proudly as he wrote his name in the careful script she had taught him. He was five now, her fair, sweet, boisterous son, a fine boy of considerable intellect and talent. There was so much of his uncle York in him, she thought.

Lady Darcy was retiring and, in her place, Elizabeth had engaged Elizabeth Denton, who had served her as wardrobe keeper since her marriage, and would now be lady mistress to Harry and governess to his sisters alongside Lady Guildford, who had also served Elizabeth for many years.

At the suggestion of the Lady Margaret, Henry had appointed the learned poet John Skelton, her protégé, as Harry's tutor. The ever-frowning, frosty-faced Skelton had great wit and a barbed tongue and made them all laugh with his satires. Henry was delighted when the respected Dutch humanist scholar, Desiderius Erasmus, visited Eltham and told Harry that Skelton was an incomparable light and ornament of letters, and that he could not have had a better teacher. But Harry looked dubious. His mentor was strict, much exercised about maintaining royal dignity, and not interested in tournaments and fighting.

Elizabeth watched, though, as her son blossomed under his tutelage. It thrilled her to see how Skelton brought out and encouraged his musical talents. The boy could play the lute like an angel, at least to her ears, and already he had begun to compose simple songs of his own.

"Young as he is, he grasps the broader points of theology," Skelton told her, as they sat in the schoolroom at Eltham, where Harry's auburn head was bent over his Latin primer. Seeing Elizabeth raise her eyebrows, he smiled. "In fact, he has opinions of his own and argues them forcibly. He's very bright, Madam, excellent at languages and loves learning for its own sake—a delightful small new rose, worthy of its stock."

She inclined her head at the compliment and continued browsing through Harry's copybooks. They were neat, with few blots. "He does seem advanced for his age," she observed.

"Most certainly. But that is to be expected, of course."

"I rather think it is down to your expert tuition," she told him.

"Ah, Madam, a tutor is only as good as the material he has to work with. It is a joy to have such an apt pupil."

It was a different story in Margaret's chamber. Rising seven, she could read and write, although not very competently. She far preferred music and dancing, and her governesses complained that she fidgeted all through her lessons, anxious to be off doing something else.

"Well, let us put away the books for today," Elizabeth said, and picked up the lute Henry had bought Margaret. "Let me hear you play," she encouraged. Thankfully, the child had some talent, and she was very good on her clavichord.

It had, overall, been a delightful afternoon. Elizabeth had spent time with her baby and marveled at how forward she was at six months, and how pretty. The child had shown no shyness, but leaped in her nurse's arms at the sight of her mother, and chuckled when Elizabeth took her and kissed her little head. It brought back memories of another little head that had lain against her shoulder, and the small ghost that still haunted these chambers. Every day, Beth was in her thoughts.

As she sat in her barge on the way back to Sheen, Elizabeth thanked God for blessing her with such beautiful children. She wished that they did not have to grow up in a world overshadowed by insecurities, threats, and intrigue, and prayed that they could continue to enjoy their childhood untroubled by the perils that beset their father.

It seemed a vain hope. She returned to find Henry in a state of high agitation, pacing his chamber like a caged lion.

"James has invaded England with Warbeck. My spies tell me that Warbeck promised him Berwick in reward."

"How dare he! It is not his to give—and it belongs to England." She did not like to remind Henry that Berwick, which had been much fought over by the Scots and the English through the centuries, had been taken by Richard during her father's reign.

He ceased his pacing and turned a resolute face to her. "I'm

sending an army north to deal with these rogues and take Warbeck. I hope soon to come face to face with this imposter!"

But, as reports filtered south, it became clear that James's army
was more interested in looting and settling old border feuds than
in placing Warbeck on the English throne.

"And as soon as he saw our army," Henry related jovially as he
carved the roast beef at dinner, "he fled back into Scotland!"

"So there was no battle?"

"No. And, by all accounts, Warbeck was disgusted at the brutality of the Scots, and angered that they were not helping him.
There was a falling-out between him and James, and I believe I
can now force James to surrender our friend Warbeck. If not, I can
count on Parliament to finance a war against Scotland."

Parliament proved most accommodating, and England poised
herself on the brink of war. But the wrangling went on—and on.

In the spring of 1497, Elizabeth was unwell, tired and breath-
less, and sometimes dizzy. One day, she had to lie down on her
bed.

"You look a little pale, my dear," the Lady Margaret said when
she came to see her, looking concerned.

"I've got a headache and my heart is pounding away," Elizabeth
told her.

"I think that all this worry over Warbeck is taking its toll."

"I fear so. I just want the matter to be settled. I was so looking
forward to our time here at Greenwich and having the children
with us, and now I am too poorly to be with them."

"Don't fret. Blessed be God, our sweet children are in good
health and enjoying the spring sunshine in the gardens. And I
trust, by His grace, that you will soon be well."

But it was June before Elizabeth fully recovered, and by then
the children were back at Eltham and she and Henry were at
Sheen. One afternoon, she and her ladies were devising ways to
refurbish old clothes when the King was announced.

"Leave us!" he commanded, and the women scattered.

Elizabeth rose anxiously from her curtsey. "Is it Warbeck?" she faltered.

"No, Bessy. The men of Cornwall have risen and are marching on London."

"But why?" She was trembling with shock. "What do they want?"

"They resent the new taxes I've had to levy for the defense of the realm. They want my head, the brutish fools. Bessy, there is no time to waste. I have ordered an armed escort to take you to Eltham to collect the children. Then you must get them to my mother's house at Coldharbour. It's within the City walls, so you will be safe there."

"And what of you, my dearest?" she cried, clinging to him.

"I am marching west with an army to deal with the rebels."

She paused, trying to still her fears. "Then may God go with you and bring you back safely to me." This new threat had come upon her so suddenly that she was still reeling, and near to tears.

Saying goodbye to him was dreadful, but she knew she had to show a brave face for his sake, for it might be the last memory he had of her. As he kissed her tenderly, his mind clearly on the task ahead, she reminded herself that he had gone into battle before and come back safely. What match would an ill-organized rabble with scythes and pitchforks be for a royal army? So she forced herself to smile as he left her, then hastened to order her women to pack and sent for her barge.

To the children, she made light of the situation. They were going to stay with Grandmother in London. That was enough for them. They capered around excitedly, gathering their favorite belongings, as their nurses stuffed their clothes into a traveling chest and Master Skelton collected up books, muttering about lessons being disrupted. If only he knew . . .

They stayed at Coldharbour for six anxious days. Elizabeth's council kept her apprised of news, and soon it became increasingly difficult to hide the seriousness of the situation from Margaret and

Harry, for the reports filtering through from the west grew ever more alarming. The rebel army had been reinforced by malcontents from the shires and, by the middle of June, she had learned that their forces numbered eighteen thousand—and that they were approaching Farnham in Surrey. It was far too close for comfort, and Elizabeth and the Lady Margaret made a snap decision to move with the children into the Tower for safety.

"Why do we have to go there?" young Margaret grumbled. "It's too gloomy and I'd rather stay here."

"I like the Tower," Harry piped up. "They've got armor there, and guns and cannon!"

Little Mary began to cry and Elizabeth took her on her lap. She knew she could hide the situation from them no longer. "We have to go," she explained. "Some men from Cornwall are marching on London because they wish to protest against what they call unfair taxes. We will be safe in the Tower, just in case there is any trouble."

"I'd like to go and fight those horrid men!" Harry cried, his eyes gleaming.

"I hope that no one will be fighting them," she said. "The King your father has gone to meet with them and parley. I hope they will listen."

"Oh." Harry looked crestfallen. "I wanted there to be a battle."

"Battles are dreadful things," she told him. "Men die; hatred is given rein; there is much savagery."

"And much chivalry!" he retorted. It was no use. His head was filled with tales of King Arthur and St. George; the reality of warfare meant nothing to him.

As they prepared to leave, Elizabeth thanked God that Arthur was far away in Ludlow, well beyond the path of the rebels. But when, later that day, she arrived at the Tower, she could not help but remember the Bastard of Fauconberg's attack and her terror as a child when the fortress was bombarded. She prayed that her own children would never know such fear.

Yet no sooner were they settled, and supper had been served, than her chamberlain arrived and whispered in her ear.

"Your Grace, I've just heard that the rebels are four miles away at Blackheath and are drawn up in battle order, ready to force an entry into the City and attack the Tower; it seems they think the King is there."

It was happening, the thing she had dreaded—just as events had played out twenty-seven years ago. She found herself shaking. "Pray excuse me," she said to the Lady Margaret and the children. "I will be back shortly."

She rose and led her chamberlain into the antechamber. "How well stocked is the Tower with munitions?" she asked urgently.

"The Constable assures me we have plenty, Madam. This is the main arsenal in the kingdom."

"Do you know where the King is?"

"Not yet, Madam. We are awaiting news."

"Keep me informed as soon as you hear anything," she said, and returned to the table. She could not face eating. She wanted to gather up her children in her arms and hide with them somewhere they would all be safe. Hopefully, the rebels would soon discover that Henry wasn't here and would turn their attention elsewhere. But it was clear now that this was no ragged mob of yokels: it was an army on a mission, prepared to fight.

She made herself engage in a game of skittles with the children, her ears straining for any undue commotion beyond the window, just as they had all those years before. But there was nothing beyond the usual sounds of the City. If only she could find out where Henry was. Did he know they were in danger? Was he marching to their assistance?

It was evening before her chamberlain returned with the Constable.

"The King is at Lambeth, your Grace, with Lord Daubeney's forces, and blocking all access to the City."

The Constable spoke. "We have reason to believe that the rebels are exhausted after their long march from Cornwall. We've had word that the King intends to surround and overcome them. But there is great fear throughout the City and the citizens are arming. Yet I think there is no part of London that remains undefended, and the magistrates are keeping continual watch lest the rebels try to invade."

"Are we in danger?" All she could think of was the children.

"Not immediately, Madam. And we are prepared for an assault. Be not disquieted. You are safe here."

But she knew her history, and she knew that the Tower's defenses had been breached before, during the Peasants' Revolt of 1381. She could not sit quietly until the rebels had been overcome. Instead, she stayed at the window with the Lady Margaret, watching and listening for any disturbance. She was still there at two in the morning, when her mother-in-law had long gone to bed, and Mistress Denton persuaded her to get some sleep.

"Madam!" said her chamberlain, coming upon her unannounced the next morning as she was praying in the oratory in the corner of her bedchamber. "The King has overcome the rebels! There is no more cause to fear!"

She sprang to her feet, hardly daring to believe it. "Tell me what happened!"

"He had them surrounded and then he himself led his army to Blackheath, where, aided by the stout hearts of the Londoners, he routed the Cornishmen in a sharp skirmish. Two thousand of their number were slain. Now, I gather, his Grace is on his way to the City to be welcomed by the Lord Mayor and to give thanks in St. Paul's Cathedral."

Elizabeth clasped her hands, marveling at how brilliantly Henry had dealt with the crisis. Truly, he was a king—and a husband—to be proud of. It had all been over far more quickly than she had expected, and he was safe. Summoning the children, she told them the news and knelt with them to give thanks. Harry could hardly contain himself.

"I wish I had been there!" he declared.

"Hush, my boy. You are meant to be praying," she chided. But she could not be cross with him. She felt like dancing.

That afternoon, Henry arrived at the Tower, folded her in his arms and kissed her heartily in front of his cheering lords and captains.

"I thank God that you have come back to me safely," she cried, tears streaming down her face.

"I would have died to defend you," he murmured. Then he bent down to kiss his children.

"Will you tell me about the battle, Father?" Harry asked.

"Of course I will," Henry smiled, ruffling his son's hair.

In July, they moved to the rural peace of Sheen.

"It's time I dealt once and for all with the threat from War-beck," Henry said, when he and Elizabeth were out hawking in the park. "I shall offer James advantageous peace terms and de-mand that he surrenders him. I'm dispatching envoys tomorrow."

But they had not been gone long when word came that James had sent Warbeck south, apparently with a view to invading En-gland from the southwest.

"His ship is called *The Cuckoo*," Henry said drily, "and never was vessel more aptly named! Well, we shall be ready for him."

They waited . . . and waited . . . and waited. Then they learned that Warbeck had surfaced in Ireland in the hope of rallying more men to his banner. But he had found no support there and had to flee across the sea to Cornwall.

"There were four Irish ships in pursuit!" Henry chuckled, but his eyes were not smiling. "It's a pity they didn't catch him." He knew, as well as Elizabeth, that Warbeck might yet attempt to invade.

King James agreed a seven-year truce, but Henry's spies in Ed-inburgh warned that he was planning another offensive across the border. Again, Elizabeth had to stifle her alarm. She did not need Henry to tell her that England stood in deep peril.

The August sun was beating down as Henry and Elizabeth arrived at Woodstock with Harry to witness Arthur's formal betrothal to the Infanta. Arthur was waiting to greet them, and Elizabeth was startled at the change in him, for he was taller than usual for a lad of nearly eleven, and the transition from child to youth was already apparent. He welcomed them with perfect courtesy, but it seemed to her that they were strangers, and she knew it had been too long since they had last seen him.

She was impressed—and she could sense that Henry was, too—by the way Arthur carried himself during the betrothal ceremony and how well he gave the Latin responses. The courtiers were watching him admiringly. It was strange to think that in a little over two years, he would be married, for it had been agreed with Ferdinand and Isabella that the Infanta would come to England when she was fourteen, in December 1499. Elizabeth longed to meet the girl who would be her son's bride.

After the betrothal, Henry and Elizabeth celebrated with a triumphant feast and much revelry, in which Arthur took part decorously—unlike Harry, who entered enthusiastically into the dancing and drew much attention on himself. Next to Arthur, he looked the picture of robust health, and the contrast was painfully obvious. Poor Arthur was still too skinny for Elizabeth's liking, but a lot of boys were at his age, she told herself, and he would fill out as he grew to manhood.

There had been no news of Warbeck for weeks, but Henry was taking no chances and was raising an army.

"For surely he will come," he had said, taking leave of Elizabeth at Westminster, "and maybe now we can trounce him for good."

In the second week of September, he wrote to her to say that Warbeck had landed near Land's End in Cornwall and taken St. Michael's Mount. He had left his wife in the monastery there, and marched to Bodmin, recruiting three thousand peasants on the way. There, he had had himself proclaimed Richard IV.

Elizabeth dropped the letter, her hands trembling. The men of Cornwall would still be smarting from their recent defeat; it was small wonder that they had rallied to Warbeck's banner. Even now—for the title Richard IV had stirred her, despite herself—a part of her was wondering if the feigned lad (although he would be about twenty-four now) had every right to call himself king. If only she could see and speak to him, she would know for certain. And it might not be long before that could happen, if Henry vanquished and captured him.

She waited in a fever of agitation for more news. It was not good. Three thousand more supporters had joined Warbeck and he had laid siege to Exeter. *But they have few weapons, no armor, and no artillery*, Henry reported. *They will not be able to hold out for long.*

It was heartening to hear, some anxious days later, that Lord William Courtenay, Katherine's husband, had joined forces with the citizens of Exeter, repelled the besiegers and cut their army to pieces. But Warbeck was not conquered yet; he was marching with his remaining supporters on Taunton, and Henry still saw him as a threat. At his command, Elizabeth and the Lady Margaret left London with the children and went on a progress through the eastern counties, reassured by the knowledge that the King had ships standing ready nearby to convey them overseas, if necessary.

Elizabeth wondered if it would have been wiser to seek the safety of the Tower, but in East Anglia they would be farther away from the coming conflict, and it would be good to remind the people there that Harry was the true Duke of York. And Harry was thrilled to be the center of attention. There was no need to bid him show a smiling face and bow to the crowds, for it came naturally to him and he charmed everyone effortlessly—to the point where his grandmother had to chide him for his conceit. But even she could not help admiring his common touch. Elizabeth wished that Arthur had just half of it.

The news was good. Warbeck's march to Taunton had ended in disaster. His remaining Cornishmen had become increasingly demoralized and hordes had deserted. *We were only twenty miles away from capturing him when he abandoned his last few supporters and fled south toward Southampton, presumably to find a ship to take him overseas,* Henry wrote from Taunton. *But I had ordered the coast to be heavily guarded, so he had no luck there, and now he has taken sanctuary in Beaulieu Abbey. I've had the abbey surrounded by soldiers and promised Warbeck a pardon if he surrenders and throws himself on my mercy. I will let you know when I receive his answer.*

Elizabeth and Margaret rejoiced together. At last, after six years of uncertainty, Warbeck was within Henry's grasp, and Elizabeth could hopefully stop tormenting herself about his identity.

"He must agree to Henry's offer," Margaret said, as they rode toward Walsingham.

"He has no choice really," Elizabeth replied, "unless he wants to stay in sanctuary forever. He could do so at Beaulieu, for it has extensive sanctuary rights. Remember, Warwick's Countess took refuge there for some time."

"I do indeed," Margaret recalled.

"I would like to meet this pretender," Elizabeth said.

"I'm sure you would," her mother-in-law replied, giving her a sideways glance. "And I'd like to give him a piece of my mind after the trouble he's caused."

They had just returned from the shrine of Our Lady when a royal messenger arrived and informed them that Warbeck had given himself up.

He handed Elizabeth a letter from Henry, who had written: *He was brought to me here at Taunton and had the effrontery to come dressed in cloth of gold! But when I confronted him with lords who had known your brother York, he had to admit that he did not recognize any of them; nor did they recognize him. In the end, he knelt before me and confessed that he was not York and pleaded for my forgiveness. I made him write out his confession and will have it printed and nailed to church doors throughout the realm. I am now taking him in my train to Exeter, where I intend to celebrate this triumph. I will not be vengeful: I mean to have only a few desperate persons hanged, the better to demonstrate my mercy to the rest. My beloved wife, it will set your mind at rest to know that Warbeck has asked to write to his real mother in Tournai.*

Elizabeth was on the road back to London when Henry's next letter reached her. He related that Warbeck's wife, Lady Catherine Gordon, had been brought to him from St. Michael's Mount. *I was told that she was in mourning, her child having died not long since, so I sent her some black apparel suitable to her rank, and she is here now. I find her to be a young woman of excellent beauty and virtue. I believe*

Warbeck to be much in love with her, but, of course, there can be no question of their being allowed to cohabit, for I do not want her giving birth to yet another pretender. I am sending the lady ahead to London, if you will be content to admit her to your household on account of her noble birth and royal connections.

"Of course, I shall welcome her," Elizabeth said, showing the letter to Margaret, and leaning out of the window of the litter to warn Harry not to ride so far ahead. "I feel sorry for her. It is not her fault that she is married to a fool."

She was now almost convinced that Warbeck was a fraud. The fact that Henry was prepared to allow the wretch's wife to associate with his Queen was proof enough that he himself had no doubts as to his true identity. But his intention was probably to keep Catherine under surveillance.

On a bright October day, Elizabeth and her party were welcomed back to London by the Lord Mayor at Bishopsgate. With the aldermen following on horseback, he escorted her to the Royal Wardrobe near Baynard's Castle, the streets being lined with representatives of the City's guilds, standing in their best liveries. Harry rode beside her, his hand raised to acknowledge the cheers, and she was moved by the people's acclaim.

The next day, she departed for Sheen. There, three days later, escorted by Windsor Herald and several gentlewomen, Catherine Gordon was brought to her. As the young woman rose from her curtsey, Elizabeth saw that she was strikingly beautiful, with perfect features, green eyes, and ebony hair.

She extended her hand to be kissed. "Welcome to court, Lady Catherine."

"It is an honor, your Grace." Catherine had a pretty Scottish accent.

"I understand that my lord the King has arranged for a pension to be paid to you." Elizabeth thought he had been extraordinarily generous in the circumstances, but reminded herself that the young woman before her was blameless and, thanks to her noble birth, would have merited high honor and been a suitable lady-in-waiting for her anyway, especially since her sisters were rarely at court these days. Over the next two weeks, she found herself enjoying Catherine's company, and it was a pleasure to see how many hearts the young woman had won over at court.

Henry had sent Warbeck under guard to London, where he was paraded through streets crammed with the crowds who had flocked to see him, and then imprisoned in the Tower.

"We can rest assured now that my son's throne is stable at last, for there is no one left to aspire to it," the Lady Margaret declared that evening. "It is a great relief to have that rogue under lock and key." She got up from her chair by the fire and held out her hands to warm them.

"Henry will be returning shortly," Elizabeth said. She was counting down the days. "We must leave for Windsor soon."

He joined them there in late November. By then, Warbeck's written confession had been circulated the length and breadth of the realm, and he had read it aloud before a commission of lords, who had visited him in the Tower.

Henry had given Elizabeth a copy. The pretender had stated that he was the son of John Warbeck, customs controller of Tournai, and that he had been lured into his imposture against his will.

"He is a foreigner, Bessy, and not my subject," Henry said, watching her from the other side of the hearth as she read the confession. "That means he cannot be charged with high treason."

"So what do you propose to do with him?" she asked, laying down the document.

"Keep him under my eye! I shall release him from the Tower and bring him to court."

Her jaw almost dropped. "That's astonishingly lenient! This is the man who has posed a serious threat to your kingdom these six years."

Henry shrugged. "I know that all too well, Bessy. But this lad was the tool of others and he has confessed to his imposture, so he can no longer be a threat to me. And I am confident that he will not try to escape. He will be shadowed by two guards at all times anyway, and confined to the precincts of the palace. Remember Lambert Simnel? He made good in my kitchens, and now I have approved his promotion to falconer."

She nodded, but still she found Henry's leniency incredible. It was as if he meant to treat Warbeck as the prince he had claimed to be. Other kings would have hanged him! She could not decide if it was folly—or statecraft of the highest order. And it made her wonder if, deep inside, Henry still feared that Warbeck really was her brother.

"On a happier note, I wanted to tell you that I am working for a treaty of perpetual peace with Scotland," Henry said, breaking the silence. "Under its terms, Margaret will be married to James, as I have long intended."

Elizabeth listened in dismay. She had expected that Margaret would one day be married to some great prince, but she was not ready to lose her yet. Her beautiful, tempestuous daughter was still so young, and the prospect of being sent so far away to that untamed northern kingdom with its turbulent nobles and its duplicitous king was unbearable.

"It is a great match for her," Henry said gently, "and it will, God willing, put an end to centuries of warfare between our two kingdoms."

"God willing," she echoed, thinking that it might take more than a marriage to do that. "But she is only eight—and he is, what, twenty-five? There is too great a disparity in their ages. And she is not robust."

"She will not be going to Scotland yet, Bessy. And age is not the prime consideration in this alliance. Plenty of marriages work despite an age gap."

"Yes, I know, but I have heard things about James that worry me. He has a bad reputation with women. And he has many bastards."

"As did your father, if I may remind you," Henry smiled. "And yet he was a great king. James has many qualities and talents, and I am assured that he will treat Margaret well when the time comes."

There was a knock on the door and Catherine Gordon entered

with some embroidery silks Elizabeth had ordered two days earlier. Seeing the King there, she hurriedly sank into a graceful curtsey. And as Henry smiled at her, Elizabeth gained the most disturbing impression. She saw that he could not take his eyes off Catherine, who had flushed under his scrutiny. Suspicion flared. She feared she could see why he had treated her kindly and given her splendid attire fit for her rank. Elizabeth had seen his accounts, in which he himself had itemized each detail of the clothing he had ordered for Catherine, even down to her hose—and thought nothing amiss of it at the time. Today, she was wearing one of the gowns, a stylish perfection of black velvet trimmed with mink, which enhanced her striking looks.

She tried to tell herself that, in decking out Catherine so lavishly, Henry wished to sweeten her kinsman, King James, with whom he was about to conclude the peace treaty that would be sealed with Margaret's hand. But a treacherous little voice in her head whispered that it no doubt pleased Henry to adorn Catherine's beauty, too, or even to fantasize about the body he was so bountifully clothing.

As Catherine curtseyed again and departed, Elizabeth watched her husband's face. His eyes had followed the young woman across the room; he seemed gripped by some enchantment.

"Henry," she said, and he started. "A penny for them! You were miles away."

He shrugged. "I was just thinking that it might be hard to stop Warbeck from contriving to see his wife, for she is very comely."

Would he be so honest with her if he was cherishing a secret infatuation for Catherine? Had she allowed her imagination to run amok for nothing?

"She has a modest demeanor," Henry went on, "but she is a singularly beautiful lady and, for all that she has borne him a child, there is an untouched look about her."

Elizabeth said nothing. It seemed an inappropriate observation, but maybe Henry was merely explaining, from a man's point of view, why Warbeck loved her. Or maybe he was indulging in fantasies of his own. But, again, he would hardly voice them to his own wife.

"I have dealt with her honorably, for she is blameless," he was saying. "Warbeck is not worthy of her. When I made him repeat his story in front of her at Exeter, she wept and raged at him for lying to her and King James. Her person, her beauty, and her dignity require a man of far greater superiority. I have assured her that her future holds many possibilities and that I will treat her as my sister."

"She has been but a pawn in this imposture," Elizabeth said. "I like her; she does deserve better."

She settled again to her embroidery, her mind in turmoil, unsure what to think. She was wishing that she was twenty-one instead of thirty-one, and that she was not putting on weight. She had been so slender before the children had come, but five pregnancies had done nothing for her figure, and she kept remembering how her father had quickly run to fat in his thirties. She really would have to look to her diet.

Had the evidence of her eyes deceived her? She had been married to Henry for nearly twelve years and they were still close, still loving. He visited her bed regularly. She had no reason to think he had ever been unfaithful to her. And it was hard to credit that he would have taken advantage of a grieving mother who had found herself in a difficult situation. Maybe it was just a case of a chivalrous king showing compassion and friendship.

But as she lay beside Henry that night and listened to his soft snoring, her mind ran riot and she found herself imagining what might have taken place between him and Catherine in the West Country and wondering if anyone else had noticed the way he looked at her. Who could she ask, without giving away her suspicions? There was no one. She really must stop thinking like this and accept that she was worrying about nothing.

Elizabeth sat enthroned next to Henry, her heart thudding violently. Today, Warbeck was to be presented to them prior to taking up residence in the gilded cage of the court, and the moment when she would finally set eyes on him was approaching. In a few minutes, she would know for certain whether or not he was her brother.

He was entering now, between the two guards who had been ordered to shadow him at all times. He was tall and fair with a prominent chin and bore a striking resemblance to her father. As he knelt before Henry, she gazed on his handsome face and felt faint.

He was not York, whatever the changes time and maturity had wrought; she knew that beyond doubt. She would have wagered much on his being one of her father's bastards, possibly sired during his exile in the Low Countries. When he uttered his gratitude for the King's lenient treatment of him, his voice was deep and manly, with a marked foreign accent.

Her heart was steadier now and she was able to incline her head graciously when Warbeck bowed to her and was escorted away. But she was suddenly filled with rage against those—King Charles, Maximilian, the Archduke Philip, Aunt Margaret, and King James—who had used this young man and perpetrated the fraud that had kept her in torment, and Henry under threat, for six long years—years of agonized hoping and fretting on her part. She blamed them too for the crushing sense of disappointment that had seized her, for she had always cherished a small hope that Warbeck might be York. Now she would never be likely to find out what had happened to her brothers. But she must look to the future. At least, with Warbeck captured, Arthur's betrothal was assured—Ferdinand and Isabella should not be able to claim there was any threat remaining to Henry's throne.

With a superhuman effort, she recovered her equilibrium and carried on with her life. Warbeck sometimes came to her chamber to see Catherine Gordon, and occasionally Henry was present and treated them both pleasantly. It was obvious that the young man was deeply smitten with his wife.

Once, Warbeck sat down next to Elizabeth and together they watched her ladies practicing dance steps. But he had eyes for only one. "Alas, Madam," he said, "take pity on a poor wretch. My lady is as brilliant as the stars. Whoever sees her cannot choose but admire and love her. But I am forbidden to do so."

He looked so dejected that Elizabeth hardly had the heart to point out that it was his own fault. "If you conduct yourself well, Master Warbeck," she said, "and prove that you are no threat to him, the King may in time relent." Privately, she doubted it, but hope might keep Warbeck on the straight path. She felt sorry for Catherine, a wife and no wife, with no more hope of children— and none of it her fault. It was clear that she was in love with her husband, even if she was hurt by his having deceived her.

All was in readiness for Christmas, which they were keeping at Sheen. The gifts had been purchased, the Yule log and the evergreens would be brought in on Christmas Eve, and the kitchens were operating at full stretch. Arthur was on his way from Ludlow and the other children had already arrived from Eltham. Elizabeth had stifled her fears about Henry fancying Catherine Gordon, for he had given her no further cause to doubt him, and was looking forward to the twelve days of revelry.

Two days before Christmas Day, around nine o'clock at night, she and Henry were hosting a gathering in her chamber when they heard shouts.

"Fire! Fire!"

Everyone leaped up as the King opened the door to the antechamber and Elizabeth peered over his shoulder. She could smell smoke. Making haste, they led their courtiers through the door to the gallery that connected with the spiral stair and—God willing—safety, but the smoke was thicker there and they could hear crackling below them.

"This way, Sire!" called a guard at the other end of the gallery. "Hurry!"

"Is it safe?" Elizabeth cried, petrified. "Where are the children? And the Lady Margaret?"

"Some guards have gone to get them," the man replied. "I beg you, make haste!"

Henry grabbed her hand and ran through the smoke. The floor felt hot beneath her feet and she bunched up her skirts and threw her train over her arm. She was in terror lest the floorboards catch light.

She was shaking as they reached the stairwell and horrified when, behind them, just as the last man reached the stair, the gallery floor collapsed and the flames roared upward.

"Get downstairs, now!" Henry shouted, and they followed the guard to the bottom. At one point, the wall was glowing and they shrank back, not daring to touch it. But, at last, they were out in the courtyard and there, to Elizabeth's profound relief, were the children, standing with the Lady Margaret, the girls clinging to her, Harry agog at the activity around him. Servants were running with buckets and bowls of water, and the yeomen of the guard had formed a chain, passing them along to the blazing building, but their frantic efforts were ineffectual, for the conflagration had spread and Henry and Elizabeth could do nothing but shepherd their family to the greater safety of the park. From there, they could see the burning palace silhouetted against the sky. The children were staring at it in awe. Elizabeth, clasping their hands, could only shudder to think what a close escape they had had.

For three hours the inferno raged, as various household officers came to the King to report what was happening. The Lord Chamberlain thought it had started in the King's lodgings.

"Can it be put out?"

"It has taken too great a hold, your Grace. People have tried to save hangings, beds, plate, clothing and jewels, but the heat is too fierce."

Henry looked grim. "They have done their best, and I appreciate it. Look, the chapel is burning!" He watched for a while, then turned to Elizabeth and his mother. "It grows late. We had best get you all to bed. It's fortunate that my old manor of Byfleet is just beyond the gardens. My Lord Chamberlain, have it prepared for us. Don't go to too much trouble, for I know the household are needed here. We just need beds for the night; the children are tired."

"I'm not, Father," said Harry.

"Well, I am!" said Henry firmly. "It's long past your bedtime."

An hour later, when the chamberlain came to escort them to the manor house, and Elizabeth, with a sleepy Mary in her arms, led the others away, Henry, exhausted as he was, insisted on staying until the fire was extinguished. But the palace was well alight, and it looked as if it would be some time before that happened.

When Elizabeth woke the next morning, in musty sheets in need of a good airing, she found Henry beside her on the bed, still wearing the clothes he had had on the night before, his face grimy with smuts. He was in a sound sleep and had evidently been too shattered to disrobe.

Later that morning, after a breakfast of new-baked bread and cheese purveyed from a nearby farm, he took her to inspect the damage. They could not get too close, as the ruins were still smoking, but it was a relief to see that the great tower was more or less intact. But the fire had done a lot of damage, and Henry stood staring gloomily at the burned-out palace.

His chief officers crowded around him. "Does anyone know how it started?" he asked.

The Lord Steward spoke. "By accident, Sir, I am sure, and not by malice. Some think a spark caught a beam."

Master Treasurer shook his head. "Others think that Perkin Warbeck set the palace on fire."

"No, he was with me when it started," Henry said.

"That's as may be." The treasurer still looked dubious. "But, Sir, the damage might run to thousands of pounds."

"There's no use weeping over it," Henry shrugged. "I will rebuild the palace, much finer and bigger than before. I pray you, offer a reward to anyone who finds some of the crown jewels in the rubble. In the meantime, my Lord Chamberlain, have the manor house prepared properly. We'll keep Christmas there."

Chapter 19

1498–1499

Warbeck had fled the court! The news traveled around Westminster as quickly as the flames that had destroyed Sheen six months earlier.

"He evaded his guards and climbed through a window in the wardrobe," Henry spluttered, angrier than Elizabeth had seen him in a long time. "And this is how he repays me for my leniency! Well, I'll not be so merciful next time. He's probably making for the coast, so I've sent men after him and given orders for the roads to be closed."

"He may be seeking sanctuary somewhere, like he did at Beaulieu," Elizabeth suggested, as Catherine Gordon burst into the room in a distraught state and stopped, seeing the King there. Henry ceased pacing and gave her that look Elizabeth had seen before.

"You are not to worry, Lady Catherine," he said kindly. "I know you are blameless. It is your husband who will suffer when my men catch him, as they will. And no"—he held up a hand—"it will do you no good to plead for him."

But Catherine fell to her knees anyway. "All I beg is that your Grace spares his life!" She held up her hands beseechingly.

"Alas, Madam, you ask too much." He looked pained. Elizabeth helped Catherine to her feet, shocked to find herself gratified that Henry had rebuffed her. She thought of interceding for Warbeck herself, but knew it would do no good.

At that moment, Derby and two other councillors appeared. "Your Grace, the Prior of the Charterhouse at Sheen is here. Warbeck claimed sanctuary there and they have detained him."

"Good," Henry replied. "Send him in. And inform Dr. de Puebla of this. If Ferdinand and Isabella have heard of his escape, tell him to reassure them that he has been speedily found and will be dealt with."

The Prior described what had happened, then he too knelt and urged the King to spare Warbeck's life.

"Father Prior," Henry answered, "I am not a bloodthirsty man, but I am no longer prepared to be lenient with him."

And there was no arguing with him. When Warbeck was taken, he was clapped into the stocks, first in Cheapside and then at Westminster, and made to read aloud his confession in both places before jeering crowds. Then he was marched under a strong guard to the Tower and imprisoned.

"I'm told that, even now, he is still asserting that he is York," Henry said tersely over a dinner that Elizabeth did not feel like eating. "He told the Constable that, when he was delivered from the Tower, he would wait for my death, then put himself into your hands, as his sister and the next heir to the crown. If he were my subject, I'd have him executed for treason. But he is not, so I've had him incarcerated in a cell where he can see neither sun nor moon and will trouble us no more. He has to be taught a lesson."

"You will not have him tried and executed then?" She was thinking of Catherine, although she could not feel much sympathy herself for Warbeck, who had acted like an imbecile and was still perpetrating his lies.

"No," Henry said.

She was taken aback. She had been certain that this would be the end for the pretender. No foreign ruler, even Aunt Margaret, could blame Henry if he put this offender to death. So why was he holding back?

She looked at him across the table. The years of uncertainty had taken their toll. He appeared old for his forty-one years. His hair had thinned and was turning gray, his complexion was pale and scored with lines of worry. Constant anxiety had done nothing for her either. She too had aged. Her mirror showed her a plump matron with pinched lips and a double chin.

Stop brooding! she admonished herself. With Warbeck securely imprisoned, the outlook for the future was bright, and the way clear for preparations for Arthur's wedding to the Infanta to proceed smoothly. And when Dr. de Puebla had an audience with Henry that afternoon, at which she was present, she was pleased to see him beaming at them.

"Your Majesty, my sovereigns will be very pleased to hear that your crown is now undisputed, and that your government is strong in all respects. I will recommend that they send envoys to England to discuss the arrangements for the Infanta's wedding to the Prince of Wales."

That was good news!

The envoys arrived in July. They were almost as grand as their sovereigns, but their courtesy was exquisite and Henry, Elizabeth, and the Lady Margaret got on so well with them that the private audience continued for four hours, with many extravagant compliments and pleasantries being exchanged.

The visitors had brought letters from Ferdinand, Isabella, and the Infanta for Elizabeth.

Henry read them reverently, clearly wishing to demonstrate to the envoys how much the marriage alliance meant to him. "Madam, I should like to have one of these letters to carry with me at all times."

Elizabeth took her cue. "Alas, my lord, I do not like to part with them, except to send one to Prince Arthur."

Their guests seemed greatly impressed.

Elizabeth now began a regular correspondence with Queen Isabella and the Infanta, stressing her keen desire for a successful outcome to the marriage preparations and assuring them that Catalina would be welcomed with open arms in England. She watched over her Latin secretary's shoulder as he wrote the letters at her dictation, and sometimes made him rewrite them three or four times, wanting to express her sentiments in the proper fashion.

When the Spanish envoys visited court in the heat of a sweltering July, Elizabeth was feeling ill. She had missed two courses and was certain that she was with child again, for she was suffering from the usual debilitating nausea. Henry had summoned Dr. Lewis that very morning, but the physick the good doctor had prescribed was not making much difference. When the envoys arrived two hours later, Elizabeth was longing for nothing but to lie down and sleep, and had to force herself to accompany the King in procession to and from Mass. She strove to be gracious when the envoys came to take their leave and kiss her hand, but she was utterly relieved when the Lady Margaret, knowing how poorly she felt, took charge of the audience.

Afterward, Margaret made Elizabeth rest and sat beside her.

"I was going to write to the Infanta," Elizabeth said. "There are certain things she should know."

"Don't bother yourself with that," Margaret said. "I can see Dr. de Puebla. What would you have me say?"

"That is most kind." Elizabeth squeezed the older woman's hand. "I'm worried about how easy it will be to converse with the Infanta when she arrives in England, and I think she should be advised always to speak French with her brother's wife, the Archduchess Margaret of Austria, in order to learn the language, because I don't understand Latin, much less Spanish."

"That's very wise advice, my dear. I will impress it on Dr. de Puebla."

"I also want the Infanta to accustom herself to drink wine. She may not know that the water here is not drinkable."

"I will tell him. Now, Elizabeth, you should get some sleep. You want to be well for our progress."

Margaret was to accompany them. But first, Henry and Elizabeth made another pilgrimage to Walsingham to pray for the safe delivery of a son. Then they joined his mother at her house at Collyweston. While they were there, they noticed that Dr. de Puebla was turning up every day, with all his servants, to dine at court.

"Has he no money for food?" Henry wondered.

The next day, he was informed that Dr. de Puebla had again arrived at Collyweston.

"Why does he keep coming here?" he asked the Lord Steward.

"To eat!" was the reply. Henry caught Elizabeth's eye and suddenly they were both helpless with laughter. It was at times like these that there was a wonderful sense of togetherness linking them, and she could forget her fears about Catherine Gordon.

Elizabeth still felt drained when they departed from Collyweston for the summer progress, but she put on a brave countenance and tried to hide the debilitating fatigue and nausea that made her crave her bed. Henry had decreed their tour be shorter this year, because of her condition, but, although she still found the pace demanding, her heart was lifted by the common people who came running to see her and pressed roses and butter and other homely offerings into her hands. The women, seeing her unlaced gown, congratulated her and wished her a happy hour. If goodwill could do the trick, she would have a fine, healthy son.

When they returned to Westminster, they found the Bishop of Cambrai, newly arrived from Burgundy and craving an audience.

"Be very wary," Henry warned Elizabeth. "He is your aunt Margaret's creature."

"I know that well!" she replied. There had once been a rumor that the Bishop and her aunt were Warbeck's real parents.

Despite feeling nauseous, she made sure she was present when Henry received the Bishop, a fleshy, expensively robed prelate who looked as if he might well be given to the lusts of the flesh.

"Your Majesty," he boomed, after courtesies had been exchanged, "her Grace the Duchess wishes to be assured that her nephew, the Duke of York, continues in good health."

Elizabeth stifled a gasp. Henry looked nonplussed for a second, then an angry flush crept up his face. "The Duke of York, my lord Bishop, is very well and residing with his sisters at Eltham Palace," he said coldly. "If you are referring to Perkin Warbeck, who is no blood kin to the Duchess, but in whom, for some unfathomable reason, she takes an interest, then I will have him brought here for your inspection."

The Bishop flushed an angry pink. "Your Majesty, her Grace has seen the young man and spent much time with him, and she is certain that he is her nephew. With the greatest of respect, you, on the other hand, never met him as a child."

"But I did, my lord Bishop." Elizabeth had to speak out. "Do you think I would not have known my own brother? I can say for certain that Warbeck is not York and can have no claim to the throne of England."

He gave her a cynical look to show that he believed she was repeating what the King had told her to say. Fury welled in her.

"The Queen speaks truth," Henry cut in. "There is so much proof of this pretender's true identity that it makes a mockery of fools who persist in clinging to the absurd notion that he is York. I will not argue with you further. The truth has been well established in this kingdom. But I will have Warbeck brought here to satisfy your mistress."

The Bishop opened his mouth to protest, but Henry silenced him with a look that would have quelled an army.

"Return this afternoon at three o'clock," he said. "The prisoner will be waiting for you."

Shortly before the appointed hour, the court assembled and Henry and Elizabeth seated themselves beneath the canopy of estate. At a nod from the King, the guards brought Warbeck before them.

Elizabeth was shocked to see him in chains and looking so altered that he was barely recognizable. He was filthy, with matted hair and stinking clothes that made her stomach churn. She shuddered to think what conditions might be like in his miserable, windowless cell, if just a few weeks of imprisonment had done this to him. If it went on for much longer, he would be dead, she was certain of it. She saw Dr. de Puebla staring at him, looking as horrified as she felt. She glanced at Henry, but he seemed unmoved.

Warbeck stood before them, his eyes dull, as if all hope had gone. How he must be regretting his imbecilic attempt to escape, if, indeed, he was still capable of rational thought. Elizabeth silently thanked God that Catherine was not in attendance on her today.

When the Bishop was announced, and saw Warbeck, he drew in his breath and visibly blanched.

"Truly, this wretch is not a prince of the blood," Henry said, in ringing tones. "Are you satisfied now, Bishop?"

"I will report back to the Duchess," the prelate said, tight-lipped, and bowed his way out.

Henry nodded at Warbeck. "Take him away," he instructed the guards.

As Elizabeth watched the young man being dragged out, she had the impulse to plead that he be better treated. Yet she knew she should not do so before the court. In private, Henry might be more amenable.

Dr. de Puebla stepped forward. "Your Majesty, might I crave an audience?"

"Certainly, my lord ambassador," Henry replied. "Come through to my closet." He rose, signed to Elizabeth to accompany him, and went ahead through the door behind the dais to the gallery that led to his apartments. In the closet he used as a study, his account books and his writing materials were laid out neatly and precisely on the table.

"Yes, Dr. de Puebla, what can I do for you?"

"Majesty, it is about the pretender. My sovereigns continue to be concerned about his power to make mischief for you and destabilize your throne. King Ferdinand never ceases pressing me to urge that you rid yourself of him. He cannot understand why you have not done so."

Elizabeth did not like the way this was going.

"For three reasons, my lord ambassador," Henry replied. "First, I have always borne in mind that Warbeck has been the tool of those who used him to overthrow me. Second, he is not my subject. Third, his wife is kinswoman to the King of Scots."

"Some princes would not be as scrupulous," Dr. de Puebla observed, "my master for one, and he would not mind my saying that. This alliance means much to King Ferdinand and Queen Isabella, but they must needs be certain that their daughter is coming to a peaceful kingdom with a stable monarchy."

Elizabeth felt another stirring of unease and Henry's response was sharp. "You have seen for yourself that Warbeck can be no threat to me now. My throne is stable, the succession assured. What more can the sovereigns demand?"

"The head of Warbeck," Dr. de Puebla replied. "Otherwise, they may have second thoughts about marrying their daughter to a prince whose future might be in jeopardy."

"Good God, man, this is England, not Italy!" Henry exploded. "The country is settled, our enemies defeated. Pray tell that to their Majesties!"

"I will, Sire," said de Puebla, evidently deciding that withdrawal was preferable to further argument. "I just pray that no other would-be claimants to the throne pit themselves against you, knowing that you deal leniently with pretenders."

He was gone before Henry could retort. When the door closed behind him, the King gave vent to his anger. "I'm not stupid, Bessy! I'm keeping Warbeck under close surveillance, and if he gets up to any more tricks, he will live just long enough to rue the day."

"I know, I know," she said soothingly. "But he may not be a threat to you for much longer. Did you see the state of him? Could he not be kept in better conditions, for our Lord's sake?"

He stared at her. "*You* are asking for clemency for *him*? This felon who has caused you so much grief, let alone threatened my throne and given me years of vexation? Bessy, I find it hard to refuse you anything, but this time I must."

"I cannot help pitying him," she admitted sadly. "It is our Christian duty to relieve those in prison." She looked into Henry's eyes and read in them only suspicion. "What?" she faltered.

"Are you asking me to show mercy because you believe that Warbeck really is your brother? Tell me the truth, Elizabeth."

She was stunned. "Did you even have to ask that? He's not my brother. I know that for a fact. But I thought that *you* still had doubts about it."

"Me?" Henry seemed to sag. "No. But that we should still suspect each other of entertaining such doubts is a sorry thing, Bessy. And yet, I cannot rid myself of the deep-seated fear that Warbeck has more cards up his sleeve, or that some other pretender will crawl out of the stonework and rise up against me. Or even, dare I say it, that York himself will appear one day and the whole damn edifice of what I have built up as king will crumble."

"I understand, Henry, oh, I do!" He opened his arms and she went into them. "Do you not know that I am torn between wanting my brother restored to me and fearing he might be, because of what it would mean for you, for us and our children?"

"I do know, cariad," Henry murmured. "But we must not let it affect us. I think your poor brother is dead, murdered by Richard. I just wish we knew for certain."

King James had professed himself eager to marry Margaret, and Henry had empowered the Bishop of Winchester to conclude negotiations for the peace treaty. Letters flew back and forth between London and Edinburgh, and Henry was in a jubilant mood, excited at the prospect of his grandson sitting on the Scottish throne.

"James wants an early wedding," he told Elizabeth and his mother as they supped together one evening in September.

"No!" they both cried in unison.

"Margaret is but a child!" Elizabeth protested, near to tears.

"It is perilous for a girl to marry too young," Henry's mother warned him. "If we are obliged to send the Princess directly to Scotland, I fear—knowing his reputation—that King James would not wait, but might injure her and endanger her health. I speak from bitter experience, my son, for I bore you at thirteen and, although I give God thanks daily for sending you to me, the birth damaged me, so that I never had another child. And that would not do when the Scottish succession depends on the birth of sons."

Henry held up his hands in mock surrender. "Fear not! I have already instructed my envoys to tell James that Margaret has not yet completed her ninth year and is so delicate that she must be married later than other young ladies. I am insisting that he agree not to demand his bride before 1503, when she will be fourteen."

"That is as well, my son," the Lady Margaret said, smiling at Elizabeth. "Give the child a few years yet with her family."

Elizabeth felt tears welling. She could not bear the thought of parting with her daughter. It would be Margaret in 1503 and doubtless Mary soon afterward. How had all those royal mothers down the ages coped?

Elizabeth stood in her chamber at Westminster, staring unseen into the dancing flames on the hearth. She could not believe her ears. Another pretender had been arrested.

"Fortunately, this one was apprehended easily," Henry said, after breaking the news.

"Who does he claim to be?" she cried.

"The young fool says he is the Earl of Warwick! But his name is Ralph Wilford. He's a student at Cambridge—and ought to be educated enough to know better! It makes me wonder what on earth they teach them at the universities these days. It seems he was encouraged in his imposture by a friar. I'm going to question him now."

"May I be present?" Elizabeth was not feeling well—she was eight months gone now, the pregnancy was dragging her down more than the others had, and her doctors were concerned—but she wanted to see Ralph Wilford for herself. Not that he was even claiming to be one of her brothers, but there was a dim spark of hope in her that this new imposture might be a cover for something else.

But Henry was firm. "You should rest, cariad. I will report back later. There is nothing to worry about; this idiot is not another Warbeck."

He returned within an hour. "He's a fantasist! He confessed that he had dreams urging him to declare himself to be Warwick, and that, by so doing, he could become king. I tell you, Bessy, my patience is exhausted. He shall hang."

"That seems very severe, in view of how you treated Warbeck."

"Bessy, Wilford is my subject. In attempting my throne, he has committed treason, and the penalty is death. I can order no less. Ferdinand and Isabella will hear of this, and I don't want it putting them off sending their daughter to England."

"I see." She was pensive for a minute. "Would it not be wise then to have the real Warwick paraded through London?"

"I don't want to make a big fuss about this, as I did with Simnel. Once I've made an example of Wilford, we can put it behind us. I just hope that the sovereigns are of the same mind."

"I pray they are. But, Henry, tell me: is there any other reason why you will not show Warwick in public? Is he in good health?" They had rarely mentioned her cousin over the years, but Elizabeth had always been painfully aware that he still languished in the Tower. He must be twenty-four now. She wondered how he had coped with the years of isolation, of being punished for nothing other than having royal blood, which he could not help. It was a cruel fate, but, given that two men had tried to impersonate him, and that he would likely always be a focus for malcontents, it was clear that Henry had no choice but to keep him close confined.

"He is well, and he does not lack for human comforts," he told her, "but, as you know, he is a simple soul—I doubt he looks for more in life than he has."

"You have seen him?"

"No, but I receive regular reports from his warders. Don't fret about him, Bessy. He is well cared for, and he is in the safest place."

Elizabeth's child would be born soon. She could not wait for this difficult pregnancy to be over, for she was worn out. She passed the short January days in her privy chamber at Greenwich, sitting by the fire, stitching a layette for the baby, or resting on her bed. Henry spent as much time with her as he could, endlessly fussing and repeatedly asking Mother Massey and the physicians if everything was proceeding as it should.

"I am all right," Elizabeth assured him. "There is no need to keep worrying."

"You have never been so unwell before," he said.

"But Mother Massey says that there's nothing unusual in that; each pregnancy is different."

Henry subsided, but still looked doubtful.

She was about to take to her chamber when Cecily arrived unexpectedly at court. When she was announced, Elizabeth rejoiced that she had come to be her gossip during her confinement, for her other sisters were unable to be present. Anne's young son Thomas was still sickly and needed her, and Katherine was far away in Devon, while Bridget was cloistered at Dartford. But when she saw Cecily, pale-faced and clad in mourning weeds, she was shocked.

"I don't want to be a burden on you at this time, but I had to come," Cecily said, her face working in distress. "They are all gone from me. My John died this morning. He had a cough and then suddenly started getting these breathing problems. The doctors could do nothing for him. And then my little girls sickened, and God has taken them, too." Her features contorted in silent agony.

Elizabeth heaved herself out of her chair and folded Cecily in her arms, remembering how she had felt when her own Beth died. "Oh, my dear, my darling sister, I am so very sorry. How dreadful for you."

"My lovely babes, my angels," Cecily sobbed. "How will I live without them? And John . . . I had grown to love him. I never thought I could love anyone after Ralph was taken from me, but John was a good man. My only comfort is that they are now all together in Heaven. And I am quite alone in the world."

"You are not, Cis. You have me, and Henry will look after you. Please stay and let me comfort you."

Cecily nodded, and they sat together and talked and wept, and she said it helped to reminisce and look back to a time before either of them were married and life at their father's court had been good.

Three days later, Lord Welles's lawyer came to see Cecily and informed her that, in his will, her husband had passed over his other heirs and directed that all his property should go to her, and that his body should be buried wherever she, with the consent of the King and Queen and the King's mother, should deem appropriate. Cecily asked the King what his pleasure in the matter was, and he commanded that Lord Welles be buried with great solemnity in Westminster Abbey, which was what she had wished. After the funeral, Elizabeth welcomed Cecily into her household as chief lady of honor.

The Lady Margaret showed Cecily great kindness and invited her to stay at Collyweston, where she intended to retire after Elizabeth's child was born. At fifty-six, Margaret was turning increasingly to religion and planning to spend more time away from the court. She was now attending Mass six times daily; she ate sparingly and observed fast days rigorously. Elizabeth knew that she wore a hair shirt next to her skin in penitence for her sins.

But this was not all. Although still married to Derby, Margaret had decided to take a vow of chastity, with her husband's blessing. Elizabeth supposed that intimacy between them had long ceased, if there had ever been any, given that childbirth had left Margaret damaged—she had never inquired too closely as to how. She was present when, wearing the somber garb she would now adopt, her mother-in-law made her vow in chapel, kneeling before the Bishop of London.

The baby was a son, to Henry's profound delight and relief.

"I have been so worried about you, cariad," he cried, leaning over the bed and taking her in his arms. "You have had a hard time of it these past months."

"Well, it has been worth it," she smiled, kissing him. "It was an easy travail. And we have another boy."

Henry leaned over the cradle where the tiny infant was sleeping peacefully, having just taken his first feed from his wet nurse.

"Shall we call him Edmund, after my father?" he asked, gazing at the child in wonder.

Elizabeth smiled. "It suits him. I like it."

"He shall be duke of Somerset and have the title that was proudly borne by my Beaufort ancestors," Henry declared.

"So tiny a creature to have so great a style!" she replied.

Little Edmund was baptized in the church of the Observant Friars in the silver font that had again been fetched from Canterbury Cathedral at the King's request. It was a splendid occasion, as lavish as if an heir to the crown had been born. The Lady Margaret stood godmother and, in her joy at being made a grandmother once more, handsomely rewarded the midwife and the nurses.

Afterward, Margaret departed with Cecily for Collyweston, where she intended to gather around her a religious community united in their devotion to God and dedicated to prayer and good works.

Elizabeth felt sad when they had gone. She had come to rely on her mother-in-law's calm and capable presence, and her affection for her had grown over the years. No longer did she resent Margaret's influence over Henry or his according her prominence at court. Margaret's heart was in the right place, and no man could ever have had a more devoted mother.

Elizabeth knew there were those who disliked Margaret and even feared her. Henry had told her that she was vigorous in enforcing her rents and dues, and it was true that she could be formidable when roused, but there was about her a touching sweetness and kindness. To see her with her grandchildren was a joy. Elizabeth was hoping that Margaret's newfound vocation would not keep her away from court too long. She hoped too that Cecily would return to her, although she understood her sister's desire for a change of scene and the spiritual support that would help her to find peace after her devastating losses.

Harry, Margaret, and Mary had been present at the christening of their new brother, Harry demanding to know when Edmund would be old enough to play soldiers with him, and the girls fussing over the baby as if he were a doll. But Arthur had not been present. Henry had not liked to interrupt his studies at Ludlow.

"It's a long and arduous journey in February, and I'd rather wait until the weather is better before summoning him to court."

Elizabeth was sorry that Arthur couldn't be with them, but she was impressed by Henry's new plans for his education, now that Dr. Rede was retiring.

"He's twelve now, old enough to imbibe the new humanist learning. He's already familiar with the classics of ancient Greece and Rome and I want that interest developed further. It's essential for a prince in this modern age. I've decided to appoint Bernard André to be Arthur's chief tutor."

She was pleased to hear that. The blind friar André had been assisting Dr. Rede for three years and Arthur liked him. Under his tutelage, the Prince had already read or committed to memory the best Latin and Greek authors.

"And he is to be joined by my physician, Dr. Thomas Linacre. He's been in Italy and has studied the new learning. My librarian, Giles Dewes, can teach the boy French, grammar, and music."

"I trust there will be time for sports and recreation. You know what they say about all work and no play?"

"Of course. Arthur must learn to be an all-round man and excel in learning and the manly exercises."

"You think he is up to it?" Elizabeth could not help thinking of her son's skinny frame and lack of robustness.

"Of course!" Henry was adamant. "By all reports, he is as sturdy as other lads his age."

She wondered if that was true, or if Henry just wanted to believe it. But Arthur's guardians would not lie about something as important as that, surely?

She did not have too long to wait to see for herself how Arthur was doing. In May, she and Henry traveled to Tickenhill to see him married to the Infanta by proxy, with the portly Dr. de Puebla standing in for the bride. The ceremony in the chapel was suitably impressive, but she was concerned to find Arthur as raw-boned as ever and looking tired. She noticed that he had a slight cough and a high color.

That night, as they lay abed, she confided her fears to Henry. "Do you think he looks well?"

"His physicians tell me he is. I could sound out Dr. Linacre, if you are worried." His hand reached out for hers.

"Yes, that would be reassuring."

"I'll speak to him tomorrow. But I was impressed with the boy. He is growing into a fine young man."

"He is." But he was too studious, too reserved, too thoughtful, too learned beyond his years. She wished there was a lighter side to Arthur. What sort of king would he make?

The next morning, Dr. Linacre saw them both. "I wouldn't worry about the cough," he said. "It will pass. And the Prince looks tired because he has been working too hard at his lessons. He is quite diligent in seeking to learn all that becomes a ruler. I will talk to Friar André about easing the curriculum a little."

"Thank you," Elizabeth said. "But I still worry that Arthur is too thin."

"A lot of boys his age are thin; it is the growth spurt; it signifies nothing. His martial exercises will help him to put on muscle."

"Then I shall not worry," she replied.

"Good," Henry smiled.

"Your Graces will be pleased to know that the Prince exchanges regular letters with the Infanta. Friar André and I supervise the writing of them and ensure that he expresses the proper sentiments. But Arthur has a way with words, and I am sure that his bride is delighted to hear that he is longing to see and embrace her, and ardently loves her already."

It was only what was expected of him. Without prompting, would a thirteen-year-old boy have written such words? And what did Arthur really think about his coming marriage, which was not far off, since the Infanta would be coming to England in December, when she reached the age of fourteen? Elizabeth doubted he would ever tell her, for he was so schooled to obedience and duty. She was thankful that the marriage would not be consummated for at least two years, for Arthur was certainly not ready for the duties of wedlock.

She left her son with a heavy heart, still fretting a little about his health. He stood stiffly as she embraced him and, for the thousandth time, she regretted that they had never been as close as she was with his siblings. It was as if she was his queen rather than his mother, to be loved dutifully and accorded all due reverence.

Their progress that summer took them to Hampshire. As soon as they returned, Elizabeth hastened to Eltham, where Harry proudly told her that he and his sisters had received a visit from the celebrated Erasmus.

"He's friends with Thomas More, and Thomas brought him, knowing that I share his love for the new learning. We were all in the hall, and I received them, and Erasmus praised my dignity and courtesy!" He paused only to draw breath. "Thomas gave me some Latin verses he had composed especially for me, and I asked Erasmus to write me some verses, too—and, Mother, he did! He sent me a ten-page poem, in which he called me, Arthur, and Edmund red roses, for our vigor, and Margaret and Mary white roses, for their maidenly innocence!"

Elizabeth was swept up by his enthusiasm, exulting in the fact that her eight-year-old son had such a passion for learning and was already proficient in Latin. She spent a happy afternoon, watching as he romped with his sisters, and laughing at his winning, mischievous way. What a king he would have made—if only God had ordained things differently. But maybe Henry, or, later, Arthur, would recognize Harry's capabilities and give him some high office in which he could put his talents to good use.

Back at court, she found Henry brooding in his study, having endured a disturbing interview with Dr. de Puebla. She was appalled to see that he seemed to have aged twenty years in the fortnight she had been away.

"What's wrong?" she asked, wrapping her arms around him.

He returned the embrace, but his heart was pounding. "You will remember that Ferdinand and Isabella expressed concern at the emergence of yet another pretender, but even though they were assured that Wilford had been speedily dealt with, Puebla keeps warning me that their faith in the security of the English throne remains shaken." He gave a despondent snort. "He reminded me that they have seen over the years how the crown can be destabilized by imposters and the continuing existence of Yorkist heirs who might yet challenge my title. Now that Warbeck has been discredited, they apparently regard Warwick as the greatest threat to England's stability, for some might think he has a strong claim to the throne, and they fear he will always be a focus for malcontents."

"What are you saying?" Elizabeth cried.

"I am saying nothing." Henry looked exasperated. "It is what Dr. de Puebla is implying, undoubtedly on the orders of Ferdinand."

"Which is?" she asked, already knowing the answer.

"That Arthur's marriage to the Infanta is conditional upon the removal of Warwick. Puebla pretty much told me that his sovereigns are averse to giving their daughter to a prince whose future crown will not be secure. And this after all I have done to establish my dynasty and rid the land of pretenders. Why must Ferdinand persist in questioning the stability of my throne?"

Elizabeth was horrified to think that Arthur's marriage would not go ahead. The shame of it. The international scandal, which would demonstrate more than anything else that England's monarchy was built on shaky foundations. It could have a serious impact on foreign relations and trade and make Henry a laughingstock in the eyes of Christendom. As her eyes met his, she could see that he too understood the implications.

"So Ferdinand has made it clear that while Warwick lives, the Infanta will not be coming to England?"

"He has. As clear as glass," Henry said heavily.

"What will you do?"

He hesitated. "I must think on it. I have been wondering— maybe Ferdinand has a point. Last week, I heard of a priest who accurately foretold the deaths of your father and the Usurper. I summoned him for a consultation and he warned me that my life would be in danger all this year, for there are two parties in the land—those who are loyal to me, and those who wish to see the House of York restored. He said that conspiracies against the throne would ensue."

"Oh, Henry, don't give ear to soothsayers!" He was too superstitious for his own good.

"But what if he's right? What if this is somehow bound up with Warwick? Maybe it's he who will plot against me, or, more likely, his supporters? Is there to be no end to these intrigues?"

"But where's the evidence that anyone is plotting?"

Henry looked defeated. She saw his stooped shoulders, and could have wept.

"In faith, Bessy, I don't know what to do. I wish that God, or rather Ferdinand, had not laid this burden on me. I am not a cruel man; I do not murder innocents, like Richard did. I act within the law. How can I proceed against Warwick, who is too stupid to hurt a fly?"

There was nothing she could say to comfort him. Presently, he said he had work to do, and dismissed her with a squeeze of the hand, reminding her not to breathe a word of what she knew.

Henry said no more until two weeks later, when he summoned Elizabeth to his study, where she found him with his astrologer.

"Dr. Parron is casting my horoscope," he said. "I thought you would be interested to hear what he says."

She tried not to show her exasperation. If only Henry would not place so much reliance on prophecies. But it was ingrained in his Welsh blood. He had grown up with his head filled with superstition. And now he was a troubled man, his face creased with lines of anxiety.

She watched as Parron laid out his charts and pointed out to Henry the positions of the constellations. Little of it made sense to her. But then he looked up, his face grave. "Sire, it is expedient that one man should die for the people, and the whole nation perish not, for no rebellion can occur without the deaths of a great part of the people and the destruction of many great families."

Elizabeth was astonished. Parron had reflected her husband's fears incredibly accurately. She saw that Henry was as amazed as she was—and she feared the implications of that.

When Parron had gone, she sat down, waiting to hear what Henry would say.

"Do you not think that was a sign?" he asked her, still looking dumbfounded.

"No. I think that, like so much else in astrology, it is open to more than one interpretation. It could be an endorsement of your treatment of Wilford."

"I asked Parron to cast for the future," Henry said quietly.

"You will not act on it, I hope?" She was beginning to fear that he would.

"I have to decide what is best for England and my own security. I dare not prejudice the Spanish alliance."

"But Warwick has never done anything to justify your doing away with him!"

"I know that, Bessy." Henry's face was gray. "But I would never just do away with him. That's not my way of doing things, having experienced, none better, what can ensue when an heir to the throne simply disappears. But while Warwick lives, there might well be others who seek to impersonate him and overthrow me. Ferdinand and Isabella understand that."

"But Warwick has no part in such treasons! He's a simple innocent who has not the guile to plot against you."

Henry was silent for a while. "Leave it, Bessy. I must think on the matter."

"You will not harm him? He is my cousin and I feel great pity for him, for his life has been a misery."

"I will not harm him. You may rest assured that I shall deal with him according to his merits."

They spoke no more on the matter. As the days, weeks, and months went by, Elizabeth began to hope that Henry had decided to placate Ferdinand and Isabella by diplomatic means. But would that be enough to safeguard the valuable Spanish alliance?

In the middle of November, she visited the children at Eltham. Edmund was crawling now and his sisters were making a great pet of him. Harry, who had loftily declared that he was too old to be playing with babies, was eager to show off his riding skills, and they spent several happy hours at the stables and in the park.

Elizabeth returned to Westminster in a buoyant mood, but there was Henry, sunk in dejection, waiting for her in his closet. She had been summoned as soon as she alighted from her barge and had not even time to take off her cloak and gloves.

"What on earth is the matter?" she cried, sketching the scantiest of curtseys.

He roused himself sufficiently to kiss her cheek. "Bad news, I'm afraid, Bessy."

"Arthur?" Her thoughts flew to Ludlow.

"No. Warwick."

She thought for a moment that she was going to hear that he was dead, and braced herself. But no.

"Warwick and Warbeck have just confessed to a plot to destroy me and all my blood—that means our children and you, too, Bessy . . . And while Warbeck appears to have believed that Warwick was helping him to my crown, Warwick intended to take it himself."

She was aghast, disbelieving. "Warwick hasn't the sense to do that!"

"It appears he has more cunning than we give him credit for," Henry observed, his eyes meeting hers. "Both of them have been examined by my judges, who have determined that they have indeed committed treason and deserve death. I've asked what they think I should do with them. Is it to be trial or attainder?"

She ought to be trembling at the thought of what might have befallen her husband and children if this plot had succeeded, but she could not believe that they had been in any real danger. It had surfaced all too conveniently for Henry, and still she doubted that Warwick had the necessary guile. But Warbeck did! She did not know what to think.

"Is it possible that Warwick was led unwittingly into treason?" she asked.

Henry shook his head. "The justices believe he knew what he was doing."

She sat down, still wearing her cloak. She could not stop thinking that this gave Henry the ideal pretext to rid himself of Warwick and Warbeck. It would render his crown more secure and preserve the Spanish alliance.

Her head was teeming with questions. "But how did they communicate with each other, with Warbeck being held so straitly?"

"Apparently there were other conspirators, two traitorous jailers called Astwood and Cleymound. The plan was to fire and seize the Tower, thus facilitating Warwick's escape to Flanders, where he would raise an army to defeat me in battle and make himself king. It would be laughable if it hadn't been orchestrated by ruthless knaves!"

Elizabeth could not imagine Warwick doing that. But if others had inveigled him into believing that he could escape and become king, he would be as putty in their hands. Who could blame him for wishing to be revenged on Henry, who had so unjustly incarcerated him for fourteen years? If, of course, he was able to reason that much.

"I doubt that Warwick understood the enormity of what he thought he was about to do or had the capacity to see it through," she said. "I can't imagine him leading an armed rebellion."

"Neither can I; he would surely have been but a figurehead, a puppet for those other traitors. It looks as if eight others were involved, jailers, prisoners, and citizens of London. Warbeck, of course, would have done anything to escape his strait confinement."

"But how did all this come to light?"

"Cleymound got cold feet and fled into sanctuary, then confessed. He did so because he feared that Warwick was about to reveal all to my lord of Oxford, the Constable of the Tower."

It was sounding more and more convincing, but Elizabeth's heart felt leaden because she knew there was no hope for Warwick. Henry had too many good reasons to want him eliminated to prevent the law from taking its course. She spared a thought, too, for Warbeck, and for Catherine, who had clung on to her love for him. How dreadful this news would be to her.

"It is a wonder how prophecies come true," she murmured.

"That is why it is best never to ignore them," Henry said, a little reprovingly.

Warbeck was tried at Westminster that month and condemned to be hanged, drawn and quartered, the punishment meted out to traitors. Two days later, at the Guildhall, eight people, including Astwood, were found guilty of conspiring to free Warwick and Warbeck. Elizabeth was surprised that Cleymound was not among them, but supposed that he either remained in sanctuary or had been pardoned for turning the others in. But she did not have leisure to ponder on that for long because she was too busy trying to comfort Catherine, who had collapsed in a storm of tears when she heard the verdict and could not be consoled.

Warwick's trial followed the next day.

"He pleaded guilty," Henry told Elizabeth at supper that evening.

"He was too simple to do other than what they told him to do," she replied, trying not to weep. "You don't need to tell me what the sentence was."

"It is what the law demands," Henry said gently. "But I will commute the sentence to beheading, in consideration of his rank and his kinship to you. It will be quick."

Quick, but brutal; a terrible way to die, especially when you didn't really understand what you had done wrong. She turned away, so that Henry should not see the tears streaming down her cheeks. Poor Warwick; poor, simple boy, who had never deliberately done anyone any harm, and whose only crime had been to have royal blood in his veins. She thought of his sister Margaret, now happily married to Sir Richard Pole, the chief gentleman of Prince Arthur's privy chamber; she would be devastated to lose her brother. Elizabeth wished that she could be at Ludlow to comfort her.

In the meantime, she had all to do to keep Catherine calm. The young woman was distraught, determined to go to Tyburn to catch a last glimpse of her husband.

"Don't go!" Elizabeth urged. "You will carry with you to the grave what you see there."

"But I must!" Catherine cried, and no one could deter her. On the morning of the execution, she was missing from her place in chapel and her cloak had gone from the peg in her chamber. Elizabeth crossed herself and prayed that Catherine might faint and be spared the sight of her husband being butchered. It was bad enough imagining it, but to see it happening . . .

But Catherine was calm when she returned. "The King had commuted the sentence," she said, as all the ladies clustered around. "He was drawn to the gallows on a hurdle—a man told me it was because he was not worthy any more to tread upon the face of the earth—but he suffered only hanging, which was mercifully over quickly. Some bystanders told me it can take more than a quarter of an hour. I thank God it was not that long. Before they put the rope around his neck, he swore that he was not the son of King Edward and asked forgiveness of God and the King for his deception. But, oh God . . ." She dissolved into racking sobs, and Elizabeth took her in her arms, as the others did their best to offer comfort where no comfort could be given. At length, Elizabeth sent for Dr. Lewis, who gave Catherine a sleeping draft that soon took effect.

Sitting beside her as she found refuge in dreams, she wondered why Henry had commuted the sentence. Was it from common humanity—or on account of Warbeck being an alien and married to King James's kinswoman? Or had he been merciful because Warbeck had unwittingly helped to send Warwick to a better world? But she could not help speculating that there might linger still, in his mind, some suspicion that he really had been of royal blood. And yet, Warbeck had denied it at the last. Expecting to face divine judgment within minutes, he was unlikely to have been lying, and she must stop torturing herself.

That evening, Henry informed her that Warwick was to suffer execution six days hence, on Tower Hill. She wanted to be there, to give her cousin some small support during his last moments, but it was out of the question, and she knew she could do more by remaining here in chapel and praying for his gentle soul. But she suffered greatly on the day he died, and stayed on her knees for hours, beseeching God to have mercy on His innocent, who had never received much in the way of earthly happiness.

She tried not to blame Henry, who had been in a very difficult position and seemed to be doing his best to placate her for the shedding of Warwick's blood. He even paid for his body to be buried in Bisham Priory near the tomb of his grandfather, the Kingmaker. But Elizabeth still wondered if there was more to the conspiracy than Henry had let on. It had surfaced so timely, so opportunely. Even so, the plotters *had* committed treason. But there was no point in saying that to Catherine, who was inconsolable.

The strain had told on Henry. He fell sick after the executions, while staying at Wanstead in Essex, and became so ill that Elizabeth feared he would die. But God did not see fit to deprive her of a husband, and England of its king, and Henry soon recovered. She was with him when Don Pedro de Ayala, a Spanish envoy who was in England to assist with the marriage arrangements, came to congratulate him on his restitution to health.

"I would have come before, your Majesty, but you were unwell. I know that my sovereigns will be overjoyed to hear that you are better. They were delighted to learn that this kingdom is now more secure than it has been for the last five hundred years, after it pleased God that the recent treasons were thoroughly purged, and I assured them that not a doubtful drop of royal blood remains here, only the true blood of your Majesties and Prince Arthur."

As Henry inclined his head in appreciation, Elizabeth began wondering afresh. Had Ferdinand been behind the late conspiracy? Had he persuaded Henry to rid the realm of traitors? Or had Henry himself taken the initiative? And yet, she could not see how he had achieved the result he desired—unless Warwick and Warbeck had somehow been lured into treasonable plotting. She wished she could ask him, but she dared not—and she did not want to know the answer.

Chapter 20

1500–1501

It was the year 1500, almost the dawn of a new century. Henry was now well established on his throne and the princes of Christendom were eager to win his friendship. He had brought peace to a kingdom torn by civil war, his treasury was full, and he had triumphed in securing the Spanish and Scottish alliances. But he was not liked; the taxes he imposed were too burdensome. His subjects wanted peace and triumphs, but they did not want to pay for them. People spoke of a golden age to come under King Arthur.

It had been a mild winter—too mild, for it had not killed off the plague that had been raging in London for months. Because of this, the Infanta's arrival had been deferred until next September, when Arthur would be fourteen and old enough—God willing—for marriage. Henry was spending enormous sums on preparations for the bride's reception and the wedding.

In the spring, to escape the contagion, Henry took Elizabeth to Calais, the last remaining outpost of England's continental empire. There, they were to meet with the Archduke Philip. Henry was still fearful that some new pretender might emerge, so they departed without fuss or fanfares, telling no one of their intended journey until two days beforehand. They had left their younger children at the Bishop of Ely's palace at Hatfield in Hertfordshire, far from the disease-ridden capital.

Elizabeth had never crossed the sea before and found the voyage from Dover exhilarating. The English Channel was calm, and they made land by nightfall. The next day, they rode to a church outside the walls of Calais, accompanied by a great train, with Catherine Gordon heading the Queen's fifty splendidly attired ladies. There, they met Philip. Elizabeth could see why he was called "the Handsome," but thought he had a dissolute air about him. She was keen to speak with him, for he was married to the Infanta's older sister Juana, and she was eager to find out more about Catalina.

The opportunity did not arise until they came face-to-face at the banquet that followed the feast in the tapestry-hung church. Holding a silver bowl of strawberries, cherries, and cream, Elizabeth smiled at her guest and congratulated him on the recent birth of his son Charles.

"I thank your Majesty," he replied. "It is a shame that I could not bring the Archduchess to meet you. She is a little indisposed after the birth."

"I understand. I have borne six children myself."

"Your Majesty is to be congratulated." He was courteous, but dispassionate, and Elizabeth could not warm to him.

"We are looking forward to the Infanta's arrival in England," she said. "Her marriage to our son will create a close bond between our houses."

"Indeed."

"Tell me, have you ever met Catalina?"

"No, but my wife speaks fondly of her. I gather that she is learned and wise—pretty, too."

He was not interested in Catalina, she could tell. And there was no point in pumping him for more information, as the musicians were starting up and the dancing was about to begin. She put down her bowl and took to the floor with Henry.

* * *

Over the next few days, there were pageants, feasts, and jousts in Philip's honor, and long conversations about politics, in which Elizabeth joined, at Henry's insistence.

"We are here to discuss Mary's marriage," he said, as they sat down at a table set up in one of the transepts of the church.

She was nonplussed, but recovered quickly. "She is but four years old," she said lightly.

"I'm aware of that," Henry responded, "but Philip and I wish to seal our friendship with a marriage between her and the Archduke Charles. It is a great match for her, my lady, for Charles is heir to the Habsburg territories and also to Spain."

"We understand that the marriage cannot take place for some years yet," Philip said, "and I would not wish to deprive your Majesty of the Princess's company in the meantime, so I would be content for her to remain in your care, for I know that she could not have a better education than her mother can give her."

Elizabeth tried to look pleased and appreciative. "Thank you. It is indeed a brilliant match for Mary." Inwardly, she was in turmoil. All she could think of was her beautiful red-haired daughter, so high-spirited, graceful, and full of promise. How could she ever bear to give her up?

They stayed at Calais, mostly at leisure, for forty days. By then, the plague was abating, and Henry deemed it safe to return to England. After disembarking at Dover, they rode to Greenwich, there to be met at the gatehouse by the Lady Margaret and Cecily, both clad in black and grave-faced.

"Oh no," Henry said, as he saw them. "Somebody has died." Elizabeth almost leaped out of her litter, full of fear. Not one of the children, please God . . .

Cecily burst into tears. "Poor Edmund is dead!" she cried. "The messenger arrived not an hour since from Hatfield. Oh, I am so sorry."

Elizabeth froze, as Henry's face crumpled. Her youngest, her sweet babe—gone forever from her. She could not believe it. "He was only fifteen months old," she whispered.

"Why?" Henry croaked. "How did he die?"

"It was a summer fever," Margaret said, clasping him to her bosom. "Do not grieve excessively, my son. Edmund is with God now and we should rejoice for him."

Everyone was crowding around. Elizabeth held her head up. "Let us go within," she said, desperate to reach the privacy of her apartments. Henry took her hand and led her there, both of them rigid with shock. In her bedchamber, he lay with her on the bed and held her as she cried out her anguish.

Clad in blue mourning robes, they summoned their courage and attended the state funeral. Standing on the steps of Westminster Hall, they waited for the cortège to arrive after it had come in procession through London. Elizabeth saw the torches approaching in the distance and braced herself for the sight of her son's coffin. She nearly collapsed when she saw Edmund's lifelike wooden effigy lying on a tiny chest covered with white damask and a cross of red velvet. It was hard to believe that her tender babe lay inside, altered in death, beyond the reach of his mother's embrace.

Leaning on Henry's arm, she followed the black-draped hearse as it was borne into Westminster Abbey, with the peers of England walking behind them, all cloaked and hooded in black. Everyone bowed their heads as a dirge was sung over the coffin, then Henry and Elizabeth left the lords to keep an overnight vigil beside it; they would observe theirs privately, in St. Stephen's Chapel. The next day, Edmund was laid to rest in the Confessor's chapel, near the sister he had never known, and Elizabeth was left to resume her existence in a world that suddenly seemed so much emptier.

Soon afterward, to cheer her, Henry summoned Arthur to court. The Prince had grown taller, but she was concerned to see that he had lost weight—weight he could ill afford to lose.

"I wasn't very well in the spring," he told her, as they strolled

along the cloisters surrounding her garden. "I felt sweaty and had
a cough, but Dr. Linacre said it was an ague. You shouldn't worry,
Mother."

"But you are better now?" she asked anxiously.

"Yes," he answered.

She was not convinced—and neither was Henry when he joined
them.

"You look flushed, my son," he said, and felt Arthur's forehead
before the boy could step away. "You are burning up."

"It's nothing," Arthur said. "Dr. Linacre told me it was no cause
for concern."

Henry frowned and, putting an arm around his son, led him a
little way off. Elizabeth sat on a bench and waited, but she could
just hear their conversation.

"Arthur," Henry was saying, "the Infanta will be here in a few
weeks, and soon it will be time for you to do your duty as a husband. You know what I'm talking about?"

Arthur's voice was low. "Yes, Sir."

"In view of this continuing ague, I think it best if you consummate your marriage, but live apart from the Infanta after that—
for a couple of years at least."

"Yes, Sir," Arthur said again.

There was a pause. "I was expecting a protest," Henry said.

"Not at all, Sir."

"We must not overtax your strength. It is dangerous for young
people to exert themselves excessively in the marriage bed. The
Infanta's brother, the heir to Spain, did so, and died."

"I heard of that, Sir. I am sure that the Infanta, of all people,
will understand."

"You're a good lad, Arthur," Henry said, and when they returned to Elizabeth, he had his arm around him again.

Arthur's cough persisted and Elizabeth could not stop worrying
about him. After he had been sent back to Ludlow, she felt worn
down with anxiety. She tried to keep it from Henry, but he knew
she was fretting and that nothing he said could reassure her, so he
wrote to Dr. Linacre, who replied that Arthur was well and looking forward to the coming of his bride. But his fourteenth birth-

day came and went, and still the Infanta did not arrive. It seemed that there were endless matters still to be arranged. Elizabeth was beginning to wonder if Catalina would ever get to England. She did not voice her secret fear that Ferdinand and Isabella might be having second thoughts.

To cheer her in her low mood, Henry invited Katherine and Lord William Courtenay to court. That autumn, the couple settled into their London house with their young children, Henry, Edward, and Margaret, and became constant presences at Westminster. Cecily visited, too, and Anne, when she was staying at the Howards' mansion at Lambeth; she had just lost another baby and looked sickly and sad. But Elizabeth loved being with her sisters; she was only sorry that Bridget was unable to join them.

Elizabeth never had lost the weight that had piled on with each pregnancy. In April 1501, when she and Henry were keeping their Easter court at Eltham with the children, she began to suspect that there might be another reason for her plumpness. For a week now, her maids had been saying that they could not lace her gowns as tightly as before and, one evening, she caught sight of her reflection in a window and was startled to see her breasts looking heavy. Could it be that she was with child yet again? She sincerely hoped not, for her last pregnancy had left her utterly drained. But she had not missed her courses, so she resolved to make a determined effort to lose weight. That double chin had to go! But it was hard, given the rich fare constantly served to her. She sent for her cook and insisted that he give her smaller portions.

From time to time, she received news of the Infanta, who had, at last, left Granada on the first stage of her journey to England. In July, she was delighted to hear that Catalina was making excellent progress in French. As Arthur spoke it well, they would be able to communicate all the more easily, which would be an advantage when it came to getting to know each other. And she herself could converse smoothly with the daughter-in-law she was looking forward to meeting.

Early in October, Henry came bounding into her chamber in the Tower palace with the glad news that the Infanta had landed at Plymouth, where she had received a lavish reception. She was now on her way to London!

Elizabeth ordered her master of horse to send five chariots and twenty palfreys for the Princess and her ladies. She had already instructed her chamberlain on the etiquette to be observed when Catalina arrived—or Katherine, as she was to be called in England. She and the Lady Margaret had spent hours drawing up lists of the ladies who were to attend them and the Infanta during the wedding celebrations.

It was heartening to read the reports of the rapturous welcome the Infanta had received from the people who had flocked to see her ride by on her way eastward. It seemed that she could not have been received with greater joy had she been the savior of the world!

Elizabeth and Henry were both busy, for there were numerous arrangements that needed their attention. The Tower was a-bustle with preparations for the wedding. There were daily jousts on the tournament ground before the White Tower, as the champions tested their skills for the contests that would follow the nuptials, and there were feasts in the King's Hall as guests began arriving. But Henry's mind was elsewhere.

"Bessy," he said, catching her arm as the master cook was offering her another dish for her approval. "I have decided that I shall go and meet the Infanta. I am impatient to see her and satisfy myself that she is as fit a bride for Arthur as I have been led to believe. I've sent messengers to Arthur, who can't be far out of Ludlow, and told him to meet me on the road."

Elizabeth was wistful. "I wish I could come with you, as I long to see her, too."

He patted her hand. "You are needed here. And I think this gentleman is waiting for your opinion on the partridge." He smiled at the hovering cook. "I will see you at Greenwich. All is in readiness for the move." He kissed her hand and strode away.

* * *

He was back a few days later, with Arthur. Elizabeth was shocked to see how thin the boy was, how hectic his complexion. And he was still coughing. But Henry seemed unconcerned. He sat by her fireside, still booted and cloaked, and bade Arthur draw up a stool.

"Well, Bessy, reports did not lie! The Infanta is everything we had hoped for, eh, Arthur?"

"She is, Sir." Elizabeth searched for some sign of enthusiasm in her son.

"We caught up with her at Dogmersfield, but her people had the effrontery to tell me that I could not see her. That fierce duenna, who guards her like a dragon, and that fool of an ambassador were adamant that Spanish protocol dictated she must remain in seclusion until she was married. You can imagine how I reacted! In fact, I was immediately suspicious, wondering if the girl was deformed or ugly. So I said they could tell the lords of Spain that I would see the Infanta, even if she were in bed." He chuckled at the memory.

"And did they agree?" Elizabeth asked, still watching Arthur. But he was listening avidly to his father.

"They did. They had no choice, for I am king here. They brought her out veiled, but I was having none of that. I lifted the veil and saw before me a very pretty girl with fair hair and fine features. Her chin is a little prominent, but it is her gentle, dignified bearing that appeals. I like her person and her behavior, and you will, too, Bessy. And Arthur is rejoicing that we have found him such a bride, are you not, my son?"

"I am indeed," Arthur chimed in, and then became a little more animated. "Mother, I never felt so much joy in my life as when I beheld the sweet face of my bride. I vow I will be a true and loving husband all my days." It was what she had wanted to hear. Maybe he wasn't as ill as she had feared. Maybe the prospect of marriage to this girl was doing him good.

"That is the happiest outcome we could have wished for," she replied, deeply moved. "May God shower you both with blessings."

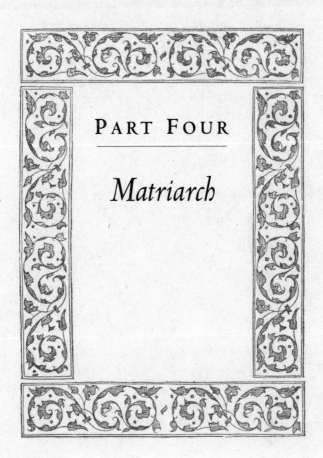

PART FOUR

Matriarch

Chapter 21

1501

It might have been Arthur's wedding, but it was Harry, ten years old and cutting a splendid figure on his horse, who was assigned the honor of riding out to Kingston-upon-Thames to welcome the Infanta and escort her to the Archbishop of Canterbury's palace at Lambeth, where she was to lodge until her marriage. Elizabeth had seen the letter Henry had had placed in Katherine's lodging, in which he had expressed their great pleasure and joy at her coming and assured her that they would treat her as their own daughter.

After Harry had gone, bursting with pride in his prominent role, Henry and Elizabeth came by barge to London and took up residence in Baynard's Castle, where Elizabeth prepared to receive Katherine. Not far along the Thames, the Lady Margaret was overseeing the renovation of Coldharbour, where the newlyweds were to stay after their marriage.

All the bells of London were ringing out when the royal family took their places at the upper windows of a haberdasher's house in Cornhill, from where they would be afforded a good view of the Infanta as she made her triumphal procession through the streets of the capital. Elizabeth opened the diamond-paned casements and leaned out. It was cold, but the children were excitedly jostling for space and craning their necks to see the pageantry. Arthur stood with the King, gravely acknowledging the cheers of the crowds below. Every window was hung with banners; the sound of minstrelsy wafted up from the street, and Elizabeth knew that pageants were being staged at various places along the route to welcome the Infanta.

And here she was, a sweet-faced young girl on a richly trapped palfrey, riding between Dr. de Puebla and the Papal Legate, and bowing graciously to left and right. She was wearing Spanish dress, with wide, stiff skirts, a coif, and a little red hat like a cardinal's, tied with a golden lace. Her long auburn hair was hanging down her back. She looked up, catching Elizabeth's eye and giving her the loveliest smile, bowed her head in reverence. Then she was gone, borne away through the crowds, leaving the impression of a reserved, dignified young lady who knew how to conduct herself and would be an asset to the royal family.

The following afternoon, on the eve of her wedding, Katherine arrived at Baynard's Castle to meet the Queen. Elizabeth sent one of her ladies to receive her and conduct her to the great chamber, and held out her hands when the Infanta was presented to her.

"I cannot welcome your Highness warmly enough," she said in French, raising Katherine from her curtsey and kissing her on both cheeks, thinking that it would be easy to love her as a daughter and that she would make Arthur a good wife.

"I have longed to see your Grace," Katherine replied in English, with a marked Castilian accent.

"And I have longed to see your Highness. Come, let us sit and get to know each other." Elizabeth indicated a chair by the hearth, concerned that Katherine would be finding the English winter hard after growing up in the warm climate of Spain. Katherine waited courteously for her to be seated, then took her place. The duenna, Doña Elvira, was hovering. Raising her eyebrows, Elizabeth signaled to her to join the other ladies at the far end of the room, which the woman did with ill-concealed grace. "I trust you are comfortably lodged."

"Yes, your Grace, thank you," Katherine said.

Elizabeth smiled at her. "From now on you must regard me as your mother, my child. If there is anything you need, come to me, and I will do my best to help. I have some influence with the King. Soon you will meet his mother, the Lady Margaret. She too has been longing for your coming. Her chief wish is to see all our children happily settled and provided for." She smiled. "Your Highness has already met my son Harry. He is a rogue! Arthur was sent away when he was small, to Ludlow Castle on the Welsh border, to be taught how to rule his principality of Wales, but Harry grew up under my care, with his sisters. You will like Margaret and Mary. Margaret is not much younger than your Highness and is to be the Queen of Scots."

"And the Princess Mary?" Katherine asked.

"She is but five," Elizabeth told her. "We must wait to see what God will provide. I had two other children, but alas, God saw fit to take them to Himself. Edmund died only last year. He was fifteen months old." She felt her voice falter.

"My mother also lost two children—two babies," Katherine ventured. "And when my brother Juan died, she mourned deeply."

"That must have been the hardest cross to bear," Elizabeth said. "We were grief-stricken ourselves to hear the news." She squeezed Katherine's hand. "But today let us speak of happier things, for you are to be married tomorrow, and there are going to be great celebrations! Lady Guildford tells me that you like to dance. She was with the King's party at Dogmersfield and saw how accomplished you are."

"I love to dance!" Katherine smiled.

"Do you know any English dances?" Elizabeth rose to her feet.

"No, your Grace."

"Then I will teach you some!" Clapping her hands, Elizabeth bade her ladies leave their embroidery and summon the musicians. There followed an enjoyable hour in which Katherine and her maids performed the stately and sedate dances of Spain, with Doña Elvira watching eagle-eyed for any hint of impropriety or levity, and Elizabeth and her ladies demonstrated the livelier English dances. There was much laughter as the Infanta's attendants tried to copy them, and the duenna looked mortified, but dared not complain, of course, for it would not be politic to criticize the Queen of England. Soon, Katherine was gliding across the tiled floor in a *basse* dance and skipping in a lively saltarello.

The evening flew by, as Elizabeth found herself enjoying her company more and more. When the time came to say farewell, she took her hand. "I know you will be a good wife to Arthur. Be patient and kind with him. He has not been well. He thinks I fuss too much, but we all pray he will amend soon."

"I know he will," Katherine replied. "At Dogmersfield, he said he was getting better. And I will have a care for his health."

Elizabeth kissed her. "God bless you for your sweet heart."

As soon as she had gone, Elizabeth departed for Lord Bergavenny's house by St. Paul's Cathedral, where she and Henry were to spend the night. As her litter carried her through the torchlit streets of London, she felt pleased that she had made a good beginning in preparing her successor for the queenly role she would one day occupy, and that Katherine was appreciative of the guidance of a mother-in-law who could initiate her into the realities and mysteries of English court life.

"You look very fine," Henry said when Elizabeth appeared in the embroidered white satin gown that (she fancied) flattered her fuller figure, and a purple velvet train. She kissed him, thinking he looked rather splendid himself in his red velvet robes, his breastplate studded with diamonds, precious stones, and pearls, and a belt of rubies at his waist.

They left early that morning to ride to the Tower, where the great procession had assembled, and waited for the Infanta to join them. When she appeared, she was royally attired in a wide-skirted wedding gown of heavy white-and-gold pleated satin. Her glorious red-gilt hair was loose beneath a jeweled coronet and a voluminous veil of silk, edged with a sparkling border of gold, pearls, and precious stones. She sank into a deep curtsey and Henry and Elizabeth embraced her.

"Your Highness makes a beautiful bride!" the Queen exclaimed.

The King was eyeing Katherine appreciatively. "We could not

have asked for better," he said. "Very becoming!" Katherine blushed.

She and Elizabeth climbed into the open chariot that was to carry them to St. Paul's Cathedral, and the King rode ahead, magnificent on his white horse. All the way to St. Paul's, the streets were dense with happy, cheering people, and Elizabeth's heart swelled to see them. Katherine looked a little bewildered, as if unable to believe that all the ovation was for her, but she smiled shyly and ventured the occasional wave, and the crowds loved her.

Elizabeth pointed out the free wine flowing from the conduits. "There will be much merrymaking today, and many sore heads tomorrow," she smiled.

When the procession drew up outside the Bishop's Palace, Henry and Elizabeth escorted Katherine within, where a beaming Lady Margaret was waiting to greet them. When Katherine refused to allow the old lady to kneel to her, Margaret's eyes glistened with emotion.

"Sweet Princess, we are blessed to have you," she said, and kissed her. The King nodded enthusiastically in agreement.

It had been decided that all eyes should be on the bridal couple on this important occasion. Henry and Elizabeth would be present, but unseen, and Harry would be giving the bride away.

"Come, my lady mother," the King said. "We must go and take our places." He escorted Elizabeth and Margaret through a door that led directly to the cathedral, leaving Katherine to await Harry's arrival. An enclosed stand had been erected for them in the nave, hung with tapestries and furnished with rich chairs. From here, they would view the ceremony through a wooden lattice that shielded them from public view.

The vast cathedral was packed with lords, ladies, dignitaries, and guests. Facing theirs was another stand for the Lord Mayor and aldermen of London. In between, along the length of the nave, had been built a raised platform, with a higher dais, or mount, in the middle, which was surrounded on all sides by steps, the entire structure being carpeted with scarlet worsted cloth; it was important that all were able to witness this prestigious marriage of the heir to the throne. And there Arthur was, engulfed in white satin, in splendid isolation, waiting at the foot of the mount. Elizabeth wondered what he was thinking. If he was nervous, there was no sign of it. She prayed that all this pageantry would not be too much for him.

"This is what I have dreamed of these thirteen years," Henry said. "Ever since I signed the Treaty of Medina del Campo. I must confess, there were times when I thought we would never see this day."

"Your careful diplomacy has triumphed!" Elizabeth told him, and he reached across and took her hand as wine was served and they waited for the nuptials to begin.

The joyful sound of trumpets, shawms, and sackbuts heralded the approach of the bride. In a stately manner, she walked along the platform, her hand resting on Harry's, her train borne by Cecily. A hundred ladies and gentlewomen, all gorgeously attired, followed. Harry was puffed up with pride, looking every inch the prince in a suit of silver tissue embroidered with gold roses.

At the mount, Arthur bowed to his bride, and she curtseyed in turn, while, with evident reluctance, Harry stepped back. Then the young couple ascended the steps to where the Archbishop of Canterbury was waiting with a host of bishops and abbots. Elizabeth watched, rapt, as the marriage was solemnized, aware of the Lady Margaret behind her, weeping with emotion. Then the Archbishop led the newly married pair to the high altar for Mass. Afterward, Arthur and Katherine—now with her face unveiled—processed back along the nave and knelt before the stand to receive the blessing of the King and Queen, who opened the lattice windows and smiled upon them. Elizabeth caught Arthur's eye and was delighted to see him smile back. Then the couple were gone, on their way to the great doors. As they passed through, a great roar of cheering could be heard outside, and voices crying, "King Henry! Prince Arthur!" Once again, the trumpets, shawms, and sackbuts blared out in celebration.

A gallant Harry led the King and Queen and their party back to the Bishop's Palace. There they embraced Arthur and Katherine and led them into the great hall, where the wedding feast was served on gold plate ornamented with precious stones. It was a marvel to see all the guests in their costly apparel and massive chains of gold. Everyone had put on a fine show.

As the short November afternoon drew on, more torches and candles were lit. Dish after dish was brought out and the wine flowed as freely as the conversation.

At the King's behest, the musicians struck up a tune and Katherine stepped down to the floor of the hall and beckoned her ladies to join her. Holding up their trains, they performed a *pavaniglia* for the company to the accompaniment of shawms and a slow, rhythmic drum beat. There were cries of "Bravo!" when the dance came to an end, and then Katherine glided into the *basse* dance she had learned the day before. Elizabeth clapped in delight and kissed and embraced her when she returned to the dais. The girl seemed to be enjoying herself, but, after a while, Henry caught Elizabeth's eye and nodded in Arthur's direction. The boy was clearly flagging.

"Time to put them to bed, I think," he murmured in her ear.

Arthur looked tired and drawn as the King summoned him to attend him. They left the hall followed by a host of lords and gentlemen, amid gusts of hearty laughter. Elizabeth rose and took Katherine by the hand, and Doña Elvira and the ladies crowded behind them. Upstairs, in the vast nuptial chamber, the great tester bed had been made up with plump pillows and fine sheets, then spread with an ermine-trimmed counterpane and strewn with dried petals and herbs. The headpiece was adorned with the royal arms of England, newly painted and gilded.

As Elizabeth assisted Doña Elvira with the disrobing, she noticed that Katherine was trembling and gave her a reassuring smile. "There is nothing to fear," she said.

Doña Elvira frowned. "The Infanta has been taught her duty, your Highness."

Elizabeth raised an eyebrow. "There should be more to it than duty, I hope," she observed. "Well, daughter, that is a strange garment you are wearing!"

"It is my farthingale," Katherine explained. "We wear them under our gowns in Spain."

"Now that you are married, you will wear English dress," Elizabeth told her.

"I will be pleased to do so," Katherine replied, but Elizabeth saw a flash of anger in Doña Elvira's eyes as the duenna tugged viciously at the ribbons holding the farthingale in place.

"Hand me the night-rail," she barked at a maid-of-honor, and pulled off Katherine's chemise, leaving her charge standing there naked and blushing until an embroidered night-rail was lifted over her head. Elizabeth turned back the bedclothes and helped Katherine into bed.

"Prop yourself up on the pillows," she said kindly. The girl obeyed, drawing up the covers over her breasts as Doña Elvira thrust forward and briskly arranged her hair like a fan over her shoulders. It was clear that she resented the Queen being there and felt that she alone was the proper person to prepare the Princess of Wales for her wedding night.

Noises outside announced the arrival of the bridegroom, and Elizabeth could hear Arthur boasting that he felt lusty and amorous, which met with a burst of earthy male laughter.

"To it, lad, to it!"

"For England and St. George!" Henry appeared in the doorway, grinning. Beside him was Arthur, dressed in a voluminous nightshirt embroidered with red-and-white roses. The men crammed into the chamber behind them, ogling the bride as she lay in bed. Her cheeks flushed a deep crimson as Arthur lifted the covers and climbed in beside her. They lay there stiffly together, two feet apart, as goblets were raised and bawdy jests made. Harry was the most incoherent of all, having drunk far too much wine. Elizabeth saw Katherine's embarrassment and caught Henry's eye. He nodded.

"Make way for his Grace of Canterbury!" he cried. Reluctantly, the men stood aside to allow the Archbishop through, and there was a semblance of hush as he raised a hand in blessing and prayed that God would make the union of the Prince and Princess fruitful.

"Amen!" said the King. "And now, my lords and ladies, we must leave these young people alone together. A hearty good night to you both!" Taking Elizabeth's hand, he escorted her away, dragging Harry with the other hand, and there was much laughter as everyone filed out.

* * *

That night, the King and Queen stayed at Baynard's Castle. Exhausted after such a momentous day, Elizabeth fell asleep as soon as her head hit the pillow, her last waking thought being of what was—hopefully—happening at the Bishop's Palace. How was Arthur faring, playing the man's part?

It was her first thought in the morning, too. She longed to find out if matters had gone well, but it was not the kind of thing a mother could ask. Henry had no such qualms, though.

"I'll speak to the lad. Ensuring the succession is vital, a matter of national importance," he said, as they broke their fast together after Mass. "And you can ask the Princess how it went."

"But not today," she reminded him. "She is in seclusion."

"Of course. Well, when you get an opportunity. Let's hope they will soon have some good news for us."

Fourteen days of celebrations had long been in the planning, not just to mark the nuptials, but also to honor the envoys sent by King James to arrange Margaret's marriage. Two days after the wedding, Henry and Elizabeth, with the Prince and Princess, sailed in state along the Thames to Westminster, to the sound of music and cheering. Trying not to be overt, Elizabeth had discreetly scrutinized the young couple for signs that all was well. Was she imagining it, or did the Princess look a little down?

As soon as she had settled into her apartments, she summoned Katherine and kissed her warmly. They sat by the fire and reminisced on the wedding. "You carried yourself so well," Elizabeth said. "We were proud of you both."

"I am grateful to your Majesties for everything," Katherine said. "I could not have wished for more. My parents will be delighted to hear of the welcome I have received and of the magnificent wedding."

"And perhaps, my dear, you can give them and us hope that your union will soon bear the desired fruits," Elizabeth said gently—and knew immediately that she had touched a sore place, for the girl's face had suddenly clouded.

"Your Majesty, I hope so, too." She hesitated.

"Is there a problem?"

Katherine blushed. "Nothing has yet passed between Prince Arthur and me."

Elizabeth was not very surprised. "Is it Arthur?"

"Your Majesty, he is not well!" Katherine burst out. "He has tried, but . . ."

"These things can take time," Elizabeth soothed, striving not to worry. "His physician assures us that there is nothing seriously wrong with him."

"Madam, I remember my brother Juan. He died of consumption four years ago. He too was thin and he coughed a lot, like Arthur."

"I don't think we should question Dr. Linacre's judgment," Elizabeth said, her sharpness disguising the alarm she felt. But she was concerned. That night, in bed, she told Henry what Katherine had said and felt him tense beside her.

"I'll talk to Linacre again," he replied. "Hopefully the other matter will resolve itself in time. Maybe we expect too much of them. Maybe we should insist they postpone the consummation of the marriage for a year or so."

"That would be wise. We do not want Arthur overtaxing his strength. Henry, you will talk to Dr. Linacre soon, won't you?"

"I will, cariad. Do not fret." But, as he took her in his arms, she felt like crying, because she was sure that there was cause for concern and that Henry was only believing what he wanted—and needed—to believe.

The following days were a whirl of tournaments, pageants, and feasting. Henry had spared no expense.

As he and Elizabeth shared a ewer of wine in her chamber before the evening's entertainments began, he told her that he had spoken to Arthur and told him to delay the consummation of his marriage.

"He looked as if a great weight had fallen from his shoulders, and I felt quite sorry for him. He's a dutiful boy. He knows I have high expectations of him, and is eager to do his duty, but I said that, for now, that means looking after his health. And I've consulted Linacre, too. He is of the opinion that Arthur caught an ague at Ludlow last year and has never quite shaken off the after-effects. But he says that things will improve with time."

"Did you ask him if it could be consumption?" She held her breath, dreading the answer.

"No, there was no need. He knew what he was talking about." Henry drained his goblet. "Come, my dear, we must go."

She took his hand, but she was crestfallen, fearing that Henry had not asked because he too had feared what Linacre might say. But, with so much as stake, the doctor would not have lied, surely? He would not have shied away from telling Henry the truth. She must hold on to that.

She tried to still her raging thoughts and keep her mind fixed on the pageant that was being performed in the White Hall. Three stages had been wheeled in by men dressed as both gold and silver lions: on one was a castle, representing Castile; the second bore a ship in which there were men dressed as sailors and a girl playing a Spanish infanta; and on the third had been erected a "Mount of Love." At the top of the castle there appeared a lady wearing Spanish dress, representing Katherine, and from its towers emerged the children of the King's Chapel in full chorus. Two gentlemen called Hope and Desire alighted from the ship and courted the infanta on the castle, but she spurned them, at which point eight knights burst from the Mount of Love and stormed the fortress, forcing her and the ladies to surrender, whereupon they stepped down from the castle and danced with the victors.

After the applause had died down, the dancing began and Arthur led his aunt Cecily onto the floor, where they performed two *basse* dances before returning to the dais to decorous clapping. Then Katherine and one of her ladies, both wearing Spanish dress, danced for the company before returning to Elizabeth's side. Harry had been sitting there fidgeting, desperate to take the floor, and as soon as Katherine was seated, he leaped up, grabbed his sister Margaret's hand and whirled her around the hall, to the delight of the onlookers. As they bowed and curtseyed to Elizabeth, there was a thunderous ovation. She had to laugh as the pair of them started up all over again, romping across the floor. Henry let out a guffaw and Katherine was smiling, but Arthur sat there stone-faced. Never had the contrast between the brothers been so evident.

"Why don't you and Katherine join them?" she suggested.

"I'm a little weary, my lady," Arthur said, in a tone that implied that his weariness had nothing to do with being fatigued, and everything to do with his brother showing off. But the court loved it. They roared their approval when Harry flung his robe to the floor and went on dancing in his doublet.

"What a boy!" Henry said, beaming. "It's a good thing I abandoned my plan to make him archbishop of Canterbury!"

The revelry went on . . . and on. Elizabeth was beginning to feel drained. On the following Sunday, there was a lavish dinner in the White Hall, at which Henry placed Katherine at his right hand with her duenna beside her, while Elizabeth hosted the Lady Margaret, her sisters and other ladies at a table set up in the King's adjacent bedchamber, and Arthur sat at a separate table with Margaret and Harry. After dinner, Katherine presented the prizes won in the jousts. Then the King and Queen led their guests into Westminster Hall, where they watched a short play and a pageant in which lords and ladies danced in celebration of the marriage. Just before midnight, eighty earls, barons, and knights came in procession to serve Henry and Elizabeth hippocras and spiced comfits, and then everyone retired to bed.

A week later, the royal family and the court left London in sixty barges, bound for Henry's new palace at Sheen, which had risen, like a phoenix, quite literally from the ashes, and was to be called Richmond, after the earldom the King had borne before his accession. Elizabeth and her ladies sat huddled in furs as they glided along the river to the sound of trumpets, clarions, shawms, tabors, and recorders wafting over from other craft in the procession, all of which were decorated and proudly displaying the crests and standards of the Lord Mayor and the City livery companies. At Mortlake everyone disembarked and took horses and chariots to Richmond.

They arrived late at night. Everyone was staring, marveling. In the flaring torchlight, it was just possible to make out the massive restored donjon towering above, and see the ornate decoration on the new river frontage. An abundance of turrets, pepper-pot domes, and pinnacles soared skyward, while the tinkling of weather vanes could be heard. Richmond was an earthly paradise.

Henry led Elizabeth to the great gatehouse, on which was emblazoned the Tudor royal arms supported by the red dragon of Cadwaladr and the greyhound of Richmond. They walked through a high arched passage and came to the Great Court, which was surrounded by galleries with large windows, their diamond panes glinting in the light of the flambeaux. Then they entered an inner court paved with marble and boasting a drinking fountain sculpted with lions and dragons guarding branches of roses, from which the water ran clear and pure.

Entering the vast great hall, Elizabeth caught her breath at the sight of the lofty timber roof decorated with hanging pendants and carved knots, the rich hangings of Arras portraying the destruction of Troy, and the massive golden statues of English kings wearing armor, with Henry's prominent among them.

Every surface, it seemed, was embellished with gold badges sporting Tudor roses and portcullises. The royal apartments in the donjon had beautiful bay windows overlooking the river or the gardens and were hung with tapestries. In the morning, Elizabeth looked out from her bedchamber and felt a swell of pride at seeing the bowling alleys, archery butts, and tennis courts below. Henry had built them at her suggestion, in the style of the palaces of Burgundy once so favored by her father. He had made Richmond his showpiece, the architectural embodiment of his dynasty, a treasure house packed with the symbols of power, wealth, and majesty.

"It's now the largest palace in England," he murmured, coming to stand beside her and kissing her neck. "I intend to spend a lot of time here!"

She turned and twined her arms around his neck, and he pulled her to him.

"We'll be late for Mass," she warned.

"The Archbishop can wait," he grinned.

* * *

After Mass, Henry led his family and favored courtiers on a walk through the palace gardens. Back in the long gallery he had built for recreation on cold or wet days, lords and ladies were playing chess, backgammon, cards, and dice. In the afternoon, for the delight of Katherine and his children, a Spanish acrobat performed great feats on a network of ropes set up in a garden.

That evening, Henry, Elizabeth, and Katherine took their places on the dais in the hall, which was lavishly furnished with carpets and gold cushions, and watched a pageant featuring sea horses and mermaids. At its climax, a rock on the stage flew open and out burst a great number of white doves and rabbits, which flew and ran about the hall, causing great merriment among the courtiers. Little Mary was beside herself, trying to catch a rabbit.

But Katherine did not join in. She had been quiet all evening. It was only natural, for tomorrow the Spanish lords and ladies who had accompanied her to England were to go home. Only her duenna and her maids were staying in England with her. When, at the end of the evening, Henry brought the wedding celebrations to a close, distributing gifts to the Spaniards in gratitude for their having brought her safely to England, Katherine looked as if she was about to burst into tears. Elizabeth was impressed to see how she recovered herself and played her part to perfection, but she feared that the Princess's composure might desert her in the morning, when the time came to take leave of her countrymen.

"Don't worry," Henry reassured her, when she confided this to him. "I know she is down, but I have something in store to cheer her."

Katherine's training in rigid Spanish etiquette stood her in good stead after all. She said a gracious, smiling farewell to the Spanish lords and ladies, as Elizabeth handed them letters to give to Ferdinand and Isabella, assuring them that their daughter was well. But after they had gone, the poor girl looked sad and pensive.

Henry led her and Elizabeth to his new library and told her to send for her ladies. He had set out some beautiful illuminated manuscripts and a selection of Mr. Caxton's printed books to divert Katherine. She was exclaiming over these when the King's jeweler appeared with a tray of his wares.

"Take your pick, child. You may choose as many pieces as you wish," Henry invited, and Katherine's eyes widened.

"Your Majesty! How kind. Thank you!" There followed an enjoyable half an hour as she tried on the jewels, her ladies marveling at their beauty. And when she had made her choices and thanked Henry again, he gave the remaining pieces to her attendants.

"That should help to take her mind off things," he said, when they had gone.

"It was a kind thought," Elizabeth smiled, loving him for it.

Chapter 22

1501–1502

Late in November, the court moved to Windsor Castle. No sooner had they settled in than Henry was talking about sending Arthur back to Ludlow. "It's best he travels while the weather's still relatively mild," he said, setting up a chess set in Elizabeth's chamber.

"But I was hoping he would stay for Christmas," she said, dismayed.

"He needs to resume his duties, cariad."

She sighed. It would have been so good to have Arthur with them for Christmas, and she could have kept a watchful eye on his health, for she was still not convinced that all was well. But it was pointless trying to make Henry change his mind. "Is Katherine to go with him?"

"I have been pondering that. I thought at first that she might stay with you, at least for the winter. Arthur knows they are to wait a while before they start living together as man and wife."

Elizabeth would be happy to keep Katherine with her. She had become very fond of her and enjoyed her company; a warmth had grown between them. By contrast, there seemed to be little rapport between Katherine and Arthur. Since the wedding, that first flush of joy the Prince had evinced on meeting his bride seemed to have evaporated into distant formality. Probably he was embarrassed by his failure in bed. "I think that, coming from the warmer climate of Spain, Katherine will find it hard wintering on the Welsh border," she said.

"Some of my councillors have raised that very point. But I have spoken to both Arthur and Katherine, and both are content that she accompany him to Ludlow. The Princess's chaplain agreed, saying it was the express wish of King Ferdinand and Queen Isabella that the Prince and Princess should not be separated, but her duenna, of course, made a fuss and said that the Princess should stay behind. I have decided that they shall both go to Ludlow."

Elizabeth gaped at him. "But you said it was best if they did not live together."

"I must bow to the wishes of the sovereigns."

She hoped he would not come to regret his decision. "At least, I pray you, tell Arthur that they must not live together as man and wife."

"I will impress that on him. Yet Ferdinand and Isabella are insisting that the marriage be consummated to seal the alliance. In view of what happened to the Infante Juan, you'd think they would be happy for that to be deferred. I would like to tell them that I am consenting to Katherine going to Ludlow, even to the danger of our son, for I do not believe that he is ready for married life. But I will be tactful and say that I am bowing to their wishes. Nothing must be allowed to jeopardize England's good relations with Spain."

"Not even our son's health?" she cried.

"I will speak to Arthur. The matter can be managed discreetly."

Elizabeth had a choking lump in her throat when she waved Arthur and Katherine goodbye on 21 December. "God go with you!" she called after them. She watched as the litter trundled out of the lower ward of Windsor Castle, straining for a last glimpse of her son's pale face and his hand raised in farewell.

There was much to distract Elizabeth from worrying in the weeks that followed: first Christmastide, and then the celebrations for

Margaret's betrothal to King James and the signing of the Treaty of Perpetual Peace between England and Scotland. The espousal took place amid lavish pageantry in the Queen's great chamber, which had been newly decorated with entwined Tudor roses and Scottish thistles in honor of the occasion.

Margaret looked gorgeous in her shimmering white gown and train, and conducted herself well, displaying none of the waywardness of spirit that had so often earned her reprimands as a child. From now on, she would be styled queen of Scots and honored as such at her father's court, ranking alongside her mother. Elizabeth was already bracing herself for the inevitable parting, yet Margaret was not to go to Scotland until September 1503. They had many months together yet.

Trumpets sounded as the King retired to his chamber to dine with the Scots and English ambassadors, and Elizabeth took Margaret by the hand and led her to the table that had been set up in the hall beneath the canopy of estate, where, two queens side by side, they were served dinner with much ceremony. There were jousts in the afternoon and a sumptuous banquet in the evening. In London, *Te Deum*s were being sung in churches, and tonight there would be bonfires in celebration, and hogsheads of wine shared in the streets.

The next day, the little Queen of Scots appeared in state in Elizabeth's chamber and presented prizes to the victors in the jousts. There was a pageant with Morris dancers, another tournament, and a final sumptuous banquet.

Elizabeth then set about preparing Margaret's trousseau, summoning mercers and tailors and arranging fittings. Margaret was particularly taken with a gown of crimson velvet with cuffs of fur and white-and-orange sleeves of sarcenet.

"I shall wear this when I meet King James," she declared. "I hope it will still fit me then."

"The tailors are all allowing for growth," Elizabeth assured her.

As well as clothing, other items were to be provided. In a palace storeroom, pewter basins, washing bowls, a fire pan, a pair of bellows, and numerous other household items were piling up. At the Lady Margaret's recommendation, Elizabeth commissioned Maynard Wewyck, the King's painter, to produce portraits of herself, Henry, and Margaret for her daughter to take to Scotland with her. Amid all the bustle, she could sometimes forget that she would not be going, too.

After Shrovetide, Henry received a letter from Sir Richard Pole, Arthur's chamberlain. He brought it to Elizabeth, his hands visibly trembling.

"Arthur is not well," he told her, putting an arm around her and drawing her over to the fire. "Pole doesn't say what the problem is, only that he and others fear that our son has overindulged himself in the marriage bed after all, and is suffering from fatigue."

"But he wasn't supposed to be bedding Katherine!" she cried. "I wish they had stayed at court. Can you not summon them back, Henry?"

"Let's not overreact, cariad. He may be better soon. He's well enough to preside over his Council and entertain local worthies, so he can't be that poorly. I'll write to Linacre and get his opinion."

Elizabeth's spirits sank. It would be days before they heard back. "Could I go to Ludlow?" she asked.

"In this weather?" Henry's eyebrows shot up. It was true: the roads were icy and the winds roaring. "Bessy, we must try not to worry too much. If Arthur was really ill, Pole would have said so. No one takes any chances with the heir to the throne."

You do! She suddenly wanted to scream at him. *You should never have let him go in the first place!* But she held her tongue. She needed Henry's emotional support and reassurance to keep her grounded and rational at this time. There could be no harsh words between them.

Days before they could expect a reply from Dr. Linacre, Henry came stamping into her apartments, scattering her ladies and ushering her into the closet that served as her oratory.

"As if the de la Poles have not caused us enough trouble!" he ranted, before she could draw breath. "I was generous! After Lincoln's death and attainder, I made his brother Edmund earl of

Suffolk, you remember? And, last year, when Suffolk murdered some mean person in a fury, I pardoned him. Some malcontents might regard him as the rightful Yorkist claimant to the throne, but I always gave him the benefit of the doubt. But now it seems he feels slighted because I have not done enough for him, and did not make him a duke, like his father. He has fled England and is now at the court of Maximilian and calling himself 'the White Rose.' What's more, Sir James Tyrell, the Governor of Guisnes, abetted him in his flight. I've ordered Tyrell home, but Suffolk is beyond my reach."

"You *were* good to him, more than you needed to be—and he treats you like this." But Elizabeth was not thinking about Suffolk. She was remembering Abbot Eastney telling her, all those years ago, that Sir James Tyrell had been at the Tower of London, on King Richard's orders, at the time of her brothers' disappearance. She had long wondered if he had had anything to do with it. And now he had turned up again, abetting a traitor.

Henry was pacing, the way he always did when he was agitated. "God knows what Ferdinand and Isabella will think of this new threat to my throne. Since the executions of Warbeck and Wilford, I've been anxious lest some other pretender stake his claim. My agents abroad think that Suffolk is dangerous. I've ordered that he be publicly condemned at Paul's Cross, and the Bishop of London is declaring him excommunicate."

Elizabeth sat down, feeling as if she had been winded. Suffolk was her cousin and had played a prominent part at her coronation and in court ceremonies. She was fond of his mother, Aunt Suffolk. His defection was shocking.

She was glad that her sisters were at court. That evening, she gathered them around the hearth and they speculated about Suffolk's motives.

"I cannot but assume the worst," Elizabeth fretted.

"It is awful that another of our blood has turned traitor," Anne said, looking wan in the firelight. She was pregnant again and sick with it.

"It reflects on us," Katherine chimed in. "The King may come to think that we are not to be trusted."

"He knows we are loyal," Elizabeth said. "It's our kinsmen he fears. Lincoln had pretensions to the crown and Suffolk apparently has similar ambitions. Maybe discontent has been festering in his mind all these years."

"He's a hothead, and his younger brother Richard is, too," Cecily added. "But I don't think he has the brains to plan a coup."

"Maximilian does," Elizabeth put in. "He's supposed to be our ally, but he could make a lot of mischief for us, as he did before when he harbored Warbeck. He's a wily fox."

She was still brooding on the matter two weeks later. Lying in bed one night, trying to read one of Mr. Caxton's romances, she found the words dancing in front of her eyes, meaningless. When would Suffolk make his move—if, indeed, he made one at all? Were they always to be plagued by pretenders? She was weary of it, sick to her heart.

The door opened and Henry walked in, dressed in his night robe and cap and carrying a candle.

"I'm glad to find you awake, Bessy."

"My dear lord, it is good to see you." It was, but she was too agitated, too tense for lovemaking.

But Henry did not join her in bed. He seated himself by the fire and was silent for a moment. "Bessy, I fear there is more bad news. I have had Suffolk's contacts traced and placed under surveillance. Tonight, I learned that Lord William Courtenay dined with him just before he fled from England. He has since been corresponding with Suffolk; one letter suggests that he invited him to invade England through Devon, where his family have their estates."

"Dear God!" Stunned, Elizabeth slid out of bed and joined Henry by the fire. "I cannot believe it."

"Neither can I. Courtenay was a captain in my army and fought against Warbeck. I believed him to be loyal. I would never have agreed to Katherine marrying him otherwise."

"She will be devastated."

Henry's eyes narrowed. "But will she be surprised?"

She gaped at him. "You surely can't believe that she was involved? She hasn't a disloyal bone in her body!"

He sighed. "Forgive me. There is no evidence of her being a party to her lord's involvement, but I feel I can trust no one these days."

"Is there any actual evidence that Lord William himself has committed treason?"

"Yes. The letters that were intercepted are enough to send him to the block."

"Oh, Blessed Mary!" Her hands flew to her mouth. "You would not, surely . . . You cannot! Think of Katherine—and their little children."

Henry reached for her hand. "I am not out for his blood. You ought to know me better, Bessy. I do not want my brother-in-law made a public spectacle on the scaffold. But I will have him where he can trouble me no more for the present. I've ordered that he be apprehended and taken to the Tower."

"Tonight?"

"Yes."

"Oh no! Poor Katherine. I must go to her." Already she was pulling on her gown over her night-rail. "Can you lace me up?"

"Bessy, it's late. You can't go chasing through London at this time of night," Henry protested.

"I am the Queen! None will dare question what I am doing." She tugged a comb through her hair and wrapped her cloak around her, then pulled on the buskins she had worn earlier. "Henry, I have to see Katherine. She will need comforting. Don't forbid me, I pray you."

"I won't, but you must take an escort. And, Bessy, I am truly sorry for your sister's trouble; but remember, it is her husband who is to blame."

Accompanied by two mounted yeomen of the guard carrying torches, Elizabeth sat impatiently in her litter as the horses drew her through the silent, shuttered streets of the City to Newgate, surprising the Watch, who was about to announce that it was midnight and all was well when he saw who it was who was passing.

All was definitely not well, and might never be so again. Courtenay's arrest could have ramifications far into the future. And how many others were involved in this latest treason? Elizabeth felt overwhelmed. What with worrying about Arthur, and feeling tired all the time, as she seemed to be these days—and now this. It was all too much. But she must not think of herself.

There were lights on in the Courtenays' house when she reached Warwick Lane.

She almost leaped out of the litter as one of the guards banged on the door. An anxious-looking steward opened it. He was probably thinking that more trouble was afoot.

"Her Grace the Queen," the guard announced.

"I would see Lady William," she said.

"Very good, Madam. She will be glad that you are here."

He led the way into the hall, where Katherine was sitting at the long table, looking disheveled and distraught.

"Bessy! Thank God you've come. I'm going out of my mind with fear."

"Oh, my dear!" Elizabeth hastened to embrace her. "Now, you are not to worry. Henry has no intention of sending William to his death. He only means to keep him in the Tower while Suffolk's treason is investigated."

Katherine closed her eyes. Her lip trembled. "I thought I would never see him again. They came without warning and seized him, and they took him away without nightclothes, body linen, or even a warm cloak."

"That can be rectified," Elizabeth said, taking refuge in practicalities.

"He's not a traitor, Bessy. He's been arrested on suspicion only; they can prove no offense because there is nothing to prove."

"Then all will be well," Elizabeth said, not wishing to dispute with her sister when she was so upset.

"Are you sure the King will not send him to the block? That's what they usually do with traitors."

"No, he has just told me that he will not, I promise you."

"But he will be attainted, yes? And then I will be in poverty and our children will be disinherited."

"Katherine, you run ahead of yourself. William has been convicted of nothing yet. He is under suspicion of conspiring with Suffolk, and the matter will be investigated further. You can depend on me to intercede for him—and for you and your little ones. Now, you must come to court tomorrow, and stay in my household, so that I can support you. And, if you are ever in want, I will be there for you, as I have always been."

She did everything she could. She had already been paying Katherine a pension, and now she augmented it with gifts. She set up a nursery household for her nephews and niece, funding the staff herself and paying for the children's food and for new coats for the boys.

She understood why Henry had imprisoned Lord William, but could not help feeling resentful toward him, which she knew was irrational. To heap this on her when she was anxious about Arthur's health seemed cruel. And yet, what else could Henry have done?

Sir James Tyrell was in the Tower now, charged with treasonably corresponding with Suffolk. He was a fool. Henry had not only confirmed him as the governor of Guisnes, but had also given him land in the Pale of Calais, and he had been living there in comfort for sixteen years. Why had he been so rash as to dabble in treason?

Henry had told her how Tyrell had refused to obey the order recalling him to England. He had eventually lured him home on the promise of a safe conduct, then had him arrested once he had boarded a ship.

"He's refusing to say anything," he said irritably. "Well, we'll give him some time to think about it, and then we'll apply a little pressure."

Maybe Tyrell knows more than we suspect, Elizabeth thought—and not all of it to do with Suffolk.

* * *

The news from Ludlow was worrying. Arthur's health was giving cause for concern.

The letter from Dr. Linacre arrived when Elizabeth herself was feeling unwell. Of late, she had felt the familiar fatigue, coupled with breathlessness and occasional giddy spells. When she saw her reflection in her mirror, she was disconcerted to see how pale she looked. Her hands were always cold. When she thought about it, she had not felt right since Edmund was born. She had made light of her ailments in the face of Henry's concern, and she had not consulted her physicians, telling herself that her symptoms were too vague to make a fuss about; the truth was that she feared what they might tell her.

And now Arthur seemed—dear God, she must face it—to be getting worse, if one read between the lines of the letter.

"I must go to him," she said, when Henry showed her Linacre's letter.

"You're not well enough, Bessy." He looked alarmed. "It's a long journey, and you get out of breath just walking in the gardens. Rest awhile, and we'll see. Arthur is in good hands. Linacre writes that there is sickness in those parts, and that Arthur may have caught it. I can't risk you catching it, too."

"It's not the plague, is it?" She drew in her breath.

"No. Just some ague that is going around."

"Then Arthur's illness might not be serious?" She leaped on that hope.

"I pray so. If it was, Linacre would surely tell us."

She badgered God to spare her son. On her knees in chapel, she recited every prayer she could think of, exhorting Him to hear her. She paid two priests to make pilgrimages and offerings on her behalf at dozens of shrines, urging them to make intercessions at every one to the Virgin, the patron of mothers, who would understand her desperate fears for her son's health. Arthur *would* recover, she told herself.

And then—praise be to God—came the most wonderful news. He was better. He had recovered sufficiently to wash the feet of fifteen poor men—one for each year of his age—on Maundy Thursday. Elizabeth herself had participated in the usual ceremonies at court, giving money and lengths of cloth to thirty-seven poor women, one for each year she had been on earth—and she had been in torment, worrying about her boy. She had gone to Greenwich for Good Friday, and then to Richmond for Easter Sunday, and there she had made an offering at the high altar after Mass, her mind in a ferment. But now, she was filled with thankfulness. Arthur was getting better. The world had righted itself.

Needing a retreat after all the emotional upheaval and the weariness that was blighting her life, she took herself off to spend a few days at the Thames-side manor of Hampton Court, as the guest of Henry's loyal chamberlain and friend, Lord Daubeney. His was a substantial house lying in the midst of a great estate that had once been put to cultivation and the farming of two thousand sheep by the Knights Hospitallers, from whom Daubeney leased it. Now it was a fashionable mansion, suitably grand for entertaining royalty.

Elizabeth enjoyed Daubeney's lavish hospitality. He was a good man, prudent, just, and honest, and loved by all. But what she had really come to Hampton Court for was its tranquillity and peace, echoes of its monastic past. For her, it was a spiritual refuge. Some of the monks' cells were still there, and she asked to occupy one rather than the splendid bedchamber that had been prepared for her. There, and in the chapel, she spent long hours in reverent meditation, and prayed for Arthur's full return to health.

Evidently word had got about that she was there, for local people came to see her and tell her their troubles or bring gifts. One poor woman gave her some almond butter, for which she was truly grateful, since it was Lent and impious to eat animal fats. Others brought chickens, pears, pippins, puddings, or cakes. She saw that none went away without a handsome reward, often more than she could afford. But it was worth it for the blessings they called down on her.

On the second day of April, feeling much restored, Elizabeth left Hampton Court and took her barge to Greenwich.

Henry welcomed her back warmly. "I trust you feel better for your rest," he said, kissing her.

"I do indeed." She felt calmer, more energized. Hampton Court had done her good. "Is there any word from Ludlow?"

"No, so I am assuming that all is well. I expect we shall hear soon."

Of course. She must stop fretting. Had she learned nothing from her retreat?

"Is there news of Suffolk?" she asked.

"Only that he is now styling himself *duke* of Suffolk," Henry told her, making a face.

"That's outrageous. Has Tyrell talked?"

"No! But he will soon. Pressure will be put on him. Now, Bessy, forget these cares and come and dine with me." He held out his hand and she took it, glad to be with him again. Life was good. She was suddenly filled with gratitude.

Two nights later, she was woken by one of her ladies.

"Madam, the King has sent for you."

"What?" She struggled to come to herself. "What time is it?"

"Four o'clock, Madam."

Suddenly, she was wide awake. It must be an urgent matter for Henry to summon her at night. *Dear God, please let it not be bad news about Arthur.*

Pulling on her night robe and slippers, she took a candle and made her way down the privy stair to Henry's bedchamber. There, she found him alone with his confessor. When he rose and turned to her, his face was pale and drawn in the candlelight.

"Oh, Bessy," he said, holding out his hands to her, and she saw that he was weeping. "Oh, God, help us. Tell her, Friar."

She knew what was coming. She had been expecting it, however often she had tried to reassure herself.

The chaplain's eyes were kind and gentle. "Madam, if we receive good things at the hands of God, why should we not endure evil things? You must be brave, my daughter. Your dearest son Prince Arthur has departed to God."

"He's dead!" A great howl broke from Henry. He crushed her to him as she struggled to take in the awful news.

"He's gone! Our boy, our boy has gone!" she cried again and again against his breast, and they clung together in a maelstrom of grief and disbelief. All she could see were her remaining years stretching out ahead of her in a world without Arthur. She would never see him again—it was impossible to believe. She did not know how she would live.

Henry was sobbing wildly. "We must bear our powerful sorrow together," he stuttered.

"Yes, my heart," she faltered. He was the only other person who could know how hard this was. How could their child be dead in the flower of his youth?

She must be strong for them both. She must draw on all the inner strength she could summon and put his needs first. "My dearest," she said, trying to stifle her tears, "we must accept God's will and be happy that Arthur has attained Heaven."

"Amen," said the friar quietly, and left them alone, quietly closing the door behind him.

Elizabeth disengaged herself and took Henry's hands. He had aged ten years in as many minutes. Her heart bled for him. He had to confront not only this devastating loss, but the knowledge that his long-cherished dream of a new Arthurian age now lay in ruins. And only one young life now stood between him and the loss of everything he had striven so carefully to build. He was forty-five and might not live to school Harry for kingship or see him grow to maturity. And that reminded her of how she had often thought—God forgive her—that Harry would be better suited to kingship than Arthur. But she would never have wanted to see him gain a crown like this—never!

"My dear, I beseech you, think of yourself and your health," she begged. "Do not give way to despair. Think of the comfort of your realm, which needs you, and of me." She knew she was asking him to do things she feared that she herself would never be able to do. But they had to go forward. Even now, with the news still raw, she understood the importance of that.

"We have but the one son now," Henry mourned. "One precious life between me and disaster. Harry is not yet eleven. We must keep him safe. We dare not lose him, too!"

"He is healthy and robust."

"But God has taken three of our children now. And there are those who plot to seize my throne. Should anything evil befall me, what would happen to Harry? Remember what Scripture warns: 'Woe to thee, O land, when thy king is a child.' We both know what can happen to child kings."

"Remember," she said, "that my lady your mother had no more children after you, yet God, by His Grace, has always preserved you. He brought you to where you are now."

"But He has taken my son, my heir." Henry's voice broke again.

Comfort came in strange ways. She had thought her childbearing days over, thought herself too unfit to risk another pregnancy. She had been so ill last time, and Henry had not loved her fully since, for fear of putting her life in danger. But now . . . Another child would surely bring succor to them both. It could never replace Arthur, but it would bring its love with it—and ensure the succession.

She took a deep breath. "Henry, be comforted. God has left you a fair prince and two fair princesses; and He is still where He was, and we are both young enough to have more children."

He stared at her through his tears. "You would risk yourself for me?"

"I doubt there would be much risk involved. Every pregnancy is different. Things might not be so bad next time. And we will find comfort in coming together."

"Oh, cariad!" He embraced her once more, as a drowning man embraces a raft.

"Another child will be a consolation to us both," she said, still feeling the need to brace him. "And, my dear, it will help to take your mind off this terrible loss. You are renowned throughout Christendom as a prudent and wise prince, and you must now give proof of it by the manner of taking this misfortune."

"Thank you, Bessy, for your good comfort," Henry said. "Now I feel the need to pray for Arthur's soul."

"I will go and lie down before I go to the chapel," she said. "I feel a little faint. It's just the shock." In fact, she could barely put one foot in front of the other, but she made it back to her bedchamber. She knew she would not sleep, so she sat by the fire, trying to still the tumult in her mind. If only she need not think.

And then, without warning, it filled her whole being, such love for her son that it took her breath away. It was deep and pure and true, and stronger than death. She had loved him. She knew it now—and now was too late. Suddenly, she was on her knees, wailing and beating her breast. Her women came running.

"Send for his Grace," Katherine ordered, as the others tried to calm her. But she was beyond consolation. The world would never again be such a happy place as when Arthur was in it. He was gone from her, completely and irrevocably. He was but a memory now. The cruel realization cut so painfully to her heart that she did not think she could go on.

But here was Henry, hastening to her, kneeling down beside her and cradling her in his arms. "Oh, my love, my cariad," he murmured. "Let me comfort *you* now. You gave me such wise counsel earlier. I have been thanking God that we had our son for fifteen years, and I pray that you will do likewise. It was His greatest blessing on us." With that, they wept together. They would face it as one. They had shared in Arthur's creation; now they would hold fast, united in their grief for him.

The days that followed passed in a blur. It was fortunate that Henry had laid down ordinances governing royal mourning, for Elizabeth was in no fit state to think of such trivial matters as etiquette. The Lady Margaret, herself devastated by the loss of her beloved grandson, ordered the Queen's ladies to dress her in a black velvet gown and surcoat with a long train and a plain hood. A cloak of black damask was made for her, and gowns of the same material were bought for the princesses. Elizabeth would stay in mourning for six months. It mattered little. She did not care what she wore.

Cecily hastened to her, the closest person who could understand her suffering, and they shed tears together, reminiscing on their lost children. "They will be with us always, forever in our hearts,"

Cecily assured her. "Embrace your grief. I cannot let mine go; I do not want to. It would be like losing my girls all over again."

"I want him back," Elizabeth wept. "I want him back for five minutes, just long enough to say how much I loved him. I never said it enough when he was alive."

"Rest assured he knows it," Cecily said, squeezing her hand.

Elizabeth found comfort in everyday things, in keeping to her usual routine. It kept her grounded. As she attended to her daily duties, she felt close to Arthur, more than ever before, and wondered if he was with her in spirit, bringing her comfort.

Everyone was kind. Messages of sympathy came flooding in. Tributes were written to the Prince who had embodied the hopes and affections of his father's subjects. It was said that his virtues equaled, if not surpassed, the fame of all former princes. The calamity and pitiful misfortune of his death had touched the entire kingdom. He was praised most eloquently as the delight of the Britons, the glorious hope of the realm and the most renowned heir of the King. But now, one verse ran, England had perforce to weep since her hope lay dead. There was small comfort in all this. If only, Elizabeth lamented with the poets, the Fates had granted Arthur a longer stay in the world.

It was heartening to be told how, at the last, he had commended his soul to God with the most fervent devotion. How she wished she had been there, to hold him in her arms and surround him with love as he departed on his final journey. Why had she not gone to him while she could? Why had she let him die in the company of strangers? She was racked with guilt and could not forgive herself.

From letters sent by those who *had* been there, she learned that Arthur had gone downhill quickly, and that Katherine had ailed, too. But Katherine's Spanish physician confirmed that, while she had contracted the ague that was in the air around Ludlow, Arthur had been suffering from something far more serious.

"Your Majesties should know," he had informed them, not

mincing his words, "that the Princess remains a virgin because the Prince had not the strength necessary to know a woman. He was like a cold piece of stone because he was in the final stages of consumption and his limbs were weak. I have never seen a man who was so thin."

Yes, Arthur had been thin; she had worried about it for a long time. And Henry had, too. But if he had been in the final stages of consumption—and if it was obvious to Katherine's doctor, it must have been to others, too—why hadn't she and Henry been informed? Then it might have been possible for them to see him one last time and be with him when he died.

But there was no point in wishing that things had been otherwise. That way lay mental torture, and her grief was enough to bear. She did not blame Henry for sending Arthur to Ludlow. He had not known what ailed the boy.

She had with her Arthur's will, drawn up on his deathbed, short and to the point. She was surprised to read that he had left all his personal possessions to his sister Margaret. There was nothing for his wife. How sad. She doubted that those two young people had ever forged a bond.

A week after Arthur died, Elizabeth woke one bleak morning to hear rapid knocks coming from the ceiling above her, as if someone was trying to get her attention. A few days later, when they came again, Henry heard them too, and she jumped out of bed to see where they were coming from. It was definitely someone rapping rhythmically on the floor above. And yet she knew that up there, there was just a lumber room to which only she had the key. There could not possibly be anyone in that room. Henry sent one of her grooms to check, just in case, but there was no one—and nothing to account for the knocking.

Then there was the strange behavior of her clock. It had been wound in the morning, but soon afterward she noticed that it had stopped. Her steward looked at it, puzzled.

"Someone has unwound the mainspring, Madam."

"But I've been here all the time. No one has touched it."

"Then I fear I cannot account for it," he said, winding it again. The knocking had not been heard again, but one evening she heard footsteps above her, walking around the lumber room. Another day, as she knelt at her prayer desk, she felt a gentle touch on her hand. Strangest of all, on several occasions when she lay reading in bed at night, it was as if someone was blowing cool air on her arms and face. There was nothing to account for it, no draft or window in that direction. And then Henry, walking in the gardens one day, heard Arthur's voice asking if he was well.

She could not explain these things, or Arthur's date of birth suddenly appearing on a blank sheet of paper in her writing chest. She knew she wanted to believe that he was trying to communicate with her and she could not help thinking back to that time after Beth's death when she had felt a child's hand in hers. How else could she account for these strange experiences?

Spring came, like a mockery. She carried her unbearable grief like a weight and could not sleep, even though she craved oblivion so that she would not have to think. She felt dragged down again, drained and weary. The old breathlessness was back. She consulted Dr. Lewis, and he put her symptoms down to sorrow and prescribed some physick to help her. It made little difference.

Henry had been advised against bringing Arthur's body to London for burial in Westminster Abbey. Consumption was contagious. So the Prince was to be buried in Worcester Cathedral. Because of the epidemic in the west of England, the grieving parents were advised to stay away, to Elizabeth's great distress. The Earl of Surrey was to represent her and the King.

They were kept abreast of events by letter. Arthur had lain in state in the great hall of Ludlow Castle before being carried with mournful pageantry to the beautiful church of St. Laurence nearby, where his coffin lay before the altar for three days. On St. George's Day, in terrible weather, it was conducted by a vast procession of mourners to Worcester. Katherine did not attend the funeral; custom would not have allowed the widow to be present, and she was too ill anyway. At Henry's wish, Arthur was interred near the high altar of the cathedral, to the sound of weeping and lamentation.

On the day of the burial, Henry and Elizabeth knelt together in her chapel, holding each other and praying for Arthur's soul. There came a point when they could pray no longer, when the tears overwhelmed them.

"We will build him a chantry chapel where prayers can be offered up in perpetuity for his soul," Henry sobbed. "We will make it more beautiful than any other royal tomb, with carvings of Tudor roses, Beaufort portcullises, Katherine's pomegranate and the falcon and fetterlock of York, to proclaim to the world who he was."

Elizabeth could envision it in her mind. "And we will go there and visit him, our beautiful boy." And then she was too choked to say any more.

Chapter 23

1502

Life had to go on. The children had to be comforted for the loss of their brother, and the young girl lying sick at Ludlow was much in Elizabeth's thoughts. Poor Katherine. A wife, yet no wife, only six months wed, and now a widow at sixteen. She was ill, far from home and in a strange land, and must be feeling utterly wretched. Elizabeth wrote to her regularly, asking after her health and assuring her that she was loved and would be looked after. They had not even begun to address the matter of what would happen to her—if she lived.

Henry had a long talk with Harry, impressing on him that he was now the heir to the throne, the future king of England, and must be even more diligent at his studies. Elizabeth suspected that Harry had long been jealous of Arthur and that his brother's death had aroused mixed feelings in him. They had not known each other well or been close, for they had grown up apart, with Arthur at Ludlow and Harry usually at Eltham. And who could blame Harry for wanting to be king and looking to a glorious future? He had been born to wear a crown.

Henry's attitude toward Harry was complicated. He loved him deeply and was proud of him, and yet at times it seemed that he disliked him, for he was often short with him. Certainly, he showed him little affection. And yet he had become intensely protective of him, knowing that the hopes of his dynasty rested on this one boy. Elizabeth wondered if Henry resented Harry just for being alive when Arthur, in whom so many of his ambitions had been invested, was dead.

Harry was quick to complain. After yet another lecture from his father on the virtues expected of a monarch, he came to Elizabeth, that prim little underlip jutting out petulantly.

"Father's being so unfair," he complained, throwing himself down on the floor at her feet and looking up at her plaintively.

"Why?" she asked, ruffling his red hair, which was cut in a pudding-basin style.

"Last year, he said he would give me my own household at Codnor Castle when Arthur was married. I've been waiting and waiting for him to do it, but now he says that I have to live at court with Margaret and Mary. It's not fair! Why should I suffer because Arthur has died?"

Elizabeth sighed. "My son, I understand how you feel. But you must realize how precious you are now to your father."

"I'd never know it," Harry muttered. "He's always lecturing me."

"But you are, I assure you. As for having your own household, he wishes to have you near him now, so that he can be assured of your health and safety. These things are so important to him. And I want you close, too. You're my only son now and you mean everything to me."

For answer, Harry leaped up and flung his arms around her neck. "I love you, Mother!" he declared. "You're the best queen in the whole world. But I *was* looking forward to going to Codnor."

"I'm very glad you're not," she countered. "Derbyshire's a long way away."

Royal duties took little account of mourning. There were the Garter ceremonies to get through, ambassadors to be received, preparations for Margaret's wedding to be made. And late in April, there came a curious request in a letter that had arrived from the Minoresses' convent at Aldgate, not far from the Tower. It was from the Abbess—Aunt Rivers's cousin, Alice FitzLewis, whom Elizabeth remembered meeting at court years before, and who had since entered religion. She had humbly requested that her kinswoman the Queen would visit her. Enclosed was a little bottle, a gift of rose water.

That same day, by coincidence, Henry told Elizabeth that they were to stay at the Tower for a few days. "Bring only a small train. I intend to question Tyrell before he is brought to trial next week. You may wish to be present."

"I would like that. There are questions I wish to ask him. It will be convenient, for my kinswoman, the Abbess of the Minories, has asked to see me." She had been surprised to receive the request. She could recall that long-ago day at Westminster, when Mother had been incensed about King Louis breaking her daughter's marriage contract and Aunt Rivers and her cousin had comforted her. About ten years ago, Alice had become a nun at the Minories, and Elizabeth had heard that she had just been elected abbess. But she and Alice had never been close—indeed, they were barely acquainted—so she was wondering why she wanted to see her.

She and Henry boarded the royal barge later that day and were soon settled in the royal apartments of the Tower. Elizabeth was very much aware that Tyrell lay imprisoned not far away and wondered if he might be persuaded to reveal what had happened to her brothers all those years ago—if he knew anything, of course. She had yearned to find out the truth for so long, but, now that she was perhaps on the brink of doing so, she feared what she might hear.

The next morning, she and Henry were escorted to the Lieutenant's lodging on Tower Green, where Tyrell was brought from his cell in the adjacent Bell Tower. He looked old, haggard, and unshaven; his clothes were grubby and gave off a sickly, stale smell. He stood before them at the other side of the table with the Constable at his elbow.

"Sir James," Henry said, "my patience is wearing thin. You have been here for some weeks now and still you have not chosen to enlighten my councillors as to why you aided and abetted the traitor Suffolk to abscond to the court of Maximilian."

Tyrell glowered at him. Elizabeth realized he would be a hard man to crack.

"Your Grace, I did not know he was absconding, so I have nothing to tell," he said. There was an infuriating nonchalance in his manner. Did he not appreciate the peril in which he stood?

"Come, Sir James," Henry retorted, "we know you were in contact with him before he left England. You may recall writing this letter." He pushed it across the table.

Tyrell took a cursory look at it. "I don't, as it happens."

"It's your handwriting." Henry produced two of Tyrell's dispatches from Guisnes.

"Maybe I did write it. But it's been misconstrued."

"I'm not sure that 'your lawful claim to the throne' is in any way ambiguous," Henry hissed, his eyes like steel.

"I was referring to the succession. Failing your Grace's heirs—which God forfend—then Suffolk would have a claim."

Henry banged the table. "Don't split hairs with me! It's quite clear in that letter that you knew Suffolk was going to Maximilian, and why. You treasonably abetted him."

"No."

"Very well, Sir James, I'll leave you to ponder on your options a little longer—but not for much longer, mind you. Take him away."

"Wait!" Elizabeth said. "I have a question for him."

Tyrell stared at her. "Your Grace?"

"I have heard," she said, looking him in the eye, "that you were at the Royal Wardrobe at the Tower in September 1483. Do you know anything about what happened to my brothers, King Edward the Fifth and the Duke of York? Did you see them there?"

He had flushed slightly. "I know nothing about them, Madam." He was lying; she was certain of it, for his gaze had flickered.

"Perhaps you would like to think about that, too," Henry said icily, and nodded to the guards.

When Tyrell had gone, she turned to Henry. "I think he knows more than he is saying."

"I'm sure of it. He's a foxy character. Well, we'll let him have some time to stew. You've given him something of far more import to worry about. Regicide is the worst kind of treason."

"Yes, you speak truth there. If it was regicide, it was not just the crime that was committed, but the concealing of it and the misery of not knowing that it inflicted on so many, not to mention the political uncertainty about my brothers reappearing one day, and the pretenders who took advantage of that. My poor mother died without ever knowing what had happened to her sons. When I think of them, all alone and frightened in the Tower, expecting death daily, I could weep even now."

Henry grasped her hand. There was a new tenderness between them these days. "Never forget that if Tyrell was involved, he was acting on orders. And we don't know for certain that he was involved at all, even if he was at the Tower at that time. I think he does know something, but there is no proof. Let us see what he says in a couple of days, when I intend to question him again."

That afternoon, still desperate to know the truth, Elizabeth rode by litter to the Minories and was shown into the Abbess's parlor. Alice FitzLewis was waiting for her; she had grown plump in the years since Elizabeth had last seen her, but had an arresting presence and a face full of wisdom.

"Your Grace, this is an honor," she said, as Elizabeth knelt to kiss her ring. "Are you in health? Your aunt sends me news of you in her letters. We were so deeply saddened to hear of the passing of Prince Arthur."

"I seem to be living my life on two levels, Reverend Mother," Elizabeth told her. "Part of me is carrying on as normal and is able to function and even laugh at times; the other part is in grief. I fall into the abyss at least once a day."

"That is normal, my child," the Abbess said, ushering her to the fine oak chair by the hearth and taking a stool herself. "You must take comfort in the knowledge that God who gave has taken Arthur to Himself and that your son has surely attained Heaven, for I have heard that he was a most virtuous and pious prince."

"He was, he was," Elizabeth breathed. "I am in turmoil when I think back on his life and on all the things I did and didn't do, or should have done. You think your children will live on after you and there will be time for everything. I, who have lost three, should know better."

"You did your very best for Arthur, I have no doubt."

"I could have loved him more!" Elizabeth burst out. "I always doubted it while he was alive; I lived with guilt. And now he is gone, I am overflowing with love for him. He was ill, and I failed to protect him. There was always a reason why I could not go to him, or why the King and I ignored the warning signs. I think Henry was in denial; neither of us saw what we should have seen. But I always had a strong urge to protect Arthur, and it's still with me, but I can't protect him now."

The Abbess had listened as it all poured out, but now she raised her hand. "God is protecting him now, and all the earthly troubles he suffered are at an end. In Heaven, there is perfect happiness. Jesus said, 'In my Father's house there are many mansions. All are welcome.' You don't have to worry about Arthur any more. God is looking after him."

Elizabeth bowed her head as the tears flowed freely. With them came a sense of comfort and peace. Maybe those strange incidents *had* been Arthur been trying to tell her that he was all right.

"Thank you, Reverend Mother," she said. "You have made me feel so much better." She took a deep breath to steady herself. "But it was not just to give comfort that you summoned me. What can I do for you?"

"I am, of course, appealing to you for money," the Abbess said, smiling apologetically. "Two of my elderly and infirm nuns have had to go into an almshouse and have barely enough to cover their food, while two of our servants here are in want."

"I will send a donation," Elizabeth promised.

"Thank you. I knew I could rely on your Grace's famous generosity." The Abbess paused. "My cousin, Lady Rivers, wishes to be remembered to you. She has been happy in her second marriage to Sir George Neville."

"So I have heard," Elizabeth said, thinking sadly of her dashing uncle Anthony, who had been so cruelly murdered by the usurper Richard.

The Abbess rose and stood by the window, looking out toward the Tower. "Another of my cousins is Sir James Tyrell, who now lies yonder accused of treason."

Elizabeth said nothing, waiting for the Abbess to reveal why she had really summoned her.

"There are several ladies who live here in a house in the close and wish to meet you," the older woman told her. "They have confided to me information about Sir James that disturbs me, and I think you should hear it, as the matter touches your Grace very closely."

Elizabeth held her breath. "Is this about my brothers?" she whispered.

"I fear it is. Shall I ask those ladies to join us? Or your Grace could visit them in their house. They chose not to leave the world, but to retire here. I think that, for various reasons, they feel safer within our holy precincts. They did not want to become embroiled in worldly controversies, but I have persuaded them that they must speak out now that Sir James is in custody."

"I will see them. Let them come here."

The Abbess rang a bell and a young nun came in. "Tell the ladies in the close that our lady the Queen wishes to see them." The little nun hastened away.

Presently, four soberly dressed women walked in, as the Abbess pulled forward a wooden bench. Looking nervous, they made their reverences to Elizabeth. She recognized the one in a widow's wimple at once.

"My lady of Norfolk! I had heard that you had retired to a nunnery. I did not realize it was here. How are you?"

"I am in tolerable health, your Grace." The Dowager Duchess looked strained. She had aged considerably since her daughter Anne's wedding to young York twenty-four years ago. Of course, she had lost both her husband and her only child—and, earlier on, her sister Eleanor, the woman Elizabeth's father was supposed to have secretly married, according to Richard. Did the Duchess know the truth of that? Did Elizabeth dare ask her? No. The implications could be far-reaching, too awful to contemplate. She reminded herself that her legitimacy was now enshrined in law.

The Abbess introduced the other ladies as Elizabeth Brackenbury and Mary and Thomasine Tyrell. Elizabeth started when she heard their names. "Brackenbury? Wasn't he the Constable of the Tower in the Usurper's time?"

"He was my father." Elizabeth Brackenbury spoke with a broad Yorkshire accent. She was a blunt-featured woman, probably in her thirties, and carelessly dressed, with strands of dark hair escaping from her cap. "I sought refuge here after he was killed at Bosworth."

"And you are both related to Sir James Tyrell?" Elizabeth asked the other ladies, feeling the tension in her mounting, for she had an instinctive feeling that these women knew the truth about her brothers.

"I am his sister," Mary said, sounding a little nervous. With her beak-like nose and thin frame, she looked like a trapped bird, Elizabeth thought.

"And I am his cousin," Thomasine added. There was a strong familial likeness between the women, but neither resembled the swarthy Tyrell very much.

"Our friend Joyce Lee, who lives with us, would have been here, too, but Thomas More, her young lawyer friend, has just come to visit her," said the Duchess stiffly. "However, she has nothing to confess to your Grace. These three ladies do. When they learned of Sir James Tyrell's arrest, they confided in me, and I said most emphatically that it was our duty to prepare you for what he might reveal under questioning."

Mary Tyrell appeared to be inwardly wrestling with herself. "Or not reveal, knowing him," she muttered, then the words came out in a rush. "The truth is, Madam, that, eighteen years ago, James confessed to me and Thomasine that he himself had been ordered to arrange the killing of your brothers, the princes."

Elizabeth began to tremble. "You know this for a certainty?" she faltered, sounding quite unlike herself.

"Why would he lie? He told us that King Richard had commanded it. It was all done in the greatest secrecy. James commandeered the keys from Sir Robert Brackenbury and dismissed him and the guards for the night. He brought with him some rough fellows and ordered them to suffocate those poor innocents as they slept and bury them within the Tower afterward."

Elizabeth closed her eyes against the pain. It was as she had feared all along. It was unbearable to think of how the lives of those young boys had been cruelly snuffed out.

"King Richard rewarded him afterward," Thomasine supplied. "My family wondered where this bounty was coming from, and why."

"Then, when we asked him and he told us what he had done, it became clear how he had earned it," Mary said. "Of course, no one could touch him then, but after Bosworth . . . Well, we were on the wrong side and James could no longer count on royal protection. He swore us to secrecy. He said we would all be in danger if the truth got out, him for treason and us for concealing it. That is why Thomasine and I sought refuge here. We just wanted to disappear. But, ever since, I have agonized about keeping what I knew to myself."

"Forgive us, Madam, for we should have spoken out earlier, especially when Perkin Warbeck claimed to be Richard, Duke of York," Thomasine whispered, looking at Elizabeth fearfully.

Elizabeth was horrified. She could hardly believe what she was hearing. These women had known . . . they had known for eighteen years! That not one of them had come forward was incredible. Had they lacked the imagination to comprehend the pain that she and her family had been suffering, or to understand how crucial it was to Henry to know what had become of her brothers? And Richard . . . He had lied to her, persistently; and he had indeed had the blood of infants on his hands. She sat there silently for a few moments, feeling quite faint and trying not to retch. "It would have saved us a lot of trouble if you had, and me a lot of heartache," she said eventually, her voice sounding strangled.

She turned to the Duchess. "You knew, too?" It came out as an accusation.

"They told me two days ago," said the Duchess. "I wish they had told me sooner. I have suffered torments over what might have happened to my son-in-law York."

"Madam, I am truly sorry," Mary said. "I know that concealing this knowledge was wrong."

"I too am to blame. I guessed the truth long ago," Elizabeth Brackenbury chimed in. "When those rumors that the princes had been murdered began to circulate, I asked my father if he knew what had happened to them. He told me that Sir James had come to him and demanded the keys, then dismissed him and the warders for the night. He showed him King Richard's warrant. He said that no harm would come to the princes. But my father always wondered. You see, he returned the next day to find them gone. There was no clue as to where they had been taken. He could not know if they were alive or dead, though he had his suspicions."

"Yet he fought for Richard at Bosworth," Elizabeth said. "He laid down his life for him. Why would he do that if he suspected him of murdering those innocents?"

"He was bound to him. He feared what might happen to him if King Henry, as he is now, took the kingdom and married your Grace. It might go ill for him if it became known that he had given the keys to Tyrell and abetted—wittingly or not—the murder of your brothers. He feared he might be accused of misprision of treason. Therefore, he fought to keep Richard on the throne."

"But you found out the truth?" Elizabeth persisted.

"After we came here, I asked Mary outright if Sir James had had anything to do with the princes' disappearance. She denied it, but I thought she was lying."

"I was afraid!" Mary cried. "You might have betrayed James—and me."

"No, I just wanted the truth! I too wanted to disappear. I had no portion, for my father was posthumously attainted after Bosworth. His lands were later restored to me, but still I preferred to hide here. The name Brackenbury will be forever associated with Richard."

"I told her the truth," Thomasine whispered. "I had to unburden myself to someone."

"You should have told the authorities!" the Duchess burst out.

The three culprits hung their heads. "We were too scared," Mary confessed. "We wanted people to forget all about us. It was only when I heard that James was in the Tower that I felt I had to confide in Mother Abbess, for I needed her advice as to what to do."

"And you have not told anyone else?" Elizabeth asked.

"Only Joyce Lee."

"She can be trusted to be discreet?"

"Oh, yes, Madam. She hopes to take the veil soon."

"Your Grace," the Abbess said, "you have heard the testimonies of these ladies. What will you do now?"

The others looked at Elizabeth fearfully. She hesitated, holding herself very still and taut, feeling an immense sense of betrayal, and not knowing quite what to say. A great wrong had been done her—and Henry, and England. But Christ had enjoined people to forgive those who sinned against them, not seven times, but seventy times seven.

"I bear you no grudge," she made herself say. "You acted only out of loyalty to your family. I know what it is to live in fear, and I will see that you are not punished for your honesty today. But the King must be told. He will wish to question Sir James about what you have told me. And I myself do, too."

Mary looked as if she was about to cry. "I am not the person to break a confidence, Madam, but I hope that my brother will understand why I had to tell you what I knew."

"It is no great matter compared with what he has done," she replied. "And he put you in an impossible position."

The Abbess rose and handed her a sealed letter. "Madam, I have written to Sir James, urging him, for the sake of his soul, to make a clean breast of this matter. I pray you will see that he gets it."

"I will," Elizabeth promised, rising herself.

"May God bless you," Alice FitzLewis said.

Elizabeth dismissed her women and sat down by a window overlooking the Thames, trying to collect her thoughts. This was all too much, coming on top of Arthur's death. For many years, she had longed to know the truth, but knowing was more painful than she had ever anticipated. She wept as she imagined how it had been for her brothers. Had they awoken and struggled in terror at the end? It was bad enough that they had been murdered as they slept, without any chance of being shriven. It did not bear thinking about. Her only consolation was that Ned had confessed his sins regularly toward the end, fearing death daily.

And Richard. It was the ultimate betrayal. While he had been giving her mother those empty assurances, and showing Elizabeth herself friendship and courting her, he had been guilty of murdering her brothers. He had lied and lied. And she had been taken in. What a fool she had been.

It was not for her to judge. God had done that. He had given Henry the victory at Bosworth. Yet still she burned with anger at Richard—and at Tyrell, who had been his henchman and committed a wicked, foul crime.

"Why the hell didn't they speak out earlier?" Henry exploded, slamming down his pen on the table. They were alone in his closet, and Elizabeth had just finished relating what she had learned at the Minories.

"I wish they had," she replied, "but Mary did not want to betray her brother. Please don't punish her."

Henry's face was livid. "If I had only known from the outset what I know now, I could have been spared years of worry about pretenders—and my throne would have been secure. Look at me! I am old before my time because of all the disquiet I have suffered. And you expect me to be merciful!"

"Henry, please! If you had been in her position, would you have broken a confidence made by your brother? Would you have risked his being sent to the block?"

He subsided, still angry. "There were greater issues at stake."

"There were. But the real culprit here is Tyrell, not his sister."

"By God, he'll talk now! I'll make him."

"Let him see the Abbess's letter first."

He sighed. "Very well. But I'll have him before us first thing tomorrow."

Tyrell stood there, ashen-faced. Gone was the bravado, the nonchalance. He would not meet Elizabeth's eye.

"Well, Sir James, what have you to say to us?" Henry barked.

The prisoner seemed to be struggling to find the words.

"Is it true what your sister has told me?" Elizabeth asked coldly.

He hesitated. "Yes, your Grace."

"And both my brothers were suffocated? Neither survived?"

"Yes."

"And this was done on the orders of the usurper Richard?" Henry interjected.

"Yes, Sir."

"Even so, you knew it was wrong. I suppose you thought to profit by it? Or are you going to say that you were intimidated into doing it?"

Tyrell hesitated again.

"Well?" Henry's face was like thunder.

"I sought preferment. When King Richard said he had a very important task he wanted done secretly, I leaped at the chance. When I learned what it was, I wanted to refuse, but I dared not. You see, Sir, I realized I was now in possession of knowledge that, if disclosed, could have cost him his throne, as was proved afterward, when those rumors that he'd murdered the princes lost him the support he needed. If I had refused him, I believed I would have been placing myself in danger, for I feared he would not have let me live to tell the tale."

Henry was giving no quarter. "So you murdered two innocents."

"I did not do it myself, Sir. My horse-keeper, John Dighton, and Miles Forrest carried out the actual deed. I was not even in the room, but without."

"And you think that exonerates you? You gave them their orders!"

"Sir, I have told you the truth."

"Did they suffer? Did they know what was happening?" Elizabeth cried, unable to hold back any longer.

"They were asleep, Madam. I heard no sounds of a struggle. It was all over quickly."

"Where were the bodies buried?" Henry asked. "I've had the Tower searched, and there is no sign of their whereabouts."

"Alas, Sir, I do not know. I left before they were buried. But Dighton can tell you."

"I'll have him summoned for questioning," Henry said. "Now, Sir James, perhaps you will tell me why you aided the traitor Suffolk."

Tyrell must have realized that he was going to die anyway, so it all came out: how he had felt sympathy for the de la Poles; how Suffolk had promised him greater rewards than he had ever received from Henry; how Tyrell had believed that helping him on his way to the Imperial court had not actually constituted anything treasonous.

Henry listened with a grim expression. "You will be tried next week at the Guildhall," he told him. "As you know, you may answer the charges but you will not mention this matter of the princes."

Elizabeth turned to him, bewildered.

"Remove the prisoner," Henry commanded.

"Why should he not mention my brothers?" she cried, as soon as they had reached the privacy of his closet.

"Because I want the story corroborated before their fate is made public. And I don't want that old controversy over your legitimacy raked up."

"But you will be more secure on your throne if people know that they are dead."

"People will know. I shall make sure of it. But I don't want the matter bandied about in court."

She understood his concerns; her legitimacy was crucial to the legitimacy of the Tudor succession. It had always been a sensitive point with Henry. He had even banned books that mentioned Richard's Act declaring her and her siblings bastards, and she had been heartily glad of it. Mention of her brothers might well revive the matter. Henry was right: it was best to maintain discretion.

He saw Dighton alone. He did not want her to suffer any more distress on hearing how her brothers had died. When he came to her that night, she feared he might not tell her all the details.

"What a knave!" he spat, accepting a goblet of wine before they retired to bed. "The lowest kind, and cunning, too. I had to wring every last word out of him. He says he buried your brothers under a stair, beneath a heap of rubble, but he doesn't think they are there now because Tyrell told him Richard meant to have them moved later. I asked him if he could show me the place, but he said he couldn't remember where it was. A likely story, but I couldn't get any more out of him. Bessy, this afternoon, I had my men examine every staircase in the Tower—and none of them could see any evidence of disturbance."

Elizabeth's shoulders sagged in disappointment. She had hoped that she could give her brothers a decent burial worthy of their rank. Now even that consolation was to be denied her. Yet she was coming to terms with her loss. Knowing the truth at last, after years of agonized uncertainty, had brought her some comfort— and a sense of relief. It was cathartic to write to her sisters and tell them the truth. She could not expect Katherine and Bridget to remember their brothers, but Cecily had lived through the pain of their loss with her, and Anne, too, to a lesser extent. Cecily would be the one most affected by the news.

She returned to Greenwich for Ascension Day, knowing that she would always carry this grief. In the week that followed, she learned that Tyrell had been arraigned for treason at the Guildhall and condemned to death. Soon afterward, he was beheaded on Tower Hill. It had been the appropriate penalty for all his crimes, especially those not mentioned in court. Justice had finally been done.

The following week, Henry had it proclaimed that Tyrell had confessed to murdering King Edward V and the Duke of York.

The proclamation caused little stir. It was yesterday's news, history now, and people's memories were short. Probably most had believed anyway that the princes had been murdered; it was no great matter to have it confirmed.

And Elizabeth believed, in her bones, that there would be no more pretenders.

Among her other cares, she was worrying about her daughter-in-law. Katherine had lain sick at Ludlow for over a month now. She was slowly getting better, but Ferdinand and Isabella had expressed concern and demanded that she be removed immediately from the unhealthy air there. Assured by Dr. Linacre that the Princess would soon be well enough to travel, Elizabeth sent an escort and a black-draped litter to convey her convalescent daughter-in-law to Richmond.

She was shocked when she saw her. Katherine had been in the bloom of health before Christmas, golden-haired, plump-cheeked, bright-eyed. Now, she was thin, and her hair and eyes looked lifeless. She thought of Arthur's will with its glaring omission. Was Katherine truly grieving for him, or was her wan appearance just the result of illness? It was impossible to tell and she did not want to probe. Best to assume that the girl was sorrowful for her loss.

"Welcome, my dear child." Elizabeth raised her from her curtsey and embraced her, feeling the bones of her spine beneath the velvet bodice. "My heart has been with you these past weeks."

"As mine has been with your Majesty," Katherine replied.

"I feel for you, widowed so young. I want to assure you that while you are here in England, you will not lack father or mother."

"I thank your Majesty." Tears glinted in the Princess's eyes.

"The King wishes to assign you a place to live until your future is decided," Elizabeth said, gesturing to her to be seated. "You are to have the choice of two residences: the Bishop of Durham's palace on the Strand, near London, or the Archbishop of Canterbury's palace at Croydon, a few miles to the south."

Katherine attempted a smile. "That is most kind of his Majesty. Which one would your Majesty recommend?"

"I would go to Croydon, for it is in the country, yet convenient for the City and Westminster. It is a fine house, most meet for a princess, and the air is healthy."

"Then I will go there. But, Madam, what is to become of me?"

"In truth, Katherine, the King and I have not discussed it. We have been in grief since Arthur's death, and we have been more concerned about your health than your future. But I will speak to his Grace tonight."

"Thank you, Madam."

"Do you want to go home to Spain?" Elizabeth asked gently.

The girl swallowed. "I wish only to do what my parents desire." It was the right, the dutiful, answer. Katherine had been well schooled.

"Of course. We will speak again tomorrow. And I will give orders for Croydon Palace to be made ready for you."

At supper that night, Elizabeth spoke to Henry. "What are your plans for Katherine?"

He sighed. "A lot depends on what Ferdinand and Isabella want. They have sent their condolences and written that the news of Arthur's passing has caused them profound sorrow, but that the will of God must be obeyed."

"However hard that is," she said sadly.

Henry reached for her hand. "The priority for me is to preserve the alliance with Spain. That could be achieved by marrying Katherine to Harry."

"But he's not yet eleven—and she is sixteen. They will be ill matched."

"Cariad, this is about England wedding Spain. In a few years, the age difference won't matter. And have you seen the way Harry looks at her? The way he looked at her at her wedding? What Arthur had, he always coveted. Now he is to have Arthur's crown—and I'll wager he wants his bride, too."

Elizabeth thought back to all the times she had seen Harry and Katherine together. Yes, he had made plain his admiration for her. It could work.

"But would such a marriage be permitted by the Church?" she wondered. "They are brother and sister-in-law. It could be seen as incestuous."

"I need to consult my bishops. But I'm waiting to see what the sovereigns want for Katherine. I hope they can see the benefits of her marrying Harry. God knows, I don't want to give back the half of her dowry she brought with her; and I want the rest of it. Above all, we need this alliance."

Elizabeth saw Katherine the next day and told her that Henry was waiting to hear from her parents. That afternoon, the Princess left for Croydon. As she watched the litter depart, Elizabeth swayed on her feet, feeling drained and a little dizzy. Dr. Lewis was away, so a London physician was sent for, who prescribed rest and a hearty diet.

Elizabeth was reluctant to spend long hours lying on her bed with time to brood about Arthur. She wanted to be up and about, keeping busy, but when she defied the doctor's orders, she felt so fatigued that a surgeon was sent for to bleed her. He ordered her to bed, and she spent three days there, trying to concentrate on her books, or her conversations with the ladies who sat with her, so that disturbing thoughts of Arthur could not intrude.

Katherine was much in her thoughts, and she sent a page to inquire after her health. He reported that the Princess had said that she was eating more and had put on weight. That set Elizabeth wondering if she was pregnant. And yet that Spanish doctor had said that Arthur had been too weak to consummate their marriage. But he could not have known for certain what had taken place—or not—in the marital bed. Would it not be wonderful if Katherine was carrying Arthur's child?

The implications were considerable. If it proved to be a boy, it would displace Harry in the line of succession; Elizabeth could imagine how upset he would be, for he was inordinately proud of his new status as the King's heir. And yet, would Henry live to see his grandson reach his majority? He was forty-five and would be over sixty by then. Harry might end up ruling England after all, as regent.

As these thoughts buzzed around in her head, Henry arrived, dismissed her ladies, and sat down by the bed. "How are you today, cariad?"

"I think I am feeling a little better. I do hope so. I can't keep lying here."

"Don't overdo things," he warned. "You must look after yourself. Especially if . . ." He looked at her hopefully. Heavens, he thought she was suffering the discomforts of early pregnancy. True to her word, she had welcomed him to her bed with arms open wide, needing the comfort of the closeness he brought as well as offering herself as a vessel for another heir to strengthen his throne. Yet, so far, there had been no sign that she had conceived.

"That's another reason why I want to get better quickly," she smiled, squeezing his hand.

"We don't have to rush things," he said. "I can contain myself in impatience!"

Their eyes met. There was a new kindness between them now. They had pulled together after Arthur's death, united in equal grief, gentle with each other. "I have some good news," Henry said. "Dr. de Puebla has just come to see me. Ferdinand and Isabella have instructed him to preserve the alliance. They are asking for the immediate return of Katherine and her dowry, but they have told Puebla to secure her betrothal to Harry. Crucially, they want to know if she is with child. If she is, their union would be incestuous and against canon law. It's a delicate matter, but we have to find out the truth. Dr. de Puebla is making inquiries."

"You will keep me informed?"

"Of course."

A week later, Elizabeth welcomed Henry to her bed, feeling greatly restored after her rest.

"There have been conflicting reports from Croydon," he said, as they lay entwined together, spent after their lovemaking, a mild breeze from the open casement playing on their bodies.

"Conflicting?"

"Aye. The Princess's chaplain told Dr. de Puebla that the marriage had been consummated, but the duenna is adamant that it was not and that Katherine remains a virgin. But, my lawyers tell me, the consummation of the marriage is not the issue. The crucial thing is whether she is with child, and it is now certain that she is not."

It was tragic that Arthur had not left something of himself behind, but Elizabeth had not held out much hope of it. "So there is no impediment to a betrothal between her and Harry?"

"No," Henry replied. "But I think we should wait a decent interval before proceeding with it. It won't create difficulties, for the sovereigns are as keen to preserve the alliance as I am." He kissed the top of her head, as she lay in the crook of his shoulder. "Now we know that Arthur left no heir, Harry can be made prince of Wales."

That, at least, was something to gladden the heart, although, as so often these days, Elizabeth could not help thinking of the boy who should still be bearing the title, the son who was meant to be king.

By the time she and Henry celebrated the feast of Corpus Christi in June, she had missed a course and suspected that she was with child. She had mixed feelings about it. Part of her was overjoyed, especially for Henry's sake and for England's—and for her own, for that matter, although no new babe could ever replace Arthur or those other little ones she had lost. The remaining part of her was in dread, fearful that this pregnancy would endanger her life. She was thirty-six now, well into middle age, and she had not felt properly well for a long time.

Trying to ignore the ever-present nausea, she ordered new clothes for William Courtenay, who still languished in the Tower. She had run out of things to say to Katherine, who was now desperate to see her husband freed. Elizabeth had badgered Henry several times on the matter, but, while he'd again assured her that he would not send Courtenay to the block, he was adamant that he must remain in the Tower.

"But he has not been tried or condemned!" she had cried.

"Nor will he be until I lay hands on Suffolk," Henry declared. "Until then, he can stay under lock and key, out of mischief. You may tell your sister, though, that not a hair on his head will be harmed, whatever the outcome."

But that was small comfort for Katherine.

The next day the court moved to Westminster. Elizabeth could not bear to see six-year-old Mary clad in deepest mourning, so she bought some orange sarcenet sleeves to enliven her black gown. Mary was thrilled—she was a vain little thing, but very winning— and enjoyed parading around in them. And then Margaret had to have a pair, too . . . Harry was all for throwing off his mourning. He hated anything to do with death and clearly did not want to talk about Arthur.

Elizabeth made an offering at the shrine of St. Edward the Confessor in Westminster Abbey, kneeling beside the tombs of Beth and Edmund. Poor little souls; they had cast their light on this world for such a short time. She sent up a prayer too for Arthur, lying so far away at Worcester. Would she ever pray by his tomb?

But life was beginning to return to normal; grief waited for no man. When they moved to Richmond, Henry commanded a disguising and Elizabeth paid a coppersmith for spangles, stars, and lace-points of silver and gold to adorn the jackets worn by the players. She also provided coats of sarcenet in the Tudor colors of white and green for the King's minstrels and trumpeters. Cecily helped with the preparations, and Elizabeth thought that her sister seemed a lot happier these days, although she was too distracted to wonder why. The performance diverted her from her grief, but it was always with her. She might be applauding the dancers, but she was dying inside. She wondered if she would ever feel normal again.

By the middle of June, she was at Windsor, where she gave money to her grooms and pages for making the traditional bonfires on St. John's Eve. She tried to take comfort in her remaining children, although the very sight of their dear little faces brought home her loss. She had nurtured Arthur as she was nurturing them—and all for what? Early in July, resolutely suppressing such thoughts, she took them for an outdoor banquet in the park. As they romped on the grass, she kept telling herself that Arthur had not lived in vain.

But then Henry came upon them, sending their offspring and the ladies scattering.

At the sight of his furious face, Elizabeth struggled to her feet, forgetting to curtsey. "My lord! Whatever is the matter?"

"Your sister Cecily is the matter! She has secretly married some unworthy varlet—and without seeking my consent, which I would have withheld had she done me that courtesy."

She stood rigid with shock. "No! What possessed her to do such a thing? And who has she married?"

"No one you or I would know! One Kyme—some say he hails from Lincolnshire, others the Isle of Wight. By God, as a princess of the blood, she should know that she cannot wed without my permission, still less disparage the royal lineage by throwing herself away on a mere esquire! She shall pay for this."

"No!" Elizabeth protested, her tears flowing fast as the enormity of Cecily's situation sank in. "Whatever she has done, she is my sister and I love her dearly. *Please* do not be harsh with her!"

"Bessy, her marriage is in my gift. I could have betrothed her to some great prince and made an alliance advantageous to myself— to England! Or I could have wed her to a great lord to keep him loyal or reward him. But I shouldn't have to spell that out to you. Sister or not, she has offended greatly. I'm banishing her from court and confiscating the lands Lord Welles left her. Be grateful that I haven't clapped her in the Tower!"

He stumped off, striding angrily back to where his horse was tethered. Elizabeth had never seen him in such a rage. She willed him to calm down soon and relent toward Cecily, who would be left destitute without her income—and it would be she, Elizabeth, who would have to step in and keep her.

Dabbing at her eyes, she called the children, who approached warily.

"Your father is cross about some matter of state," she told them.

"Don't worry. He needed to get it off his chest. Come, let us go back to the castle."

As soon as they returned, she hastened to the Lady Margaret's lodging. Margaret had been a good friend to Cecily in her widowhood. Surely, she would help.

When she entered Margaret's chamber, she found Cecily there in floods of tears, with Margaret holding her hand and exhorting her not to give way to despair.

"Oh, my dear!" Elizabeth said, and ran to embrace her sister.

"You have heard, then," Margaret said.

"Henry told me. He means to banish Cecily from the court and confiscate her lands."

"Probably he spoke in the heat of the moment," the old lady said, "and he will rescind the orders soon, or at least ordain a more merciful punishment. He is not a vindictive man."

"No, but he is very angry," Elizabeth said.

"Bessy, I love Thomas!" Cecily cried. "I have dutifully married two husbands for policy and lost them both. I do not see why I should not now make my own choice and follow my heart."

"God knows, Henry will not see it like that," Elizabeth said distractedly. "I wish you had come to me first. I would have moved Heaven and earth to help you. But to present Henry with a *fait accompli*—that was unbelievably rash. You have only made things worse for yourself. Tell me, what is it about Thomas that made you do it?"

"He loves me. He makes me feel beautiful and special. And he is kind. I know you will like him!" Cecily was suddenly radiant.

"I dare say I will, but what I think of him is not the issue. Cis, please don't worry. I will see what I can do to soften Henry."

She tried, over supper that evening. She used every weapon in her armory: pleading, persuasion, tears, begging him to relent for the sake of the little one she carried . . . None of it made any difference. In the end, she grew shrill and flung down her spoon. "Haven't we got enough to cope with at this time, without you being so harsh to Cecily? I live with grief, Henry. We are mourning our son; I am having to come to terms with the murder of my brothers. Do not add to our woes. I need my sister with me. I need all the support and comfort I can get."

Henry looked away. "Bessy, I have to be a king first and a husband and father second. Cecily is to blame for this trouble; it was not of my making. If I do not make an example of her, others will think they can flout me with impunity, and I will not have it!"

Her pleas had fallen on deaf ears. She was shocked herself at Cecily's rash marriage, but her anger was now directed solely at Henry, who was being so stubborn. She was deeply hurt that he had ignored her appeal, and her feelings.

"I am exhausted," she said. "With your leave I will retire."

"Good night," Henry said, draining his goblet.

She left, seething. What was wrong with him? Did he have no feelings?

Chapter 24

1502–1503

As her ladies prepared her for bed, Elizabeth's mind was churning with resentment, and it was not just connected with Cecily. She burned to think of how much grief the unresolved issue of William Courtenay's fate was causing Katherine—and that was Henry's doing too. With him, it seemed, policy came before pity—or any human feelings, for that matter! Look how he had sent Arthur to Ludlow in the depth of winter, insisting that the boy was up to it. It was a risk he should never, ever have taken. They had both had concerns about Arthur's health, but no, Henry had ignored her maternal instincts and chosen to rely on Dr. Linacre's advice. She was finding it hard to forgive him for the devastation he had wrought in her life, not to mention those of her sisters.

She could sit there no longer while her hair was being combed. She waved her ladies away and took herself to bed, fuming. She had thought that she and Henry had come together as never before in their terrible loss, but she had been wrong. It seemed to have hardened him. Why was he being so unkind?

The answer might lie in another matter that had been troubling her. She was still painfully aware of the admiring way he looked at Catherine Gordon and the respect with which he treated her. She had long believed that her marriage was one of fidelity and mutual support, but Henry's recent behavior had made her doubt it. Every time she looked in a mirror, she saw an over-plump, sad-faced reflection, a woman well past her youth, worn down with seven pregnancies. How could any man not prefer the lovely, youthful Catherine, with her striking coloring and gentle manner? She kept telling herself there was no evidence that Henry's interest in the young woman had ever strayed beyond a chivalrous fancy. Even so, she felt threatened by it.

She had to get away by herself for a while. She wanted to make Henry aware of how deeply he had hurt her. They had rarely traveled separately, apart from when she had gone on pilgrimage. They had always hated being apart; she recalled how Henry had come home early from that campaign in France because he had missed her so much. Now, she meant to make him miss her again and make plain to him what he was doing to their marriage. And, while she was away, she would try to make sense of her own feelings. She loved him, there was no doubt about that. Yet hatred was the natural obverse of that, and it was proving destructive. She was rational enough to understand that. So it was better that she spend some time apart from Henry.

She could not leave immediately. In the morning, before she faced him with her decision, she returned to the Lady Margaret's lodging and found Cecily, who was desperate to hear what Henry had said.

"I'm so sorry," Elizabeth apologized. "I tried my utmost, but he would not listen."

Cecily looked as if she had been punched.

"You have done your best," Margaret said. "You cannot do more. Cecily and I have come to an arrangement. I am giving her and Kyme the use of Collyweston, and I hope to persuade the King to restore her income."

"I trust you will have more success than I did," Elizabeth sighed, suspecting that her mother-in-law's persuasions might carry more weight than hers. "But, Cis, this is an incredibly kind offer. Collyweston is a beautiful house. Few newlyweds could have a better start to their married life."

Cecily hugged her. "My Lady Margaret has been so kind to me. And my disgrace will be leavened by having the freedom to be with Thomas. I do hope that you will be able to receive him some day, Bessy."

"So do I. You've been a fool, but a fool for love, and who can blame you for that? At least I am leaving you in safe hands."

"You are leaving us?"

"I intend to make a progress and take Katherine with me. After everything that has happened, I feel a need to get away and have a change of scene."

"Is that wise, in your condition?" Margaret asked. "I would not travel far if I were you, Bessy."

"I feel quite well," Elizabeth lied, "and I have yet to decide where I will go. But I will take great care of myself, I assure you."

"It seems an extraordinary thing to do." Margaret gave her a shrewd look. Had she guessed that there was something wrong? "What does Henry have to say about it?"

"I haven't discussed it with him yet. I am on my way to do so now."

"I suspect he will not be very pleased. But you must sort the matter out between you."

"I will miss you," Cecily said.

"We both will," Margaret echoed.

As she walked along the gallery that led to Henry's apartments, Elizabeth's heart was sinking. Her anger was still lively, yet she hated confrontations. But he had put her in this horrible situation.

An usher led her to his closet, where she found him going through a great pile of accounts, his pet monkey on his shoulder. He looked up warily.

"Bessy. Good day. What brings you here?"

She sat down. "I wish to go on a summer progress, if you will give me leave."

He laid down his pen and gave her a sorrowful look. "On your own?"

She held his gaze. "Yes."

"But we usually go on progress together."

"It has been a terribly difficult year. I feel weighted down with grief and cares, and I need to get away."

"From me?"

"From everything."

"Is this to do with Cecily?"

"Cecily—and everything else that has happened. I can't take any more, Henry. Travel will help to take my mind off things."

"And where do you propose to go?"

"To Wales, in easy stages."

"Wales? Bessy, are you mad? Have you seen yourself in the mirror lately? You look ill. You're with child and your life was despaired of last time. And yet you are bent on journeying hundreds of miles. Frankly, I think you've taken leave of your senses."

"Not at all. It's essential that I go. Don't gainsay me."

"You'll be away from me for most of the summer."

"Well, that should be a relief for both of us."

He exhaled, exasperated. "And all this because I have justly punished Cecily for her grave offense!"

Be careful, her inner voice was warning her. *Don't make things worse than they already are. Accusations hurled at him now can never be unsaid.*

"It's not just that. I need time to grieve. I pray you, let me go."

He looked at her heavily. "Very well. But it is against my better judgment."

"Thank you," she said stiffly. He raised hurt eyes to her.

"There is something else." The idea had come to her as she lay wakeful in the small hours, and she had been thinking about it all morning. "When I come back, I want a place of my own to retire to when the world gets me down. It will do me a power of good to have a project to divert me, something for me to look forward to when I return."

Henry swallowed. It seemed that a great gulf had opened up between them, and it was her doing—no, it was his!

"Where do you envisage building this place?" His voice was hoarse.

"There's that space on the waterfront at Greenwich. I thought a small house of red brick with battlements, perhaps a tower, but certainly a garden and some fruit trees."

There was a pause as he stared at her. "By God, you've thought it all out, haven't you?"

"I only had the idea in the night."

"And you want this house built so that you can live apart from me?"

"I did not say that. I just want a place to call my own."

"You didn't need to say it."

She made a huge effort. "Look, Henry, this is not the best time to talk about the future. I need time to think. I may feel differently after the progress. But right now, I feel very alone, and that's down to you."

His eyes flashed. "What else have I done—or not done? You must tell me."

"There's the delay over Courtenay's fate. You have no idea what it's doing to Katherine, or to me, seeing her so distressed. And—" She shut up. Some things could never be said.

"It's Arthur, isn't it? You resent me for not realizing earlier that something was amiss and for making all the wrong decisions."

"You knew, well before last December, that Arthur was not well. You feared the consequences of his consummating the marriage—you told me. But my worries were dismissed. Instead of heeding my instincts, you relied on Dr. Linacre—and look how wrong he was!"

"And don't you think that I will regret that every day of my life? I'm crucifying myself for it, and for not going to him when he needed us." There were tears in Henry's eyes. But she was frozen in her anger and resentment. She had nothing to give him, as he had done nothing to help her.

He rose and moved around the table. She stepped back and he stopped. "I believed what I wanted to believe. I could not face the alternative. I clung on to what Linacre was saying. Do not blame me for that. I was living on hope."

"As was I. Henry, I know you are grieving, too. But that should make you receptive to my pain. Yet you have only added to it."

He placed his hands on her shoulders, but she shrugged him off. "Bessy, you, of all people, should know that, for a king, considerations of state must come before all others. Do not ask me to show more leniency in your sisters' cases than I already have."

She flung him a look. "I thought I meant more to you than that. Certainly, we need time apart. I will go and make ready for my progress and ask Katherine to accompany me."

"Bessy—" Henry began.

"And while I'm away," she went on, "I will draw some rough plans for my house at Greenwich." With that, she left him, her heart breaking.

The July sun was blazing when she and Katherine, with a small retinue, left Windsor for Woodstock. They had both wept a little to leave their children behind, but hoped to return to them in a stronger frame of mind. They boarded the Thames ferry at Datchet and rode north to Notley Abbey, where they stayed that night in the Abbot's luxurious house. Elizabeth was heavy-hearted, yet she felt well physically, apart from a little nausea in the morning. She trusted that the coming changes of scene would lift her spirits. But that hope was dashed when, the next day, a messenger caught up with them with a letter from Havering, where Katherine's children were staying in the care of Lady Cotton.

"Edward is dead!" Katherine wailed, letting it drop to the floor. "Dear God, how will I bear it?"

Elizabeth took her in her arms and let her cry, weeping herself, knowing—who better?—what her sister was going through. Had there not been enough tragedy? Little Edward had been but five years old.

She picked up the letter and read it. Lady Cotton had written that a summer fever had carried him off with alarming speed.

"I must go to Havering," Katherine sobbed. "I must see him once more before he is chested. You should not come, because this malady might be infectious and you have the child to think of."

Elizabeth saw the sense in this. "Are you sure you'll be all right?"

"I have my ladies to comfort me. Do not worry."

Elizabeth returned to the letter. "Lady Cotton is asking to know my pleasure as to where he should be buried. My dear, I will write this day to the Abbot of Westminster and ask that he be found a place in the abbey. And do not worry about the cost; I will defray it. Here, take some money to give as gifts to Edward's nurse and his rocker." She reached for her purse.

Katherine left that day in a litter provided by the Abbot, and Elizabeth rode on alone to Woodstock. There, she began to feel ill. It was the effect of the shocking news of her nephew's death, coming on top of everything else, she told herself—but she felt bad enough to take to her bed, feeling as poorly as she had done in the spring. She found herself wishing that Henry was with her, but it was too soon to mend what had gone wrong between them, and her feelings for him were deeply confused. Oh, but she felt so drained; her head ached and her heart was pounding wildly. When she got up to use the privy, she was assailed by breathlessness and dizziness. What was wrong with her?

She wondered if she should send for a doctor. There would be several in Oxford, and the steward must know of them. It had been foolish not to bring Dr. Lewis. But she had had these symptoms before and got better. She decided to wait a while and hope that rest did the trick. In the meantime, she lay there praying for a speedy recovery and a successful outcome to her pregnancy, and to that end sent offerings to various local shrines and churches.

By August, she was well enough to travel and decided to press on with her journey. To turn back at this stage would not be wise. She was feeling less hostile toward Henry, but she still needed time alone.

A week later, she was in Wales. The weather had been good and the roads free of mud and mire. It seemed a long way from Henry and the court. At Monmouth, she presented two beautifully embroidered vestments to the priory. Then it was on to Raglan Castle, where her cousin, Lord Herbert, made her very welcome. He was the natural son of the last Duke of Somerset, who had been beheaded in the late wars, and the last male descendant of the Beauforts.

Over dinner in the great hall, he spoke of Raglan's former owner, his father-in-law, William Herbert, Earl of Huntingdon.

"He married one of your Grace's cousins, Dame Katherine Plantagenet."

The Usurper's bastard. She had heard of Katherine, but never met her.

"They are both dead now. The castle came to me through my good lady, Huntingdon's daughter by his first wife." He patted Lady Herbert's hand.

"I remember attending your wedding—when was it, ten years ago?" Elizabeth smiled, feeling that horrible lassitude coming over her again and longing for the comfortable bed that was awaiting her upstairs.

"Yes, Madam. We felt so honored to have your Grace and the King there."

They chatted on until she excused herself, feeling faint with exhaustion.

Ludlow was only fifty miles from Raglan, but Elizabeth could not have faced visiting the place where Arthur had died and, anyway, he was not there. He had gone where she could not reach him, and there had been no more strange occurrences for some time now.

She rode south instead to Chepstow. After taking a ferry across the Severn, she arrived at Berkeley Castle, where she stayed as the guest of the delightful old Lord Berkeley and his wife. They feasted on venison she had sent for from London, wine she had ordered from Bristol, and oranges and candied fruits, a costly gift delivered by a well-wisher. Afterward, she had her minstrels entertain the company.

From Berkeley, she made her way in slow stages to the palace at King's Langley, realizing that she had overreached herself. By the time she reached Langley in September, she was feeling very ill indeed and had to summon her apothecary to bring her some physick. While she waited, she had her accounts brought to her for checking, as she had done meticulously all her married life, but had to abandon the task because she was too exhausted to hold the pen. The physick was beneficial, however, and within days she was able to leave her bed and enjoy the venison and the Rhenish wine sent by the Lord Mayor of London. She had had a craving for venison during this pregnancy and could not get enough of it.

She still felt fatigued. Everything was an effort. She kept her apothecary with her in case she needed more medicine. Her pregnancy was draining her. She was longing for the birth to be over and, at the same time, dreading it, for how would she find the strength to undergo the rigors of labor if her health did not improve? But there were several months still to wait. Hopefully, she would soon feel better, as she had in her earlier pregnancies, although not with Edmund, which worried her.

She had kept in touch by letter with Cecily, Anne, and Katherine, doing her best to offer comfort to her two younger sisters, for Anne had just lost another child in infancy. But Cecily seemed very happy with her Thomas and less bothered now by being in disgrace; no doubt she had the Lady Margaret to thank for that. Elizabeth usually wrote regularly to Bridget, although she did not often get a reply. It was as if Bridget had put worldly ties behind her. She was twenty-one now and appeared to have settled into the religious life, for which Elizabeth was most thankful. Now she wrote, asking after Bridget's health and craving her prayers for her own speedy recovery. Every small intercession would help, she was sure.

One afternoon, as she was resting, she heard a clattering of hooves, running footsteps, and a small commotion in the courtyard below her window. Heaving herself off the bed, she looked out, but whoever had arrived had gone within, and she could see only grooms leading the horses away. Pray God it was not some local dignitary come to interrupt her rest.

It was not. To her utter surprise, the door of her chamber opened and there stood Henry. "Bessy! I was at Woodstock and heard that you were at Langley. I had to come." He crossed to the bed in three strides, looking at her as lovingly as ever. It was only now that she realized how much she had missed him, how empty her existence had been without him.

"Henry!" she said, rising hastily, and would have curtseyed, but he caught her in his arms and crushed her to him. As she stood there, thinking how good it was to be close to him again, she realized that her anger had spent itself. He had done what he thought to be right at the time in sending Arthur to Ludlow. He had not punished Courtenay and Cecily to hurt her, but because he had to make an example of them. And, feeling his heart pounding against hers, how could she ever have thought that he was drawn to Catherine Gordon? It was nonsense—she knew it now.

She had been selfish, thinking only of herself. She had been too bound up with grief and resentment to think clearly. Maybe she had been right to get away after all, to see her responses as irrational. Sometimes, you just had to let go of things. "I'm sorry," she wept, her cheek against Henry's riding gown. "I should not have left you. You are grieving, too."

He drew back and tilted her chin up so that they were facing each other. "No, Bessy. I was unkind. I acted like a blundering fool. I know I hurt you."

"I am not hurting now," she said. "I can only feel the greatest joy at seeing you. I'm so glad you came."

"So am I," he smiled, and kissed her most tenderly. "But they tell me you have not been well."

"I'm all the better for seeing you," she said, determined to make light of it and let nothing spoil their reunion. "I've just been feeling tired. I'm sure that it will pass as the child grows larger."

"Then you must return to your rest, cariad, and I'll sit with you and you can tell me about your adventures."

There was great tenderness between them now. They could not make love because of her condition, but she lay in Henry's arms every night, savoring the intimacy, and he stayed with her for the rest of the progress. It was as if there had never been any rift between them.

They visited Minster Lovell Hall, where more memories of her Yorkist past awaited her. It had been the residence of Lord Lovell, one of Richard's chief advisers, who had disappeared after fighting on the wrong side at Stoke and never been seen again. The manor was now owned by Harry, although he had never been there, and it was looked after by royal officials. As she strolled arm in arm with Henry along the banks of the nearby River Windrush, Elizabeth could not help but wonder where Lovell was.

"Do you think he's dead?" she asked.

"He's probably abroad," Henry replied. "But I'd still like to get my hands on him. By the way, I have had some plans drawn up for your house at Greenwich." He cast her a wry look. "If you still want it, that is."

"I dare say I shall use it occasionally, but it will be something for all of us, especially Harry."

He bent and kissed her. "I'm glad you're not leaving me."

"I never was. I was in a bad place, Henry. I think I was running from my grief as much as from you and all our troubles." She squeezed his hand. "But I feel better now. I will always mourn Arthur and our other little ones—that loss will never leave me—but I feel more positive about life now. And this babe will help." She patted her stomach.

They arrived at Richmond late in October. Soon afterward, Elizabeth hired embroiderers to work on a set of rich hangings for the bed in which she intended to be confined, for Henry wanted this child to be born in the palace that symbolized more than any other the Tudor dynasty. The finished hangings were gorgeous, patterned with white-and-red roses and edged with red satin. Elizabeth also ordered a new truckle bed on which to give birth, a counterpane and curtains of crimson and blue velvet, and a beautiful cloth of estate in crimson taffeta.

As the weeks raced by, she began to feel better, which did wonders for her peace of mind. She interviewed suitable staff for the baby's household. She kept in touch with Cecily, who was enjoying married life at Collyweston, and supported Katherine and her children.

Once a week, she visited Harry, Margaret, and Mary at Eltham and spent many happy hours with them making preparations for Christmas. She was aware that they were growing up fast. At eleven, her beautiful boy Harry was very conscious of his elevated status as the heir and was becoming a little pompous. Yet he was so vital, so clever, and so like her father—handsome, open-handed, affable—and while not a little devious, he was still a very affectionate son, and for Elizabeth the light shone out of his eyes. God forbid that anything evil befall this precious, favorite child.

Margaret, just turned thirteen, was quite the young lady now, still headstrong, but more sedate, and blossoming in looks and charm. Elizabeth dreaded the thought of her leaving for Scotland next year, and Margaret herself seemed torn. Part of her was excited at the prospect of becoming a queen, but the little girl in her wanted to stay with her doting parents. Mary, at six, was as exquisite as ever, the most enchanting child. One day, she would make some lucky prince a beautiful wife. But would it be the Archduke Charles? Matters had not progressed very far in that direction, and Elizabeth was content for now that this should be so.

In December, she stayed for a few days at the Tower, hoping she would feel close to her brothers there. They must be lying somewhere nearby. If only she knew where. She was great with child now, but still she tramped all over the palace, looking for some sign that the masonry around the staircases had been disturbed. She should have known that it would all be in vain.

When she returned to her chamber, she found a monk of Westminster waiting for her with one of the abbey's precious relics. "My lord Abbot has sent your Grace Our Lady's girdle," he said. "It will afford you special protection during your confinement."

Elizabeth took the beautiful, fragile thing reverently, fearing that it would crumble in her hands. It would be a great comfort to wear this during her travail, and she was conscious of being highly privileged, for the abbey did not lightly lend out its relics, and then only to the highest in the land. She rewarded the monk with a handsome donation and laid the girdle in her treasure chest, wrapped in silk.

They kept Christmas at Richmond. Elizabeth had been dreading this first Yuletide without Arthur, but her other children and her daughter-in-law were there to comfort her, and Henry allowed Harry to join the two of them when they went in state to Mass on Christmas Day. The children of the King's Chapel sang carols and Harry sat rapt as his father's minstrels played a beautiful accompaniment. In the twelve days of merriment that followed, the tables groaned with lavish spreads of food, the wine flowed as if from bottomless ewers, and there were revels, disguisings, plays, and dancing girls, all under the governance of the Lord of Misrule. There was plenty to take Elizabeth's mind off her grief, yet she could not help seeing, among the merrymakers, three lost little ghosts who should have been here, joining in the revelry they would have enjoyed so much.

She was touched that Henry had allowed Katherine to celebrate Christmas Day with Courtenay in the Tower. Afterward, Katherine had reported that he was in good spirits, but very bored with his monotonous existence within the four walls of his prison, although it was a comfortable enough chamber, for prisoners of rank were allowed to have luxuries sent in, and Elizabeth had provided tapestries, rugs, cushions, books, and a chess set. She had also paid an inn near the Tower to send in choice food daily. She was hoping that Henry might relent soon and free Courtenay, for there seemed to be very little evidence against him.

At New Year, Henry's astrologer, Dr. Parron, told fortunes to divert the courtiers.

Elizabeth gave him her palm and he studied it, then lifted his face and smiled. "This year, your Grace will live in wealth and delight."

Henry was sitting there listening, his hands resting on the exquisitely bound almanac Parron had given him. He grinned. "It says in here, my lady, that you will live until you are eighty or ninety and will bear me many sons!"

"That's reassuring," she laughed. "And they'll be lusty, if this little one's kicking is anything to go by!" She felt heartened by Parron's prediction; he had been reliable in the past. Everything would be all right.

After Twelfth Night, she felt the need for another retreat.

Henry looked alarmed when she told him. "You're not ill?" he asked anxiously.

"The doctors say that all is well," she told him.

"Hmm," he said. "I hope they are right." He had not trusted doctors since Linacre had misled him with such terrible consequences.

"I'm sure they are. But I would like time to myself for some quiet prayer, and to rest untroubled by the demands of the court for a short space."

"Very well," he said, taking her in his arms. "But I will miss you."

"I will not be gone long," she assured him.

Lord Daubeney was delighted to see her at Hampton Court again and did not demur when she asked for the same cell she had occupied on her last visit. She stayed for ten days, still buoyed up by Dr. Parron's prophecy. But when she returned to Richmond, she had an unpleasant dizzy turn, and Henry sent for her surgeon, who bled her.

"We just need to balance the humors in the body, Madam," he said soothingly, opening his jar of leeches. Afterward, she felt that horrible drained feeling again. Well, it would not be long now until the child was born, please God, and then hopefully she would feel much better. She only had until March to wait, by her reckoning.

Weary as she was, she ordered that money be paid out for medicines for young Henry Courtenay, who was ill, and sent gifts to cheer her aunt Suffolk, who must be worrying herself to a frazzle over her son, who was still eluding the King's agents abroad.

Henry often came and sat with her in the afternoons when she was resting on her bed. He was full of plans.

"You remember that I was going to rebuild Henry the Third's old chapel at Windsor as a tomb house for Henry the Sixth?"

He had been planning it for years. And he had been trying—as yet without success—to persuade the Pope to make poor, feeble Henry of Lancaster a saint. The new chapel, which stood next to the still-unfinished St. George's, which her father had begun building, was to house his shrine and the royal tombs of the House of Tudor. One day, she herself would lie there.

"Well," Henry was saying, "after much thought, I've changed my mind and decided to build a new Lady Chapel at Westminster Abbey instead. The monks have been pestering me to do so for years now; they want the bones of Henry the Sixth." Of course they did. Saints were lucrative assets. "Every English king has been crowned in Westminster Abbey. It houses the shrine of the sainted King Edward the Confessor, around which many kings and queens are buried. My grandmother, Queen Katherine, the widow of Henry the Fifth, lies there. My plan, Bessy, is to build a magnificent tomb for us in the center of the new Lady Chapel, before the altar; King Henry's shrine will be at the east end. Our descendants will lie there in glory for all eternity."

His eyes were shining. "I'll have the whole chapel painted and adorned with our arms and badges—the leopards of England, Tudor roses, the red dragon of Cadwaladr, crowned fleurs-de-lis, your Yorkist falcons and fetterlocks, the Richmond greyhounds, the Lancastrian collars of SS knots, the Beaufort portcullises and hawthorn bushes, to commemorate the finding of my crown on Bosworth field. And I will procure sacred relics for the altar that will stand at the foot of our tomb. The chapel will be magnificent when it's finished."

Elizabeth was carried along by his enthusiasm, but found it a little chilling to think about tombs and burial when she was so near her time. She knew, though, that, as ever, Henry was concerned to perpetuate his dynasty and his greatness, and she was pleased that he intended her to be given equal prominence. After all, he owed his crown to her.

Chapter 25

1503

Her retreat did her good. Soon, she was feeling more herself and suffering only the lumbering discomforts of late pregnancy. As the child was not due for some weeks, Henry decided that they would spend Candlemas together at the Tower, and that Katherine could accompany them. They traveled there together by barge at the end of January. When they arrived, he gave Katherine leave to visit her husband daily.

Elizabeth settled gratefully into the Queen's Lodgings, where her great chamber was newly hung with her favorite tapestries, the ones embellished with fleurs-de-lis of gold. Here, soon after she arrived, she received a poor woman who had brought her a gift of capons and was trembling in awe as she offered them. Elizabeth thanked her kindly and sent her away with a reward. She had the capons served to her and Henry at supper, along with the costly oranges and pomegranates she had sent her fool, Patch, to buy, when he told her that they were to be had in the market at Borough.

It was on Candlemas Day that she felt the first tightening of her womb. She and Henry had just returned from the chapel of St. John the Evangelist in the White Tower, having donned their robes of state and gone in procession to Mass to celebrate the feast of the Purification of the Virgin Mary. When she returned to her lodgings, she was glad to be divested of her heavy, ermine-lined mantle and her crown, and was looking forward to the venison that had been delivered for her dinner. Suddenly, she felt the familiar pain in her womb. No, it could not be; it was too soon. Dear God, the child could not be born here in the Tower without everything needful to hand; she must get to Richmond, where all was in readiness. But the pains came again, and again, and soon it was clear that there would be no time to get to Richmond.

It was a hard travail, and it seemed to go on forever. Fortunately, Mother Massey had been installed in the Queen's household for two weeks now, and she took charge amid a flurry of frantic makeshift preparations. But Elizabeth was soon beyond caring. Had her belly not been so large, she would have been doubled up with pain.

That evening, she was brought to bed of a daughter, a tiny little cherub who gave a weak wail and then sank into a peaceful slumber.

Henry came at once, but Mother Massey made him wait until Elizabeth had been washed and tidied.

"Oh, my cariad, you have come through it safely," he breathed, bending over the bed and kissing her. "I thank God!"

Sleepy as she was, Elizabeth was utterly glad to see him, and so thankful just to be here.

"I have been in good hands." She smiled at Mother Massey, who had just finished swaddling the baby. Henry reached out and she laid it in his arms.

"A pretty little maid," he observed, kissing the tiny forehead. "May God bless you, my little one, all the days of your life."

"I had hoped to gladden you with a son," Elizabeth said weakly. She was aware of a sense of disappointment and failure—dread, too, because she might have to go through this all over again.

"It is no matter. I love our daughter already. She is as beautiful as her mother. I will make an offering to the Virgin in gratitude for her safe arrival. I'm sure that she was watching over you."

"And I didn't even have her girdle with me. It's at Richmond."

She smiled at him, thinking what a loving husband he was. How could she ever have doubted his feelings for her?

They called their daughter Katherine, after the Spanish princess they had come to love and Elizabeth's sister, who was to be one of the godmothers. But the little mite was slow to take suck and did not thrive. Looking distressed, Mother Massey recommended that they waste no time in having her christened. The ceremony took place in the Chapel Royal of St. Peter ad Vincula, and afterward, the infant was brought to Henry and Elizabeth to receive their blessings and be called by her Christian name for the first time. Henry kissed her and laid her gently in the great state cradle, which had been brought by barge from Richmond and made up with a soft woolen mattress and down pillows that he himself had hastily purchased from a London mercer.

"I fancy that little Katherine has a better color today," Elizabeth said hopefully, lying back on her pillows and willing her daughter to live.

"You're right," Henry smiled. "And I'm told that she has begun to take more milk."

"That's a good sign," she replied, filled with relief. As soon as she regained her strength, she would give thanks and offerings to God for His great blessings and supervise the baby's care herself. If a mother's will could prevail, this little one would thrive.

Elizabeth made a steady recovery and Mother Massey pronounced herself pleased with her progress. But a week after the birth, she began to experience pains low down in her belly.

Mother Massey felt the place where her womb was.

"Ooh!" Elizabeth drew in her breath.

"It's painful there, Madam?"

"Yes."

"And does your Grace have a discharge?"

"Yes, I have noticed that. It's not very pleasant."

"No, I imagine not." The midwife felt her forehead and frowned. "You are a little hot, Madam."

"I actually feel cold and a little shivery. What do you think is the matter?"

"It's too early to say, but I wish my brother was here to attend you. He is a physician and very good at treating childbed conditions, but he is away visiting family in Plymouth."

"Will you send for him?" Elizabeth pleaded. "Before this malady, whatever it is, gets worse."

The King was summoned. After a hurried consultation with Mother Massey outside the door, he hastened to Elizabeth's bedside, looking concerned. "Cariad, you are not to worry. The midwife says this kind of reaction is common. But, to be on the safe side, I have summoned her brother. With fast horses, he could be here in four days."

"Four days?" She started up in the bed. "I could be dead by then!"

"Who's talking about dying?" Henry answered sharply. "Mother Massey says there is no great urgency. Had there been, she would have sent for your own Dr. Hallysworth, since Dr. Lewis is unwell. But she does not see the necessity. And you're not looking too poorly, Bessy. Try not to fret. If there is any cause for concern, I will send for Hallysworth."

She lay back, reassured. Mother Massey was highly experienced. If she thought there was nothing to worry about, then there wasn't. She picked up her Book of Hours and tried to concentrate on the prayers. Soon, she was asleep. When she awoke, she felt refreshed and not so shivery. She sat up and ate some hearty broth and a little white fish, and Mother Massey declared herself pleased with her progress.

"I doubt my brother will be needed," she smiled.

Elizabeth maintained her progress and her spirits revived. She was going to get better. Soon, she would be churched and then she could see her children again. She spent the next day sitting up in bed, cradling her baby, embroidering clothes for her, and playing chess with Henry. Her appetite was improving. She still felt a little shivery, but Mother Massey assured her that would ease.

The night drew in. Katherine sat by the bed, reading aloud a romance of Tristan and Yseult, one of Elizabeth's favorite tales. After supper, Henry arrived, and Katherine sped off to see her husband. Later that evening, Henry lay down on the bed and took Elizabeth in his arms. She lay there, savoring the closeness between them, remembering that tomorrow would be her birthday. She would be thirty-seven. There could not be much in the way of celebrations, of course, but there might be some gifts.

Presently, she fell asleep.

She awoke in agony. It was still dark. Henry was beside her, snoring rhythmically, still fully dressed. She clutched at her stomach. "Henry! Wake up! Help me!"

He was instantly alert.

"Henry, I'm bleeding!" She could feel the blood pouring out of her. "Get Mother Massey! Hurry!" She was beside herself with fear.

Henry leaped up and crashed through the door. In seconds, it seemed, he returned, pulling the midwife by the hand. She was in her night robe and coif, but her feet were bare. She flung back the bedclothes. Elizabeth screamed in horror when she saw the spreading pool of blood. She felt sick and clammy and was finding it hard to focus.

She must be dying! "Oh, God, help me!" she wailed.

"There is no time to lose," Mother Massey cried. "Your Grace must send for a doctor."

As Henry ran from the room, the midwife shouted for the maids to come, and packed a rolled-up sheet between Elizabeth's legs to stem the blood. Then she gripped her hand. "It will be all right, Madam. The doctor will be here soon."

Elizabeth was aware of Henry returning and speaking to Mother Massey. "I've sent a fast messenger to summon Dr. Hallysworth, with spare horses and guides to speed his way with lighted torches.

He's at his home at Gravesend, so I've ordered that a barge be sent to collect him. How is she?"

"Poorly, Sire." Mother Massey sounded panicky. "She is losing a lot of blood and she's in shock."

"No, dear God, not my Bessy!" Henry's voice seemed to come from a long way off. "Cariad, speak to me! Cariad!"

Elizabeth felt strong arms encircling her. But she was beyond answering; the world was slipping away. Yet she was still aware that Henry was here. That was all that mattered. In fact, they were all here, all those she had loved: Father, Mother, Ned, York, her lost children, and Arthur, her beloved Arthur, coming toward her like a golden knight out of legend, well and strong as he had never been in life. She felt herself lifted up on a tide of their love and borne away down a long, long tunnel, at the end of which beckoned a dazzling light and a Heaven more glorious than she had ever dreamed of.

Author's Note

This novel is closely based on the research I undertook for my biography, *Elizabeth of York: The First Tudor Queen* (2013). Occasionally, for the sake of clarity and a smooth narrative, I have used a little dramatic license; for example, Avice Welles was not appointed Prince Edward's wet nurse until June 1471, but I have her in post in May!

Historically, Elizabeth of York was very important. She was the daughter, sister, niece, wife, mother, and grandmother of monarchs, and the ancestress of every English monarch since 1509, every Scottish monarch since 1513, and every British monarch since 1603. She should have been England's first reigning queen, but in fifteenth-century England it was unthinkable that a female should rule, for it was believed to be against the laws of God and Nature for a woman to wield dominion over men.

Elizabeth lived through a turbulent period of history that saw the beginning of the transition from the medieval to the modern world. She was closely connected to some of England's most controversial figures, among them Richard III, Henry VII, Henry VIII, and the notorious—or possibly misunderstood—Wydevilles, her mother's family.

Despite the wealth of source material for Elizabeth's story, history does not always record her thoughts, emotions, motives, hopes and fears. There is evidence to show that she was passionate and proactive in intriguing behind the scenes to become queen.

Once she was crowned, her voice was silent, so we can only specu-late on how events affected her.

There are two sources for Elizabeth's intrigues, both controver-sial, the first being a letter she sent to John Howard, Duke of Norfolk, which was seen by Sir George Buck in the seventeenth century, but is now lost. Buck's manuscript was damaged by fire in 1731, but his summary of the letter was reconstructed in 1979 by A. N. Kincaid from the manuscript copy closest to the origi-nal. In it, Elizabeth asked Norfolk to act as mediator in negotiat-ing her marriage to Richard III, who was, she wrote, "her only joy and maker in [this] world, and that she was his in heart and in thoughts, in [body] and in all."

The evidence for the letter being genuine is discussed in my biography of Elizabeth. It seems she probably regarded marriage to the King as the best means of safeguarding her future and her family's security. Her statement is not so much romantic as a declaration of fealty. Her pursuance of the union is in keeping with the Elizabeth in *The Song of Lady Bessy*, a near-contemporary metrical chronicle that describes her involvement in the momen-tous events of 1485. It was written by Humphrey Brereton, an agent of Lord Stanley, Henry VII's stepfather. Parts are demon-strably inventions, probably because Brereton was not always as close to events as he pretended. There is no way of proving that the poem is based on fact, as no other source mentions Elizabeth's role in the events it describes, yet it has been said that there is "a great deal of truth" in it. What is striking is that the Elizabeth portrayed in *The Song of Lady Bessy* is as proactive as the Elizabeth who wrote to Norfolk urging his help in progressing her marriage with Richard III.

Central to Elizabeth's story is that of the Princes in the Tower. They were her brothers, and we can only imagine the distress that their disappearance in 1483, and rumors that they had been mur-dered, caused her. Later, when a pretender surfaced claiming to be the younger Prince, that must have impacted profoundly on her.

What happened to Edward V and Richard, Duke of York, remains the subject of lively debate. The evidence is discussed in my book *The Princes in the Tower* (published in 1992 and reissued as *Richard III and the Princes in the Tower* in 2014), and I revisited the subject in my biography of Elizabeth of York.

In a work of history, it is possible to state that the evidence suggests one theory or another, and to lay out the facts and weigh the arguments. In fiction, you have to decide where you are going with the story. Here, I have offered what I believe to be the most credible explanation of what happened to the Princes. The fact that Henry and Elizabeth both visited the Tower at the time when Sir James Tyrell made his confession suggests that it was authentic, which many have doubted. And it was probably from the ladies at the Minories that Sir Thomas More learned of the fate of the Princes, as recounted in his *History of King Richard III*.

I refer the reader to my biography of Elizabeth of York for her relations with Henry VII; her health and the likelihood that iron-deficiency anemia led to her death; the probability that an agent provocateur (Cleymound) lured Warwick and Warbeck into a treasonable conspiracy; the evidence for Prince Arthur's failure to consummate his marriage to Katherine of Aragon; and the possible effects on Elizabeth of the long separation from her premature, fragile son Arthur. Tragically, I was in a position to comprehend her grief when Arthur died, for my own son passed away in 2020. Her doubts about her love for Arthur in no way mirror my feelings for my son, whom I adored, but it occurred to me that such grief must be even more painful for a mother who felt that she had not loved her child as much as she felt she should have.

A note on names. *The Song of Lady Bessy* inspired the nickname by which those close to Elizabeth call her in the novel. She calls her sister Cecily "Cis," because that was the diminutive in the nickname—"Proud Cis"—by which their grandmother, Cecily Neville, Duchess of York, was known. I have called Elizabeth's brother Edward "Ned" to avoid confusion with his father, Edward IV; her brother Richard "York" to avoid confusion with Richard III; and her son Henry "Harry" to avoid confusion with his father,

Henry VII. After Henry VII's accession, Richard III is sometimes called "the Usurper," because that is how many people would have regarded him.

I wish to extend my warmest thanks to my fabulous teams at Headline and Ballantine for commissioning this book and for their invaluable professional, editorial, and creative support. It really is a joy to work with such wonderful publishers. Special thanks, as ever, go to my amazing agent, Julian Alexander, for bringing us together. Lastly, but never least, I want to express my loving appreciation of my dear husband, Rankin, for always being there for me.

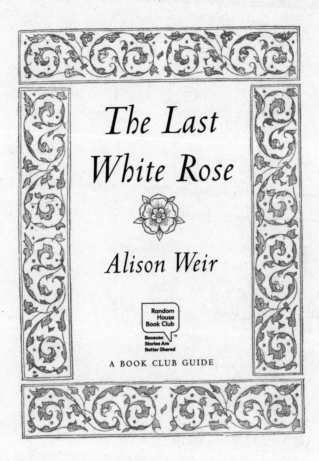

The Last White Rose

Alison Weir

Random House Book Club

Because Stories Are Better Shared

A BOOK CLUB GUIDE

FIRSTBORN

February 1466

I

ELIZABETH

The Queen of England lay in her gilded bedchamber in the Palace of Westminster, exhausted after her labor, and full of trepidation. Her firstborn child, who should have been a son, the longed-for heir to York, and to England, was a girl. A pretty babe—but a girl.

How would Edward react? As the nurse swaddled the infant, Elizabeth lay tense, praying that his great love for her would outweigh his disappointment. And though all her instincts were screaming *never again*, after the ordeal through which she had just safely come, she braced herself to assure him that next time it would be a son.

She flushed to think what people would be saying when the news got out. My lord of Warwick would be smirking, reveling in the fact that the upstart Wydeville queen had failed in her primary duty. He had made no secret of the fact that he despised her, that he thought Edward had thrown himself away on the impoverished widow of a knight who had fallen fighting for the wrong side in the recent wars between the royal Houses of York and Lancaster. Warwick had wanted the King to marry a French princess and thereby gain a great alliance and political advantages. Like most of the nobility, he had been shocked and angered when Edward announced his marriage.

She remembered clearly the day the Council had met at Reading. They had raised the matter of the French marriage, and it was then, Edward had later told her, that he'd broken the news, to an appalled silence, that he was already wed. But he had not cared. He was the King, twenty-two years old and headstrong. He had insisted on presenting Elizabeth to his lords, watching them hawk-like as they reluctantly bent the knee to her. She could tell they thought it preposterous that a king would marry for love. But marry for love he had, and lustily!

She could recall the day of their first meeting as clearly as if it were yesterday, although it was nearly two years ago now. Penniless and desperate, she had been staying with her parents at their manor house at Grafton when they heard that the King was coming to hunt in Whittlewood Forest.

"Go and petition him!" her mother urged, the mother who was nowhere near as lowborn as Warwick liked to think, for she was a princess of the House of Luxembourg. "Use your wiles! I hear he finds women irresistible. With your beauty, you should be able to charm him."

Elizabeth had stared at her reflection in her mother's silver mirror. John had called her beautiful and she knew she was, with her perfect features, rosy skin and gilt-blond hair. But John had been killed at the Battle of St. Albans three years ago, and she still mourned him.

At twenty-seven, and a mother twice over, she still had the gloss of youth, although there was now something glacial about her beauty. She supposed it had evolved as a form of protection against those who despised her for her poverty. Would her face melt the King's heart? Or would he see before him just another Lancastrian widow undeserving of his pity? Worse, would he expect something in return for listening to her plea? His reputation with women was notorious.

She had armored herself, taking her two young sons for protection, reasoning that surely the King would not attempt to seduce her when she had a child on either side of her.

She raised herself in the opulent bed, gazing down at her new daughter, who lay sleeping peacefully in the great gilded cradle. Nearby, the flames leaped in the hearth, warming the room against the February chill. Elizabeth lay back again.

She had vivid memories of hurrying through the forest. It had been April and the woodland floor was carpeted with bluebells, a most glorious sight. Tom, then eight, and Dickon, six, had run ahead of her, jumping over tree roots and jostling each other, heeding her call only when she reached the place by the roadside where the King was expected to ride by.

She had dressed with care. Her good black gown was high-waisted and low-cut, revealing her creamy bosom. She had shaved her forehead in the fashionable mode, bound up her fair hair around her head, and draped over it a black veil. She wore no jewelry save her wedding ring. The effect was very becoming, she decided.

They waited for hours. They had got there early; they could not have missed him, surely?

At last, at long last, she heard hoofbeats. A party of riders, by the sound of it. And yes, there was the royal standard bearer, riding ahead of the rest, who were led by a young man whose bearing alone proclaimed who he was. Elizabeth sank into her curtsey, suddenly fearful that ambushing him in such a dramatic fashion was a step too far. She bowed her head, feeling herself blush, and clutched her kneeling boys' hands.

"Madam!" the King's voice rang out from above her. "Are you in distress?"

She dared to lift her face. A great golden god stood before her. Her eyes met his, and she saw in them a look she recognized as lust.

"Your Grace . . ." she faltered, but he stayed her with a gesture. He waved his escort on to the appointed hunting ground. After they had departed, exchanging knowing glances, he dismounted and raised her to her feet.

"You were waiting to see me," he said, his eyes raking her face, her bosom, the whole of her.

"Sir, forgive me. I am a poor widow, deprived of my dower because my late husband's mother has remarried, and her lord has claimed it for himself."

"Who was your husband?" he asked, melting her with his gentleness.

"Sir John Grey of Groby," she said.

"Ah. He died fighting for Henry of Lancaster, as I recall." She braced herself for rejection, now that he knew who she was. "And your lady mother was once married to Henry's uncle, the Duke of Bedford." She was amazed that he should know all this.

"She was, Sir. I realize I am not worthy of your Grace's pity . . ."

"On the contrary, Lady Grey, you are worthy of much more than that." He took her hand and, to her surprise, raised it to his lips. "I will look into the matter of your dower—on one condition."

"Yes, Sir?" she faltered, fearing that she knew what was coming next.

"That you will consent to walk with me, so that I may get to know you better. I must confess I have never met such a comely widow."

He tethered his horse and led her off in the direction of a nearby church. Ever after, she remembered it as a magical place.

Thus it had begun, his covert courtship, their secret trysts, which were few and far between, for he was constantly on the move around his realm, and distance often separated them.

Her parents were delighted and proud. Ambitious, seasoned courtiers, they could now see a gilded future opening up for their family. "If you play your cards right," Mother urged.

Elizabeth did not need telling.

At first, Edward had pressed her to be his mistress.

"No, Sir," she said, and kept on saying it. But he was ardent and insistent, and she found it increasingly hard to resist him. Once, when they were sitting in her mother's chamber at Grafton, he tried to take her, pulling at her skirts. Deftly, she unsheathed his dagger and held it to her throat, forcing him to let her go.

"I know I am unworthy to be your queen, Sir, but I value my honor more than my life!" she cried, only half jesting.

Edward had stared at her, then he fell to his knees before her, abasing himself before his humble subject—and he had said the words she had never thought to hear. "Forgive me, Beth. You are so beautiful, and I forgot myself in my passion. And you are not unworthy to be my queen. They want me to marry a French princess, but, sweetheart, my heart is yours. I want *you* to be my wife!"

It was incredible, unbelievable. No king, to her knowledge, had ever married a commoner, or married for love. Most people would dismiss it as craziness. Kings married princesses, making grand alliances. It was amazing what love could do to a man.

And so she found herself, one fresh August morning, wearing a chaplet of flowers, walking with Edward through the woods at Grafton to the little chapel they called the Hermitage. There, in the presence of her mother and two of the King's gentlemen, they were married.

As soon as they returned to the manor, Edward took her to bed. It was the headiest day of her life. She smiled at the memory.

2

EDWARD

Edward had been pacing his apartments at Westminster, praying that Beth would come safely through her ordeal and be spared to him, and that God would vouchsafe him a son. The birth of an heir would be a vindication of his unpopular marriage. It would show Warwick and those others, especially his brother Clarence, who had been so hostile to it. God, let them bring him news soon!

He sat down and tried to concentrate on the state papers before him. He had won his throne by right of conquest, avenging his late father's death and quelling all opposition. Henry of Lancaster, the pretender he had overthrown, had fled up north. The birth of a prince would ensure the Yorkist succession and surely bring over any whose loyalty was wavering. Even Warwick. Especially Warwick.

It must be a prince. The Queen's physician had assured him of it. He could only pray that the doctor was right.

He rose and unlocked the coffer beneath the window. Lifting from it a velvet bag, he drew out the jewel he had lovingly bought for Beth some weeks earlier; it was to be a token of his gratitude for the birth of their son. Within hours, minutes, even, he could be giving it to her, flushed with joy at having his heir. He was looking forward to lavishing honors on the boy, teaching him to hunt and how to be a king . . .

His happy reverie was broken by a tap on the door.

He opened the door to the Queen's bedchamber and waved away the women. In spite of her ordeal, Beth looked lovely, her gorgeous golden tresses spread out on the pillow. She smiled nervously at him. In a few short weeks, he could claim her again. He waited for desire to rise in him, but it didn't. It was the measure of how disappointed he was, in her, in her physician and in Providence, God Himself even. A daughter! Instead of triumphing, he would now be shamed in the face of his critics. Lusty Edward, unable to get himself a son . . .

"Beth?" He moved to the bed and took her hand. Her eyes were dark shadows, full of anxiety.

"Edward, I am so sorry. I have failed you. Next time . . ."

He hushed her with a finger on her lips. "Let's not think of that now. We have a healthy child. You have not failed me, for this little one's birth augurs well for the future." He bent to kiss her, glad he had found the words to comfort her and had hidden his disappointment.

He bent over the cradle. His daughter lay looking up at him with big blue eyes and lips like a rosebud. Tufts of auburn hair, just like his, were escaping from her tiny bonnet. She was so new, so perfect. He took one look—and was lost. Suddenly, having a son did not seem so important. What did matter was that this precious firstborn be loved, protected and nurtured as no child ever before.

"Elizabeth," he said, smiling. "She shall be called Elizabeth after her beautiful, clever mother!" He picked up the babe and kissed her tenderly, giving her his blessing. Then he drew the jewel from his pocket and gave it to Beth anyway.

3

RICHARD

He dreamed he was standing on the battlements of Middleham Castle, his dark hair blowing about his face. In his dream Anne was standing beside him, the wind whipping her pale gold tresses against her thin face.

When he awoke and found himself back in the Palace of Westminster, he thought of her, something he rarely did these days. How was she faring at Middleham? She had wept so much when he was summoned south to court last year. She was a sweet child, but sometimes he thought her an encumbrance. What fourteen-year-old boy, who had already led an army to battle, wanted to keep company with an eight-year-old girl? And yet he could never have been discourteous to her, for she was the daughter of his revered and beloved guardian and mentor, Warwick.

He sighed and rose from his bed. He missed Middleham; he found the court stifling and longed for the green dales of Yorkshire.

His sister Margaret, at nineteen, five and a half years his senior, was already at the breakfast table.

"The Queen's had her baby," she said.

Richard turned sharply. "Yes?"

"A princess."

"Oh." He knew that Edward had wanted a son to succeed him, and Richard had wanted that for him too. It meant that the House of York would be firmly established on the throne, which would mean peace and prosperity for all his blood—and for England.

"Oh, well, she can have another child," he said.

"The Princess is to be called Elizabeth," she told him. "After the Queen."

The Queen. Richard had never liked her, nor her horde of Wydeville kinsfolk, all of them greedy for offices, power and grand marriages. And Edward, the fool, had been liberal-handed with these, advancing those jumped-up, good-for-nothing parvenus. It made Richard feel sick to think of it. Why couldn't his brother have married that French princess Warwick had worked so hard to secure for him?

As ever, these days, the thought of Warwick made Richard uneasy. He had never forgotten the Earl's explosion of anger when Edward had announced his marriage, how he had raged against the foolishness, the inappropriateness of it. Richard had always worshipped his brother, but he had been at one with Warwick on this, unable to believe that Edward had acted so stupidly. To marry for love? Even peasants thought twice about that.

Yet even he had to admit that Elizabeth had performed her duties as Queen faultlessly, as if she had been born to it. But she was too haughty, too much on her dignity, too insistent on being paid the proper deference. And now she had failed in her first duty, that of ensuring the succession by bearing the King a son. It would be laughable if it wasn't such a serious disappointment.

"Keep on frowning like that, and you'll get lines on your forehead," Margaret teased.

"I was thinking." He laid some cold beef on a slice of bread. He wished that Edward would pay more heed to Warwick, who was wise and experienced. But Warwick's influence, once almighty, had waned as the Wydevilles swept all before them. Richard was torn between his beloved brother and his beloved guardian. He hoped he would never be called upon to make a choice between them.

* * *

Later that day, he went to pay his respects to his new niece. The Queen received him coolly. He bent to look at the infant, noticing that she had red hair. Babies held no attraction for him, but he praised her prettiness and congratulated her mother. Then he made his escape, knowing that his presence was unwelcome. The Queen knew that he was Warwick's man. And if you were Warwick's man, you couldn't be her friend. For the thousandth time, he wondered what Edward had seen in her.

As he walked back to his apartment, he felt the familiar pain in his back. It had become an occasional companion over the past year or so. He felt as if his body was listing to one side, and he could feel a small prominence there. But it wasn't noticeable beneath his clothes, and he was convinced that it was the result of an injury from the martial exercises in which Warwick had regularly had him drilled. As usual, he shrugged off the discomfort.

That night, he dreamed of a golden crown and an alluring flame-haired beauty. The morning found him depressed and despondent. Unless he had another growth spurt, and suddenly became handsome, such a woman would never desire him. And definitely—for he had two older brothers—he would never wear a crown.

Questions and Topics
for Discussion

1. *Princess, Bastard, Queen, Matriarch.* Elizabeth's tumultuous life lasted just thirty-seven years, yet she and Henry VII united the two great families of England to create the Tudor line, founding an intricate, conflicted dynasty. How does Elizabeth demonstrate strong leadership in the plot to bring Henry Tudor to England, along with a powerful belief in her divine right to the throne? While she asserts that women "are not fitted by Nature to wield dominion over men," how does she find other ways to influence the political sphere?

2. This is the first in a new trilogy that will take us through the reigns of seven monarchs, and be woven into the stories explored in the Six Tudor Queens series. How did you feel the court of Edward IV compares to that of his grandson, Henry VIII? How does this novel show the development of the culture and self-belief that will mark the future Tudor monarchs—both male and female?

3. Elizabeth's family flees twice into sanctuary. She loses beloved relations and friends to sudden execution, and sees her mother influence the death of an uncle. Even after

Henry's victory, her life is punctuated by uprisings and threats to the crown. How is this constant sense of threat conveyed in the novel, and how does it affect Elizabeth? What makes her family believe so strongly that they have the right and obligation to rule?

4. *"It's a sad fact that the Wydevilles are not liked by the nobility or the people."* A significant backdrop is the antagonism between the Wydevilles and Edward IV's family and courtiers. How does Alison Weir show Elizabeth's gradual growth of understanding of the danger of political intrigue, the need for compromise, and the realization that perhaps her mother was not always right? What impact does this have on Elizabeth's own approach to life at court?

5. Motherhood is a constant theme in *The Last White Rose*, focusing particularly on the difficult dynamics of royal families. Complicated parental relationships are represented through many characters—Lady Stanley and Henry Tudor have as complex and interesting a relationship as Elizabeth and her mother—and Elizabeth's differing emotions toward her own children are powerfully shown. Loss also casts a shadow over the narrative. How do these very human relationships bring authenticity and depth to the book, and did you find they helped you develop empathy with people living centuries before us?

6. *"The overwhelming likelihood is that the princes in the Tower have been murdered on the King's orders."* In telling Elizabeth of York's story, offering an answer to the mystery of Ned and York's fate is unavoidable. Alison Weir's version, including Elizabeth's meeting in the Minories, is based on recorded events, though she keeps Elizabeth, and us, in the dark until almost the end of the novel before delivering an explosive resolution. How did you react to the author's approach to the tale, and did it convince you?

7. The competition between royal brothers is reflected in three generations, with the book opening as Clarence attacks Edward IV's right to reign and closing as Harry takes over Arthur's destiny. Through Elizabeth's eyes, Arthur and Harry seem to mirror the characteristics of their murdered uncles. Does an accident of birth bestow the brothers with roles to which perhaps they may not be best suited? What insight did you gain into the childhood of princes?

8. From an early age, Elizabeth expects to marry strategically rather than for love. How did you respond to her decision to accept Richard's proposal, and her ability to justify it for the good of her family and the wider world? What was your impression of Richard, who is first introduced as a serious and kindly man, and very different from his historical reputation? After leaving sanctuary, was Elizabeth too naïve in her desire to believe his reasoning and explanations for his actions?

9. *"Would that I had been born a boy,"* Elizabeth sighed. *"Although, if I had, I would likely be dead!"* It is intriguing to wonder what would have happened had Elizabeth been the longed-for male heir—what might England have become? She is just old enough to have reigned, but do you think she is right—that her ambitious relatives would never have stood for one of Edward IV's children taking the reins of power?

10. *"I think you and I are going to accord well together."* Elizabeth chooses to pursue a marriage to Henry in order to cement her position as the true heir to the throne. The marriage develops into one of genuine attraction and affection, but do you feel it is underscored by her discomfort at his assumption of the crown in his own right, rather than hers? What power does Elizabeth manage to wield in their relationship, and how does Alison Weir show this?

11. There is a huge supporting cast in *The Last White Rose*, ranging across the years and many walks of life, from Lord and Lady Stanley, Elizabeth's sisters and relations and the young Katherine of Aragon, to those who support her in sanctuary and beyond. Which ones play key roles in developing Elizabeth's story? Who particularly stood out for you, and why?

12. With characters whose lives overlap with the Six Tudor Queens series, such as Warwick and Perkin Warbeck, we see a different side of the story. Are there any particular historical people whom you were excited to learn more about and will enjoy revisiting in the next books? What are you most looking forward to as Alison Weir's new trilogy moves into Henry's and then Mary's reigns?

ABOUT THE AUTHOR

ALISON WEIR is the *New York Times* bestselling author of the novels *Katherine of Aragon, The True Queen; Anne Boleyn, A King's Obsession; Jane Seymour, The Haunted Queen; Anna of Kleve, The Princess in the Portrait; Katheryn Howard, The Scandalous Queen; Katharine Parr, The Sixth Wife; The Marriage Game; A Dangerous Inheritance; Captive Queen; The Lady Elizabeth;* and *Innocent Traitor,* as well as numerous historical biographies, including *Queens of the Conquest, Queens of the Crusades, The Lost Tudor Princess, Elizabeth of York, Mary Boleyn, The Lady in the Tower, Mistress of the Monarchy, Henry VIII, Eleanor of Aquitaine, The Life of Elizabeth I,* and *The Six Wives of Henry VIII.* She lives in Surrey, England.

alisonweir.org.uk
alisonweirtours.com
Facebook.com/AlisonWeirAuthor
Twitter: @AlisonWeirBooks